The Western Literary Tradition

An Introduction in Texts

VOLUME 2
Jonathan Swift to George Orwell

The Western Literary Tradition

An Introduction in Texts

VOLUME 2
Jonathan Swift to George Orwell

Edited, with Introductions and Notes, by

MARGARET L. KING

Hackett Publishing Company, Inc.
Indianapolis/Cambridge

For further information, please address
  Hackett Publishing Company, Inc.
  P.O. Box 44937
  Indianapolis, Indiana 46244-0937

  www.hackettpublishing.com

Interior design by Laura Clark
Composition by Aptara, Inc.

Library of Congress Control Number: 2020933148

ISBN-13: 978-1-64792-034-0 (pbk.)
ISBN-13: 978-1-64792-036-4 (PDF ebook)

The paper used in this publication meets the minimum requirements of American
National Standard for Information Sciences—Permanence of Paper for Printed
Library Materials, ANSI Z39.48–1984.

∞

For my grandchildren,
a troubled heritage rich in thoughts not to be forgotten on the journey ahead

CONTENTS

Section II
Realism and Naturalism

Section III
Modernism and the Crisis

CHRONOLOGY

Reason and Romanticism

Realism and Naturalism

Modernism and the Crisis

1893	William Butler Yeats, *When You Are Old*
1903	Thomas Mann, *Tonio Kröger*
1903	W. E. B. Du Bois, *The Souls of Black Folk*
1914	James Joyce, *The Sisters*
1915	T. S. Eliot, *The Love Song of J. Alfred Prufrock*
1915	Franz Kafka, *The Metamorphosis*
1916	William Butler Yeats, *Easter, 1916*
1915	Mariano Azuela, *The Underdogs*
1917–1918	Wilfred Owen, *The Send-Off; Anthem for Doomed Youth; Dulce et Decorum Est*
1918	Siegfried Sassoon, *Counter-Attack; The Rear-Guard; Dreamers; Suicide in the Trenches*
1919	William Butler Yeats, *The Second Coming*
1919	John Reed, *Ten Days That Shook the World*
1921	Luigi Pirandello, *Six Characters in Search of an Author*
1925	Osip Mandelstam, *The Noise of Time*
1925	T. S. Eliot, *The Hollow Men*
1925	Ernest Hemingway, *Indian Camp*
1929	Virginia Woolf, *A Room of One's Own*
1929	Erich Maria Remarque, *All Quiet on the Western Front*
1930	William Faulkner, *A Rose for Emily*
1931	Emma Goldman, *Living My Life*
1935–1940	Anna Akhmatova, *Requiem*
1936	Federico García Lorca, *The House of Bernarda Alba*
1936	Victor Serge, *Open Letter to André Gide*
1939	Bertolt Brecht, *Mother Courage and Her Children*
1940	Arthur Koestler, *Darkness at Noon*
1940	Winston Churchill, *We Shall Fight on the Beaches*
1941	Simone Weil, *The* Iliad *or the Poem of Force*
1942–1944	Anne Frank, *The Diary of a Young Girl*
1944	Jean-Paul Sartre, *No Exit*
1946	John Hersey, *Hiroshima*
1947	Pablo Neruda, *The Heights of Macchu Picchu*
1949	George Orwell, *1984*
1958	Elie Wiesel, *Night*

GLOSSARY

abolitionism: Movement to end slavery, originating in Britain in the late eighteenth century, and emergent in the United States soon after the American Revolution.

Acmeism: Pre-revolutionary Russian literary movement, advocating a sparse, clear Modernist style in contrast to what the Acmeists saw as the elaborately metaphysical and uncommunicative approach of their contemporaries.

Allies: In World War II, the coalition of the United Kingdom, the United States, the Soviet Union, and many allies worldwide.

American Revolution (1775–1783): Rebellion of thirteen American colonies against the British Empire, resulting in their gaining independence and forming a new nation, the United States of America.

anarchism: A political philosophy that rejects all forms of coercion by any authority, especially that of the state, and accordingly opposes all wars.

authoritarianism: An ideology or regime demanding complete obedience at the expense of personal freedom.

autobiography: The account of a life written by its subject, generally a formal work, often published, in contrast to more intimate forms of life writing such as diary or memoir.

Axis: In World War II, the coalition of Germany, Italy, and Japan, with many allies worldwide.

Bolshevik Revolution (1917): Bolshevik-led takeover of Russian state by leftist revolutionaries in November 1917, followed by the era from 1917 through 1923 of establishment of power under head of state Vladimir Lenin.

Bolsheviks: Members of the radical Marxist political party, a faction of the Social Democratic Labor Party, which took over the Russian state in the revolution of November 1917.

bourgeoisie: A middling social group between the strata of workers and aristocracy, associated in the modern era with private-property interests in a capitalist economy.

Cheka: First Soviet secret police organization, which investigated alleged counter-revolutionary activity, responsible for the execution of many perceived enemies of the regime.

Civil War, American (1861–1865): Fought between northern and southern states of the United States over the institution of slavery and the preservation of the union.

Civil War, Russian (1918–1920): War fought between the Red (Bolshevik) and White (various counter-revolutionary and foreign interventionist) armies.

Civil War, Spanish (1936–1939): See Spanish Civil War.

collectivization: The coerced restructuring of agricultural production in the Soviet Union, especially between 1928 and 1933, in which the land of peasant proprietors was confiscated and all workers were forced to join collective farms.

Comintern (1919–1943): Abbreviation for the Communist International, or Third International, an organization committed to achieving worldwide communism.

communism: Political philosophy based on Marxist theory calling for the elimination of private property, concretized in the Soviet system in which the Communist Party controls all aspects of the economy, politics, and culture.

Communist Party: Political party advocating the political philosophy of Marxist-Leninism and its realization by revolutionary change and the institution of a strong state.

concentration camp: A fortified place where political prisoners, ethnic minorities, and members of other targeted groups are held under brutal conditions and subject to forced labor, punitive abuse, and sometimes mass extermination; especially associated with the Nazi regime from 1933–1945.

Crimean War (1853–1856): A war fought mainly between Great Britain, France, and the Ottoman Empire on one side, and Russia on the other, primarily concerning Russia's protectionist claims over Orthodox Christians in the Middle East.

D-Day (June 6, 1944): Day of Allied invasion of Normandy (France) and beginning of military march to Berlin and victory in World War II.

drama: A verse or prose composition telling a story through characters experiencing conflicts and reactions to the events described, usually intended for performance.

Easter Rising (1916): Irish rebellion against British rule during World War I, which began on Easter Monday (April 24) and lasted six days before it was brutally suppressed.

Enlightenment: A cultural movement affecting most European nations, characterized by confidence in reason as a guide to thought and action and in the progress of humankind, and advocating such values as religious tolerance, free speech, and constitutional government.

essay: A nonfiction composition, often informal and brief, offering an analysis or interpretation of a subject from a personal viewpoint.

existentialism: Twentieth-century philosophical theory that individuals are completely free agents who determine their own existence.

fascism: Political philosophy vaunting nation or race, concretized in an autocratic, dictatorial, and militarist regime repressive of opposition.

Final Solution: Nazi effort to exterminate European Jewry, to be realized in a network of concentration camps in Germany and Poland.

French Revolution (1789–1799): A revolution against monarchical rule that began with a liberal phase in 1789 focused on securing civil rights, becoming increasingly violent and repressive of dissent from 1792 to 1795, and ending finally with the overthrow of its leadership in 1799 by the consul, later emperor, Napoleon Bonaparte.

genocide: The targeted killing of a group of people, defined by such markers as ethnicity, nationality, or religion.

Great Purge (1936–1938): Also called "Great Terror"; Stalin's intense campaign to rid the Soviet leadership of persons with dissenting opinions or viewed as a threat to the regime, marked by show trials, executions, and deportations to punitive forced-labor camps.

Holocaust: The mass slaughter of European Jews by Nazi Germany, the goal of the planned Final Solution, effected in a network of concentration camps in Germany and Poland.

imperialism: The theory and practice of expanding a nation's dominion beyond its boundaries by territorial acquisition of other regions or by indirect control of their political, economic, and cultural life.

Industrial Revolution: In the eighteenth and nineteenth century, the shift from an economy based primarily on agriculture to one directed by industrial manufacturing, generating enormous social change and conflict.

journalism (genre): Nonfiction prose writing that attempts to convey a series of facts without interpretation to inform a public of ongoing events.

letter: A message directed to a person or group, often brief and informal, variously offering personal reflections, a narrative account, or an analysis of ideas or events.

lyric (poetry): The genre of poetry most often encountered in modern literature, often expressive of personal feelings or outlooks.

Marxism: Philosophical foundation of communism, elaborated in the works of Karl Marx and his collaborator Friedrich Engels, highlighting the value of labor, the inevitability of class struggle, and the dictatorship of the proletariat as a transitional phase before the achievement of a classless and stateless society.

memoir: A narrative of a series of events composed by the participant and based on personal experience; generally less formal than an autobiography.

Mexican Revolution (1910–1920): Protracted and violent struggle of competing factions, marked by exile and assassination, ending in the abolition of the prior dictatorship and the establishment of a constitutional republic in Mexico.

Mexican War of Independence (1810–1821): Inspired by the American and French Revolutions, a struggle in which colonial Mexico won its independence from Spain.

Modernism: A cultural movement of the late nineteenth to early twentieth century, in literature rejecting the understanding of the text as a nexus of words whose meaning is self-evident; involves the disruption of meaning, the indulgence in ambiguity and allusive references, and the proliferation of symbols.

Napoleonic era (1799–1815): Defined by the rise to power of Napoleon Bonaparte in 1799 and his ultimate defeat in 1815, during which time the consul, then emperor, imposed a new Civil Code in France and engaged in a series of wars to extend the principles of the French Revolution and French political dominance through much of Europe.

nationalism: An intense awareness of national identity, whether or not the nation exists as an autonomous state, accompanied by intense loyalty to the nation's people, culture, and goals.

Naturalism: An outlook that assumes the natural and material causation of all human events, and rejects any divine or spiritual intervention in human activity or consciousness.

Nazi: Abbreviation of National Socialist German Workers Party, German fascist political party in power 1933–1945, led by Adolf Hitler.

Nazism: Ideology and movement led by German Nazi party.

Nobel Peace Prize: Swedish prize awarded annually to persons of any nationality who have contributed notably to fraternity between nations, limitations on standing armies, and hosting of peace congresses; selected by a five-person committee appointed by the Norwegian Parliament.

Nobel Prize in Literature: Swedish prize awarded annually since 1901 to one or more authors from any country or countries for the excellence of the whole body of their work.

novel: An extended fictional prose narrative exploring the experience of characters impacted by a complex series of events.

October Revolution (1917): Bolshevik-led takeover of Russian state by leftist revolutionaries on November 7, 1917, equivalent to October 25 in the traditional Russian calendar. See also Bolshevik Revolution, Russian Revolution.

Old Bolsheviks: Unofficial designation of Russian politicians and theorists who had belonged to the Bolshevik Party prior to the 1917 revolution, of whom many were later persecuted under Stalin in the 1930s.

poetry: A form of imaginative writing that evokes a strong emotional response by the deliberate and concentrated use of language, meaning, images, and rhythm.

Puritanism: A religious reform movement of the sixteenth and seventeenth centuries, an outgrowth of the Calvinist strand of the Protestant Reformation, which flourished in England and was carried to the New England colonies of North America, where it had a lasting impact on culture, society, and politics.

race, racialism: For most of the authors represented in this volume, *race* means either the entirety of the human race, or it refers to a group of people identified by nation or religion: thus Poles or Spaniards (where *race* means *nation*), or Hindus or Muslims (where *race* means those embracing a particular religious faith). During this period (eighteenth to twentieth centuries), however, people of European descent had significant contact with two groups that today are often considered to constitute different races: those descended from Africans, often called black or Black; and the indigenous peoples of the Western hemisphere, often called Amerindians, Indians, or Native Americans, inhabiting South, Central, and North America, the last including the island systems of the Caribbean Sea. Index entries for "race, racialism" refer to this latter sense of race and its accompanying racial attitudes.

Realism: Following upon the Enlightenment's embrace of reason, an outlook that entails the close description, without idealization or exaggeration, of the actual people, events, and material objects that are immediately perceived.

Romanticism: A cultural movement repudiating the rationalism and secularism of the Enlightenment and affirming the importance of imagination, inspiration, and the passions.

Russian Revolution (1905): The wave of mass anti-government worker strikes, peasant uprisings, and military mutinies which, though suppressed, occasioned the institution of some constitutional reforms.

Russian Revolution (1917): Bolshevik-led takeover of Russian state by leftist revolutionaries in November, 1917, followed by the era from 1917 through 1923 of establishment of power under head of state Vladimir Lenin.

socialism: An economic or political system based on the public or collective ownership of the means of production, resulting in an equitable distribution of good and maximal social equality.

Soviet state: The communist state resulting from the Russian Revolution of 1917 until the establishment of the formal constitution of the Soviet Union in 1923.

Soviet Union: Short form for Union of Soviet Socialist Republics; socialist state existent 1923–1991, successor to the former Russian Empire following the Russian Revolution and Civil War; theoretically a federation of multiple soviet republics but actually highly centralized and dictatorial.

Spanish Civil War (1936–1939): Fierce conflict following a military coup, supported by conservatives, nationalists, and fascists, against the Second Spanish Republic, supported by an array of liberal, socialist, anarchist, and communist entities, with involvement by both Nazi and Soviet governments seemingly predictive of World War II.

speech: A prose composition generally delivered to an audience commenting on events or ideas of current interest, often seeking to motivate listeners to a particular action or understanding.

St. Petersburg: The city of St. Petersburg, Russia's cultural capital, founded by Tsar Peter the Great in the eighteenth century; renamed Petrograd from

1914 to 1924, and Leningrad from 1924 to 1991, when it was again renamed St. Petersburg.

story (short story): A brief fictional prose narrative exploring the thoughts or behavior of a limited group of characters involved in a series of events or problematic situations.

Sturm und Drang: The "storm and stress" movement of the 1770s, viewed as the first phase of German Romanticism.

Third International: See Comintern.

Thirty Years' War (1618–1648): Disastrous war involving France, Sweden, and the German states among others, devolving into a struggle for power in central Europe, and resulting in about eight million deaths, among them 20 percent of the German population; seen by some to prefigure the world wars of the twentieth century.

totalitarianism: A highly centralized and dictatorial system of government exercising total power over politics, culture, and private life.

treatise: Nonfiction, expository prose writing, formal in tone and methodical in approach, intended to analyze, interpret, or instruct an educated public about a specific matter.

Western Front: Main military theater during World War I, a 400-mile-plus line of parallel fortified trenches held by facing enemy forces, crossing through Belgium and France from the North Sea to the Swiss border.

World War I (1914–1918): War fought between the Entente powers (France, the United Kingdom, and Russia, joined late by the United States and other allies) and Central powers (Germany, Austria–Hungary, the Ottoman Empire, and Bulgaria, and their allies).

World War II (1939–1945): Global war fought between the Allied (principally the United Kingdom, the United States, and the Soviet Union) and Axis (principally Germany, Italy, and Japan) powers.

PREFACE TO VOLUME TWO

This volume introduces students to eighty literary texts of the Western tradition over the span of 250 years from 1700 to 1950. Highlighting significant themes and tracing prominent trends, it samples a range of genres, among them poetry, drama, short story, and the novel; and, in nonfiction prose, essay, letter, speech, treatise, journalism, and life writing, including autobiography and memoir.[1] Most major European languages are represented, including English, Danish, Dutch, French, German, Italian, Polish, Portuguese, Russian, Spanish, and Swedish. The authors—sixty-three male and seventeen female—come from the European nations where those languages are spoken and from American regions, northern and southern, of European settlement. Students may use this collection of eighty texts to familiarize themselves with the contours of the modern Western outlook and sensibility, while extending their knowledge of particular authors and problems by a collateral reading of full-length works as guided by their teachers.

Literature is affected by ongoing social, economic, and political development, as are the works included in this volume. In Volume Two, covering an era of rapid change, those developments include industrialization, nationalism, imperialism, abolitionism, and revolution. Although the primary emphasis is on the evolution of literary expression, this volume necessarily explores the impact upon it of these external dynamics—for literary creation never occurs in a vacuum, but always in relation to present contexts.

A unique intersection of literary activity and catastrophic political and military events occurred in the first half of the twentieth century. Chapter 8, the last in Volume Two, considers how fifteen authors are imbricated in these events, and respond to them in kaleidoscopic ways. It offers a wide array of voices, including some that were not in their time, or remain in ours, popular or congenial. They must not be excluded, for they, too, are part of the Western literary tradition.

Volume Two ends at about 1950: one year after the publication of the eightieth, and last text, George Orwell's *1984*, and eight years before the publication, in 1958, of Elie Wiesel's *Night*—a work based on the author's memory of wartime experiences in 1944–1945. After 1950, authors whose work lies within the Western tradition will continue, naturally, to publish. The literary landscape, however, becomes vastly more complex and inevitably global, as authors from other world regions address and grapple with Western culture

---

1. See the Glossary in this volume for definitions of these literary genres.

while at the same time, employing the theoretical approach known as post-colonialism, they criticize it from the vantage point of peoples who had been subjugated to European occupation or domination. The study of the later twentieth century and the first decades of the twenty-first constitute, therefore, an endeavor beyond the scope of this project.

SECTION I

Reason and Romanticism

Introduction to Section I

The modern era opens with the Enlightenment (the 1700s), which wielded the razor of reason against what were seen as the inherited prejudice and intolerance of earlier phases of Western culture.[1] It is followed quickly by the era of Romanticism (the 1770s to 1830s), a repudiation of Enlightenment rationalism and secularism. These cultural shifts play out against a background of volatile events both political—revolution, imperialism, nationalism; and economic—mercantilist competition and the first stages of industrialization.

The Enlightenment was an insurgent movement that pitted the Moderns against the Ancients, as the contestants were termed: the ancient past of classical authors, now to be superseded, and the recent past of religious conflict and abusive monarchical and ecclesiastical institutions. Writing in the prose genres of essay, letter, and treatise, and as poets, playwrights, storytellers, and novelists, Enlightenment authors challenge the validity of authoritative texts, ideologies, and personalities, seeking to dismantle, in tones often ironic and satiric and sometimes openly hostile, the stubborn fortress of tradition.

Chapter 1 of Section I presents eight such authors, writing mainly in English and French (just one in German), whose critical glance falls on state, church, and social and cultural norms. It opens with the satirist Jonathan Swift who offers a deliberately absurd solution for poverty in Ireland, then under English domination, and the aristocratic traveler Lady Mary Wortley Montagu, who finds some of the customs she observes in the Ottoman Empire not only admirable but, she implies, even superior to those at home. The French-speaking Swiss author Jean-Jacques Rousseau inquires into the cause of social inequality and finds that it is not rooted in nature, but is rather the creation of the selfish rich who deliberately deceive, and thereby subjugate the poor. The Frenchman Voltaire targets what he sees as the false ideology that God, or providence, works purposively to benefit humankind, ignoring the myriad natural, institutional, and personal agents inimical to human welfare. His contemporary Denis Diderot, also French, mocking the whole panoply of social and moral norms, advocates a cultural nihilism that, arguably, leads inevitably to paralysis.

---

1. See Glossary for important persons, events, places, and concepts that recur throughout Section I.

1

More optimistically, the German dramatist Gotthold Ephraim Lessing presents the case for religious toleration by denying the uniqueness and superiority of Christianity. Amid the first rumblings of the American Revolution, the Englishman Thomas Paine makes the case against Britain's right to control its North American colonies, and delineates a new American entity that will be grounded in freedom and offer asylum to the victims of European political and religious repression. The Englishwoman Mary Wollstonecraft, finally, takes up the defense of women: another group disadvantaged by contemporary institutions. Women have been enslaved, she argues, by a marriage system that makes them valuable only as prospective brides—only, therefore, if they are beautiful and the purveyors of paternal wealth—and as bearers of children.

Before long, a reaction set in against the corrosive approach of Enlightenment writers, who littered the cultural terrain with the detritus of their destructive critiques. That reaction was embodied in Romanticism, the cultural movement the Enlightenment called forth. The Romantics revered not reason, but imagination, inspiration, and the passions; they valued the power of nature over the discipline of reason, the spontaneity of the child over the adult, the mystic truths of religion over the encyclopedias and almanacs of compilers of fact, and the rootedness of human identity in nation and history rather than in the polite networks of salons and drawing rooms where Enlightenment wits vied to disparage the ideas and values they detested.

Chapter 2 of Section I presents works by twelve Romantic authors, writing from the 1770s to the 1830s in English, German, French, Italian, Polish, and Russian. The three English authors, all poets, emerged in the early years of that movement. William Blake, a professional engraver who copiously illustrated his own works, is represented here by ten of his forty-five *Songs of Innocence and Experience*, which offer contrasting views of nature and humanity while exploring the inner world of mind and feeling that lay at the core of Romanticism. William Wordsworth and Samuel Taylor Coleridge, sometime friends who collaborated on the important collection of *Lyrical Ballads* (1798), are represented here by the former's *Ode: Intimations of Immortality*, a celebration of childhood, and the latter's *Kubla Khan* and *Frost at Midnight*, celebrations, respectively, of the imagination and of nature.

Johann Wolfgang von Goethe and Friedrich von Schiller, predating these English authors, are among the leaders of the *Sturm und Drang* (storm and stress) movement of the 1770s, generally seen as the first phase of German Romanticism. Goethe's *The Sorrows of Young Werther*, narrating the experience, mostly in the first person, of a young man desperately in love, announces Romanticism's major themes: love, interiority, and nature. Schiller's early historical drama *Don Carlos* also focuses on a desperate lover, but delivers as well a plea for political liberation that will be heard in later nationalist literature. The poet Novalis, a third German author, articulates in his *Hymns to the Night* the virtual manifesto of Romanticism, juxtaposing the Night—the realm of imagination, love, and truth—against the Light—the dry, soulless rationalism, as Novalis viewed it, of the Enlightenment.

Chapter 2 next presents two French novelists. The first is Madame de Staël, whose *Delphine* not only celebrates the enduring love of the two young protagonists, but excoriates the legal institutions (an echo of Wollstonecraft) that restricted women from pursuing their own desires in love and marriage. The second is Victor Hugo, whose *The Hunchback of Notre Dame*, while it tells tales of hopeless and thwarted loves, even more strikingly, opposing the Enlightenment disdain for earlier eras, celebrates the medieval past of the city of Paris, concretized in its great Gothic cathedral, Notre Dame.

Next to be considered are two Italian authors: Giacomo Leopardi, with three of his *Canti* (*Poems*), and Alessandro Manzoni, with his acclaimed novel *The Betrothed*, often termed the most important Italian novel of the century. Both are noblemen (as was the German Novalis by birth, and both Goethe and Schiller by fiat), reflecting the dominance in that setting of an aristocracy that had acquired the immense inheritance of both classical and Renaissance culture. Both, too, are nationalists, although when they wrote, there was not yet an Italian nation: in a region of multiple states and a hodgepodge of dialects, they envisioned national and linguistic unification and liberation. And both write about love: Leopardi intimately, of his own feelings; and Manzoni, at a distance, as the narrator of a betrothed couple's struggle against malicious adversaries and natural calamities to achieve their longed-for marriage.

Nationalism was the overwhelming impetus to the poetic genius of Adam Mickiewicz, a Polish nobleman of Lithuanian ancestry, writing in a country whose political existence, by 1795, had been eradicated by its neighboring states. Considered the foremost Polish-Romantic author, Mickiewicz also writes powerfully about nature and the imagination. But superseding these is the pain of national loss and humiliation, felt in the two poems included here: his *Ode to Youth* and *To a Polish Mother*, summoning the younger generation to action and mothers to raise their sons for sacrifice.

The poet Alexander Pushkin, finally, generally considered the architect of Russian as a literary language, is represented by his short narrative poem, *The Bronze Horseman*. Unlike fragmented Italy or occupied Poland, Russia was a unified state under totalitarian rule; and although it is not the principal thrust of his poem, the figure of the Tsar Peter the Great, whose equestrian statue dominates a principal square of St. Petersburg, the city he built and named after himself, is certainly a ponderous presence. Still Pushkin does not criticize Tsar Peter—he could not, as he spent his entire career under the surveillance of the tsarist police. Yet the hero—or rather the antihero—of the poem, a dismal clerk, is destroyed by the combined force of violent nature and the indomitable horseman's statue.

Both the Enlightenment and Romanticism had immense consequence for the development of nineteenth-century culture. The Enlightenment would especially impact political, economic, and scientific thought, while Romanticism would shape the literary, philosophical, musical, and artistic currents of the nineteenth century and beyond. In tension with each other, together they constitute the pivotal moment in the birth of modernity.

Chapter 1

The Age of Reason

Introduction

Wedged between the English Revolution (1642–1688) of the previous century and the American (1775–1783) and French (1789–1799) Revolutions that capped their own, Enlightenment writers waged a cultural rebellion against inherited ideas and institutions, as did the eight authors appearing in this chapter. They critiqued the tyrannical state (Jonathan Swift, Thomas Paine; the British government in both cases), social injustice (Jean-Jacques Rousseau), cultural (Lady Mary Wortley Montagu, Denis Diderot) and religious (Voltaire, Gotthold Ephraim Lessing) norms, and male dominion over women (Mary Wollstonecraft). They did so in a range of genres—pamphlet (Swift, Paine), treatise (Rousseau, Wollstonecraft), letter (Montagu), drama (Lessing), and novel (Voltaire, Diderot)—and in tones ranging from satiric to defiant. In opposing nearly the whole of the cultural legacy of earlier times, the cohort of writers they represent opened up the modern age.

In his Latin epitaph, which he took care to compose some years before he died, Jonathan Swift (1667–1745) called himself a "valiant fighter for liberty" (*strenuum . . . vindicatorem libertatis*). And so he was; but his weapon was his pen. A Whig in his youth, he supported the Protestant monarchy against a Catholic resurgence; a Tory in his maturity, he was a member of the inner circle of Tory leadership and the editor of that party's newspaper, the *Examiner*; and Irish by birth, though of English lineage, and in his later years, though an ordained priest of the established Protestant church of Ireland resented by the native Catholic majority, he championed Irish causes against British rule.[1]

Swift was a prolific author of works in prose and verse—most published anonymously or under a pseudonym—filling nearly twenty volumes in modern editions. His most famous work is the novel *Gulliver's Travels* (1726), which in the guise of a travel narrative parodies the culture, society, and politics of contemporary England. He is represented here by his last major work, published in

---

1. England's Glorious Revolution (1688) had established a Protestant constitutional monarchy following the deposition of a Catholic king. The Whigs were the parliamentary party that achieved this end; their opponents were the Tories. England had ruled Ireland since the twelfth century, a dominion made harsher when, following the Reformation, England established its own Protestant Anglican Church in Ireland, while the Irish population remained largely Catholic.

1729, a brief pamphlet with a lengthy title: *A Modest Proposal for Preventing the Children of Poor People in Ireland from Being a Burden on Their Parents or Country, and for Making Them Beneficial to the Public.* In this bitterly satirical essay, a deadpan Swift (as an anonymous Proposer), proffers a solution for Irish over-population, a principal cause of that island's tenacious poverty: Irish mothers, he recommends, should be encouraged to sell their superfluous infants who, tastily seasoned and roasted, could supply the tables of the wealthy. All parties would benefit: Irish families would have fewer mouths to feed and a source of ready cash, and those able to pay for savory human flesh might enjoy a new delicacy while redressing a knotty social problem. The crisp rationality of his argument contrasts brilliantly with the gruesomeness of his proposed remedy, sure to electrify an audience already horrified by reports of cannibalism among New World natives. His point, unstated, is unmistakable: the British regime was already devouring Irish flesh.

Where Swift the satirist confronts the dire state of Ireland, the English-woman Lady Mary Wortley Montagu (1689–1762) explores Turkish customs as an instructive antithesis to European norms. The daughter of an aristocratic member of Parliament and the wife of another, she journeyed with her husband to the Ottoman Empire, an Islamic state on Europe's southeastern border, where he would serve as ambassador. His presence there indicated that the aggressive phase of Ottoman expansion that had extended from the fifteenth through the seventeenth centuries was over. Whereas the Ottoman Turks had been seen in those earlier times as ferocious invaders, they now presented to Western visitors an exotic social and cultural tableau inviting curious assessment and even imitation.

A self-taught classicist who had devoured the works of the Latin poet Ovid and translated those of the Greek philosopher Epictetus, Montagu was a prolific author of poems and letters, her correspondence from 1709 to 1762 filling three volumes in its 1837 edition. That correspondence includes her famous "embassy letters" of 1716–1718, often published separately, written when as a young wife and mother she accompanied her husband to Constantinople (now Istanbul), the Ottoman capital. Her letters, of which excerpts appear in this chapter, vividly describe the Turkish milieu, with a special focus on Turkish women, whose lives were both more restricted and less fettered than those of their English counterparts.

Just as Montagu suggests that Turkish women may in some ways fare better than their European contemporaries, the Swiss-born Francophone author Jean-Jacques Rousseau (1712–1778) suggests that human beings might do better to live in accord with nature rather than with reason. This is the provocative theme that runs through his many works: his discussions of politics and education, his novel *Julie, or the New Heloise*, and his autobiographical *Confessions*. Rousseau's elevation of nature over reason and related to it, his celebration of the passions, makes him an eccentric figure in an era that disliked eccentricity. An Enlightenment thinker in an age of reason, he wields the tool of reason to probe and reveal its limits.

In an important early work, the *Discourse on the Origin and Foundations of Human Inequality* (1754)—selections from which are given in this chapter—Rousseau persuasively argues that the progress of civilization, and the ever-expanding realm of rational thought, leads not to greater human well-being but rather to misery. The human journey, in fact, from its beginnings in a "state of nature"[2] to the present social and political order, traces a downward trajectory from freedom to corruption, dependency, and slavery. As human beings move from their original state into society—learning new skills, building complex relationships, and acquiring property—natural inequality, previously of little importance, explodes into social inequality, causing the subservience of some and the domination of others; these, driven by greed and ambition, set off in pursuit of property and power, reducing the unwitting many who have not seized those advantages to poverty and impotence. The dispossessed turn violently on their new masters, who respond in kind, triggering a "state of war." To settle it, the rich trick the multitude into accepting the rule of law, promising security and justice for all. The poor "[race] to meet their chains," the rich having succeeded in their scheme to subject "the whole human race to perpetual labor, servitude, and wretchedness."

While Rousseau challenges in the *Discourse on Inequality* the core Enlightenment notion of the superiority of modern to past times, Voltaire (born François-Marie Arouet; 1694–1778) confronts in his novel *Candide* (1759) an essential assumption of Christianity, the religion virtually coterminous with premodern European civilization: that God's providence, his benevolent governance of all of creation, is always active, even though evil exists. That assumption had recently been defended in the *Theodicy* (literally, "God's justice") of German philosopher Gottfried Wilhelm Leibniz (1646–1716), whose message Voltaire distorts somewhat and utterly eviscerates. *Candide* bears the subtitle "or Optimism," for that is what it is about: the absurdity of an optimistic outlook in a world gone so horribly wrong and the absurdity, specifically, of Leibniz's optimistic defense in the face of conspicuous evil, of God's benevolence—an argument Voltaire sums up devastatingly in the recurrent pronouncement that "all is for the best in this best of all possible worlds."

This is the message taught the young hero Candide by his tutor and mentor Dr. Pangloss, a man learned in "all tongues," as his name declares, and all branches of philosophy. In his many adventures, Candide finds out how

---

2. "state of nature": In *Discourse on Inequality*, Rousseau elaborates upon, and really inverts, the notions of the "state of nature" and, below, the "state of war," that had earlier been key points in the political theories of seventeenth-century English thinkers Thomas Hobbes and John Locke.

wrong Pangloss is: he is wounded in the Seven Years' War (1756–1763); nearly drowned in the tsunami raised by the catastrophic Lisbon earthquake of 1755, as told in the excerpt given here; tortured by the Inquisition; nearly killed many times on his journeys through South America and Europe and on to the Ottoman Empire. All the while Candide searches for his first love Cunegonde, now hideously deformed, whom he rescues more than once and settles with at last, together with Pangloss and his other companions. Exhausted by all they have suffered, they are now intent only on the cultivation of the little farm that is their last refuge—"we must cultivate our garden," Candide famously concludes.

Voltaire's war against Leibniz is of a piece with his larger vision. Standing at the midpoint of the Enlightenment era, he is, arguably, its voice, his message summing up all the rest: impatience with unjust authority, superstition, and triviality; a strike for freedom of thought, speech, and worship; a reevaluation of the past and new orientation toward the future; and a hatred, above all, of the institutions that burden and torment the human spirit, especially the Catholic Church, but a few others as well. Ranging over every inch of the cultural universe in seven-league boots, he is not deep or difficult (he is a *philosophe*, as Enlightenment figures termed themselves,[3] not a systematic philosopher), but quick, ruthless, and entertaining. *Ecrasez l'infâme!* ("Crush that infamous thing!") is his famous watchword.

Voltaire's indictment of "that infamous thing" is angry and brash. In his play *Nathan der Weise* (*Nathan the Wise*), the German writer Gotthold Ephraim Lessing (1729–1781) employs a quieter tone to level a neat blow against Christian hegemony which, even though splintered in Protestant and Catholic institutions as it had been since the Reformation, was still the dominant cultural ideology, supported by the state and administered by an entrenched and privileged bureaucracy. Demonstrating to his audience the equivalence of the three world theisms—Christianity, Judaism, and Islam—Lessing goes further than the plea for tolerance and skepticism that the deist Voltaire had made: Lessing's argument decenters Christianity, and indeed religion, within the cultural sphere.

A poet, philosopher, and literary critic, Lessing is known especially for his many plays—the first of which was written in 1748, when he was nineteen years old—and his *Laocoön, An Essay on the Limits of Painting and Poetry* (1767). *Nathan the Wise* was one of his last works, published two years before his death, and first performed posthumously in Berlin in 1783. Its hero Nathan is modeled on Lessing's close friend, the Jewish philosopher Moses Mendelssohn, who led German Jewry into the cultural mainstream of the Enlightenment.

---

3. *philosophe*: French for "philosopher," although the *philosophes* were thinkers who considered questions of aesthetics, politics, and moral philosophy in works geared to a general reading public. The term is applied, as well, to both Rousseau and Diderot.

Set in exotic twelfth-century Jerusalem during the Third Crusade, inscribed in iambic pentameters modeled after Shakespeare's, *Nathan the Wise* is a celebration of good people of all kinds: the Muslim ruler Saladin and his brothers and sisters, dead and alive; a heroic knight Templar and a kindly friar; an adopted daughter and her loyal companion; and the generous, wise, and wealthy Nathan, a deeply decent man who happens to be a Jew. A momentary confusion entangling Christians, Jews, and Muslims is sorted out by the closing scene of the play, when all are united in a harmonious, familial whole. That is the ecumenical message of the play and of the famous scene at its center, when Nathan tells Saladin the story of the three rings, excerpted here. A story that had circulated for centuries before this retelling, which had been featured by the Renaissance author Giovanni Boccaccio (see Volume One, Chapter 7, Text 3) among the one hundred stories of the *Decameron*, it argues that Christianity, Judaism, and Islam—minor and trivial points of doctrine aside—are essentially indistinguishable, the superior truth of any one of them never to be determined.

The *philosophe* Denis Diderot (1713–1784) would likely have dismissed as impossible, as well as unnecessary, the notion of any superior truth. Diderot is especially famous as the principal editor of the *Encyclopedia*, a compilation of more than seventy thousand articles on all areas of learning including the natural sciences and practical arts, published between 1751 and 1772, by which latter date it totaled twenty-eight volumes. His own contributions to the *Encyclopedia* fill three volumes of the more than twenty of his published works. In the others are his correspondence, his essays on many subjects, and his novels—for like Voltaire and Rousseau, he wrote fiction alongside his other endeavors. Like many of Diderot's works, *Rameau's Nephew*, which he began to compose in 1761/1762 and continued to revise thereafter, was not published in his lifetime. Indeed, its publication in the form it left his hand was delayed for more than a century. One manuscript, since lost, was transferred on his death, as he had arranged, to Catherine the Great of Russia. A copy of that original reached the German author Johann Wolfgang von Goethe (see Chapter 2, Text 4), who translated and published it in German in 1805, a version then retranslated into French and published in 1821. In 1891, another manuscript, an authoritative autograph in the original French, was adventitiously discovered and subsequently served as the basis of the modern critical edition published in 1950.

Diderot was the *philosophe* most subversive of the contemporary order, and he often suffered for transgressing cultural norms. *Rameau's Nephew*, one of several he allowed to circulate only to an intimate circle of friends, was apparently too incendiary a work to bring to light while he still lived. It is a fictive dialogue between a narrator identified only as *Moi* (Me or Myself), who should not be assumed to be Diderot himself; and an interlocutor identified only as *Lui* (He or Him), characterized as odd and eccentric, a parasite who circulates in Parisian high society, cadging dinners and seducing women while engaging flamboyantly in conversations on ideas, personalities, and the arts—especially music; he is a musician, and the nephew, as the title informs us, of the great composer and musicologist Jean-Philippe Rameau (1683–1764). This intriguing but repellent character denigrates everything—philosophical truth, intellectual merit, musical and dramatic performance, the duty to meet one's obligations and educate one's children—and claims to value only wealth, status, and pleasure. His preferences and aversions are pronounced in a torrent of words responding at times, but in no orderly way, to the questions posed to him by Myself. Diderot presents, in effect, the portrait of a nihilist: an inhabitant of the age of reason who defies the standard of reason; a character, and a novel, that is hard to like and hard to forget.

When speaking through his character He, Diderot was a cultural revolutionary: intent on dismantling conventions, customs, and traditions. Thomas Paine (1737–1809) was committed to political revolution, a cause he advocated in the British colonies in America against the king of England, and later, straddling the two great political eruptions of the late eighteenth century, in France against that nation's king and government. He fought two revolutions by the force of his pen, employing language that was fresh, provocative, and highly effective.

Son of a Quaker father and Anglican mother, Paine received only an elementary schooling in his native England. In 1774, he arrived in America on the cusp of the revolution that he would promote and celebrate. It took him only two years to identify fully with the American colonial insurgency against imperial Britain. In January 1776—at the midpoint of the interlude between the battles of Lexington and Concord in April 1775 and the ratification of the *Declaration of Independence* on July 4, 1776—the pamphlet *Common Sense* appeared, or rather exploded, into print, its authorship attributed to "Tom Paine, an Englishman." Paine's pamphlet, running to seventy-nine pages in its third edition (February 1776), not only presented a logical case for American independence, drawing on the wellsprings of Enlightenment thought supported by historical and biblical example, but couched it in scintillating language: it is virtually a prose poem. It argues the fundamental injustice of hereditary monarchy, calling for a new political entity where the law, and not an individual, is king; the greater commercial prospects of the American colonies once they were freed from Britain's mercantilist regulations; the difficulty of communication across the Atlantic; and the role of America as an "asylum for mankind," a place offering freedom and opportunity to emigrants from all over Europe.

Paine was prescient, foreseeing not only an independent United States but identifying many of its enduring ideals. His other works—notably the pamphlet series, *The Crisis* (1776–1783), written during the American struggle, and *The Rights of Man* (1791–1792) and *The Age of Reason* (1794–1807), on the French Revolution—similarly disseminated Enlightenment political and religious ideas; but none equaled *Common Sense* in immediate and long-term impact.

Mary Wollstonecraft (1759–1797) was a revolutionary as well: a supporter of the political revolution in France, which she had witnessed firsthand; and a fierce advocate of women's rights. No sooner had the English statesman Edmund Burke published *Reflections on the Revolution in France* (1790), his famous critique of the French Revolution, Wollstonecraft responded to Burke in *A Vindication of the Rights of Men* (1790). She followed it up promptly with her most famous work, its complementary feminist manifesto, the *A Vindication of the Rights of Woman* (1792). It is a foundational text of the modern feminist movement.

Wollstonecraft's message was not, in fact, new. Her assumption of women's moral and intellectual equality with men had already been argued by women authors of the fifteenth through seventeenth centuries (see especially Volume One, Introduction to Chapter 13), as had been their aptitude for advanced education; and their capacity as writers and thinkers had been demonstrated in many works of prose and verse—however much their writings had often been ignored. Even her focus on marriage, an institution in service to dynastic strategies for property accumulation that necessarily limited women's freedom of choice and potential for growth, had been anticipated a century earlier by the stalwart Anglican and Tory thinker Mary Astell.[4] But Wollstonecraft's contribution is significant: she not only develops these views in a lengthy (if rambling) and impassioned manifesto couched in the rhetoric of the Enlightenment, but she also links them explicitly to the political revolution then underway—her "vindication of the rights of woman," after all, announced in her title, explicitly references the key document of the French Revolution, the *Declaration of the Rights of Man*.

The daughter of a violent father, the patriarch of her downwardly mobile middle-class family, Wollstonecraft was vividly aware of the predicament faced by women in a society governed by men for their financial and sexual advantage. She was an early supporter of women's education, working first as a governess in private employ and then as the head of a school for girls. Later, she moved to London and flourished in its literary circles, writing essays, treatises, and novels. Engaged notoriously in two affairs and giving birth to an illegitimate child, at the late age of thirty-eight Wollstonecraft married the man by whom she was pregnant, the English political thinker William Godwin. Months later, she died giving birth to their daughter, the future Mary Shelley, author of *Frankenstein*. Wollstonecraft's unconventional marital and sexual life was itself a comment on the traditional system of marriage.

---

4. In *A Serious Proposal to the Ladies* (1694) and *Some Reflections Upon Marriage* (1700), among other works.

In Wollstonecraft's *A Vindication of the Rights of Woman*, the political liberalism that she espoused in her *Rights of Men* expands into a broad and assertive feminism. She assails a marriage system that confines and infantilizes women and rears them to value only beauty and trinkets, and to trade a brief moment of glory during their youth, as they experience courtship and marriage, for later decades of tedium, constraint, and subordination.

1. Jonathan Swift, *A Modest Proposal* (1729)

Swift—as the anonymous Proposer—deplores as a "melancholy object" the plight of the poor mothers seen begging in the streets of Dublin with "three, four, or six children" for whom they are unable to provide. He argues that a "fair, cheap, and easy method" should be found for making these uncared-for children useful to society. He calculates the number of children born each year for whom provision must be made (after some twenty thousand are set aside to propagate the species) to be one hundred thousand. The solution is for the mothers to sell them once they have been weaned, at which point, having been adequately fed by their mothers' milk, they will be plump and ready for consumption. The payment received from wealthy buyers will assist the parents who have sold infants to pay their rent and provide for their remaining children. Granted, infant flesh will be rather expensive, yet affordable by English landlords who, Swift mordantly observes, "as they have already devoured most of the parents, seem to have the best title to the children."

A Modest Proposal

A Modest Proposal for Preventing the Children of Poor People in Ireland from Being a Burden on Their Parents or Country, and for Making Them Beneficial to the Public

It is a melancholy object to those who walk through this great town, or travel in the country, when they see the streets, the roads and cabin-doors crowded with beggars of the female sex, followed by three, four, or six children, all in rags, and importuning every passenger [passerby] for alms. These mothers, instead of being able to work for their honest livelihood, are forced to employ all their time in strolling to beg sustenance for their helpless infants who, as they grow up, either turn thieves for want of work, or leave their dear native country to fight for the Pretender[5] in Spain, or sell themselves to the Barbados.[6]

---

5. Pretender: a son of the former English king James II, deposed in the Glorious Revolution of 1688; James's supporters hoped he would regain the throne.

6. Barbados: at this time, a British colony in the West Indies.

I think it is agreed by all parties that this prodigious number of children in the arms, or on the backs, or at the heels of their mothers, and frequently of their fathers, is in the present deplorable state of the kingdom a very great additional grievance; and therefore whoever could find out a fair, cheap, and easy method of making these children sound and useful members of the commonwealth[7] would deserve so well of the public as to have his statue set up for a preserver of the nation.

But my intention is very far from being confined to provide only for the children of professed beggars: it is of a much greater extent, and shall take in the whole number of infants at a certain age who are born of parents in effect as little able to support them as those who demand our charity in the streets.

As to my own part, having turned my thoughts for many years upon this important subject, and maturely weighed the several schemes of our projectors [policy-makers], I have always found them grossly mistaken in their computation. It is true that a [newborn] child . . . may be supported by [a mother's] milk for a solar year with little other nourishment . . . ; and it is exactly at one year old that I propose to provide for them in such a manner, as, instead of being a charge upon their parents, . . . or wanting food and raiment for the rest of their lives, they shall, on the contrary, contribute to the feeding and partly to the clothing of many thousands.

There is likewise another great advantage in my scheme, that it will prevent those voluntary abortions, and that horrid practice of women murdering their bastard children, alas! too frequent among us, sacrificing the poor innocent babes I doubt [suspect] more to avoid the expense than the shame, which would move tears and pity in the most savage and inhuman breast.

The number of souls in this kingdom being usually reckoned one million and a half, of these I calculate there may be about two hundred thousand couples whose wives are breeders;[8] from which number I subtract thirty thousand couples, who are able to maintain their own children, . . . there will remain one hundred and seventy thousand breeders. I again subtract fifty thousand for those women who miscarry, or whose children die by accident or disease within the year. There only remain one hundred and twenty thousand children of poor parents annually born. The question therefore is how this number shall be reared, and provided for? which, as I have already said, under the present situation of affairs, is utterly impossible by all the methods hitherto proposed. For we can neither employ them in handicraft or agriculture; they neither build houses . . . nor cultivate lands; they can very seldom pick up a livelihood by stealing till they arrive at six years old. . . .

---

7. commonwealth: the republic, or as here, the nation.
8. breeders: able to bear children.

I shall now therefore humbly propose my own thoughts, which I hope will not be liable to the least objection.

I have been assured by a very knowing American of my acquaintance in London, that a young healthy child, well-nursed, is, at a year old, a most delicious nourishing and wholesome food, whether stewed, roasted, baked, or boiled; and I make no doubt that it will equally serve in a fricassee, or a ragout.[9]

I do therefore humbly offer it to public consideration, that of the hundred and twenty thousand children already computed, twenty thousand may be reserved for breeding; . . . [but] that the remaining hundred thousand may, at a year old, be offered in sale to the persons of quality and fortune through the kingdom, always advising the mother to let them suck plentifully in the last month, so as to render them plump and fat for a good table. A child will make two dishes at an entertainment for friends, and when the family dines alone, the fore or hind quarter will make a reasonable dish, and seasoned with a little pepper or salt, will be very good boiled on the fourth day, especially in winter. . . .

I grant this food will be somewhat dear [expensive], and therefore very proper for landlords, who, as they have already devoured most of the parents, seem to have the best title to the children. . . . I have already computed the charge of nursing a beggar's child . . . to be about two shillings[10] per annum,[11] rags included; and I believe no gentleman would repine [hesitate] to give ten shillings for the carcass of a good fat child, which, as I have said, will make four dishes of excellent nutritive meat, when he has only some particular friend, or his own family to dine with him. Thus the squire will learn to be a good landlord, and grow popular among his tenants, the mother will have eight shillings neat profit, and be fit for work till she produces another child. . . . As to our city of Dublin, shambles [slaughterhouses] may be appointed for this purpose, in the most convenient parts of it, and butchers we may be assured will not be wanting. . . .

After a digression, Swift lays out the main benefits of his plan.

I think the advantages by the proposal which I have made are obvious and many, as well as of the highest importance.

For first, as I have already observed, it would greatly lessen the number of papists,[12] with whom we are yearly overrun, being the principal breeders of the nation, as well as our most dangerous enemies. . . .

---

9. fricassee . . . ragout: meat served in a sauce or highly seasoned stew.

10. shillings: Swift gives monetary values in traditional British units of shillings and, below, pounds sterling.

11. per annum: per year.

12. papists: a derogatory term for Catholics, who were the great majority of the Irish population.

Secondly, the poorer tenants will have something valuable of their own, which . . . [may] help to pay their landlord's rent, their corn[13] and cattle being already seized,[14] and money a thing unknown.

Thirdly, whereas the maintenance of a hundred thousand children, from two years old and upwards cannot be computed at less than ten shillings apiece per annum, the nation's stock will be thereby increased fifty thousand pounds per annum, besides the profit of a new dish, introduced to the tables of all gentlemen of fortune in the kingdom, who have any refinement in taste. . . .

Fourthly, the constant breeders, besides the gain of eight shillings sterling per annum by the sale of their children, will be rid of the charge of maintaining them after the first year.

Fifthly, this food would likewise bring great custom[15] to taverns, where the vintners [proprietors] will certainly be so prudent as to procure the best receipts [recipes] for dressing it to perfection; and consequently have their houses frequented by all the fine gentlemen who justly value themselves upon their knowledge in good eating. . . .

Sixthly, this would be a great inducement to marriage, which all wise nations have either encouraged by rewards or enforced by laws and penalties. It would increase the care and tenderness of mothers towards their children when they were sure of a settlement for life to the poor babes, provided in some sort by the public, to their annual profit instead of expense. We should soon see an honest emulation [competition] among the married women, which of them could bring the fattest child to the market. Men would become as fond of their wives during the time of their pregnancy as they are now of their mares in foal, their cows in calf, or sow when they are ready to farrow; nor offer [dare] to beat or kick them (as is too frequent a practice) for fear of a miscarriage. . . .

I can think of no one objection that will possibly be raised against this proposal, unless it should be urged that the number of people will be thereby much lessened in the kingdom. This I freely own, and it was indeed one principal design [intention] in offering it to the world. . . .

But, as to myself, having been wearied out for many years with offering vain, idle, visionary thoughts, and at length utterly despairing of success, I fortunately fell upon this proposal, which, as it is wholly new, so it has something solid and real, of no expense and little trouble, full in our own power, and whereby we can incur no danger in disobliging England.[16] For this kind of commodity will not bear exportation, and flesh being of too tender a consistency to admit a long continuance in salt.[17] . . .

---

13. corn: wheat and, in this sense, other agricultural products.

14. seized: that is, by the landlords for payment of the rent.

15. great custom: many customers.

16. disobliging England: arousing the opposition of the English by creating an export that would compete with their own commodities.

17. Infant flesh would not be suited to salting for preservation and export.

After all, I am not so violently bent upon my own opinion as to reject any offer, proposed by wise men, which shall be found equally innocent, cheap, easy, and effectual. But before something of that kind shall be advanced in contradiction to my scheme, and offering a better, I desire the author or authors will be pleased maturely to consider two points. First, as things now stand, how they will be able to find food and raiment for a hundred thousand useless mouths and backs. And secondly, there being a round million of creatures in human figure[18] throughout this kingdom, whose whole subsistence put into a common stock would leave them in debt two million of pounds sterling, adding those who are beggars by profession to the bulk of farmers, cottagers and laborers, with their wives and children, who are beggars in effect; I desire those politicians who dislike my overture, and may perhaps be so bold to attempt an answer, that they will first ask the parents of these mortals, whether they would not at this day think it a great happiness to have been sold for food at a year old, in the manner I prescribe, and thereby have avoided such a perpetual scene of misfortunes as they have since gone through by the oppression of landlords, the impossibility of paying rent without money or trade, the want of common sustenance, . . . or greater miseries, upon their breed forever.

I profess, in the sincerity of my heart, that I have not the least personal interest in endeavoring to promote this necessary work, having no other motive than the public good of my country, by advancing our trade, providing for infants, relieving the poor, and giving some pleasure to the rich. I have no children by which I can propose to get a single penny; the youngest being nine years old, and my wife past childbearing.

2. Lady Mary Wortley Montagu, *Embassy Letters* (1716–1718)

In the three letters written on April 1, 1717, from which excerpts appear below, Montagu introduces her female correspondents in England to her impressions of life in the Ottoman Empire. In the first letter, she describes an all-female bath-house, a space where women could speak and relax among themselves—one of a sort unavailable to Englishwomen, whose gatherings were tightly bound by social conventions. In the second, she details not only what garments Turkish women wore, but notes the freedom to venture upon secret affairs that their concealing dress afforded Ottoman ladies. In the third, famously, she reports on the Turkish practice of vaccination against smallpox, pursued in domestic settings and administered by untrained female healers—a practice that she would

---

18. creatures in human figure: human beings.

bring back to England. She displays a remarkable openness to Turkish customs that are wholly foreign to her experience as an English aristocrat. "The Turkish ladies don't commit one sin the less for not being Christian," Montagu writes slyly with a tangle of negatives about women engulfed in robes designed to ensure their modesty, but which instead, by ensuring anonymity, permit their illicit sexual ventures.

EMBASSY LETTERS

To the Lady ————
Adrianople, April 1, 1717

I am now got into a new world, where everything I see appears to me a change of scene; and I write to your ladyship with some content of mind, hoping at least that you will find the charm of novelty in my letters, and no longer reproach me that I tell you nothing extraordinary.

I won't trouble you with a relation of our tedious journey; but I must not omit what I saw remarkable at Sophia [modern Sofia, Bulgaria], one of the most beautiful towns in the Turkish empire, and famous for its hot baths, that are resorted to both for diversion and health. I stopped here one day on purpose to see them. Designing to go *incognita* [unseen], I hired a Turkish coach. . . . They are covered all over with scarlet cloth, lined with silk, and very often richly embroidered and fringed. This covering entirely hides the persons in them, but may be thrown back at pleasure, and the ladies peep through the lattices. . . .

In one of these covered wagons, I went to the *bagnio* [bath house] about ten o'clock. It was already full of women. It is built of stone, in the shape of a dome, with no windows but in the roof, which gives light enough. There were five of these domes joined together, the outermost being less than the rest, and serving only as a hall, where the porteress stood at the door. . . .

The next room is a very large one paved with marble, and all round it, raised, two sofas of marble, one above another. There were four fountains of cold water in this room, falling first into marble basins, and then running on the floor in little channels made for that purpose, which carried the streams into the next room, . . . with the same sort of marble sofas, but so hot with steams of sulfur proceeding from the baths adjoining it, it was impossible to stay there with one's clothes on. The two other domes were the hot baths, one of which had cocks [pipes controlled by valves] of cold water turning into it, to temper it to what degree of warmth the bathers have a mind to.

I was in my traveling habit, which is a riding dress, and certainly appeared very extraordinary to them. Yet there was not one of them that showed the least surprise or impertinent curiosity, but received me with all the obliging civility possible. I know no European court where the ladies would have behaved themselves in so polite a manner to a stranger. I believe in all there were two hundred women, and yet none of those disdainful smiles, or satiric whispers, that never fail in our assemblies when anybody appears that is not dressed exactly in the fashion. . . .

The first sofas were covered with cushions and rich carpets, on which sat the ladies; and on the second, their slaves behind them, but without any distinction of rank by their dress, all being in the state of nature, that is, in plain English, stark naked, without any beauty or defect concealed. Yet there was not the least wanton smile or immodest gesture among them. . . . There were many amongst them as exactly proportioned as any goddess . . . and most of their skins shiningly white, only adorned by their beautiful hair divided into many tresses, hanging on their shoulders, braided either with pearl or ribbon. . . .

I was here convinced of the truth of a reflection I had often made, that if it was the fashion to go naked, the face would be hardly observed. I perceived that the ladies with the finest skins and most delicate shapes had the greatest share of my admiration, though their faces were sometimes less beautiful than those of their companions. . . .

They generally take this diversion once a week, and stay there at least four or five hours. . . . The lady that seemed the most considerable among them entreated me to sit by her, and was ready to undress me for the bath. I excused myself with some difficulty. They being all so earnest in persuading me, I was at last forced to open my shirt, and show them my stays [corset]; which satisfied them very well for, I saw, they believed I was so locked up in that machine, that it was not in my own power to open it, which contrivance they attributed to my husband. I was charmed with their civility and beauty, and should have been very glad to pass more time with them. . . .

Adieu, madam: I am sure I have now entertained you with an account of such a sight as you never saw in your life, and what no book of travels could inform you of. It is no less than death for a man to be found in one of these places.

To the Countess of —————
Adrianople, April 1, 1717

I wish to God, dear sister, that you were as regular in letting me have the pleasure of knowing what passes on your side of the globe, as I am careful in endeavoring to amuse you . . . by giving you a full and true relation of the novelties of this place, none of which would surprise you more than a sight of my person, as I am now in my Turkish habit, though I believe you would be of my opinion, that it is admirably becoming. I intend to send you my picture; in the meantime, accept it here.

The first piece of my dress is a pair of drawers [long underpants], very full, that reach to my shoes, and conceal the legs more modestly than your petticoats. They are of a thin rose-colored damask, brocaded with silver flowers, my shoes of white kid leather, embroidered with gold. Over this hangs my smock [slip] of a fine white silk gauze, edged with embroidery. This smock has wide sleeves, hanging half way down the arm, and is closed at the neck with a diamond button. . . . My caftan, of the same stuff [fabric] with my drawers, is a robe exactly fitted to my shape, and reaching to my feet, with very long strait falling sleeves. Over this is the girdle [belt] of about four fingers broad, which all that can afford have entirely of diamonds or other precious stones. . . . The headdress is composed of a cap . . . which is in winter of fine velvet embroidered with pearls or diamonds, and in summer of a light shining silver stuff. This is fixed on one side of the head, hanging a little way down with a gold tassel, and bound on either with a circle of diamond (as I have seen several) or a rich embroidered handkerchief. . . .

As to their morality or good conduct, I can say . . . the Turkish ladies don't commit one sin the less for not being Christian. . . . It is very easy to see they have more liberty than we have. No woman, of whatever rank, is permitted to go into the street without two muslins [veils]: one that covers her face all but her eyes, and another that hides the whole dress of her head, and half way down her back; and their shapes are wholly concealed by a thing they call a *ferigee*, which no woman of any sort appears without. . . . You may guess how effectually this disguises them, so that there is no distinguishing the great lady from her slave. It is impossible for the most jealous husband to know his wife when he meets her; and no man dare either touch or follow a woman in the street. This perpetual masquerade gives them entire liberty of following their inclinations without danger of discovery. . . .

To Miss Sarah Chiswell
Adrianople, April 1, 1717

In my opinion, dear Sarah, I ought rather to quarrel with you for not answering my . . . letter of August till December, than to excuse my not writing again till now. I am sure there is on my side a very good excuse for silence. . . .

A propos of distempers [illnesses], I am going to tell you a thing that I am sure will make you wish yourself here. The smallpox, so fatal, and so general amongst us, is here entirely harmless by the invention of engrafting, which is the term they give it. There is a set of old women who make it their business to perform the operation every autumn, in the month of September, when the great heat is abated. People send to one another to know if any of their family has a mind to have the smallpox; they make parties for this purpose, and when they are met (commonly fifteen or sixteen together), the old woman comes with a nutshell full of the matter of the best sort of smallpox, and asks what veins you please to have opened. She immediately rips open that you offer to her with a large needle (which gives you no more pain than a common scratch), and puts into the vein as much venom as can lie upon the head of her needle, and after binds up the little wound with a hollow bit of shell; and in this manner opens four or five veins. . . .

The children or young patients play together all the rest of the day, and are in perfect health to the eighth. Then the fever begins to seize them, and they keep [to] their beds two days, very seldom three. They have very rarely above twenty or thirty [lesions] in their faces, which never mark; and in eight days' time they are as well as before their illness. Where they are wounded, there remain running sores during the distemper [illness], which I don't doubt is a great relief to it. Every year thousands undergo this operation; and the French ambassador says pleasantly, that they take the smallpox here by way of diversion, as they take the waters in other countries. There is no example of any one that has died in it; and you may believe I am very well satisfied of the safety of the experiment, since I intend to try it on my dear little son.

I am patriot enough to take pains to bring this useful invention into fashion in England; and I should not fail to write to some of our doctors very particularly about it, if I knew any one of them that I thought had virtue enough to destroy such a considerable branch of their revenue for the good of mankind. But that distemper [illness] is too beneficial to them not to expose to all their resentment the hardy wight [person] that should undertake to put an end to it. Perhaps, if I live to return, I may, however, have courage to war with them. . . .

3. Jean-Jacques Rousseau, *Discourse on the Origin and Foundations of Human Inequality* (1754)

Social inequality is not a natural human condition, according to Rousseau, but emerges in historical time. In the immense span of early history, when, as he sees it, there was scarcely any development of human society or culture, the human being lived alone, unknowing, and unattached, not recognizing even his own children, existing simply to fulfill his simple needs. Inequality begins to emerge in that state of nature with the invention of the arts, especially, of metallurgy and agriculture. At this point, the ownership of property begins as well, and with it, inevitably, human inequality. The possessors and the dispossessed devolve into the nightmarish state of war that Thomas Hobbes and John Locke had imagined. At last, the rich, seeking to secure their wealth, undertake "the most cunning project ever to enter the human mind": they convince the desperate and predatory multitude to agree to the establishment of a state that—as the rich deceitfully promise—would be governed by just laws and would protect all equally. The gullible masses accept the bait, "rac[ing] to meet their chains," their liberty irretrievably lost, their perpetual enslavement ensured.

DISCOURSE ON THE ORIGIN AND FOUNDATIONS OF HUMAN INEQUALITY

Introduction

I conceive of two kinds of inequality in the human species: one that I call natural or physical, because it is established by nature, and consists in the difference of age, health, the strength of the body, and qualities of mind or soul; the other that may be called moral or political inequality, because it depends on some sort of convention . . . that other people have authorized. This consists in the different privileges that some may enjoy more than others, such as being wealthier, more respected, or more powerful, so compelling others to obedience. . . .

What then is the purpose of this *Discourse*? To mark that moment in the progress of things when, law putting an end to violence, nature was subjected to law; and to explain by what amazing chain of events the strong agreed to serve the weak, and people bought an imaginary peace at the cost of real contentment. . . .

My friend, from whatever country you come, whatever you may think, listen. Here is your history as I believe it can be read not in those books like those you have, which lie, but in nature itself, which never lies. . . . I shall speak to you of a time long gone. How much you have changed from what you were!

Part One

Rousseau depicts the life of human beings in a state of nature, a wilderness in which only the simplest wants are satisfied, and the instinct for self-preservation is moderated by a natural compassion for others.

And so we see the human being in a state of nature, wandering through the forests, without tools, without speech, without a home, without war, without ties, and with no need of these, and with no desire to have them . . . ; subject to few passions and sufficient to himself, having nothing but the feelings and the thoughts proper to his condition, sensing only his true needs, noting only what he cared to see. . . . If he chanced to make some discovery, he could not communicate it, as he did not know even his own children. Art perished with its inventor, there being no transmission of knowledge nor progress, as generations replicated themselves; for each one beginning at the same point, the ages rolled on each with all the rudeness of those that came before. The species had already grown old, while the human being was still an infant. . . .

In this unchanging state of nature, there was little inequality among humans.

After having proved that inequality is barely noticeable in the state of nature, and that its influence is virtually null, it now remains for me to reveal the origin of inequality, and its progress in the successive developments of the human mind . . . , [considering] the accidental changes that, while they advanced human reason, debased the species, achieving, in adapting him to society, the corruption of the human being, and so bring both the world and humankind from that time long ago to the point where we see them now.

Part Two

The first person who, having enclosed a plot of land, had a mind to say "This is mine," and found people simple enough to believe him, was the true founder of civil society. How many crimes, wars, and murders, how much misery and horror would he have spared humankind who, tearing down the fence or filling the ditch, had cried to his companions: "Do not listen to this imposter! You are lost if you forget that the fruits of the earth belong to all, but the earth to no one!" But it seems certain that things had already come to that point where they could not continue as before: for the idea of property depends on many earlier notions that could only have emerged over time, and was not formed all at once in the human mind. . . .

Rousseau traces the development of a more complex society within the state of nature.

So long as people were content with their rustic huts, so long as they were satisfied with clothes made from animal skins sewn with thorns or fish-bones, to adorn themselves with feathers and shells, to paint their bodies in assorted colors, . . . their lives were free, healthy, good and happy as could be for as long as they lived. . . . But as soon as one person needed the help of another, or realized that it was beneficial for one person to have provisions for two, equality disappeared, property was instituted, labor became necessary, and the vast forests were transformed into pleasant fields watered by human sweat, in which slavery and misery could soon be seen to take root and sprout alongside the harvest. . . .

The arts of metallurgy and agriculture flourish, and with them the ownership of property.

Things in this state could have remained equal, if talents had been equal, and if, for example, a perfect balance was always reached between need for iron and the consumption of foodstuffs; but nothing sustained that balance, and it failed. The strongest did most of the work; the more skilled accomplished more by theirs; the cleverest found ways to lighten his load; the farmer had more need of iron or the blacksmith more of wheat, so that by the same labor, one prospered while the other barely survived. Thus natural inequality advances imperceptibly . . . and the effects of human differences, combined with those of circumstance, become more visible and durable. . . . Matters having come to this point, it is easy to imagine the rest. I shall not pause to describe the successive invention of the other arts, the progress of languages, the use and exercise of talents, the inequality of fortune, the use or abuse of wealth, nor all the consequences that follow upon these, which each reader can easily supply for himself. . . .

With the further development of skills and knowledge, given innate differences between people and other circumstantial factors, property accumulation continues, wealth is used and abused, and human inequality increases.

Before the signs that represent wealth were invented, it could only be measured in land and livestock, the only real possessions that humans possessed. But now when inheritances had grown in number and extent to the point where they covered the whole of the earth and encompassed everything, no one could acquire more except by taking it from others. Those who due to their weakness or laziness had been unable to acquire any now became poor, although they had lost nothing, everything around them changing while they changed not at all; they were obliged either to accept their subsistence from the hands of the rich, or to seize it, thus giving birth to . . . either domination and servitude, or violence and robbery. The rich for their part having once tasted the pleasure of ruling soon disdained all others, and . . . designed nothing other than to subjugate and enslave their neighbors. . . .

Thus the usurpations of the rich and the brigandage of the poor unleashed passions stifling all natural compassion and the still weak voice of justice, and reduced them all to greed, ambition, and wickedness. There broke out a perpetual conflict between the right of the strongest and the right of the first occupant which would end only with warfare and murder. Society, not yet formed, devolved to the most horrible state of war. . . .

It is not possible that people did not at last reflect on so miserable a situation, and on the calamities that had overcome them. The rich especially must soon have felt how disadvantageous to them was a perpetual war in which they bore all the cost. . . . Besides, . . . they knew that their [usurpations] rested on only a precarious and improper foundation, and that having acquired them only by force, force could remove them without their having any recourse. Even those who had become wealthy by their own industry could scarcely claim a better basis for their ownership. They could boast, "It is I who built this wall; I earned this land by my own labor." To which their critics could respond: "Who gave you its boundaries? And by what right do you demand payment from us for labor we never imposed on you? Do you not know that a multitude of your brothers perish, or suffer from need of what you have an excess, and that you should have sought the explicit and unanimous consent of humankind to appropriate for yourself from the bounty belonging to all anything that exceeded your share?"

Lacking valid reasons to justify himself and sufficient strength to defend himself, . . . the rich man, pressed by necessity, conceived at length the most cunning project ever to enter the human mind: he would use in his own behalf the very weapons of those who attacked him, making allies of his adversaries, filling their heads with alien ideas, and giving them different institutions that were as favorable to him as the law of nature was unfavorable.

With this intention, having explained to his neighbors the horror of a situation that armed each of them against all others and rendered their possessions as onerous as their wants, and where no one was secure either in poverty nor in wealth, he freely invented specious reasons to lead them to his goal. "Let us unite," he said to them, "to guard the weak from oppression, restrain the ambitious, and assure to each the possession of what belongs to him. Let us institute rules of justice and peace that all without exception would be obliged to obey, and which will in some way repair the blows of fortune by subjecting equally the weak and the strong to mutual responsibilities. In a word, instead of turning our forces against ourselves, let us gather them into one supreme power that may govern us by wise laws, protect and defend all the members of the group, repulse common enemies, and maintain us in eternal concord."

Much less than a discourse of this sort was sufficient to deceive ordinary people, easily seduced, . . . who were in any case . . . too greedy and ambitious to manage for long without masters. All raced to meet their chains believing they had secured their liberty; for although they had sufficient sense to recognize the advantages of a political settlement, they did not have enough experience to foresee its dangers. . . .

Such was, or must have been, the origin of society and of laws, which gave new shackles to the weak and new strength to the rich, irretrievably destroyed natural liberty, established forever the law of property and inequality, changed a clever usurpation into an irrevocable right, and for the profit of a few ambitious individuals subjected the whole human race to perpetual labor, servitude, and wretchedness.

4. Voltaire, *Candide* (1759/1761)

The whole of Candide responds to Leibniz's *Theodicy*, but the episode of the Lisbon earthquake of November 1, 1755, which took some thirty thousand lives and left the city in ruins, does so most pointedly. Voltaire saw the Lisbon earthquake as the very embodiment of inexplicable evil and testimony to the failure of divine providence. As such, it permits him to mock the Leibnizian argument for the justice of God in the outlandish pronouncements of Dr. Pangloss, tutor and companion to the innocent Candide. In Chapter 5, given here in full, Candide and Pangloss are on a ship in Lisbon harbor when the earth shakes, their ship sinks, and the next stage of their adventures begins. Arrived in Lisbon, Pangloss discourses amid the wreckage on sufficient causes and universal reason in the hearing of an agent of the Inquisition,[19] who tests the philosopher's views on free will—a doctrine of the church that seems to contradict the Leibnizian argument for the divine determination of all events. Pangloss replies cheerfully, doubling down on his explanations. But he has said too much, and at the close of the chapter, both he and Candide, though they live in the best of all possible worlds, are about to be arrested by the Inquisition.

CANDIDE

Chapter 5: The storm, the shipwreck, the earthquake, and what became of Dr. Pangloss, of Candide, and of Jacques the Anabaptist

Half of those on board, struck down, dying of those inconceivable agonies that the rolling of a vessel conveys to the nerves and to all the fluids of a body when it is shaken in opposing directions, didn't even have the strength to worry about the danger they faced. The other half cried out and prayed aloud; the sails were torn, the masts broken, the vessel took on water. Those who could work did

---

19. Inquisition: The Portuguese judicial institution in this case, modeled on the Spanish Inquisition and set up to investigate and prosecute heresy, which it did with notorious brutality.

what they could; but they were all at cross purposes, and no one took command. The Anabaptist[20] lent a hand; he was on the prow; a furious sailor hit him hard and laid him out on the deck; but the blow he gave him was so hard that he lost his balance and fell overboard head first. He was hanging upside down, caught up in a section of the broken mast. The good Jacques ran to his assistance, helped him get back on board, but in his struggles he slipped into the sea himself, in full view of the sailor, who left him to drown without even bothering to watch him go down.

Candide ran to the side, and caught sight of his benefactor, who came up to the surface for a moment before being swallowed forever. He wanted to throw himself into the sea after him, but the philosopher Pangloss prevented him, proving to him that the Bay of Lisbon had been especially made so that the Anabaptist could drown in it. While he was proving this by logical deduction, the vessel foundered and everyone died, with the exception of Pangloss, of Candide, and of the brutal sailor who had drowned the virtuous Anabaptist; the wretch swam successfully to the shore, while Pangloss and Candide were carried ashore clinging to a plank.

When they had recovered a little they set out on foot for Lisbon; they had some money in their pockets with which they hoped to save themselves from starvation now that they had escaped drowning.

No sooner had they passed through the gates of the town, weeping over the death of their benefactor, than they felt the earth tremble under their feet; the sea in the port began to boil, and the ships at anchor were smashed to pieces. Gusts of wind showered sparks and glowing cinders over the streets and squares of the city; the houses collapsed, the roofs leveled with their foundations, and their foundations shattered; thirty thousand inhabitants, randomly selected without regard to age or sex, were crushed in the ruins. The sailor said to himself, with a whistle and a swear word, "There'll be good pickings here!" "What can be the sufficient reason[21] of this phenomenon?" asked Pangloss. "This is the end of the world!" cried Candide. The sailor at once ran into the middle of the ruins, risked death looking for money, found some, took it, got drunk, and having slept it off, bought the favors of the first willing woman that he met among the ruins of the shattered houses, surrounded by the dying and the dead. Pangloss, however, caught hold of his sleeve: "My friend," he said to him, "that's no good, you're falling short of the standard set by universal reason, you're not spending your time as you should." "Christ!" said the sailor.

---

20. The Anabaptist assists Candide earlier in the narrative, and is thus referred to as the latter's "benefactor." Voltaire here honors a member of a radical Protestant movement dating from the early sixteenth century that had been repudiated and viciously persecuted by both Catholics and mainstream Protestants.

21. sufficient reason: the philosophical principle which posits that everything must have a reason, cause, or basis.

"I'm a sailor and I was born in the colonies. I've made four voyages to Japan, and four times I walked on the crucifix.[22] I'm just the man to talk to about universal reason!"

Some falling rocks had wounded Candide, who was stretched out in the street and covered in debris. He said to Pangloss, "Alas! Get me a little wine and some oil; I'm dying." "This earthquake isn't something new," replied Pangloss. "The city of Lima in South America felt the same shocks last year. The same causes, the same effects. There must be a fissure of sulfur underground that stretches from Lima to Lisbon."[23] "There is no better explanation," said Candide. "But for God's sake, get me a little oil and some wine." "What do you mean there is no better explanation!" replied the philosopher. "I maintain that my answer is proven and there could be no better explanation." Candide fainted and Pangloss brought him a little water from a nearby fountain.

Next day, having found some bits and pieces to eat while picking their way between the ruins, they recovered some of their strength. Then they worked alongside everyone else to give what help they could to their companions who had escaped death. A few residents, whom they had helped, gave them as good a lunch as one could hope for after such a disaster. It is true that the meal was mournful; the guests mingled tears with their food, but Pangloss consoled them, assuring them that things could not be otherwise. "For," said he, "all this is the best there could be; for if there is a volcano under Lisbon, then it couldn't be anywhere else. For it is impossible that things could be placed anywhere except where they are. For all is well."

A little dark man, an agent of the Inquisition, who was sitting beside him, politely joined in the conversation, and said: "I gather, sir, that you do not believe in original sin; for if all is as good as could be, then there has not been a fall, nor are we punished for it."[24]

"I very humbly beg pardon of Your Excellency," replied Pangloss even more politely, "for the fall of mankind and their punishment were necessary events in the best of all possible worlds."[25] "Good sir, then you don't believe in free will?" asked the agent. "Your Excellency will excuse me," said Pangloss, "but free will is compatible with inflexible necessity; for it was necessary that we should be

---

22. Trampling on the crucifix was a demonstration of the repudiation of Christianity required at this time of all Europeans entering Japan.

23. As a philosopher, Pangloss is happy, even in the absence of material evidence, to supply explanations for natural events as much as for metaphysical ones.

24. "Original sin" is the sin borne by all humans for the acts of Adam and Eve in the Garden of Eden that contravened God's commands, as presented in Genesis 3. As a result of those acts, committed freely—for God had given both man and woman free will—both were expelled from the Garden and that expulsion constituting the fall of humankind.

25. In this conversation, Pangloss is explicating, and at the same time parodying Leibniz's explanation that the necessary determination of all things is compatible with the exercise of free will—and indeed, many Christian theologians maintain that position today.

free; since after all the will is determined . . ." Pangloss was in the middle of his phrase when the agent gave a nod of his head to his guard, who poured him a glass of port to drink.

5. Gotthold Ephraim Lessing, *Nathan the Wise* (1779)

In Act III Scene 7 of *Nathan the Wise*, midway through the play, a gripping encounter unfolds between Nathan, the Jew, and the sultan Saladin, a Muslim. Saladin has inquired about the three religions of Judaism, Islam, and Christianity, and Nathan responds with a story of a ring with mystical powers passed through generations from father to favorite son. In time, a father who loves his three sons equally has duplicates made, and gives one ring to each. The rings represent the three faiths; and just as the father's love for his children prevents him from valuing one over the others, so God, the tale implies, leaves unknown which of the three faiths is true.

Both Nathan and Saladin know the meaning of the allegory even as Nathan relates it—hence Saladin's discomfort, explicit in Lessing's stage directions. Saladin resists the truth that Nathan delivers—the truth of the equivalency of the three faiths, and the unknowability of God's will—as it would undermine his legitimacy. But he loves and respects Nathan, and knows that truth has been told.[26]

NATHAN THE WISE

NATHAN:
Long ago in the East there lived a man
To whom a loving hand had given a ring
Of immeasurable worth. The stone was an opal,
That flashed a hundred sparkling colors,
And had the special power to make
Whoever wore this ring in true faith
Beloved of God and all humankind. No wonder
That the man from the East never took that ring
Off his finger, and was determined
To keep it ever after within his house.[27]
And so it was. He willed the ring at first

---

26. The iambic pentameters of Lessing's text are rendered here as blank verse lines of irregular pulse. Stage directions, in italics, are in Lessing's original.

27. "House" here and henceforth has the meaning of family, household, and lineage.

To that one of his sons he loved the best,
Instructing him in turn to leave the ring
To the most beloved of his sons,
And so again, setting birthright aside,
The most beloved son might always be,
By power of the ring, the foremost of his house.
Sultan, do you understand what I am saying?

SALADIN:
I understand you. Go on!

NATHAN:
So this ring descended from son to son,
To a father of three sons, in time,
All three of whom were equally devoted
To their father, who could not help but
Love them all alike. At times the first,
At times the second, or then the third,
Seemed worthier of the ring—
And so each in turn tugged at his heart,
But he could not slight the others,
But giving in to pious weakness,
Promised the ring to each of them.
And so it went—until the kindly father,
His death approaching, faced a dilemma.
It grieved him to deceive two of his sons
To whom he had made a promise—what could be done?
He sends in secret for a jeweler,
Instructing him to make two other rings
Just like the first, and to spare neither cost nor toil
To make sure each new ring he made
Was like—just like—the first. This the jeweler did.
He brought the two rings to the father,
Who could not tell them from the ring he had.
Relieved and joyful he called his sons to him,
One at a time, and gave them each his blessing,
And to each his ring—and died.
Do you hear this, Sultan?

SALADIN, *who turns away from him, distraught*:
I hear you, I hear you! Get on with your story
And bring it to a close, please!

NATHAN:

It is concluded.
What happened next, you know as well as I.
As soon as the father died, each son showed up
With his ring, and each one claimed to be master
Of the house. They examined the rings—they quarreled—
They complained. To no avail. It could not be discerned
Which ring was real . . .

After a pause, Nathan awaiting the sultan's response. . . .

No more can we determine
Which faith is the true faith.

SALADIN:

What? Is this the answer to my question?

NATHAN:

Forgive me, I beg you—but how can I
Make distinction between three rings
Which the father took deliberate care to make
In such a way they could not be distinguished?

SALADIN:

The rings! Don't play games with me! I would have thought
That the three religions that I named to you
Could easily be distinguished—by vestments worn,
By what may be eaten and what drunk!

NATHAN:

But not at all by their fundamental truths.
For are they not all rooted in their history,
Inscribed on paper, or told by word of mouth?
And history surely must be accepted wholly
In good faith—must it not?
Of whose good faith then are we least in doubt?
Of our own kin? Of those whose blood we share?
Of those who from our infancy gave proof of love?
Of those who have never failed us? . . .
How could I trust my forefathers less
Than you do yours? Or to put it otherwise,
Shall I ask you to declare your ancestors liars
So as not to say the same of mine?
Or those of Christians? Is it not so?

SALADIN, *under his breath*:
By the living God! He is right! I must say nothing.

NATHAN:
Now let us return to our rings.
The three sons each complained to the Judge,
Each swearing he had received the ring
Directly from his father's hand—which was the truth!
And with the ring the promise was received,
To enjoy one day the primacy it bequeathed—
As was no less the truth! The father, each swore,
Could not have been false to him; and rather than
Suspect so beloved a father, he would first—
Although inclined to think the best of them—
Charge his brothers with deception. . . .

SALADIN:
And now, the Judge?—I must hear
What you will have the Judge declare. Speak!

NATHAN:
The Judge declares: if you do not now produce
The father here before my judgment seat,
I cannot rule. Do you think that I am here
To work out riddles? Or do you expect
The real ring to open its mouth and speak?
But wait! I heard you say the real ring
Has the miraculous power to render the wearer beloved
Of God and men. This the false ring cannot do.
The ring will decide! Now which one of you is loved
The best by the other two? Go ahead, which?
You have nothing to say? . . . Does each love only himself?
Then all of you are frauds, and have been defrauded!
Not one of your rings is real. . . .

SALADIN:
Splendid! Splendid!

NATHAN:
And so, the Judge continued, though not my judgment,
I offer my advice: Do this—
Let things stand as they are. Each of you
Has his ring, given to him by his father.
Let each believe that his own ring is real.

Perhaps the father wished to bear no longer
The tyranny of a single ring.
And surely he loved all three of you,
And loved you all alike, so did not wish
To disadvantage two of you
To privilege just one. So on with it!
Let each rejoice in his father's love . . .
Let each one strive to prove
His ring's stone's great power. . . .
And if the stone still works its power
For the children of your children's children,
Then come again in a thousand thousand years
Before this judgment seat,
When a greater One than I will sit and speak.
Now go! Said the prudent Judge.

SALADIN:
God! God!

NATHAN:
Saladin,
Do you feel yourself to be this great, awaited One?

SALADIN, *hurling himself upon Nathan, grabbing his hand, which he does not release for the remainder of the scene*:
Am I dust? Am I nothing? God!

NATHAN:
What is it, Sultan?

SALADIN:
Nathan, dear Nathan!
The thousand thousand years of your Judge
Have not yet come. His judgment seat is not mine.
Go! Go! But be my friend.

NATHAN:
Has Saladin nothing more to say to me?

SALADIN:
Nothing.

6. Denis Diderot, *Rameau's Nephew* (c. 1761–1772)

Diderot's novel *Rameau's Nephew* purports to be the record of a conversation held in a Paris café on a single evening, perhaps in 1761, between the narrator, *Moi* (Myself), and his interlocutor, *Lui* (He). Their conversation ranges at random over matters much discussed during the Enlightenment: literature, music, the theater, education, morality, high society, and, loosely, philosophy, or the meaning of life. He, the principal character, challenges with vivacity the whole roster of social and cultural norms, which Myself, with somewhat less passion and eloquence, defends. The selections given here relate the discussion while avoiding the numerous references to contemporary literary, stage, and political personalities.

RAMEAU'S NEPHEW

"Myself" introduces himself and the nephew of Rameau, "one of the oddest characters in this country."

Rain or shine, it is my regular habit every day about five to go and take a walk around the Palais-Royal. . . . If the weather is too cold or rainy, I take shelter in the Regency Café, where I entertain myself by watching chess being played. . . . One day I was there after dinner, looking hard, saying little, and listening the least amount possible, when I was accosted by one of the oddest characters in this country, where God has not stinted us. The fellow is a compound of elevation and abjectness, of good sense and lunacy. The ideas of decency and depravity must be strangely scrambled in his head, for he shows without ostentation the good qualities that nature has bestowed upon him, just as he does the bad ones without shame. . . . He has no greater opposite than himself. . . . Today his linen is filthy, his clothes torn to rags, he is virtually barefoot, and he hangs his head furtively; one is tempted to hail him and toss him a coin. Tomorrow he is powdered, curled, well dressed; he holds his head high, shows himself off—you would take him for a man of quality. He lives from day to day, sad or cheerful according to luck. His first care on arising in the morning is to ascertain where he will dine; after dinner he ponders supper. . . .

I have no great esteem for such eccentrics. Some people take them on as regular acquaintances or even friends. But for my part it is only once a year that I stop and fall in with them, largely because their character stands out from the rest and breaks that tedious uniformity which our education, our social conventions, and our customary good manners have brought about. . . . He is the nephew of the famous musician who delivered us from the plainsong of Lully[28] that we had intoned for over a century, and who wrote so much visionary

---

28. Jean-Baptiste Lully (1632–1687): the leading composer of seventeenth-century France. "Plainsong," the musical style of the medieval church, is here used disparagingly.

gibberish and apocalyptic truth about the theory of music—writings that neither he nor anyone else ever understood. . . .

HE accosts me: Ha ha! So there you are, master Philosopher! And what are
you up to among all these idlers? Do you waste your time, too, pushing wood?
(That is the contemptuous way of describing chess and checkers.) . . .

They chat and come to the subject of genius.

MYSELF: Speaking of the uncle, do you ever see him?

HE: I see him pass in the street.

MYSELF: Doesn't he do anything for you?

HE: If he has ever has done anything for anybody, it must be without knowing
it. He is a philosopher after a fashion: he thinks of no one but himself; the rest
of the universe doesn't matter a tinker's damn to him. His wife, his daughter,
may die as soon as they please. Provided the parish bells that toll for them continue to sound the intervals of the twelfth and the seventeenth, all will be well.
It's lucky for him and that's what I envy especially in men of genius. They are
good for only one thing—apart from that, zero. They don't know what it is to
be citizens, fathers, mothers, cousins, friends. Between you and me, one should
try to be like them in every way, but without multiplying the breed. The world
needs men, but men of genius, no; I say, no! No need of them. They are the
ones who change the face of the earth. . . .

*The conversation turns to the narrator's eight-year-old daughter and the education
she will receive—giving an opening for the Nephew's thoughts on knowledge.*

HE: But I limit myself for the moment to one question: won't she need a master
or two?

MYSELF: Of course.

HE: There we are, then. You'll expect those masters to know grammar, mythology, history, geography, and morals, and to give lessons in them. Twaddle, my
dear philosopher, twaddle: if they knew these subjects well enough to teach
them, they wouldn't teach them.

MYSELF: Why not?

HE: Because they would have spent their whole life learning them. A man
must have gone deep into art or science to master the elements. Classic works
are written only by white-haired practitioners. The darkness of the beginnings
lights up only toward the middle or the end. . . . Not before thirty or forty
years of application did my uncle begin to see the glimmer of musical theory. . . .
[U]ntil one knows everything one knows nothing worth knowing, ignorant of
the origin of this, the purpose of that and the place of either. Which should come

first? Can one teach without method? And where does method spring from? I tell you, Philosopher mine, I have an idea physics will always be a puny science, a drop of water picked up from the great ocean on the point of a needle, a grain of dust from the Alps. Take the causes of phenomena—what about them? Really, it would be as well to know nothing as to know so little and so poorly. That's the conclusion I had reached when I took up music teaching. What are you thinking about?

MYSELF: I'm thinking that everything you've just said is more specious than solid. Let's drop it. You've been teaching, you say, composition and thoroughbass?[29]

HE: Yes.

MYSELF: And you were entirely ignorant of both?

HE: Not really. That's why others were worse than I, namely those who thought they knew something. I at least never spoiled the minds or the hands of children. When they went from me to a good master, having learnt nothing they had nothing to unlearn, which was time and money saved. . . .

The conversation turns to wealth and poverty and the values worth living for.

HE: And think of poverty! The voice of conscience and honor is pretty feeble when the guts cry out. Isn't it enough that if I ever get rich I shall be bound to make restitution? I am prepared to do this in every conceivable way—through gorging, through gambling, through guzzling, and through wenching.

MYSELF: But I'm afraid you will never get rich.

HE: I suspect it too.

MYSELF: Suppose it did work out, what then?

HE: I would act like all beggars on horseback.[30] I'd be the most insolent ruffian ever seen. I'd remember every last thing they made me go through and pay them back with slings and arrows. I love bossing people and I will boss them. I love being praised and they will praise me. . . .

MYSELF: Knowing what worthy use you would make of wealth, I see how deplorable it is that you are poor. . . .

HE: I almost think you're making fun of me, Master Philosopher. But you don't even suspect with whom you're tangling. . . . The well-to-do of every description have either said or not said to themselves the words I've just confided to you; the fact remains that the life I would lead in their position is precisely

---

29. thoroughbass: a kind of musical notation indicating to the performer the accompanying bass line.
30. beggars on horseback: that is, worthless aristocrats.

theirs. That's where you fellows are behind the times. You think everybody aims at the same happiness. What an idea! . . . But virtue and philosophy are not made for everybody. The few who can, have it; the few who can, keep it. Just imagine the universe philosophical and wise, and tell me if it would not be devilishly dull. Listen! I say hurrah for wisdom and philosophy—the wisdom of Solomon:[31] to drink good wines, gorge on choice food, tumble pretty women, sleep in downy beds—outside of that, all is vanity.

MYSELF: What! And fighting for your country?

HE: Vanity! There are not countries left. All I see from pole to pole is tyrants and slaves.

MYSELF: What of helping your friends?

HE: Vanity! No one has any friends. And even if one had, should one risk making them ungrateful? . . .

MYSELF: To hold a position in society and discharge its duties?

HE: Vanity! What difference whether you hold a position or not, provided you have means, since you only seek a position in order to get wealth. Discharge one's duties—what does that bring you?—jealousy, worries, persecution. Is that the way to get on? Nonsense! Pay court, pay court, know the right people, flatter their tastes and fall in with their whims, serve their vices and second their misdeeds—that's the secret. . . .

After a discussion of music theory and contemporary composers, Myself returns to the issue of morality and the values the Nephew will teach his own son.

MYSELF: How is it that with such fineness of feeling, so much sensibility where musical beauty is concerned, you are so blind to the beauties of morality, so insensible to the charm of virtue?

HE: It must be that virtue requires a special sense that I lack, a fiber that has not been granted me. . . . And then there is heredity. My father's blood is the same as my uncle's; my blood is like my father's. The paternal molecule was hard and obtuse, and like a primordial germ it has affected all the rest.

MYSELF: Do you love your son?

HE: Do I love the little savage? I am crazy about him!

---

31. Wisdom of Solomon is a deuterocanonical (apocryphal to Protestants) biblical book written in Greek in the intertestamentary period urging the practice of righteousness; but Diderot here confuses it, perhaps purposely, with the biblical book *Ecclesiastes*, influential and much read, which repeatedly holds that "all is vanity."

MYSELF: And will you do nothing to thwart in him the effect of his accursed paternal molecule?

HE: I'll try it, but (I think) in vain. If he is fated to become a good man, trying won't do any harm. But if the molecule decides that he shall be a ne'er-do-well like his father, the pains I might take to make him an honest man would be very dangerous. Education would work continually at cross-purposes with the natural bent of the molecule, and he would be pulled by two contrary forces that would make him go askew down the path of life. . . . He would waste his best years. So at the moment I hold my hand, I simply observe him and let him come along. He is already greedy, cozening, rascally, lazy, and a liar: I am afraid he is a pedigreed beast.

MYSELF: And you will make him a musician so that the likeness can be complete?

HE: A musician! A musician! Sometimes I look at him and grind my teeth and say to myself "If you ever learn a note, I really think I'll twist your neck."

MYSELF: But why, if you don't mind telling me?

HE: It leads nowhere.

MYSELF: It leads everywhere.

HE: Yes, if you excel. But who can guarantee that his child will excel? It's ten thousand to one that he will be a wretched note-scraper like me. Do you know that it would be easier to find a child able to govern a kingdom and be a great king than a great violinist? . . .

The real goal, the Nephew maintains, is to be rich—a principle Myself rejects.

HE: Gold, gold is everything; and everything without gold, is nothing. Therefore, instead of having my son's head stuffed with grand maxims which he would have to forget under pain of being a pauper, this is what I do whenever I have a gold piece—not often, to be sure: I plant myself in front of him, draw the piece from my pocket, show it to him with admiring looks, raise my eyes to heaven, kiss the gold in front of him, and to show him still more forcibly the importance of the sacred coin, I stammer out the names and point out with the finger all the things one can buy with it—a beautiful gown, a beautiful hat, a good cake; next I put the coin in my pocket, parade before him proudly, pull up my coat tails and strike my waistcoat where the money lies. Thus do I make him understand that it is from that coin I draw the self-assurance he beholds. . . . I want my child happy, or what amounts to the same thing, honored, rich, powerful. I know the easiest ways to accomplish this, and I mean to teach them to my son early in life. If you wise men blame me, the majority (and success itself) will absolve me. He will have gold—it's I who tell you so,

I guarantee it—and if he has a great deal, he will lack nothing, not even your admiration and respect.

MYSELF: You might be wrong about those.

HE: If so, he can do without, like many other people. . . .

The conversation winds down, and the Nephew takes his leave.

HE: Farewell, Master Philosopher, isn't it true that I am ever the same?

MYSELF: Alas! Yes, unfortunately.

HE: Here's hoping this ill fortune lasts me another forty years. He laughs best who laughs last.

7. Thomas Paine, *Common Sense* (1776)

In these passages from Part Three of *Common Sense*, which opens with the author's famous claim that he offers only "simple facts, plain arguments, and common sense," Paine proposes that the tie between England and America be severed and a new form of government created. He denies, as some believed, that the American colonies have flourished under English rule, arguing instead that they have been held back by selfish regulations and will prosper more greatly if freed from the mother country. Far from having enjoyed England's protection, religious refugees from both England and the rest of Europe have fled to safety and freedom in America. England's entanglements with other European countries, moreover, with whom Americans would rather be at peace, have often drawn them into war.

Another issue is the relative size of England and America: it "reverses the common order of nature" that England, a small island off the northwest corner of Europe, should pretend to rule the vast expanse of America: "[T]here is something very absurd in supposing a continent to be perpetually governed by an island." Instead, American must form its own government: one in which "the Law is king," and not the flawed heir to some fortunate dynasty. This section closes with a rousing plea for action: "Every spot of the old world is overrun with oppression. Freedom has been hunted round the globe. . . . O! receive the fugitive, and prepare in time an asylum for mankind."

COMMON SENSE

Thoughts on the Present State of American Affairs

In the following pages I offer nothing more than simple facts, plain arguments, and common sense: and have no other preliminaries to settle with the reader, than that he will divest himself of prejudice and prepossession, . . . and generously enlarge his views beyond the present day.

Volumes have been written on the subject of the struggle between England and America. Men of all ranks have embarked in the controversy . . . ; but all have been ineffectual, and the period of debate is closed. Arms as the last resource decide the contest; the appeal was the choice of the King, and the Continent [i.e., America] has accepted the challenge.

. . .

The sun never shined on a cause of greater worth. It is not the affair of a city, a county, a province, or a kingdom; but of a continent—of at least one-eighth part of the habitable globe. It is not the concern of a day, a year, or an age; posterity is virtually involved in the contest, and will be more or less affected even to the end of time, by the proceedings now. Now is the seed-time of Continental union, faith and honor. The least fracture now will be like a name engraved with the point of a pin on the tender rind of a young oak; the wound would enlarge with the tree, and posterity read in it full grown characters.

. . .

As much has been said of the advantages of reconciliation, which, like an agreeable dream, has passed away and left us as we were, it is but right that we should examine the contrary side of the argument, and inquire into some of the many material injuries which these Colonies sustain, and always will sustain, by being connected with and dependent on Great Britain. To examine that connection and dependence, on the principles of nature and common sense, to see what we have to trust to, if separated, and what we are to expect, if dependent.

I have heard it asserted by some, that as America has flourished under her former connection with Great Britain, the same connection is necessary towards her future happiness. . . . Nothing can be more fallacious than this kind of argument. We may as well assert that because a child has thrived upon milk, that it is never to have meat. . . . But . . . I answer roundly that America would have flourished as much, and probably much more, had no European power taken any notice of her. The commerce by which she has enriched herself are the necessaries of life, and will always have a market while eating is the custom of Europe.

But she has protected us, say some. That she has engrossed us is true, and defended the Continent at our expense as well as her own, is admitted; and she would have defended Turkey from the same motive, that is—for the sake of trade and dominion.

Alas! we have been long led away by ancient prejudices and made large sacrifices to superstition. We have boasted the protection of Great Britain, without considering, that her motive was interest not attachment; and that she did not protect us from our enemies on our account; but from her enemies on her own account, from those who had no quarrel with us on any other account, and who will always be our enemies on the same account. Let Britain waive her pretensions to the Continent, or the Continent throw off the dependence, and we should be at peace with France and Spain, were they at war with Britain. . . .

It has lately been asserted in parliament, that the Colonies have no relation to each other but through the Parent Country, i.e., that Pennsylvania and the Jerseys and so on for the rest, are sister Colonies by the way of England; this is certainly a very roundabout way of proving relationship, but it is the nearest and only true way of proving enmity (or enemyship, if I may so call it). France and Spain never were, nor perhaps ever will be, our enemies as Americans, but as our being the subjects of Great Britain.

. . .

But Britain is the parent country, say some. Then the more shame upon her conduct. Even brutes do not devour their young, nor savages make war upon their families. . . . Europe, and not England, is the parent country of America. This new world has been the asylum for the persecuted lovers of civil and religious liberty from every part of Europe. Hither have they fled, not from the tender embraces of the mother, but from the cruelty of the monster; and it is so far true of England, that the same tyranny which drove the first emigrants from home, pursues their descendants still. . . .

It is pleasant to observe by what regular gradations we surmount the force of local prejudices, as we enlarge our acquaintance with the world. A man born in any town in England divided into parishes, will naturally associate most with his fellow parishioners (because their interests in many cases will be common) and distinguish him by the name of neighbor; if he meets him but a few miles from home, he drops the narrow idea of a street, and salutes him by the name of townsman; . . . but if in their foreign excursions they should associate in France, or any other part of Europe, their local remembrance would be enlarged into that of Englishmen. And by a just parity of reasoning, all Europeans meeting in America, or any other quarter of the globe, are countrymen; for England, Holland, Germany, or Sweden, when compared with the whole, stand in the same places on the larger scale, which the divisions of street, town, and county do on the smaller ones; distinctions too limited for Continental minds. Not one third of the inhabitants, even of this province [Pennsylvania], are of English descent. Wherefore, I reprobate [challenge] the phrase of Parent or Mother Country applied to England only, as being false, selfish, narrow and ungenerous.

But, admitting that we were all of English descent, what does it amount to? Nothing. Britain, being now an open enemy, extinguishes every other name and title: and to say that reconciliation is our duty, is truly farcical. . . .

Much has been said of the united strength of Britain and the Colonies, that in conjunction they might bid defiance to the world. But this is mere presumption; the fate of war is uncertain, neither do the expressions mean anything; for this continent would never suffer itself to be drained of inhabitants, to support the British arms in either Asia, Africa, or Europe.

Besides, what have we to do with setting the world at defiance? Our plan is commerce, and that, well attended to, will secure us the peace and friendship of all Europe; because it is the interest of all Europe to have America a free port. Her trade will always be a protection, and her barrenness of gold and silver secure her from invaders.

I challenge the warmest advocate for reconciliation to show a single advantage that this continent can reap by being connected with Great Britain. . . . Our corn [grain] will fetch its price in any market in Europe, and our imported goods must be paid for, buy them where we will.

But the injuries and disadvantages which we sustain by that connection, are without number; and our duty to mankind at large, as well as to ourselves, instruct us to renounce the alliance: because any submission to or dependence on Great Britain, tends directly to involve this Continent in European wars and quarrels, and set us at variance with nations who would otherwise seek our friendship, and against whom we have neither anger nor complaint. . . .

Europe is too thickly planted with kingdoms to be long at peace, and whenever a war breaks out between England and any foreign power, the trade of America goes to ruin, because of her connection with Britain. The next war may not turn out like the last, and should it not, the advocates for reconciliation now will be wishing for separation then, because neutrality in that case would be a safer convoy than a man of war. Everything that is right or reasonable pleads for separation. The blood of the slain, the weeping voice of nature cries, 'tis time to part. Even the distance at which the Almighty has placed England and America is a strong and natural proof that the authority of the one over the other, was never the design of Heaven. . . .

. . .

As to government matters, it is not in the power of Britain to do this continent justice: The business of it will soon be too weighty and intricate to be managed with any tolerable degree of convenience, by a power so distant from us, and so very ignorant of us; for if they cannot conquer us, they cannot govern us. To be always running three or four thousand miles with a tale or a petition, waiting four or five months for an answer, which when obtained requires five or six more to explain it in, will in a few years be looked upon as folly and childishness—There was a time when it was proper, and there is a proper time for it to cease.

Small islands not capable of protecting themselves are the proper objects for kingdoms to take under their care; but there is something very absurd in supposing a continent to be perpetually governed by an island. In no instance has nature made the satellite larger than its primary planet, and as England and America, with respect to each other, reverses the common order of nature, it is evident they belong to different systems: England to Europe, America to itself.

. . .

Paine expands on the matter of Britain's inability to rule the colonies and sketches a plan for colonial self-government.

But where says some is the king of America? I'll tell you, friend, he [i.e., God] reigns above, and does not make havoc of mankind like the Royal Brute [i.e., king] of Britain. Yet that we may not appear to be defective even in earthly honors, let a day be solemnly set apart for proclaiming the charter [i.e., a constitution]; let it be brought forth [and] a crown be placed thereon, by which the world may know . . . that in America the Law is king. . . .

A government of our own is our natural right: And . . . it is infinitely wiser and safer, to form a constitution of our own in a cool deliberate manner, while we have it in our power, than to trust such an interesting event to time and chance. . . .

. . .

You that tell us of harmony and reconciliation, can you restore to us the time that is past? Can you give to prostitution its former innocence? Neither can you reconcile Britain and America. The last cord now is broken, the people of England are presenting addresses against us. There are injuries which nature cannot forgive; she would cease to be nature if she did. As well can the lover forgive the ravisher of his mistress, as the continent [can] forgive the murders of Britain. The Almighty has implanted in us these inextinguishable feelings for good and wise purposes. They are the guardians of his image in our hearts. They distinguish us from the herd of common animals. The social compact would dissolve, and justice be extirpated from the earth, or have only a casual existence were we callous to the touches of affection. The robber and the murderer would often escape unpunished, did not the injuries which our tempers sustain provoke us into justice.

O you that love mankind! You that dare oppose, not only the tyranny, but the tyrant, stand forth! Every spot of the old world is overrun with oppression. Freedom has been hunted round the globe. Asia, and Africa, have long expelled her.—Europe regards her like a stranger, and England has given her warning to depart. O! receive the fugitive, and prepare in time an asylum for mankind.

8. Mary Wollstonecraft, *A Vindication of the Rights of Woman* (1792)

The excerpts presented here are taken from Chapter 2 of the *Vindication*, entitled "The Prevailing Opinion of a Sexual Character Discussed"—a discussion, that is, of the commonly held assumptions about the nature of women. Among the observations raised are these: Women's domination by men has been ascribed to the different capacities of either sex, with men attaining to a standard of excellence of mind and character not achieved by women. To the extent that is true, Wollstonecraft argues, it is because women have been kept in ignorance, and taught "from their infancy" and by their mothers that if they are only beautiful, "everything else is needless for, at least, twenty years of their lives." Docile and obedient, they entertain their husbands: "[C]reated to be the toy of man, his rattle, [she] must jingle in his ears whenever, dismissing reason, he chooses to be amused."

The "arbitrary" and "illegitimate power" over men that beauty gives to women, allowing them to exercise "a short-lived tyranny" while they are young is, however, obtained by self-degradation; and it is a power which, if they sought true equality with men, they would need to surrender. Rather than cling to the illegitimate power afforded by beauty, women should seek to better themselves: "[T]he grand end of their exertions should be to unfold their own faculties and acquire the dignity of conscious virtue," which, as for men, is the only acquisition that "can satisfy an immortal soul," such as Wollstonecraft believes the human being possesses. Moreover, by improving herself and committing to the management of her family rather than simply to "adorn[ing] her person," she will gain her liberty and with it, her self-worth; for "[l]iberty is the mother of virtue," enabling both men and women to "become more wise and virtuous."

A VINDICATION OF THE RIGHTS OF WOMAN

Chapter 2: The Prevailing Opinion of a Sexual Character Discussed

To account for, and excuse the tyranny of man, many ingenious arguments have been brought forward to prove, that the two sexes, in the acquirement of virtue, ought to aim at attaining a very different character: or, to speak explicitly, women are not allowed to have sufficient strength of mind to acquire what really deserves the name of virtue. Yet it should seem, allowing them to have souls, that there is but one way appointed by Providence to lead mankind to either virtue or happiness.

If then women are not a swarm of ephemeral triflers, why should they be kept in ignorance under the specious name of innocence? Men complain, and with reason, of the follies and caprices of our sex, when they do not keenly satirize our headstrong passions and groveling vices. Behold, I should answer, the natural effect of ignorance! . . . Women are told from their infancy, and taught by the example of their mothers, that a little knowledge of human weakness, justly termed cunning, softness of temper, outward obedience, and a scrupulous attention to a puerile kind of propriety, will obtain for them the protection of man; and should they be beautiful, everything else is needless for, at least, twenty years of their lives. . . .

Men, indeed, appear to me to act in a very unphilosophical manner, when they try to secure the good conduct of women by attempting to keep them always in a state of childhood. . . . Children, I grant, should be innocent; but when the epithet is applied to men, or women, it is but a civil term for weakness. For if it be allowed that women were destined by Providence to acquire human virtues, and by the exercise of their understandings, that stability of character which is the firmest ground to rest our future hopes upon, they must be permitted to turn to the fountain of light, and not forced to shape their course by the twinkling of a mere satellite. . . .

Consequently, the most perfect education, in my opinion, is such an exercise of the understanding as is best calculated to strengthen the body and form the heart; or, in other words, to enable the individual to attain such habits of virtue as will render it independent. In fact, it is a farce to call any being virtuous whose virtues do not result from the exercise of its own reason. . . . Still the regal homage which [women] receive is so intoxicating, that till the manners of the times are changed, and formed on more reasonable principles, it may be impossible to convince them that the illegitimate power which they obtain, by degrading themselves, is a curse, and that they must return to nature and equality, if they wish to secure the placid satisfaction that unsophisticated affections impart. But for this epoch we must wait—wait, perhaps, till kings and nobles, enlightened by reason, and, preferring the real dignity of man to childish state, throw off their gaudy hereditary trappings: and if then women do not resign the arbitrary power of beauty—they will prove that they have less mind than man. . . .

Connected with man as daughters, wives, and mothers, their moral character may be estimated by their manner of fulfilling those simple duties; but the end, the grand end of their exertions should be to unfold their own faculties and acquire the dignity of conscious virtue. They may try to render their road pleasant; but ought never to forget, in common with man, that life yields not the felicity which can satisfy an immortal soul. I do not mean to insinuate, that either sex should be so lost, in abstract reflections or distant views, as to forget the affections and duties that lie before them, and are, in truth, the means appointed to produce the fruit of life; on the contrary, I would warmly recommend them, even while I assert, that they afford most satisfaction when they are considered in their true subordinate light. . . .

Youth is the season for love in both sexes; but in those days of thoughtless enjoyment, provision should be made for the more important years of life, when reflection takes place of sensation. But [. . . most] male writers . . . have warmly inculcated that the whole tendency of female education ought to be directed to one point—to render them pleasing.

Let me reason with the supporters of this opinion, who have any knowledge of human nature, do they imagine that marriage can eradicate the habitude of life? The woman who has only been taught to please will soon find that her charms are oblique sunbeams, and that they cannot have much effect on her husband's heart when they are seen every day, when the summer is passed and gone. Will she then have sufficient native energy to look into herself for comfort, and cultivate her dormant faculties? Or, is it not more rational to expect that she will try to please other men; and, in the emotions raised by the expectation of new conquests, endeavor to forget the mortification her love or pride has received? When the husband ceases to be a lover—and the time will inevitably come, her desire of pleasing will then grow languid, or become a spring of bitterness; and love, perhaps, the most evanescent of all passions, gives place to jealousy or vanity.

I now speak of women who are restrained by principle or prejudice; such women though they would shrink from an intrigue with real abhorrence, yet, nevertheless, wish to be convinced by the homage of gallantry, that they are cruelly neglected by their husbands; or, days and weeks are spent in dreaming of the happiness enjoyed by congenial souls, till the health is undermined and the spirits broken by discontent. How then can the great art of pleasing be such a necessary study? it is only useful to a mistress; the chaste wife, and serious mother, should only consider her power to please as the polish of her virtues, and the affection of her husband as one of the comforts that render her task less difficult, and her life happier. But, whether she be loved or neglected, her first wish should be to make herself respectable, and not rely for all her happiness on a being subject to like infirmities with herself. . . .

Nature has given woman a weaker frame than man; but, to ensure her husband's affections, must a wife, who, by the exercise of her mind and body, whilst she was discharging the duties of a daughter, wife, and mother, has allowed her constitution to retain its natural strength, and her nerves a healthy tone, is she, I say, to condescend, to use art, and feign a sickly delicacy, in order to secure her husband's affection? Weakness may excite tenderness, and gratify the arrogant pride of man; but the lordly caresses of a protector will not gratify a noble mind that pants for and deserves to be respected. . . .

In a seraglio [harem], I grant, that all these arts [of seduction] are necessary; . . . but have women so little ambition as to be satisfied with such a condition? Can they supinely dream life away in the lap of pleasure, or the languor of weariness, rather than assert their claim to pursue reasonable pleasures and render themselves conspicuous by practicing the virtues which dignify mankind? Surely she has not an immortal soul who can loiter life away merely employed to adorn her person, that she may amuse the languid hours, and soften the cares of a fellow-creature who is willing to be enlivened by her smiles and tricks, when the serious business of life is over.

Besides, the woman who strengthens her body and exercises her mind will, by managing her family and practicing various virtues, become the friend, and not the humble dependent of her husband, and if she deserves his regard by possessing such substantial qualities, she will not find it necessary to conceal her affection, nor to pretend to an unnatural coldness of constitution to excite her husband's passions. In fact, if we revert to history, we shall find that the women who have distinguished themselves have neither been the most beautiful nor the most gentle of their sex. . . .

How women are to exist in that state where there is to be neither marrying nor giving in marriage, we are not told.—For though moralists have agreed that the tenor of life seems to prove that *man* is prepared by various circumstances for a future state, they constantly concur in advising *woman* only to provide for the present. Gentleness, docility, and a spaniel-like affection are, on this ground, consistently recommended as the cardinal virtues of the sex; and, disregarding the arbitrary economy of nature, one writer has declared that it is masculine for a woman to be melancholy. She was created to be the toy of man, his rattle, and it must jingle in his ears whenever, dismissing reason, he chooses to be amused. . . .

I love man as my fellow; but his scepter, real or usurped, extends not to me, unless the reason of an individual demands my homage; and even then the submission is to reason, and not to man. In fact, the conduct of an accountable being must be regulated by the operations of its own reason; or on what foundation rests the throne of God?

It appears to me necessary to dwell on these obvious truths, because females have been insulated, as it were; and, while they have been stripped of the virtues that should clothe humanity, they have been decked with artificial graces that enable them to exercise a short-lived tyranny. Love, in their bosoms, taking place of every nobler passion, their sole ambition is to be fair [i.e., beautiful], to raise emotion instead of inspiring respect; and this ignoble desire, like the servility in absolute monarchies, destroys all strength of character. Liberty is the mother of virtue, and if women are, by their very constitution, slaves, and not allowed to breathe the sharp invigorating air of freedom, they must ever languish like exotics, and be reckoned beautiful flaws in nature. . . .

As to the argument respecting the subjection in which the sex has ever been held, it retorts [reflects] on man. The many have always been enthralled by the few; and, monsters who have scarcely shown any discernment of human excellence, have tyrannized over thousands of their fellow creatures. Why have men of superior endowments submitted to such degradation? For, is it not universally acknowledged that kings, viewed collectively, have ever been inferior, in abilities and virtue, to the same number of men taken from the common mass of mankind—yet, have they not, and are they not still treated with a degree of reverence, that is an insult to reason? China is not the only country where a living man has been made a God. Men have submitted to superior strength, to enjoy with impunity the pleasure of the moment—women have only done the same, and therefore . . . it cannot be demonstrated that woman is essentially inferior to man, because she has always been subjugated.

Brutal force has hitherto governed the world, and that the science of politics is in its infancy, is evident from philosophers scrupling to give the knowledge most useful to man that determinate distinction.

I shall not pursue this argument any further than to establish an obvious inference, that as sound politics diffuse liberty, mankind, including woman, will become more wise and virtuous.

Chapter 2

The Romantic Era

Introduction

The Enlightenment was a brief era, lasting about a century; the Romantic era is still briefer. It spans the last three decades of the eighteenth century, so over-lapping the last phase of the Enlightenment, and the first three of the next. Thereafter, having left its impress permanently on the literary process, it does not disappear, but is absorbed by later tendencies of realism and naturalism, as seen in the next section (see Introduction to Section II). This chapter looks at twelve authors whose works illustrate a range of Romantic features: three English, three German, two French, two Italian, one Polish, and one Russian.

The chapter opens with the three English poets William Blake (1757–1827), William Wordsworth (1770–1850), and Samuel Taylor Coleridge (1772–1834), all pioneers of Romanticism in that language. They celebrate nature, the imagination, the exotic, and the freshness of childhood as opposed to the wisdom of the sage. In their verse, they abandon the classicism of earlier poets, employing irregular rhythms and rhyme schemes that are not only more flexible, but also more aligned with human speech and thought, and more suited to the emotional range of Romantic poetry.

The Blake poems included here are from his early collection of nineteen *Songs of Innocence* (1789), and his expanded volume published five years later, the *Songs of Innocence and Experience* (1794), which adds twenty-six poems to the original nineteen. Blake, who was an engraver and painter before he was a poet, exuberantly illustrated both volumes. Nature, time, death, nurture, and other themes appear in both categories, although in different tonalities: the poems of innocence are hopeful, playful, and comforting; while those of experience speak of darkness, labor, and danger. These contrasts are deliberate, as announced in the subtitle of the 1794 volume: *Shewing the Two Contrary States of the Human Soul*. Some of the poems, indeed, bear the same title in their "innocent" and "experienced" manifestations, as does, for instance, *The Chimney Sweeper*: in the first version, the child laborer goes cheerfully to work; in the second, he laments his abandonment by his parents.

Unusually for writers in this era, Blake's origins were artisan, not bour-geois, professional, official, or aristocratic. Beyond some rudimentary school-ing, his chief teacher was his mother, from whom he imbibed a deep knowledge of the Bible, conspicuous in his later verse. His father was prosperous enough to provide him with materials for drawing and reading, and apprenticed him to a capable engraver from whose tutelage he emerged, at age twenty-one, a professional of that craft. Both parents were Dissenters from the established Anglican Church, and it was their beliefs that informed the adult Blake's most unorthodox, yet Christian beliefs, and enabled his exploration of unconventional religious alternatives. He was born in London and lived there almost without interruption, together with his wife: an illiterate woman whom he taught to read, to write, and to engrave, and who assisted him in his work. He wrote, and illustrated, prolifically: beyond the early poems of innocence and experience, he is known especially for *The Marriage of Heaven and Hell*, *Milton: A Poem*, and *Jerusalem*.

Blake's genius was not recognized during his lifetime, but subsequently many scholars have come to consider him the founder of English Romanticism. Wordsworth and Coleridge, whose first works follow soon after Blake's, are unequivocally recognized as early Romantic authors, their jointly authored *Lyrical Ballads* of 1798 seen as the cornerstone of that movement.

The son of an estate manager for a local nobleman in England's Lake District, Wordsworth was sent to a fine grammar school[1] and on to Cambridge University, where he languished as a scholar. After some shiftless years that included a stay in France during the early stages of its Revolution, he collaborated with Coleridge on the *Lyrical Ballads*. Supported initially by patrons, Wordsworth eventually received a monetary settlement in 1802, which permitted him to marry, and in 1813, a position that provided a steady income. He was named England's poet laureate in 1843, a title attesting to his high reputation.

In addition to the *Lyrical Ballads*, Wordsworth is best known for the 1807 collection of his *Poems, in Two Volumes*, which contains the *Ode: Intimations of Immortality* (probably composed in 1802–1804) included in this chapter. His autobiographical *Prelude*, the masterpiece upon which he had worked for much of his career, was published posthumously by his widow in 1850.

Coleridge, the third English Romantic poet considered here, is the intellectual leader of the group. His father, a vicar of the Anglican Church and the headmaster of a grammar school, possessed an ample library and encouraged his son's early and voluminous reading. Nine years old when his father died, Coleridge went on to school and to Cambridge University, where—unlike Wordsworth—he distinguished himself as a scholar. He later became not only a poet, but also a dramatist, essayist, philosopher, theologian, and literary critic. As a poet, he is best known for his two long poems, the exceptionally original *Rime of the Ancient Mariner*, which appeared with Wordsworth's poems in the

---

1. A grammar school would teach a classical curriculum, grounded in Latin grammar, and typically educated the sons of the elite.

Lyrical Ballads of 1798, and the Gothic ballad *Christabel* (composed 1797 and 1800, published 1816); and for the brief and unfinished *Kubla Khan* (composed 1797, published 1816), composed while under the influence of laudanum, to which he had a lifelong addiction. For Coleridge led a turbulent and unhappy life. He had married young and fathered four children, whom he abandoned in 1808. The wild-eyed Blake and the laggard student Wordsworth finished their years alongside their wives in domestic comfort. Coleridge, in contrast, spent his later years living in other people's households, and finally, from 1816–1834, in Highgate, London, with the physician James Gillman.

Romanticism came earlier to Germany than to England, inaugurated by the *Sturm und Drang* (storm and stress) movement of the 1770s, which energetically repudiated the rationalism of the late Enlightenment. Johann Wolfgang von Goethe (1749–1832),[2] among the early leaders of *Sturm und Drang*, published in 1774 the first novel to embody its motifs: *The Sorrows of Young Werther*. A young artist on no particular career course resides in the small village of Wahlheim (an invention). Werther befriends, then falls in love with, a young woman who is, at first, pledged to another man, and soon thereafter marries him. But Werther cannot stop loving Charlotte, whom he affectionately calls Lotte, even as he remains friends with Albert, her husband. The sequence of letters Werther writes to his friend Wilhelm that comprise most of the book[3] explore the young man's inner turmoil and mental disintegration. After a single moment of passion, when Werther reveals his feelings to Lotte, he kills himself with Albert's pistol, which Lotte herself has conveyed to him.

The Sorrows of Young Werther was an instant success, circulating in multiple languages, and spawning a tourist industry. Not only did it bring fame to the twenty-four-year-old author, it also remained Goethe's best-known work, prompting the issuance of a revised edition in 1787. Its potency derived in part from the circumstances of its composition: for the events described in the book as occurring in 1771 and 1772, trace with some exactitude Goethe's own experiences of 1773 and 1774 when resident in the village of Wetzlar. He had been in love with a woman, also named Charlotte, who had married his friend; and soon thereafter, in the same milieu, another friend suffering from unrequited love had committed suicide. In *Werther*, Goethe weaves his own story together with that of his fictional characters—although Goethe himself, once the impossibility of the situation became apparent, left Wetzlar, cleanly cutting his ties.

In 1774, following the publication of *Werther*, Goethe became the right-hand aide of Karl August, duke of Saxe-Weimar, attending to his

---

2. Goethe's patron, Karl August, the Duke of Saxe-Weimar, raised Goethe to the nobility in 1782, from which point "von" is added to his birth name.

3. The epistolary novel was a popular genre in this period, exemplified by Samuel Richardson's *Clarissa* (1748) and Jean-Jacques Rousseau's *Julie, or the New Heloise* (1761).

patron's bureaucratic, military, and cultural affairs. During the next five decades, spent mostly in Weimar, Goethe wrote novels, plays, poems, and an autobiography—culminating in the verse drama *Faust*, which revisits the protean character Christopher Marlowe had heroized (see Volume One, Chapter 11, Text 2), and which was subsequently reinvented in musical and dramatic productions by Hector Berlioz, Charles Gounod, and others. Germany's most celebrated intellectual, he influenced an entire generation of writers as well as several nineteenth-century philosophers, including Hegel, Schopenhauer, Kierkegaard, and Nietzsche.

One of those whom Goethe inspired was Friedrich von Schiller (1759–1805).[4] In Weimar, from 1794 until 1805, when Schiller died, Goethe produced his plays that gave expression to the aesthetic values they shared. The son of a military doctor, Schiller attended an elite military academy where, following in his father's path, he studied medicine. But he also engaged in literary discussions at school, immersing himself in the works of Rousseau (see Chapter 1, Text 3) and Goethe. He was still at school when he wrote his first play, *The Robbers* (1781), a dark critique of social hypocrisy and political oppression. A powerful statement of *Sturm und Drang* motifs, it caused a sensation—as had Goethe's *Werther* seven years earlier—and in 1782, Schiller left his regiment and his intended military career. For five years, he made a circuit of major German courts and cities, and wrote three more plays. The last of these, produced in Hamburg in 1787, was *Don Carlos*, an excerpt of which appears in this chapter. Like many of Schiller's plays, *Don Carlos* utilized historical events as a scaffolding for the enactment of the author's major theme: the liberation of the individual from the intersecting tyrannies of political despotism, religious repression, and social convention.

Encumbered by a ceaselessly unfolding plot that scrambles the historical record, *Don Carlos* nonetheless stands out for its electric confrontation of the essential conflict between tyranny and freedom. At the end of the third of five acts, the pivotal moment of the play, the king of Spain, the most powerful monarch of his age, who wields not only political power but also, in the service of religious conformity, the repressive machinery of the Inquisition, faces a lone and honest man who speaks forcefully of a future age when the mission of the state will be to advance the welfare of its citizens. Schiller's European audience, unnerved by the savagery of the wars of religion that the Reformation had spurred and poised, having witnessed the English and American revolutions, to see one explode in France, was exquisitely alert to Schiller's trumpeted message.

Fresh from the publication of *Don Carlos*, Schiller came to Weimar, where Goethe presided as cultural arbiter as well as personal assistant to the ruler.

---

4. As he had previously raised Goethe to the nobility, in 1802, the Duke of Saxe-Weimar so honored Schiller, adding "von" to his birth name.

Through this connection, Schiller was made a professor of history and philosophy at the nearby University of Jena, where he wrote works of literary criticism, philosophy, and history, as well as poetry. In 1799, married and stricken with the illness that would end his life, he returned to Weimar, the hub of German civilization, and to playwriting. From then until his death, Goethe produced Schiller's great dramas—notably *Wallenstein* (1799); *Maria Stuart* (1800); *The Maid of Orleans* (1801); and *William Tell* (1804). These plays and others entitle Schiller to recognition, many critics agree, as one of the greatest playwrights in the European tradition; second only, perhaps, to Shakespeare.

Georg Philipp Friedrich von Hardenberg (1772–1801)—whose pen name Novalis (adopted in 1798) recalls a forgotten name of his noble family with roots in the twelfth century—also died young: in 1801, four years before Schiller, not yet thirty years old. By that time, alongside a career as a philosopher, as the manager of a salt-mining enterprise, and as a Thuringian magistrate, he had achieved the status of a great poet, arguably the most important of the German Romantic movement among whose leading minds he passed his brief existence.

Born to a struggling noble family deeply committed to late-Reformation Pietism, Novalis was a brilliant university student at Jena, Leipzig, and Wittenberg, obtaining a law degree, but more significantly immersing himself in the pantheism of Baruch Spinoza, the idealism of Immanuel Kant, the post-Kantian philosophy of his contemporaries Johann Gottlieb Fichte and Friedrich Schlegel, and the mysticism of the seventeenth-century Christian thinker Jakob Böhme [Jacob Boehme], among others. He developed a philosophical vision that fused these traditions; and with it, an understanding of Romanticism as a movement that reached for the spiritualization of the world and the recovery of the individual's unity with a perfect, infinite, and undifferentiated cosmos, the poet or the artist being the agent of that harmonization of all things. And he wrote: philosophical essays and fragments; novels finished and unfinished; and poems, including the six prose-and-verse poems that constitute his masterful *Hymns to the Night*, the paradigmatic work of German Romantic poetry, excerpts of which are included in this chapter.

Novalis wrote the *Hymns to the Night* following the death of his fiancée, Sophie von Kühn, whom he had met when she was twelve, to whom he was betrothed when she was thirteen, and who died of tuberculosis at fifteen, when Novalis himself was twenty-six. In poetic prose with interpolated verse passages, the six *Hymns to the Night* constitute a manifesto against the guiding principles of the Enlightenment: the supreme value of reason; the denial of (or at least indifference to) soul, spirit, and the divine; and the assumption of earthly progress toward a secular utopia. Against these—in their sum, the "Light"—Novalis contraposes the "Night": the eternal realm of spirit, Nature, love, and God. His program is not mere nihilism, the negation of life: rather, life *is* the Night, eternal slumber, and death in the arms of the Mother—Nature herself, embodied in the Virgin Mother of Jesus—and the Father—roughly, the Christian God. Associated with these eternals is Novalis's dead beloved, Sophie, a vision of whom he experienced at her gravesite, as told in the third *Hymn*. Like Beatrice for Dante (see Volume One, Introduction to Chapter 7), or Laura for Petrarch (see Volume One, Introduction to Chapter 8), she is an intermediary between the poet and the world of the spirit.

A salon hostess, a political liberal, a novelist and literary critic, Germaine de Staël-Holstein, known as Madame de Staël (1766–1817), was one of the leading writers of early Romanticism in France. The only daughter of two Swiss Protestants, whose father was finance minister both to King Louis XVI and, on his deposition, to the early Revolutionary government, she was married in 1786 to the much older Baron Eric Magnus Staël-Holstein, the Swedish ambassador to France. As the ambassador's wife, she enjoyed the protection of diplomatic immunity during the early stages of the Revolution that broke out in 1789, although she was forced to flee in 1792 when the Revolution descended into violence. Upon the downfall of the dictator Robespierre in 1795, she returned to Paris, hopeful of a return to the Revolution's originally liberal program, but watched in horror as Napoleon Bonaparte gained power.

In August 1802, Napoleon became First Consul for Life; and four months later, in December 1802, Staël's first novel, *Delphine*, appeared. Set a decade earlier in the period from April 1790 to October 1792, *Delphine* says little about the Revolution, and nothing whatsoever about Napoleon. Yet Napoleon recognized the work as a threat to his sovereignty, and exiled Staël from Paris—she was not to approach nearer than forty leagues, about 120 miles, to the city—and later, from all of France.

Napoleon detested Staël, as she did him, but that detestation alone is not sufficient to explain Napoleon's response to *Delphine*. He viewed it as an assault on his policies regarding women, marriage, and family that would reverse the changes the Revolution had initiated. Addressed provocatively to *la France silencieuse*—silent France? the France of silence? the France that has been silenced?—Staël's novel is about the suffering to which such policies subjected women, presenting on the one hand a litany of failed, mercenary, and thwarted marriages, and on the other, the fearsome consequences for women—but not for men—who defied social conventions in search of love and personal choice.[5] Staël herself defied those conventions flamboyantly: in 1800, she separated formally from her husband, and both before and after that event, lived openly with a series of lovers whose children she bore and assiduously educated. The eldest of her surviving children, Auguste de Staël, published his mother's complete works in 1820, three years after her death.

---

5. Staël's attack on marriage conventions, especially burdensome for women of the elites, continues the arguments raised earlier by María de Zayas y Sotomayor and Moderata Fonte (see Volume One, Introduction to Chapter 13).

Delphine is an epistolary novel,[6] a format that permits first-person communication of feelings unmediated by a narrator. Staël explores those feelings with exquisite precision and at length, tracing the profound relationship between Delphine and Léonce, two human beings in love.[7] Their love is foiled by many forces—a scheming mother, obligations owed to friends and relatives, the code of honor, the laws of morality, and above all, the iron grip of public opinion. They surmount all these hurdles, but their love is impossible in the end: they cannot marry. They die tragically, within moments of each other, one by suicide, one by firing squad, victims of the Revolution as it devolves to its savage end.

In his youth, Victor Hugo (1802–1885), the son of a general active in the Napoleonic wars, was no friend of the French Revolution, although in later years he supported republicanism. The prolific author of novels, plays, poetry, and essays, the first of his two greatest novels (as many rank them), *Notre-Dame de Paris (The Hunchback of Notre Dame,*[8] 1831), excerpted here, reflects his early views, and the second, *Les Misérables*[9] (1862), his mature outlook. In the forefront of French Romanticism, Hugo lamented the destruction of the monuments and memory of French civilization wrought by the revolutionary wave. Set in Paris in 1482, *The Hunchback* brings to life the vibrant city of that era and celebrates its prize work of architecture, the cathedral of Notre Dame, built in Gothic style between the twelfth and fourteenth centuries.[10] The Revolution detested Gothic, associated, it was thought, with an era of Christian intolerance and monarchical tyranny. The Romantics, in contrast, saw in the vertical dynamic, luxuriant tracery, and shifting patterns of light and color characteristic of Gothic the artistic and imaginative achievement of a more innocent world. Hugo's *Hunchback* is a work as much about the cathedral as the extraordinary characters who enact its narrative.

Those characters include the evil Archdeacon of the cathedral Frollo, the abject poet Gringoire, the arrogant Captain Phoebus, as secondary figures; and as principals, the captivating street dancer Esmeralda and the fabulously ugly bell ringer of Notre Dame, Quasimodo: huge, hunchbacked, one-eyed, and deaf. The Archdeacon and the poet are in love with the dancer, but she is in love with Phoebus, whom she is accused of killing after he had been stabbed,

---

6. Staël was acquainted with the earlier epistolary novels by Richardson, Rousseau, and Goethe, all of which she commends in her essays on literature.

7. Readers today will ask: Was there a sexual relationship? The issue does not arise, although the author herself was certainly aware of the power of sexual love.

8. As, from 1833, it was generally translated in English.

9. The title is often not translated into English, or translated variously as *The Miserables, The Wretched Ones*, etc.

10. Gothic: originally a derogatory term first used by Renaissance advocates of a renewal of classicism, the name derives from that of the Gothic barbarians whose invasions hastened the fall of the Roman Empire.

but not fatally, by the Archdeacon. Quasimodo rescues Esmeralda, for he, too, is in love with her, minutes before her execution. But she is captured again and hanged; he claims her body and dies holding it in his embrace.

Like Goethe's *Werther* and Staël's *Delphine*, Hugo's *Hunchback* is a love story. It differs from these predecessors, however. It is not an epistolary novel, but one told by an omniscient narrator given to disquisitions on history and architecture. It does not dwell on the beauties of nature, but on those of the stone cathedral and the cityscape. It does not feature elegant and articulate members of the elite, but two outcasts, orphaned by civilization. Nevertheless, they love.

Love escaped the grasp of Giacomo Leopardi (1798–1837), regarded by many as the greatest Italian poet of the nineteenth century, and indeed, as one of the greatest European poets of that century. His disappointment in love fueled some of his most intense later poems, reminiscent of Novalis, while his earlier ones assail Italy's cultural despondency and lost national purpose, recalling Hugo, and engage in philosophical questions. For he was a philosopher as well as a poet, his *Zibaldone*, or philosophical notebooks, admired by Schopenhauer and Nietzsche, filling seven volumes on their posthumous publication by national commission in 1898–1890. In addition, he was a classical scholar: a fluent reader, translator, and editor of ancient Hebrew, Greek, and Latin, and an author of tragedies on ancient models. He achieved his immense learning under private tutelage, but mainly at his own initiation,[11] in his father's library of 16,000 volumes—a testimony to humanism's weighty stamp on Italian culture—housed in his noble family's otherwise forbidding palace in the town of Recanati, part of what was then the Papal States.[12]

Blighted from childhood by ill health, Leopardi died not yet thirty-nine years old in the cholera epidemic of 1837 in Naples, Italy. Spared burial in a common grave that was normally the fate of that disease's victims, he was eventually entombed in 1939 in a monument overlooking the Bay of Naples, not far from the presumed gravesite of Roman epic poet Virgil (see Volume One, Introduction to Chapter 3)—a proximity that undoubtedly would have pleased him.

Selections from three of Leopardi's *Canti* (*Poems*)[13] appear in this chapter: two closely related early poems composed in 1818, *All'Italia* (*To Italy*) and *Sopra il monument di Dante* (*On Dante's Monument*), lamenting his country's dismal state; and from 1833 the later poem *A se stesso* (*To Himself*), recording his suffering from a failed romance.

---

11. When Leopardi was fourteen years old, his father dismissed his tutor because there was "nothing left to teach him." Quoted by Jonathan Galassi, ed. of Leopardi, *Canti*, trans. Galassi (New York: Farrar Straus Giroux, 2010), 363.

12. Papal States: territories of central Italy under papal sovereignty from the eighth century until Italian unification in 1870.

13. Leopardi published the *Canti* in two editions in 1831 and 1835, while a close friend gathered his complete works in a posthumous edition of 1845.

In 1828, Leopardi had read the just-published novel by Alessandro Manzoni, *I promessi sposi* (*The Betrothed*, 1827/1840), which many regard as the greatest Italian novel of the century. Set in the seventeenth century, it is a tale of Lucia and Renzo, two peasant villagers, whose wedding, moments before it is to take place, is foiled by the cruel intervention of the villainous Don Rodrigo; the Baron Rodrigo, who intends to seize Lucia for himself, represents for Manzoni the tyranny both of foreign overlordship of Italy and of the nobility as a social class. The two lovers flee, assisted by the saintly Capuchin priest Father Christopher, who arranges for their nighttime escape by boat across Lake Como. During that journey, in the most famous passage of the novel (included in this chapter), Lucia looks back on her village, nestled in the familiar Alpine mountains of her birthplace. The two fugitives then travel along separate highways, to be reunited at last after long and perilous adventures.

The poet and novelist Alessandro Manzoni (1785–1873) was born within the elite circles of northern Italy: his father, his maternal grandfather (the Enlightenment thinker and judicial reformer Cesare Beccaria), and his mother's lover (for whom she had deserted his father when Manzoni was seven years old and from whom he inherited considerable property) were all nobles. Yet in his youth, like many of his generation, he was a liberal: spurning the church, welcoming the French Revolution, and hailing Napoleon as a liberator—to be disillusioned by that liberator's turn to dictatorship, his fall, and the consequent subjection of Italy once again to a foreign power. During the Renaissance, much of Italy had fallen, bit by bit, to the Spanish and then Austrian Habsburgs; Manzoni had made a close study of the history of that era, even incorporating in *The Betrothed* eyewitness accounts of those events. He incorporates, as well, his vision of a compassionate Catholicism, to which he had returned after his earlier rejection of the church.

In the second edition of the novel, moreover, which appeared in 1840 and is now authoritative, Manzoni revised all the passages of the first version that had been in different dialects—for Italy was not only a political patchwork, but also a linguistic one—according to the Tuscan standard that Dante (see Volume One, Introduction to Chapter 7) and his successors had urged, thereby contributing to the linguistic unification of Italian culture not long before its political unification was achieved. Manzoni's death in 1873 was a grand cultural event in Risorgimento Italy,[14] to be followed by an anniversary commemoration the following year, for which the great musician Giuseppe Verdi composed his famous *Requiem*.

Just as Manzoni had yearned for the liberation of Italy, so Adam Mickiewicz (1798–1855), his contemporary, yearned for that of Poland—and of all

---

14. Risorgimento: "resurgence" or "rising," signifying the cultural and political movement preliminary to the unification of Italy that Manzoni had advocated, accomplished in 1870, three years before Manzoni's death.

nations subjugated to imperialist regimes. Like Schiller, too, he looked to a time when states were governed for the benefit of their citizens. Like Leopardi, he hoped that the new generation would wake up from the prevailing dormancy and sacrifice themselves for the nation. These were Mickiewicz's concerns as his century's principal figure of Polish nationalism, and equally of Polish Romanticism.

Mickiewicz was born to an ancient Lithuanian noble family that was aggregated to the Polish *szlachta* (nobility) during the two centuries that the regions of Lithuania, Poland, Belarus, and Ukraine, plus adjacent areas, had been unified under the Polish-Lithuanian Commonwealth. That unity was fractured by three partitions of Poland (in 1772, 1793, and 1795) by neighboring states—the Russian Empire, the Kingdom of Prussia, and the Habsburg monarchy (Austria)—effecting, three years before Mickiewicz's birth, the complete disappearance of Poland as an entity from the map of Europe.

This astounding political datum shaped Polish culture for the next century and more, as it did the life and work of Adam Mickiewicz. Although, like other Romantic poets, he wrote widely admired poems about nature (his *Crimean Sonnets* won special praise) and love, he wrote mainly about the liberation of his homeland. He did so in lyric poems, in drama, and in narrative verse, most notably in *Konrad Wallenrod* (1828) and the epic *Pan Tadeusz* (*Master Thaddeus*, 1834). His literary production was remarkable given his complex career as an exile in Russia (1824–1829), as a professor of Slavic literature (mainly in Paris, 1840–1844), and as a political activist, especially after 1830, the year of an attempted Polish uprising. He died in 1855 in Constantinople, the capital of the Ottoman Empire, where he had gone to raise Polish and Jewish regiments to fight Russia during the Crimean War (1853–1856). Numerous monuments celebrate his towering presence as a "national poet," including those in the Polish cities Warsaw and Kraków, where he was eventually interred, and museums in Constantinople (now Istanbul), Paris, and Warsaw.

Two of Mickiewicz's poems are included in this chapter: the early *Ode to Youth* (1820) and, a decade later, *To a Polish Mother* (1830). The first poem calls on the youth of Poland to rise up to liberate their nation. The second calls on the mothers of Poland to prepare their sons for resistance and martyrdom. In the latter, the Polish mother is likened to Mary, the mother of Jesus, who tragically witnessed the crucifixion of her son, who died for the salvation of all—as Poland's sons must die for their nation.

During his Russian exile, Mickiewicz had written a poem on the extraordinary bronze statue in Peter's Square,[15] St. Petersburg, of Tsar Peter the Great

---

15. Peter's Square: as it was known until 1825; and thereafter Senate Square until 1925, when it was renamed Decembrists' Square to commemorate the Decembrist Revolt against the tsarist regime following the death of Tsar Alexander I; and Senate Square again since 2008. Mickiewicz's poem was entitled *The Monument of Peter the Great*.

(r. 1682–1725) on his rearing horse, poised on its own stone promontory[16] overlooking the Neva River. Catherine the Great, empress of Russia (r. 1762–1796),
who commissioned the famous statue,[17] had it inscribed "to Peter the First
from Catherine the Second," as a tribute to the ruler who opened Russia to the
West and to modernity. Mickiewicz, however, saw in Peter, and in his bronze
representation, not a forward-looking ruler, but a tyrant—one brandishing a
whip and trampling people in his way. Mickiewicz's Russian contemporary
Alexander Pushkin (1798–1837), in contrast, although he admired the Pole
as a poet, avoided his politics—if only because he was under constant scrutiny by the tsarist police and the tsar, Nicholas I, in person. In 1833, Pushkin
composed his own longer poem on the statue, entitled *The Bronze Horseman*—
the title of the poem, and thenceforth, the name of the monument. Although
Pushkin carefully sidesteps the political issues the Polish poet had raised, certain intonations of his poem betray skepticism of autocratic power—as Tsar
Nicholas recognized and forbade its publication. A censored version was permitted in 1837, after Pushkin's death, but the original poem did not appear
until 1904, when Russia, on the verge of revolution, was no longer invested in
protecting tsarist sensibilities.

In this poem and in other works, Pushkin played with fire and was rewarded
for his provocations by long spells of exile (in the Caucasus and Crimea, 1821–
1824) and house arrest (at his aristocratic family's comfortable country estate).
Narrowly escaping destruction following the Decembrist Revolt, which took
several of his friends, he nevertheless died young, ingloriously, in a duel over a
matter of honor. Amid this political maelstrom, he managed in his brief two
decades of mature productivity to reconstruct Russian as a literary language[18]
and bestow upon the Russian literary tradition its foundational texts and
themes. Alongside the brief narrative *The Bronze Horseman* and the verse novel
Eugene Onegin, often considered his principal achievements, Pushkin wrote
lyric and narrative poems, verse drama and fairy tales, and short stories—a
legacy of works that served as a storehouse of materials to be developed by later
Russian authors.

---

16. stone promontory: an immense natural boulder, called the "Thunder Stone," which had been
transported to the site.
17. famous statue: the creation of the French sculptor Etienne Maurice Falconet (1768–1782),
who labored on it fourteen years.
18. Russian as a literary language: the Russian aristocracy spoke and wrote in French, while
Russian was the language of the people, unrefined by literary use outside of church-related materials. Pushkin would develop and refine Russian in his precise, polished poetry, accomplishing for
that language what Dante, Shakespeare, and Cervantes had done for Italian, English, and Spanish.

1. William Blake, *Songs of Innocence* and *Experience* (1789, 1794)

Presented here are five of Blake's nineteen *Songs of Innocence* and five of his twenty-six *Songs of Experience*, giving voice in their sum to key Blakean themes: childhood, love, gentleness, safety, and of course, innocence; and then betrayal, lovelessness, darkness, fear, and the fruits of experience. They appear here in the order encountered in some editions, but as there are variant editions ordered differently, the sequence of the components does not seem to reflect a narrative principle. Some of the poems form pairs: both *Innocence* and *Experience* include the poems *Holy Thursday* and *The Chimney Sweeper*, while *Infant Joy* in *Innocence* corresponds to *Infant Sorrow* in *Experience*, and *The Lamb* in *Innocence* is often juxtaposed with *The Tyger* [Tiger] in *Experience*. *The Laughing Song* in *Innocence*, however, has no direct counterpart in *Experience*; lacking a clear match, the brief and gripping poem *The Clod and the Pebble*, which contrasts selfless and selfish love, is supplied in its stead. Even in this condensed sampling of Blake's poems, their essential paradox is displayed: the utter simplicity of the language, and the rich profundity of the thought.[19]

SONGS OF INNOCENCE (1789)

The Lamb

The poet asks the lamb about God: Do you know who made thee? And then he explains: Jesus, who came from heaven to earth and was made incarnate as a human child, made the lamb and was the lamb, who was sacrificed for the sake of humankind. Both the child and the lamb are figurations of God.

Little Lamb, who made thee?
Dost thou know who made thee?
Gave thee life & bid thee feed
By the stream & o'er the mead;
Gave thee clothing of delight,
Softest clothing, wooly, bright;
Gave thee such a tender voice,
Making all the vales rejoice?
Little Lamb, who made thee?
Dost thou know who made thee?

Little Lamb, I'll tell thee,
Little Lamb, I'll tell thee:
He is callèd by thy name,
For he calls himself a Lamb.
He is meek, & he is mild;
He became a little child.
I a child, & thou a lamb,
We are callèd by his name.
Little Lamb, God bless thee!
Little Lamb, God bless thee!

---

19. The archaisms and contractions present in the original are retained, as they affect rhythm, rhyme, and sense.

The Chimney Sweeper

Little boys, sold (the euphemism might be "apprenticed" or "indentured") by a father or a mother to an adult chimneysweep, climbed up inside and cleaned the chimneys that exhausted the coal fires of London in the early stages of industrialization. Blake empathizes with their wretchedness; and here, as a song of Innocence, *portrays Tom, an orphaned chimneysweep, who dreams of being rescued by an angel to romp in the clouds and who wakes the next morning still filled with his dream's delight and the angel's promise that "[h]e'd have God for his father."*

When my mother died I was very young,
And my father sold me while yet my tongue
Could scarcely cry 'weep! weep! weep! weep!'
So your chimneys I sweep, and in soot I sleep.

There's little Tom Dacre, who cried when his head,
That curl'd like a lamb's back, was shav'd: so I said
'Hush, Tom! never mind it, for when your head's bare
You know that the soot cannot spoil your white hair.'

And so he was quiet, and that very night,
As Tom was a-sleeping, he had such a sight!—
That thousands of sweepers, Dick, Joe, Ned, and Jack,
Were all of them lock'd up in coffins of black.

And by came an Angel who had a bright key,
And he open'd the coffins & set them all free;
Then down a green plain leaping, laughing, they run
And wash in a river, and shine in the Sun.

Then naked & white, all their bags left behind,
They rise upon clouds, and sport in the wind;
And the Angel told Tom, if he'd be a good boy,
He'd have God for his father, & never want joy.

And so Tom awoke; and we rose in the dark,
And got with our bags & our brushes to work.
Tho' the morning was cold, Tom was happy & warm;
So if all do their duty, they need not fear harm.

The Laughing Song

At some future time—evoked by the "When . . . When . . . When . . . When . . . When . . ." that initiate five of the twelve lines of the poem—then the woods, the stream, the air, the green hill, the meadows, the grasshopper, the birds, and the children, will all be united in a song of pure joy, a celebration of life itself.

When the green woods laugh with the voice of joy,
And the dimpling stream runs laughing by;
When the air does laugh with our merry wit,
And the green hill laughs with the noise of it;

When the meadows laugh with lively green,
And the grasshopper laughs in the merry scene,
When Mary and Susan and Emily
With their sweet round mouths sing 'Ha, ha, he!'

When the painted birds laugh in the shade,
Where our table with cherries and nuts is spread:
Come live, and be merry, and join with me,
To sing the sweet chorus of 'Ha, ha, he!'

Holy Thursday

On Holy Thursday, Ascension Day in the Anglican Church calendar, commemorating Christ's ascension into heaven, the brightly clad orphan children of London are led into St. Paul's Cathedral by the church servitors called beadles. The children raise their voices in song, and like a "mighty wind," their song rises straight up to heaven.

'Twas on a Holy Thursday, their innocent faces clean,
The children walking two and two, in red and blue and green,
Grey headed beadles walk'd before, with wands as white as snow,
Till into the high dome of Paul's they like Thames' waters flow.

Oh what a multitude they seem'd, these flowers of London town!
Seated in companies they sit with radiance all their own.
The hum of multitudes was there, but multitudes of lambs,
Thousands of little boys and girls raising their innocent hands.

Now like a mighty wind they raise to heaven the voice of song,
Or like harmonious thunderings the seats of Heaven among.
Beneath them sit the aged men, wise guardians of the poor;
Then cherish pity, lest you drive an angel from your door.

Infant Joy

But two days old, the infant lies in the space between eternity and civilization; he has no name to limit his existence, and so is happiness itself—"Joy" is his name.

'I have no name: Pretty joy!
I am but two days old.'   Sweet joy, but two days old.
What shall I call thee?   Sweet joy I call thee:
'I happy am,   I sing the while,
Joy is my name.'   Sweet joy befall thee!
Sweet joy befall thee!

SONGS OF EXPERIENCE (1794)

The Clod and the Pebble

*Even as it suffers under the pounding of bovine hooves, the soft and vulnerable "little
clod of clay" sings of the joy that comes from selfless love—a "heaven" in the midst of
"hell." But the wiser, hard, tough, pebble in the brook corrects the clod: "love" seeks
only to enslave others, and "builds a hell" that heaven deplores.*

'Love seeketh not itself to please,   'Love seeketh only Self to please,
Nor for itself hath any care,   To bind another to its delight,
But for another gives its ease,   Joys in another's loss of ease,
And builds a heaven in hell's despair.'   And builds a hell in heaven's despite.'

So sung a little clod of clay,
Trodden with the cattle's feet,
But a pebble of the brook
Warbled out these metres meet:

Holy Thursday

As in the corresponding song of Innocence, *it is again Holy Thursday, the day
of Christ's ascension; but in this case, infants are "reduced to misery," and the
song the children sing is a mere "trembling cry" and no "song of joy." For they live
in "a land of poverty," where the sun never shines, and it is always winter.*

Is this a holy thing to see   And their sun does never shine.
In a rich and fruitful land,   And their fields are bleak & bare.
Babes reduced to misery   And their ways are fill'd with thorns.
Fed with cold and usurous hand?   It is eternal winter there.

Is that trembling cry a song?   For where'er the sun does shine,
Can it be a song of joy?   And where'er the rain does fall:
And so many children poor?   Babe can never hunger there,
It is a land of poverty!   Nor poverty the mind appall.

The Chimney Sweeper

The child chimney sweeper of Innocence *was rescued from misery by a visit from an angel. But in* Experience, *the little boy is a "little black thing among the snow" who weeps and weeps "in notes of woe." He seems to laugh and play, so father and mother take no notice of him, having gone to church to pray, their holiness a posture won at the cost of the child's misery.*

A little black thing among the snow:
Crying weep, weep, in notes of woe!
Where are thy father & mother? say?
They are both gone up to the church to pray.

Because I was happy upon the heath,
And smil'd among the winters snow:
They clothed me in the clothes of death,
And taught me to sing the notes of woe.

And because I am happy & dance & sing,
They think they have done me no injury:
And are gone to praise God & his Priest & King,
Who make up a heaven of our misery.

The Tyger

The splendid tiger, "burning bright," possesses a "fearful symmetry," the awful orderliness and rationality that for Blake bespeaks repression, cruelty, and the stifling of imagination. How could God have created such a terrifying beast, one that makes the stars weep and "[throw] down their spears"? In stark, searching monosyllables, the poet wonders: "Did he who made the Lamb make thee?" It is an open question: Could the same creator have fashioned the kindly Lamb and the fierce Tyger? Or were there two creators—one beneficent, one diabolic?

Tyger Tyger, burning bright,
In the forests of the night;
What immortal hand or eye,
Could frame thy fearful symmetry?

In what distant deeps or skies,
Burnt the fire of thine eyes?
On what wings dare he aspire?
What the hand, dare seize the fire?

And what shoulder, & what art,
Could twist the sinews of thy heart?
And when thy heart began to beat,
What dread hand? & what dread feet?

What the hammer? what the chain,
In what furnace was thy brain?
What the anvil? what dread grasp,
Dare its deadly terrors clasp!

When the stars threw down their spears
And water'd heaven with their tears:
Did he smile his work to see?
Did he who made the Lamb make thee?

Tyger Tyger burning bright.
In the forests of the night:
What immortal hand or eye,
Dare frame thy fearful symmetry?

Infant Sorrow

In sharp contrast to the Infant Joy *of the* Innocence *poems, here the infant leaps into a "dangerous world"; he is a "fiend hid in a cloud," who resists both his father's hands and the swaddling clothes used to wrap newborns tight. Exhausted by his struggle to be free, he does not rest, but "sulk[s]" on his mother's breast.*

My mother groan'd! my father wept.
Into the dangerous world I leapt:
Helpless, naked, piping loud;
Like a fiend hid in a cloud.

Struggling in my father's hands,
Striving against my swadling bands,
Bound and weary I thought best
To sulk upon my mother's breast.

2. William Wordsworth, *Ode: Intimations of Immortality from Recollections of Early Childhood* (1807)

Composed in stages, at first titled only *Ode*, with the explanatory subtitle added some years later, the *Intimations of Immortality* can be seen as a culminating statement of Wordsworth's poetic message. The poet himself recognized its significance, as may be inferred from his deliberate placement of the work in his 1807 and 1820 collections, in each case, as the final poem:[20] in effect, a summation of the whole. The poem celebrates infancy as a condition close to the divine, a state barely emerged from a preexistent reality—the "immortality" of the title—exceeding that of the present world. As the child grows and approaches adulthood, that original exaltation is diminished and finally lost. The adult's philosophical mind can only approximate the truth that the child by nature apprehends. Although critics have objected to some qualities of the *Ode*, it was greatly popular on it first publication and is generally considered to be one of Wordsworth's greatest works.

---

20. William Wordsworth, *Poems, In Two Volumes* (London: Longman, Hurst, Rees, and Orme, 1807), 2:145–58; *The Miscellaneous Poems of William Wordsworth*, 4 vols. (London: Longman, Hurst, Rees, Orme, and Brown, 1820), 4:273–84. In both cases, the poem appears with a separate title page and is entitled simply *Ode*. I have not been able to examine the second volume of the 1815 collection in two volumes (London: Longman, Hurst, Rees, Orme, and Brown), but in the table of contents of vol. 2 printed in the early pages of vol. 1, the *Ode* is again listed as the closing poem.

ODE: INTIMATIONS OF IMMORTALITY[21]

Stanzas 1–4, originally composed before the remaining seven, develop the theme of the child's fresh apprehension of nature, more vivid than that of an adult, as the poet himself remembers: "The things which I have seen I now can see no more," he comments; and it is a painful loss, for "there hath past away a glory from the earth." Where has it gone? "Where is it now, the glory and the dream?"

1.

There was a time when meadow, grove, and stream,
The earth, and every common sight,
To me did seem
Apparelled in celestial light,
The glory and the freshness of a dream.
It is not now as it hath been of yore;—
Turn wheresoe'er I may,
By night or day.
The things which I have seen I now can see no more.

2.

The Rainbow comes and goes,
And lovely is the Rose,
The Moon doth with delight
Look round her when the heavens are bare,
Waters on a starry night
Are beautiful and fair;
The sunshine is a glorious birth;
But yet I know, where'er I go,
That there hath past away a glory from the earth.

3.

Now, while the birds thus sing a joyous song,
And while the young lambs bound
As to the tabor's sound,
To me alone there came a thought of grief:
A timely utterance gave that thought relief,
And I again am strong:
The cataracts blow their trumpets from the steep;
No more shall grief of mine the season wrong;
I hear the Echoes through the mountains throng,
The Winds come to me from the fields of sleep,

---

21. Omitted is the epigraph first added in the 1815 collection, containing the well-known phrase "the child is father to the man."

And all the earth is gay;
Land and sea
Give themselves up to jollity,
And with the heart of May
Doth every Beast keep holiday;—
Thou Child of Joy,
Shout round me, let me hear thy shouts, thou happy Shepherd-boy.

4.

Ye blessèd creatures, I have heard the call
Ye to each other make; I see
The heavens laugh with you in your jubilee;
My heart is at your festival,
My head hath its coronal,
The fulness of your bliss, I feel—I feel it all.
Oh evil day! if I were sullen
While Earth herself is adorning,
This sweet May-morning,
And the Children are culling
On every side,
In a thousand valleys far and wide,
Fresh flowers; while the sun shines warm,
And the Babe leaps up on his Mother's arm:—
I hear, I hear, with joy I hear!
—But there's a Tree, of many, one,
A single field which I have looked upon,
Both of them speak of something that is gone;
The Pansy at my feet
Doth the same tale repeat:
Whither is fled the visionary gleam?
Where is it now, the glory and the dream?

In stanza 5, the poet explores the ancient idea, one that Plato among others had proposed, that the human self exists prior to birth, so that birth is not the beginning but rather the final moment of reality, after which comes "a sleep and a forgetting." We do not come into the world, as commonly thought, naked and unformed, but splendidly and powerfully: "trailing clouds of glory do we come / From God, who is our home." But as the infant becomes a child, "shades of the prison-house begin to close" about him; the young man "still is Nature's Priest," and has access to the original vibrancy of things; but the grown man lives in disenchantment: the "vision splendid" dies away, and "fade[s] into the light of common day."

5.

Our birth is but a sleep and a forgetting:
The Soul that rises with us, our life's Star,
Hath had elsewhere its setting,
And cometh from afar:
Not in entire forgetfulness,
And not in utter nakedness,
But trailing clouds of glory do we come
From God, who is our home:
Heaven lies about us in our infancy!
Shades of the prison-house begin to close
Upon the growing Boy,
But he beholds the light, and whence it flows,
He sees it in his joy;
The Youth, who daily farther from the east
Must travel, still is Nature's Priest,
And by the vision splendid
Is on his way attended;
At length the Man perceives it die away,
And fade into the light of common day.

The poet remarks in stanzas 6–8 on the child's development. Mothers and nurses help the child forget his glorious past. With his playthings, the child imitates and incorporates into himself the business of ordinary life—"As if his whole vocation / Were endless imitation" is the sour assessment—distancing himself from his "heaven-born freedom," and taking upon himself the weight of mere existence, that "earthly freight."

6.

Earth fills her lap with pleasures of her own;
Yearnings she hath in her own natural kind,
And, even with something of a Mother's mind,
And no unworthy aim,
The homely Nurse doth all she can
To make her Foster-child, her Inmate Man,
Forget the glories he hath known,
And that imperial palace whence he came.

7.

Behold the Child among his new-born blisses,
A six years' Darling of a pigmy size!
See, where 'mid work of his own hand he lies,
Fretted by sallies of his mother's kisses,
With light upon him from his father's eyes!

See, at his feet, some little plan or chart,
Some fragment from his dream of human life,
Shaped by himself with newly-learnèd art
A wedding or a festival,
A mourning or a funeral;
And this hath now his heart,
And unto this he frames his song:
Then will he fit his tongue
To dialogues of business, love, or strife;
But it will not be long
Ere this be thrown aside,
And with new joy and pride
The little Actor cons another part;
Filling from time to time his "humorous stage"
With all the Persons, down to palsied Age,
That Life brings with her in her equipage;
As if his whole vocation
Were endless imitation.

8.

Thou, whose exterior semblance doth belie
Thy Soul's immensity;
Thou best Philosopher, who yet dost keep
Thy heritage, thou Eye among the blind,
That, deaf and silent, read'st the eternal deep,
Haunted for ever by the eternal mind,—
Mighty Prophet! Seer blest!
On whom those truths do rest,
Which we are toiling all our lives to find,
In darkness lost, the darkness of the grave;
Thou, over whom thy Immortality
Broods like the Day, a Master o'er a Slave,
A Presence which is not to be put by;
Thou little Child, yet glorious in the might
Of heaven-born freedom on thy being's height,
Why with such earnest pains dost thou provoke
The years to bring the inevitable yoke,
Thus blindly with thy blessedness at strife?
Full soon thy Soul shall have her earthly freight,
And custom lie upon thee with a weight,
Heavy as frost, and deep almost as life!

In stanza 9, the poet muses that we can sometimes, somehow, still apprehend that vision we have lost: "Our Souls have sight of that immortal sea / Which brought us hither. . . ." And so, in stanzas 10 and 11, we may rejoice: though we can never regain "the hour / Of splendour in the grass, of glory in the flower," we shall not grieve; "The innocent brightness of a new-born Day / Is lovely yet. . . ."

9.

O joy! that in our embers
Is something that doth live,
That Nature yet remembers
What was so fugitive!
The thought of our past years in me doth breed
Perpetual benediction: not indeed
For that which is most worthy to be blest;
Delight and liberty, the simple creed
Of Childhood, whether busy or at rest,
With new-fledged hope still fluttering in his breast:—
Not for these I raise
The song of thanks and praise
But for those obstinate questionings
Of sense and outward things,
Fallings from us, vanishings;
Blank misgivings of a Creature
Moving about in worlds not realised,
High instincts before which our mortal Nature
Did tremble like a guilty thing surprised:
But for those first affections,
Those shadowy recollections,
Which, be they what they may
Are yet the fountain-light of all our day,
Are yet a master-light of all our seeing;
Uphold us, cherish, and have power to make
Our noisy years seem moments in the being
Of the eternal Silence: truths that wake,
To perish never;
Which neither listlessness, nor mad endeavour,
Nor Man nor Boy,
Nor all that is at enmity with joy,
Can utterly abolish or destroy!
Hence in a season of calm weather
Though inland far we be,
Our Souls have sight of that immortal sea

Which brought us hither,
Can in a moment travel thither,
And see the Children sport upon the shore,
And hear the mighty waters rolling evermore.

Then sing, ye Birds, sing, sing a joyous song!
And let the young Lambs bound
As to the tabor's sound!
We in thought will join your throng,
Ye that pipe and ye that play,
Ye that through your hearts to-day
Feel the gladness of the May!
What though the radiance which was once so bright
Be now for ever taken from my sight,
Though nothing can bring back the hour
Of splendour in the grass, of glory in the flower;
We will grieve not, rather find
Strength in what remains behind;
In the primal sympathy
Which having been must ever be;
In the soothing thoughts that spring
Out of human suffering;
In the faith that looks through death,
In years that bring the philosophic mind.
And O, ye Fountains, Meadows, Hills, and Groves,
Forebode not any severing of our loves!
Yet in my heart of hearts I feel your might;
I only have relinquished one delight
To live beneath your more habitual sway.
I love the Brooks which down their channels fret,
Even more than when I tripped lightly as they;
The innocent brightness of a new-born Day
Is lovely yet;
The Clouds that gather round the setting sun
Do take a sober colouring from an eye
That hath kept watch o'er man's mortality;
Another race hath been, and other palms are won.
Thanks to the human heart by which we live,
Thanks to its tenderness, its joys, and fears,
To me the meanest flower that blows can give
Thoughts that do often lie too deep for tears.

3. Samuel Taylor Coleridge, *Kubla Khan* (1797/1816) and *Frost at Midnight* (1798/1817)

A voracious reader as a child, Coleridge had feasted his imagination on the *Arabian Nights*[22] and Marco Polo's *Description of the World* (see Volume One, Chapter 7, Text 1), from which and similar sources he assembled the building blocks of the vision in *Kubla Khan*[23] of a "stately pleasure-dome," along which ran a "sacred river" through "caves of ice" and "measureless" caverns on to a "sunless sea." In the pleasure-dome may be recognized the realm of the imagination. Its exotic setting, wild natural features, and hint of dangers—"[a]ncestral voices prophesying war"—menacing the poet's vulnerable world are all characteristically Romantic, if exceptionally stirring and vivid, an effect achieved by robust rhythms and resounding, variably structured rhymes. The poet of this compelling fragment is depicted in its final lines: "Beware! Beware! / His flashing eyes, his floating hair! . . . For he on honey-dew hath fed, / And drunk the milk of Paradise." It is an apt description: for Coleridge wrote the work fueled by laudanum, an opiate, to which he was irreparably addicted. The poet himself describes the circumstances in the preface to the 1816 collection of the poems in which *Kubla Khan*, composed in 1797, was published.[24]

Frost at Midnight, first written in 1798, not long after *Kubla Khan*, and published in 1817 in Coleridge's collection *Sybilline Lines*, is a very different poem. It is composed in blank verse, unadorned by rhyme, and its organic rhythms emerge from the flow of words, a hallmark of the "conversational" poetry the poet had recommended to his friend Wordsworth. The poet is alone in the middle of the night, his infant child cradled at his side, perceiving the forms and messages of the beautiful Lake District landscape outside his cottage, on whose eaves hang the icicles formed by the "secret ministry" of frost—a phrase appearing in the first line of the poem and repeated in the third-from-last. He imagines that, unlike himself, who grew up a lonely child in a school outside of London, his child will grow up amid the lush and sumptuous "shapes and sounds" of lakes, mountains, and clouds of the natural world, which are God's "eternal language." "Therefore," he concludes, in a last ten-line sentence ending with the image of icicles "shining to the quiet Moon," "all seasons shall be sweet to thee." Nature, God, childhood, and the poetic imagination, are fused together as one.

---

22. *Arabian Nights* or the *One Thousand and One Nights*, a collection of Middle Eastern tales in Arabic compiled during the Middle Ages and first translated into English in the early eighteenth century.

23. The full title of the poem is *Kubla Khan, or, A Vision in a Dream: A Fragment.* It is named for Kublai or Qubilai Khan, Mongol emperor of China (r. 1260–1294), and Marco Polo's employer during the latter's stay there in 1275–1292.

24. Samuel Taylor Coleridge, *Christabel: Kubla Khan: A Vision; The Pains of Sleep* (London: Bulmer, 1816), preface at 51–54.

KUBLA KHAN

In Xanadu did Kubla Khan
A stately pleasure-dome decree:
Where Alph, the sacred river, ran
Through caverns measureless to man
Down to a sunless sea.
So twice five miles of fertile ground
With walls and towers were girdled round:
And there were gardens bright with sinuous rills
Where blossom'd many an incense-bearing tree;
And here were forests ancient as the hills,
Enfolding sunny spots of greenery.

But O, that deep romantic chasm which slanted
Down the green hill athwart a cedarn cover!
A savage place! as holy and enchanted
As e'er beneath a waning moon was haunted
By woman wailing for her demon-lover!
And from this chasm, with ceaseless turmoil seething,
As if this earth in fast thick pants were breathing,
A mighty fountain momently was forced;
Amid whose swift half-intermitted burst
Huge fragments vaulted like rebounding hail,
Or chaffy grain beneath the thresher's flail:
And 'mid these dancing rocks at once and ever
It flung up momently the sacred river.
Five miles meandering with a mazy motion
Through wood and dale the sacred river ran,
Then reach'd the caverns measureless to man,
And sank in tumult to a lifeless ocean:
And 'mid this tumult Kubla heard from far
Ancestral voices prophesying war!

The shadow of the dome of pleasure
Floated midway on the waves;
Where was heard the mingled measure
From the fountain and the caves.
It was a miracle of rare device,
A sunny pleasure-dome with caves of ice!

A damsel with a dulcimer
In a vision once I saw:
It was an Abyssinian maid,

And on her dulcimer she play'd,
Singing of Mount Abora.
Could I revive within me,
Her symphony and song,
To such a deep delight 'twould win me,
That with music loud and long,
I would build that dome in air,
That sunny dome! those caves of ice!
And all who heard should see them there,
And all should cry, Beware! Beware!
His flashing eyes, his floating hair!
Weave a circle round him thrice,
And close your eyes with holy dread,
For he on honey-dew hath fed,
And drunk the milk of Paradise.

FROST AT MIDNIGHT

The frost performs its secret ministry,
Unhelped by any wind. The owlet's cry
Came loud—and hark, again! loud as before.
The inmates of my cottage, all at rest,
Have left me to that solitude, which suits
Abstruser musings: save that at my side
My cradled infant slumbers peacefully.
'Tis calm indeed! so calm, that it disturbs
And vexes meditation with its strange
And extreme silentness. Sea, hill, and wood,
This populous village! Sea, and hill, and wood,
With all the numberless goings-on of life,
Inaudible as dreams! the thin blue flame
Lies on my low-burnt fire, and quivers not;
Only that film, which fluttered on the grate,
Still flutters there, the sole unquiet thing.
Methinks, its motion in this hush of nature
Gives it dim sympathies with me who live,
Making it a companionable form,
Whose puny flaps and freaks the idling Spirit
By its own moods interprets, everywhere
Echo or mirror seeking of itself,
And makes a toy of Thought.

But O! how oft,
How oft, at school, with most believing mind,
Presageful, have I gazed upon the bars,
To watch that fluttering stranger! and as oft
With unclosed lids, already had I dreamt
Of my sweet birthplace, and the old church-tower,
Whose bells, the poor man's only music, rang
From morn to evening, all the hot Fair-day,
So sweetly, that they stirred and haunted me
With a wild pleasure, falling on mine ear
Most like articulate sounds of things to come!
So gazed I, till the soothing things I dreamt
Lulled me to sleep, and sleep prolonged my dreams!
And so I brooded all the following morn,
Awed by the stern preceptor's face, mine eye
Fixed with mock study on my swimming book:
Save if the door half opened, and I snatched
A hasty glance, and still my heart leaped up,
For still I hoped to see the stranger's face,
Townsman, or aunt, or sister more beloved,
My playmate when we both were clothed alike!

Dear babe, that sleepest cradled by my side,
Whose gentle breathings, heard in this deep calm,
Fill up the interspersed vacancies
And momentary pauses of the thought!
My babe so beautiful! it thrills my heart
With tender gladness, thus to look at thee,
And think that thou shalt learn far other lore
And in far other scenes! For I was reared
In the great city, pent 'mid cloisters dim,
And saw nought lovely but the sky and stars.
But thou, my babe! shalt wander like a breeze
By lakes and sandy shores, beneath the crags
Of ancient mountain, and beneath the clouds,
Which image in their bulk both lakes and shores
And mountain crags: so shalt thou see and hear
The lovely shapes and sounds intelligible
Of that eternal language, which thy God
Utters, who from eternity doth teach
Himself in all, and all things in himself.
Great universal Teacher! he shall mould
Thy spirit, and by giving make it ask.

Therefore all seasons shall be sweet to thee,
Whether the summer clothe the general earth
With greenness, or the redbreast sit and sing
Betwixt the tufts of snow on the bare branch
Of mossy apple-tree, while the nigh thatch
Smokes in the sunthaw; whether the eve-drops fall
Heard only in the trances of the blast,
Or if the secret ministry of frost
Shall hang them up in silent icicles,
Quietly shining to the quiet Moon.

4. Johann Wolfgang von Goethe,
The Sorrows of Young Werther (1774)

Lotte (as he affectionately calls Charlotte) and Albert have married, but Werther continues to live nearby and visit frequently—Lotte, not forbidding him to do so, and Albert, a little dubious, but willing. As the impossibility of a relationship with Charlotte becomes increasingly clear to Werther and ever more unbearable, he considers suicide. The excerpts that follow tell the story of his last twelve days on earth, December 12 to 23, 1772.

THE SORROWS OF YOUNG WERTHER

In the weeks before Christmas, Werther moves to a decision for suicide, which he sees as the only possible resolution of his hopeless love.

December 12

Dear Wilhelm, I am in the state that those unlucky fellows must have suffered who were thought to be possessed by an evil spirit. Sometimes it seizes me: not fear, not desire, but an inner, mysterious turbulence that chokes back my breath and threatens to burst open my heart. Such pain! Such pain! And then I plunge forth into the fearful dark night of this most hateful season.

Yesterday evening I had to go out. A sudden thaw had arrived—I was told that the river had overflowed its banks, the streams were all swollen, and Wahlheim, my beloved valley, lay under water. It was nearly midnight, and I rushed outside. It was a frightening scene. Roaring torrents crashed down the cliffs in the moonlight, sweeping up trees, fields, hedgerows, and all that lay below, and the whole valley from end to end was a stormy lake battered by the wind! And then when the moon shone forth again, sitting calmly above the black clouds, mirrored in the fierce and splendid waters that roared and thundered before me, then a shudder came upon me, and then, a longing. Ah, with arms extended, I stood above the abyss and breathed "dive in, dive in!" And enraptured, I thought to rid myself of my sorrows and suffering, to lose myself in the waves. Ah—but my foot would not be lifted from the ground, and so end my desolation. My hour has not yet come, I feel it has not.[25] O Wilhelm! How gladly would I have given up this existence, to fly through those clouds on the winds of the storm, to hold fast to the waters! Ha!—may not perhaps this imprisoned soul one day know this ecstasy? . . .

December 14

What is happening, my dear friend? I terrify myself! Is not my love for her utterly pure, sacred, and fraternal? Have I ever felt in my soul a forbidden desire?—I will say no more—but now, dreams! O how right they were, they who believed such chaotic visions were caused by malign powers! This night! I tremble to say it: I held her in my arms, pressed her to my heart, and with countless kisses covered her lips that whispered her love; my eyes swam to see hers giddily swim. God! Do I sin, that even now I am still in ecstasy, that deep within my soul I relive these rapturous moments? Lotte! Lotte!—I am done for! My mind is confused, for a week I have been unable to think, my eyes are full of tears. I am not at all well, I am entirely well. There is nothing I wish, nothing I desire. It would be better if I were gone. . . .

On December 21, Werther writes the following letter to Lotte, to which he will make further additions. When it is done, it will be left sealed on his desk to be given to her after his death.

It is decided, Lotte, I will die, and I write you these words without any romantic excess, but calmly, on the morning of the day on which I shall see you for the last time. When you read this, my darling, the cold grave will already hold the rigid corpse of that restless and luckless man who has no sweeter prospect than in the last moments of his life to be able to talk to you. I have spent a frightful night, and yet, ah, a salutary night; for it has determined my firm decision. I am resolved to die!

When I tore myself away from you yesterday, my mind overcome with a terrifying turbulence that bore down upon my heart, the hopelessness and joylessness of my existence in your presence seized me with deathly coldness. I could scarcely reach my room, and beside myself, threw myself on my knees, and O God! you granted me the ultimate solace of bitter tears. A thousand plans, a thousand possibilities, raged within my soul, until at last it stood there firm, whole, one final, singular thought: I must die! I lay down to sleep, and

---

25. Cf. John 2:4, Jesus's words to Mary.

in the morning, in the quietude of awakening, there it stood still firm, still strongly fixed in my heart: I must die! It is not despair, it is a certitude that I have served my purpose, and must sacrifice myself for you.

Yes, Lotte! Why should I not speak out? One of us three must depart, and that one will be me. O my darling! Into this ravaged heart has often entered the terrible urge—to murder your husband! You! and me! So let it be then. When you climb the mountainside on some pleasant summer evening, remember me then, how I came up so often from the valley; then look toward the churchyard and on to my grave, overgrown by the tall grass which, in the glow of the setting sun, is blown here and there by the wind.

I was at peace when I began this letter, but now, seeing it all so vividly, now I weep like a child. . . .

Lotte, meanwhile, is beginning to suspect she is in love with Werther. She had instructed him not to return until Christmas Eve—to give them both a bit of space—but he returns on December 21, and loiters aimlessly. He had left with her some pages of his own translation of Ossian,[26] and she asks him to read them to her—pages of profound emotional force. The two can go on no further and embrace passionately. Overcome, she tells him he must see her no more; he must go and never return. He asks her for a last word of farewell, but she gives none. He says farewell forever. The next morning, on December 22, he returns to his final letter to Lotte and writes some more.

For the last time, for the last time then do I open up my eyes. They can no longer see the sun, for ah, gloom and mist have hidden it away. Weep, then, Nature! For your son, your friend, your lover is coming to his end. . . .

Forgive me! Oh forgive me! Yesterday! That should have been the last moment of my life. O you angel! For the first time, unmistakably, for the very first time, deep inside my innermost being there surged a rapturous joy! She loves me! She loves me! That sacred fire still burns on my lips, lit by the fire on yours, and in my heart burns a new, fierce delight. Forgive me! Forgive me! . . .

All things pass away, but even eternity cannot extinguish the living fire that I tasted yesterday on your lips, that I feel inside me! She loves me! These arms have held her tight, these quivering lips have touched hers, this trembling mouth her mouth. She is mine! You are mine! Yes, Lotte, forever! . . .

Werther sends a note to Albert: "Would you be so kind as to lend me your pistols for a journey? Farewell." Lotte advises Albert to give them to the servant who had brought the note, to whom she conveys the pistols by her own hands, with her wishes

---

26. Ossian: epic verse with other fragments purportedly by the legendary third-century Gaelic bard Ossian, but actually the invention of eighteenth-century scholar and poet James Macpherson. Goethe and his contemporaries were not aware of the forgery.

for Werther's good journey. Werther learns from his servant that Lotte had handed them over without saying a word of farewell. He writes some last notes and arranges his papers, then resumes his letter to Lotte.

Past eleven

Everything around me is silent, and my soul is at peace. Thanks be to God, who for these last moments grants me this power, this strength.

I go to the window, my darling, and I see, even through the stormy, wind-driven clouds, I still see a few of the stars of the eternal heavens. No, you will not fall from the sky! The Almighty holds you in his heart, as he holds me. . . . What is there that does not remind me of you? Do you not everywhere enfold me? And have I not, like a child, held fast hungrily to every little thing that you have made sacred by your touch? . . .

I have sent your father a note asking him to see to my remains. In the churchyard there are two linden trees, in the far corner near the field; I would like to be laid to rest there. He can, and he will do this for his friend. You must also ask him to do so. I will not discomfit pious Christians who do not wish their bodies to lie alongside an unfortunate wretch such as myself.[27] . . .

Here now, Lotte! I do not flinch from taking the cold, fearsome cup, from which I shall drink death's potion. You handed it to me, and I do not fear it. All, all of the hopes and wishes of my life, all are now fulfilled! And so I knock with a cool and steady hand at death's bronze door. . . .

I wish to be buried in these clothes, Lotte, which you sanctified by your touch. I have also asked this of your father. My soul soars over my grave. . . . This pink ribbon that you wore on your bosom when I first saw you among the children. . . . This ribbon must be buried with me—you gave it to me on my birthday! . . . Ah, I did not think then that the road ahead would have led to this.—Be at peace! I beg you, be at peace!

They are loaded. The clock strikes twelve. So let it be then. Lotte! Lotte, farewell! Farewell!

The narrator, in the guise of editor of Werther's letters, tells the rest of the story. Werther dies a lingering death on December 23. He is a suicide; no clergyman officiates at his burial; no friends are present.

A neighbor saw the flash of the powder and heard the gunshot. But afterward all was still, so he gave it no more thought.

Around six in the morning a servant entered the room with a candle. He found his master stretched out on the floor, the pistols, and the blood. He called to Werther, and shook him; no answer but a rattling in his throat. He ran to get a doctor and Albert. Lotte heard the doorbell ring, and her whole body

---

27. Those who had committed suicide were not buried in sacred ground.

shook to hear it. She woke her husband, they both rose up, the servant sobbed and stammered out the news, and Lotte, stricken, fell at Albert's feet.

When the doctor reached the unfortunate Werther, he found him on the floor, beyond hope, his blood still pulsing, but his limbs motionless. He had shot himself over his right eye and blown out his brains. Yet blood still flowed from a vein that had burst in his arm, and still he breathed.

It could be seen from the bloodstains on the back of the chair that he had shot himself while seated at his desk, then fell convulsing to the ground. He lay on his back near the window, all strength gone. He was fully dressed in his blue coat and buff waistcoat, with his boots on.

The household, the neighborhood, the town were in an uproar. Albert arrived. Werther lay on the bed, his head bandaged, his face like that of one already dead, his limbs motionless. His lungs still gave forth horrible rattling breaths, some weak, some stronger. His end was coming. . . . Of Albert's dismay, of Lotte's lamentation, I had best say nothing.

The old custodian came as soon as he heard the news and kissed the dying man, weeping hot tears. His eldest sons came soon after him on foot. . . . Werther died at twelve midday. The custodian's presence and his arrangements restored calm. That night at eleven, he had the body buried at the spot Werther had chosen. The old man, with his sons, followed the body to the grave. Albert could not come. Lotte's life was despaired of. Laborers bore the coffin. No clergyman attended.

5. Friedrich von Schiller, *Don Carlos* (1787)

Hearing from his courtiers rumors of the queen's infidelity with his son Carlos, King Philip searches through his records for an adviser he can trust—and finds the Marquis Posa, a military hero, who has never approached the king for reward or advancement. Philip summons Posa, who enters the royal presence modestly but firmly, and gives an extraordinary response to the king's inquiry. He has not approached the king because he will not serve the king: he serves humanity, he longs for liberty, he looks to the future. He would gladly assist the king in changing course: to abandon his policies of political control and religious repression and, instead, to "new create / The earth," to create a new kind of state that serves the cause of human prosperity and happiness. This, of course, the king cannot accept; but he recognizes in Posa an authentic man and wants his assistance in probing the matter of the queen's alleged adultery.[28]

---

28. Explanations are given in the notes for archaisms or obscure terms in this verse translation, which closely follows Schiller's original. The italicized stage directions within the dialogue are Schiller's. To distinguish my notes from the stage directions, I have set them within brackets.

DON CARLOS

Act III, Scene 10

The KING and MARQUIS POSA. The MARQUIS, as soon as he observes the KING, comes forward and sinks on one knee; then rises and remains standing before him without any sign of confusion.

KING *(looks at him with surprise)*:
We've met before then?

MARQUIS:
No.

KING:
You did my crown
Some service? Why then do you shun my thanks?
My memory is thronged with suitor's claims.
One only[29] is omniscient. 'Twas your duty
To seek your monarch's eye! Why did you not? . . .

[Posa explains that he has long been abroad—and that, with all respect, he has decided to leave the court and the royal service altogether. He explains that he wishes to serve humanity, and as a courtier, he would need to abandon his aspirations.]

MARQUIS:
I cannot be the servant of a prince.

The KING looks at him with astonishment.

I will not cheat the buyer. Should you deem
Me worthy of your service, you prescribe
A course of duty for me; you command
My arm in battle and my head in council.
Then, not my actions, but the applause they meet
At court becomes their object. But for me,
Virtue possesses an intrinsic worth.
I would, myself, create that happiness
A monarch, with my hand, would seek to plant,
And duty's task would prove an inward joy,
And be my willing choice. Say, like you this?
And in your own creation could you hear
A new creator? For I ne'er[30] could stoop
To be the chisel where I fain[31] would be—

---

29. one only: that is, God.
30. ne'er: never.
31. fain: willingly.

The sculptor's self. I dearly love mankind,
My gracious liege, but in a monarchy
I dare not love another than myself.

KING:
This ardor is most laudable. You wish
To do good deeds to others; how you do them
Is but of small account to patriots,
Or to the wise. Choose then within these realms
The office where you best may satisfy
This noble impulse.

MARQUIS:
     'Tis not to be found.

KING:
     How!

MARQUIS:
What your majesty would spread abroad,
Through these my hands—is it the good of men?
Is it the happiness that my pure love
Would to mankind impart? Before such bliss
Monarchs would tremble. No! Court policy
Has raised up new enjoyments[32] for mankind. . . .
     But is that
Which can content the court enough for me?
Must my affection for my brother pledge
Itself to work my brother injury?
To call him happy when he dare not think?
Sire, choose not me to spread the happiness
Which you have stamped[33] for us. I must decline
To circulate such coin. I cannot be
The servant of a prince.

KING (*suddenly*):
     You are, perhaps,
A Protestant?[34]

MARQUIS (*after some reflection*):
     Our creeds, my liege,[35] are one.

---

32. new enjoyments: that is, other, and for Posa inferior aspirations.

33. stamped: that is, impressed with the royal insignia, as for coinage.

34. Posa's lofty vision and confident rejection of conventional norms leads the king to suspect he is a Protestant—which would have been intolerable in Spain at that time, where religious conformity was strictly monitored by the Spanish Inquisition.

35. liege: a term of respect for a noble or royal superior.

A pause.

I am misunderstood. I feared as much. . . .
I may seem dangerous, because I think
Above myself. I am not so, my liege;
My wishes lie corroding here *(laying his hand on his breast).* . . .
      The world is yet
Unripe for my ideal; and I live
A citizen of ages yet to come. . . .

KING:
      Say,[36] am I
The first to whom your views are known?

MARQUIS:
      You are.

KING *(Rises, walks a few paces and then stops opposite the MARQUIS. . . .):*
This tone, at least, is new; but flattery
Exhausts itself. And men of talent still
Disdain to imitate. So let us test
Its opposite for once. Why should I not?
There is a charm in novelty. Should we
Be so agreed, I will bethink me[37] now
Of some new state employment, in whose duties
Your powerful mind———

MARQUIS:
      Sire, I perceive how small,
How mean, your notions are of manly worth.
Suspecting, in an honest man's discourse,
Naught but a flatterer's artifice—methinks[38]
I can explain the cause of this your error.
Mankind compel you to it. With free choice
They have disclaimed their true nobility,
Lowered themselves to their degraded state.
Before man's inward worth, as from a phantom,
They fly in terror—and contented with
Their poverty, they ornament their chains
With slavish prudence; and they call it virtue
To bear them[39] with a show of resignation.

---

36. say: tell me.
37. bethink me: give thought to.
38. methinks: I think.
39. to bear them: that is, to bear themselves.

Thus did you find the world, and thus it was
By your great father[40] handed o'er[41] to you.
In this debased connection—how could you
Respect mankind?

KING:
       Your words contain some truth. . . .

[The king is moved by Posa's vision and authenticity and urges him to continue.]

MARQUIS:
       Your majesty,
I lately passed through Flanders and Brabant,
So many rich and blooming provinces,
Filled with a valiant, great, and honest people.
To be the father of a race like this
I thought must be divine indeed; and then
I stumbled on a heap of burnt men's bones.[42]

He stops, he fixes a penetrating look on the KING, who endeavors to return his glance; but he looks on the ground, embarrassed and confused.

True, you are forced to act so; but that you
Could dare fulfill your task—this fills my soul
With shuddering horror!. . .
       But soon
A milder age will follow that of Philip,
An age of truer wisdom; hand in hand,
The subjects' welfare and the sovereign's greatness
Will walk in union. Then the careful state[43]
Will spare her children, and necessity
No longer glory to be thus inhuman.

KING:
When, think you, would that blessed age arrive,
If I had shrunk before the curse of this?
Behold my Spain, see here the burgher's[44] good
Blooms in eternal and unclouded peace.
A peace like this will I bestow on Flanders.

---

40. your great father: King Philip's father, Holy Roman Emperor Charles V.
41. o'er: over.
42. a heap of burnt men's bones: that is, the telltale residue of the brutal Spanish suppression of the Dutch Revolt.
43. careful state: the state that cares for its subjects.
44. burgher: townsman or citizen.

MARQUIS (*hastily*):
The churchyard's peace![45] And do you hope to end
What you have now begun? Say, do you hope
To check the ripening change of Christendom,[46]
The universal spring, that shall renew
The earth's fair form? Would you alone, in Europe,
Fling yourself down before the rapid wheel
Of destiny, which rolls its ceaseless course,
And seize its spokes with human arm. Vain thought!
Already thousands have your kingdom fled
In joyful poverty: the honest burgher
For his faith exiled, was your noblest subject!
See! with a mother's arms, Elizabeth[47]
Welcomes the fugitives, and Britain blooms
In rich luxuriance, from our country's arts.
Bereft of the new Christian's[48] industry,
Granada[49] lies forsaken, and all Europe
Exulting, sees his foe oppressed with wounds,
By its own hands inflicted![50]

The KING is moved; the MARQUIS observes it, and advances a step nearer.

       You would plant
For all eternity, and yet the seeds
You sow around you are the seeds of death!. . .
In vain you waste your high and royal life
In projects of destruction. Man is greater
Than you esteem him. He will burst the chains
Of a long slumber, and reclaim once more
His just and hallowed rights. . . .
Restore us all you have deprived us of,
And, generous as strong, let happiness
Flow from your horn of plenty—let man's mind
Ripen in your vast empire—give us back
All you have taken from us—and become,
Amidst a thousand kings, a king indeed!

---

45. The churchyard's peace: that is, the false peace of a graveyard, enjoyed only by the dead.
46. ripening change of Christendom: the Protestant Reformation.
47. Elizabeth I: Elizabeth the Great, queen of England (r. 1558–1603) and Philip's enemy, who will welcome refugees from Spain.
48. new Christian: term referring to the *conversos*, converts to Christianity from Islam or Judaism, now victims of the Spanish Inquisition.
49. Granada: the last Muslim stronghold, captured by the Spanish in 1492.
50. Europe rejoices that Spain, its enemy, suffers from the self-inflicted wounds of tyranny and religious repression.

He advances boldly and fixes on him a look of earnestness and enthusiasm.

Oh, that the eloquence of all those myriads,
Whose fate depends on this momentous hour,
Could hover on my lips and fan the spark
That lights thine eye into a glorious flame!
Renounce the mimicry of godlike powers,
Which level us to nothing. Be, in truth,
An image of the Deity himself!
Never did mortal man possess so much
For purpose so divine. The kings of Europe
Pay homage to the name of Spain. Be you
The leader of these kings. One pen-stroke now,
One motion of your hand, can new create
The earth![51] but[52] grant us liberty of thought. . . .

[In earnest entreaty, Posa throws himself at the king's feet, surprising the monarch. The king asks Posa what his hopes are for Spain. His plans are preposterous, but the king is impressed, and demands Posa's service.]

MARQUIS:
      You can do it, sire.
Who else? Devote to your own people's bliss
The kingly power, which has too long enriched
The greatness of the throne alone. Restore
The prostrate dignity of human nature,
And let the subject be, what once he was,
The end and object of the monarch's care,
Bound by no duty, save a brother's love.
And when mankind is to itself restored,
Roused to a sense of its own innate worth,
When freedom's lofty virtues proudly flourish—
Then, sire, when you have made your own wide realms
The happiest in the world, it then may be
Your duty to subdue the universe.

KING *(after a long pause)*:
I've heard you to the end. Far differently
I find, than in the minds of other men,
The world exists in yours. And you shall not
By foreign laws be judged. I am the first
To whom you have your secret self-disclosed;
I know it—so believe it—for the sake

---

51. can new create the earth: can create the earth anew.
52. but: only.

Of this forbearance—that you have till now
Concealed these sentiments, although embraced
With so much ardor—for this cautious prudence.
I will forget, young man, that I have learned them,
And how I learned them. Rise! I will confute
Your youthful dreams by my matured experience,
Not by my power as king. Such is my will,
And therefore act I thus. Poison itself
May, in a worthy nature, be transformed
To some benignant use. . . .

MARQUIS (*quickly*):
And, sire, my fellow-subjects? Not for me,
Nor my own cause, I pleaded. Sire! your subjects——

KING:
Nay, if you know so well how future times
Will judge me, let them learn at least from you,
That when I found a man, I could respect him.

MARQUIS:
Oh, let not the most just of kings at once
Be the most unjust! In your realm of Flanders
There are a thousand better men than I.
But you—sire! may I dare to say so much—
For the first time, perhaps, see liberty
In milder form portrayed.

KING (*with gentle severity*):
            No more of this,
Young man! You would, I know, think otherwise
Had you but learned to understand mankind
As I. But truly—I would not this meeting
Should prove our last. How can I hope to win you?

MARQUIS:
Pray leave me as I am. What value, sire,
Should I be to you were you to corrupt me?

KING:
This pride I will not bear. From this day forth
I hold you in my service. No remonstrance—
For I will have it so. . . .

*[The king raises the delicate matter of the queen, whose purity of character Posa defends.
The king assigns Posa the task of ferreting out the truth, instructing the courtier Count
Lerma that henceforth, Posa is to have privileged access to the royal presence.]*

KING: . . . .
Marquis, you know mankind. Just such a man
As you I long have wished for—you are kind—
Cheerful—and deeply versed in human nature—
Therefore I've chosen you———

MARQUIS (surprised and alarmed):
        Me, sire!

KING:
        You stand
Before your king and ask no special favor—
For yourself nothing!—that is new to me—
You will be just—ne'er weakly swayed by passion.
Watch my son close—search the queen's inmost heart.
You shall have power to speak with her in private.
Retire.

He rings a bell.

MARQUIS:
        And if with but one hope fulfilled
I now depart, then is this day indeed
The happiest of my life.

KING *(holds out his hand to him to kiss)*:
        I hold it not
Amongst my days a lost one.

The MARQUIS rises and goes. COUNT LERMA enters.

        Count, in future,
The marquis is to enter, unannounced.

6. Novalis, *Hymns to the Night* (1800)

Of Novalis's six *Hymns*, the first and third are given here in full, followed by excerpts from the fifth and sixth. The first Hymn introduces the opposition of Light and Night; the third, autobiographical in origin, reports a vision of his dead beloved experienced at her gravesite; the fifth identifies the birth of Christ with the era of the Night, when eternity is opened to all humankind; and the sixth rejoices in that fulfillment.[53]

---

53. The translation here is by the nineteenth-century English poet and theologian George MacDonald, a learned disciple of Novalis. It is slightly modified for readability: orthography is Americanized; the pronouns "thee," "thou," "thy," and "thine" have been replaced with "you" and "your"; and in a few cases, phrases are transposed for greater clarity.

Hymn to the Night

First Hymn

The day is glorious, but even more the night. Viewed by a "lordly stranger," the king over nature, Night's "hidden power affects [the] soul," bringing him to his beloved, and an eternal bridal night.

Before all the wondrous shows of the widespread space around him, what living, sentient thing loves not the all-joyous light, with its colors, its rays and undulations, its gentle omnipresence in the form of the wakening Day? The giant world of the unresting[54] constellations inhales it as the innermost soul of life, and floats dancing in its azure flood; the sparkling, ever-tranquil stone, the thoughtful, imbibing plant, and the wild, burning, multiform beast-world inhales it; but more than all, the lordly stranger with the meaning eyes, the swaying walk, and the sweetly closed, melodious lips. Like a king over earthly nature, it rouses every force to countless transformations, binds and unbinds innumerable alliances, hangs its heavenly form around every earthly substance. Its presence alone reveals the marvelous splendor of the kingdoms of the world.

Aside I turn to the holy, unspeakable, mysterious Night. Afar lies the world, sunk in a deep grave; waste and lonely is its place. In the chords of the bosom blows a deep sadness. I am ready to sink away in drops of dew, and mingle with the ashes.—The distances of memory, the wishes of youth, the dreams of childhood, the brief joys and vain hopes of a whole long life, arise in gray garments, like an evening vapor after the sunset. In other regions the light has pitched its joyous tents: what if it should never return to its children, who wait for it with the faith of innocence?

What springs up all at once so sweetly boding in my heart, and stills the soft air of sadness? Do you also take a pleasure in us, dusky Night? What do you hold under your mantle, that with hidden power affects my soul? Precious balm drips from your hand out of its bundle of poppies. You uplift the heavy-laden pinions[55] of the soul. Darkly and inexpressibly are we moved: joy-startled, I see a grave countenance that, tender and worshipful, inclines toward me, and, amid manifold entangled locks, reveals the youthful loveliness of the Mother. How poor and childish a thing seems to me now the light! how joyous and welcome the departure of the day!—Did you not only therefore, because the Night turns your servants away from you, strew in the gulfs of space those flashing globes, to proclaim, in seasons of your absence, your omnipotence, and your return?

More heavenly than those glittering stars we hold the eternal eyes which the Night has opened within us. Farther they see than the palest of those countless

---

54. unresting: that is, restless.
55. pinions: wings.

hosts. Needing no aid from the light, they penetrate the depths of a loving soul that fills a loftier region with bliss ineffable. Glory to the queen of the world, to the great prophetess of holier worlds, to the foster-mother of blissful love! she sends you to me, you, the tenderly beloved, the gracious sun of the Night. Now am I awake, for now am I yours and mine. You have made me know the Night, and brought her to me to be my life; you have made of me a man. Consume my body with the ardor of my soul, that I, turned to finer air, may mingle more closely with you, and then our bridal night [may] endure forever.

Third Hymn

Solitary and weeping, I[56] *see a "shiver of twilight," which dissolves the chains of the Light; "[a]way fled the glory of the world." The narrator beholds a vision of the beloved,*[57] *in whose eyes "eternity reposed." The beloved is the "sun" of the Night.*

Once when I was shedding bitter tears, when, dissolved in pain, my hope was melting away, and I stood alone by the barren hillock which in its narrow dark bosom hid the vanished form of my Life, lonely as never yet was lonely man, driven by anguish unspeakable, powerless, and no longer aught but a conscious misery;—as there I looked about me for help, unable to go on or to turn back, and clung to the fleeting, extinguished life with an endless longing: then, out of the blue distances, from the hills of my ancient bliss, came a shiver of twilight, and at once snapped the bond of birth, the fetter of the Light.[58] Away fled the glory of the world, and with it my mourning; the sadness flowed together into a new, unfathomable world. You, soul of the Night, heavenly Slumber, did come upon me; the region gently upheaved itself, and over it hovered my unbound, new-born spirit. The hillock became a cloud of dust, and through the cloud I saw the glorified face of my beloved. In her eyes eternity reposed. I laid hold of her hands, and the tears became a sparkling chain that could not be broken. Into the distance swept by, like a tempest, thousands of years. On her neck I welcomed the new life with ecstatic tears. Never was such another dream; then first and ever since I hold fast an eternal, unchangeable faith in the heaven of the Night, and its sun, the Beloved.

Fifth Hymn

Novalis's mysticism is tied to his vision of history. From an ancient pagan Iron Age—echoes are heard here of Hesiod (see Volume One, Chapter 2, Text 2) and

---

56. In the first hymn, the human spectator is a "lordly stranger"; in the third, he is the narrator, the "lyrical 'I.'"
57. Sophie, the poet's deceased fiancée, plays the role here of a *Mittler,* or intercessor, between the human and divine realms, as had Beatrice for Dante and Laura for Petrarch (see in Volume One, respectively, Chapter 7, Text 2 and Chapter 8, Text 1).
58. the fetter of the Light: the imprisonment of soul by the principle of the Light, in contrast to its freedom by the principle of the Night.

Schiller, in his studies of ancient paganism—in which all worshiped the Sun, to a bright new age heralded by the birth of Christ to a virgin mother, embodying the eternal mother principle earlier identified with the night. The possibility now emerges of eternity and universal salvation.

In ancient times an iron Fate lorded it, with dumb force, over the widespread families of men. A gloomy oppression swathed their anxious souls: the Earth was boundless, the abode of the gods and their home. From eternal ages stood its mysterious structure. . . . Life reveled through the centuries like one spring-time, an ever-variegated festival of the children of heaven and the dwellers on the earth. All races childlike adored the ethereal, thousandfold flame,[59] as the one sublimest thing in the world. . . .

After long centuries, the old gods vanish and are transformed. A new age is born with the birth of "a son of the first maid and mother, the eternal fruit of mysterious embrace."

The old world began to decline. The pleasure-garden of the young race withered away; up into opener regions and desolate, forsaking his childhood, struggled the growing man. The gods vanished with their retinue. Nature stood alone and lifeless. Dry Number and rigid Measure bound her with iron chains. . . . No longer was the Light the abode of the gods, and the heavenly token of their presence: they cast over them the veil of the Night. The Night became the mighty womb of revelations; into it the gods went back, and fell asleep, to go abroad in new and more glorious shapes over the transfigured world. Among the people which, untimely ripe, was become of all the most scornful and insolently hostile to the blessed innocence of youth, appeared the New World, in guise never seen before, in the song-favoring hut of poverty,[60] a son of the first maid and mother, the eternal fruit of mysterious embrace. The foresee-ing, rich-blossoming wisdom of the East at once recognized the beginning of the new age; a star showed it the way to the lowly cradle of the king. In the name of the far-reaching future, they did him homage with luster and odor, the highest wonders of Nature. In solitude the heavenly heart unfolded itself to a flower-chalice of almighty love, upturned to the supreme face of the father, and resting on the bliss-boding bosom of the sweetly solemn mother. With deify-ing fervor the prophetic eye of the blooming child beheld the years to come, foresaw, untroubled over the earthly lot of his own days, the beloved offspring of his divine stem.[61] . . .

---

59. thousandfold flame: that is, the sun.

60. hut of poverty: the manger in which Jesus was born: cf. Luke 2:6–7. The following state-ments also allude to biblical verses in which the Magi arrive, guided by a star to the manger in Bethlehem; cf. Matthew 2:1–2 and 9–11.

61. stem: lineage; in Christian theology, Jesus is begotten of the Father; Jesus, the Father, and the Holy Spirit form the Trinity of the coequal persons of God.

Jesus is resurrected and restored to his Mother, who follows him in ascension to heaven.[62] *All humankind is saved.*

Your loved ones weep tears of joy over your grave, tears of emotion, tears of endless thanksgiving; ever afresh, with joyous start, see you rise again, and themselves with you; behold you weep with soft fervor on the blessed bosom of your mother, walk in thoughtful communion with your friends, uttering words plucked as from the tree of life; see you hasten, full of longing, into your father's arms, bearing with you youthful Humanity, and the inexhaustible cup of the golden Future. Soon the mother hastened after you in heavenly triumph; she was the first with you in the new home. Since then, long ages have flowed past, and in splendor ever increasing your new creation has bestirred itself, and thousands have, out of pangs and tortures, followed you, filled with faith and longing and truth, and are walking about with you and the heavenly virgin[63] in the kingdom of Love, minister in the temple of heavenly Death, and are yours forever.

The rhymed verses that follow celebrate resurrected humanity, who drink golden wines shed by the stars and live as stars in the sky. Entering eternal night, we behold the face of God, which is the sun of the night.

Uplifted is the stone,	Free, from the tomb emerges
And all mankind is risen;	Love, to die never more;
We all remain your own,	Fulfilled, life heaves and surges
And vanished is our prison.	A sea without a shore!
All troubles flee away	All night! all blissful leisure!
Before your golden cup;	One jubilating ode!
For Earth nor Life can stay	And the sun of all our pleasure
When with our Lord we sup.[64] . . .	The countenance of God!

Courage! for life is striding
To endless life along;
The Sense, in love abiding,
Grows clearer and more strong.
One day the stars, down dripping,
Shall flow in golden wine:
We, of that nectar sipping,
As living stars shall shine!

---

62. Cf. Luke 24:50–51 for the ascension of Jesus. There is no explicit biblical passage affirming the ascension, or bodily assumption of Mary into heaven, although several passages have been so interpreted, and that event is accepted by the Catholic and Eastern Orthodox churches.
63. heavenly virgin: Jesus's mother, Mary.
64. When with our Lord we sup: a reference to the Lord's Supper on the night before Jesus's crucifixion, for which see the Gospels of Matthew 26:26–29; Mark 14:22–25; Luke 22:14–20; John 6:53–59; and several references in Acts and 1 Corinthians.

Sixth Hymn: Longing for Death

Here Novalis celebrates Death, by which we return to the eternal life of the Night.
We are going home to the father, no longer as the "lordly stranger" of the first hymn,
but as a risen child.

Into the bosom of the earth!
Out of the Light's dominions!
Death's pains are but the bursting forth
Of glad Departure's pinions!
Swift in the narrow little boat,
Swift to the heavenly shore we float!

Blest be the everlasting Night,
And blest the endless Slumber!
We are heated with the day too bright,
And withered up with cumber![65]
We're weary of that life abroad:
Come, we will now go home to God! . . .

With anxious yearning now we see
That Past in darkness drenched;
With this world's water never we
Shall find our hot thirst quenched:
To our old home we have to go
That blessed time again to know.

What yet doth hinder our return?
Long since repose our precious!
Their grave is of our life the bourn;[66]
We shrink from times ungracious!
By not a hope are we decoyed:
The heart is full; the world is void!

Infinite and mysterious,
Thrills through me a sweet trembling,
As if from far there echoed thus
A sigh, our grief resembling:
The dear ones long as well as I,
And send to me their waiting sigh.

Down to the sweet bride,[67] and away
To the beloved Jesus!
Courage! the evening shades grow gray,
Of all our griefs to ease us!
A dream will dash our chains apart,
And lay us on the Father's heart.

7. Madame de Staël, *Delphine* (1802)

Excerpts follow from nine of the 220 letters[68] that make up Staël's novel, distributed across the volume, illustrating the stages of the doomed romance between
Delphine and Léonce. Even these brief samplings display Staël's exquisite delineation of personal feelings and viewpoints, conveyed in the precise and elegant
language that might be heard in lively conversation in her salon.

---

65. cumber: that is, we are encumbered with burdens that cause us to wither.
66. bourn: that is, boundary.
67. sweet bride: both the Virgin Mary and the beloved.
68. In addition to these letters, some of which contain quoted letters within them, there are seven
narrative fragments by Delphine and a narrative conclusion.

DELPHINE

Letters 1.26 and 27: June 20 and 29, 1790

A rich and generous widow, Delphine d'Albémar has contributed to her relative Mme de Vernon a sum of money that will enable Vernon to marry her daughter Matilde to Léonce de Mondoville. But Delphine and Léonce meet at a Paris gathering—where Matilde is also present—and they fall in love. Léonce will propose to Delphine.

1.26: Delphine to Louise, her sister-in-law

Delphine is asked to sing with Matilde and a gentleman an aria about Dido: I was assigned the role of Dido. Léonce was seated opposite us, leaning on the piano. I could scarcely utter the first sounds, but in looking at him, . . . all my strength revived. . . . The loveliness of the aria and the agitation of my heart lent to my performance the full emotional force and meaning of the moment. Léonce, dear Léonce, laid his head on the piano; I heard his rapid breathing, and when at times he looked up at me, his eyes were full of tears. Never, never before had I felt so beyond myself; I found in the music, in the poetry, a power and magic as yet unknown to me, . . . and I felt an enthusiasm and elevation of my soul of which love was the first cause, but which was purer still than love itself. . . .

Léonce speaks with Delphine on the balcony, assured by her performance that she had sung for him and not another man; then they return to the company: Léonce displayed the extraordinary joy . . . of a man who had just escaped a great torment. His mood and mine were one; we invented a thousand games, each of us filled with an inner sense of overflowing happiness. He mocked me gently for what he called my philosophy, the independence of my conduct, my disregard for social convention; but he was happy, and forged between us that inward familiarity, the most intimate expression of the affections of the soul. It seemed to me that all had been said between us, that all obstacles had been removed, all vows uttered. Though I knew nothing of his plans, . . . I was sure that he loved me, and so nothing in the world seemed uncertain to me.

1.27: Léonce to his tutor, M. Barton

My fate is decided, my dear teacher, no one but Delphine shall rule over my heart: yesterday at a ball, yesterday she virtually promised herself to me. . . . I have no more doubts, no uncertainties. It remains only for me to act on my decision, and I consult you only about the means of obtaining my goal. . . .

Yesterday then. . . . But how can I describe that day? It would be to plunge my soul again into confusion. What a feeling love is! It is in life another life! In my heart live thoughts and memories of happiness so vivid that with every breath, I delight in my existence. . . . Can you believe it? I fear that I will die before tomorrow, before an hour, before that instant when I will see her again.

Letter 3.1–2 and 5–6: December 4, 1790

The unscrupulous Mme de Vernon, to protect her daughter's interests, has informed Léonce that Delphine has entertained the attentions of another man. Léonce repudiates her and on July 13, without affection, marries Matilde. But some months later, he is still in love with Delphine and professes his love to her. An exchange of letters ensues, in which Delphine tells Léonce that it is his duty now to stay with his wife and ensure her happiness.

3.1: Léonce to Delphine

The perfidy of others has separated us, my Delphine; now may love reunite us. Let us erase the past from our memory—what matter to us the external circumstances that surround us? Do you not view all those objects around us as though through a fog? Are you convinced they are real? I believe in nothing but you. In my confusion, I know that I have been wrongfully deceived; that I have accused a dying woman; that her daughter calls herself my wife. I know this. But one image only stands out from the dark maelstrom of my memories: it is you, Delphine. I see you at the foot of that deathbed, seeking to staunch my fury, regarding me sweetly, with love. . . .

Barton, my dear friend, did he not propose yesterday that your intention was to leave, and to leave without seeing me? I could not have believed it, my love; what pleasure could your sweet soul find in making me run after you like a madman? You do not believe, never could you have believed that I would resign myself to live without you! No, though an abominable plot has prevented me from being your husband, I shall in no way consent to see you one day, one hour less than if we had been united as one. We are one; all my other ties are lies; there is nothing true but my love, than your love—because you love me, Delphine!

Tell me, I beg you, the day, that day when I consented to that marriage that exists only in the eyes of the world, that marriage sealed by vows that are null, . . . were you not there behind a column, a witness to that fatal ceremony? I thought at the time that you were there only in my imagination; but if it is true, if it was really you that I saw, why did you not rush into my arms? . . . Ah! I would have recognized your voice; your tone would have sufficed to convince me of your innocence; and before that same altar, placing your hand on my heart, it is to you that I would have sworn the love that I felt only for you.

3.2: Delphine to Léonce

How unhappy we are: oh, Léonce, do you not believe that I feel it? Everything pointed a few months ago to our obtaining the purest joy. I was free, my situation and my fortune assured me a perfect independence. I saw you, and I loved you with every fiber of my being—and a mortal blow . . . has separated us for ever. My love, you must not reproach yourself for this outcome. It is destiny, destiny alone, that has destroyed us both. . . . Perhaps, my love, Providence has deemed us worthy of that which is most noble in the world: the sacrifice of love to virtue.

3.5: Léonce to Delphine

Delphine has fled, but Léonce will follow: If you will not tell me where you are, if you continue to refuse to see me, my decision is firm . . . : I shall reveal to Matilde the parade of lies that caused me to be her spouse; and declare to her at the same time that from the bottom of my heart I view our marriage as void. I will leave to her half of my fortune, she will retain my name, and will see me no more. I shall spend the rest of my life with my mother, in Spain; and she to whom you have thought it proper to sacrifice me will hear no more of me but of my death. . . .

You see, it is done. I shall instruct Matilde, by a letter, of the circumstances of our marriage, of my love for you, and of my decision to live far from her. Within twenty-four hours she will know all, unless you write me that you have changed your mind, or if you say nothing. What my letter will say, once said, is irrevocable. If the words I shall use are harsh, you will know who has dictated them; and if like a dagger to the breast they torment Matilde, it is not my crazed hand that must be accused, but the coldness and tyrannical reason by which you drive me mad.

3.6: Delphine to Léonce

You thought you would frighten me with a threat unworthy of you. Since I have known you, I have felt myself to be opposed to you one sole time, after having read your last letter. For some moments, I thought that you could do what you have proposed, and I thought it of you easily, because I had ceased to respect you.

Léonce, that moment of cruel tranquility is gone. I blush that I feared you would be capable of committing an act more harsh and immoral than any man ever considered. You, Léonce, you would condemn a woman as virtuous as Matilde to such cruel isolation! She has just lost her mother, and you would rob her of her husband! You would leave her, you say, your name and your property— that is to say that you would be without fault in the eyes of the world, which weighs so differently the duties of husbands and wives. But what would you really be doing to Matilde? . . . What crime has she committed, that you should punish her in this way? . . .

And I, good heavens! And I, who understands all too well what suffering your loss can cause, I would bring upon Matilde a sorrow beyond all other sorrows! Because, do not deceive yourself, Léonce, if you make yourself guilty of the deed you threaten, it is I who must be accused—not for refusing to see you, not for having tried to overcome my weakness, but for having allowed you to read my heart, which should have been closed off forever from the moment you were no longer free.

Léonce remains with Matilde, but he and Delphine see each other daily at her country estate. She is told that she is jeopardizing her chances of salvation, and worse—tongues are beginning to wag about her relationship to Léonce. He takes Delphine to the church where he married Matilde, and threatening his death if she refuses, demands that she pledge her undying love to him. Both collapse and fall ill.

Letter 4.35: December 4, 1791

Léonce and Delphine are still in love, even as gossip continues. Their friend, the Protestant M. de Lebensei, argues the possibility of divorce for Léonce: the French revolutionary legislature was planning to legalize it (and would do so the following year). At long last, Matilde has learned that Léonce is in love with Delphine and confronts her. Delphine decides that she must go away, so as not to undermine Matilde's marriage to Léonce. She pledges Matilde to secrecy.

4.35: Delphine to Matilde

Tomorrow night, Matilde, I shall leave Paris, and but a few days later, France. Léonce will know nothing about where I shall hide myself. Nor will he know, whatever happens, that it is for your happiness that I have sacrificed mine. I am bold to tell you, Matilde, your religion has not demanded from you a sacrifice greater than this I have made for you. . . . Yes, and again I speak boldly, that while I would rather die than have to blame myself for your sorrows, I have more than expiated my faults. . . .

Farewell, Matilde. You will hear no more of me—your childhood companion, your mother's friend, she who made your marriage possible, she, at the last, who could not bear your pain, she exists no more for you, or for anyone. Pray for her, not because she was guilty, for never has she been less so. . . . But pray for an unhappy woman, the most unhappy of all women, for her who is willing to rip out her heart to spare you the merest portion of what she is resigned to suffer.

Letter 6.10: August 9, 1792

Delphine has fled to Switzerland where, having been compromised by a vengeful old suitor whom she had meant to assist, she is forced to take formal vows as a nun. Meanwhile, Matilde has given birth to a son, and both she and the infant have died. Léonce, having grieved for his son, is now free. He comes in search of Delphine and finds that she is bound by conventual vows. Their friend M. de Lebensei describes their encounter.

6.10: M. de Lebensei to Louise, Delphine's sister-in-law

When Léonce entered the parlor, he saw Delphine behind the deadly grill,[69] covered by her black veil, at which spectacle, he was seized by a fearsome trembling. He looked back and forth between Delphine and me, his face signaling almost at the same moment that he understood and that he denied the truth before him. "Is she a nun," he cried; "is she?" At these words, Delphine knew it was Léonce. She reached out her arms toward him; he threw himself at the grill . . . and said with a voice the sound of which I shall never forget: "Matilde is dead; Delphine, can you be mine?" "No," she replied, "but I can die!" And she fell to the floor, motionless. . . .

Delphine is permitted to exit from behind the grill into the outer room.

When the grill was opened, Delphine rushed to kneel before Léonce, took his ice-cold hands in hers, and spoke most tenderly to him. Léonce, still beside himself, now recognized his beloved, and taking her in his arms pressed her to his heart. . . . Clasping Delphine's trembling hands in his own, already in the delirium of the fever that has not yet left him, Léonce said to her: "How has it come to be, my beloved, that I see you covered in this veil? . . . Oh! Throw off these dark garments that enclose you, come to me dressed in white, in all the splendor of your youth and your beauty; come, bride of my heart, you in whom my life reposes. But why are you crying? . . . Are you not mine, forever mine, mine alone!" His voice became ever weaker while uttering these terrible words; he rested his head on my shoulder, and fell unconscious.

Letter 6.12: August 13, 1792

M. de Lebensei, a Protestant, urges on Léonce the solution that Delphine should renounce her vows, an abomination in a Catholic regime, but a course that both universal morality and the laws of the revolutionary French republic allow. Delphine has already agreed to do so. Léonce reluctantly agrees.

6.12: Léonce to M. de Lebensei[70]

Delphine has consented to your proposal, and I accept it. She changes my destiny, she changes her own; we shall live, and we shall live together—a future

---

69. Nuns were allowed to speak to visitors through a grill that separated the convent's public rooms from the interior.
70. This brief letter is quoted within Letter 6.12, from M. de Lebensei to Louise, Delphine's sister-in-law.

unforeseen! Tomorrow was to be the last day of my life; it will be the first of a
new existence, when Delphine will be happy at last! Farewell, my friend; I owe
you my life; I owe you much more, because you may be sure that otherwise
Delphine would not have survived my death. . . .

Letters 6.18 and 6.19: September 8 and 9, 1792

*They are both free, but Léonce is disquieted: their marriage would be forever over-
shadowed by their violation of social and religious norms. He will join the foreign
armies at war with France, with which many noble French émigrés[71] now serve,
and he will die on the battlefield. Delphine writes in despair, but he has already
left, and her last letter never reaches him.*

6.18: Léonce to Delphine

O my beloved! Do not think that my love for you is lessened by this struggle
between my character and my feelings. I can reconcile them only by the sacrifice of my life, but that does not mean I love you less. But how can I unite
myself to you while dishonoring you, unable to save you from the cruel assault
of public censure? . . .

Ah, then, it is done, and by my will we are separated. Could I have an
enemy more cruel than myself? How can I ever make you understand how it
can be that I leave you and that I adore you, that I seek death when a happiness I so desired had been offered, and that my passion for you has reached the
zenith of its vigor at the same moment it cannot defeat my nature? O, you who
are so sweet and so tender, you who have always known how to read my heart:
see in the depths of this heart the turmoil that destroys it, see what it is I cannot
say, and what it is I cannot bear. . . .

Onward then. . . . Farewell. . . . When I am no more, seek out my tomb,
come and rest at that place where my heart will be buried. I shall feel you near
me, and held in the arms of death, I shall tremble.

6.19: Delphine to Léonce[72]

You are leaving me, you are going away . . . I shall follow you . . . but, you brute,
you have not said where you are going . . . I do not know where on the earth
to seek you—never has there been such cruelty! . . . the wretch, no, he is not
cruel, he goes away to die . . . I want to find you . . . I want to tell you . . . but
I am alone, whither shall I run? What a fearsome solitude! ah, my God! my
God! help me! . . .

---

71. émigrés: emigrants from revolutionary France, mostly of the nobility.

72. Delphine's last letter is the penultimate of the novel, followed by her last to Louise, her sister-
in-law. The remainder of the tale is told in the Conclusion by a nameless narrator.

Narrator's conclusion: September–October, 1792

Léonce has left, but Delphine's old friend M. de Serbellane comes to her aid. They learn that he is with the Prussian army at Verdun and has been arrested: although he had not yet joined the ranks, he was found in violation of the law that any émigré found armed was subject to execution.[73] Delphine and Léonce spend a last night in prison together. The next morning Delphine takes poison. She survives long enough to accompany the cart that carries Léonce to the site of his execution. At that spot, she dies. He holds her in a last embrace, and then, lest she be disfigured by the shots that will be aimed at him, hands her body to Serbellane. Léonce dies only seconds after Delphine. They will be united at last, buried in the same tomb.

8. Victor Hugo, *The Hunchback of Notre Dame* (1831)

The following three passages from Hugo's novel spotlight the climactic moment when Quasimodo, the deaf, one-eyed, hunchbacked bell-ringer of Notre Dame, snatches the captivating Esmeralda from the hands of the executioner and settles her safely in the upper reaches of the cathedral. In the first passage, to the intense delight of the crowd before whom the drama unfolds, Quasimodo holds the girl's body aloft, shouting "sanctuary"—for once within the walls of the cathedral, she is safe from her persecutors. In the second and third, the bewildered Esmeralda and the monstrous Quasimodo, whose kindness and restraint are exemplary, engage in a dialogue remarkable for its directness, its bare monosyllables contrasting markedly to the lofty style of the novel's all-knowing narrator.

THE HUNCHBACK OF NOTRE DAME

Book 8, Chapter 6: Three Hearts Differently Formed

The exotic Esmeralda, thought to be a Gypsy,[74] has been condemned for the murder of Captain Phoebus—when it was not she, but the Archdeacon Claude Frollo, who had struck him and although Phoebus was not in fact dead. She has been charged, tortured, and condemned to death, a sentence to be executed immediately.

---

73. A law that had just been passed on October 6, 1792.

74. Gypsy: a derogatory term for one of the Roma people, unassimilated migrants in Europe perhaps from northern India; also called "Egyptian," from which the word "gypsy" derives. She was neither Roma nor Egyptian, but the child of a Parisian prostitute kidnapped by a group of Roma who at the same time abandoned the infant Quasimodo at Notre Dame Cathedral.

No one noticed, in the gallery of the kings of France above the portal,[75] an odd spectator who had observed all these events so impassively, his neck so distended, his face so deformed, that had he not been dressed in parti-colored red and violet, he could have been taken for one of the stone monsters from whose throats had spouted, for the last six hundred years, the contents of the cathedral's long gutters.[76] This spectator had missed nothing of what had happened since midday in front of Notre Dame's portal. And from the first moment, unobserved by anyone, he had sturdily attached a thick-knotted rope to one of the colonnettes of the gallery, the end of which stretched down along the entrance steps. This done, he proceeded to watch calmly. . . .

Suddenly, just as the hangman's assistants were prepared to execute Charmolue's cold order,[77] he climbed over the balustrade of the gallery, gripped the rope with his feet, knees, and hands, and glided down along the façade . . . toward the two executioners, quick as a cat fallen from a roof, downed them with his two massive fists, swept up the gypsy in his hand as a child would a doll, sprang with a single leap back to the church, and holding the girl raised above his head, cried in a formidable voice, "Sanctuary."[78] . . .

"Sanctuary! Sanctuary!" the crowd repeated, and the clapping of their ten thousand hands caused Quasimodo's one eye to sparkle with joy and pride.

At this uproar, the condemned girl came to her senses. She opened her eyes, looked at Quasimodo, then quickly closed them as though terrified by her savior.

Charmolue, along with his henchmen and followers, was stupefied. It was true: within the perimeters of Notre Dame, the condemned girl was inviolable. The cathedral was a place of refuge. All claims of human justice expired on its doorstep.

Quasimodo stood before the great portal, his giant feet as solidly planted on the church's pavement as the massive Romanesque pillars. His huge hairy head sat on his shoulders like that of a lion which, like him, has a mane but no neck. He held the girl, palpitating, suspended from his calloused hands like a swath of white linen . . . as though she was something delicate, exquisite, and precious, made for other hands than his. . . . Then suddenly, he clasped her tightly in his arms against his craggy chest as his possession, as his treasure, like the mother of the child, his monster's eye, bent down on her, overflowing with

---

75. gallery of the kings of France: a row of twenty-eight statues of the kings of France carved on the façade of the Notre Dame Cathedral above the pointed arches of the portal.

76. stone monsters: the gargoyles, a frequent feature of Gothic architecture, functional as they are striking.

77. Jacques Charmolue, Frollo's associate, had tortured Esmeralda, obtained a confession, and sentenced her to death.

78. Sanctuary: in the Middle Ages, churches were sanctuary sites, in which an accused or condemned person was safe from pursuit.

tenderness, sorrow, and compassion, then raised up again, like a flash of lightning. The women cheered and cried, the crowd stamped with delight, because in this moment Quasimodo had achieved true beauty. He was beautiful—he, this orphan, this foundling, this outcast; he felt strong and majestic, squarely facing this world from which he had been banished, in which he had intervened so mightily, facing this phantom of human justice whose prey he had seized, all those tigers forced to bite the air, these lawmen, these judges, these executioners, this whole royal battalion that he had smashed—he, who was nothing—with the power of God. . . .

Then after some minutes of triumph, Quasimodo swiftly charged into the church with his burden. The people, who loved a show of strength, searched for him with their eyes through the dark nave,[79] regretful that he had so quickly neglected their acclamations. Suddenly, he reappeared at one end of the gallery of the kings of France, then raced along it like a madman, holding his conquest aloft in his arms, shouting "Sanctuary!" The crowd burst out again in applause.

Reaching the far end of the gallery, he plunged again into the interior of the church, reappearing a moment later on the upper platform, still running wildly, the gypsy still in his arms, still crying "Sanctuary!" And the crowd applauded. Finally, he made a third appearance at the peak of the great bell tower. From there it seemed he proudly displayed to the whole city the girl whom he had saved, and three times his voice thundered—that voice that was rarely heard, and that he himself heard never[80]—frenziedly to the clouds: "Sanctuary! Sanctuary! Sanctuary!" . . .

Book 9, Chapter 2: Hunchbacked, One-Eyed, Lame

Quasimodo brings Esmeralda to a small cell under the flying buttresses[81] traditionally reserved for asylum-seekers.

There it was that after his wild and triumphal sprint through galleries and towers, Quasimodo deposited Esmeralda. So long as that sprint lasted, she had not recovered her senses; half asleep, half awake, she felt only that, when she was lifted up in the air, when she floated, when she flew, something had raised her beyond the earth. From time to time, she heard Quasimodo's piercing laugh, his booming voice in her ear; she opened her eyes, and beneath her saw Paris in speckled confusion, its thousand roofs of slate and tile like a red and blue mosaic, and above her saw the awful but joyous face of Quasimodo. Then her eyes closed; she imagined that it was all over, that they had executed her while

---

79. nave: the large central space of the cathedral.
80. heard never: Quasimodo was deaf.
81. flying buttresses: characteristic feature of Gothic architecture, external vertical supports for the cathedral's tall walls, connected to them by an arch.

unconscious, and that the deformed spirit who governed her destiny had taken her and borne her away. She dared not look at him, and turned away.

But when the bell-ringer, disheveled and breathless, brought her to the sanctuary cell, when she felt his huge hands gently unloose the rope that tortured her arms, . . . her mind awoke, and her thoughts returned to her one by one. She saw that she was in Notre Dame, she remembered that she had been whisked from the executioner's grasp, that Phoebus was still alive, that Phoebus loved her no more; and these last two ideas arriving at once, one of which embittered the other, the poor condemned girl turned toward Quasimodo who stood before her, and who frightened her. She asked: "Why did you save me?"

He looked at her anxiously, as though trying to guess what she had said. She repeated her question. At that he shot her a look of profound sadness, and vanished. She remained, astonished. Some moments later, he returned, carrying a package that he laid at her feet. It contained clothes that kindly women had left for her at the door of the church. She then looked down at herself, realized she was nearly naked, and blushed. . . . Quasimodo felt for her modesty, covered his one eye with his capacious hand, and left again, but slowly.

She dressed herself quickly. It was a white robe with a white veil—the habit of a novice of the Hôtel-Dieu.[82] Scarcely had she finished when Quasimodo returned, carrying a basket under one arm and a mattress under the other. The basket held a bottle, some bread, and other provisions. He placed the basket on the floor and said, "Eat." He stretched the mattress out on the flagstones and said, "Sleep." It was his own dinner, and his own bed, that the ringer of the bells had brought her.

The gypsy raised her eyes to thank him, but could not utter a word. The poor devil was truly hideous. She lowered her head, trembling in fear. He said to her, "I terrify you. I am quite ugly, am I not? Don't look at me; just listen. By day, you will remain here; at night, you may walk through the whole of the church. But don't leave the church, neither by day nor by night. You would be lost. They would kill you and I would die."

Moved, she raised her head to respond, but he had disappeared. She was alone again, mulling over the remarkable words of this almost monstrous being, and struck by the sound of his voice, so harsh and yet so kind. . . .

Book 9, Chapter 3: Deaf

The next morning, she realized upon awakening that she had slept. This was remarkable and it astonished her. For so long she had been unaccustomed to

---

82. Hôtel-Dieu: the oldest hospital in Paris, adjacent to Notre Dame cathedral, and staffed by conventual nuns. A novice, who had not yet taken conventual vows, would wear a white habit.

sleep. A joyous ray from the rising sun had come through the attic window and fallen on her face. At the same time, she saw through this window an object that frightened her: the face of unlucky Quasimodo. Involuntarily, she closed her eyes, but in vain: she still imagined she saw, through her shut eyes, the face of the monster, one-eyed and gap-toothed. Then, her eyes still closed, she heard a rough voice say very gently: "Don't be afraid. I am your friend. I came to see you sleep—that does not harm you, does it, if I come to see you sleep? . . . Now I shall go way. See, I have placed myself behind the wall. You can open your eyes." . . .

Quasimodo leaves, but Esmeralda calls him back.

The two stayed unmoving for some time, considering each other in silence, he viewing such grace, she such ugliness. . . . He was first to break the silence: "You told me to return then?" She nodded affirmatively and said, "Yes." He understood her nod. "Alas," he said, hesitant to proceed, "it is that . . . I am deaf." . . .

"Never have I seen my ugliness as I do at this moment. When I compare myself to you, I pity myself, poor unhappy monster that I am! To you, I am a beast, am I not? You, you are a ray of sunshine, a drop of dew, the song of a bird! As for me, I am something frightful, neither man nor animal, I do not know what—something harder, more shapeless, more downtrodden than a stone." Then he began to laugh, and his laugh was the most agonized sound in the world. He continued: "Yes, I am deaf. But you can speak to me with gestures, with signs. . . . And then, I shall easily know your will by the movement of your lips, from the way you look."

"Very well!" she replied, smiling; "tell me why you saved me?" He looked at her attentively as she spoke. "I understand," he replied. "You ask me why I saved you. You have forgotten a wretch . . . to whom, on their hateful pillory, you brought solace the very next morning. A drop of water and a look of pity, those were more than I could repay with my life. You have forgotten this wretch. But he—he remembers."

She listened with profound sorrow. A tear rolled down the bell-ringer's eye, but it did not fall. . . . "Listen," he continued when he no longer feared that the tear would escape, "we have here some very high towers. A man who fell from one would be dead before he reached the ground. When you wish that I fall in this way, you do not even need to say a word, a look will suffice."

Then he rose. However distressed the gypsy was herself, this bizarre creature still aroused her compassion. She signaled him to stay. "No, no," he said. "I must not stay here too long. I am not at my ease when you look at me. It is out of pity that you cast your eyes upon me. I will go somewhere where I shall be able to see you, without your seeing me. That will be better."

He took a small metal whistle out of his pocket. "Take this," he said. "When you need me, when you want me to come, when you are not terrified to see me, whistle with this. That sound I can hear."

He laid the whistle on the ground, and fled.

9. Giacomo Leopardi, *To Italy; On Dante's Monument; To Himself* (1818, 1833)

In the poems included here, Leopardi reflects on his national past and on his own existence. The two early poems, written in tandem in 1818—*To Italy* and *On Dante's Monument*—express his distress at what was to him his nation's devastation: its cultural despair, witnessed by the neglect and ruination of its material, moral, and literary legacy.[83] They are followed by a poem from his later years, more personal and philosophical, written probably in 1833 following a final rejection by the woman he loved: *To Himself*. Between his first poems and his last, Leopardi gradually shed the Petrarchan model he had earlier imitated, his verse becoming increasingly free of rhyme and metrical limits, thus anticipating modern poetic practice. His minimalist verse, intense and tightly packed, echoes ancient models and the more recent ones of Dante and Petrarch (see in Volume One, respectively, Introduction to Chapter 7 and Introduction to Chapter 8).

To Italy (1818)

In To Italy, *Leopardi expresses the anguish he feels as a man thrust into an unfeeling modern world, destined to live with only the memories of past greatness. By the fourth stanza, despairing of Italy, he turns to the battle of Thermopylae where in 480 BCE, three hundred Spartan warriors with their allies held off the vast armies of the Persian emperor Xerxes, intent on the conquest of the Greek cities. Their heroism contrasts with the lassitude and ineffectiveness of Leopardi's Italian contemporaries.*

O my fatherland, I see the walls, the arches,
the columns, statues, and lonely
towers of our forebears,
but their glory I do not see;

---

83. Leopardi himself provided ample notes on his views, which were printed in the early editions of his *Canti*. The discussion of the battle of Thermopylae, defended to the death by Spartan warriors, is familiar to Leopardi from the poetic account of the Greek poet Simonides, an eyewitness to the event.

I do not see the laurel and the iron[84] that crowned
our ancient fathers. Now disarmed,
your face, your chest, are bared.
Ah, what wounds! what blood,
what bruises! What state you are in now,
most beautiful woman![85] I ask heaven,
I ask the world: tell me, tell me;
who has reduced her so? worse yet,
both her arms are bound in chains,
her hair in disarray, without her veil,[86]
she sits on the ground, dejected, spurned,
she hides her face between her knees,
and cries.
Cry, Italia, you have good reason,
you who were born to outdo other peoples,
in fortune and misfortune.

If your eyes were two surging fountains,
never could your grief be equal
to your suffering and disgrace;
once a queen, now you are a slave.
Whoever speaks or writes of you,
remembering your past glory,
does he not say: she was great once, but no more?
Why, why? Where is the ancient power,
Where the might, the courage, and the strength?
Who took your sword away?
Who betrayed you? What skill or stratagem,
what overwhelming force sufficed
to strip you of your robe and golden crown?
How did you fall, and when,
from such a height to such diminishment?
Does no one fight for you? Not even one
defends you? To arms, to arms! I alone
shall fight, and fall, alone, for you.
May it be, O heaven! that my blood
will light a fire in Italian hearts.

---

84. the laurel and the iron: the laurel wreath denoted a victor in war or other competition; the Iron Crown of Lombardy was used in the Middle Ages in the coronation of kings of Italy.
85. woman: Italia, symbolizing the nation of Italy, is female.
86. veil: in Roman times, the veil signified a woman's respectability.

Where are your sons? I hear the sound,
of weapons, wagons, shouts, and drums:
your sons are fighting
far away, in other lands.[87]
Hearken, Italia, hear me. I see flags,
a flourish of troops and cavalry,
and smoke and dust, the glittering of swords
like lightning in the mist.
Are you consoled? do the trembling flashes
summon you to this uncertain field?
For what end does the youth of Italy
fight these battles? O powers above!
Italian arms fight for another country.
Oh wretched is he who is spent in war
not for his fatherland, for his
dear wife and sons,
but is slain by another's enemy,
by another nation, and cannot say,
dying: land of my birth,
the life you gave me, I yield it back to you.

Oh bold and beloved and blessed
the ancient times, when in their battalions
men rushed to die for the fatherland;
and you, Thessalian mountain passes,
forever glorious and revered,
where a few brave and eager souls
outmastered Persian strength, and fate's![88]
The trees, the rocks, the waves,
I think the very mountains tell
the passer-by with muted voice
how that entire shore
was covered with unconquered ranks
of corpses that had died for Greece.
Then Xerxes, the cruel coward,

---

87. other lands: Leopardi alludes to the Italian forces fighting for Napoleon in his Russian invasion of 1812.

88. With this stanza, Leonardi's attention shifts to the events of 480 BCE, when a huge army under the Persian emperor Xerxes invaded Greece, passing south from Macedon through Thessaly, on the Aegean coast in central Greece, and were halted by a small force of Spartans and allies at the narrow pass near Thermopylae.

fled across the Hellespont,[89]
remembered evermore for his disgrace;
and to the peak at Antela,[90] where dying,
the sacred band fell deathless,
Simonides[91] ascended,
to view that sky, that sea, that earth.

And both cheeks wet with tears,
with quaking foot, and short of breath,
he took his lyre in his hand.
"You, most blessed of men,
who turned your breast to the enemy's spears
for love of her who gave you life,
you whom Greece honors, whom the world reveres:
What mighty love could lead
young souls to war and peril?
What love could lead you to so harsh an end?
How was that final hour, O sons,
so joyous? when smiling you ran
to that dire, tearful pass?
As though each one of you
went to a dance, or to a splendid banquet,
and not to death?

But dark Tartarus[92] awaits you,
and the dreadful river.
You died on that fearsome shore
without your wives or children,
without kisses and without tears."
. . . .[93]

"Before your memory and our love for you
can fade or pass away,
the stars will be ripped from the sky, shrieking,
fall into the sea, and go dark forever.

---

89. Xerxes did so following the naval battle of Salamis, near Athens, which occurred shortly after the encounter at Thermopylae.
90. Antela: a hilltop town near the pass.
91. Simonides: the contemporary poet who commemorated the Spartan feat at Thermopylae.
92. Tartarus: In Greek mythology, a pit beneath the earth and below Hades, fed by Phlegethon, the "river of fire." Here the Titans were imprisoned, however, but not heroes; Greek heroes spent the afterlife in Elysium.
93. One stanza is omitted here. Simonides continues to speak through the last stanza of the poem.

Your tomb is an altar. Here mothers will come
to show their little ones the beautiful drops
of your blood. And here I kneel down,
O blessed ones, to the earth,
and kiss these stones and this soil,
which shall be praised and glorified
forevermore from pole to pole.
If only I could be with you, down below,
this soulful earth soaked with my blood.
But if fate denies, does not consent
that I, fallen in war,
close my dying eyes for Greece,
then, if the gods are willing,
may your poet's modest fame
endure in ages yet to come
so long as your fame endures."

On Dante's Monument Being Planned in Florence (1818)

On the death in 1321 of the great Italian poet Dante, his body, as his contemporary Boccaccio had lamented, lay buried in Ravenna, and not in his native Florence (see Volume One, Introduction to Chapter 7). Centuries later, some Florentines took action to repatriate his remains in a suitable monument in the church of Santa Croce, a plan that Leonardi commends here. But just as in To Italy, *Leopardi digresses to celebrate the Spartan heroes at Thermopylae; here he digresses to lament the Italian lives lost in service to Napoleon Bonaparte, Italy's new master, during his disastrous 1812 Russian campaign. Italy, personified as Italia, does not defend itself; she is a widow, bereft and alone.*

This is why our people huddle
under the white wings of peace:
Italian minds cannot break loose
from their ancient torpor
until this cursed land returns
to its ancestral ways.
O Italia, honor from your heart
those forebears; for now your towns
are widowed of any like them,
any worthy of your tribute.
Turn, look behind you, my fatherland,
see that unending train of immortal spirits,
and weep, and be ashamed;
for senseless is your grief if without shame.

Turn, be ashamed, and awaken,
stabbed to the heart at last
remembering our ancestors, and our progeny.

Long has the eager visitor,
alien in mind and speech and outlook,
sought to find on Tuscan soil
the grave of him whose verse
rivals Homer, unrivaled no more.
But oh, for shame! Not only, he is told,
do his cold ashes and naked bones
lie exiled still,
interred in foreign soil,
but Florence, within your walls,
not even a stone is raised to him
for whose sake the whole world extols you.
You who care, your deed will cleanse our country
of this sad and base ignominy.
A noble task you undertake, you valiant few,
to be repaid in love
from every loving Italian heart.
. . . .[94]

Will we perish thus forever?
Is there no limit to our shame?
So long as I live, I shall cry out:
"Turn back to your ancestors, your lost lineage;[95]
Look at these ruins—
books, paintings, statues, temples;
consider on what soil it is you tread;
do these memories not arouse you?
Why linger then? get up and go!
Such corruption has no place here,[96]
this home and bosom of the greatest spirits.
If she houses only cowards,
she'd be better widowed and alone."

---

94. Stanzas 3 to 11, omitted here, digress to lament the sacrifice of Italian troops in Napoleon's Russian campaign.
95. lost lineage: Leopardi writes *guasto legnaggio*, "stunted wood" or "dead stumps," signifying a lineage (expressed graphically in a genealogical tree) that has expired; but more likely, playing on the word, he means also *guasto lignaggio*, "dead" or "ruined," or "lost lineage," as given here.
96. here . . . alone: that is, Italy, or Italia, the female subject of the two last lines; if only cowards live here, then Italia is better widowed and childless, alone.

To Himself (1833)

Leopardi fell in love with several women—and clearly loved several men—but his rejection by one woman in particular moved him to write a series of profoundly pessimistic poems, including To Himself, *in which he despairs of love and longs only for death.*

Now I'll let you rest forever,
my tired heart. The last illusion died—
one meant to be eternal. It died.
Now gone, I know, is not only the hope
for sweet illusion, but even the desire.
Rest forever. You have throbbed
enough. All your beating
is futile; the earth does not deserve
your sighs. Life is agony and tedium,
nothing more; and the world is filth.
Be still now. Surrender to despair.
Fate gave to our kind
nothing but death. Nature, in the end,
despises you—that brute power
which, hidden, ordains the pain we suffer,
and the infinite emptiness of everything.[97]

10. Alessandro Manzoni, *The Betrothed* (1827/1840)

Lucia, her fiancé Renzo, and her mother Agnese flee from their village, where seeking to claim Lucia for himself, the villainous Don Rodrigo has interrupted the wedding plans of the two young people. They take refuge with the saintly Capuchin[98] friar and priest Father Christopher, who advises them that they must depart their native homeland, and has already arranged for their safe escape. As instructed, the three cross Lake Como[99] on a little rowboat, to where they will seek their different paths of safety before, as they all hope, their eventual reunion and the couple's marriage. Gliding across the lake, as reported

---

97. infinite emptiness of everything: Leopardi writes *infinita vanità del tutto*, alluding to the "all is vanity" theme of Ecclesiastes 12.8. "Emptiness" is preferred to "vanity" here, however, as being more accessible to a modern audience; and "everything" to "the whole," the literal translation of the poet's *del tutto*.

98. Capuchin: the Capuchin Order of Friars Minor, an offshoot of the Franciscan Order founded by Saint Francis of Assisi.

99. Lake Como: one of several famous lakes in Lombardy (northern Italy) in the foothills of the Alps; the city of Lecco near its southern tip, just west of the village that is home to Manzoni's characters, is some thirty-five miles north of the metropolis of Milan.

in a famous lyrical passage, Lucia views the mountains of her birthplace—mountains that stretch, now as then, to the edge of the shore of the lake, along which they rise immediately skyward; and nestling amid them, the villagers' cottages, her own home and garden, the window of her bedroom, and not far away, the ominous castle of Don Rodrigo. And she weeps.

THE BETROTHED

Our fugitives proceeded in silence for some distance at a good pace, now one, now another turning to see if anyone was following. They were wholly overcome by the strain of their flight, by their anxiety given the uncertainty of their situation, by their sorrow at what had happened, and by their fear, in their confusion, of some new unknown danger. Still more troubling was the continuous tolling of the bells[100] which, while they became more dull and muted the further they went, seemed to have an ever more lugubrious and sinister effect. At last the ringing stopped. Then finding themselves in an open field, and hearing not a whisper, they slowed their pace. . . .

Lucia held her mother's arm tightly, and gently declined, with some delicacy, the arm the young man offered her on the rough woodland path. She was embarrassed somewhat, even in some distress, at having been alone with him so much, and with such familiarity, given that she had expected, within a few moments, to become his wife. Now with that dream having so tragically vanished, she regretted having been so forward, and among so many other reasons for anxiety, she suffered as well from that sense of shame that is not born of any shameful act, but that knows no cause, like the fear of a child who trembles in the darkness, not knowing why.

"And the cottage?" Agnese suddenly asked. But although the question was important, no one responded, since no one could give her a satisfactory response. They continued their journey in silence, and soon after arrived at the little courtyard in front of the church attached to the monastery.

Renzo approached the door and gave it a firm push—and indeed, it opened; and the moonlight, entering through the aperture, lit up the pale face and silver beard of Father Christopher, who stood right there in expectation of their arrival. Noting that no one was missing, he said "Thanks be to God!" and signaled them to enter. Another Capuchin stood next to him: the sacristan, a lay brother,[101] whom Father Christopher had persuaded to stand watch with him, to leave the door half-open, and to stand guard over it so as to receive these poor endangered refugees. It had required the full authority of the priest's

---

100. bells: the bells sounded the alarm at their escape.
101. sacristan, a lay brother: The sacristan was responsible for the ceremonial objects and vestments housed adjacent to the main church sacristy. In a monastery, the role was often filled by a layperson attached to the institution.

saintly reputation to obtain the sacristan's hesitant cooperation in this perilous and irregular situation.

Once they had entered, Father Christopher closed the door very gently. Now the sacristan could contain himself no longer, and calling the priest aside, he hissed into his ear: "but Father, Father! at night . . . in the church . . . with women . . . closing the door . . . the rules . . . but Father!" . . . "*Omnia munda mundis,*"[102] Father Christopher replied, . . . forgetting that the sacristan did not understand Latin. . . . But hearing these solemn words uttered in a mysterious tone, offered with such resolution, he concluded that they must constitute the answer to all his doubts. He calmed himself and said: "Enough! You know more about this than I do."

"Trust me," responded Father Christopher. Then, by the uncertain light of a lamp that burned before the altar, he turned to the fugitives, who stood eagerly waiting, and said to them: "My children! Thank the Lord who has preserved you from great danger. . . . But that said, my children," he continued, "understand that this country is not safe for you. It is your home; you were born here; you have wronged no one; but God wills it so. It is a trial, my children: endure it with patience, with faith, without bitterness, and be assured that there will come a time when you will accept all that will now come to pass.

"As a start, I have thought about finding a refuge for you. Soon, I hope, you will be able to return safely to your home. In any case, God will provide, and do what is best for you—and I will certainly not fail to be worthy of the grace he has bestowed on me, choosing me as his agent in assisting you poor dear persecuted children." Turning to the two women, he continued: "You will be able to stay at ——,[103] where you will be well out of danger yet still not too far from home. Look for our convent, ask for the Father Superior, and give him this letter; he will be for you another Father Christopher. And you, my dear Renzo, you, too, must for now find a safe refuge from the rage of others, and your own. Carry this letter to Father Bonaventure of Lodi, in our monastery at the Porta Orientale[104] in Milan. He will treat you like a son: he will guide you, find work for you, for as long as you are unable to return here and live in peace.

"Now go to the shore of the lake, by the mouth of the Bione.[105] . . . There you will see a small boat anchored. You will call 'boat,' and will be asked, 'for whom,' to which you will reply, 'Saint Francis.'[106] You will now get in the boat, which will take you to the far shore, where you will find a cart which will take you directly to ——."[107]

---

102. *Omnia munda mundis*: to those who are pure, all things are pure.

103. ——: a convent, not named in the original.

104. Porta Orientale: one of the main gates to the city of Milan, currently known as the Porta Venezia.

105. Bione: a stream near the convent that ran into Lake Como.

106. Saint Francis of Assisi: founder of the Franciscan Order from which the Capuchins derive.

107. ——: the location is not identified in the original.

Anyone who asks how Father Christopher had so readily at hand these means of transport over water and land would betray his ignorance of the power possessed by a Capuchin with the reputation of a saint. . . .

"Before you leave," Father Christopher said, "let us pray together to the Lord that he may be with you in this journey, and always; and above all that he give you the courage and the will to follow the path he has ordained for you." So saying, he fell to his knees in the middle of the church, and the others did likewise. After they had prayed for some moments in silence, the priest added these words in tones subdued but distinct: "We pray as well for that poor sinner who has brought us to this state. We ourselves would be unworthy of your mercy if we did not wholeheartedly ask it for him—who has such need of it! We, in our tribulation, have this comfort, that we are on the path that you have set for us: we can offer up to you our troubles, and they are made a blessing. But he! He is your enemy. Unlucky man! He dares to defy you! Have pity on him, O Lord, touch his heart, make him yours, and grant him all those blessings that we desire for ourselves."

Then hastily, he stood up and said: "Away, my children, there is no time to lose. May God keep you, may his angel stay by your side. Now go." And while they were going, overflowing with feelings that do not find words, but are expressed without them, he added, in a different intonation: "My heart tell me that we shall meet again soon."

The heart, of course, to those who consult it, always has something to say about what will be. But what does the heart know? Only an iota of what has already happened.

Not waiting for a response, Father Christopher went toward the sacristy,[108] the travelers left the church, and the sacristan closed the door, saying goodbye in a voice—his, too—in a different timbre. Without a sound, they went to the shore as instructed and saw the waiting boat; the watchword given and accepted, they climbed in. The boatman, wielding an oar at the prow, came down and grabbed the other oar, and rowing with both oars, headed across the lake toward the opposite shore.

Not even a breath of wind disturbed the surface of the lake, which spread out smooth and polished and would have seemed completely still except for the shimmering, wavering light of the moon that looked down from the summit of the sky. The only sounds heard were the slow, somber splash of waves breaking on the graveled shore, the more distant sloshing of water between the piers of the bridge, and the rhythmic fall of those two oars, which sliced the blue surface of the lake, streaming water as they rose and plunged again below. The boat's wake, which formed behind it as the prow cleaved the still surface, left a rippling streak stretching back to the shore.

---

108. sacristy: or vestry; the room where vestments and ceremonial objects are kept in a church.

The silent passengers turned back to see the mountains and the moonlit countryside, streaked here and there by dark shadows. They could make out the villages, the houses, the cottages. The huge palace of Don Rodrigo, with its stubby tower, loomed above the cottages heaped at the foot of the promontory, looking like a wild beast erect in the darkness surveying a multitude of sleeping innocents, planning his assault. Lucia saw it, and shivered. She then cast her eye downward along the slope to her own little village, discerned its outlines, found her own little house, found the tangled branches of the fig tree that spilled over the wall of the courtyard, and found the window of her bedroom. Seated in the bottom of the boat, she leaned her arm on its edge, and leaned her forehead on her arm, as though to sleep; and she wept hidden tears.

Farewell, mountains soaring from the waters upward to the sky; we who were raised among you know your jagged peaks, impressed on our minds as clearly as the faces of our closest kin. Farewell, streams; we recognize the special sound each one makes, like the voice of a dear friend. Farewell, snow-covered houses scattered along the hills like flocks of grazing sheep.

How sad the step of the man who, raised among you, now departs! He has left eagerly, dreaming that elsewhere there is hope of better fortune, but his dreams of wealth now collapse; how could he have left? He would turn back again if he did not believe that he will return one day, pockets full of cash. As he advances down the valley, he looks around, wearied and dismayed by that featureless expanse; and the air is heavy and dead. Dejected and dispirited, he arrives in the turbulent city, where houses press against houses, streets lead to other streets, and he can scarcely breathe. In front of fine buildings admired by visitors, he recalls with anxious longing the little field, the humble cottage on which he has already set his heart, which he will buy when he comes home, a rich man, to his mountains.

But what of her, she who had never looked beyond their precinct, never felt the least desire to leave, who had formed in their shadow all plans for the future, but had been expelled by a demonic power! Who at once torn away from her dearest pursuits, and denied her fondest hopes, must leave these mountains to seek out persons unknown whom she has never wished to know, and cannot even guess when it will be that she can return!

Farewell, house where she was born, where sitting and nursing a secret thought, she learned to tell the sound of ordinary footsteps from the sound of one particular step, which she awaited with an obscure timidity. Farewell, house where she is still a stranger, a house secretly eyed so many times in passing, and not without blushing; that house that had offered, in her mind, a life as a wife, peaceful and perpetual. Farewell, church, where her soul so often found serenity, singing praises to the Lord; where her marriage had been promised and planned; where the secret longing of her heart was to be solemnly blessed, her love sanctioned and made holy—farewell! He who gave you such great joy is everywhere; and he does not disrupt the joy of his children, except to provide them a greater and more certain happiness.

Of such sort, if not exactly these, were the thoughts of Lucia, not unlike those of the other two voyagers, as the boat neared the right bank of the Adda.[109]

11. Adam Mickiewicz, *Ode to Youth* (1820) and *To a Polish Mother* (1830)

The two poems that follow concern Mickiewicz's lifelong struggle to free Poland from foreign domination: a perilous task, as Russia defended its sovereignty with a program of assiduous censorship and espionage, backed up by relentless force. *Ode to Youth*, an early poem, celebrates the young, the generation who will have the vision and the courage to forge a new creation, dismissing the old who have surrendered to a world without hope. *To a Polish Mother* is darker, composed soon before the Polish uprising of 1830, and after Mickiewicz had experienced five years in exile in Russia. It paints a grim picture of the fate of those who, fired by love of country, are bold enough to confront the tyranny that now controls it. The poet instructs the Polish mother to prepare her son for torture, martyrdom, and death, though it will pierce her heart—as it pierced the heart of Mary, mother of Jesus, who died on the cross. Her son will not die gloriously on the battlefield but in obscurity, sentenced by the decree of faceless autocrats. His only monument will be the gallows on which he dies, his only memorial his mother's tears and the gratitude of his comrades. The Polish mother is, for Mickiewicz, the key to national survival: it is she who will transmit the memory of past glory to her sons, to ready them for sacrifice and victory.

ODE TO YOUTH

No heart, no soul, they're crowds of skeletons,
O Youth! Bestow upon me wings!
I'll rise over the world that's lifeless
To heaven's realm of rare illusions,
Where rapture creates dream visions,
Stirs up the flower of freshness,
And covers it with hope's golden paintings.

Let him who is dazed by years' sway,
His furrowed brow bending down low,

---

109. the Adda: an Italian river rising in the Alps near the Swiss border, flowing in a mainly southerly direction through Lake Como to join the Po River upstream from Cremona.

Of this world's sphere only as much know
As his feeble eyes can survey.

   O Youth! Soar above the earth's flatness,
   And with the sun's piercing eye,
   All mankind's gigantic vastness
   From end to end probe as you fly.

. . . .

   Together as one, my young friends!
In common happiness each man's goal blends;
Strong in accord, prudent yet with passion,
Together as one, my young friends!
And he is happy who in battle fell,
If only his body, death-stricken,
Gave others a rung to Fame's citadel.
Together as one, my young friends!
Although the road is slippery and steep,
Violence and weakness defend the fortress:
Let violence with violence meet,
And let's learn in youth to struggle with weakness!

   A child in the crib that tore off Hydra's head,[110]
   In youth will strangle the Centaurs;[111]
   He will from hell wrest out the dead,
   To heaven will go for laurels.[112]
   Reach far beyond the range of your sight,
   Conquer what reason can't conquer;
   Youth! Strong as an eagle in flight,
   As a thunderbolt is your shoulder.

So shoulder to shoulder! As with a common chain
Let us encircle the whole planet!
Let's swiftly aim our thoughts at one target
And spirits into one domain!
Terrestrial globe, away from your base!
We will push you onto a new lane,
Until freed from moldy bark once again,
You will recall your verdant days.

---

110. Hydra: in Greek mythology, a many-headed serpent, slain by the hero Hercules.
111. Centaurs: legendary creatures, half human, half horse.
112. laurels: in antiquity, a crown of laurels was granted in recognition of great achievement.

As in the regions of chaos and night
Beset by the strife of elements,
By one 'Let there be' of God's might
The world off living things arose;
The storm blusters, deep water flows,
And stars throw light upon the heavens.

In our lands dead night still lies:
Human desires are still at war;
But love emits its fire beacon;
The spirit's world from chaos will rise:
Youth will conceive it in its bosom
And friendship bond it forevermore.

The numb icecaps suddenly quail,
So does prejudice that dims light's radiance.
O morning star of freedom, hail,
Behind you the sun of deliverance!

To a Polish Mother

O Polish mother! If in your son's eyes
   There ever gleams the genius's greatness,
If on his childish brow there will arise
   Of the ancient Poles pride and nobleness;

If turning his back on his playmates' crowd,
   He runs to the bard[113] who sings of past deeds,
If he listens heedfully, his head bowed,
   When they tell him of his forefathers' feats:

O Polish mother! Your son plays the wrong part!
   Kneel before Our Lady of Sorrows
And look at the sword which pierces Her heart: [114]
   The foe will strike your breast with the same blows.

For though the whole world may in peace flower,
   Though powers, peoples, minds, may join in action,
Your son is called to a fight without splendor
   And to martyrdom . . . without resurrection.

---

113. bard: a poet; especially one who tells epic tales of a community's forebears.
114. Lady of Sorrows: Mickiewicz imagines the Polish mother before an image, or icon, of Jesus's mother, the Virgin Mary. Called the *mater dolorosa* (sorrowful mother), she watched and suffered to see the crucifixion of her son: cf. John 19:25–27.

Soon bid him go to a solitary lair
    To ponder long . . . on rushes rest his head,
Breathe damp and putrid vapors in the air,
    And with the venomous serpent share his bed.

There he will learn to conceal his anger,
    Keep his thoughts unfathomed, like a deep lake,
Poison with soft talk, as with putrid vapor,
    Cut a lowly figure like the cold snake.

A child in Nazareth, our Redeemer
    Cared for a small cross[115] on which He saved mankind.
I would have your child, O Polish mother,
    Play with the toys which he will later find.

Bind tight his hands with chains without delay
    And have him harnessed to a wheelbarrow,[116]
So that before the headsman's ax he won't pale,
    Nor when he sees the rope let his face glow.

For he will not go like the knights of old
    To plant victorious cross in Jerusalem,
Neither like the soldiers in the New World,
    To toil and drench soil with his blood for freedom.

A nameless spy will send him a cartel,[117]
    A perjured court will struggle with him hence;
A hidden pit will be the field of battle,
    A powerful foe will pass his sentence.

Dry wood of gallows for him who lost his fight
    Will be left behind as a monument,
For all his glory woman's short lament
    And his countrymen's long talks in the night.

---

115. a small cross: another reference to religious art, which sometimes portrayed the child Jesus playing with a miniature cross, alluding to his future crucifixion.
116. wheelbarrow: Mickiewicz writes "wheelbarrow," but implicitly the reference is to the wheeled cart, or tumbril, by which prisoners during the French Revolution were brought to the place of execution by guillotine.
117. cartel: a note summoning him to the place where he will be captured.

12. Alexander Pushkin, *The Bronze Horseman* (1833)

This brief narrative poem, about one-half of which appears below, has three protagonists. The first is the horseman himself, Tsar Peter the Great, commemorated in the bronze equestrian statue after which the poem is named. At great cost of treasure and human life, Peter had constructed his city, St. Petersburg, along the Neva River's final sweep through swampland and forest to its mouth in the Gulf of Finland. The second protagonist is the Neva, which in the well-documented cataclysm of 1824, whipped by furious winds, overflowed its banks and left destruction behind. The third is Yevgeny, a clerk, whose family's social rank had been reduced by Peter's strategic decimation of the *boyar* nobility.[118] He now yearns only for married respectability, children who will carry on his line, and a decent burial alongside his beloved Parasha, whom he will make his wife.

This dream will not be realized. Amid the chaos of the storm, seated in Peter's Square astride one of two bronze lions positioned before a palace, Yevgeny sees in the distance, where Parasha's cottage had stood on an island off the far shore, nothing but ruination. When the storm subsides, he goes to the island to view the devastation. He goes mad, and never goes home: the "bleak abode" he has abandoned, Pushkin tells us in a laconic aside, is rented to an impecunious poet.

One night, the crazed vagrant goes to Peter's Square, and vents his fury at the bronze horseman—who looks on him with "derision." Yevgeny runs; the bronze steed, stamping and snorting, pursues him. He falls and dies of exposure on the embankment of the Neva. His body is washed up on an island, the same on which the husk of Parasha's ravaged cottage has beached. He is not laid to rest by his grandchildren and alongside his wife, as he had hoped, but is buried by workmen, alone and unnamed— "as fitting." The simple, amiable Yevgeny, "my poor, hapless brother," has been the toy of nature and the tsar, who have crushed his mind and his world.

THE BRONZE HORSEMAN

Prologue

Tsar Peter looks out at the forlorn shore, occupied only by the huts of Finnish fishermen. Here he will construct a city to confront his enemies, to whose harbor will come ships of all nations, bearing treasure. Now, one hundred years later, a city,

---

118. *boyar* nobility: an aristocratic class next in rank after the princes, which Peter had destroyed to make way for a service nobility directly loyal to him. Pushkin's own paternal family descended from the *boyars*; his mother from the latter group, through her grandfather, a military engineer of African birth.

"sumptuous and stately," has risen. Its river crossed by beautiful bridges has been contained in granite embankments. "O how I love you, Peter's daughter!" says the poet. But now he will tell the "somber tale" of the "dreadful time"—the 1824 flood, that is—"its imprint" still deep "on our generation."

Part One

The storm is rising when Yevgeny returns home. He is aware of the coming storm, but settling down to sleep, dreams of a simple life with his beloved Parasha.

November's chilly breath pervaded
The city's streets, as daylight faded.
Dull waves mouthed malice as they ran
To break against ornate defences:
Nevá[119] was tossing, like a man
Confined to bed with fevered senses.
Now it was late, and dark; fierce rains
Beat churlishly on window panes,
While mournfully the wind lamented.
Just at this time a young man came
Back home from seeing friends. His name?
Yevgeny—let us be contented
To call our hero this: its sound
Is pleasing, and my pen has found
It an agreeable convention.[120]
His surname we don't need to mention:
In ancient times it may have been
A shining object of devotion
And eulogized by Karamzin[121]
In native annals—but what notion
Do people have of it today?
Our hero earns his honest pay
As clerk, lives somewhere as a boarder,
Shuns those ordained to rule and order,
Gives his dead ancestors no thought
And sets the vanished past at naught.

---

119. Nevá: as in the original Russian, voiced with the accent on the second syllable.
120. Yevgeny: Eugene in Russian; the same name—but without surname as he is a humble clerk—as the hero of Pushkin's verse novel *Eugene Onegin*, also published in 1833.
121. Nikolay Karamzin (1766–1828): author of a twelve-volume *History of the Russian State*. Yevgeny's ancestors would have been mentioned by Karamzin as part of the *boyar* class, now downgraded.

Yevgeny came home and, undressing
Got into bed. He tossed and turned,
But could not sleep, for in him burned
All those concerns he found most pressing.
What did he think about? That he
Was poor, condemned to drudgery:
For work he must, to make a living
And still maintain his self-respect;
That God had shown great thrift when giving
Him brains and wealth, while that select
Fraternity of men set over
The common folk could live in clover,
Though lazy, not to say inept;
That he had been a clerk for merely
Two years. He also thought that clearly
The weather, turning worse, had kept
The river rising in proportion.
All bridges would, as a precaution,
Have been removed, so he'd not see
Parasha for some days, maybe.
Yevgeny sighed, and conjured visions,
As poets do when they compose:

"Get married? Why not? I suppose
It's not the lightest of decisions.
But then I'm young; my health is strong;
I'm ready to work hard and long;
We'll find a place that can be rented
And build a simple, homely nest:
Parasha will be well contented.
And after some time, if we're blessed
With children, and I get promotion,
I can entrust to her devotion
Child-rearing and the household tasks . . .
And so until we meet our Maker,
When our grandchildren in God's acre
Will bury us—that's all one asks . . ."
. . . .

The storm strikes. Yevgeny wakes, ventures out, crosses to Peter's Square, where he sits on the back of a monumental lion, paws raised "in admonition," looking out upon the bronze statue of horse and rider—and beyond it, in the distance, sees that his beloved's house has been destroyed. He sits "[a]s if chained" to the lion, and all

*around him is water; but Tsar Peter, indifferent to the flood, sits "[o]n high," his
arm stretched out as though in command, "[t]he great bronze idol on its horse."*

With paws upraised in admonition
As they fulfill their guardian mission
Upon a lofty portico
In Peter's Square, two life-like lions
Stand watch outside a noble scion's
New mansion.[122] Here Yevgeny, so
Pale-faced, sat motionless. Although
The tempest howled, he sat unhearing
Upon the marble creature, fearing,
Poor fellow, for another. Quite
Unmindful of the water's height—
Though, soaked by waves, his feet were freezing—
Dead to the rain's chastising might,
Unheeding of the wind which, seizing
His hat, had flung it out of sight,
Yevgeny gazed into the distance,
His eyes in desperation fixed
On one point. Meeting no resistance,
Immense waves raging there had mixed
The depths into a deadly potion;
There wreckage in erratic motion
Was drifting, aimless . . . There: yes, there—
O God!—right by the waves, near where
The Gulf begins: a fence, untended;
A lonely willow; the unmended
Clapboarding of a battered hut—
And there: the widow and her daughter,
His love, his dear Parasha . . . But
Was this a dream in which he sought her?—
Is all our life, devoid of sense,
A dream: Fate's jest at Man's expense?

And he, transfixed in every feature,
As if chained to the marble creature,
Could not dismount: on every side
Was water, water, far and wide.
And turned away from him, in splendid

---

122. two life-like lions: at the time, two such lions stood before a house standing at that point
in the square.

Indifference to Nevá's blind force,
Unshakeable, as if suspended
On high, there sat with arms extended
The great bronze idol on its horse.

Part Two

It is over; the storm subsides, the streets emerge, and Yevgeny goes off to find his beloved. Her house is gone, all is in ruins; "he started shaking / With sudden laughter."

   Yevgeny hastened
To the familiar neighbourhood
Along familiar streets he could
But scarcely recognize. So, chastened
By fearful sights, he hurried on,
Poor fellow! Here a house was gone:
Uprooted; here debris lay scattered
About; here still stood, mauled and battered,
Some crippled houses. All around,
As if upon a battleground,
Lay corpses. Feeble from the scourging
Of thoughts too hard for him to bear,
He gasped and in distraction verging
On frenzy ran headlong to where
Fate stood with tidings, uninvited,
As with a letter, stamped and sealed.
Now he was near: the Gulf was sighted,
And soon their house would be revealed . . .
But what was this?
   He stopped. Retracing
His steps, he turned—continued pacing.
He looked . . . walked on . . . and looked once more . . .
There was the willow. He was sure
Their gate was here. Could it have vanished?
Where was their house—not washed away?
And dark thoughts which would not be banished
Beset him. Like a beast at bay
He circled, muttering; then, taking
Hold of his brow, he started shaking
With sudden laughter. . . .

All else has returned to normal, but Yevgeny has gone mad.

But as for my poor, hapless brother . . .
His frail mind could withstand no more
Such harsh blows, dealt one on another
By Fate. The wild, tumultuous roar
Of wind and waves reverberated
Inside his head. Withdrawn, unsure,
He roamed, his poor mind lacerated
By nightmare thoughts of death and doom.   .
Time passed: a week, a month . . . His room
Was taken to have been vacated;
And when our hero's lease expired,
His bleak abode was soon acquired
As lodging by a needy poet.
Yevgeny's things remained still there.
As for the world, he ceased to know it,
But wandered all day, sleeping where
He could upon the quay. Donated
Odd scraps of food made up his fare.
His shabby clothes began to tear
And fall to pieces. He was baited
By spiteful children pelting him
With stones. . . .

So he dragged out the mortal span
Left to him, neither beast nor man,
Not this nor that, without a station
In this world or the next . . .

*One night, he awakes . . . and goes to Peter's Square. The marble lions are there. So
is the bronze horse, which leaves his pedestal to pursue Yevgeny at a gallop through
the streets of St. Petersburg.*

Yevgeny started up, the stirring
Of memories like old wounds spurring
Him on. He set off hastily
And roamed the streets. Then, suddenly,
He stopped and, full of apprehension,
Looked all around. He stood below
Some columns, stately in dimension.
Two lions on a portico
Stood, paws upraised in admonition
As they fulfilled their guardian mission;

And nearby—awesome sight indeed—
A granite bluff: as if suspended
On high, there sat with arm extended
The great bronze idol on its steed.

    Yevgeny shuddered. He was troubled
By painful clarity of thought.
He knew this place, where once in sport
The flood had played and waves had bubbled,
Defiant in their fierce despair;
He knew these lions, and this square,
And him whose bronze head dominated
The darkness from its lofty height—
Whose fateful will had on this site
Decreed a city be created.
His figure awesome to behold!
Upon that brow what thought untold!
What armoured might, aloofly ample!
And in that steed what fire, what force!
Where are you galloping, proud horse,
And where will those hooves plunge and trample? . . .

    Yevgeny paced in agitation
Around the statue's massive base
And wildly gazed upon the face
Of him who straddled half creation.
His chest was tight. His brow was chilled,
Pressed to the railings. Darkness filled
His eyes. The prey of passions blazing
Within him, he stood sullenly
Before the royal effigy;
And quivering with fury, raising
His fist, as if compelled by some
Dark force to blind, impulsive action,
He hissed through teeth clenched in distraction:
"You . . . builder of grand schemes! I'll come
And get you!"—and then ran off, numb
With terror from a sudden vision:
He thought the fearsome tsar had turned
By slow degrees his face, which burned
With righteous anger and derision . . .
And through that dark, deserted square
Yevgeny ran, and was aware

Of cumbrous hooves behind him pounding
The roadway, crashing and resounding
Like thunder in the still night air;
For after him, with arm extended,
The Bronze Colossus on its steed
Charged at the gallop and offended
The moonlit calm with its stampede.
And then, no matter where he wended
His way, he found that all night through—
Poor, hapless wretch—he was attended
By bronze hooves beating their tattoo. . . .

*Yevgeny collapses. His body will be found on an island offshore, alongside the ruins
of Parasha's hut. He is buried, alone.*

        Some distance
Offshore a little island can
Be seen. . . .
In that forlorn place not a blade
Of grass grows. Here had drifted, floating
Unhindered as the floods had played,
A battered hut. It stayed there, stranded:
Like a black bush. A barge moored there
Last year in spring, and workmen landed
To cart the hut off. It was bare
And almost wrecked. Outside, unwitting,
They stumbled on Yevgeny near
The threshold. His remains were here
Interred with simple rites, as fitting.

SECTION II

Realism and Naturalism

Introduction to Section II

Section I has taken us from the rationalism of the Enlightenment (beginning and ending in the eighteenth century) to its repudiation (just a few years later, straddling the turn of the century) in the Romantic era. In Section II, we are introduced to the Realism and the Naturalism of the nineteenth century.[1] Realism, embracing the clear-eyed outlook of the Enlightenment and shunning Romanticism's flights of fancy, entails the close description of what actually is: the people and objects that the author immediately perceives. Naturalism, honing even more closely to verifiable, material reality, insists on the natural and material causation of all human events, and explicitly rejects any divine or spiritual intervention in human activity or consciousness.

These assumptions, styles, and outlooks were accompanied by—and responded to—momentous concurrent events. Among those events were the political repercussions of the earlier French Revolution, principally the Napoleonic takeover and aggression, and the multiple revolutions in 1830 and 1848. Exploding alongside these political disruptions was the economic cataclysm of the Industrial Revolution, which produced a large and restive working class overseen by a dominant entrepreneurial class, the bourgeoisie. As nationalism mounted at home, in a third set of developments, European power and culture expanded worldwide in a surge of global imperialism.

Meanwhile, as in the intellectual realm philosophical thought and scientific investigation flourished and the methods of modern scholarship advanced, authors writing in European languages at home and in colonial settings abroad poured forth rivers of poetry and prose, drama, stories, and novels. Of these genres, the novel reigns supreme. Readers (who constituted, with advancing rates of literacy, a mass audience) devoured not only long narratives with multiple characters involved in complex plots, but even multivolume sets of novels that pursued their characters across generations. The short story and the longer novella were also popular genres. Drama engaged growing audiences as it took a new turn away from classical and historical themes to examine contemporary, middle-class existence.

---

1. See Glossary for important persons, events, places, and concepts that recur throughout Section II.

In all these genres, characters were often drawn from middling or even laboring classes, and love, marriage, and childhood were prominent themes—especially as women authors, and even more so women readers, became an increasingly prominent sector of the literary scene. Lyric poetry continued its path from formal to freer patterns, as its themes expanded in directions similar to those pursued in other genres. The thirty texts offered in Section II represent these various trends, considered in four geographical arenas: England; the Continent (France, Germany, Italy, and Spain); Scandinavia and Russia; and Anglo- and Latin America.

Chapter 3 considers seven English authors of texts composed between 1813 and 1899. It opens with novels by two women authors, Jane Austen and Elizabeth Gaskell, writing about love and marriage in very different settings, and in a tone distinctly changed from that of Goethe's Werther or Staël's *Delphine* in the Romantic era. The characters of Austen's *Pride and Prejudice* are drawn from higher and lower strata of the English gentry, an elite landowning class, while those of Gaskell's *North and South*, inhabiting an industrial city, are drawn from the managerial and laboring sectors. In both settings, however, a new standard is set: the female protagonists both marry the men they come, somewhat reluctantly, to love, but without sacrificing their personal independence and consciousness. Charles Dickens, arguably the greatest English novelist of the century, and Charlotte Brontë, a woman author along with Austen and Gaskell, write about children, the most vulnerable members of modern society, respectively, in *Oliver Twist* and *Jane Eyre*. Twist's Oliver, born a nonentity, will through a series of adventures recover the social and domestic comfort that were his genetic inheritance, eclipsed by circumstances; and Brontë's Jane, repudiated by her family, will after tremendous struggle achieve the love and security that her character and steadfastness warrant.

The Realist outlook in these four English novels is not shared by Alfred, Lord Tennyson, who would be named England's Poet Laureate (succeeding Wordsworth; see Introduction to Chapter 2) by Queen Victoria. A master craftsman, Tennyson preferred themes drawn from literature and history, as evidenced in the two poems included in this chapter: his *Ulysses* (about the character of Odysseus as portrayed in Dante's *Inferno*; see Volume One, Chapter 7, Text 2) and the bravado *The Charge of the Light Brigade* (about an episode in the recent Crimean War). Rudyard Kipling's poems, in contrast, give expression to the tensions arising from Britain's imperialistic ventures (even as he idealizes them), as in the two famous poems given here: *Gunga Din* and *The White Man's Burden*. In his short story, *Outpost of Progress* (which preceded and anticipated his famous novel *Heart of Darkness*), Joseph Conrad is less forgiving about the imperial mission. Stripping away its pretensions, in the Naturalist mode, and even approaching a Modernist exploration of the psyche contorted by imperialism (for Modernism, see Introduction to Section III and Introduction to Chapter 7), he unmasks the ideals that Kipling had celebrated.

Chapter 4 looks at six Continental authors—four French, one Spanish, one Italian—of works composed between 1832 and 1906. The first two selections, from the novel *Père Goriot* by Honoré de Balzac and the prose poems by Charles Baudelaire gathered in *Paris Spleen*, center on the city of Paris, much as had Hugo's Romantic novel *The Hunchback of Notre Dame* (see Chapter 2, Text 8). The prototypical Realist, Balzac inexorably maps old Goriot's decline during his residency in a Parisian boarding house from prosperous grain merchant to penniless nonentity, vanquished by his love for his two daughters and their utter selfishness. Baudelaire depicts scenes from Parisian life, using its human and material bits and pieces to symbolize, in a style anticipating the Modernist, his larger message of meaninglessness and despair. Like Balzac, the novelist George Sand—the male pseudonym adopted by a woman author to advance, as she believed, her career opportunities—is the relentless investigator of the life of the eponymous heroine of her novel *Indiana*. Unthinkable in that era, she renounces her marriage to a brutal husband, is deceived by an aristocratic lover, and is determined to commit suicide, before finding peace with a very ordinary man. Émile Zola, the fourth French author and third novelist whose work is included here, depicts in his Naturalist novel *Germinal* the debased conditions of existence of the mine laborers of France's industrial north. Despite the conscientious efforts of the hero, their plight is unrelieved by a strike that devolves from failure to tragedy by an act of sabotage.

Following in the footsteps of Sand's *Indiana* (and in contrast to the works of the English writers Austen, Gaskell, and Brontë, which have happier outcomes), two women novelists from Spain and Italy respectively depict the failed marriages of two wives, the consequences of which are dreadful: the protagonists of Emilia Pardo Bazán's *The House of Ulloa* and Sibilla Aleramo's (pseudonym of Rina Faccio) *A Woman*. These tales of forced matches, brutal husbands, and financial exploitation, with their negative impact on children, reach the nadir of the Realist exploration by women authors of the institution of marriage; an institution that was, in this era, the central fact of female existence.

Although they could draw on an older tradition of folklore, epic, and saga, Russia and the Scandinavian nations on the northern fringe of the European continent had not yet, by 1800, created a modern literary tradition, as their neighbors south and west had done from the fourteenth to sixteenth centuries. It was the task of great nineteenth-century authors from these regions to create that modern tradition, reconstructing their national languages for the purpose and producing novels, stories, poems, and drama that won the enthusiastic admiration of a discriminating European audience. Chapter 5 offers selections from the work of six of these vanguard authors.

Henrik Ibsen and August Strindberg, playwrights from Norway and Sweden, respectively, not only expanded the range of their spoken vernaculars to
achieve a vehicle for complex literary expression, but also altered the thrust of
European drama from the representation of high classical themes and historical
figures to that of contemporary middle-class life. Ibsen's internationally popular *A Doll's House* presents a conventionally married woman who, by a series
of circumstances, recognizes that she has been not her husband's wife but his
"doll," a showpiece, and in a fierce moment of decision, leaves him, her household, and her children. Strindberg's *Miss Julie*, even more shocking, depicts a
spoiled aristocrat who invites the sexual advances of a household servant, and
in the end, as the consequences of her action unfold, kills herself. *The Overcoat*
by Russian author Nikolay Gogol (a follower of the Romantic poet Pushkin;
see Introduction to Chapter 2 and Text 12) explores the mental world of a
lowly civil servant whose whole existence is centered on a coat he needs to keep
warm in St. Petersburg, and who dies when, once he has obtained it, it is then
stolen. Works by the three literary giants Fyodor Dostoevsky, Leo Tolstoy, and
Anton Chekhov likewise delve into the psychological crises of their protagonists: Dostoevsky into the mind of a middle-class retiree who rejects the scientific rationalism of his age; Tolstoy into that of a complacent and self-centered
bureaucrat who finally, on his deathbed, gains insight into who he really is; and
Chekhov into the minds of two aristocrats, a sister and brother, who persist in
denying the reality of the extinction of their social class and way of life until
the moment that they hear the sound of axes cutting down the cherry orchard
that was the pride and the symbol of their ancestral estate.

Chapter 6 looks across the Atlantic Ocean to the emergent American civilizations, European in origin and outlook, of Anglophone and Latin America.
Here, too, a modern literary tradition takes form no earlier than the nineteenth
century, and is roughly coincident, in both American zones, with the creation
of independent nations. Although American authors built upon the European
cultural achievements they had inherited, they also responded to circumstances
unique to the American context: the memory of religious persecution; the
detestation of political tyranny; the presence of a vast frontier; and the large
role played by the institutions of slavery (of African captives), especially in the
North, and peonage (of indigenous peoples), especially in the South.

The works selected here by eight Anglophone authors deal with the Puritan
heritage of colonial America (Nathaniel Hawthorne, Henry David Thoreau,
Walt Whitman, and Emily Dickinson); address black-white racial tensions and
the move toward the abolition of slavery (Herman Melville, Harriet Beecher
Stowe, and Frederick Douglass); and trace the development of an American
(Whitman) and female self-consciousness (Dickinson and Charlotte Perkins
Gilman). They address these matters in novels (Hawthorne's *The Scarlet Letter*,
Stowe's *Uncle Tom's Cabin*); in short stories (Melville's *Benito Cereno*, Gilman's

The Yellow Wallpaper); in essays (Thoreau's *Walden*); in speeches (Douglass's *What to the Slave Is the Fourth of July?*); and poetry (Whitman's *Leaves of Grass*, Dickinson's *Poems*). By the end of nineteenth century, the prolific works of these and other authors of the young United States had created a rich tradition of literary expression comparable to those of the European nations.[2]

The literary expanse of Latin America, consisting of thirty-three nations and five "official" languages derived from colonial forebears,[3] is far vaster and more varied than that of Anglophone America. Here, as farther north, a native literature only emerges after 1800, roughly in concert with struggles for independence from former European masters. Of this literature, a sampling of three appears in Chapter 6. The earliest, *The Mangy Parrot* by José Joaquín Fernández de Lizardi, portraying the sometimes shocking adventures of a young Mexican during the period of the Mexican War of Independence (1810–1821), is considered the first Mexican, and also the first Latin American, novel. Written later in the century, the novelistic biography by the Argentine journalist Eduardo Gutiérrez celebrates the exploits of the gaucho Juan Moreira on that nation's cattle range frontier. Soon after, the Brazilian mulatto Joaquim Maria Machado de Assis wrote the brief short story *To Be Twenty Years Old!*, one small item among the fifteen volumes of his works, conveying in a nutshell the carefree world of the youthful elite of Rio de Janeiro.

In less than a century, in the eleven nations whose literary achievements are represented here as well as in others that could not be included, in a multitude of styles and genres, in works by thirty authors, there can be observed the making of the modern consciousness—a consciousness that would soon be shattered by the events and insights of the century that follows.

---

2. By the same time, an independent literature had taken form in Canada, a second Anglophone-American nation, which did not, however, become a self-governing dominion until 1867.

3. Those five languages are principally the Romance languages Spanish, Portuguese, and French, plus the non-Romance languages English and Dutch. They do not count the numerous indigenous languages, spoken by some eleven million inhabitants of South America, Mexico, and the Caribbean.

Chapter 3

England

Introduction

The selections[1] included in this chapter from the novels, stories, and poetry of seven English authors[2] exemplify some major themes of nineteenth-century literature. Novels by Jane Austen and Elizabeth Gaskell feature lovers who, after resolving tensions in their relationships, are united in marriage, reconfiguring the Romantic treatment of love by placing it squarely in a realistic social setting. Novels by Charles Dickens and Charlotte Brontë deal, among other matters, with childhood, another theme of interest to Romantic authors, but once again considering the child in a realistic setting—here, in both cases, in harsh and threatening situations. Poems by the highly popular Alfred, Lord Tennyson and Rudyard Kipling, whose works reflect values widely held in nineteenth-century England, describe heroic action and the conflicts and opportunities presented by imperialist ventures abroad, at a time when the British Empire was approaching its greatest extent. A short story by the seventh author, Joseph Conrad, explores as do many of his important longer works, the tragic conflicts and consequences arising from European colonialism.

Like many of the Romantics, Jane Austen and Elizabeth Gaskell wrote about love, but their love stories were of a different sort. The desperately impassioned rhetoric of Goethe's Werther or Staël's Delphine (see Chapter 2, Texts 4 and 7) has no echo in Austen or Gaskell, whose female protagonists are slow to fall in love, and will do so only cautiously and on their own terms. Not only are the female characters invented by these English authors assertive and self-willed, but also the love affairs into which they enter (and which end in marriage, as was then deemed proper) unfold amid a social network that is itself a topic of interest and which conditions the behavior of the participants.

Jane Austen (1775–1817) published six novels in her brief lifetime, all of which were about marriage in the gentry class to which she belonged. In England, the gentry were a landowning elite, often holding positions as clergymen, military officers, or academics; it was of lesser standing than the nobility,

---

1. The selections in this chapter retain the orthography, capitalization, and punctuation of the original English editions published in the nineteenth through early twentieth centuries.
2. English authors: all those named here are English natives except Conrad; Conrad was of Polish descent and Russian citizenship until, in 1886, before writing his major works, he became a naturalized British citizen.

which was small, but ranked well ahead of the class of entrepreneurs and manufacturers. In that world, much as Mary Wollstonecraft had lamented not long before (see Chapter 1, Text 8), a woman's destiny depended on a successful marriage, understood as one in which the wife secured lifelong security and respect. Austen's heroines defy those norms, the never-married author gently mocking the triviality, artificiality, and ambition that they engendered in both the men and the women who must conform to them. Yet these heroines accept marriage in the end, but only after negotiating satisfactory terms: after they have chosen partners, that is, who allow them full autonomy in a relationship of equals.

In Austen's second novel, *Pride and Prejudice* (1813), selections of which appear in this chapter, the witty and determined Elizabeth Bennett scorns, rejects, loves, and finally marries the self-confident, wealthy, and higher-ranking Mr. Darcy, the grandson of an earl; while Darcy in turn learns in stages to recognize that what he loves in Elizabeth can be realized only if he accepts, in the fullest sense, all that she is. *Pride and Prejudice* was spectacularly successful, winning a wide readership at the time; its popularity not only as a printed work, but also in television and film adaptations, has continued to this day.

Elizabeth Gaskell (1810–1865), unlike the celibate Austen, was already married and a mother when she turned to a career in writing, during which she produced six novels, more than thirty short stories and novellas, and, among nonfiction works, the first biography of her friend Charlotte Brontë, also featured in this chapter. Although she was, like Austen, born to a gentry family, her marriage to a Unitarian minister brought her to Manchester, one of the northern manufacturing centers of a rapidly industrializing Britain. The entrepreneurs and laborers of that milieu figure prominently in her novels, and notably so in *North and South* (1854), excerpted here.

North and South belongs to the genre of the industrial, or social novel: one in which social conflict is part of the story, intertwined with the individuals who enact the narrative. The conflict between manufacturers and their "hands," as they were called—their employees—lies at the center of the novel, which depicts a strike that threatens to turn to a riot. Margaret Hale, the protagonist, a southerner of the gentry elite who finds herself in a northern textile-manufacturing city (rather like Manchester), has come to know, and at first to deplore but in time to respect and to desire, the master of Marlborough Mills, John Thornton, a self-made man who had risen from poverty. She demands that he cast off his selfishness and deal compassionately with the laboring poor. He will do so, and they will marry, but not until he has lost all he had, and she has by a turn of fate inherited great wealth, and the very enterprise that had been his.

While Austen and Gaskell speak of love, Charles Dickens and Charlotte Brontë pick up the theme of childhood that the Romantics had also highlighted.

Where it was childhood innocence that intrigued the Romantics, however, Dickens and Brontë examine the lives of children placed in a social world that sacrifices them to adult priorities.

The author of fifteen novels, all published in weekly or monthly serial installments, in addition to journalistic works (filling four volumes in a recent edition), plays, poetry, travel books, speeches, public lectures, and letters (filling twelve volumes), Charles Dickens (1812–1870) is arguably the foremost nineteenth-century English writer, and the one most often mentioned in tandem with Shakespeare and Milton (see in Volume One, respectively, Chapter 11, Text 3 and Chapter 14, Text 3). Among the multifarious themes that he explores—including poverty, crime, the city, the plight of abandoned women, slavery, industrialization, capitalism, and empire—is that of childhood, highlighted here. Dickens portrays the neglect, abuse, and utter loneliness suffered by children, in contrast to the Romantic authors considered in the previous chapter, who conceived the child as a precious innocent or a prophetic seer—as do Blake, Wordsworth, and Coleridge (see Chapter 2, Texts 1, 2, and 3), although Blake, anticipating Dickens, addresses the cruelty inflicted upon them. Nowhere does he do so more poignantly than in his early novel, *Oliver Twist* (1838), of which excerpts appear in this chapter.

The child's name blazons the message Dickens conveys in this picaresque novel tracing the life of an abandoned orphan from infancy to eventual vindication and triumph:[3] it is assigned to him randomly by the parish beadle working his way through the alphabet, the exemplification of a corrupt and mindless bureaucracy charged to care for the helpless. The excerpts from the early chapters of the novel convey, as well, Dickens's condemnation of the workhouse system for the relief of poverty instituted a few years before by the Poor Law Act of 1834. That legislation removed the burden of care from the parish, which had since Elizabethan times distributed assistance to the needy, to a national system administered by boards of directors. Those directors oversaw the institution of the workhouse, where resident women and children, removed from family and male kin and subsisting on starvation rations, performed onerous labor tasks. The consequence was horrific abuse, beyond the coercion implicit from the start in the institutionalization of poor relief.[4] Oliver Twist—whose essential goodness was never scarred by his experiences—was a victim of this system, branded from his first moment of life as a "workhouse boy."

A fitting counterpart to the workhouse boy is the charity-school girl who is the eponymous heroine of the novel *Jane Eyre* (1847) by Charlotte Brontë

---

3. picaresque: from the *picaro* character who first appeared in the sixteenth-century novella, *The Life of Lazarillo de Tormes;* see Volume One, Chapter 13, Text 2.

4. The system was subsequently reformed, but not with total success; the problem of the institutionalization of poverty is still with us.

(1812–1855). Unlike Dickens, who had himself undergone hardships similar to those of his child heroes,[5] Brontë was raised in security, if not wealth, as the daughter of an Anglican pastor. Yet she encountered circumstances that echo in *Jane Eyre*: her mother died when she was five, and when she was nine, her two older sisters died in a tuberculosis outbreak at the school that she also, with another sister, attended. Brontë's heroine Jane perseveres at the bleak institution to which she was sent when she was nine years old and boldly sets out on her own, another nine years later, to take up the position of governess—an employment in which her author, too, had briefly labored.

Jane Eyre was Brontë's second novel, written after an earlier career alternating between schooling in England and abroad, employment as teacher and governess, and study and writing at home in the company of her several siblings—especially her two younger sisters Emily and Anne who also, in their brief lifetimes, wrote novels.[6] Unlike Charlotte's first novel, which had been rejected for publication (and would be published posthumously), *Jane Eyre* was a great success, hailed immediately by the reading public as something gripping and new: the story of an intelligent, passionate, and authentic young woman who defied adversity and won, in the end, all that she had sought. Although *Jane Eyre* held pride of place among the four novels Brontë produced in quick succession in the decade before her death, the others had similar themes, and have since won serious critical attention.

If marriage, childhood, and labor tensions are major themes of nineteenth-century English literature, so too is empire. Of the many outstanding poets of that age, two especially, Alfred, Lord Tennyson and Rudyard Kipling, give particular voice to the imperial urge. Both were, not surprisingly, establishment poets: they were embraced by the powerful—Tennyson by none less than Queen Victoria, holding the lofty title of Poet Laureate for forty-two years, from 1850 until his death—and celebrated in elite cultural circles.

In a lustrous career (after a difficult youth) spanning much of the nineteenth century, Tennyson (1809–1892) proved himself an elegant craftsman of lyric verse, inheriting and extending the legacy of the Romantic poets. The range of his poems, characterized by ravishing, polished rhythms, was broad. In two lengthy poems, *In Memoriam* (1842) and *Maud* (1855), he laments a deceased friend and narrates a failed love affair. In the lyrical ballad *Lady of Shalott* (1832) and in the twelve segments of *Idylls of the King* (1859–1885), which narrate the story of King Arthur, he summons up a nostalgic vision of the medieval past. In the brief elegiac poems *Break, Break, Break* (1842) and

---

5. His father was imprisoned for debt when Dickens was twelve years old, and to help sustain his family, he worked for some years in a blacking factory, affixing labels to jars of boot polish.
6. In 1847, all three sisters published their first novels. A year later, Emily and Anne both died, probably of tuberculosis, as did their brother Branwell.

Crossing the Bar (1889), he evokes in succinct and restrained verse a powerful mood of melancholy. The two poems included in this chapter, however, describe and admire bold action, in assertive statements suited to an age of imperial expansion. In *Ulysses* (1833), which recalls not only Homer's Odysseus (see Volume One, Introduction to Chapter 2), but also more specifically, Dante's Ulysses (*Inferno*, Canto 26; see Volume One, Chapter 7, Text 2), Tennyson portrays a hero whose quest for knowledge and meaning take him beyond the limits of the known world. In *The Charge of the Light Brigade* (1854), he celebrates the heroic young men who sacrificed themselves in the cause of national honor—a cause that to them seemed worthy, although to a later generation it was nonsensical: "Theirs not to make reply, / Theirs not to reason why, / Theirs but to do and die."

Where Tennyson admired the pluck and daring of British action abroad, Rudyard Kipling (1865–1936) was an out-and-out, unblushing imperialist. Tennyson was already in his fifties when Kipling was born in India to parents who belonged to the resident British elite of managers and military officers. He lived in that milieu as a small child and returned as a young adult, employed as a journalist as he launched his meteorically successful literary career, crowned by a Nobel Prize in Literature in 1907. Many of his works reflect the Indian milieu or that of South Africa, where he ventured in later years. Immersed in the culture of British imperialism, he knew its brutality, but also its capacity to bring about (as he viewed it) positive civilizational change.

Kipling was admired in the earlier phase of his career as a superb prose stylist, but detested subsequently for his pro-imperialist stance. Although his fortunes shifted, his literary legacy is undeniable. It featured: novels, especially *Kim* (1901), the tale of an Irish orphan caught up in the Great Game, the competition for primacy between Russia and Britain, as it played out in India; short stories portraying ordinary British soldiers and sailors, such as *The Man Who Would Be King* (1888); works for children in his *Jungle Books* (1894 and 1895) and *Just So Stories* (1902); and poems, many about distant lands and British ventures abroad, but also, as in *If* (1895), about the dignity of the human condition, and compellingly, in *My Boy Jack* (1916), about the death of sons of grieving parents during World War I. The two poems chosen to represent his work in this chapter exemplify two dimensions of his imperialist outlook. The first, *Gunga Din* (1892), profiles a rank-and-file soldier who recognizes the moral superiority of the native servant who has saved his life. The second, *The White Man's Burden* (1899), presents the case for European imperialism: "Take up the White Man's burden," he urges; send forth the most-promising of your youth to serve the needs of your wild and vulnerable new subjects, "[h]alf-devil and half-child."

In contrast to Tennyson and Kipling, the Polish-born Joseph Conrad (1857–1924) was a critic of imperialism, which he had observed at close quarters during the two decades he spent at sea. Conrad was born Józef Teodor Konrad Korzeniowski in 1857 in Berdychiv, Ukraine, then part of the Russian Empire, which had absorbed a huge swath of the former Polish kingdom. His father, a poet and translator of Hugo and Shakespeare, was a descendant of the Polish *szlachta* (nobility), and a Polish nationalist who died, as did his wife, of tuberculosis he contracted in a Russian labor camp. Raised and educated from age eleven in Kraków, Poland, by his wealthy uncle, Conrad went to Marseilles at age sixteen, in part to fulfill his ambition to go to sea and in part to evade compulsory service in the Russian army. His seaman's career on French ships from 1874, and on British ships from 1878, took him to all the major ports of the global commercial system.

In 1886, Conrad achieved certification as a master mariner in the British merchant navy, changed his name from Korzeniowski to Conrad, and became a British citizen. Eight years later, in 1894, suffering from ill health partly due to his 1890 stint in Africa as a captain on a Congo River steamboat, he retired to become a professional writer—in English, his third language.

Conrad wrote prolifically but struggled financially, achieving wealth and acclaim only with the publication of his 1913 novel, *Chance.* By that time, he had published several novels that are now considered classics, among them *Lord Jim* (1900), *Typhoon* (1902), and *The Secret Agent* (1907), as well as the novella *Heart of Darkness* (1899), based on his 1890 Congo experience. Two years earlier, he had written the succinct *An Outpost of Progress,* also set on the Congo River and dealing with many of the same themes of the later volume. This chapter includes selections from that 1897 short story in which, as in *Heart of Darkness* whose mysterious character Kurtz went mad, Conrad observes the deterioration in body and mind of Europeans stationed at a trading depot on the Congo River.

1. Jane Austen, *Pride and Prejudice* (1813)

In a brilliant scene from the ball at Meryton, attended by the local gentry families along with the party of Mr. Darcy and his friend Mr. Charles Bingley, Austen captures the tensions of the relationship that will develop between the skeptical but desirous Elizabeth Bennett and her haughty admirer, the aristocrat Darcy. Darcy had asked her to dance, and confusedly, despite herself, Elizabeth has accepted. The dancers take their places in two rows, with the ladies facing their gentlemen partners. Pair by pair, they approach each other, execute their steps, and move down the line, making way for the next couple to perform. Together the participants perform an intricate courtship ritual—and as Elizabeth and Darcy participate, they, too, perform theirs in words.

Elizabeth first challenges Darcy to enter into conversation, suggesting formulaic statements they might make to break the anxious silence; he parries, amiably, testing her. She proposes a similarity in their characters, a seeking for ascendancy; he evades cleverly, flattering her, but admitting nothing for his part. She probes again, asking whether he is not inclined to prejudice in judging other people; he eludes her question, but challenges her attempt to analyze his character.

The dance they have danced is over. Elizabeth's attraction to Darcy is as clear as his to her, but both are silenced. For the remainder of the ball, she must deal with the embarrassment caused her by her two relations—her distant cousin, the sycophantic clergyman Mr. Collins, the servitor of ladies related to Darcy; and her mother, a woman without subtlety or polish. Collins presumptuously approaches Darcy, who is cold but civil. Mrs. Bennett loudly and boorishly, in Darcy's hearing, boasts of her elder daughter's Jane prospects for marriage with Darcy's friend Bingley.

PRIDE AND PREJUDICE

[Elizabeth] danced next with an officer, and had the refreshment of talking of Wickham,[7] and of hearing that he was universally liked. When those dances were over she returned to Charlotte Lucas,[8] and was in conversation with her, when she found herself suddenly addressed by Mr. Darcy, who took her so much by surprise in his application for her hand, that, without knowing what she did, she accepted him. He walked away again immediately, and she was left to fret over her own want of presence of mind; Charlotte tried to console her.

"I dare say you will find him very agreeable."

"Heaven forbid!—*That* would be the greatest misfortune of all!—To find a man agreeable whom one is determined to hate!—Do not wish me such an evil."

When the dancing recommenced, however, and Darcy approached to claim her hand, Charlotte could not help cautioning her in a whisper not to be a simpleton and allow her fancy for Wickham to make her appear unpleasant in the eyes of a man of ten times his consequence. Elizabeth made no answer, and took her place in the set, amazed at the dignity to which she was arrived in being allowed to stand opposite to Mr. Darcy, and reading in her neighbours' looks their equal amazement in beholding it. They stood for some time without speaking a word; and she began to imagine that their silence was to last through

---

7. George Wickham: a military officer on the make, who has been courting Elizabeth; Elizabeth is not yet aware of his unscrupulous character, of which Darcy is fully cognizant.

8. Charlotte Lucas: Elizabeth's friend, and the daughter of Sir William Lucas who will appear shortly.

the two dances,[9] and at first was resolved not to break it; till suddenly fancying that it would be the greater punishment to her partner to oblige him to talk, she made some slight observation on the dance. He replied, and was again silent. After a pause of some minutes she addressed him a second time with:

"It is *your* turn to say something now, Mr. Darcy.—*I* talked about the dance, and *you* ought to make some kind of remark on the size of the room, or the number of couples."

He smiled, and assured her that whatever she wished him to say should be said.

"Very well.—That reply will do for the present.—Perhaps by and by I may observe that private balls are much pleasanter than public ones.—But *now* we may be silent."

"Do you talk by rule then, while you are dancing?"

"Sometimes. One must speak a little, you know. It would look odd to be entirely silent for half an hour together, and yet for the advantage of *some*, conversation ought to be so arranged as that they may have the trouble of saying as little as possible."

"Are you consulting your own feelings in the present case, or do you imagine that you are gratifying mine?"

"Both," replied Elizabeth archly; "for I have always seen a great similarity in the turn of our minds.—We are each of an unsocial, taciturn disposition, unwilling to speak, unless we expect to say something that will amaze the whole room, and be handed down to posterity with all the éclat of a proverb."

"This is no very striking resemblance of your own character, I am sure," said he. "How near it may be to *mine*, I cannot pretend to say.—*You* think it a faithful portrait undoubtedly."

"I must not decide on my own performance."

He made no answer, and they were again silent till they had gone down the dance,[10] when he asked her if she and her sisters did not very often walk to Meryton. She answered in the affirmative, and, unable to resist the temptation, added, "When you met us there the other day, we had just been forming a new acquaintance."[11]

The effect was immediate. A deeper shade of hauteur overspread his features, but he said not a word, and Elizabeth, though blaming herself for her own weakness, could not go on. At length Darcy spoke, and in a constrained manner said,

"Mr. Wickham is blessed with such happy manners as may ensure his *making* friends—whether he may be equally capable of *retaining* them, is less certain."

---

9. two dances: a gentleman asked a lady for the pleasure of two dances.

10. gone down the dance: moved down the row of dancers, at the end of the first dance; they will then dance a second.

11. acquaintance: on this occasion they had met Mr. Wickham.

"He has been so unlucky as to lose *your* friendship," replied Elizabeth with emphasis, "and in a manner which he is likely to suffer from all his life."

Darcy made no answer, and seemed desirous of changing the subject. At that moment Sir William Lucas appeared close to them, meaning to pass through the set to the other side of the room; but on perceiving Mr. Darcy he stopped with a bow of superior courtesy to compliment him on his dancing and his partner.

"I have been most highly gratified indeed, my dear Sir. Such very superior dancing is not often seen. . . . Allow me to say, however, that your fair partner does not disgrace you, and that I must hope to have this pleasure often repeated, especially when a certain desirable event, my dear Miss Eliza (glancing at her sister and Bingley), shall take place. . . . but let me not interrupt you, Sir.—You will not thank me for detaining you from the bewitching converse of that young lady, whose bright eyes are also upbraiding me."

The latter part of this address was scarcely heard by Darcy; but Sir William's allusion to his friend seemed to strike him forcibly, and his eyes were directed with a very serious expression towards Bingley and Jane, who were dancing together. Recovering himself, however, shortly, he turned to his partner, and said,

"Sir William's interruption has made me forget what we were talking of."

"I do not think we were speaking at all. Sir William could not have interrupted any two people in the room who had less to say for themselves.—We have tried two or three subjects already without success, and what we are to talk of next I cannot imagine."

"What think you of books?" said he, smiling. . . .

"No—I cannot talk of books in a ball-room; my head is always full of something else."

"The *present* always occupies you in such scenes—does it?" said he, with a look of doubt.

"Yes, always," she replied. . . . "I remember hearing you once say, Mr. Darcy, that you hardly ever forgave, that your resentment once created was unappeasable. You are very cautious, I suppose, as to its *being created*."

"I am," said he, with a firm voice.

"And never allow yourself to be blinded by prejudice?"

"I hope not."

"It is particularly incumbent on those who never change their opinion, to be secure of judging properly at first."

"May I ask to what these questions tend?"

"Merely to the illustration of *your* character," said she, endeavouring to shake off her gravity. "I am trying to make it out."

"And what is your success?"

She shook her head. "I do not get on at all. I hear such different accounts of you as puzzle me exceedingly."

"I can readily believe," answered he gravely, "that report may vary greatly with respect to me; and I could wish, Miss Bennet, that you were not to sketch my character at the present moment, as there is reason to fear that the performance would reflect no credit on either."

"But if I do not take your likeness now, I may never have another opportunity."

"I would by no means suspend any pleasure of yours," he coldly replied. She said no more, and they went down the other dance and parted in silence; on each side dissatisfied, though not to an equal degree, for in Darcy's breast there was a tolerable powerful feeling towards her, which soon procured her pardon, and directed all his anger against another.[12] . . .

The dance over, Elizabeth returns to converse with the others present.

Elizabeth listened with delight to the happy, though modest hopes which Jane entertained of Bingley's regard, and said all in her power to heighten her confidence in it. On their being joined by Mr. Bingley himself, Elizabeth withdrew to Miss Lucas; to whose inquiry after the pleasantness of her last partner she had scarcely replied, before Mr. Collins came up to them and told her with great exultation that he had just been so fortunate as to make a most important discovery.

"I have found out," said he, "by a singular accident, that there is now in the room a near relation of my patroness. I happened to overhear the gentleman himself mentioning to the young lady who does the honours of this house the names of his cousin Miss de Bourgh, and of her mother Lady Catherine. How wonderfully these sort of things occur! Who would have thought of my meeting with—perhaps—a nephew of Lady Catherine de Bourgh in this assembly!—I am most thankful that the discovery is made in time for me to pay my respects to him, which I am now going to do, and trust he will excuse my not having done it before. My total ignorance of the connection must plead my apology."

"You are not going to introduce yourself to Mr. Darcy?"

"Indeed I am. I shall entreat his pardon for not having done it earlier." . . .

Elizabeth tried hard to dissuade him from such a scheme; assuring him that Mr. Darcy would consider his addressing him without introduction as an impertinent freedom, rather than a compliment to his aunt. . . . Mr. Collins listened to her with the determined air of following his own inclination, and when she ceased speaking, replied thus,

"My dear Miss Elizabeth, I have the highest opinion in the world of your excellent judgment in all matters within the scope of your understanding, but permit me to say that there must be a wide difference between the established

---

12. another: that is, Wickham.

forms of ceremony amongst the laity, and those which regulate the clergy; forgive me leave to observe that I consider the clerical office as equal in point of
dignity with the highest rank in the kingdom—provided that a proper humil-
ity of behaviour is at the same time maintained. You must therefore allow me
to follow the dictates of my conscience on this occasion. . . ." And with a low
bow he left her to attack Mr. Darcy, whose reception of his advances she eagerly
watched, and whose astonishment at being so addressed was very evident. Her
cousin prefaced his speech with a solemn bow, and though she could not hear
a word of it, she felt as if hearing it all, and saw in the motion of his lips the
words "apology," "Hunsford," and "Lady Catherine de Bourgh."—It vexed her
to see him expose himself to such a man. Mr. Darcy was eyeing him with
unrestrained wonder, and when at last Mr. Collins allowed him time to speak,
replied with an air of distant civility. . . .

As Elizabeth had no longer any interest of her own to pursue, she turned
her attention almost entirely on her sister and Mr. Bingley, and the train of
agreeable reflections which her observations gave birth to, made her perhaps
almost as happy as Jane. She saw her in idea settled in that very house in all
the felicity which a marriage of true affection could bestow. . . . Her mother's
thoughts she plainly saw were bent the same way, and she determined not to
venture near her, lest she might hear too much.

*Nonetheless, Elizabeth is placed near her mother at the dinner table, and hears her
indiscreet talk.*

When they sat down to supper, therefore, she considered it a most unlucky
perverseness which placed them within one of each other; and deeply was she
vexed to find that her mother was talking to that one person (Lady Lucas)
freely, openly, and of nothing else but of her expectation that Jane would be
soon married to Mr. Bingley. . . .

In vain did Elizabeth endeavour to check the rapidity of her mother's
words, or persuade her to describe her felicity in a less audible whisper; for to
her inexpressible vexation, she could perceive that the chief of it was overheard
by Mr. Darcy, who sat opposite to them. Her mother only scolded her for being
nonsensical.

"What is Mr. Darcy to me, pray, that I should be afraid of him? I am sure
we owe him no such particular civility as to be obliged to say nothing *he* may
not like to hear."

"For heaven's sake, madam, speak lower.—What advantage can it be to
you to offend Mr. Darcy?—You will never recommend yourself to his friend
by so doing."

Nothing that she could say, however, had any influence. Her mother would
talk of her views in the same intelligible tone. Elizabeth blushed and blushed
again with shame and vexation. She could not help frequently glancing her

eye at Mr. Darcy, though every glance convinced her of what she dreaded; for though he was not always looking at her mother, she was convinced that his attention was invariably fixed by her. The expression of his face changed gradually from indignant contempt to a composed and steady gravity. . . .

To Elizabeth it appeared, that had her family made an agreement to expose themselves as much as they could during the evening, it would have been impossible for them to play their parts with more spirit, or finer success; and happy did she think it for Bingley and her sister that some of the exhibition had escaped his notice, and that his feelings were not of a sort to be much distressed by the folly which he must have witnessed. That his two sisters and Mr. Darcy, however, should have such an opportunity of ridiculing her relations was bad enough, and she could not determine whether the silent contempt of the gentleman, or the insolent smiles of the ladies, were more intolerable. . . .

2. Elizabeth Gaskell, *North and South* (1854)

Rushing from her father's house, where her mother lies near death, to borrow a waterbed for the invalid, Margaret Hale is aware of gathering crowds of laborers, tense and menacing, and realizes that the ongoing strike may be approaching a dangerous climax. She arrives at the Thornton compound to find that John, the manager, has sheltered on the premises the crew of Irish strike-breakers he has recruited, while his mother, sister, and servants watch the scene outside unfold, terrified. As the workers approach in a violent mood, he has summoned a detachment of soldiers, stationed some twenty minutes away, to come and maintain order. Margaret insists that Thornton go out and confront the angry workers, warning them of the approach of the soldiers and promising a resolution. He does so and she follows. When stones are hurled at the hated manager, she throws her arms around him and shields him with her body—displaying to all present her attachment to him—and is herself struck. Thornton carries the unconscious Margaret inside and though she cannot hear him, professes his own love to her. In contrast to the disciplined emotions displayed in Austen's description of the Meryton ball (see Chapter 3, Text 1), the emotional tenor of Gaskell's narrative is tumultuous and compelling.

NORTH AND SOUTH

Chapter 22: A Blow and Its Consequences

The Thornton women, now joined by Margaret, watch the angry crowd that has gathered below from the windows of their house within the factory compound.

The women gathered round the windows, fascinated to look on the scene which terrified them. Mrs. Thornton, the women-servants, Margaret,—all were there. . . . Mrs. Thornton watched for her son, who was still in the mill. He came out, looked up at them—the pale cluster of faces—and smiled good courage to them, before he locked the factory door. . . . And the sound of his well-known and commanding voice, seemed to have been like the taste of blood to the infuriated multitude outside. Hitherto they had been voice-less, wordless, needing all their breath for their hard-laboured efforts to break down the gates. But now, hearing him speak inside, they set up such a fierce, unearthly groan, that even Mrs. Thornton was white with fear as she preceded him into the room. He came in a little flushed, but his eyes gleamed, as in answer to the trumpet-call of danger, and with a proud look of defiance on his face, that made him a noble, if not a handsome man. Margaret had always dreaded lest her courage should fail her in any emergency, and she should be proved to be, what she dreaded lest she was—a coward. But now, in this real great time of reasonable fear and nearness of terror, she forgot herself, and felt only an intense sympathy—intense to painfulness—in the interests of the moment.

Mr. Thornton came frankly forwards:

"I'm sorry, Miss Hale, you have visited us at this unfortunate moment, when, I fear, you may be involved in whatever risk we have to bear. Mother! hadn't you better go into the back rooms?. . . Go, Jane!" continued he, address-ing the upper-servant. And she went, followed by the others.

"I stop here!" said his mother. "Where you are, there I stay." And indeed, retreat into the back rooms was of no avail; the crowd had surrounded the outbuildings at the rear, and were sending forth their awful threatening roar behind. . . . Mr. Thornton . . . glanced at Margaret, standing all by herself at the window nearest the factory. . . . As if she felt his look, she turned to him and asked a question that had been for some time in her mind:

"Where are the poor imported workpeople? In the factory there?"

"Yes! I left them cowed up in a small room, at the head of a back flight of stairs; bidding them run all risks, and escape down there, if they heard any attack made on the mill doors. But it is not them—it is me they want."

"When can the soldiers be here?" asked his mother, in a low but not unsteady voice.

He took out his watch with the same steady composure with which he did everything. He made some little calculation . . . "[I]t must be twenty minutes yet."

"Twenty minutes!" said his mother, for the first time showing her terror in the tones of her voice.

"Shut down the windows instantly, mother," exclaimed he: "the gates won't bear such another shock. Shut down that window, Miss Hale."

Margaret shut down her window, and then went to assist Mrs. Thornton's trembling fingers.

From some cause or other, there was a pause of several minutes in the unseen street. Mrs. Thornton looked with wild anxiety at her son's countenance, as if to gain the interpretation of the sudden stillness from him. His face was set into rigid lines of contemptuous defiance; neither hope nor fear could be read there. . . .

"Had you not better go upstairs, Miss Hale?" [said Mr. Thornton].

Margaret's lips formed a "No!"—but he could not hear her speak, for the tramp of innumerable steps right under the very wall of the house, and the fierce growl of low deep angry voices that had a ferocious murmur of satisfaction in them, more dreadful than their baffled cries not many minutes before.

"Never mind!" said he, thinking to encourage her. "I am very sorry that you should have been entrapped into all this alarm; but it cannot last long now; a few minutes more, and the soldiers will be here." . . .

He moves to a window to look out. As soon as they saw Mr. Thornton, they set up a yell, to call it not human is nothing,—it was as the demoniac desire of some terrible wild beast for the food that is withheld from his ravening. Even he drew back for a moment, dismayed at the intensity of hatred he had provoked.

"Let them yell!" said he. "In five minutes more—. I only hope my poor Irishmen are not terrified out of their wits by such a fiendlike noise. Keep up your courage for five minutes, Miss Hale."

"Don't be afraid for me," she said hastily. "But what in five minutes? Can you do nothing to soothe these poor creatures? It is awful to see them."

"The soldiers will be here directly, and that will bring them to reason."

"To reason!" said Margaret, quickly. "What kind of reason?"

"The only reason that does with men that make themselves into wild beasts. By heaven! they've turned to the mill-door!"

"Mr. Thornton," said Margaret, shaking all over with her passion, "go down this instant, if you are not a coward. Go down and face them like a man. Save these poor strangers, whom you have decoyed here. Speak to your workmen as if they were human beings. Speak to them kindly. Don't let the soldiers come in and cut down poor creatures who are driven mad. . . . If you have any courage or noble quality in you, go out and speak to them, man to man!"

He turned and looked at her while she spoke. A dark cloud came over his face while he listened. . . .

"I will go. Perhaps I may ask you to accompany me downstairs, and bar the door behind me; my mother and sister will need that protection."

"Oh! Mr. Thornton! I do not know—I may be wrong—only—"

But he was gone; he was downstairs in the hall; he had unbarred the front door; all she could do, was to follow him quickly, and fasten it behind him, and clamber up the stairs again with a sick heart and a dizzy head. Again she took her place by the farthest window. He was on the steps below. . . She threw the window wide open. Many in the crowd were mere boys; cruel and thoughtless . . . some were men, gaunt as wolves, and mad for prey . . . with starving children at home [they were] relying on ultimate success in their efforts to get higher wages, and enraged beyond measure at discovering that Irishmen were to be brought in to rob their little ones of bread. Margaret knew it all. . . . If Mr. Thornton would but say something to them—let them hear his voice only—it seemed as if it would be better than this wild beating and raging against the stony silence that vouchsafed them no word, even of anger or reproach. But perhaps he was speaking now; there was a momentary hush of their noise, inarticulate as that of a troop of animals. She tore her bonnet off, and bent forward to hear. She could only see; for if Mr. Thornton had indeed made the attempt to speak, the momentary instinct to listen to him was past and gone, and the people were raging worse than ever. He stood with his arms folded; still as a statue; his face pale with repressed excitement. . . . Margaret felt intuitively, that in an instant all would be uproar; the first touch would cause an explosion, in which, among such hundreds of infuriated men and reckless boys, even Mr. Thornton's life would be unsafe,—that in another instant the stormy passions would have passed their bounds, and swept away all barriers of reason, or apprehension of consequence. Even while she looked, she saw lads in the background stooping to take off their heavy wooden clogs[13]—the readiest missile they could find; she saw it was the spark to the gunpowder, and, with a cry, which no one heard, she rushed out of the room, down stairs,—she had lifted the great iron bar of the door with an imperious force—had thrown the door open wide—and was there, in face of that angry sea of men, her eyes smiting them with flaming arrows of reproach. The clogs were arrested in the hands that held them—the countenances, so fell not a moment before, now looked irresolute, and as if asking what this meant. For she stood between them and their enemy. She could not speak, but held out her arms towards them till she could recover breath.

"Oh, do not use violence! He is one man, and you are many;" but her words died away, for there was no tone in her voice; it was but a hoarse whisper. . . .

"Go!" said she, once more (and now her voice was like a cry). "The soldiers are sent for—are coming. Go peaceably. Go away. You shall have relief from your complaints, whatever they are."

"Shall them Irish blackguards be packed back again?" asked one from out the crowd, with fierce threatening in his voice.

"Never, for your bidding!" exclaimed Mr. Thornton. And instantly the storm broke. The hootings rose and filled the air,—but Margaret did not

---

13. wooden clogs: *sabots*, the signature footwear of industrial laborers, who could not afford leather shoes.

hear them. Her eye was on the group of lads who had armed themselves with their clogs some time before. She saw their gesture—she knew its meaning— she read their aim. Another moment, and Mr. Thornton might be smitten down,—he whom she had urged and goaded to come to this perilous place. She only thought how she could save him. She threw her arms around him; she made her body into a shield from the fierce people beyond. Still, with his arms folded, he shook her off.

"Go away," said he, in his deep voice. "This is no place for you."

"It is," said she. "You did not see what I saw." . . . A clog whizzed through the air. Margaret's fascinated eyes watched its progress; it missed its aim, and she turned sick with affright, but changed not her position, only hid her face on Mr. Thornton's arm. Then she turned and spoke again:

"For God's sake! do not damage your cause by this violence. You do not know what you are doing." She strove to make her words distinct.

A sharp pebble flew by her, grazing forehead and cheek, and drawing a blinding sheet of light before her eyes. She lay like one dead on Mr. Thornton's shoulder. Then he unfolded his arms, and held her encircled in one for an instant:

"You do well!" said he. "You come to oust the innocent stranger. You fall— you hundreds—on one man; and when a woman comes before you, to ask you for your own sakes to be reasonable creatures, your cowardly wrath falls upon her! You do well!" They were silent while he spoke. They were watching, open-eyed and open-mouthed, the thread of dark-red blood which wakened them up from their trance of passion. Those nearest the gate stole out ashamed; there was a movement through all the crowd—a retreating movement. Only one voice called out:

"Th' stone was meant for thee; but thou wert sheltered behind a woman!"

Mr. Thornton quivered with rage. . . . [H]e went slowly down the steps right into the middle of the crowd. "Now kill me, if it is your brutal will. There is no woman to shield me here. You may beat me to death—you will never move me from what I have determined upon—not you!" He stood amongst them with his arms folded, in precisely the same attitude as he had been in on the steps.

But the retrograde movement towards the gate had begun—as unreasoningly, perhaps as blindly, as the simultaneous anger. Or, perhaps, the idea of the approach of the soldiers, and the sight of that pale, upturned face, with closed eyes, still and sad as marble, though the tears welled out of the long entanglement of eyelashes, and dropped down; and, heavier, slower plash than even tears, came the drip of blood from her wound. Even the most desperate . . . drew back, faltered away, scowled, and finally went off, muttering curses on the master, who stood in his unchanging attitude, looking after their retreat with defiant eyes. The moment that retreat had changed into a flight . . . , he darted up the steps to Margaret.

She tried to rise without his help.

"It is nothing," she said, with a sickly smile. "The skin is grazed, and I was stunned at the moment. Oh, I am so thankful they are gone!" And she cried without restraint.

He could not sympathise with her. His anger had not abated; it was rising the more as his sense of immediate danger was passing away. The distant clank of the soldiers was heard: just five minutes too late to make this vanished mob feel the power of authority and order. He hoped they would see the troops, and be quelled by the thought of their narrow escape. While these thoughts crossed his mind, Margaret clung to the doorpost to steady herself: but a film came over her eyes—he was only just in time to catch her. "Mother—mother!" cried he; "Come down—they are gone, and Miss Hale is hurt!" He bore her into the dining-room, and laid her on the sofa there; laid her down softly, and looking on her pure white face, the sense of what she was to him came upon him so keenly that he spoke it out in his pain:

"Oh, my Margaret—my Margaret! no one can tell what you are to me! Dead—cold as you lie there, you are the only woman I ever loved! Oh, Margaret—Margaret!"

3. Charles Dickens, *Oliver Twist* (1838)

The English Poor Law Act of 1834 nationalized poor relief, replacing the earlier system of parish-based relief. Now able-bodied men were denied assistance, while women and children, separated from their kinsmen, were removed to workhouses. A network of these workhouses sprawled over the country, their supervision entrusted to boards of directors—composed of deep "philosophical" sages, Dickens observes sardonically, alluding to the principles of Utilitarianism that guided them. The workhouse regime was not only cold and impersonal, but also negligent, punitive, and cruel, especially so in its parsimonious allowance of food, barely sufficient to sustain life.

Dickens voices his condemnation of this regime in his dramatic portrayal of the little boy Oliver Twist. The three scenes that follow, taken from the first, second, and fourth chapters of the novel, tell of Oliver's birth to a vagrant, unwed mother, assisted by an uncaring doctor and a drunken pauper; his initiation into the workhouse regime after an infancy passed in the equally grim environs of a baby farm;[14] and his apprenticeship—after

---

14. baby farm: orphaned and abandoned children were sent out to be nursed and weaned by mercenary wet nurses, who as in this case, might be tasked to rear a number of children at once.

the potentially fatal one as a chimneysweep had been averted—to a coffin maker. From that placement, freed at last from the workhouse, Oliver will escape to London, to spend the next phase of his young life amid that city's criminal underground.

OLIVER TWIST

Chapter 1: Treats of the Place Where Oliver Twist Was Born and of the Circumstances Attending His Birth

Among other public buildings in a certain town, which for many reasons it will be prudent to refrain from mentioning, . . . there is one anciently common to most towns, great or small: to wit, a workhouse; and in this workhouse was born . . . the item of mortality whose name is prefixed to the head of this chapter.

For a long time after it was ushered into this world of sorrow and trouble, by the parish surgeon, it remained a matter of considerable doubt whether the child would survive to bear any name at all. . . . The fact is, that there was considerable difficulty in inducing Oliver to take upon himself the office of respiration. . . . Now, if, during this brief period, Oliver had been surrounded by careful grandmothers, anxious aunts, experienced nurses, and doctors of profound wisdom, he would most inevitably and indubitably have been killed in no time. There being nobody by, however, but a pauper old woman, who was rendered rather misty by an unwonted allowance of beer; and a parish surgeon who did such matters by contract; Oliver and Nature fought out the point between them. The result was, that, after a few struggles, Oliver breathed, sneezed, and proceeded to advertise to the inmates of the workhouse the fact of a new burden having been imposed upon the parish, by setting up as loud a cry as could reasonably have been expected from a male infant who had not been possessed of that very useful appendage, a voice, for a much longer space of time than three minutes and a quarter.

As Oliver gave this first proof of the free and proper action of his lungs, the patchwork coverlet which was carelessly flung over the iron bedstead, rustled; the pale face of a young woman was raised feebly from the pillow; and a faint voice imperfectly articulated the words, 'Let me see the child, and die.'

The surgeon had been sitting with his face turned towards the fire: giving the palms of his hands a warm and a rub alternately. As the young woman spoke, he rose, and advancing to the bed's head, said, with more kindness than might have been expected of him:

'Oh, you must not talk about dying yet.'

'Lor bless her dear heart, no!' interposed the nurse, hastily depositing in her pocket a green glass bottle, the contents of which she had been tasting in a corner with evident satisfaction. . . . 'Think what it is to be a mother, there's a dear young lamb do.'

Apparently this consolatory perspective of a mother's prospects failed in producing its due effect. The patient shook her head, and stretched out her hand towards the child.

The surgeon deposited it in her arms. She imprinted her cold white lips passionately on its forehead; passed her hands over her face; gazed wildly round; shuddered; fell back—and died. . . .

'It's all over, Mrs. Thingummy!' said the surgeon at last. . . . The surgeon leaned over the body, and raised the left hand. 'The old story,' he said, shaking his head: 'no wedding-ring, I see. Ah! Good-night!'

The medical gentleman walked away to dinner; and the nurse, having once more applied herself to the green bottle, sat down on a low chair before the fire, and proceeded to dress the infant.

What an excellent example of the power of dress, young Oliver Twist was! Wrapped in the blanket which had hitherto formed his only covering, he might have been the child of a nobleman or a beggar; it would have been hard for the haughtiest stranger to have assigned him his proper station in society. But now that he was enveloped in the old calico robes which had grown yellow in the same service, he was badged and ticketed, and fell into his place at once—a parish child—the orphan of a workhouse—the humble, half-starved drudge—to be cuffed and buffeted through the world—despised by all, and pitied by none.

Oliver cried lustily. If he could have known that he was an orphan, left to the tender mercies of church-wardens and overseers, perhaps he would have cried the louder. . . .

Chapter 2: Treats of Oliver Twist's Growth, Education, and Board

Mr. Bumble, formerly the parish beadle and now an agent of the workhouse, brings Oliver from the baby farm, where he has spent a wretched infancy, back to the workhouse. The night he arrives, he is interviewed by the board of directors, who inform him that he is to be educated in the workhouse and taught a "useful trade." The next day, he will begin his career picking oakum,[15] sustained on starvation rations.

Oliver . . . was then hurried away to a large ward; where, on a rough, hard bed, he sobbed himself to sleep. What a novel illustration of the tender laws of England! They let the paupers go to sleep!

The room in which the boys were fed, was a large stone hall, with a copper at one end: out of which the master, dressed in an apron for the purpose, and

---

15. oakum: a fiber obtained by untwisting old ropes, used especially for caulking ships and sealing pipe joints.

assisted by one or two women, ladled the gruel at mealtimes. Of this festive composition each boy had one porringer, and no more—except on occasions of great public rejoicing, when he had two ounces and a quarter of bread besides.

The bowls never wanted washing. The boys polished them with their spoons till they shone again; and when they had performed this operation . . . , they would sit staring at the copper, with such eager eyes, as if they could have devoured the very bricks of which it was composed; employing themselves, meanwhile, in sucking their fingers most assiduously, with the view of catching up any stray splashes of gruel that might have been cast thereon. Boys have generally excellent appetites. Oliver Twist and his companions suffered the tortures of slow starvation for three months: at last they got so voracious and wild with hunger, that one boy, . . . hinted darkly to his companions, that unless he had another basin of gruel per diem, he was afraid he might some night happen to eat the boy who slept next him, who happened to be a weakly youth of tender age. He had a wild, hungry eye; and they implicitly believed him. A council was held; lots were cast who should walk up to the master after supper that evening, and ask for more; and it fell to Oliver Twist.

The evening arrived; the boys took their places. The master, in his cook's uniform, stationed himself at the copper; his pauper assistants ranged themselves behind him; the gruel was served out; and a long grace was said over the short commons.[16] The gruel disappeared; the boys whispered each other, and winked at Oliver; while his next neighbors nudged him. Child as he was, he was desperate with hunger, and reckless with misery. He rose from the table; and advancing to the master, basin and spoon in hand, said: somewhat alarmed at his own temerity:

'Please, sir, I want some more.'

The master was a fat, healthy man; but he turned very pale. He gazed in stupefied astonishment on the small rebel for some seconds, and then clung for support to the copper. The assistants were paralysed with wonder; the boys with fear.

'What!' said the master at length, in a faint voice.

'Please, sir,' replied Oliver, 'I want some more.'

The master aimed a blow at Oliver's head with the ladle; pinioned him in his arm; and shrieked aloud for the beadle.

The board were sitting in solemn conclave, when Mr. Bumble rushed into the room in great excitement, and addressing the gentleman in the high chair, said,

'Mr. Limbkins, I beg your pardon, sir! Oliver Twist has asked for more!'

There was a general start. Horror was depicted on every countenance.

---

16. long grace . . . short commons: Dickens contrasts the excessive length of the prayer with the insufficiency of food.

'For *more!*' said Mr. Limbkins. 'Compose yourself, Bumble, and answer me distinctly. Do I understand that he asked for more, after he had eaten the supper allotted by the dietary?'

'He did, sir,' replied Bumble.

'That boy will be hung,' said the gentleman in the white waistcoat. 'I know that boy will be hung.'

Nobody controverted the prophetic gentleman's opinion. An animated discussion took place. Oliver was ordered into instant confinement; and a bill was next morning pasted on the outside of the gate, offering a reward of five pounds to anybody who would take Oliver Twist off the hands of the parish. In other words, five pounds and Oliver Twist were offered to any man or woman who wanted an apprentice to any trade, business, or calling. . . .

Chapter 4: Oliver, Being Offered Another Place, Makes His First Entry into Public Life

In Chapter 3, Oliver is sent out to be apprenticed as a chimneysweep, an occupation in early industrial England that engaged many derelict children, who often died in the perilous business—a horrific situation that William Blake, too, had deplored in his Songs of Innocence and Experience *(see Chapter 2, Text 1). But the magistrate who was to sign the papers of indenture, seeing Oliver's horrified expression, declined to do so. Oliver was again offered, with a bonus of five pounds, to anyone who would take him as an apprentice, the offer accepted by Mr. Sowerberry, the parish undertaker. It is an ironic placement, as Sowerberry, a beneficiary of the workhouse system, makes the coffins for the emaciated victims of the workhouse, which are especially profitable as they needn't be very large or sturdy.*

Mr. Bumble grasped the undertaker by the arm, and led him into the building. Mr. Sowerberry was closeted with the board for five minutes; and it was arranged that Oliver should go to him that evening 'upon liking'—a phrase which means, in the case of a parish apprentice, that if the master find, upon a short trial, that he can get enough work out of a boy without putting too much food into him, he shall have him for a term of years, to do what he likes with. . . .

Mr. Bumble leads the sobbing Oliver, stricken by his helplessness, to Mr. Sowerberry's shop.

The undertaker, who had just put up the shutters of his shop, was making some entries in his day-book by the light of a most appropriate dismal candle, when Mr. Bumble entered.

'Aha!' said the undertaker; looking up from the book, and pausing in the middle of a word; 'is that you, Bumble?'

'No one else, Mr. Sowerberry,' replied the beadle. 'Here! I've brought the boy.' Oliver made a bow.

'Oh! that's the boy, is it?' said the undertaker: raising the candle above his head, to get a better view of Oliver. 'Mrs. Sowerberry, will you have the goodness to come here a moment, my dear?'

Mrs. Sowerberry emerged from a little room behind the shop, and presented the form of a short, then, squeezed-up woman, with a vixenish countenance.

'My dear,' said Mr. Sowerberry, deferentially, 'this is the boy from the workhouse that I told you of.' Oliver bowed again.

'Dear me!' said the undertaker's wife, 'he's very small.'

'Why, he *is* rather small,' replied Mr. Bumble: looking at Oliver as if it were his fault that he was no bigger; 'he is small. There's no denying it. But he'll grow, Mrs. Sowerberry—he'll grow.'

'Ah! I dare say he will,' replied the lady pettishly, 'on our victuals and our drink. I see no saving in parish children, not I; for they always cost more to keep, than they're worth. However, men always think they know best. There! Get downstairs, little bag o' bones.' With this, the undertaker's wife opened a side door, and pushed Oliver down a steep flight of stairs into a stone cell, damp and dark: forming the ante-room to the coal-cellar, and denominated 'kitchen'; wherein sat a slatternly girl, in shoes down at heel, and blue worsted stockings very much out of repair.

'Here, Charlotte,' said Mr. Sowerberry, who had followed Oliver down, 'give this boy some of the cold bits that were put by for Trip. He hasn't come home since the morning, so he may go without 'em. I dare say the boy isn't too dainty to eat 'em—are you, boy?'

Oliver, whose eyes had glistened at the mention of meat, and who was trembling with eagerness to devour it, replied in the negative; and a plateful of coarse broken victuals was set before him.

I wish some well-fed philosopher, whose meat and drink turn to gall within him; whose blood is ice, whose heart is iron; could have seen Oliver Twist clutching at the dainty viands that the dog had neglected. I wish he could have witnessed the horrible avidity with which Oliver tore the bits asunder with all the ferocity of famine. There is only one thing I should like better; and that would be to see the Philosopher making the same sort of meal himself, with the same relish.

'Well,' said the undertaker's wife, when Oliver had finished his supper: which she had regarded in silent horror, and with fearful auguries of his future appetite: 'have you done?'

There being nothing eatable within his reach, Oliver replied in the affirmative.

'Then come with me,' said Mrs. Sowerberry: taking up a dim and dirty lamp, and leading the way upstairs; 'your bed's under the counter. You don't mind sleeping among the coffins, I suppose? But it doesn't much matter whether you do or don't, for you can't sleep anywhere else. Come; don't keep me here all night!'

Oliver lingered no longer, but meekly followed his new mistress.

Oliver takes up his residence among the coffins in Mr. Sowerberry's dark shop, and serves his master as a laborer and professional mourner—a mourning child in a funeral procession making a very powerful impression—until, abused and exploited, he runs away to London where, free of the institutions set up to care for him, he will pursue further adventures.

4. Charlotte Brontë, *Jane Eyre* (1847)

Dispatched by the unloving family to which she had been consigned after the death of her mother and in the absence of her father, the nine-year-old Jane Eyre enters Lowood Institution, which she will not leave until she is eighteen. During her nine-year stay, she is neglected, abused, and starved; but makes some friends and acquires an education sufficient for her to be employed as a governess—one of the few careers available to a young woman without family or fortune.

JANE EYRE

Chapter 5

Jane Eyre embarks on her fifty-mile journey to Lowood Institution, where she will be reared and educated, with austerity and without compassion. About eighty girls are in residence; all dressed in identical brown uniforms, fed meager meals in a bare refectory, sent to bed in a common dormitory, instructed in a rudimentary curriculum, and subjected to harsh discipline. During a period allowed for recreation in the garden, Jane encounters one of the girls, whose name, she later learns, is Helen Burns. Helen is reading Rasselas, *a novel by the eighteenth-century author Samuel Johnson.*

I saw a girl sitting on a stone bench near; she was bent over a book, on the perusal of which she seemed intent: from where I stood I could see the title—it was "Rasselas;" a name that struck me as strange, and consequently attractive. In turning a leaf she happened to look up, and I said to her directly—

"Is your book interesting?" I had already formed the intention of asking her to lend it to me some day.

"I like it," she answered, after a pause of a second or two, during which she examined me.

"What is it about?" I continued. I hardly know where I found the hardihood thus to open a conversation with a stranger; the step was contrary to my nature and habits. . . .

"You may look at it," replied the girl, offering me the book.

I did so; a brief examination convinced me that the contents were less taking than the title. . . . I returned it to her; she received it quietly, and without saying anything she was about to relapse into her former studious mood: again I ventured to disturb her—

"Can you tell me what the writing on that stone over the door means? What is Lowood Institution?"

"This house where you are come to live."

"And why do they call it Institution? Is it in any way different from other schools?"

"It is partly a charity-school: you and I, and all the rest of us, are charity-children. I suppose you are an orphan: are not either your father or your mother dead?"

"Both died before I can remember."

"Well, all the girls here have lost either one or both parents, and this is called an institution for educating orphans."

"Do we pay no money? Do they keep us for nothing?"

"We pay, or our friends pay, fifteen pounds a year for each."

"Then why do they call us charity-children?"

"Because fifteen pounds is not enough for board and teaching, and the deficiency is supplied by subscription." . . .

Chapter 7

Jane had been at Lowood some three weeks when the overseer, the clergyman Mr. Brocklehurst, comes for a visit, accompanied by his lavishly accoutered wife and daughters.

One afternoon (I had then been three weeks at Lowood), as I was sitting with a slate[17] in my hand, puzzling over a sum in long division, my eyes, raised in abstraction to the window, caught sight of a figure just passing. . . . It was Mr. Brocklehurst, buttoned up in a surtout,[18] and looking longer, narrower, and more rigid than ever.[19]

---

17. slate: a tablet used for writing on, such that what is written can be erased and the surface can be used repeatedly. Although a slate is an expensive tool, because it is reusable, it is ultimately cheaper than paper.

18. surtout: an overcoat.

19. Jane had met him before; Brocklehurst had proposed Lowood to Jane's hostile guardian as a solution to her problem of keeping Jane.

Brocklehurst criticizes the management of the place and the luxury, as he saw it, allowed some of the girls, while Jane stayed in the background, hiding behind her slate.

I might have escaped notice, had not my treacherous slate somehow happened to slip from my hand, and falling with an obtrusive crash, directly drawn every eye upon me; I knew it was all over now, and, as I stooped to pick up the two fragments of slate, I rallied my forces for the worst. It came.

"A careless girl!" said Mr. Brocklehurst, and immediately after—"It is the new pupil, I perceive." . . . "Let the child who broke her slate come forward!"

Of my own accord I could not have stirred; I was paralysed: but the two great girls who sit on each side of me, set me on my legs and pushed me towards the dread judge, and then Miss Temple[20] gently assisted me to his very feet, and I caught her whispered counsel—

"Don't be afraid, Jane, I saw it was an accident; you shall not be punished."

The kind whisper went to my heart like a dagger. . . .

"Fetch that stool," said Mr. Brocklehurst, pointing to a very high one from which a monitor had just risen: it was brought.

"Place the child upon it."

And I was placed there, by whom I don't know: I was in no condition to note particulars; I was only aware that they had hoisted me up to the height of Mr. Brocklehurst's nose. . . .

"Ladies," said he, turning to his family, "Miss Temple, teachers, and children, you all see this girl?"

Of course they did; for I felt their eyes directed like burning-glasses against my scorched skin.

"You see she is yet young; you observe she possesses the ordinary form of childhood. . . . Who would think that the Evil One[21] had already found a servant and agent in her? Yet such, I grieve to say, is the case." . . .

"My dear children," pursued the black marble clergyman, with pathos, "this is a sad, a melancholy occasion; for it becomes my duty to warn you, that this girl . . . is . . . evidently an interloper and an alien. You must be on your guard against her; you must shun her example; if necessary, avoid her company, exclude her from your sports, and shut her out from your converse. Teachers, you must watch her: keep your eyes on her movements, weigh well her words, scrutinise her actions, punish her body to save her soul: if, indeed, such salvation be possible, for (my tongue falters while I tell it) this girl, this child, . . . is—a liar!" . . .

---

20. Miss Temple: a sympathetic member of the Lowood staff.
21. Evil One: the devil.

With this sublime conclusion, Mr. Brocklehurst adjusted the top button of his surtout, . . . bowed to Miss Temple, and then all the great people sailed in state from the room. Turning at the door, my judge said—

"Let her stand half-an-hour longer on that stool, and let no one speak to her during the remainder of the day."

There was I, then, mounted aloft; I . . . was now exposed to general view on a pedestal of infamy. What my sensations were no language can describe; but just as they all rose, stifling my breath and constricting my throat, a girl came up and passed me: in passing, she lifted her eyes. What a strange light inspired them! What an extraordinary sensation that ray sent through me! . . . It was as if a martyr, a hero, had passed a slave or victim, and imparted strength in the transit. I mastered the rising hysteria, lifted up my head, and took a firm stand on the stool. Helen Burns . . . [then] returned to her place, and smiled at me as she again went by. What a smile! I remember it now . . . ; it lit up her marked lineaments, her thin face, her sunken grey eye, like a reflection from the aspect of an angel. . . .

Chapter 9

Jane becomes habituated to the hardships at Lowood and relishes the natural beauty of the place. But the poorly nourished girls were subject to infection and many fell sick—among them, Helen Burns. The nurse tells her it is the doctor's judgment that "she'll not be here long."

This phrase, uttered in my hearing yesterday, would have only conveyed the notion that she was about to be removed to Northumberland, to her own home. I should not have suspected that it meant she was dying; but I knew instantly now! It opened clear on my comprehension that Helen Burns was numbering her last days in this world. . . .

Jane rises in the night to find her friend.

Coming near, I found the door slightly ajar; probably to admit some fresh air into the close abode of sickness. Indisposed to hesitate, and full of impatient impulses—soul and senses quivering with keen throes—I put it back and looked in. My eye sought Helen, and feared to find death. . . . I advanced; then paused by the crib[22] side: my hand was on the curtain, but I preferred speaking before I withdrew it. I still recoiled at the dread of seeing a corpse.

"Helen!" I whispered softly, "are you awake?" . . .

"Can it be you, Jane?" she asked, in her own gentle voice. . . .

---

22. crib: that is, cot, narrow bed.

I got on to her crib and kissed her: her forehead was cold, and her cheek both cold and thin, and so were her hand and wrist; but she smiled as of old.

"Why are you come here, Jane? It is past eleven o'clock: I heard it strike some minutes since."

"I came to see you, Helen: I heard you were very ill, and I could not sleep till I had spoken to you."

"You came to bid me good-bye, then: you are just in time probably."

"Are you going somewhere, Helen? Are you going home?"

"Yes; to my long home—my last home."

"No, no, Helen!" I stopped, distressed. While I tried to devour my tears, a fit of coughing seized Helen; . . . when it was over, she lay some minutes exhausted; then she whispered—

"Jane, your little feet are bare; lie down and cover yourself with my quilt."

I did so: she put her arm over me, and I nestled close to her. After a long silence, she resumed, still whispering—

"I am very happy, Jane; and when you hear that I am dead, you must be sure and not grieve: there is nothing to grieve about. We all must die one day, and the illness which is removing me is not painful; it is gentle and gradual: my mind is at rest. I leave no one to regret me much: I have only a father; and he is lately married, and will not miss me. By dying young, I shall escape great sufferings. . . ."

"But where are you going to, Helen? Can you see? Do you know?"

"I believe; I have faith: I am going to God."

"Where is God? What is God?"

"My Maker and yours, who will never destroy what He created. . . ."

And I clasped my arms closer round Helen; she seemed dearer to me than ever; I felt as if I could not let her go; I lay with my face hidden on her neck. . . . She kissed me, and I her, and we both soon slumbered.

When I awoke it was day: an unusual movement roused me; I looked up; I was in somebody's arms; the nurse held me; she was carrying me through the passage back to the dormitory. . . . A day or two afterwards I learned that Miss Temple, on returning to her own room at dawn, had found me laid in the little crib; my face against Helen Burns's shoulder, my arms round her neck. I was asleep, and Helen was—dead.

Chapter 10

Hitherto I have recorded in detail the events of my insignificant existence: to the first ten years of my life I have given almost as many chapters. But this is not to be a regular autobiography . . . ; therefore I now pass a space of eight years almost in silence: a few lines only are necessary to keep up the links of connection. . . .

Jane has spent six of those eight years as a pupil and two as a teacher. Now it is time for her to leave Lowood and make her way in the world. She boldly—unprecedentedly—advertises for a position.

I had my advertisement written, enclosed, and directed before the bell rang to rouse the school; it ran thus:—

"A young lady accustomed to tuition" (had I not been a teacher two years?) "is desirous of meeting with a situation in a private family where the children are under fourteen" (I thought that as I was barely eighteen, it would not do to undertake the guidance of pupils nearer my own age). "She is qualified to teach the usual branches of a good English education, together with French, Drawing, and Music" (in those days, reader, this now narrow catalogue of accomplishments, would have been held tolerably comprehensive). "Address, J.E., Post-office, Lowton, —shire." . . .

Gaining permission to perform some errands in town, Jane sends the letter from the post office. A week later, she returns and inquires of the postmistress:

"Are there any letters for J.E.?" I asked.

She peered at me over her spectacles, and then she opened a drawer and fumbled among its contents for a long time, so long that my hopes began to falter. At last, having held a document before her glasses for nearly five minutes, she presented it across the counter, accompanying the act by another inquisitive and mistrustful glance—it was for J.E.

"Is there only one?" I demanded.

"There are no more," said she; and I put it in my pocket and turned my face homeward: I could not open it then; rules obliged me to be back by eight, and it was already half-past seven.

Various duties awaited me on my arrival. . . . *[But later that evening:]* There still remained an inch of candle: I now took out my letter; the seal was an initial F.; I broke it; the contents were brief.

"If J.E., who advertised in the —shire Herald of last Thursday, possesses the acquirements mentioned, and if she is in a position to give satisfactory references as to character and competency, a situation can be offered her where there is but one pupil, a little girl, under ten years of age; and where the salary is thirty pounds per annum. J.E. is requested to send references, name, address, and all particulars to the direction:—

"Mrs. Fairfax, Thornfield, near Millcote, —shire."

I examined the document long: the writing was old-fashioned and rather uncertain, like that of an elderly lady. . . . I now felt that an elderly lady was no bad ingredient in the business I had on hand. Mrs. Fairfax! I saw her in a black gown and widow's cap; . . . a model of elderly English respectability. Thornfield! that, doubtless, was the name of her house: a neat orderly spot,

I was sure; . . . Millcote, —shire; I brushed up my recollections of the map of England, yes, I saw it; both the shire and the town. —shire was seventy miles nearer London than the remote county where I now resided: that was a recommendation to me. . . .

Jane receives all necessary permissions and makes all arrangements to take up her position as a governess at Thornfield.

The box was corded, the card nailed on. In half-an-hour the carrier was to call for it to take it to Lowton, whither I myself was to repair at an early hour the next morning to meet the coach. . . . *[At last,]* I mounted the vehicle which was to bear me to new duties and a new life in the unknown environs of Millcote.

5. Alfred, Lord Tennyson, *Ulysses* (1833) and *The Charge of the Light Brigade* (1854)

Two of Tennyson's most famous poems are given below, both exalting the nobility of valiant action in the face of death. In *Ulysses*, the actors, inspired by their leader, are old, but still desirous of searching for something greater—for simply to draw breath is not life. In *The Charge of the Light Brigade*, inadequately armed mounted soldiers sent on a suicidal mission, probably in error, nobly execute the task they have been assigned. Tennyson's masterful use of rhythm is evident in both poems. Equally apparent is his skilled management of tone as he evokes longing and purpose in *Ulysses*, the pace and ferocity of hopeless action in *The Charge*.

ULYSSES

Ulysses (Homer's Odysseus) has returned from the Trojan War to Ithaca, but is eager to resume his adventures, wishing to "drink / Life to the lees." He has seen much of the world, "always roaming with a hungry heart"; but he yearns to roam still, and find "that untravell'd world whose margin fades / [f]or ever. . . ." Though he is old, his spirit yearns to "follow knowledge like a sinking star, / Beyond the utmost bound of human thought." And so he leaves his kingdom to his son Telemachus and sets out with his ship's crew, with whom, before death comes, "[s]ome work of noble note, may yet be done." They will sail west through the Mediterranean Sea and then "beyond the sunset," their "heroic hearts" determined "[t]o strive, to seek, to find, and not to yield." Tennyson's profile of Ulysses reprises and develops Dante's in the Inferno, Canto 26 (see Volume One, Chapter 7, Text 2).

It little profits that an idle king,
By this still hearth, among these barren crags,
Match'd with an aged wife, I mete and dole
Unequal laws unto a savage race,
That hoard, and sleep, and feed, and know not me.
I cannot rest from travel: I will drink
Life to the lees: All times I have enjoy'd
Greatly, have suffer'd greatly, both with those
That loved me, and alone, on shore, and when
Thro' scudding drifts the rainy Hyades[23]
Vext the dim sea: I am become a name;
For always roaming with a hungry heart
Much have I seen and known; cities of men
And manners, climates, councils, governments,
Myself not least, but honour'd of them all;
And drunk delight of battle with my peers,
Far on the ringing plains of windy Troy.
I am a part of all that I have met;
Yet all experience is an arch wherethro'
Gleams that untravell'd world whose margin fades
For ever and for ever when I move.
How dull it is to pause, to make an end,
To rust unburnish'd, not to shine in use!
As tho' to breathe were life! Life piled on life
Were all too little, and of one to me
Little remains: but every hour is saved
From that eternal silence, something more,
A bringer of new things; and vile it were
For some three suns to store and hoard myself,
And this gray spirit yearning in desire
To follow knowledge like a sinking star,
Beyond the utmost bound of human thought.

This is my son, mine own Telemachus,
To whom I leave the sceptre and the isle,—
Well-loved of me, discerning to fulfil
This labour, by slow prudence to make mild
A rugged people, and thro' soft degrees
Subdue them to the useful and the good.

---

23. Hyades: a group of stars in the constellation Taurus signaling the rainy season and turbulent seas.

Most blameless is he, centred in the sphere
Of common duties, decent not to fail
In offices of tenderness, and pay
Meet adoration to my household gods,
When I am gone. He works his work, I mine.

    There lies the port; the vessel puffs her sail:
There gloom the dark, broad seas. My mariners,
Souls that have toil'd, and wrought, and thought with me—
That ever with a frolic welcome took
The thunder and the sunshine, and opposed
Free hearts, free foreheads—you and I are old;
Old age hath yet his honour and his toil;
Death closes all: but something ere the end,
Some work of noble note, may yet be done,
Not unbecoming men that strove with Gods.
The lights begin to twinkle from the rocks:
The long day wanes: the slow moon climbs: the deep
Moans round with many voices. Come, my friends,
'Tis not too late to seek a newer world.
Push off, and sitting well in order smite
The sounding furrows; for my purpose holds
To sail beyond the sunset, and the baths
Of all the western stars, until I die.
It may be that the gulfs will wash us down:
It may be we shall touch the Happy Isles,
And see the great Achilles, whom we knew.
Tho' much is taken, much abides; and tho'
We are not now that strength which in old days
Moved earth and heaven, that which we are, we are;
One equal temper of heroic hearts,
Made weak by time and fate, but strong in will
To strive, to seek, to find, and not to yield.

THE CHARGE OF THE LIGHT BRIGADE

Like Tennyson's Ulysses, the men of the Light Brigade—though they are young—will strive and not yield, obeying the command given them without question, serving the nation that gave them birth. The Light Brigade was a British light cavalry force mounted on fast, unarmored horses, the riders armed with lances and sabers. In the battle of Balaclava on October 25, 1854, an engagement in the Crimean War (1853–1856), they charged valiantly but uselessly against the Russian enemy and were devastated. There were survivors, but half of the six hundred participants Tennyson celebrates were killed or wounded in the futile charge into the "valley of Death."

I

Half a league, half a league,
Half a league onward,
All in the valley of Death
   Rode the six hundred.
"Forward, the Light Brigade!
Charge for the guns!" he said.
Into the valley of Death
   Rode the six hundred.

II

"Forward, the Light Brigade!"
Was there a man dismayed?
Not though the soldier knew
   Someone had blundered.
   Theirs not to make reply,
   Theirs not to reason why,
   Theirs but to do and die.
   Into the valley of Death
   Rode the six hundred.

III

Cannon to right of them,
Cannon to left of them,
Cannon in front of them
   Volleyed and thundered;
Stormed at with shot and shell,
Boldly they rode and well,
Into the jaws of Death,
Into the mouth of hell
   Rode the six hundred.

IV

Flashed all their sabres bare,
Flashed as they turned in air
Sabring the gunners there,
Charging an army, while
   All the world wondered.
Plunged in the battery-smoke
Right through the line they broke;
Cossack and Russian
Reeled from the sabre stroke
   Shattered and sundered.
Then they rode back, but not
   Not the six hundred.

V

Cannon to right of them,
Cannon to left of them,
Cannon behind them
   Volleyed and thundered;
Stormed at with shot and shell,
While horse and hero fell.
They that had fought so well
Came through the jaws of Death,
Back from the mouth of hell,
All that was left of them,
   Left of six hundred.

VI

When can their glory fade?
O the wild charge they made!
   All the world wondered.
Honour the charge they made!
Honour the Light Brigade,
   Noble six hundred!

6. Rudyard Kipling, *Gunga Din* (1892) and *The White Man's Burden* (1899)

In the very different age in which we live, the imperialist phase of modern history is often seen as regrettable and culpable, and its supporters are often condemned as the heartless destroyers of other peoples and cultures. The poet Kipling was unmistakably a supporter of British imperialism. But he is no mere aggressor, as seen in the poems given here. In *Gunga Din*, he tells the story of a British soldier saved by an Indian native, who was himself killed in the process. He does not merely express gratitude, but acknowledges that Gunga Din, not he, was the greater man. In *The White Man's Burden*, in a more theoretical vein, Kipling argues that it is the imperialist's duty and right-ful mission to bring European civilization, technically and, for Kipling and his generation, intellectually more advanced, to fellow human beings around the globe.

GUNGA DIN

Gunga Din is an Indian servant to a regiment of British soldiers, who consider themselves the natural superiors to the native people of India—although they are no aristocrats, but children of the poor, as the narrator's colloquialisms attest. Din is poorer still, having nothing but the rags he wears and a water bucket, which he fills and brings to the thirsty soldiers suffering in the heat—and in the midst of battle, to the fallen wounded, showing himself to be as "white" as his masters: "An' for all 'is dirty 'ide / 'E was white, clear white, inside / When 'e went to tend the wounded under fire!" In a skirmish between the British force and a detachment of Indian natives, Gunga Din saves the narrator's life and in doing so, is shot and killed. The soldier who has denigrated his loyal servant recognizes Din's humanity in the end, and indeed his superiority to his purported master. The colorful lan-guage and rhythmic pulse—notably the drumbeat of "Din! Din! Din!"— evoke the rough, pitiless life of the soldiers abroad, framing the sacrificial nobility of the native.

You may talk o' gin and beer
When you're quartered safe out 'ere,
An' you're sent to penny-fights an' Aldershot it;
But when it comes to slaughter
You will do your work on water,
An' you'll lick the bloomin' boots of 'im that's got it.
Now in Injia's sunny clime,
Where I used to spend my time
A-servin' of 'Er Majesty the Queen,
Of all them blackfaced crew

The finest man I knew
Was our regimental bhisti, Gunga Din,
       He was 'Din! Din! Din!
    'You limpin' lump o' brick-dust, Gunga Din!
       'Hi! Slippy *hitherao*
       'Water, get it! *Panee lao,*
    'You squidgy-nosed old idol, Gunga Din.'

The uniform 'e wore
Was nothin' much before,
An' rather less than 'arf o' that be'ind,
For a piece o' twisty rag
An' a goatskin water-bag
Was all the field-equipment 'e could find.
When the sweatin' troop-train lay
In a sidin' through the day,
Where the 'eat would make your bloomin' eyebrows crawl,
We shouted 'Harry By!'
Till our throats were bricky-dry,
Then we wopped 'im 'cause 'e couldn't serve us all.
       It was 'Din! Din! Din!
    'You 'eathen, where the mischief 'ave you been?
       'You put some *juldee* in it
       'Or I'll *marrow* you this minute
    'If you don't fill up my helmet, Gunga Din!'

'E would dot an' carry one
Till the longest day was done;
An' 'e didn't seem to know the use o' fear.
If we charged or broke or cut,
You could bet your bloomin' nut,
'E'd be waitin' fifty paces right flank rear.
With 'is mussick on 'is back,
'E would skip with our attack,
An' watch us till the bugles made 'Retire,'
An' for all 'is dirty 'ide
'E was white, clear white, inside
When 'e went to tend the wounded under fire!
       It was 'Din! Din! Din!'
    With the bullets kickin' dust-spots on the green.
       When the cartridges ran out,
       You could hear the front-ranks shout,
    'Hi! ammunition-mules an' Gunga Din!'

I shan't forgit the night
When I dropped be'ind the fight
With a bullet where my belt-plate should 'a' been.
I was chokin' mad with thirst,
An' the man that spied me first
Was our good old grinnin', gruntin' Gunga Din.
'E lifted up my 'ead,
An' he plugged me where I bled,
An' 'e guv me 'arf-a-pint o' water green.
It was crawlin' and it stunk,
But of all the drinks I've drunk,
I'm gratefullest to one from Gunga Din.
      It was Din! Din! Din!
  'Ere's a beggar with a bullet through 'is spleen;
  'E's chawin' up the ground,
      'An' 'e's kickin' all around:
  'For Gawd's sake git the water, Gunga Din!'

'E carried me away
To where a dooli lay,
An' a bullet come an' drilled the beggar clean.
'E put me safe inside,
An' just before 'e died,
'I 'ope you liked your drink,' sez Gunga Din.
So I'll meet 'im later on
At the place where 'e is gone—
Where it's always double drill and no canteen.
'E'll be squattin' on the coals
Givin' drink to poor damned souls,
An' I'll get a swig in hell from Gunga Din!
      Yes, Din! Din! Din!
  You Lazarushian-leather Gunga Din!
  Though I've belted you and flayed you,
      By the livin' Gawd that made you,
  You're a better man than I am, Gunga Din!

THE WHITE MAN'S BURDEN

It is not the white man's rapacity that Kipling discerns in the imperial ventures of Europeans in all the regions of the globe, but his compassion and generosity. It is the "White Man's burden" to send their youth to distant lands to serve the needs of "new-caught, sullen peoples" abroad; to "seek another's profit, / [a]nd work another's gain"; to feed the hungry and tend the sick; to live and die building roads and opening ports, while facing the resentment of those they serve, who will judge them harshly if they fail; but they will be judged at home, as well, by their peers, by the work that they do. Lending solemnity and intensity to the message, the refrain "Take up the White Man's burden" is repeated at the head of each verse.

Take up the White Man's burden—
   Send forth the best ye breed—
Go bind your sons to exile
   To serve your captives' need;
To wait in heavy harness,
   On fluttered folk and wild—
Your new-caught, sullen peoples,
   Half-devil and half-child.

Take up the White Man's burden—
   In patience to abide,
To veil the threat of terror
   And check the show of pride;
By open speech and simple,
   An hundred times made plain,
To seek another's profit,
   And work another's gain.

Take up the White Man's burden—
   The savage wars of peace—
Fill full the mouth of Famine
   And bid the sickness cease;
And when your goal is nearest
   The end for others sought,
Watch Sloth and heathen Folly
   Bring all your hope to nought.

Take up the White Man's burden—
   No tawdry rule of kings,
But toil of serf and sweeper—
   The tale of common things.
The ports ye shall not enter,
   The roads ye shall not tread,
Go make them with your living,
   And mark them with your dead.

Take up the White Man's burden—
   And reap his old reward:
The blame of those ye better,
   The hate of those ye guard—
The cry of hosts ye humour
   (Ah, slowly!) toward the light:—
"Why brought ye us from bondage,
   Our loved Egyptian night?"

Take up the White Man's burden—
   Ye dare not stoop to less—
Nor call too loud on Freedom
   To cloak your weariness;
By all ye cry or whisper,
   By all ye leave or do,
The silent, sullen peoples
   Shall weigh your Gods and you.

Take up the White Man's burden—
   Have done with childish days—
The lightly proffered laurel,
   The easy, ungrudged praise.
Comes now, to search your manhood
   Through all the thankless years,
Cold, edged with dear-bought wisdom,
   The judgment of your peers!

❊ ❊ ❊

7. Joseph Conrad, *An Outpost of Progress* (1897)

The title of Conrad's story is, of course, ironic: no progress is achieved at the trading outpost staffed by the two ineffectual white Europeans, Kayerts and Carlier, and their team of ineffectual African workers; only malfeasance and degradation. Only their subordinate, the self-starting African Makola, exerts himself to rake in the profits the company expects, trading European goods for elephant tusks[24] extracted from the jungle by African hunters. When a menacing band of African slave-traders appears, brandishing guns, the terrified but wily Makola covertly sells the outpost's workers and some local villagers as slaves in exchange for an enormous haul of ivory tusks. Kayerts and Carlier won't touch the tusks at first, which they recognize—briefly evincing conscience—as the sordid gains of slave-trafficking. But they yield to Makola's scheme, and store the tusks in the depot to impress the director—whose steamer is long overdue—when he returns.

Before that moment comes, Kayerts and Carlier, weakened by hunger (the provisions left them long exhausted and the villagers no longer providing supplements) and mentally distressed, clash violently over a triviality. Kayerts shoots Carlier, who was, as Makola determines, unarmed. At this fraught moment, the steamer of the Great Civilizing Company (as Conrad sardonically names it) approaches. Anticipating the director's imminent arrival, Kayerts hangs himself from the cross that had been erected over the grave of the previous manager of the "outpost of progress."

AN OUTPOST OF PROGRESS

There were two white men in charge of the trading station. Kayerts, the chief, was short and fat; Carlier, the assistant, was tall, with a large head and a very broad trunk perched upon a long pair of thin legs. The third man on the staff was [the African native] . . . Makola . . . [who] spoke English and French with a warbling accent, wrote a beautiful hand, understood bookkeeping, and cherished in his innermost heart the worship of evil spirits. His wife was a negress from Loanda, very large and very noisy. . . . Makola, taciturn and impenetrable, despised the two white men. He had charge of a small clay storehouse with a dried-grass roof, and pretended to keep a correct account of beads, cotton cloth, red kerchiefs, brass wire, and other trade goods it contained. . . .

The previous manager of the trading station had been a failed artist who mysteriously died. He was buried near the manager's house and a cross, now leaning, was planted over his grave.

---

24. elephant tusks: the source of ivory used for luxury products, a major commodity in colonial commerce in Africa and Asia. The ivory trade is now mostly illegal.

Makola had watched the energetic artist die of fever in the just finished house with his usual kind of "I told you so" indifference. Then, for a time, he dwelt alone with his family, his account books, and the Evil Spirit that rules the lands under the equator. He got on very well with his god. Perhaps he had propitiated him by a promise of more white men to play with, by and by. At any rate the director of the Great Trading Company, coming up in a steamer that resembled an enormous sardine box with a flat-roofed shed erected on it, found the station in good order, and Makola as usual quietly diligent. The director had the cross put up over the first agent's grave, and appointed Kayerts to the post. Carlier was told off as second in charge. . . .

They were two perfectly insignificant and incapable individuals, whose existence is only rendered possible through the high organization of civilized crowds. . . . But the contact with pure unmitigated savagery, with primitive nature and primitive man, brings sudden and profound trouble into the heart. . . . No two beings could have been more unfitted for such a struggle. Society, not from any tenderness, but because of its strange needs, had taken care of those two men, forbidding them all independent thought, all initiative, all departure from routine; and forbidding it under pain of death. . . . But the two men got on well together in the fellowship of their stupidity and laziness. Together they did nothing, absolutely nothing, and enjoyed the sense of the idleness for which they were paid. . . .

One day, out of nowhere, dangerous strangers arrive.

Then, one morning, as Kayerts and Carlier, lounging in their chairs under the verandah, talked about the approaching visit of the steamer, a knot of armed men came out of the forest and advanced towards the station. They were strangers to that part of the country. They were tall, slight, draped classically from neck to heel in blue fringed cloths, and carried percussion muskets over their bare right shoulders. Makola showed signs of excitement, and ran out of the storehouse (where he spent all his days) to meet these visitors. They came into the courtyard and looked about them with steady, scornful glances. Their leader, a powerful and determined-looking negro with bloodshot eyes, stood in front of the verandah and made a long speech. . . .

"What lingo is that?" said the amazed Carlier. "In the first moment I fancied the fellow was going to speak French. Anyway, it is a different kind of gibberish to what we ever heard."

"Yes," replied Kayerts. "Hey, Makola, what does he say? Where do they come from? Who are they?"

But Makola, who seemed to be standing on hot bricks, answered hurriedly, "I don't know. They come from very far. Perhaps Mrs. [Makola] will understand. They are perhaps bad men."

The leader, after waiting for a while, said something sharply to Makola, who shook his head. Then the man, after looking round, noticed Makola's hut and walked over there. The next moment Mrs. Makola was heard speaking with great volubility. . . .

"I don't like those chaps—and, I say, Kayerts, they must be from the coast; they've got firearms," observed the sagacious Carlier.

Kayerts also did not like those chaps. . . . They became uneasy, went in and loaded their revolvers. Kayerts said, "We must order Makola to tell them to go away before dark."

The strangers left in the afternoon, after eating a meal prepared for them by Mrs. Makola. The immense woman was excited, and talked much with the visitors. . . . Makola sat apart and watched. . . . He accompanied the strangers across the ravine at the back of the station-ground, and returned slowly looking very thoughtful. When questioned by the white men he was very strange, seemed not to understand, seemed to have forgotten French—seemed to have forgotten how to speak altogether. . . .

Carlier and Kayerts slept badly. They both thought they had heard shots fired during the night—but they could not agree as to the direction. In the morning Makola was gone somewhere. He returned about noon with one of yesterday's strangers, and eluded all Kayerts's attempts to close with him: had become deaf apparently. Kayerts wondered . . . [and] worried, said, "Isn't this Makola very queer to-day?" Carlier advised, "Keep all our men together in case of some trouble." . . .

In the afternoon Makola came over to the big house and found Kayerts watching three heavy columns of smoke rising above the forests. "What is that?" asked Kayerts. "Some villages burn," answered Makola, who seemed to have regained his wits. Then he said abruptly: "We have got very little ivory; bad six months' trading. Do you like get a little more ivory? . . . Those men who came yesterday are traders from Loanda who have got more ivory than they can carry home. Shall I buy? I know their camp."

"Certainly," said Kayerts. "What are those traders?"

"Bad fellows," said Makola, indifferently. "They fight with people, and catch women and children. They are bad men, and got guns. There is a great disturbance in the country. Do you want ivory?"

"Yes," said Kayerts. Makola said nothing for a while. Then: "Those workmen of ours are no good at all," he muttered, looking round. "Station in very bad order, sir. Director will growl. Better get a fine lot of ivory, then he say nothing."

"I can't help it; the men won't work," said Kayerts. "When will you get that ivory?"

"Very soon," said Makola. "Perhaps to-night. You leave it to me, and keep indoors, sir. I think you had better give some palm wine to our men to make a dance this evening. Enjoy themselves. Work better to-morrow. There's plenty palm wine—gone a little sour."

Kayerts said "yes," and Makola, with his own hands carried big calabashes to the door of his hut. . . . The men got them at sunset. When Kayerts and Carlier retired, a big bonfire was flaring before the men's huts. They could hear their shouts and drumming. . . .

In the middle of the night, Carlier waking suddenly, heard a man shout loudly; then a shot was fired. Only one. Carlier ran out and met Kayerts on the verandah. They were both startled. As they went across the yard to call Makola. . . . Then Makola appeared close to them. "Go back, go back, please," he urged, "you spoil all." "There are strange men about," said Carlier. "Never mind; I know," said Makola. Then he whispered, "All right. Bring ivory. Say nothing! I know my business." The two white men reluctantly went back to the house, but did not sleep. . . . They lay on their hard beds and thought: "This Makola is invaluable." In the morning Carlier came out, very sleepy, and pulled at the cord of the big bell. The station hands mustered every morning to the sound of the bell. That morning nobody came. Kayerts turned out also, yawning. Across the yard they saw Makola come out of his hut, [and] . . . shouted from the distance, "All the men gone last night!"

They heard him plainly, but in their surprise they both yelled out together: "What!" Then they stared at one another. "We are in a proper fix now," growled Carlier. "It's incredible!" muttered Kayerts. "I will go to the huts and see," said Carlier, striding off. Makola coming up found Kayerts standing alone.

"I can hardly believe it," said Kayerts, tearfully. "We took care of them as if they had been our children."

"They went with the coast people," said Makola after a moment of hesitation. . . . Then [Kayerts asked]: "What do you know about it?"

Makola moved his shoulders, looking down on the ground. "What do I know? I think only. Will you come and look at the ivory I've got there? It is a fine lot. You never saw such."

He moved towards the store. . . . On the ground . . . lay six splendid tusks.

"What did you give for it?" asked Kayerts, after surveying the lot with satisfaction.

"No regular trade," said Makola. "They brought the ivory and gave it to me. I told them to take what they most wanted in the station. It is a beautiful lot. No station can show such tusks. Those traders wanted carriers badly, and our men were no good here. No trade, no entry in books: all correct."

Kayerts nearly burst with indignation. "Why!" he shouted, "I believe you have sold our men for these tusks!" Makola stood impassive and silent. "I—I—will—I," stuttered Kayerts. "You fiend!" he yelled out.

"I did the best for you and the Company," said Makola, imperturbably. "Why you shout so much? Look at this tusk."

"I dismiss you! I will report you—I won't look at the tusk. I forbid you to touch them. I order you to throw them into the river. You—you!"

"You very red, Mr. Kayerts. If you are so irritable in the sun, you will get fever and die—like the first chief!" pronounced Makola impressively. . . .

Makola had meant no more than he said, but his words seemed to Kayerts full of ominous menace! He turned sharply and went away to the house. Makola retired into the bosom of his family; and the tusks, left lying before the store, looked very large and valuable in the sunshine. . . .

Next morning they saw Makola very busy setting up in the yard the big scales used for weighing ivory. By and by Carlier said: "What's that filthy scoundrel up to?" and lounged out into the yard. Kayerts followed. They stood watching. Makola took no notice. When the balance was swung true, he tried to lift a tusk into the scale. It was too heavy. He looked up helplessly without a word, and for a minute they stood round that balance as mute and still as three statues. Suddenly Carlier said: "Catch hold of the other end, Makola—you beast!" and together they swung the tusk up. Kayerts trembled in every limb. He muttered, "I say! O! I say!" and putting his hand in his pocket found there a dirty bit of paper and the stump of a pencil. He turned his back on the others, . . . and noted stealthily the weights which Carlier shouted out to him with unnecessary loudness. When all was over Makola whispered to himself: "The sun's very strong here for the tusks." Carlier said to Kayerts in a careless tone: "I say, chief, I might just as well give him a lift with this lot into the store."

As they were going back to the house Kayerts observed with a sigh: "It had to be done." And Carlier said: "It's deplorable, but, the men being Company's men the ivory is Company's ivory. We must look after it." "I will report to the Director, of course," said Kayerts. "Of course; let him decide," approved Carlier. . . .

After the slave-trading incident, the villagers no longer bring food to the Europeans, whose own provisions have run dry, while the expected company steamer is long overdue. The two men become sick and disoriented. A violent fight breaks out between them. Kayerts imagines himself at risk from Carlier; amid the confusion, he shoots.

After a few moments of an agony frightful and absurd, he decided to go and meet his doom. . . . He turned the corner, steadying himself with one hand on the wall; made a few paces, and nearly swooned. He had seen on the floor, protruding past the other corner, a pair of turned-up feet. A pair of white naked feet in red slippers. He felt deadly sick, and stood for a time in profound darkness. Then Makola appeared before him, saying quietly: "Come along, Mr. Kayerts. He is dead." He burst into tears of gratitude; a loud, sobbing fit of crying. After a time he found himself sitting in a chair and looking at Carlier, who lay stretched on his back. Makola was kneeling over the body.

"Is this your revolver?" asked Makola, getting up.

"Yes," said Kayerts; then he added very quickly, "He ran after me to shoot me—you saw!"

"Yes, I saw," said Makola. "There is only one revolver; where's his?"

"Don't know," whispered Kayerts in a voice that had become suddenly very faint.

"I will go and look for it," said the other, gently. He made the round along the verandah, while Kayerts sat still and looked at the corpse. Makola came back empty-handed, stood in deep thought, then stepped quietly into the dead man's room, and came out directly with a revolver, which he held up before Kayerts. Kayerts shut his eyes. Everything was going round. . . . He had shot an unarmed man.

After meditating for a while, Makola said softly, pointing at the dead man who lay there with his right eye blown out—

"He died of fever." Kayerts looked at him with a stony stare. "Yes," repeated Makola, thoughtfully, stepping over the corpse, "I think he died of fever. Bury him to-morrow." . . .

The next morning, a dense fog settled. In the distance can be heard the whistling of an approaching steamboat.

Kayerts heard and understood. He stumbled out of the verandah, leaving the other man quite alone for the first time since they had been thrown there together. He groped his way through the fog, calling in his ignorance upon the invisible heaven to undo its work. Makola flitted by in the mist, shouting as he ran—

"Steamer! Steamer! They can't see. They whistle for the station. I go ring the bell. Go down to the landing, sir. I ring."

He disappeared. Kayerts stood still. He looked upwards; the fog rolled low over his head. He looked round like a man who has lost his way; and he saw a dark smudge, a cross-shaped stain, upon the shifting purity of the mist. As he began to stumble towards it, the station bell rang in a tumultuous peal its answer to the impatient clamour of the steamer. . . .

Kayerts hangs himself from the cross that stood over the former manager's grave. The director arrives and cuts down his body.

Chapter 4

The Continent

Introduction

The six authors whose works are sampled in this chapter—four French, one Spanish, and one Italian—exemplify the literary trends of Realism and Naturalism that prevailed in European Continental literature in the wake of Romanticism, whose innocence and vibrancy could not survive an era shaken by Revolution, dictatorship, and industrialization. The novels of Honoré de Balzac and George Sand baldly depict the real world they perceive, from pretentious furnishings to shameless self-promotion to the brutal exploitation of others. Émile Zola discards all lingering illusions and mystifications as he journeys beyond Realism to Naturalism, which posits that only material existence is real, along with the psychological conditions it engenders. In the mode of a Realist or Naturalist, Charles Baudelaire astutely observes the world of Paris, while at the same time translating the phenomena he observes into a new language of symbols, thus anticipating the Modernist[1] trend that could be glimpsed on the horizon. Author of an acclaimed novel detailing the moral and physical collapse of an old aristocratic house, Emilia Pardo Bazán imports Zola's Naturalism to a region where such thinking was starkly unfamiliar. In the same vein, the searingly personal autobiographical novel by Italian author Sibilla Aleramo scrutinizes a woman's entrapment in a failed marriage that could only be resolved by her abandonment of the child she loved.

Honoré de Balzac (1799–1850)[2] is the paragon of Realism. Unlike Romantic authors whose imagination shapes their descriptions of things, Balzac tells readers what it is that sits before their eyes: the exact coloration of wall paneling, the precise substance of a mantelpiece, the veracious facial expression of a character, told in skin texture, the arch of an eyebrow, and a tilt of the head. A cast of characters, delineated with that precision, populate his many novels and novellas which, in the 1830s, he began to gather in a multivolume compilation called the *The Human Comedy* (*La comédie humaine*)—a nod to Dante's

---

1. Modernism: the cultural movement of Modernism that flourished from the late nineteenth to early twentieth century that vigorously rejected traditional forms in art, literature, philosophy, and other creative endeavors.

2. Born Honoré Balzac to a respectable but middling family, he himself added "de" to his name in an act of self-ennoblement that he complemented by marrying, only months before his death, a Polish countess he had courted for years.

Divine Comedy (see Volume One, Chapter 7, Text 2), which also, with different intent, featured a multitude of players. In the component parts of Balzac's enormous drama (the complete, posthumous edition of 1869–1876 comprised more than ninety works in twenty-four volumes), these characters appear and reappear at different stages of life, enmeshed in ever-shifting situations, exiting the stage and reappearing as summoned by the author.

Père Goriot (in English, variously "Father" or "Old" or, untranslated, simply Père Goriot), selections from which are included in this chapter, appeared in 1835 before the larger project of *The Human Comedy* was launched. Generally considered one of Balzac's finest novels, it opens with a meticulous description of an ordinary boarding house in a dismal corner of Paris, the central place to which all the major characters and a mare's nest of plots and subplots relate. Colors, shadows, noises, odors abound, nothing is omitted, but, as the author himself assures us in the opening paragraphs of the novel, all he reports is true. The residents of the boarding house are given an equally close look, as are those with whom they interact in the different sectors of Paris that are specified as though on a map. A cluster of stories intersect, diverge, and come together in the end, always focusing on Père Goriot himself, who arrives at Mme. Vauquer's boarding house as a portly retired merchant, but having divested himself for the benefit of his two grasping daughters, will die there in a wretched garret, a pauper and alone.

A child of privilege who wasted his inheritance, consorted with courtesans, and eased his existence with opiates and alcohol, Charles Baudelaire (1821–1867) was an exquisite craftsman of the French language, composing tightly structured, endlessly inventive, and lyrically rich poems in verse and prose. He scorned what he viewed as the illusions of the Romantics: human innocence, the bounties of nature, the actuality of things, the lodestar of beauty, and the chimera of happiness. An anguished man who met an awful death—paralyzed and silenced by a massive stroke at the age of forty-five—he was the most innovative French poet of his era.

Baudelaire's best-known work is his collection *The Flowers of Evil* (1857)—a shocking title, but an exact translation of the French *Les fleurs du mal*. In these lyric poems, the author speaks sardonically of sex and death, moral dissolution, and the ugliness that, in an industrial age, scarred the splendors of Paris. Remarkable as these lyrics are, they do not outshine the fifty luminous prose poems collected in *Paris Spleen* (*Le spleen de Paris*, composed over more than a decade and published posthumously in 1869). Here the English translation of the title, although quite literal, does not exactly convey the French notion of "spleen": its sense is closer to melancholy than the English, which is closer to "anger."

And melancholy they are, evoking a world where nothing is to be hoped for, where what is valued is not real, where what is real does not endure. Ranging in length from some one hundred words to some two thousand, they are not narratives, but extended apperceptions, told in elaborate symbols and a purposive patterning of words. Without rhyme or formal rhythmic scheme (although the words weave their own rhythm), they cast the lyric aside, yet are most definitely poems. As Baudelaire wrote in his dedication to his publisher, he had dreamed "of the miracle of a poetic prose, musical without rhythm or rhyme, supple enough and jarring enough to be adapted to the soul's lyrical movements, to the undulations of reverie, to the twists and turns that consciousness takes."[3] A sampling of six of the fifty is given in this chapter.

Both Balzac and Baudelaire write about Paris—much as Hugo had in *The Hunchback of Notre Dame* (see Chapter 2, Text 8). George Sand (pseudonym of Amantine-Lucile-Aurore Dupin; 1804–1876), in contrast, a woman writer who fascinated the public by her male pseudonym, her cross-dressing, and her cigar-smoking, sets her novels of love and romance in the country. Yet she addresses in them matters of concern to the Paris elite, who had in recent memory experienced the Revolution of 1789, Napoleon's autocracy, the Bourbon restoration, and further revolutionary explosions in 1830 and 1848. For Sand, whose understanding of history and politics was profound, the consequence of these events was that women as wives, daughters, and mothers were returned to the subordination to men that the revolutionary age, as it dawned, promised to terminate. Mary Wollstonecraft and Madame de Staël, as has been seen (see Chapter 1, Text 8; Chapter 2, Text 7), like their predecessors, had addressed this injustice, but to no avail: in the middle of the nineteenth century, it persisted.

Born with "the blood of kings" in her veins, as she wrote in her autobiography,[4] the daughter of an aristocratic father and a commoner mother, Sand wrote prolifically—nearly seventy novels, some dozen plays, a five-volume autobiography, and twenty-five volumes of correspondence along with literary criticism and political essays—and won an enthusiastic readership, as well as admirers among France's literary greats, among them Balzac, who pronounced her funeral eulogy and declared her a "great woman." Sand attracted critics as well, who denounced her for promoting immorality and undermining the institution of marriage. Her own behavior fueled their criticism: for she had defiantly left her husband and taken a long series of lovers, most famously the composer Frédéric Chopin.

Sand's first sole-authored novel, *Indiana* (1832), champions the search for love and independence of an unhappily married woman who, by the laws of the land, cannot own property in her own right, divorce her husband, or claim

---

3. Charles Baudelaire, *Paris Spleen and La Fanfarlo,* ed. and trans. Raymond N. MacKenzie (Indianapolis: Hackett, 2008), 3.
4. George Sand, *Story of My Life: The Autobiography of George Sand,* group translation ed. Thelma Jurgrau (Albany: State University of New York Press, 1991), 82.

custody of her children.[5] Sand depicts the young Indiana surrounded by towering male figures: a brutal husband, her husband's colorless but always-helpful
brother, and a conscienceless aristocrat who would seduce and then reject her.
Spurned by her lover, disgraced, and desperate, she decides to kill herself—and
is supported in that intention by her loyal brother-in-law, pledged to join her in
that martyrdom. On the point of self-destruction, she discovers that he is the
man she loves, as he had always loved her. They retire to live together delight-
edly and at peace.

Indiana's repudiation of her marriage and search for sexual fulfillment outside its bounds both shocked and fascinated the public. The selections given in
this chapter are taken not from the novel itself, but from Sand's three prefatory
writings reprinted in the 1856 edition, the last of her lifetime, in which she
staunchly defends her advocacy of women's liberation: an Introduction written
in 1852, and the prefaces to the first (1832) and second (1842) editions.

Whereas George Sand focused on one form of social injustice—one that
was suffered by women enslaved by law and custom—Émile Zola (1840–1902)
addressed many. Famously, he came to the defense of Captain Alfred Dreyfus,
framed for a crime he did not commit and victimized because he was Jewish.
On the front page of the Paris newspaper *L'Aurore* on January 13, 1898, Zola
addressed his scathing "J'Accuse. . . !" (I accuse you) to Félix Faure, president of the French Republic, laying bare the deception. Although in this case
he entered into the political fray directly, it is primarily in his literary work,
consisting of nearly forty novels along with numerous short stories, plays, and
essays, that Zola exposed the hypocrisy and cruelty of contemporary society. In
Germinal (1885), the novel that many consider to be his masterpiece, selections
from which appear in this chapter, Zola turned his attention to the suffering
of the laboring poor and their victimization by a predatory bourgeoisie. It is,
as one critic has written, "a timeless cry of protest against oppression and the
misery of the poor who never inherit the Earth."[6]

Zola researched his novels exhaustively, creating a "dossier" of facts and
documents for each one. In 1884, he journeyed to the mining town of Anzin in
northern France, a region that in 1869 had seen fierce strikes that were violently
suppressed. There he studied all facets of the mining industry, descending in
the shafts to observe boilers, carts, and ladders, and talking with the workers whose voices are vividly heard in *Germinal*. Étienne Lantier, the novel's
principal character, emerges as the leader of a strike that wreaks chaos and
destruction, leaving the miners worse off than before and forced by hunger
to return to work. Disgusted and convinced that only the annihilation of the

---

5. Yet notably, Sand herself, before the novel was written, had already separated from her husband, gained custody of her children, and acquired the management of her own wealth.
6. Ruth Scurr, "Rereading Zola's *Germinal*," *The Guardian* (June 18, 2010).

capitalist class can better the workers' condition, the Russian anarchist Souvarine then sabotages one of the mines. Étienne, trapped at the bottom of the shaft, is eventually rescued, although many others die, including the woman he loves. Six weeks later, barely recovered, Étienne sets out for Paris, now dedicated to leading a revolution that will shatter the old world and bring forth a new.

When Zola died in 1902, prematurely and, it was said, accidentally, his Spanish contemporary Emilia Pardo Bazán (1851–1921) had transported his literary naturalism to the unlikely soil of her homeland, where it infused her nineteen novels, hundreds of short stories, plays, works of literary criticism, and political commentary. She had acquired her education in her aristocratic father's library, studying with his encouragement a course that ranged from German philosophy to feminist manifestoes. Married at age seventeen, she had three children by a man who, opposing her intellectual ambitions, quietly retired to the country in 1886, leaving her free to conduct a long-term affair with the renowned author Benito Pérez Galdós. Acquiring the title of countess in her own right upon her father's death in 1908, she capped off her career with an appointment in 1916 to a professorship at the University of Madrid, a position she held until her death at age seventy.

Pardo Bazán's *The House of Ulloa* (*Los pazos de Ulloa*; 1886), a selection from which appears in this chapter, is often seen as her greatest work and one of the greatest Spanish novels of the century. In it she chronicles the corruption and decay of an aristocratic house: the material house and its living inhabitants. The hero, the priest Julián, has been sent by clerical superiors to bring order to the life and finances of the Marquis Don Pedro of Moscoso, husband of his unloved wife, Nucha, and father of his unwanted daughter. Don Pedro needs a son to carry on his line—that fatal need that powers so much tragedy in the history of Europe's ruling elites. One is available: an illegitimate son Perucho, whom he has fathered with a slovenly servant, his huntsman's daughter. Nucha's child stands in the way of Perucho's legitimation and inheritance. With reason, Nucha fears for her life and her daughter's. She enlists Julián to help her wrest "a woman from her legal master and a daughter from her father."

Like the heroine of Pardo Bazán's novel, Sibilla Aleramo (pseudonym of Rina Faccio; 1876–1960) was the mother of a child she loved, a son fathered by the man who raped her when she was fifteen and then, as was obligatory, married her. She tells the story of her life in the autobiographical novel *A Woman* (*Una donna*; 1906), excerpted here, completed five years after having left her husband and—painfully, the laws not permitting her to assume custody—abandoning her son. She had begun writing stories and essays during her hopeless marriage, but *A Woman* was her first major literary work and her finest. It caused a sensation in European literary circles, appearing in multiple editions and translations into several European languages. Like Pardo Bazán's work in Spain, Aleramo's in Italy, where traditional and repressive attitudes toward women's roles prevailed, was profoundly shocking.

Aleramo continued writing while engaging in numerous romantic relationships, among them, notoriously, a lesbian affair that also resulted in a novel, *The Crossing* (*Il passaggio*; 1919), and a platonic friendship with the renowned and notorious writer Gabriele D'Annunzio. Over the early decades of a terrible century, she witnessed World War I and the Russian Revolution, tolerated Mussolini, and embraced communism; all while she wrote more than a dozen novels, along with poetry, plays, and other works, and circulated in avant-garde literary circles. But it is for her unique capture of a particular moment in her own life late in the prior century, illustrating the plight of an Italian woman caught between the cultural and legal barriers to freedom and her devotion to her child, that she is best known.

1. Honoré de Balzac, *Père Goriot* (1835)

The selections that follow trace Père Goriot's deterioration over the seven years in which he lives in Mme. Vauquer's boarding house, the topographical core of the novel: from his arrival in 1813, when he occupies expensive quarters on the first floor; to his removal year-by-year to cheaper accommodations on the second and third floors; and eventually to the attic, alongside the servants. Finally, having given away the last of his possessions to pay the debts of his daughter's lover, he dies in his attic room, attended only by two poor students. It is the students who arrange a pauper's funeral—a funeral Père Goriot's daughters fail to attend, sending instead their empty carriages in hollow tribute to the man who had ruined himself for them.[7]

PÈRE GORIOT

Mme. Vauquer (*nee* de Conflans) is an elderly person, who for the past forty years has kept a lodging-house in the Rue Neuve-Sainte-Genevieve, in the district that lies between the Latin Quarter and the Faubourg Saint-Marcel. Her house (known in the neighborhood as the *Maison Vauquer*) receives men and women, old and young, and no word has ever been breathed against her respectable establishment. . . .

---

7. The translation used here gives "Father Goriot" for "Père Goriot," *père* meaning "father" in French; but the latter name, used in many translations, is preferred throughout as more precisely conveying the author's tone. Minor emendations in orthography and punctuation are made to the text, with interpolated terms placed in brackets.

Balzac describes the house, exterior and interior, in meticulous detail, here turning to the sitting room and dining room.

The house might have been built on purpose for its present uses. Access is given by a French window to the first room on the ground floor, a sitting-room which looks out upon the street through the two barred windows. . . . Another door opens out of it into the dining-room. . . . Nothing can be more depressing than the sight of that sitting-room. The furniture is covered with horse hair woven in alternate dull and glossy stripes. There is a round table in the middle, . . . on which there stands, by way of ornament, the inevitable white china tea-service, covered with a half-effaced gilt network. . . . The hearth is always so clean and neat that it is evident that a fire is only kindled there on great occasions; the stone chimney-piece is adorned by a couple of vases filled with faded artificial flowers imprisoned under glass shades. . . .

Yet, in spite of these stale horrors, the sitting-room is as charming and as delicately perfumed as a boudoir, when compared with the adjoining dining-room. . . . The paneled walls of that apartment were once painted some color, now a matter of conjecture, for the surface is encrusted with accumulated layers of grimy deposit, which cover it with fantastic outlines. . . . The oilcloth which covers the long table is so greasy that a waggish [student] will write his name on the surface, using his thumb-nail as a style. . . . In short, there is no illusory grace left to the poverty that reigns here; it is dire, parsimonious, concentrated, threadbare poverty. . . .

At the time when this story begins, the lodging-house contained seven inmates. The best rooms in the house were on the first story, Mme. Vauquer herself occupying the least important. . . .

The allotment of the remainder of the rooms on the first through third stories is detailed, the residents at each level paying a lower fee than those on the level below. Among the third-story residents is Monsieur Goriot, "a retired manufacturer of vermicelli, Italian paste and starch," and Eugene de Rastignac, a law student. The attic rooms above the third story house the servants Christophe and Sylvie.

These seven lodgers were Mme. Vauquer's spoiled children. Among them she distributed, with astronomical precision, the exact proportion of respect and attention due to the varying amounts they paid for their board. . . . Such a gathering contained, as might have been expected, the elements out of which a complete society might be constructed. . . .

We now take a closer look at Père Goriot.

In the year 1813, at the age of sixty-nine or thereabouts, Père Goriot had sold his business and retired—to Mme. Vauquer's boarding house. When he first came there he had taken the rooms [on the first story] . . . ; he had paid twelve hundred francs a year like a man to whom five louis[8] more or less was a mere trifle. For him Mme. Vauquer had made various improvements in the three rooms destined for his use, in consideration of a certain sum paid in advance . . . for some yellow cotton curtains, a few chairs of stained wood covered with Utrecht velvet, . . . and wall papers that a little suburban tavern would have disdained. . . .

Goriot had brought with him a considerable wardrobe, the gorgeous outfit of a retired tradesman who denies himself nothing. . . . He usually wore a coat of corn-flower blue; his rotund and portly person was still further set off by a clean white waistcoat, and a gold chain and seals which dangled over that broad expanse. . . . His cupboards . . . were filled with a quantity of plate that he brought with him. The widow's eyes gleamed as she obligingly helped him to unpack the soup ladles, table-spoons, forks, cruet-stands, tureens, dishes, and breakfast services—all of silver . . . ; he could not bring himself to part with these gifts that reminded him of past domestic festivals.

Goriot's initial affluence soon fades, however, toward the end of his second year of residence.

He asked Mme. Vauquer to give him a room on the second floor, and to make a corresponding reduction in her charges. Apparently, such strict economy was called for, that he did without a fire all through the winter. Mme. Vauquer asked to be paid in advance, an arrangement to which [Monsieur] Goriot consented, and thenceforward she spoke of him as "Père Goriot."

Yet oddly, Goriot was often visited by fashionably dressed young women, whom he identified as his "daughters."[9]

At that time Goriot was paying twelve hundred francs a year to his landlady, and Mme. Vauquer saw nothing out of the common in the fact that a rich man had four or five mistresses; nay, she thought it very knowing of him to pass them off as his daughters. . . . When at length her boarder declined to nine hundred francs a year, she asked him very insolently what he took her house to be, after meeting one of these ladies on the stairs. Père Goriot answered that the lady was his eldest daughter.

"So you have two or three dozen daughters, have you?" said Mme. Vauquer sharply.

"I have only two," her boarder answered meekly, like a ruined man who is broken in to all the cruel usage of misfortune.

---

8. franc and louis: the franc was the standard French unit of currency; the *louis d'or* or *louis tournois*, a coin of higher but fluctuating value.

9. Mme. Vauquer assumes that a parade of fashionably dressed women come to visit Goriot, when they are only his two daughters sporting their ever-changing wardrobe of elegant outfits.

Towards the end of the third year Père Goriot reduced his expenses still further; he went up to the third story, and now paid forty-five francs a month. . . . He had grown sadder day by day under the influence of some hidden trouble; among all the faces round the table, his was the most woebegone. . . . His diamonds, his gold snuff-box, watch-chain and trinkets, disappeared one by one. He had left off wearing the corn-flower blue coat, and was sumptuously arrayed, summer as well as winter, in a coarse chestnut-brown coat, a plush waistcoat, and doeskin breeches. He grew thinner and thinner; his legs were shrunken, his cheeks, once so puffed out by contented bourgeois prosperity, were covered with wrinkles. . . . In the fourth year of his residence, . . . [the] hale vermicelli manufacturer, sixty-two years of age, who had looked scarce forty . . . , had suddenly sunk into his dotage, and had become a feeble, vacillating septuagenarian. . . .

One evening after dinner Mme. Vauquer said half banteringly to him, "So those daughters of yours don't come to see you any more, eh?" meaning to imply her doubts as to his paternity; but Père Goriot shrank as if his hostess had touched him with a sword-point.

"They come sometimes," he said in a tremulous voice.

"Aha! you still see them sometimes?" cried the students. "Bravo, Père Goriot!"

The old man scarcely seemed to hear the witticisms at his expense that followed on the words; he had relapsed into the dreamy state of mind that these superficial observers took for senile torpor, due to his lack of intelligence. If they had only known, they might have been deeply interested by the problem of his condition; but few problems were more obscure. . . .

Meanwhile, the student Rastignac, engaged on a vigorous program of social climbing, visiting his cousin, a vicomtesse, and with her a duchess, her friend, learns that Goriot is the father of the Baroness Delphine de Nucingen and the Countess Anastasie de Restaud; and that the father had sacrificed himself for the welfare of his daughters, who cut him off, seeing him only in private, to which he acceded so as not to embarrass their husbands. The duchess explained:

"Their father had given them all he had. For twenty years he had given his whole heart to them; then, one day, he gave them all his fortune too. The lemon was squeezed; the girls left the rest in the gutter."

Rastignac is impressed: "Père Goriot is sublime!" he says to himself. Back at the boarding house, his colleagues know now that Père Goriot is the father of a baroness and a countess. Determined to know more before he approaches Delphine de Nucingen—who will become his mistress—Rastignac locates the man to whom Goriot had sold his vermicelli business and learns the whole story.

In the days before the Revolution,[10] Jean-Joachim Goriot was simply a workman in the employ of a vermicelli maker. He was a skillful, thrifty workman,

---

10. Revolution: the French Revolution of 1789–1795.

sufficiently enterprising to buy his master's business when the latter fell a chance victim to the disturbances of 1789. . . .

Goriot made out well when the price of grain surged in Paris.

He excited no one's envy, it was not even suspected that he was rich till the peril of being rich was over, and all his intelligence was concentrated, not on political, but on commercial speculations. Goriot was an authority second to none on all questions relating to corn, flour, . . . and the production, storage, and quality of grain. He could estimate the yield of the harvest, and foresee market prices. . . .

Besides his business, Goriot was absorbed by his love for his wife and on her death, for his daughters.

Two all-absorbing affections filled the vermicelli maker's heart to the exclusion of every other feeling. . . . He had regarded his wife, the only daughter of a rich farmer of La Brie, with a devout admiration; his love for her had been boundless. . . .

After seven years of unclouded happiness, Goriot lost his wife. . . . All the affection balked by death seemed to turn to his daughters, and he found full satisfaction for his heart in loving them. More or less brilliant proposals were made to him from time to time; wealthy merchants or farmers with daughters vied with each other in offering inducements to him to marry again; but he determined to remain a widower. . . .

As might have been expected, the two girls were spoiled. With an income of sixty thousand francs, Goriot scarcely spent twelve hundred on himself, and found all his happiness in satisfying the whims of the two girls. The best masters were engaged, that Anastasie and Delphine might be endowed with all the accomplishments which distinguish a good education. They . . . learned to ride; they had a carriage for their use . . . ; they had only to express a wish, their father would hasten to give them their most extravagant desires, and asked nothing of them in return but a kiss. . . .

When the girls were old enough to be married, they were left free to choose for themselves. Each had half her father's fortune as her dowry; and when the Comte de Restaud came to woo Anastasie for her beauty, her social aspirations led her to leave her father's house for a more exalted sphere. Delphine wished for money; she married Nucingen, a banker of German extraction, who became a Baron of the Holy Roman Empire. Goriot remained a vermicelli maker as before. His daughters and his sons-in-law began to demur; they did not like to see him still engaged in trade, though his whole life was bound up with his business. For five years he stood out against their entreaties, then he yielded, and consented to retire on the amount realized by the sale of his business and the savings of the last few years. . . . He had taken refuge in Mme. Vauquer's lodging-house, driven there by despair when he knew that his daughters were compelled by their husbands not only to refuse to receive him as an inmate in their houses, but even to see him no more, except in private.

The final tragedy came when, having given up all that remained to him to his daughter Anastasie, Goriot had a stroke and died, attended only by Rastignac and Bianchon, another student. They pay for a pauper's funeral, which his daughters do not attend. Of Goriot's boarding-house colleagues, only Rastignac and the servant Christophe are present.

Rastignac and Christophe and the two undertaker's men were the only followers of the funeral. . . . When the coffin had been deposited in a low, dark, little chapel, the law student looked round in vain for Goriot's two daughters or their husbands. Christophe was his only fellow-mourner; Christophe, who appeared to think it was his duty to attend the funeral of the man who had put him in the way of such handsome tips. . . . The two priests, the chorister, and the beadle came, and said and did as much as could be expected for seventy francs in an age when religion cannot afford to say prayers for nothing. . . . The whole service lasted about twenty minutes. There was but one mourning coach, which the priest and chorister agreed to share with Eugene and Christophe. . . .

But just as the coffin was put in the hearse, two empty carriages, with the armorial bearings of the Comte de Restaud and the Baron de Nucingen, arrived and followed in the procession to [the cemetery] Père-Lachaise. At six o'clock Goriot's coffin was lowered into the grave, his daughters' servants standing round the while. The ecclesiastic recited the short prayer that the students could afford to pay for, and then both priest and lackeys disappeared at once. The two gravediggers flung in several spadefuls of earth, and then stopped and asked Rastignac for their fee. Eugene felt in vain in his pocket, and was obliged to borrow five francs of Christophe. This thing, so trifling in itself, gave Rastignac a terrible pang of distress. It was growing dusk, the damp twilight fretted his nerves; he gazed down into the grave and the tears he shed were drawn from him by the sacred emotion, a single-hearted sorrow. When such tears fall on earth, their radiance reaches heaven. And with that tear that fell on Père Goriot's grave, Eugene Rastignac's youth ended. He folded his arms and gazed at the clouded sky; and Christophe, after a glance at him, turned and went—Rastignac was left alone.

2. Charles Baudelaire, *Paris Spleen* (1869)

This sampling of six of the fifty prose poems in *Paris Spleen* hints at the range of Baudelaire's themes and approaches. In the first, #2 in the volume, a "shriveled" old woman takes delight in observing an infant, who rejects her. In #7, a jester petitions the statue of Venus, avowing his love of beauty—but she, beauty incarnate, does not care. In #17, the poet immerses himself in the "ocean" of his beloved's hair, whose odor, texture, and taste bring forth the ecstasy of memory. In #19, a rich child delights in a poor child's toy, although his own is a sparkling prize, while the other's is a live rat his parents plucked from the street, "from life itself." In #33, the poet instructs the reader to "get yourself drunk," as that is the only point of things: "[O]n wine, on poetry, or on virtue, whatever you like." In #48, the poet inquires of his disconsolate soul where it would like to settle down: In Lisbon? In Batavia? In the Arctic Circle? "Anywhere," his soul responds, "[a]s long as it's out of this world!"

Paris Spleen

2. The Old Woman's Despair

The shriveled little old woman felt delight in seeing the pretty baby everyone fussed over, the one everyone wanted to please; this pretty creature as fragile as she, the little old woman, and—also like her—without teeth or hair.

And she went up to the child, planning to make little smiles and cheerful faces for him.

But the frightened child struggled under the caresses of the decrepit good woman, and filled the whole house with his yelps.

Then the good old woman turned back to her eternal solitude, and she wept in a corner, saying to herself:

"Ah, for us miserable old females, the era of pleasing even the innocent ones is over; and we arouse only horror in the little children we want to love!"

7. The Fool and Venus

What a fine day! The vast park grew faint under the burning eye of the sun like youth under the domination of Love.

The universal ecstasy of things was not expressed by any sound; the waters themselves seemed to be asleep. Entirely unlike human celebrations, here the orgy was a silent one.

It was as if a steadily expanding light made objects sparkle more and more; as if the excited flowers burned with the desire to rival the sky's azure with the energy of their own colors, and as if the heat, making scents visible, caused them to mount up toward the stars like steam.

However, amid this universal enjoyment, I caught sight of one afflicted creature.

At the feet of a colossal Venus, one of those artificial fools, one of those voluntary buffoons assigned to amuse kings when Remorse or Ennui have overcome them, tricked out in a gaudy, ridiculous costume, wearing horns and bells on his head, pressed up against the pedestal and raised his tear-filled eyes to the immortal Goddess.

And his eyes said: "I am the least of humans and the most solitary, deprived of love and friendship, and thus inferior to the most imperfect of animals. But still I was created, I too, to perceive and feel immortal Beauty! Ah, Goddess! Have pity on my sorrow and my madness!"

But the implacable Venus with her eyes of marble only gazed out at something, I don't know what, in the distance.

17. A Hemisphere in Her Hair

Let me breathe in long, long the fragrance of your hair, plunge my face entirely into it like a thirsty man into spring water, wave it in my hand like a scented handkerchief, to shake out memories into the air.

If you could know all that I see—all that I sense—all that I hear in your hair! My soul voyages on this perfume the way the souls of other men voyage on music.

Your hair contains a whole dream, full of sails and masts; it contains great seas, where monsoons carry me to enchanted climates, where the sky is bluer and more profound, where the atmosphere is perfumed by fruits, by leaves, and by human skin.

In the ocean of your hair, I can just glimpse a port swarming with melancholy songs, with vigorous men of all nations, with vessels of every shape outlining their subtle and complicated architectures against an immense sky of lazing, eternal heat.

In the caresses of your hair I recover the languors of long hours passed on a divan, in a room on a fine vessel, gently rocked by the imperceptible swellings of the port, among pots of flowers and casks of refreshing water.

In the hearth fire of your hair, I breathe in the odor of tobacco, mixed with opium and sugar; in the night of your hair, I see the sheen of the infinite tropical azure; on the downy banks of your hair, I grow drunk with combined odors of tar, of musk, and of coconut oil.

Let me bite your heavy black tresses slowly. When I chew on your elastic, rebellious hair, I feel I am eating memories.

19. The Toy of the Poor

I want to suggest an innocent diversion. So few amusements involve no guilt!

When you go out in the morning, determined only to wander up and down the highways, fill your pockets with little gadgets that cost no more than a sou[11]—like the flat puppet worked by a single string, the blacksmith beating on an anvil, the rider and his horse, with a tail that works as a whistle—and in front of taverns, or under the trees, give them out as gifts to the unknown poor children you encounter. At first, they won't dare to take them; they won't believe their good fortune. But then their hands will eagerly snatch up the present, and off they will flee, as cats do when they go far away to eat the morsel you have given them, having learned to distrust people.

Down one road, behind the gate of an enormous garden, at the back of which could be seen the whiteness of a pretty chateau[12] struck by the sun, stood a fine and fresh child, dressed in those country clothes that are so coyly attractive.

Luxury, the absence of worry, and the habitual spectacle of wealth make these children so pretty that one would think them made from a different mold than the children of mediocrity or poverty.

Next to him on the grass lay a splendid toy, as fresh as its master, gleaming and gilded, wearing a purple outfit, covered with little feathers and glass beads. But the child was not playing with his favorite toy; instead, this is what he was watching:

On the other side of the gate, on the road, among the thistles and nettles, there was another child, dirty, puny, soot-covered, one of those pariah-animals in which an impartial eye would detect beauty if, like the eye of the connoisseur detecting an ideal painting beneath a layer of varnish, he could wash off the repulsive patina of poverty.

Through this symbolic barrier separating two worlds, that of the highway and that of the chateau, the poor child was showing his own toy to the rich one, who examined it eagerly as if it were some rare and unknown object. Now, this toy that the dirty little child was provoking, tossing and shaking in a box with a grate—was a live rat! The parents, through economy no doubt, had taken the toy directly from life itself.

And the two children laughed with each other fraternally, smiling with teeth of an *equal* whiteness.

33. Get Yourself Drunk

You should always be drunk. This is the whole point, the only question. In order not to feel the horrible burden of Time that breaks your shoulders and bends you down toward the ground, you must get yourself relentlessly drunk.

But drunk on what? On wine, on poetry, or on virtue, whatever you like. But get yourself drunk.

---

11. sou: a French coin obsolete by the nineteenth century, but surviving as a slang term for a value of a fraction of the franc, the principal unit of currency at this time.
12. chateau: large French country house or castle.

And if at some point, on the steps of a palace or on the green grass of a ditch or in the sad solitude of your room, you awaken with your drunkenness already diminished or vanished, ask the wind, the wave, the star, the bird, the clock, everything that flees, everything that groans, everything that rolls, everything that signs, everything that speaks, ask them what time it is, and the wind, the wave, the star, the bird, the clock will reply: "It's time to get drunk! So as not to be one of the martyred slaves of Time, get yourself drunk; get yourself drunk always! On wine, on poetry, or on virtue, whatever you like."

48. Any Where Out of the World

This life is a hospital where each patient is obsessed with switching beds. This one wants to go suffer facing the stove, and that one thinks he'll get better if he's next to the window.

It always seems to me that I would be better off in any place but the one where I am, and this question of moving on is one I endlessly discuss with my soul.

"Tell me, my soul, my poor cold soul, what would you think of living in Lisbon? It must be warm there, and you would cheer up there like a lizard. The city is on the water's edge; they say it's built of marble, and that the people there have such a hatred for vegetation that they cut down all the trees. Now there's a country to your taste: a landscape made of light and of mineral, and liquid to reflect them!"

My soul does not respond.

"Since you have such a love of repose and of watching the spectacle of movement, would you like to go live in Holland, that enchanting land? Perhaps you would be entertained in that country whose image you've so often admired in museums. What would you think of Rotterdam, you who love forests of masts, and boats moored outside houses?"

My soul remains mute.

"Would Batavia [Jakarta, Indonesia] make you smile more? We would find there the European spirit wedded with tropical beauty."

Not a word.—Is my soul dead?

"So, have you become so benumbed that you'll only take pleasure in your own disease? If that's the way it is, let's flee to those countries that resemble Death.—I know what you need, poor soul! We'll pack up our trunks for Torneo [Tornio, Finland]. We'll go even farther, to the extreme end of the Baltic; even farther from life, if that's possible; we'll set up house at the Pole. There, the sun only nears the earth obliquely, and the slow alterations of light and night suppress variety and augment monotony, that other kind of nothingness. There, we can take long baths of shadows, except when, from time to time, the Northern Lights will entertain us with their pink sprays, like a reflection of Hell's fireworks!"

At last, my wise soul bursts out and cries: "Anywhere! Anywhere! As long as it's out of this world!"

3. George Sand, *Indiana* (1832)

Sand's novel *Indiana* was an instant success, but it horrified many critics—critics to whom the author responded. Rather than an excerpt from the novel itself, the selections that follow are from three prefatory writings reprinted in the 1856 edition of *Indiana*, the last to appear in Sand's lifetime: the *Introduction* to the 1852 edition; the *Preface* to the 1832 edition; and the *Preface* to the 1842 edition. In these, at three junctures of her career, Sand defends what she—writing as "he," the presumed author—has done.

In the 1852 *Introduction*, written in the first person, Sand rebuffs those critics who chose "to see in the book a deliberate argument against marriage" or to pen "an incendiary proclamation against the repose of society." Nothing of the sort: she had simply followed her "instincts" and "having no theory of art or philosophy in my mind." The 1832 *Preface* likewise insists that the author (identifying herself as George Sand and writing as a male author) has written "a very simple tale, in which the author has invented almost nothing." In the Realist vein, she has merely copied life, or so she claims. If he (the male author) has portrayed the inequalities that exist in society, he should incur no blame: "The author is merely a mirror which reflects them, . . . and he has no reason for self-reproach if the impression is exact, if the reflection is true." The 1842 *Preface*, written ten years after the original publication, during which there was time for reflection upon a mountain of criticism, Sand goes further: "[H]aving advanced on life's highway and watched the horizon broaden around me, . . . I find myself so entirely in accord with myself with respect to the sentiment which dictated *Indiana* and which would dictate it now if I had that story to tell to-day for the first time. . . ." The cause he has sought to defend "is the cause of half of the human race, nay, of the whole human race; for the unhappiness of woman involves that of man. . ."[13]

INDIANA

Introduction (1852)

I wrote *Indiana* during the autumn of 1831. It was my first novel; I wrote it without any fixed plan, having no theory of art or philosophy in my mind. I

---

13. Minor emendations in orthography and punctuation are made to the text of the translation used here, with interpolated terms placed in brackets.

was at the age when one writes with one's instincts, and when reflection serves only to confirm our natural tendencies. Some people chose to see in the book a deliberate argument against marriage. I was not so ambitious, and I was surprised to the last degree at all the fine things that the critics found to say concerning my subversive purposes. Under all régimes and in all times there has been a race of critics, who, in contempt of their own talent, have fancied that it was their duty to ply the trade of denouncers. . . if [whose] advice were followed, some of us would be forbidden to write anything whatsoever.

At the time that I wrote *Indiana*, the cry of Saint Simonism[14] was raised on every pretext. Later they shouted all sorts of other things. . . . If a writer puts noble sentiments in the mouth of a mechanic, it is an attack on the bourgeoisie; if a girl who has gone astray is rehabilitated after expiating her sin, it is an attack on virtuous women; if an impostor assumes titles of nobility, it is an attack on the patrician caste; if a bully plays the swashbuckling soldier, it is an insult to the army; if a woman is maltreated by her husband, it is an argument in favor of promiscuous love. And so with everything.

Thank God, I have forgotten the names of those who tried to discourage me at my first appearance, and who, being unable to say that my first attempt had fallen completely flat, tried to distort it into an incendiary proclamation against the repose of society. I did not expect so much honor. . . .

GEORGE SAND.

Nohant, May, 1852.

Preface to the edition of 1832

If certain pages of this book should incur the serious reproach of tending toward novel beliefs, if unbending judges shall consider their tone imprudent and perilous, I should be obliged to reply to the criticism that it does too much honor to a work of no importance; that, in order to attack the great questions of social order, one must either be conscious of great strength of purpose or pride one's self upon great talent, and that such presumption is altogether foreign to a very simple tale, in which the author has invented almost nothing. If, in the course of his task, he has happened to set forth the lamentations extorted from his characters by the social malady with which they were assailed; if he has not shrunk from recording their aspirations after a happier existence, let the blame be laid upon society for its inequalities, upon destiny for its caprices! The author is merely a mirror which reflects them, . . . and he has no reason for self-reproach if the impression is exact, if the reflection is true. . . .

---

14. Saint Simonism: alluding to the ideas of Claude Henri de Rouvroy, Comte de Saint-Simon, denotes a socialistic system where the state owns all property, and citizens share in the wealth according to their contributions.

[The author] . . . being still a young man, he simply tells you to-day what he has seen. . . . He plies with exactitude his trade of narrator. He will tell you everything, even painful truths; but, if you should wrap him in the philosopher's robe, you would find that he was exceedingly confused, simple storyteller that he is, whose mission is to amuse and not to instruct. . . .

These facts, it seems to me, are sufficient to protect this book from the reproach of immorality; but . . . you will perhaps chide me on account of the last pages; you will think that I have done wrong in not casting into misery and destitution the character who has transgressed the laws of mankind through two volumes. In this regard, the author will reply that before being moral he chose to be true; he will say again, that, feeling that he was too new to the trade to compose a philosophical treatise on the manner of enduring life, he has restricted himself to telling you the story of *Indiana,* a story of the human heart, with its weaknesses, its passions, its rights and its wrongs, its good qualities and its evil qualities.

Indiana, if you insist upon an explanation of everything in the book, is a type; she is woman, the feeble being whose mission it is to represent *passions* repressed, or, if you prefer, suppressed by *the law*; she is desire at odds with necessity; she is love dashing her head blindly against all the obstacles of civilization. But . . . the powers of the soul become exhausted in trying to struggle against the positive facts of life. That is the conclusion you may draw from this tale, and it was in that light that it was told to him who transmits it to you. . . .

Preface to the edition of 1842

In allowing the foregoing pages to be reprinted, I do not mean to imply that they form a clear and complete summary of the beliefs which I hold today concerning the rights of society over individuals. I do it simply because I regard opinions freely put forth in the past as something sacred, which we should neither retract nor cry down nor attempt to interpret as our fancy directs. But today, having advanced on life's highway and watched the horizon broaden around me, I deem it my duty to tell the reader what I think of my book.

When I wrote *Indiana,* I was young; I acted in obedience to feelings of great strength and sincerity which overflowed thereafter in a series of novels, almost all of which were based on the same idea: the ill-defined relations between the sexes, attributable to the constitution of our society. These novels were all more or less inveighed against by the critics, as making unwise assaults upon the institution of marriage. *Indiana* . . . did not escape the indignation of several self-styled serious minds, whom I was strongly disposed at that time to believe upon their simple statement and to listen to with docility. But, although my reasoning powers were developed hardly enough to write upon so grave a subject, I was not so much of a child that I could not pass judgment in my turn on the thoughts of those persons who passed judgment on mine. . . .

Certain journalists of our day who set themselves up as representatives and guardians of public morals . . . pronounced judgment pitilessly against my poor tale, and, by representing it as an argument against social order, gave it an importance and a sort of echo which it would not otherwise have obtained. They thereby imposed a very serious and weighty rôle upon a young author hardly initiated in the most elementary social ideas, whose whole literary and philosophical baggage consisted of a little imagination, courage, and love of the truth. Sensitive to the reproofs and almost grateful for the lessons which they were pleased to administer, he examined the arguments which arraigned the moral character of his thoughts before the bar of public opinion, and, by virtue of that examination, which he conducted entirely without pride, he gradually acquired convictions which were mere feelings at the outset of his career and which to-day are fundamental principles. . . .

A long while after I wrote the [original] preface to *Indiana* under the influence of a remnant of respect for constituted society, I was still seeking to solve this insoluble problem: *the method of reconciling the welfare and the dignity of individuals oppressed by that same society without modifying society itself.* Leaning over the victims and mingling his tears with theirs, making himself their interpreter with his readers, but, like a prudent advocate, not striving overmuch to palliate the wrongdoing of his clients, . . . the novelist is really the advocate of the abstract beings who represent our passions and our sufferings before the tribunal of superior force and the jury of public opinion. It is a task which has a gravity of its own beneath its trivial exterior. . . .

I do not flatter myself that I performed this task skillfully; but I am sure that I attempted it in all seriousness, amid inward hesitations wherein my conscience . . . marched forward to its goal, without swerving too far from the straight road and without too many backward steps. . . .

After this novitiate of ten years, being initiated at last in broader ideas which I derived not from myself but from the philosophical progress which had taken place around me. . . , I realized at last that, although I may have done well to distrust myself and to hesitate to put forth my views at the epoch of ignorance and inexperience when I wrote *Indiana*, my present duty is to congratulate myself on the bold utterances to which I allowed myself to be impelled then and afterwards; bold utterances for which I have been reproached so bitterly, and which would have been bolder still had I known how legitimate and honest and sacred they were.

Today therefore, having reread the first novel of my youth with as much severity and impartiality as if it were the work of another person, on the eve of giving it a publicity which it has not yet derived from the popular edition, . . . I find myself so entirely in accord with myself with respect to the sentiment which dictated *Indiana* and which would dictate it now if I had that story to tell to-day for the first time, that I have not chosen to change anything in it save a few ungrammatical sentences and some inappropriate words. . . .

I repeat then, I wrote *Indiana,* and I was justified in writing it; I yielded to an overpowering instinct of outcry and rebellion which God had implanted in me, God who . . . interposes in the most trivial as well as in great causes. But what am I saying? is this cause that I am defending so very trivial, pray? It is the cause of half of the human race, nay, of the whole human race; for the unhappiness of woman involves that of man, . . . and I strove to demonstrate it in *Indiana.* . . .

They who have read me without prejudice understand that I wrote *Indiana* with a feeling, not deliberately reasoned out, to be sure, but a deep and genuine feeling that the laws which still govern woman's existence in wedlock, in the family, and in society are unjust and barbarous. I had not to write a treatise on jurisprudence but to fight against public opinion; for it is that which postpones or advances social reforms. The war will be long and bitter; but I am neither the first nor the last nor the only champion of so noble a cause, and I will defend it so long as the breath of life remains in my body. . . .

4. Émile Zola, *Germinal* (1885)

The excerpts from *Germinal* that follow depict three critical moments in the novel: first, the miners' strike and riot; second, Étienne Lantier's emergence from hiding following the strike; and third, his setting forth in the bright springtime, following his recuperation from his harrowing experience in the depths of the exploded mine, to pursue the task he now sets for himself: to lead a revolution that will "shatter the earth."[15]

GERMINAL

The workers of village Two Hundred and Forty, attached to the mine Le Voreux, have ceased to work, and race throughout the region from mine to mine summoning their fellow workers to join them in a strike. They look to Étienne, who had urged them to strike against the bourgeois mine owners, and he now takes command. But contrary to his wishes, they wreak chaos and destruction, beginning at the mine at Jean-Bart, managed by Deneulin, who will be ruined by the striker's assault.

---

15. La Brûlé, Maheu, Levaque, Jeanlin (a child), Catherine, and Chaval are workers at Le Voreux mine; Deneulin is the manager of the Jean-Bart mine; Souvarine is a Russian anarchist; Montsou is a bleak mining town in northeastern France.

Early that morning, before daybreak, a kind of shudder had passed through the mining villages, a tremor that grew and spread and spilled out over the roads and the entire countryside. . . .

Miners were arriving from every direction, . . . women from across the fields, all leaderless, all unarmed, flowing there naturally like water flowing downhill. Étienne . . . got in along with the first ones to arrive. There were scarcely three hundred present.

There was a moment's hesitation, when Deneulin appeared, standing at the top of a stairway leading to the receiving area.

"What do you want?" he asked in a powerful voice. . . .

There were some mutterings and some elbowing in the crowd. Finally, Étienne stepped forward, saying:

"Monsieur, we mean you no harm. But work must stop here immediately."

Deneulin treated him like some kind of imbecile.

"So you think it's doing me some kind of favor to make the work stop at my place? Why don't you just shoot me in the back?" . . .

Étienne was trembling, but he still restrained himself. He lowered his voice.

"I beg you, sir, give the order for your men to come up. I can't promise to control my comrades. And you can avoid a disaster if you do."

"No, to hell with your peace offering! Do I even know you? You don't work here, and I have nothing to debate with you. . . . You're just a gang of thieves wandering around the countryside to loot houses." . . .

"Please, Monsieur! . . . There's going to be a massacre. What's the good in letting people get killed for nothing?"

He struggled and protested, and hurled one last shout at the crowd:

"You heap of criminals, you'll see what's what when we come back for you, and we're the stronger ones!"

They led him away, as a surge from the crowd pushed those in the front up against the staircase, twisting its front railing. It was the women doing the pushing, their shouts goading on the men. The door gave all at once, a door without a lock, only fastened with a latch. But the stairway was too narrow, and the crowd would never have got in if some of the besiegers had not found other openings. Then, they poured in from all sides—from the changing room, the screening shed, the boiler room. They had overrun the mine in less than five minutes, and they were swarming at every landing, with angry gestures and shouts, carried away by their victory over this boss who had resisted them. . . .

"To the boilers!" howled La Brûlé. "Let's put out the fires!"

Levaque had found a large file, and he was brandishing it like a sword, shouting out over the tumult:

"Let's cut the cables! Let's cut the cables!"

Everyone took up the call except for Étienne and Maheu, who continued to protest in a daze, trying to be heard above the roar. At last, Étienne was able to say:

"But there are men down there, comrades!"

The tumult seemed to double, with voices shouting out from all sides.

"Too bad! They shouldn't have gone down! . . . It's what traitors deserve! . . . Yes, let them stay down there! . . . Anyway, they have the ladders!"

Thinking of the ladders made them all the more stubbornly insist on the idea, and Étienne realized he would have to give in on the point. Fearing the worst kind of disaster, he hurried over to the winding machine, wanting at least to get the cages up so that the cables wouldn't crush them with their enormous weight if they fell down upon them. The machine operator had disappeared . . . so he took hold of the lever to start it up, and maneuvered it while Levaque and two others climbed up the iron framework supporting the pulleys. The cages were scarcely fixed on their bolts when they heard the grinding sound of the file chewing away at the steel. There was a great silence . . . ; everyone lifted up their heads, watching and listening, seized with emotion . . . as if the teeth of the file were delivering from evil by grinding through the cable of one of these misery pits, turning this one into a place where no man would ever descend again.

But La Brûlé had disappeared up the stairs to the changing room, continuing to shout: "We have to put out the fires! To the boilers! To the boilers!"

Some women followed her. . . . La Brûlé, armed with a large shovel, was hunched down in front of one of the fireboxes and emptying it violently, throwing the glowing coals onto the brick floor, where they continued burning and giving off black smoke. . . . The heaps of burning coals mounted higher, and the powerful heat cracked the ceiling of the huge room. . . .

Just then, they heard the high-pitched voice of Jeanlin.

"Look out! I'm going to put out the fires! I'll let it all out!"

One of the first ones in, he had kicked around in the crowd for a while, . . . on the lookout for any harm he could do, and he hit upon the idea of opening the steam valves. Jets of steam burst out as violently as gunshots, and the five boilers emptied themselves in a storm of steam, making a deep hissing sound like rolling thunder. . . . Everything had disappeared in the steam. . . .

This lasted about a quarter of an hour. Some buckets of water were thrown to extinguish the piles of cinders; all danger of a fire was past. But the crowd's rage had not cooled; on the contrary, it was whipped up even more. Men were heading down with hammers, and the women armed themselves with iron bars, and there was talk of wrecking the boilers, destroying the engines, and demolishing the whole mine.

"Down with the traitors! . . . Oh, the dirty cowards! . . . Down with them!"

The workers were emerging from the mine. . . . Then they moved off, trying to find the road in order to flee. . . .

And suddenly, [the mine] Jean-Bart fell into a great silence. Not a soul, not a breath. Deneulin came out of the foremen's room, . . . and all alone he went to see the mine. First, he stopped in front of the shaft, raised his eyes, and saw the cut cables: the steel ends hung down useless. . . . Then, he went up to the engine, and looked at the motionless piston road. . . . Then, he went down to the boilers, walking slowly in front of the extinguished fireboxes, gaping open and flooded, and gave a kick to one of the boilers, hearing its empty echo. That was enough! It was all over; he was ruined. . . . And despite the certainty of his disaster, he felt no hatred for the Montsou vandals. . . . They were brutes, no doubt; but they were brutes who couldn't even read, and who were dying of hunger.

The strike has failed. The mine owners have identified the troublemakers, Étienne among them; and he has gone into hiding—in a mine shaft. At last he emerges, and looks to a new day.

Across the whole region, there was one disaster after another. At night, as he wandered through the black countryside, like a wolf venturing out of his forest, he imagined he could hear the sound of one company after another going bankrupt. Bordering the roads now were nothing but closed factories, buildings rotting away under the pale night sky. . . .

Étienne would often stop at a bend in the road to listen to the melancholy sound of buildings decaying. He breathed the darkness in deeply, and he felt a joy in the annihilation going on around him, a hope that the sun would rise on the extermination of the old world—not one fortune left standing, everything cut down to the same level as if by a scythe sweeping across the earth. But what especially intrigued him amid the general massacre was the Company and its mines. Blinded in the darkness, he would nonetheless set off to visit them all, one after another, happy whenever he heard of some further damage. . . . Thus, hour by hour, the costs of repairs were going up and the mines were rapidly becoming useless, blowing holes in the shareholders' dividends and leading eventually to the annihilation of the famous [wealth] of Montsou, whose value had grown a hundredfold over the preceding century.

Hearing about all these endless blows, Étienne felt hope surging up within him again, and he began to think that a third month of the strike would finish off the monster, the weary, satiated beast squatting down there somewhere like an idol in its mysterious tabernacle. . . .

When the anarchist Souvarine blows up Le Voreux, the mine served by the workers of village Two Hundred and Forty, Étienne is trapped at the bottom with Catherine, the young girl he has desired, and her pimp Chaval, his rival. In the last of several struggles between the two men, Étienne kills Chaval. Trapped for days as the icy waters rise around them, Etienne and Catherine at last consummate their long-denied passion. But Catherine dies in his arms, where she is found when Étienne, white-haired, starved, and senseless, is rescued. After a hospital stay of six weeks, he

*sets off for Paris. It is Germinal, the month in the French Revolutionary calendar[16]
spanning March and April, when the seeds in the field and the buds on the trees
burst forth with new life. He has found his path forward: he will lead a revolution,
which will come, and which will convulse the earth.*

Outside, Étienne followed the road for a while, absorbed in his thoughts. All
sorts of ideas were buzzing within him. But then he suddenly felt the fresh air
and looked up at the clear sky, and he took a deep breath. On the horizon, the
rising sun looked glorious; it was a joyous dawn, spreading across the entire
countryside. A stream of gold washed over the entire immense plain, from east
to west. This life-giving warmth expanded and extended itself, like a tremor of
youth pulsating with the signs of the earth, the song of the birds, all the murmurings of the waters and the woods. It was good to be alive, and the old world
seemed to want to live on for one more springtime.

Imbued with all that hope, Étienne slackened his pace, his gaze wandering
from left to right, taking in the joy of the new season. He turned his thoughts
to himself, and he thought that he was strong, matured by his harrowing experience down in the depths of the mine. His education was complete now, and
he was going forth into the world well armed, an intellectual soldier of the
revolution who had declared war on society, society as he saw it and condemned
it. . . . [He] felt a need to glorify [these workers], to depict them as the only
noble creatures, the flawless, the true aristocracy of the earth, and humanity's
only hope for regeneration. He could already see himself standing at the ros-
trum, triumphing along with the people—as long as the people didn't turn and
destroy him. . . .

If one class had to be devoured, why shouldn't it be the people, so full of
life continually renewed, who devoured the bourgeoisie, effete and worn out
from their luxurious lives? The new society would arise out of new blood. And
in waiting for and expecting this new barbarian invasion that would regener-
ate the old, exhausted nations of the world, he reverted to his absolute faith in
the coming revolution, the real one, the workers' revolution, whose fires would
burn away the end of this century with the same purple color that he could see
before him in the rising sun, spreading its blood red hues across the sky. . . .

Far off, in the bright sunlight, he saw the belfries of several mines. . . .
Work was grinding on everywhere, and he imagined he could hear the blows of
the pickaxes deep below the earth. . . . One blow, then another, then another,
under the fields, under the roads and the villages basking in the light: all the
obscure labor down in that underground prison. . . . And now he considered
that, perhaps, the violence hadn't helped hurry things along. The broken cables,

16. French revolutionary calendar: in effect from 1793 to 1805 and again during the Paris Com-
mune of 1871.

the torn-up rails, the smashed lamps—what a futile effort it had been! What had been the good of it, that crowd of three thousand racing around destroying things? He vaguely perceived that legal methods might, one day, prove far more terrible. His thinking was maturing; he had sown the wild oats of his anger. . . .

Now, the April sun up in the clear sky was shining in all its glory, warming the fecund earth. And life was spring forth from her fertile womb, the buds bursting into green leaves, the fields quivering as the new grass pushed its way forth. . . . Again, and again, more and more distinctly, as if they were themselves approaching the earth above them, the comrades were tapping. . . . Men were pushing their way upward, a blackened, vengeful army, germinating slowly in the furrows, rising up for the harvests of the coming century, and it was their germination that would shatter the earth.

5. Emilia Pardo Bazán, *The House of Ulloa* (1886)

At the climactic moment in *The House of Ulloa*, Nucha, the wife of the Marquis Don Pedro de Moscoso, meets clandestinely with the priest Julián, who had been sent by his superiors to bring order to the marquis's unruly household. She is delirious with fear: "[T]hey"—her husband and his villainous entourage— will kill her and they will kill her baby girl, so that the master's illegitimate son Perucho may inherit the estate.[17] She must get away, taking the child, and she needs Julián's help. Julián listens to her astonishing plan, and is resolved to assist.[18]

THE HOUSE OF ULLOA

Nucha regularly attended mass in the renovated chapel, kneeling the whole time, and slipping out as Julián gave the blessing. Without turning around or losing track of his prayer, Julián knew the very moment when the señorita rose and sensed the imperceptible tap of her footsteps on the new wooden floor. But one morning he did not hear her. This mere fact disrupted the serenity of his prayer. When he stood up, he saw Nucha standing by him, signaling silence with her finger on her lips. Perucho, who assisted at mass with impressive ease, was putting out the candles, wielding a long rod. The lady's eyes said eloquently: "Send that boy away." The priest told the altar boy to leave him.

---

17. Ulloa, like most aristocratic estates, is entailed so that females are barred from the inheritance of real property.

18. The ellipses in the translation that follows are in the original, except for those enclosed in brackets, interpolated by the present editor.

The boy procrastinated, puttering as he folded a towel for the washbasin. At last, reluctantly, he left. The fragrance of flowers and fresh varnish filled the chapel; a warm light entered by the windows, filtering through the curtains of crimson taffeta, making the statues of the saints on the altar seem to come alive and contriving to brighten Nucha's pallor with a rosy hue.

"Julián?" she asked in an imperious tone, unusual for her.

"Señorita," he responded quietly, respecting the sacred place. His lips quivered and his hands shook with cold, for he thought the terrible moment of confession had arrived.

"We must talk. And we must talk here, of necessity. Anywhere else someone will be watching us."

"Indeed, they would watch."

"Will you do what I ask of you?"

"You know I will . . ."

"Whatever it may be?"

"I . . ."

His consternation grew. His heart beat in a muffled roar. He leaned on the altar.

"Here is what I ask of you," Nucha announced, looking at him fixedly with eyes not merely vague but wholly indeterminate; "you must help me get away from here. From this house."

"To . . . to get away," Julián stammered, thunderstruck.

"I need to leave. And take my child with me. I want to go back to my father. For this to happen, it must be kept secret. If those here know of it, they will take a key and lock me up. They will tear me from my little one. They will kill her. I know for certain they will kill her."

Her tone, her demeanor, the expression on her face, were those of someone not in possession of her full mental faculties; of a woman driven by a nervous excitation that verges on delirium.

"Señorita," sputtered the priest, not a little shaken, "you mustn't stand, you mustn't stand . . . Sit down on this bench. We shall talk calmly. I know you have problems, señorita. You must have patience, prudence. Calm yourself."

Nucha let herself sink down on the bench. She breathed laboriously, like one whose pulmonary functions are gravely impaired. . . . Once she caught her breath, she spoke composedly.

"Patience and prudence! I have these as much as a woman can have. Let's not hide from the facts. You know yourself when the nail began to hammer me—since that day when I decided to learn the truth, and it did not cost me . . . too much effort. Well, it cost . . . a battle. But that matters little. For myself I would think nothing of leaving, since I am not well and I do not expect to live much longer; but—my baby?"

"Your baby . . ."

"They are going to kill her, Julián, these . . . persons. Do you not see that she is in their way? You really do not see it?"

"For God's sake, I beg you to calm yourself . . . We shall talk quietly and sensibly . . ."

"I am tired of staying calm!" Nucha exclaimed angrily, like one who has been toyed with. "I have prayed, I have pleaded. I have exhausted every possibility. I will not wait, I cannot wait any longer. I hoped that the elections would turn out well,[19] thinking then we could leave this house, and then I would no longer fear. I am afraid in this house, as you yourself know, Julián; horribly afraid . . . especially at night."

By the light of the sun, which sifted through the crimson curtains, Julián saw the señorita's dilated pupils, half-opened lips, arched eyebrows, and an expression of mortal terror painted on her face.

"I am very frightened," she repeated, trembling.

Julián felt helpless. How he wished he knew what to say! But nothing came to mind, nothing. The mystical counsels that he had ready at hand [. . .] all of that vanished when he faced this relentless, throbbing, and boundless sorrow.

"As soon as I came here to this house that is so large and so ancient," Nucha continued, "a chill ran down my spine. It is only that now . . . these are not the trifling thoughts of a spoiled girl, no. . . . They are going to kill my baby. You will see! Whenever I leave her with the wet nurse, I am on hot coals. We must act quickly. It must all be resolved this very hour. I turn to you, because I cannot trust anyone else . . . You love my little girl."

"To see her is to love her . . . ," Julián stammered, overcome by emotion and nearly speechless.

"I am alone, alone," Nucha repeated, brushing her cheeks with her hand to wipe away the tears that choked off the sound of her voice. "I thought I would make my confession with you, but . . . it is God who hears my confession . . . I would not have obeyed if you had sent me away from here. For I know what my duty is: the wife must never separate from her husband. When I married, my intention was . . ."

All of a sudden, she stopped, and looking right into Julián's face, she asked him: "Does it not seem to you, as it does to me, that this marriage would end badly? My sister Rita was almost engaged to my cousin when he asked for my hand. . . . Through no fault of mine, Rita and I have been estranged ever since. I don't know how this happened. God knows I did nothing to cause Pedro to choose me. Papa advised me that, all the same, I should marry my cousin. I did what he said. I was resolved to be a good wife, to love him much, to obey

---

19. The marquis had participated unsuccessfully in a local election, marred by corruption on both sides.

him, to care for his children. . . . Tell me, Julián, have I fallen short in any way?"

Julián crossed his hands. His knees shook, and he nearly fell to the floor. He declared rapturously: "You are an angel, Señorita Marcelina."[20]

"No . . . ," she replied, "not an angel, but I do not recall having harmed anyone. I cared much for my little cousin Gabriel,[21] who was sickly and had no mother . . ." On saying these words, the dam burst, and her tears finally ran free. Nucha breathed better, as if those memories of her childhood settled her nerves and crying gave her relief [. . .]

"Why did I need to marry? I had Papa and Gabriel with whom I could live always. If they died, I could enter a convent. In short, I am not to blame for Rita's anger. When Papa told me of my cousin's intentions, I told him that I did not wish to rob my sister of her suitor; then Papa . . . kissed me all over on my cheeks, as he used to do when I was little, and, in words I seem to still hear him say, replied: 'Rita is . . . a fool. Be quiet.' But for all that Papa said . . ., my cousin had preferred Rita!"

She continued after some seconds of silence: "As you have seen, I do not have much for which my sister should envy me! . . . What sorrows I have borne, Julián! When I think about it, my stomach churns in knots." . . .

At last the priest could express a portion of his feelings. "Those knots do not surprise me. . . . I have them as well, and day and night, I ponder your misfortunes, señorita. . . . When I saw that mark, the bruise on your wrist. . ."

For the first time in their conversation, Nucha's pale face reddened, and her eyes were veiled beneath the fringe of her eyelashes. She did not respond directly.

"You see," she whispered with the trace of a bitter smile, "these misfortunes always happen to me through no fault of my own. . . . Pedro insisted that I claim from Papa the portion owing me from Mama's estate, because Papa wouldn't give him a penny to campaign in the elections. Also he was furious that my aunt Marcelina, who had intended to leave her property to me, now intends, I understand, to leave it to Rita. . . . I have nothing to do with any of this. . . . Why will they kill me? I know I am poor; there is no need to remind me of it. But all of that means nothing. . . . What really pained me was my husband's saying that because of me the house of Moscoso was left without an heir![22] . . . Without an heir! And my daughter? the little angel of my womb?"

20. Marcelina: her proper name; Nucha is the abbreviation of the diminutive Marcelinucha. Julián is underscoring the declaration he makes on his knees by using her baptismal name.

21. cousin Gabriel: Nucha's frail, younger cousin on her mother's side, although here she names him her *hermanito,* or little brother.

22. the house of Moscoso was left without an heir: Don Pedro de Moscoso, Marquis of Ulloa, is without an heir who can succeed to the title and the property, because the only legitimate offspring is a female, Nucha's daughter.

The unhappy woman wept, slowly, without sobbing. Her eyelids now had the reddish hue that painters give to the eyelids of their *Dolorosas.*[23]

"What happens to me," she added, "means nothing. I can endure until the end. If they treat me . . . one way . . . or another, if . . . that servant . . . takes my place, . . . well, then, . . . patience, it would be a question of being patient, of suffering, of surrendering to death. . . . But this involves my little girl—he has another child, a son, a bastard. . . . My daughter is the obstacle! . . . They will kill her!" . . .

She said it again solemnly, with great deliberation: "They will kill her. Don't look at me that way. I am not mad, but I am overwrought. I have decided to leave and go live with my father. I do not believe that is a sin, even if I take the baby with me. And if I sin, don't tell me so, Julianciño![24] . . . It is an irrevocable decision. You will come with me, because I cannot execute my plan alone. You will come with me?"

Julián wanted to object to something—but what? He did not know himself. He was won over by the sweet diminutive by which the señorita called him to her aid, and the feverish determination with which she spoke. Deny help to the unfortunate woman? Impossible. Consider the risk the project posed of difficulty and inconvenience? That didn't occur to him for a moment. In his innocence, so absurd a flight seemed almost easy. Oppose the journey? He too had been and was at every moment fearful, with mortal terror, not only for the child but also for the mother; had it not occurred to him one thousand times that both lived in imminent danger? Besides, what in the world would deter him from trying to dry those pure eyes, to soothe that labored breath, to see the señorita once again secure, honored, respected, surrounded by kindness in her father's house?

He imagined the escape scene. It would be at daybreak. Nucha would be wrapped in many coats and scarves. He would take charge of the infant, asleep and wrapped in blankets as well. In case she awoke, he would carry in his pocket a bottle of warm milk. [. . .] The baby would not go hungry. They would ride comfortably in a big carriage with an enclosed compartment. Each turn of the wheels would take them further away from the dread house of Ulloa. . .

Very quietly, they began to discuss and resolve the details. A ray of sun burst from the clouds, and the saints, in their niches, seemed to smile benevolently at the group on the bench [. . .] [displaying] on their painted faces not the slightest displeasure at the priest engaged in planning the details of an abduction—for that is what it was: wresting a woman from her legal master and a daughter from her father.

---

23. *Dolorosas*: The images of the *mater dolorosa*, the grieving Virgin Mary at the crucifixion of her son Jesus.

24. Julianciño: a diminutive of Julián, a tender endearment, used here to add force to her plea.

This scene, placed within pages of the end of the novel, promises a daring and successful adventure to liberate the señorita. But that promise unravels quickly. Perucho, who had seen the señorita[25] and the priest in close discussion, reveals that fact to the household. The marquis summons the two conspirators, terrifies Nucha, and, accusing Julián of illicit relations with his wife, summarily dismisses him. Julián is banished to a distant parish. Soon after, he learns of Nucha's death—a great relief, for she has escaped her marital dungeon. Ten years later, he returns, and finds her grave. At play nearby are the smartly-clad Perucho and Nucha's daughter, now eleven, clothed in peasant rags. The girl has survived, but Perucho is the heir apparent, the next señorito of the house of Ulloa.

6. Sibilla Aleramo, *A Woman* (1906)

Aleramo's husband has returned infected with a venereal disease, which increases her revulsion for him. She establishes a separate bedroom, and focuses obsessively on her son. By the terms of the will of her recently deceased uncle, she will receive a modest inheritance—enough to let her think of claiming her independence. She plans her departure, and at last, she leaves, alone; her husband will not allow her to take her son with her. A year later, she has not seen him, and even his messages to her have been intercepted. She begins to write the book we read, an account of her life, for her son. The selections that follow are from the closing chapters of *A Woman*, which tell of a mother's agonizing and irrevocable abandonment of her child.

A WOMAN

I contemplated my son. Our intimacy seemed to increase as his intelligence revealed itself in those early stirrings of thought. While he did his homework at a little table, I wrote or read, pausing to respond to his questions. Minutes passed by sweetly and peaceably. But when he left me to go out and play, a chill came over me . . . .

In long intervals of leisure, Aleramo read. Was she not, like the heroines she read about, denying her feelings, and failing to act on them?

I had continued to belong to a man I despised and who did not love me. To the world, I wore the mask of a contented woman, legitimating in some way an

---

25. *señorita:* in this context, the lady of the house and counterpart of the master, the *señorito*, terms that would be used by members of the household.

ignoble servitude, and sanctifying a monstrous lie. For my son—so as not to
run the risk of losing my son.

And now, the final shame that has vanquished so many women, I conceived
of death as liberation. I abased myself to that extent that, by dying, I would
abandon my son. But I did not have the courage, while living, to lose him.

At times a wind of madness swept over me. In the evening . . . I was left
alone facing the man who disgusted me by his glances and his feints at reconciliation. I took refuge in arguments, responding sarcastically when he bemoaned
the industrial crisis and the attitude of the workers. . . . Then suddenly a little
voice would interject: "Mamma!"; and after a moment: "Come here, Mamma!"
I arose and went to the darkened little room where I had put the child to sleep.
He saw my shadow in the open doorway, and called me again, more gently:
"Mamma!" And when he sensed I was near his little bed, he would reach out
his arms, clasp my neck, and pull my head down next to his. Silently, he stroked
my eyes and cheeks; I felt the soft, warm tremor of his fingers. . . .

What did this dear soul want? To be certain that I was not crying, that his
Papa had not made me cry? . . . . I threw myself across his bed and my sobs rose,
irrepressibly. I muffled them in the bedcovers, hearing again the tremulous
word: "Mamma!" My face was bathed in tears, mine and his. . . . In my heart
I prayed: "Pardon me, pardon me, my son!" And then for a long time I stayed
there, prostrate, wordless, waiting for a merciful sleep to embrace the little boy,
and for me, the paralysis that follows the crisis. . . .

Aleramo receives a telegram from her father telling her that a beloved uncle was
near death. She leaves immediately for Turin, but on arrival, learns that he has
died. He has left her a small legacy as well—five times larger than that left to her
siblings, and sufficient to allow her to plan an independent life for her and her
child. For now, she returns home, and tells her husband that they must separate—
and she will take their child.

He stood near the French doors leading to the garden. . . . His face was swollen
and livid.

"My son?" he burst out. "Just try it!"

His shout of rage must have passed through the door and out to the street.
The child's body at my side, shaking and trembling, clung to me, choking back
his sobs.

"And you, get up! Come with to the factory! Get up!"

But the little tremulous voice refused: "I have to do my homework. . . ."

His pure blue eyes confronted the turbid, frightening eyes of his father. A
moment of silence passed. I stood motionless; I felt only the pressure of a small,
damp hand.

I heard him slam the door closed, and his footsteps on the gravel receding
into the distance.

We were alone in the house, on a gloomy afternoon. . . . The hand of the heartbroken little boy dried the tears that slipped slowly from my eyes, and asked me: "What did he want? What was Papa talking about? Why does he shout so, Mamma, why does he always make you cry?"

"I must get away from here, my darling son; you see, I must leave. . . ."

What was I saying? He put his hands on my shoulders, with all the tumultuous force of his tiny being.

"Mamma, Mamma, and I come with you, don't I? Tell me it is so, tell me!. . . I don't want to stay here with Papa, I don't want to be parted from you. . . . I don't want it, Mamma! You will take me away with you, tell me you will take me away?. . ."

And he fell into my arms, bursting into tears, a lament that tore through my flesh, the lament of a man and of an infant at the same time, which seemed to encompass all the sorrow in the world. . . . My son, my little son! I held you tight, I wept with you, so desperately, feeling I had been merged with you, as if I had gathered you back into my womb and launched you a second time into life in an infinite spasm of pain and joy that matched the overwhelming sovereignty of the bond that is between us, the eternal bond. . . .

Aleramo writes her father about her decision to leave, and explores her legal situation, which is dire. She must leave now, or she will never escape.

Chance, or destiny, or perhaps the obscure logic of things had determined that, finally, I was forced to show the man to whom I was enslaved how great was the horror I felt of his embrace. After ten years—of misery! . . . .

To leave, to leave forever. No longer to live a lie. For my son even more than for me! To suffer everything, his absence, his forgetting, my death; but never again to know self-loathing, nor to lie to the boy, luring him into the circuit of my dishonor!. . . .

While pondering her escape, she asks her son:

"You will remember me always, won't you? If I were to die, if I had to part from you. . .?"

"Yes."

His heart was in that affirmation, amid the tears. . . . He had made a promise to himself that, buried within, would rise up one day and empower him. . . .

Aleramo tells her husband she is leaving that night. He goes to his room, and she sits at her son's bedside.

Midnight. Only three hours more. . . . Seated in an armchair, I felt cold . . . . Suddenly I felt all my strength failing me. Was I falling asleep? I was so tired; would I have the strength to leave?

The clock struck three. I jumped up, put on my coat, and got ready to leave. Then I turned to the little bed, and woke him up. "I am going," I said softly, "and the hour is now; be good, be good, love me, I will always be your Mamma. . . ." And I kissed him, hesitating, unable to shed one tear. Then I heard his little sleepy voice saying: "Yes, always good. . . . Send grandfather to take me, Mamma. . . . So I can be with you. . . ." He turned his face to the wall, peacefully. Then, at that moment, I knew that I would not return, I felt a force outside of me that ruled over me, I was going forth to meet a new destiny—and that all the pain that lay before me could not surpass the pain that I felt then. . . .

She has made that decisive journey. Her story resumes a year later.

Much time has passed. By now, a year.

I did not go back there. I have not seen my son again. The dark presentiment was correct. For how many months have I struggled to preserve the illusion that I might recover my son?

The first days were a hiatus, spent under the silent and fearful surveillance of my sister. Then the weeks followed in an ever more violent exchange of letters between my husband and myself, between him and my father, and finally between our lawyers. His surprise at my resistance became increasingly evident. He believed I would return in the end—did he not have my son as hostage?

And the child, with the help of a maidservant, sent me little notes in which his uncertain fingers had written words of love and anguish: ". . . . I want to run away, Mamma, but how can I? Here they tell me terrible things about you. . . . I love you so much, I will never forget you, not even in a hundred years. . . . But what are you doing? Can't you send someone to get me?" . . . .

More and more I came to realize that I would obtain nothing from my husband, that his vendetta would be inexorable. First he sent me threats, then mockeries; he knew that I had no grounds on which to initiate a legal case for separation. My father, tired out, no longer intervened; he had told me from the start not to hope, and ever since. I received the rejection of my request to collect my inheritance from my uncle, denied for lack of marital authorization. Finally, even my lawyer said nothing more could be done. I remained the property of that man, and I was to consider myself fortunate that he had not had me brought back by force. That was the law.

My husband fired the maidservant, so I no longer received my son's little messages. A young governess had been hired to teach him. I wrote her, but she did not reply.

No one could do anything for me. Why did death wait so long? Or I was already dead, and nothing of me survived but a memory? . . . .

Is there any hope left for me? No. Tomorrow, perhaps, there will come to me a new reason for existence. . . . But I do not expect anything. Tomorrow, it may be, I shall die. And the final throes of this life of mine will be what has been written in these pages.

They are written for him.

My son, my son! Perhaps his father believes he is happy! He bestows on him a pile of things. He will give him toys, books, teachers. He will surround him with comforts and luxuries. My son will forget me and hate me.

Hate me then—but don't forget me!

And he will be raised to respect the law, a useful thing to those who are powerful. He will love authority and tranquility and well-being. Whenever I look at his picture now, the childish features seem to me to represent, in his eyes, my sorrow, and in the curve of his lips, the harshness of his father. But he is mine. He is mine, he must be like me! To hold him, to embrace him, to enclose him in me! And I would disappear, because he would entirely be *me*!

One day, he will be twenty. Will he set off then, perchance, to search for his mother? Or will he already have the picture of a different woman in his heart? Will he not sense then that my arms will reach out to him across the vacancy, and that I will call to him, call to him by name?

Or perhaps I shall exist no longer. I shall not be able any more to tell him about my life, the story of my soul—and to tell him that I have waited for him so long!

And it is for this reason I have written. My words will reach him, and he will hear them.

Chapter 5

Scandinavia and Russia

Introduction

By the sixteenth or seventeenth centuries, European literature could be written in modern vernacular languages including French, Italian, Spanish, English, and German—greatly broadening the audience for books, whose appetites were fed by a constellation of busy printing houses and a burgeoning population of authors. That maturation of the languages of Scandinavia and Russia came later, however, only after 1800. Alexander Pushkin, as has been seen (see Introduction to Chapter 2), reconstructed Russian as a literary language in the 1820s and 1830s, a task continued by Nikolay Gogol in the following decade, as seen in this chapter. It will be seen here, too, that Henrik Ibsen and August Strindberg play a similar role in the construction of the modern Danish and Swedish literary traditions. Authors from these peripheral regions were necessarily familiar with other European languages and generally spent years on end traveling through western Europe, residing at major cultural centers, and absorbing the literature, philosophy, and social thought of their Western contemporaries. Westerners, in turn, readily recognized the talents of their counterparts from Europe's northern and eastern borders, and translated and performed their works that thereupon reached an international audience. Not only did the periphery join the European mainland in a cultural union, but also Europe itself, as a civilization, grew larger.

Discussion here turns first to Henrik Ibsen and August Strindberg, dramatists from Norway and Sweden, respectively, whose innovative work impacted on playwriting far beyond the borders of their native lands. Familiar with the realist and naturalist approaches then current in western Europe, they employ them in exploring the psychological experience of the contemporary bourgeoisie and especially of women.

Seen by some as the greatest playwright since Shakespeare, Henrik Ibsen (1828–1906) early sought out a career in the theater, working as an actor, a director, and a writer. Writing in Danish, the literary language of the political entity of Denmark-Norway that was dissolved shortly before Ibsen's birth, he created the language that modern Norwegian literature would employ. From 1864 to 1891, he lived abroad, mostly in Italy and Germany, absorbing the traditions of international European culture, and producing a sequence of dramas that won enthusiastic acclaim: among them, *Peer Gynt* (1867), with musical accompaniment by Edvard Grieg; *A Doll's House* (1879), one of the most popular plays of the European tradition, selections from which appear in this chapter; *An Enemy of the People* (1882); *The Wild Duck* (1884); and *Hedda Gabler* (1890). Over these years, his focus shifted from classical and historical subjects to "problem plays"—plays that addressed current issues of concern to middle-class audiences, including poverty and privilege, the struggle of individuals facing public pressure, and the role of women in the family. In 1891, Ibsen returned to Norway as a famed and honored national figure.

Ibsen was the son of a prominent entrepreneur who went bankrupt when the future playwright was a young boy. His younger Swedish contemporary, August Strindberg (1849–1912), the son of a prosperous shipping agent, also faced familial difficulties: his mother had been his father's maidservant and he was their fourth child, but first legitimate son. The imprint of that socially awkward parentage, exacerbated by his mother's early death and father's subsequent marriage to his children's governess, was lasting. It is documented in his autobiographical novel, *Son of a Servant*, and leaves its traces in *Miss Julie* (1888), selections from which appear in this chapter, one of the most important of his more than sixty plays. Strindberg overcame many other obstacles in the course of a brilliant and erratic career as playwright, novelist, short story writer, historian, social theorist, scientist, and occultist, much of it, like Ibsen's, spent abroad in major European capitals. Like Ibsen, as well, Strindberg confronted contemporary issues in his tense, daring dramas—and in stories that occasioned a charge of blasphemy, of which he was acquitted—often centered on women and marriage. Too daring to be awarded conventional honors, Strindberg was awarded in 1912, just prior to his death, what his supporters called the "Anti-Nobel Prize," funded largely by public subscription.

The brief excerpts given in this chapter from Ibsen's *A Doll's House* and Strindberg's *Miss Julie*, both examining the "woman question," pose a compelling contrast. Ibsen portrays a bourgeois woman trapped in a conventional marriage—playing the part of a doll in a doll's house—who suddenly and cleanly, spurred by the unmistakable unmasking of her husband's weakness and narcissism, leaves to begin a new and independent life, making a bold decision that will convince the audience of its justice. Strindberg's *Miss Julie*, a one-act play involving only three actors, will shock more and convince less, but will equally challenge the audience's understanding of the norms of contemporary family life—although it is by no means as pro-woman a drama as Ibsen's. Julie is the daughter of a count, whose forward-looking, emancipated mother has left her a legacy of confused sexual identity and mental instability. The action occurs on Midsummer's Night, a holiday surviving from pagan times that is an occasion for excess. Julie tempts Jean, a handsome male servant of her household, to seduce her—and finds, when her father returns home, that the consequences of that act are inevitable and fatal. As the curtain closes, she holds Jean's razor and is heading to the hayloft to cut her throat.

The "woman question," although a matter also of interest to contemporary Russian authors, is not so pressing for them as for the Norwegian Ibsen or the Swedish Strindberg. The four selections included here by the Russian writers Nikolay Gogol, Fyodor Dostoevsky, Leo Tolstoy, and Anton Chekhov—all figures of first importance in what many consider the "Golden Age" of Russian literature—dwell more on individual and cultural identity: identities that in each case are poised for disintegration in the face of the omnivorous forces of a tyrannical state, modernization, and secularization.

If Strindberg presents a tragic portrait of a person, a woman, whose existence was rendered meaningless by social norms and customs, the Ukrainian-born Russian author Nikolay Gogol (1809–1852), in his short story *The Overcoat* (1842), presents a comedic portrait of such a person, a man. Gogol's Akaky Akakiyevich is a lower-level civil servant, locked immovably in a rank of scant importance, whose service to the state is to copy documents without emendation and embellishment, and whose whole being is determined by that function. He dies, consumed by the fruitlessness of his labors and the fierce St. Petersburg cold, the victim of his one desire: his yearning for an overcoat that can keep him warm. In this story, abridged here, as in his eighteen other short stories, the genre to which he gravitated—although Gogol is also highly regarded for his play, *The Government Inspector* (1836) and his novel, *Dead Souls* (1842)—the anonymous, lost civil servant, a cog in the wheel of the Russian tsarist state, personifies modern existence. Gogol's realistic portrayal of contemporary society is deeply pessimistic: there is no escape.

Gogol's Akaky Akakiyevich will remind the reader of Pushkin's Yevgeny (see *The Bronze Horseman*, Chapter 2, Text 12), also a lower-level civil servant, who is consumed in the aftermath of the St. Petersburg flood that is identified with the narcissism of the bronze horseman, Tsar Peter the Great. He has some kinship, as well, with the Underground Man, the purported narrator of the novella *Notes from the Underground* (1864) by Fyodor Dostoevsky (1821–1881).

We meet the Underground Man twice. In the first part of the novella, excerpted here, he is a retired civil servant in his forties, who has chosen to live, as he prefers, in a miserable "mousehole," subsisting on the pittance he has by happenstance inherited. From this perch, he denounces the scientism, determinism, and grim utopianism of his generation. Intelligent and imaginative—possessing, that is, aptitudes that Pushkin's Yevgeny and Gogol's Akakiyevich lack—the Underground Man understands the promises made by those who insist on a rational and, in concept, benevolent reordering of society, but willfully repudiates those promises: for he will not accept a world where facts are everything, where the dream is to house, feed, and groom everyone to a bland uniformity, where two times two are self-evidently four. They are not. There is more.

Notes from the Underground is an early work of Dostoevsky's, written before his greatest novels—among them, *Crime and Punishment* (1866); *The Idiot* (1869); *The Possessed* (1872); and the magnum opus, *The Brothers Karamazov* (1880). Considered one of the great Russian authors, whose legacy includes translations and essays as well as numerous short stories and novels, he is remembered especially as an astute student of human psychology, and as an advocate—even as the testimony of the philosophers of his era, whose work he knew, pointed in the other direction—of Russian Christian Orthodoxy.

In Dostoevsky's novella, Gogol's short story, and Pushkin's poem, three Russian authors depict the impact of the conscienceless state, philosophical nihilism, and rife secularization on the ordinary men subject to those overmastering powers. The forces that beset Ivan Ilyich, in contrast, who was also a civil servant—although a wealthier, more capable, and more ambitious one—are his own limitations as a human being. He is the protagonist of *The Death of Ivan Ilyich* (1886), a short story written by Leo Tolstoy in his later years, when he had himself experienced much death and spiritual torment.

Descended on his father's side from an ancestor granted hereditary nobility by Tsar Peter the Great and on his mother's from an eminent aristocratic family, Leo Tolstoy (1828–1910) was haunted by his wealth and status. These encumbrances appear not only as themes in his many novels and stories (a collection of his works made by his wife during his lifetime extended to ninety volumes), but as a recurrent theme in his career as well. For this landowner devoted himself to many worthy causes: among others, the education of the peasantry, famine relief, and the rights of dissident religious groups. He had seen military service in the Crimean War (1853–1856) and wrote about it powerfully, but subsequently became a pacifist. In his later years, he opposed private property and, to his wife's distress, renounced copyright on the works he wrote from that point forward. He was profoundly religious, having undergone a life-altering spiritual crisis, although his heterodox beliefs resulted in his excommunication by the Russian Orthodox clerisy.

Tolstoy's most famous works are two novels considered to be among the greatest in the European tradition: *War and Peace* (1869) and *Anna Karenina* (1878). Among his other works, however, and especially among his later ones most marked by his religious experiences, the short story *The Death of Ivan Ilyich* stands out. The protagonist Ivan Ilyich is the model of a successful civil servant. As a young man, he had studied the law dutifully and successively won posts as special assistant to a provincial governor, as examining magistrate, and up the ladder, finally, to chief prosecutor. He married a pretty woman of his set, with some wealth, who liked his dancing, although he felt no love for her—and when marital tensions ensued, he handled them by distancing himself from the disruptive household involvements. Upon his final promotion, his purse now bursting, he decorated his new home with all the luxuries befitting his station, so that it resembled that of all others in his circle; at the same time, he shed old acquaintances who did not meet the standard of the rank to which he was now elevated. At work, he labored assiduously, ensuring that no personal matters intervened in his judicial deliberations, as a stream of terrified accused malefactors appeared before him to be deemed deserving of punishment or death. His only delights were his adolescent son, his peasant manservant, and his games of whist, which he played skillfully and with modest profit. He was not an evil man, but worse: a man who had never reflected on who he was—until, that is, when at age forty-five, torn with pain, he must confront death. The selections given here from the closing chapters of the story detail his final agony and illumination.

Whereas Tolstoy explores the human soul, Anton Chekhov (1860–1904), with equal acuity and compassion, investigates the shaping of human experience by social and cultural conditions—a concern arising from his own past. One of six children of a father, the son of a serf, who became a grocer and then went bankrupt, Chekhov supported and sustained the other members of his family for the whole of his brief life, cut short at age forty-four by chronic tuberculosis. He did so by writing daily pieces for newspapers, even as he pursued his medical degree and established a practice. Especially known at first for his crisp, effective short stories, he turned in time to playwriting, producing within the space of a decade, among others, four dramas hailed as masterpieces: *The Seagull* (1895); *Uncle Vanya* (1897); *The Three Sisters* (1900); and *The Cherry Orchard* (1903). Selections from *The Cherry Orchard*, written months before its debut and the author's death, appear in this chapter.

Chekhov named *The Cherry Orchard* "a comedy"; his friend, the famous impresario and director Konstantin Stanislavski, produced it as a tragedy. It is both. It is a tragedy because it dramatizes the end of an era, the world of landowners and serfs, symbolized by the cherry orchard destined for destruction that flourished on the estate where the siblings Lyubov Andreyevna Ranyevskaya and Leonid Andreyevich Gayev were born and raised. It is a comedy, as Chekhov intended, because with two exceptions—the housekeeper Varya (the "adopted daughter" of Lyubov Andreyevna, thus not an aristocrat by birth) and the wealthy merchant Lopakhin (the son of a serf, like Chekhov's father)— the characters are virtually incoherent, hilariously unaware of what is plainly occurring, absurdly unable and unwilling to hear what is said to them with perfect clarity. These lovable but useless aristocrats are blind to the fate that will befall them if they cannot adapt to the modern world: dispossession of their ancestral home and loss of their wealth and status. Lopakhin, a loyal friend of the family and savvy entrepreneur, insistently proposes to them a way forward, but they ignore him. In the end, their estate is auctioned—and purchased by

Lopakhin, the new proprietor. As the household members exit their doomed home for an unpromising future, the sound is heard in the distance of axes at work, felling the splendid cherry orchard.

1. Henrik Ibsen, *A Doll's House* (1879)

The final scenes of Act III respond to the receipt of two items of mail. The first is a letter from the clerk Krogstad to bank manager Torvald Helmer, informing him of the forged signature Helmer's wife Nora had affixed to a bond years ago when Krogstad lent her the money to bring Torvald to Italy for his health—money she has been over time scrimping to repay. Thus Helmer learns of his wife's crime, committed though it was for his sake, but in the moment, dishonoring him. The second is a missive from Krogstad to Nora, which Helmer intercepts and opens. Krogstad makes amends; his own precarious situation has been remedied in another way. He returns the bond, which Helmer now destroys along with the earlier letter. Helmer is relieved: Nora will be found guilty of no crime, his own position is safe, and all may return to normal.

Self-importantly, Helmer tells Nora he forgives her. But Nora cannot forgive him for that patronizing gift of forgiveness: Torvald does not understand what she had done for him or the sacrifice she would have made—for she was prepared to kill herself—in order to save his reputation. She realizes at last that he is shallow and hypocritical, and that their marriage has been a lie. She will leave, in a massive assertion of pride and independence. The last sound heard before the curtain falls is from offstage: the sound of the front door slamming behind her.[1]

A DOLL'S HOUSE

HELMER (*standing at the open door*): . . . What is this? Not gone to bed? Have you changed your things?

NORA (*in everyday dress*): Yes, Torvald, I have changed my things now.

HELMER: But what for?—so late as this.

NORA: I shall not sleep tonight.

HELMER: But, my dear Nora—

---

1. Minor emendations have been made to the translation used here as needed. Italicized stage directions are in the original. All ellipses have been interpolated by the present editor.

NORA (*looking at her watch*): It is not so very late. Sit down here, Torvald. You and I have much to say to one another. (*She sits down at one side of the table.*)

HELMER: Nora—what is this?—this cold, set face?

NORA: Sit down. It will take some time; I have a lot to talk over with you.

HELMER (*sits down at the opposite side of the table*): You alarm me, Nora!— and I don't understand you.

NORA: No, that is just it. You don't understand me, and I have never understood you either—before tonight. No, you mustn't interrupt me. You must simply listen to what I say. Torvald, this is a settling of accounts.

HELMER: What do you mean by that?

NORA (*after a short silence*): Isn't there one thing that strikes you as strange in our sitting here like this?

HELMER: What is that?

NORA: We have been married now eight years. Does it not occur to you that this is the first time we two, you and I, husband and wife, have had a serious conversation?

HELMER: What do you mean by serious?

NORA: In all these eight years—longer than that—from the very beginning of our acquaintance, we have never exchanged a word on any serious subject.

HELMER: Was it likely that I would be continually and forever telling you about worries that you could not help me to bear?

NORA: I am not speaking about business matters. I say that we have never sat down in earnest together to try and get at the bottom of anything.

HELMER: But, dearest Nora, would it have been any good to you?

NORA: That is just it; you have never understood me. I have been greatly wronged, Torvald—first by papa and then by you.

HELMER: What! By us two—by us two, who have loved you better than anyone else in in the world?

NORA (*shaking her head*): You have never loved me. You have only thought it pleasant to be in love with me.

HELMER: Nora, what do I hear you saying?

NORA: It is perfectly true, Torvald. When I was at home with papa, he told me his opinion about everything, and so I had the same opinions; and if I differed from him I concealed the fact, because he would not have liked it. He called me his doll-child, and he played with me just as I used to play with my dolls. And when I came to live with you—

HELMER: What sort of an expression is that to use about our marriage?

NORA (*undisturbed*): I mean that I was simply transferred from papa's hands into yours. You arranged everything according to your own taste, and so I got the same tastes as you—or else I pretended to, I am really not quite sure which—I think sometimes the one and sometimes the other. When I look back on it, it seems to me as if I had been living here like a poor woman—just from hand to mouth. I have existed merely to perform tricks for you, Torvald. But you would have it so. You and papa have committed a great sin against me. It is your fault that I have made nothing of my life.

HELMER: How unreasonable and how ungrateful you are, Nora! Have you not been happy here?

NORA: No, I have never been happy. I thought I was, but it has never really been so.

HELMER: Not—not happy!

NORA: No, only merry. And you have always been so kind to me. But our home has been nothing but a playroom. I have been your doll-wife, just as at home I was papa's doll-child; and here the children have been my dolls. I thought it great fun when you played with me, just as they thought it great fun when I played with them. That is what our marriage has been, Torvald.

HELMER: There is some truth in what you say—exaggerated and strained as your view of it is. But for the future it shall be different. Playtime shall be over, and lesson-time shall begin.

NORA: Whose lessons? Mine, or the children's?

HELMER: Both yours and the children's, my darling Nora.

NORA: Alas, Torvald, you are not the man to educate me into being a proper wife for you.

HELMER: And you can say that!

NORA: And I—how am I fitted to bring up the children?

HELMER: Nora!

NORA: Didn't you say so yourself a little while ago—that you dare not trust me to bring them up?

HELMER: In a moment of anger! Why do you pay any heed to that?

NORA: Indeed, you were perfectly right. I am not fit for the task. There is another task I must undertake first. I must try and educate myself—you are not the man to help me in that. I must do that for myself. And that is why I am going to leave you now.

HELMER (*springing up*): What do you say?

NORA: I must stand quite alone, if I am to understand myself and everything about me. It is for that reason that I cannot remain with you any longer. . . .

HELMER: To desert your home, your husband and your children! And you don't consider what people will say!

NORA: I cannot consider that at all. I only know that it is necessary for me.

HELMER: It's shocking. This is how you would neglect your most sacred duties.

NORA: What do you consider my most sacred duties?

HELMER: Do I need to tell you that? Are they not your duties to your husband and your children?

NORA: I have other duties just as sacred.

HELMER: That you have not. What duties could those be?

NORA: Duties to myself. . . .

HELMER: And can you tell me what I have done to forfeit your love?

NORA: Yes, indeed I can. It was to-night, when the wonderful thing did not happen; then I saw you were not the man I had thought you.

HELMER: Explain yourself better—I don't understand you.

NORA: I have waited so patiently for eight years; for, goodness knows, I knew very well that wonderful things don't happen every day. Then this horrible misfortune came upon me; and then I felt quite certain that the wonderful thing was going to happen at last. When Krogstad's letter was lying out there, never for a moment did I imagine that you would consent to accept this man's conditions. I was so absolutely certain that you would say to him: Publish the thing to the whole world. And when that was done—

HELMER: Yes, what then?—when I had exposed my wife to shame and disgrace?

NORA: When that was done, I was so absolutely certain, you would come forward and take everything upon yourself, and say: I am the guilty one.

HELMER: Nora—!

NORA: You mean that I would never have accepted such a sacrifice on your part? No, of course not. But what would my assurances have been worth against yours? That was the wonderful thing which I hoped for and feared; and it was to prevent that, that I wanted to kill myself.

HELMER: I would gladly work night and day for you, Nora—bear sorrow and want for your sake. But no man would sacrifice his honor for the one he loves.

NORA: It is a thing hundreds of thousands of women have done.

HELMER: Oh, you think and talk like a heedless child.

NORA: Maybe. But you neither think nor talk like the man I could bind myself to. As soon as your fear was over—and it was not fear for what threatened me, but for what might happen to you—when the whole thing was past, as far as you were concerned it was exactly as if nothing at all had happened. Exactly as before, I was your little skylark, your doll, which you would in future treat with doubly gentle care, because it was so brittle and fragile. (*Getting up.*) Torvald—it was then it dawned upon me that for eight years I had been living here with a strange man, and had borne him three children—. Oh! I can't bear to think of it! I could tear myself into little bits!

HELMER (*sadly*): I see, I see. An abyss has opened between us—there is no denying it. But, Nora, would it not be possible to fill it up?

NORA: As I am now, I am no wife for you.

HELMER: I have it in me to become a different man.

NORA: Perhaps—if your doll is taken away from you.

HELMER: But to part!—to part from you! No, no, Nora, I can't understand that idea.

NORA (*going out to the right*): That makes it all the more certain that it must be done. (*She comes back with her cloak and hat and a small bag which she puts on a chair by the table.*)

HELMER: Nora, Nora, not now! Wait till tomorrow.

NORA (*putting on her cloak*): I cannot spend the night in a strange man's room.

HELMER: But can't we live here like brother and sister—?

NORA (*putting on her hat*): You know very well that would not last long. (*Puts the shawl round her.*) Good-bye, Torvald. I won't see the little ones. I know they are in better hands than mine. As I am now, I can be of no use to them.

HELMER: But some day, Nora—some day?

NORA: How can I tell? I have no idea what is going to become of me.

HELMER: But you are my wife, whatever becomes of you.

NORA: Listen, Torvald. I have heard that when a wife deserts her husband's house, as I am doing now, he is legally freed from all obligations towards her. In any case I set you free from all your obligations. You are not to feel yourself bound in the slightest way, any more than I shall. There must be perfect freedom on both sides. See, here is your ring back. Give me mine.

HELMER: That too?

NORA: That too.

HELMER: Here it is.

NORA: That's right. Now it is all over. I have put the keys here. The maids know all about everything in the house—better than I do. Tomorrow, after I have left her, Christine will come here and pack up my own things that I brought with me from home. I will have them sent after me.

HELMER: All over! All over!—Nora, shall you never think of me again?

NORA: I know I shall often think of you and the children and this house.

HELMER: May I write to you, Nora?

NORA: No—never. You must not do that.

HELMER: But at least let me send you—

NORA: Nothing—nothing—

HELMER: Let me help you if you are in want.

NORA: No. I can receive nothing from a stranger.

HELMER: Nora—can I never be anything more than a stranger to you?

NORA (*taking her bag*): Ah, Torvald, the most wonderful thing of all would have to happen.

HELMER: Tell me what that would be!

NORA: Both you and I would have to be so changed that—. Oh, Torvald, I don't believe any longer in wonderful things happening.

HELMER: But I will believe in it. Tell me? So changed that—?

NORA: That our life together would be a real wedlock. Good-bye. (*She goes out through the hall.*)

HELMER (*sinks down on a chair at the door and buries his face in his hands*): Nora! Nora! (*Looks round, and rises.*) Empty. She is gone. (*A hope flashes across his mind.*) The most wonderful thing of all—?

The sound of a door shutting is heard from below.

2. August Strindberg, *Miss Julie* (1888)

Much action is condensed into the slim limits of *Miss Julie's* one act. Julie is "crazy"—by nature, and because it is Midsummer's Night, traditionally a night of abandon. She has just broken off her engagement to a man she was last seen pretending to train with a dog whip. She is the child of an unstable mother, who had married her father only with reluctance, sequestering property beyond his control—and who was the likely arsonist who destroyed the family's barns and houses. Her father, the count, is a typical aristocrat. Julie loves him—but she has also learned, from her mother, to hate him.

On this night, Julie approaches with sexual overtures the handsome servant Jean, who is in turn casually pledged to the cook Kristin—opportunely asleep when the key moment arrives. Julie and Jean take refuge in his room lest they be seen alone together by revelers—and he responds to her invitation; the deed is done. Julie is fatally dishonored. Now they must go away, Julie insists; doesn't he love her? Jean fantasizes a bit about opening a hotel with her in Italy's Lake Como, but without money, the dream remains a dream.

Julie rifles her father's desk, comes downstairs dressed for travel and equipped with cash, carrying a birdcage holding her pet canary. The canary cannot come, and Jean kills it. Kristin returns, planning to take Jean off to church with her, and explains her faith to Julie: Jesus will save those upon whom he sheds grace and the last shall be the first. But she is shocked by the dead bird. Meanwhile, the count has returned. Soon, he will discover the theft; and soon, the police will arrive. There is no escape. The brief final scene of the play follows. Jean guides Julie, by suggestion, to take her own life. The curtain closes as she exits to do so.[2]

---

2. In the translation used here, the title is given as *Countess Julie*; here *Miss Julie*, as it is more normally translated, is substituted. Minor typographical emendations are made for consistency. Italicized stage directions are as they appear in the original.

MISS JULIE

JEAN: Such a devil. And all this on account of your confounded canary!

JULIE (*tired*): Oh, don't speak of the canary—do you see any way out—any end to this?

JEAN (*thinking*): No.

JULIE: What would you do in my place?

JEAN: In your place—wait. As a noble lady, as a woman—fallen—I don't know. Yes, now I know.

JULIE (*she takes up razor from table and makes gestures saying*): This?

JEAN: Yes. But *I* should not do it, mark you, for there is a difference between us.

JULIE: Because you are a man and I am a woman? What other difference is there?

JEAN: That very difference—of man and woman.

JULIE (*razor in hand*): I want to do it—but I can't. My father couldn't either that time when he should have done it.

JEAN: No, he was right, not to do it—he had to avenge himself first.

JULIE: And now my mother revenges herself again through me.

JEAN: Haven't you loved your father, Miss Julie?

JULIE: Yes, deeply. But I have probably hated him too, I must have—without being aware of it. And it is due to my father's training that I have learned to scorn my own sex. Between them both they have made me half man, half woman. Whose is the fault for what has happened—my father's? My mother's? My own? I haven't anything of my own. I haven't a thought which was not my father's—not a passion that wasn't my mother's. And last of all from my betrothed the idea that all people are equal. For that I now call him a wretch. How can it be my own fault them? Throw the burden on Jesus as Kristin did? No, I am too proud, too intelligent, thanks to my father's teaching.—And that a rich man cannot enter the Kingdom of Heaven—that is a lie, and Kristin, who has money in the savings bank—she surely cannot enter there. Whose is the fault? What does it concern us whose fault it is? It is I who must bear the burden and the consequences.

JEAN: Yes, but—

Two sharp rings on a bell are heard. Julie starts to her feet. Jean changes his coat.

JEAN: The Count—has returned. Think if Kristin has—

Goes up to speaking tube and listens.

JULIE: Now he has seen the desk!

JEAN (*speaking in the tube*): It is Jean, Excellency. (*Listens*) Yes, Excellency. (*Listens*) Yes, Excellency,—right away—immediately, Excellency. Yes—in half an hour.

JULIE (*in great agitation*): What did he say? In heaven's name, what did he say?

JEAN: He wants his boots and coffee in a half hour.

JULIE: In half an hour then. Oh, I'm so tired—I'm incapable of feeling, not able to be sorry, not able to go, not able to stay, not able to live—not able to die. Help me now. Command me—I will obey like a dog. Do me this last service—save my honor. Save his name. You know what I have the will to do—but cannot do. You will it and command me to execute your will.

JEAN: I don't know why—but no I can't either.—I don't understand myself. It is absolutely as though this coat does it—but I can't command you now. And since the Count spoke to me—I can't account for it—but oh, it is that damned servant in my back—I believe if the Count came in here now and told me to cut my throat I would do it on the spot.

JULIE: Make believe you are he—and I you. You could act so well a little while ago when you knelt at my feet. Then you were a nobleman—or haven't you ever been at the theatre and seen the hypnotist—. (*Jean nods*) He says to his subject "Take the broom," and he takes it; he says, "Sweep," and he sweeps.

JEAN: Then the subject must be asleep!

JULIE (*ecstatically*): I sleep already. The whole room is like smoke before me—and you are like a tall black stove, like a man clad in black clothes with a high hat; and your eyes gleam like the hot coals when the fire is dying; and your face is a white spot like fallen ashes.

The sunshine is coming in through the windows and falls on Jean. Julie rubs her hands as though warming them before a fire.

It is so warm and good—and so bright and quiet!

JEAN (*takes the razor and puts it in her hand*): There is the broom, go now while it's bright—out to the hay loft—and—

He whispers in her ear.

JULIE (*rousing herself*): Thanks. And now I go to rest. But tell me this—the foremost may receive the gift of Grace?[3] Say it, even if you don't believe it.

JEAN: The foremost? No, I can't say that. But wait, Miss Julie—you are no longer among the foremost since you are of the lowliest.

JULIE: That's true, I am the lowliest—the lowliest of the lowly. Oh, now I can't go. Tell me once more that I must go.

JEAN: No, now I cannot either—I cannot.

JULIE: And the first shall be last—

JEAN: Don't think. You take my strength from me, too, so that I become cowardly.—What—I thought I heard the bell!—No! To be afraid of the sound of a bell! But it's not the bell—it's someone behind the bell, the hand that sets the bell in motion—and something else that sets the hand in motion. But stop your ears, stop your ears. Then he will only ring louder and keep on ringing until it's answered—and then it is too late! Then come the police—and then—

Two loud rings on a bell are heard, Jean falls in a heap for a moment, but straightens up immediately.

It is horrible! But there is no other way. Go!

Julie goes out resolutely.

3. Nikolay Gogol, *The Overcoat* (1842)

Akaky Akakiyevich[4] is a lowly civil servant in the St. Petersburg bureaucracy, locked perpetually into Rank Nine of the fourteen slots on the Table of Ranks established by Tsar Peter the Great, earning a meager four hundred rubles[5] annually for his labors as a copyist. Impoverished, without friends or family, he subsists on little, and can barely renew his meager wardrobe, of which his battered overcoat is the special butt of his officemates' mockery. He takes it for repair to the skilled but drunken tailor Petrovich, who pronounces it unsalvageable—Akaky Akakiyevich must have a new one.

---

3. Julie is asking a theological question, prompted by Kristin's earlier sermonizing: Will she find salvation?

4. Akaky Akakiyevich: "Akaky son of Akaky"; the English equivalent would be the bland "John Johnson."

5. rubles: the standard currency of the Russian Empire.

An outrageous 150 rubles is negotiated down to 80, but 80 rubles the civil servant does not have. He denies himself, and saves.

At last, the goal is met and Petrovich brings the precious overcoat, whose fabric and style, in anticipation, they have been discussing for months. Akaky Akakiyevich proudly wears it to the office and to the evening party at a coworker's home mounted in celebration of the overcoat's magnificence. Returning home, however, he is assaulted—and the precious overcoat is stolen. He pursues justice, obtaining an audience with "a very prominent personage," a district chief, who brutally rejects the petition. Akaky Akakiyevich stumbles out of the office; coatless, he catches a fatal cold in the frigid St. Petersburg wind, and dies within days. But he will be avenged—by his ghost.[6]

THE OVERCOAT

In the department of ———, but it is better not to mention the department. The touchiest things in the world are departments, regiments, courts of justice, in a word, all branches of public service. Each individual nowadays thinks all society insulted in his person. . . .

So, in a certain department there was a certain official—not a very notable one, it must be allowed—short of stature, somewhat pock-marked, red-haired, and mole-eyed, with a bald forehead, wrinkled cheeks, and a complexion of the kind known as sanguine. The St. Petersburg climate was responsible for this. As for his official rank—with us Russians the rank comes first—he was what is called a perpetual titular councilor, over which, as is well known, some writers make merry and crack their jokes, obeying the praiseworthy custom of attacking those who cannot bite back. . . .

When and how he entered the department, and who appointed him, no one could remember. However much the directors and chiefs of all kinds were changed, he was always to be seen in the same place, the same attitude, the same occupation—always the letter-copying clerk. . . . No respect was shown him in the department. The porter not only did not rise from his seat when he passed, but never even glanced at him, any more than if a fly had flown through the reception-room. . . . Some insignificant assistant to the head clerk would thrust a paper under his nose without so much as saying, "Copy," or, "Here's an interesting little case," or anything else agreeable, as is customary amongst well-bred officials. And he took it, looking only at the paper, and not observing who handed it to him, or whether he had the right to do so; simply took it, and set about copying it. . . .

---

6. The translation is emended slightly to Americanize spelling and substitute the more familiar term "overcoat" for "cloak," the consensus of many translations.

It would be difficult to find another man who lived so entirely for his duties. It is not enough to say that Akaky labored with zeal; no, he labored with love. In his copying, he found a varied and agreeable employment. . . . Having written to his heart's content, he lay down to sleep, smiling at the thought of the coming day—of what God might send him to copy on the morrow. . . . Thus flowed on the peaceful life of the man, who, with a salary of four hundred rubles, understood how to be content with his lot. . . .

There exists in St. Petersburg a powerful foe of all who receive a salary of four hundred rubles a year, or thereabouts. This foe is no other than the Northern cold. . . . At nine o'clock in the morning, . . . it begins to bestow such powerful and piercing nips on all noses impartially, that the poor officials really do not know what to do with them. . . . Their only salvation lies in traversing as quickly as possible, in their thin little overcoats, five or six streets, and then warming their feet in the porter's room, and so thawing all their talents and qualifications for official service, which had become frozen on the way.

Akaky Akakiyevich had felt for some time that his back and shoulders were [suffering] with peculiar poignancy, in spite of the fact that he tried to traverse the distance with all possible speed. He began finally to wonder whether the fault did not lie in his overcoat. He examined it thoroughly at home, and discovered that . . . it had become thin as gauze. The cloth was worn to such a degree that he could see through it, and the lining had fallen into pieces. . . .

Akaky Akakiyevich takes his worn-out overcoat to be repaired by the tailor Petrovich.

Ascending the staircase which led to Petrovich's room . . . , Akaky Akakiyevich pondered how much Petrovich would ask, and mentally resolved not to give more than two rubles. . . . [He] at length reached a room where he beheld Petrovich seated on a large unpainted table, with his legs tucked under him like a Turkish pasha. His feet were bare, after the fashion of tailors as they sit at work. . . . About Petrovich's neck hung a skein of silk and thread, and upon his knees lay some old garment. He had been trying unsuccessfully for three minutes to thread his needle, and was enraged at the darkness and even at the thread, growling in a low voice, "It won't go through, the barbarian! you pricked me, you rascal!"

Akaky Akakiyevich was vexed at arriving at the precise moment when Petrovich was angry. He liked to order something of Petrovich when he was a little downhearted . . . [when he] generally came down in his price very readily, and even bowed and returned thanks. . . . But now it appeared that Petrovich was in a sober condition, and therefore rough, taciturn, and inclined to demand, Satan only knows what price. . . . Petrovich screwed up his one eye very intently at him, and Akaky Akakiyevich involuntarily said, "How do you do, Petrovich?"

"I wish you a good morning, sir," said Petrovich squinting at Akaky Aka-kiyevich's hands, to see what sort of booty he had brought.

"Ah! I—to you, Petrovich, this—" . . .

Akaky Akakiyevich struggles to find the words to define his predicament.

"But I, here, this—Petrovich—an overcoat, cloth—here you see, everywhere, in different places, it is quite strong—it is a little dusty and looks old, but it is new, only here in one place it is a little—on the back, and here on one of the shoulders, it is a little worn, yes, here on this shoulder it is a little—do you see? That is all. And a little work—"

Petrovich took the overcoat, spread it out, to begin with, on the table, looked at it hard, shook his head . . . , held up the overcoat, and inspected it against the light, and again shook his head. Then he turned it, lining upwards, and shook his head once more. . . . "No, it is impossible to mend it. It is a wretched garment!"

Akaky Akakiyevich's heart sank at these words.

"Why is it impossible, Petrovich?" he said, almost in the pleading voice of a child. "All that ails it is, that it is worn on the shoulders. You must have some pieces—"

"Yes, patches could be found, patches are easily found," said Petrovich, "but there's nothing to sew them to. The thing is completely rotten. If you put a needle to it—see, it will give way."

"Let it give way, and you can put on another patch at once." . . .

"No," said Petrovich decisively, "there is nothing to be done with it. . . . But it is plain you must have a new overcoat."

At the word "new" all grew dark before Akaky Akakiyevich's eyes, and everything in the room began to whirl round. . . . "A new one?" said he, as if still in a dream. "Why, I have no money for that."

"Yes, a new one," said Petrovich, with barbarous composure.

"Well, if it came to a new one, how—it—"

"You mean how much would it cost?"

"Yes."

"Well, you would have to lay out a hundred and fifty or more," said Petro-vich, and pursed up his lips significantly. He liked to produce powerful effects, liked to stun utterly and suddenly, and then to glance sideways to see what face the stunned person would put on the matter.

"A hundred and fifty rubles for an overcoat!" shrieked poor Akaky Aka-kiyevich, perhaps for the first time in his life, for his voice had always been distinguished for softness.

"Yes, sir," said Petrovich, "for any kind of overcoat. If you have a mar-ten fur on the collar, or a silk-lined hood, it will mount up to two hundred."

. . .

Akaky Akakiyevich goes home to reflect on the problem of the overcoat.

Then Akaky Akakiyevich saw that it was impossible to get along without a new overcoat, and his spirit sank utterly. How, in fact, was it to be done? Where was the money to come from? He must have some new trousers, and pay a debt of long standing to the shoemaker for putting new tops to his old boots. . . . In short, all his money must be spent. And even if the director should be so kind as to order him to receive forty-five or even fifty rubles instead of forty, it would be a mere nothing, a mere drop in the ocean toward the funds necessary for an overcoat. . . .

But although he knew that Petrovich would undertake to make an overcoat for eighty rubles, still, where was he to get the eighty rubles from? He might possibly manage half. Yes, half might be procured, but where was the other half to come from? But the reader must first be told where the first half came from.

Akaky Akakiyevich had a habit of putting, for every ruble he spent, a groschen[7] into a small box, fastened with lock and key, and with a slit in the top for the reception of money. At the end of every half-year he counted over the heap of coppers, and changed it for silver. This he had done for a long time, and in the course of years, the sum had mounted up to over forty rubles. Thus he had one half on hand. But where was he to find the other half? . . . Akaky Akakiyevich thought and thought, and decided that it would be necessary to curtail his ordinary expenses, for the space of one year at least, to dispense with tea in the evening, to burn no candles, and, if there was anything which he must do, to go into his landlady's room, and work by her light. . . .

To tell the truth, it was a little hard for him at first to accustom himself to these deprivations. But he got used to them at length, after a fashion, and all went smoothly. He even got used to being hungry in the evening, but he made up for it by treating himself, so to say, in spirit, by bearing ever in mind the idea of his future overcoat. From that time forth, his existence seemed to become, in some way, fuller, . . . and even his character grew firmer, like that of a man who has made up his mind, and set himself a goal. . . . Fire gleamed in his eyes, and occasionally the boldest and most daring ideas flitted through his mind. Why not, for instance, have marten fur on the collar? . . .

At last, the rubles are assembled and the overcoat is made.

It was—it is difficult to say precisely on what day, but probably the most glorious one in Akaky Akakiyevich's life, when Petrovich at length brought home the overcoat. He brought it in the morning. . . . Never did an overcoat arrive so exactly in the nick of time, for the severe cold had set in, and it seemed to

---

7. groschen: a small coin.

threaten to increase. Petrovich brought the overcoat himself as befits a good tailor. On his countenance was a significant expression, such as Akaky Akakiyevich had never beheld there. . . . Taking out the overcoat, he gazed proudly at it, held it up with both hands, and flung it skillfully over the shoulders of Akaky Akakiyevich [who] . . . , like an experienced man, wished to try the sleeves. Petrovich helped him on with them, and it turned out that the sleeves were satisfactory also. In short, the overcoat appeared to be perfect, and most seasonable. . . . Akaky Akakiyevich . . . paid him, thanked him, and set out at once in his new overcoat for the department. . . .

That whole day was truly a most triumphant festival for Akaky Akakiyevich. He returned home in the most happy frame of mind, took off his overcoat, and hung it carefully on the wall, admiring afresh the cloth and the lining. Then he brought out his old, worn-out overcoat, for comparison. He looked at it, and laughed, so vast was the difference. . . . He dined cheerfully, and after dinner wrote nothing, but took his ease for a while on the bed, until it got dark. Then he dressed himself leisurely, put on his overcoat, and stepped out into the street. . . .

Unaccustomed to going out in the evening, still Akaky Akakiyevich greatly enjoyed the cheerful party his coworkers hosted in honor of his overcoat. But returning home, he is assaulted and the overcoat is stolen. He seeks the aid of a senior official who could help to recover it, but that dignitary ejects him from his office. In the frigid St. Petersburg cold, without the protection of an overcoat, he falls deathly ill.

The next day a violent fever developed. Thanks to the generous assistance of the St. Petersburg climate, the malady progressed more rapidly than could have been expected, and when the doctor arrived, he found, on feeling the sick man's pulse, that there was nothing to be done, . . . [and] he predicted his end in thirty-six hours. After this he turned to the landlady, and said, "And as for you, don't waste your time on him. Order his pine coffin now, for an oak one will be too expensive for him." . . .

And St. Petersburg was left without Akaky Akakiyevich, as though he had never lived there. A being disappeared, who was protected by none, dear to none, interesting to none. . . . A being who . . . went to his grave without having done one unusual deed, but to whom, nevertheless, at the close of his life, appeared a bright visitant in the form of an overcoat, which momentarily cheered his poor life, and upon him, thereafter, an intolerable misfortune descended, just as it descends upon the heads of the mighty of this world! . . .

After the death of Akaky Akakiyevich, his ghost wanders the streets of St. Petersburg, snatching overcoats. Its appetite is satisfied at last when it acquires the overcoat of the prominent personage who had rebuffed the civil servant's desperate plea for redress.

4. Fyodor Dostoevsky, *Notes from the Underground* (1864)

The samplings given here of the "notes" written by the Underground Man are taken from Part One, written when the author was a retired civil servant in his forties for an unspecified audience of learned "gentlemen." They exemplify the author's refusal to conform to social norms and expectations, and especially his decision to resist the passionless, mathematically precise, and inalterable "Laws of Nature,"[8] obedience to which, experts of the day claimed, could lead to the rectification of human nature and the attainment of human well-being.[9] To confound these supposed goods, the Underground Man proposes willful resistance, chaos, suffering, and destruction—which painful though they may be, do not eradicate human freedom and independence.[10]

NOTES FROM THE UNDERGROUND

Prologue

The author of the Notes and the Notes themselves are, of course, imaginary. Nevertheless it is clear that such persons as the writer of these notes not only may, but positively must, exist in our society, when we consider the circumstances in the midst of which our society is formed. [. . .]

—Fyodor Dostoevsky

1.1

I am a sick man. . . . I am a spiteful man. I am an unattractive man. I believe my liver is diseased. However, I know nothing at all about my disease, and do not know for certain what ails me. I don't consult a doctor for it, and never have [. . .]. No, I refuse to consult a doctor from spite. [. . .] My liver is bad, well—let it get worse!

---

8. Laws of Nature: inheriting ancient concepts of "natural law," early modern philosophers posited the existence of "laws of nature" that determined events, as Thomas Hobbes and John Locke used the term; as used by Isaac Newton and Robert Boyle, the "laws of nature" become equivalent to physical processes, as with Newton's "laws of motion." In mocking these concepts, Dostoevsky rejects much of the intellectual endeavor of the previous two centuries.

9. Here Dostoevsky refers to a bundle of contemporary socialist theories, notably that of Charles Fourier, who envisioned the reconstruction of human society and consequent restructuring of human personality.

10. The version of Dostoevsky's work employed here is itself based on the classic translation by Constance Garnett, with adjustments of orthography and some modernization of terminology. The present editor's additional emendations are given in brackets, as are ellipses supplied by the present editor that do not appear in the original; the latter are retained.

I have been going on like that for a long time—twenty years. Now I am forty. I used to be in the government service, but am no longer. I was a spiteful official. I was rude and took pleasure in being so. [. . .]

I was lying when I said just now that I was a spiteful official. I was lying from spite. I was simply amusing myself with the petitioners and with the officer, and in reality I never could become spiteful. [. . .]

You imagine no doubt, gentlemen, that I want to amuse you. You are mistaken in that, too [. . . .]; however, irritated by all this babble (and I feel that you are irritated) you think fit to ask me who I am—then my answer is, I am a Collegiate Assessor.[11] I was in the civil service that I might have something to eat (and solely for that reason), and when last year a distant relation left me six thousand [rubles][12] in his will I immediately retired from the service and settled down in my corner. [. . .] My room is a wretched, horrid one in the outskirts of the town. [. . .] I am told that the Petersburg[13] climate is bad for me, and that with my small means it is very expensive to live in Petersburg. I know all that better than all these sage and experienced counselors and advisors. . . . But I am remaining in Petersburg; I am not going away from Petersburg! I am not going away because . . . ech! Why, it is absolutely no matter whether I am going away or not going away. [. . .]

But what does a decent man like to talk about most?

Answer: About himself.

Well, so I will talk about myself. [. . .]

1.3 [. . .]

I will continue calmly [considering] persons with strong nerves who [. . .] in certain circumstances [. . .] bellow their loudest like bulls, [. . .] yet, [. . .] confronted with the impossible they subside at once. The impossible means the stone wall! What stone wall? Why, of course, the laws of nature, the deductions of natural science, mathematics. As soon as they prove to you, for instance, that you are descended from a monkey, then it is no use scowling, accept it for a fact. When they prove to you that in reality one drop of your own fat must be dearer to you than a hundred thousand of your fellow creatures, [. . .] then you have just to accept it, there is no help for it, for twice two is a law of mathematics. Just try refuting it.

---

11. The rank of Collegiate Assessor (also held by Dostoevsky's father) is the eighth of fourteen ranks of civil servants given in the Table of Ranks established under Tsar Peter the Great.

12. rubles: also roubles; the Russian currency.

13. Petersburg: the city of St. Petersburg, hub of the Russian state, which also figures as a character in Pushkin's *The Bronze Horseman* (see Chapter 2, Text 12) and Gogol's *The Overcoat* (see Chapter 5, Text 3).

"Upon my word," they will shout at you, "it is no use protesting: it is a case of twice two makes four! Nature does not ask your permission, she has nothing to do with your wishes, and whether you like her laws or dislike them, you are bound to accept her as she is, and consequently all her conclusions. A wall, you see, is a wall . . . and so on, and so on."

Merciful heavens! But what do I care for the Laws of Nature and arithmetic, when, for some reason I dislike those laws and the fact that twice two makes four? Of course I cannot break through the wall by battering my head against it if I really have not the strength to knock it down, but I am not going to be reconciled to it simply because it is a stone wall and I have not the strength.

As though such a stone wall really were a consolation, and really did contain some word of conciliation, simply because it is as true as twice two makes four. Oh, absurdity of absurdities! How much better it is to understand it all, to recognize it all, all the impossibilities and the stone wall; not to be reconciled to one of those impossibilities and stone walls if it disgusts you to be reconciled to it [. . .], that it is a sleight of hand, a bit of juggling, a conjurer's trick [. . .].

1.7 [. . .]

Oh, tell me, who was it first announced, who was it first proclaimed, that man only [behaves badly] because he does not know his own interests; and that if he were enlightened, if his eyes were opened to his real normal interests, man would at once cease to [act badly], would at once become good and noble because, being enlightened and understanding his real advantage, he would see his own advantage in the good and nothing else [. . .]. Oh, the babe! Oh, the pure, innocent child! Why, in the first place, when in all these thousands of years has there been a time when man has acted only from his own interest? What is to be done with the millions of facts that bear witness that men, *consciously*, that is fully understanding their real interests, have left them in the background and have rushed headlong on another path, to meet peril and danger, compelled to this course by nobody and by nothing, but, as it were, simply disliking the beaten track, and have obstinately, willfully, struck out another difficult, absurd way, seeking it almost in the darkness. So, I suppose, this obstinacy and perversity were pleasanter to them than any advantage. . . . Advantage! What is advantage?

And will you take it upon yourself to define with perfect accuracy in what the advantage of man consists? And what if it so happens that a man's advantage, *sometimes*, not only may, but even must, consist in his desiring in certain cases what is harmful to himself and not advantageous. And if so, if there can be such a case, the whole principle falls into dust. [. . .]

But yet you are fully convinced that [man] will be sure to learn when he gets rid of certain old bad habits and when common sense and science have completely re-educated human nature and turned it in a normal direction. [. . .] That is not all; then, you say, science itself will teach man . . . that he never has really had any caprice or will of his own, [. . .] and that there are, besides, things called the Laws of Nature; so that everything he does is not done by his willing it, but is done of itself, by the Laws of Nature. Consequently we have only to discover these Laws of Nature, and man will no longer have to answer for his actions and life will become exceedingly easy for him. All human actions will then, of course, be tabulated according to these laws, mathematically, like tables of logarithms up to 108,000, and entered in an index; or, better still, there would be published certain edifying works of the nature of encyclopedic dictionaries, in which everything will be so clearly calculated and explained that there will be no more incidents or adventures in the world.

Then—this is all what you say—new economic relations will be established, all ready-made and worked out with mathematical exactitude, so that every possible question will vanish in the twinkling of an eye, simply because every possible answer to it will be provided. Then the Crystal Palace[14] will be built. [. . .] Of course there is no guaranteeing (this is my comment) that it will not be, for instance, frightfully dull then (for what will one have to do when everything will be calculated and tabulated?), but on the other hand everything will be extraordinarily rational. [. . .]

I, for instance, would not be in the least surprised if all of a sudden, apropos of nothing, in the midst of general prosperity a gentleman [. . .] were to arise and, putting his hands on his hips, say to us all: "I say, gentleman, hadn't we better kick over the whole show and scatter rationalism to the winds, simply to send these logarithms to the devil, and to enable us to live once more at our own sweet foolish will!" [. . .] And all that for the most foolish reason, which, one would think, was hardly worth mentioning: that is, that man everywhere and at all times, whoever he may be, has preferred to act as he chose and not in the least as his reason and advantage dictated. [. . .] One's own free unfettered choice, one's own caprice—however wild it may be, one's own fancy worked up at times to frenzy—is that very "most advantageous advantage" which we have overlooked, which comes under no classification and against which all systems and theories are continually being shattered to atoms. [. . .] What man wants is simply *independent* choice, whatever that independence may cost and wherever it may lead. [. . .]

---

14. Crystal Palace: Dostoevsky refers to the Crystal Palace (later, "palace of crystal"), a building of iron and glass erected in London to house the Great Exhibition of 1851, showcasing recent industrial and technological advances. For many Russian thinkers, it represented the summit of human creativity and aspiration—but quite the opposite for Dostoevsky.

1.9 [. . .]

Gentlemen, I am tormented by questions; answer them for me. You, for instance, want to cure men of their old habits and reform their will in accordance with science and good sense. But how do you know, not only that it is possible, but also that it is *desirable* to reform man in that way? And what leads you to the conclusion that man's inclinations *need* reforming? In short, how do you know that such a reformation will be a benefit to man? And to go to the root of the matter, why are you so positively convinced that not to act against his real normal interests guaranteed by the conclusions of reason and arithmetic is certainly always advantageous for man and must always be a law for mankind? [. . .] Man likes to make roads and to create, that is a fact beyond dispute. But why has he such a passionate love for destruction and chaos also? Tell me that! [. . .]

And why are you so firmly, so triumphantly, convinced that only the normal and the positive—in other words, only what is conducive to welfare—is for the advantage of man? [. . .] Perhaps suffering is just as great a benefit to him as well-being? Man is sometimes extraordinarily, passionately, in love with suffering, and that is a fact. There is no need to appeal to universal history to prove that; only ask yourself, if you are a man and have lived at all. [. . .] Why, suffering is the sole origin of consciousness. Though I did lay it down at the beginning that consciousness is the greatest misfortune for man, yet I know man prizes it and would not give it up for any satisfaction. Consciousness, for instance, is infinitely superior to twice two makes four. [. . .]

1.10

You believe in a palace of crystal that can never be destroyed [. . .]. And perhaps that is just why I am afraid of this edifice, that it is of crystal and can never be destroyed and that one cannot stick one's tongue out at it even on the sly.

You see, if it were not a palace, but a henhouse, I might creep into it to avoid getting wet, and yet I would not call the henhouse a palace out of gratitude to it for keeping me dry. You laugh and say that in such circumstances a henhouse is as good as a mansion. Yes, I answer, if one had to live simply to keep out of the rain.

But what is to be done if I have taken it into my head that that is not the only object in life, and that if one must live, one had better live in a mansion? That is my choice, my desire. You will only eradicate it when you have changed my preference. [. . .] I know, anyway, that I will not be put off with a compromise, with a recurring zero, simply because it is consistent with the Laws of Nature and actually exists. I will not accept as the crown of my desires a block of buildings with tenements for the poor on a lease of a thousand years, and perhaps with a signboard of a dentist hanging out. Destroy my desires, eradicate my ideals, show me something better, and I will follow you. [. . .]

But while I am alive and have desires I would rather my hand were cut off than bring one brick to such a building!

5. Leo Tolstoy, *The Death of Ivan Ilyich* (1886)

The pain that had begun with an ordinary household injury persisted and grew worse, despite consultations with a raft of doctors and the ingestion of a heap of medications. The prosecutor Ivan Ilyich, forty-five years old, is dying and in terrible pain. In his suffering, he reflects on his past life—and realizes it has been all wrong. Only his childhood memories are bright; the recent past is grim, and in it "there was nothing to defend." The man whose role it has been to pronounce guilt and sentence others to imprisonment and death now judges his own life, which he had seen as pleasant and blameless, and finds it to have been a lie. As Ivan Ilyich begins to understand the falsity of the life he has lived, he begins to hear a voice—The voice of his soul? The voice of God?—and to see a light. In his last torments, horrible to those who heard the screams they evoked, he no longer feels pain, and no longer fears death.[15]

THE DEATH OF IVAN ILYICH

Chapter 9 [. . .]

Ivan Ilyich's wife returns from an evening out, asks if he is in pain, and urges him to take some opium. He does and awakes with an awareness of his utter helplessness.

Till about three in the morning he was in a state of stupefied misery. It seemed to him that he and his pain were being thrust into a narrow, deep black sack, but though they were pushed further and further in they could not be pushed to the bottom. And this, terrible enough in itself, was accompanied by suffering. He was frightened yet wanted to fall through the sack, he struggled but yet cooperated. And suddenly he broke through, fell, and regained consciousness. [. . .] He wept on account of his helplessness, his terrible loneliness, the cruelty of man, the cruelty of God, and the absence of God. "Why have you

---

15. The classic translation of Louise and Aylmer Maude is modified slightly here: paragraphing and punctuation are adjusted; the terms "Thee" and "Thou" used to address God are emended to "you"; and the spelling of the protagonist's name, "Ilych" in the original transcription from the Russian, is changed to the more familiar form "Ilyich." The present editor's additional emendations are given in brackets, as are ellipses supplied by the present editor that do not appear in the original; the latter are retained.

done all this? Why have you brought me here? Why, why do you torment me so terribly?"

He did not expect an answer and yet wept because there was no answer and could be none. The pain again grew more acute, but he did not stir and did not call. He said to himself: "Go on! Strike me! But what is it for? What have I done to you? What is it for?" Then he grew quiet and not only ceased weeping but even held his breath and became all attention. It was as though he were listening not to an audible voice but to the voice of his soul, to the current of thoughts arising within him.

"What is it you want?" was the first clear conception, capable of expression in words, that he heard. "What do you want? What do you want?" he repeated to himself.

"What do I want? To live and not to suffer," he answered. And again he listened with such concentrated attention that even his pain did not distract him.

"To live? How?" asked his inner voice.

"Why, to live as I used to—well and pleasantly."

"As you lived before, well and pleasantly?" the voice repeated.

And in imagination he began to recall the best moments of his pleasant life. But strange to say none of those best moments of his pleasant life now seemed at all what they had then seemed—none of them except the first recollections of childhood. There, in childhood, there had been something really pleasant with which it would be possible to live if it could return. But the child who had experienced that happiness existed no longer; it was like a reminiscence of somebody else.

As soon as the period began which had produced the present Ivan Ilyich, all that had then seemed joys now melted before his sight and turned into something trivial and often [revolting]. And the further he departed from childhood and the nearer he came to the present the more worthless and doubtful were the joys. This began with the School of Law. A little that was really good was still found there—there was light-heartedness, friendship, and hope. But in the upper classes there had already been fewer of such good moments. Then during the first years of his official career, when he was in the service of the governor, some pleasant moments again occurred: they were the memories of love for a woman. Then all became confused and there was still less of what was good; later on again there was still less that was good, and the further he went the less there was. [. . .]

"It is as if I had been going downhill while I imagined I was going up. And that is really what it was. I was going up in public opinion, but to the same extent life was ebbing away from me. And now it is all done and there is only death."

"Then what does it mean? Why? It can't be that life is so senseless and horrible. But if it really has been so horrible and senseless, why must I die and die in agony? There is something wrong! Maybe I did not live as I ought to have done," it suddenly occurred to him. "But how could that be, when I did every-thing properly?" he replied, and immediately dismissed from his mind this, the sole solution of all the riddles of life and death, as something quite impossible.

"Then what do you want now? To live? Live how? Live as you lived in the law courts when the usher proclaimed 'The judge is coming!' The judge is coming, the judge!" he repeated to himself. "Here he is, the judge. But I am not guilty!" he exclaimed angrily. "What is it for?" And he ceased crying, but turning his face to the wall continued to ponder on the same question: Why, and for what purpose, is there all this horror?

But however much he pondered he found no answer. And whenever the thought occurred to him, as it often did, that it all resulted from his not having lived as he ought to have done, he at once recalled the correctness of his whole life and dismissed so strange an idea.

Chapter 10

Another [two weeks] passed. Ivan Ilyich now no longer left his sofa. He would not lie in bed but lay on the sofa, facing the wall nearly all the time. He suffered ever the same unceasing agonies and in his loneliness pondered always on the same insoluble question: "What is this? Can it be that it is Death?" And the inner voice answered: "Yes, it is Death." "Why these sufferings?" And the voice answered, "For no reason—they just are so." Beyond and besides this there was nothing. [. . .]

[Recently] during the loneliness in which he found himself as he lay fac-ing the back of the sofa, a loneliness in the midst of a populous town and sur-rounded by numerous acquaintances and relations but that yet could not have been more complete anywhere—either at the bottom of the sea or under the earth—during that terrible loneliness Ivan Ilyich had lived only in memories of the past. Pictures of his past rose before him one after another. They always began with what was nearest in time and then went back to what was most remote—to his childhood—and [halted] there. [. . .]

Then again together with that chain of memories another series passed through his mind—of how his illness had progressed and grown worse. There also the further back he looked the more life there had been. There had been more of what was good in life and more of life itself. The two merged together. "Just as the pain went on getting worse and worse, so my life grew worse and worse," he thought. "There is one bright spot there at the back, at the begin-ning of life, and afterwards all becomes blacker and blacker and proceeds more and more rapidly—in inverse ratio to the square of the distance from death," thought Ivan Ilyich. And the example of a stone falling downwards with increas-ing velocity entered his mind. Life, a series of increasing sufferings, flies further and further towards its end—the most terrible suffering. [. . .] He shuddered, shifted himself, and tried to resist, but was already aware that resistance was impossible, and again with eyes weary of gazing but unable to cease seeing what was before them, he stared at the back of the sofa and waited—awaiting that dreadful fall and shock and destruction.

"Resistance is impossible!" he said to himself. "If I could only understand what it is all for! But that too is impossible. An explanation would be possible if it could be said that I have not lived as I ought to. But it is impossible to say that," and he remembered all the legality, correctitude, and propriety of his life. "That at any rate can certainly not be admitted," he thought, and his lips smiled ironically as if someone could see that smile and be taken in by it. "There is no explanation! Agony, death. . . . What for?"

Chapter 11 [. . .]

The doctor visits, and tells Ivan Ilyich's wife that things are very bad and that the pain must be terrible.

It was true, as the doctor said, that Ivan Ilyich's physical sufferings were terrible, but worse than the physical sufferings were his mental sufferings which were his chief torture. His mental sufferings were due to the fact that that night, [. . .] the question suddenly occurred to him: "What if my whole life has been wrong?"

It occurred to him that what had appeared perfectly impossible before, namely that he had not spent his life as he should have done, might after all be true. It occurred to him that his scarcely perceptible attempts to struggle against what was considered good by the most highly placed people, those scarcely noticeable impulses which he had immediately suppressed, might have been the real thing, and all the rest false. And his professional duties and the whole arrangement of his life and of his family, and all his social and official interests, might all have been false. He tried to defend all those things to himself and suddenly felt the weakness of what he was defending. There was nothing to defend. [. . .]

Chapter 12

[Then] the screaming began that continued for three days, and was so terrible that one could not hear it through two closed doors without horror. [. . .] [He] realized that he was lost, that there was no return, that the end had come, the very end, and his doubts were still unsolved and remained doubts.

"Oh! Oh! Oh!" he cried in various intonations. He had begun by screaming "I won't!" and continued screaming on the letter "O."

For three whole days, during which time did not exist for him, he struggled in that black sack into which he was being thrust by an invisible, resistless force. He struggled as a man condemned to death struggles in the hands of the executioner, knowing that he cannot save himself. And every moment he felt that despite all his efforts he was drawing nearer and nearer to what terrified him. He felt that his agony was due to his being thrust into that black hole and still more to his not being able to get right into it. He was hindered from getting into it by his conviction that his life had been a good one. That very justification of his life held him fast and prevented his moving forward, and it caused him most torment of all.

Suddenly some force struck him in the chest and side, making it still harder to breathe, and he fell through the hole and there at the bottom was a light. What had happened to him was like the sensation one sometimes experiences in a railway carriage when one thinks one is going backwards while one is really going forwards and suddenly becomes aware of the real direction.

"Yes, it was not the right thing," he said to himself, "but that's no matter. It can be done. But what *is* the right thing? he asked himself, and suddenly grew quiet.

This occurred at the end of the third day, two hours before his death. [. . .]

His son, all tears, comes to see him and then his wife. He realizes that, in dying, he is hurting them.

And suddenly it grew clear to him that what had been oppressing him, and would not leave him, was all dropping away at once from two sides, from ten sides, and from all sides. He was sorry for them, he must act so as not to hurt them: release them and free himself from these sufferings. "How good and how simple!" he thought. "And the pain?" he asked himself. "What has become of it? Where are you, pain?"

He turned his attention to it.

"Yes, here it is. Well, what of it? Let the pain be."

"And death . . . where is it?"

He sought his former accustomed fear of death and did not find it. "Where is it? What death?" There was no fear because there was no death.

In place of death there was light.

"So that's what it is!" he suddenly exclaimed aloud. "What joy!"

To him all this happened in a single instant, and the meaning of that instant did not change. For those present his agony continued for another two hours. Something rattled in his throat, his emaciated body twitched, then the gasping and rattle became less and less frequent.

"It is finished!" said someone near him.

He heard these words and repeated them in his soul. "Death is finished," he said to himself. "It is no more!"

He drew in a breath, stopped in the midst of a sigh, stretched out, and died.

6. Anton Chekhov, *The Cherry Orchard* (1903)

As *The Cherry Orchard* opens, Lyubov Andreyevna and her brother Gayev must pay the interest on the mortgage that burdens their estate or the estate must be sold at auction. They cannot do so, beyond obtaining as a gift from a wealthy kinswoman a mere fraction of the sum that is needed. Their friend and neighbor Lopakhin is eager to help them, proposing an entrepreneur's solution: they must cut down the cherry orchard, allow the property to be developed with modest cottages to be rented to summer sojourners, and so live comfortably on the rental income. They disparage the plan and ignore him.

Inevitably, the day of the auction comes. Although Gayev and Lopakhin attend, the family stays home celebrating, oddly, its outcome, as though a miracle will occur to prevent the sale. Lopakhin outbids a rival buyer, and purchases the estate. The family members and their dependents must now leave for bleak and uncharted futures. As they gather their belongings, only minutes before their train is due to depart, they hear the sound of an axe tearing down the cherry trees—for Lopakhin is the owner now and he will do what must be done.[16]

THE CHERRY ORCHARD

Act I [. . .]

[Lyubov Andreyevna has just arrived from Paris after a five-year absence, and greets friends and family at her old home. She has been summoned to deal with the problem of the impending interest payment on the mortgage; failure to pay means the auctioning off of the estate. Lopakhin has come to greet her, and to propose a plan to avert that calamity.]

---

16. The characters named in these excerpts are Lyubov Andreyevna Ranyevskaya, called Lyuba, the owner of the estate; her brother Leonid Andreyevich Gayev, called Lyonya; their merchant friend Yermolay Alekseyevich Lopakhin; and Firs, Gayev's elderly servant. Ellipses in the original text are retained; those interpolated by the present editor are given in brackets. Stage directions italicized in the original, similarly, are retained; transitions and explanations supplied by the present editor appear italicized, but in brackets.

LOPAKHIN: I have to go now, at five o'clock in the morning I have to leave for Kharkov.[17] Damn it! I wanted to look at you, talk to you [. . .]. Your brother here, Leonid Andreyevich, says that I am a boor and a peasant, but it's all the same to me. Let him say what he wants. I only want you to trust me as you did before [. . .]. God have mercy! My father was your father's and grandfather's serf, but you, particularly you, have done so much for me that I can forget all that. I love you like my own family . . . More than my family. . . .

[The others carry on an unrelated conversation.]

LOPAKHIN: I want to tell you something pleasant, happy. (*Looks at his watch.*) I'm going now. I don't have time to chat . . . Well, so, I'll just say two or three words. You already know that the cherry orchard is to be sold to pay your debts. The auction is set for August 22nd. But don't worry, my dear one, sleep easy, there is a way out. . . . Here is my plan. Pay attention now! Your estate is located only thirteen miles from town, and the railroad runs close by, so if the cherry orchard and the land near the river were cleared for small plots and leased for summer houses, then you would have at the least twenty-five thousand rubles a year income.

GAYEV: Excuse me, but that's nonsense!

LYUBOV ANDREYEVNA: I don't quite understand you, Yermolay Alekseyevich.

LOPAKHIN: You could get at the least twenty-five rubles a year for every two-and-a-half-acre plot, and if you advertise now, I guarantee you that by autumn you won't have one free scrap of land, everything will be snapped up. In short, congratulations, you are saved. The site is wonderful, the river is deep. But you'll have to tidy it up, of course, clear the land . . . For example, you'll have to take down the old structures, like this house, which isn't really needed now, and cut down the old cherry orchard . . .

LYUBOV ANDREYEVNA: Cut it down? Darling, forgive me, but you don't understand at all. If there's anything in the county you can point to as interesting, even remarkable, it can only be our cherry orchard.

LOPAKHIN: The only remarkable thing about this orchard is that it is very big. You get cherries only once every two years and then you can't get rid of them, nobody buys them.

GAYEV: But this orchard is so remarkable, it's even mentioned in the encyclopedia.

LOPAKHIN: (*Looking at this watch.*) If we don't think of anything or come to any conclusion, then on August 22nd, both the cherry orchard and the whole

_____
17. Kharkov: a major center in Ukraine, then part of Russian Empire.

estate will be sold at auction. Make up your minds! There's no other way out, I swear to you. None, none. [. . .]

[As Lopakhin leaves, he says goodbye to the family.]

LOPAKHIN: In three weeks, we'll see each other again. [. . .] Goodbye for now. It's time to go [. . .]. If you think about the summer houses and decide to do it, then let me know, and I'll get you a loan of fifty thousand. Think it over seriously. [. . .]

Act II [. . .]

[The family has gathered outdoors as the sun is about to set. Lopakhin presses Lyubov Andreyevna and Gayev for a response to his proposal, but they evade the issue. He presses them again.]

LOPAKHIN: The rich Deriganov plans to buy your estate. He's going himself, personally, they say, to the sale.

LYUBOV ANDREYEVNA: And where did you hear that?

LOPAKHIN: They're talking about it in town.

GAYEV: Our aunt from Yaroslavl promised to send something, but when and how much we don't know.

LOPAKHIN: How much will she send? One hundred thousand? Two hundred thousand?

LYUBOV ANDREYEVNA: Well . . . Ten thousand . . . or fifteen, and for that we'll be grateful.

LOPAKHIN: Excuse me, I've never met such frivolous people as you, such unbusiness-like, strange people. I'm telling you plainly that your estate will be sold, and you simply don't understand.

LYUBOV ANDREYEVNA: What can we do? Teach us what?

LOPAKHIN: I teach you every day. Every day I tell you one and the same thing . . . Both the cherry orchard and the land by the river must be rented for summer houses. Do that now, immediately, the auction is on top of you! Understand? Once you decide, once and for all, that there should be summer houses, then you'll get all the money you need, and then you'll be saved.

LYUBOV ANDREYEVNA: Summer houses and summer folk—it's so vulgar, forgive me.

GAYEV: I completely agree with you.

LOPAKHIN: I'll either sob, or I'll yell, or I'll faint. I can't stand it! You're torturing me! [. . .]

[They return to idle conversation, with Lyubov Andreyevna reflecting at length on her disordered life. It is getting late, and Firs, the old faithful servant, enters with Gayev's coat. Firs longs for the old days, before the emancipation of the serfs,[18] a nostalgia Lopakhin scorns. Gayev suggests that an old acquaintance will make him a loan—a possibility Lopakhin mocks, with even Lyubov Andreyevna sharing his skepticism.]

LYUBOV ANDREYEVNA: How old you've gotten, Firs!

FIRS: Excuse me?

LOPAKHIN: She said, "How very old you've gotten!"

FIRS: I've lived a long time. They wanted to marry me off before your papa was even born . . . (*Laughs.*) When they set us free, I was already a senior valet. But I didn't agree to freedom, stayed with the masters . . . (*Pause.*) I remember everyone was glad for some reason, but why they were glad, they didn't know.

LOPAKHIN: It was so very good in the old days. They flogged you at least.

FIRS: (*Who has not heard.*) I should think so. The peasants and the masters, the masters and the peasants, but now everything's mixed up, you can't understand anything.

GAYEV: Be quiet, Firs. Tomorrow I have to go into the city. I'm supposed to meet a certain general who can give me a promissory note.

LOPAKHIN: Nothing will come of it. And you won't pay the interest, don't worry.

LYUBOV ANDREYEVNA: He's delirious. There are no generals. [. . .]

[After more pointless conversation, as Act II nears its close, Lopakhin utters yet another warning.]

LOPAKHIN: Let me remind you, ladies and gentlemen: on August 22nd, the cherry orchard will be sold. Think about that! . . . Think about it! . . .

Act III [. . .]

[While Gayev and Lopakhin have gone off to the auction at which the estate will be sold—unless some miracle intervenes—the family is enjoying a ball, in the company of assorted neighbors, including a postal clerk and the station master, whose

---

18. The serfs were emancipated in 1861 by act of Tsar Alexander II.

*presence betrays the household's downward social trajectory. Gayev and Lopakhin
return with news.]*

LYUBOV ANDREYEVNA: Is it you, Yermolay Alekseyevich? Why did it
take you so long? Where's Leonid?

LOPAKHIN: Leonid Andreyevich arrived with me, he's coming . . .

LYUBOV ANDREYEVNA: (*Excited.*) Well, what happened? Was there an
auction? Tell me!

LOPAKHIN: (*Confused, afraid to destroy his own joy.*) The auction was over at
four o'clock . . . We missed the train, had to wait until nine thirty. [. . .]

LYUBOV ANDREYEVNA: Lyonya, what is it? Lyonya, what? (*Impatiently,
with tears in her eyes.*) Quickly, for God's sake . . .

GAYEV: (*Doesn't answer her, only waves his hand; to Firs, crying.*) Here take this
. . . There's some anchovies [. . .]. I didn't eat anything today . . . How much
I've suffered! [. . .]. I'm awfully tired. Help me, Firs, to get undressed. (*Exits to
his room, Firs following him.*) [. . .]

LYUBOV ANDREYEVNA: Was the cherry orchard sold?

LOPAKHIN: It was sold.

LYUBOV ANDREYEVNA: Who bought it?

LOPAKHIIN: I bought it. (*Pause.*)

*Lyubov Andreyevna is overcome; she would fall if she weren't standing near an
armchair or table. [. . .]*

LOPAKHIN: I bought it. Wait a minute, ladies and gentlemen, be so kind, my
head is swimming, I can't talk . . . (*Laughs.*) We got to the auction. Deriganov
was there. Leonid Andreyevich had only fifteen thousand and Deriganov had
already put down thirty thousand over and above the debt. I saw how the business stood, so I jumped in and put down forty . . . He put down forty-five. I
made it fifty-five. You see he kept adding five thousand and I added ten each
time . . . Well, it came to a finish. I put down ninety thousand over and above
the debt, and it was mine. Now the cherry orchard is mine! Mine! (*Laughs
out loud.*) My god, Lord in Heaven, the cherry orchard is mine! Tell me that
I'm drunk, not in my right mind, that I've imagined all of this . . . (*Stamps his
feet.*) Don't laugh at me. If my father and grandfather were to get up out of
their graves and look at everything that's happened, how their Yermolay, their
beaten, half-literate Yermolay, who ran around barefoot in the winter, how this
very same Yermolay bought an estate, the most beautiful one in the whole
world. I bought the estate where my grandfather and father were slaves, where

they weren't allowed into the kitchen. I'm asleep, this is a mirage for me, it only seems to be [. . .]. (*The orchestra is heard tuning up.*) Hey musicians, play, I want to hear you! Everyone, come look at how Yermolay Lopakhin will take the axe to the cherry orchard, how the trees will fall to the ground! We'll build summer houses and our grandchildren and their grandchildren will see a new life . . . Music, play! (*The music plays. Lyubov Andreyevna lowers herself to a chair and bitterly cries. To her reproachfully.*) Why, why didn't you listen to me? My poor, good woman, you can't go back now. (*With tears.*) Oh if only all this would pass quickly, if only our incoherent, unhappy lives would change quickly!

[The celebration is over. In the final Act IV, the family has packed its belong-ings, stripping bare the house that is slated for destruction. As they share parting embraces, they hear in the distance the sound of busy axes demolishing the cherry orchard. Firs, the ancient and ailing servitor for whom the emancipation of the serfs was history's greatest calamity, is left behind in the boarded-up house. There he dies, entombed, the last witness to the world that is no more.]

Chapter 6

The Americas

Introduction

For the three centuries after 1492, when Christopher Columbus opened
the western hemisphere to European exploration, encounter, and conquest,
Europeans settled in the Americas north and south, bringing with them European cultural traditions in an array of languages: Spanish, Portuguese, French,
English, Dutch, and German, among others. In the southern regions, by the
sixteenth century, Europeans established a dominion over densely populated
indigenous communities and states, some of which had achieved advanced levels of civilization. Here new literary currents emerged over time expressive of
the American experience, yielding works mainly in Spanish and Portuguese. To
the north, where indigenous populations were more thinly spread, Europeans
from the seventeenth century settled a narrow strip of territory on the eastern
coast and pushed westward from that anchorage over the next two centuries.
Here a distinctively new American literary production, written in English,
developed fully only after the revolutionary era (1775–1783).[1] In both northern and southern regions, colonial civilization almost from its birth was shaped
by the importation from Africa of a slave labor force and the establishment of
a plantation economy, which existed alongside a commercial economy based
on the exportation of natural resources: furs, fish, agricultural products, and,
especially, gold and silver. It is in this context that the eleven texts appearing
in this chapter were composed over the course of the nineteenth century: eight
in English, the contributions of authors born in the United States of America;
and three in Spanish or Portuguese, the contributions of Mexican, Argentinian, and Brazilian authors.

The first of the Anglophone authors is Nathaniel Hawthorne (1804–
1864), who writes in *The Scarlet Letter* (1850), selections from which appear
in this chapter, of the early Puritan experience of the North American set-
tlers. The two hubs of the original Anglo-American colonies were Virginia,
settled by planters, and Massachusetts, settled by refugees from the wars
and persecutions fueled by the European Reformations (see Volume One,

---

1. The representative texts of Anglo-American literature included in this chapter are all by US
authors, but Canadian literature, as well, written in both French and English, also emerged in
the nineteenth century and even before Canada's national confederation.

Introduction to Section III). Many of those Massachusetts refugees were Puritans, members of a sect of English Protestants resisting the established Church of England and adopting an austere and conscientious form of life—a form of life and a set of beliefs that shaped some of the most important intellectual and political leaders of colonial and revolutionary America. Hawthorne himself was descended from a leader of Puritan Massachusetts, and although he repudiated the harshness of the Puritan regime, its legacy of moral earnestness and high ideals remained important for him as well as other early authors in the modern American tradition. The shadows of the American Puritan experience fall on his many short stories and five novels, among other writings, but especially on *The Scarlet Letter*.

The beautiful Hester Prynne, living alone in Boston while her husband traveled, has given birth to an illegitimate daughter, the child of an adulterous relationship, and is condemned as her punishment—a more merciful one than the death sentence that could have been enacted—to wear forevermore on her chest a red letter "A," the emblem of her adultery. The novel opens with its exhibition to the public: she emerges from prison, her infant in her arms, and a brilliantly embroidered scarlet letter affixed to her coarse gray gown, blazing defiantly on her bosom. She retires to a cottage on the outer edge of the city, and supports herself and her daughter by the labor of her hands—the labor of that same needlework that crafted the brilliant scarlet letter, now applied to ordinary tasks for her fellow citizens. She willingly accepts this penitential existence, caring only for the welfare of her daughter, whom she has named Pearl: a name, ironically, evoking purity and perfection.

But there are two men who haunt her solitary existence: her husband Chillingworth, a much older, ill, and twisted man, who has returned to Boston and is determined to wreak vengeance on his wife's seducer; and the charismatic and beloved minister Dimmesdale, her secret lover, whom she has spared from ignominy, but who lives consumed by guilt and wracked by pain from a hidden, invisible, and perhaps imaginary scarlet letter that burns on his breast, underneath his ministerial robes. In her dignified self-sufficiency, Hester far outshines, in moral stature and psychological well-being, the two men who encircle her, both consumed by their passions and fatally ill. In the end Dimmesdale, in full public view, stands on the scaffold where Hester first displayed to all gathered the symbol of her sinfulness, and with his last breath, confesses his own. Having no more reason to live, for he has lost the opportunity to avenge himself, Chillingworth soon dies—leaving his fortune to Pearl, now, as Hawthorne describes her, "the richest heiress of her day, in the New World." Hester and Pearl disappear for some years to unknown European sites, where Pearl, now grown, apparently marries. Hester returns to her cottage on the edge of town, dons her gray gown and the scarlet letter, and resumes her life of penitential solitude.

Like Hawthorne, Herman Melville (1819–1891) had inherited deep connections to Anglo-American origins: two of his grandfathers were heroes of the Revolutionary War. He writes broadly about the American experience, from that of whale-hunters on an impossible global quest, as in his epic novel *Moby Dick* (1851); to that of a Wall Street clerk, in his celebrated short story *Bartleby the Scrivener* (1853); to that of a slave mutiny on a marooned ship off the Chilean coast in a second story, his *Benito Cereno* (1855), excerpts of which appear in this chapter. His career was erratic: it lurched from an opulent existence in early childhood to financial hardship and a disrupted education to adventures as a sailor in tropical seas to some twenty years (1866–1885) of routine labor as the deputy inspector in New York's Custom House. So, too, was his literary production: after early successes won by his tales of exotic places, his masterpiece, *Moby Dick*, failed to please the critics, and his later writings met with an indifferent reception, the author's genius only winning recognition after his death.

Benito Cereno tells the story of a Spanish captain of that name, the master of a ship marooned without water or supplies just north of Cape Horn at the southern tip of the South American continent. The slaves have mutinied and killed all the Spanish officers on board except Cereno himself, who, physically threatened and psychologically manipulated by one of the African leaders masquerading as his body servant, cannot speak the truth to the American captain who boards the ship to investigate its situation. These events, which Melville sets in 1799, some years before the British acts of 1807 and 1833 abolishing, respectively, the slave trade and slavery itself, are based on an actual occurrence of some years later. It was documented by the 1817 memoir of Amasa Delano, the American ship's captain, who led the eventual capture of the ship, followed by the punishment of the mutineers.

Clearly, the attitudes toward the Africans involved expressed by Melville's characters, and implicit in the author's narrative of their rebellious and violent behavior, reflect cultural attitudes regarding slavery that precede the American Civil War (1861–1865), and which would erupt only six years after the story was published. But these are not Melville's main concern; rather, the story centers on the American captain Delano, whose obstinate innocence, sustained for the first three-quarters of the novella-length story, prevents his recognizing what has actually occurred. He thinks, perhaps, the Spanish captain is rude, or ill, or insane, or an imposter; he admires the solicitous loyalty of the African Babo, who watchfully shadows Cereno, and each day, while expertly shaving his supposed master, holds a razor to his throat; Delano accepts the absurd notion that the Africans cleaning and sharpening the pile of hatchets brought up from the hold are engaged in housekeeping and not preparing for an assault. Absurdly optimistic, the American denies, until the truth is unmistakable, the discordant reality that lies before him: that black slaves have seized power and have enslaved the whites.

Slavery would come to an end in the United States, although not until eighty-seven years after that nation's birth in 1776 (the "four score years and seven" that President Abraham Lincoln famously named). The causes of its extinction were multifarious, but perhaps none was more important than the surge of abolitionist sentiment in the northern states, especially in Puritan and Quaker communities, guided by Great Britain's example—for having previously been the world's greatest slave trader, that nation would lead the drive for abolition. *Uncle Tom's Cabin*, a novel portraying the evils of slavery published in 1852, just nine years before outbreak of the Civil War, fueled the American abolitionist movement. Written by Harriet Beecher Stowe (1811–1896), the daughter and wife of Protestant clergymen, it was an immediate success: it became the best-selling novel in the United States, and the second most popular book after the Bible; it sold millions of copies in Britain, where Queen Victoria read and approved it (as did, in Russia, the future Bolshevik leader Vladimir Lenin); and it was swiftly translated into, first, the major European languages and, eventually, into more than sixty world languages.

And yet Stowe's novel had its critics, and not just for what literary scholars considered excessive sentimentality. In the later nineteenth and twentieth centuries, Black leaders condemned the novel for constructing stereotypes that undermined the cause of Black liberation and social advancement. The figure of Uncle Tom, a benevolent older slave and committed Christian who accommodated the slaveholding culture, though he died its victim, was deemed especially harmful. So, too, was that of the slave Sambo, depicted as lazy and shiftless. Perhaps worse, the successful Black hero George Harris, like his wife, the heroine Eliza, were both mulattoes,[2] a choice seen to insinuate that the most capable former slaves were those of mixed race. Moreover, some found it offensive that a white woman who had never experienced life in the slave south should have presumed to write about it.

Nonetheless, whatever judgments may be passed in retrospect on *Uncle Tom's Cabin*, in its day it changed minds and the abolitionist sentiment it supported was critical in the ideological struggle, and eventually, the epochal war that led to slavery's end. Its rhetorical force is observed in the selection included in this chapter depicting the desperate escape made by Eliza Harris, carrying her young son Harry, across the frozen Ohio River to freedom.

In 1852, the same year that saw the publication of Stowe's *Uncle Tom's Cabin*, Frederick Douglass (1818–1895), who had himself escaped slavery, delivered to the Rochester Ladies' Anti-Slavery Society in Rochester, New York, the speech that has come to be entitled *What to the Slave Is the Fourth of July?* Delivered on July 5, one day after the joyous celebration of the seventy-sixth year of American independence, the speech Douglass gave, excerpted here, is a

---

2. mulatto: a person of mixed race, generally African and white (Caucasian).

crucial statement of the tension between the ideals of America's founding and the fact of the continued existence in its midst of the institution of slavery; and it continues to be a reminder of the essential contradiction between the goals of liberation and self-determination embraced by the nation's founders and the heritage of racism their descendants still bear.

Douglass had described the cruelty of slavery and his stunning escape in his *Narrative of the Life of Frederick Douglass* (1845), the first of the three autobiographies he would write over his long career. His story was extraordinary. He had been born to a black slave mother and a white father (it was rumored, the plantation master), and had witnessed and suffered the cruelty of slavery. By the time he escaped in 1838, at about twenty years of age, self-taught and gifted with eloquence, he possessed the wisdom and compassion of a gray-haired sage. Supported by white abolitionists in America and abroad, he took up the leadership of the Black abolitionist movement, launching the publication of its first newspaper, the *North Star*, in Rochester, New York, to whose abolitionist community he delivered the speech excerpted in this chapter. Nine years later, the Civil War broke out—a war in which two of his sons fought—resulting in the emancipation of the slaves by Abraham Lincoln's order and extended and confirmed by three constitutional amendments. Douglass moved to Washington, DC, where he served the government in administrative and diplomatic positions, while continuing his speaking tours supporting, in addition to the cause of Black emancipation, that of women's rights. When his first wife—a free Black woman who had helped him escape from bondage—died in 1882, after forty-four years of marriage, Douglass married, scandalously, a white woman, his junior by twenty years and a radical feminist, the daughter of abolitionists.

Like Stowe and Douglass, Henry David Thoreau (1817–1862) was an abolitionist. He supported, as they had, the Underground Railroad, the network of safe houses and pathways that facilitated escaped slaves to reach the northern United States and Canada; and he opposed both the Mexican War (1846–1848), which would have extended the slaveholding domain, and the Fugitive Slave Act (1850), which required free states to return slave refugees to their slave masters. Most eloquently, upon the execution on December 2, 1859 of the anti-slavery insurgent John Brown, Thoreau celebrated Brown's sacrifice, thus helping to create a martyr for the swelling abolitionist movement.

As an abolitionist, however, Thoreau was driven not by an urge for social activism, but because the freedom of the slave was an object consistent with the freedom he cared most about: his own—and that of any human being. Born to a modest entrepreneurial family in Concord, Massachusetts, never marrying and never bothering to collect the Harvard diploma he had earned in 1837, he lived without profession or occupation. After Harvard, he had taught; later (1841–1844), he tutored the children of the family of the towering thinker Ralph Waldo Emerson; for a brief spell, he worked in his family's pencil factory; but his preferred career was his own spiritual development. To pursue it, he created a one-man religion, without God or doctrine: the religion he practiced between 1845 and 1847, living in a small, plain cabin in the woods bordering Walden Pond, not far from Concord, Massachusetts, accompanied only by his thoughts and conversing only with the ambient trees, forest creatures, and sky, water, and wind.

Thoreau describes this episode in *Walden, or Life in the Woods*, and in the chapter *Where I Lived, and What I Lived For*, selections from which appear here. Bound in the same volume in its original 1854 edition was his essay *Resistance to Civil Government* (originally published 1849), a declaration of the right of the citizen to disobey the state that would influence the philanthropist Leo Tolstoy, the champion of Indian independence Mohandas Gandhi, and the leader of the American civil rights movement, Martin Luther King Jr. His other books, travelogues, essays, and journals, many published posthumously, totaled some twenty volumes—an immense achievement for a man who had been ill with tuberculosis for more than two decades before his death, in 1862, at age forty-four.

Thoreau's equal in his sense of himself, Walt Whitman (1819–1892) was, like Thoreau, itinerant, but unlike his contemporary, unsupported by family wealth. Schooled only to the age of eleven, he worked as printer's assistant and later as printer, editor, publisher, journalist, government clerk, and even as a volunteer nurse tending to wounded soldiers during the Civil War. Like Thoreau, once again, he never married, both authors posing a contrast to Hawthorne, Melville, Stowe, and Douglass, all of whom adhered to conventional household arrangements. Whitman's sexuality, moreover, is a factor; and it is an unknown one—Was he bisexual? Homoerotic? Autoerotic? Intimations of all are found in his verse.

Whitman's poetic masterpiece (or perhaps masterpieces) is his *Leaves of Grass*. That collection began as a handful of poems he self-published in 1855, to mixed and sometimes horrified reviews. He then constantly reworked and expanded it until it reached, in the "deathbed" edition of 1892, some four hundred poems of novel forms and various lengths. The significance of the title is not to be passed over. "Leaves of Grass" is in itself a paradox, as grass is not a leaf, nor does it grow leaves; "leaves" may refer not only to those on trees but to the pages of a book; and grass suggests a sprawling expanse of single blades, each blade representing an individual human life in the multitude that is humanity. Finally, grass means flesh. That equivalence is drawn in a biblical verse that he, as the son of pious Quakers, knew well: Isaiah 40:6–8, "All flesh is grass. . . . The grass withereth, the flower fadeth: but the word of our God shall stand for ever."[3] The grass dies, the flowers fade and fall, but God's words, and Walt Whitman's, will "stand for ever."

---

3. In the King James Version, the one Whitman would have used. The Isaiahan theme recurs in 1 Peter 1:24.

Whitman's *Leaves of Grass*—containing within it the fifty-two sections of *Song of Myself*, a sequence running close to one hundred pages—includes poems about himself and his consciousness; the universe, God, essential truth, and nature; the American people and American democracy. Whitman, "America's poet," did not just write about America, but is, according to critic Harold Bloom, "the central voice of American literature."[4]

If Whitman had not been dubbed "America's poet," Emily Dickinson (1830–1886) might well have claimed the title. Descended from an old Puritan family, educated in the best schools available to girls, Dickinson lived in Amherst, Massachusetts nearly all her life. There, when not managing her disabled mother's care, she was dedicated to her house, her garden, and her friends, to whom she wrote innumerable letters (a mere fraction of which survive, filling three volumes in a modern edition), and was intent on everyday things: birds, flowers, butterflies, and baking bread. Like Whitman, her personal life was unconventional, her eccentricity marked by her increasing isolation and, in later years, her costume: in those later years, she dressed only in white. Of uncertain sexuality, she never married, although she had profound and even passionate relationships, largely epistolary, both with female friends and male mentors.

Widely read, Dickinson was especially influenced by Shakespeare and the Bible (notably the Book of Revelation), the seventeenth-century metaphysical poets, and the English Dissenter and hymnist Isaac Watts. Thus grounded— and little concerned, as were her contemporaries, with slavery, the abolitionist cause, or the Civil War—her thoughts were intense and speculative, focused on nature, death, the soul, and immortality. These themes recur constantly in her nearly 1,800 poems; most published only posthumously, the first editions by rival members of the two warring factions of her family. Her first poems date from the 1850s, when she was in her twenties. By 1865, she had assembled more than one thousand poems, in mostly clean copies, on leaves of fine paper sewn together at the spine in forty-six fascicles, or "packets"; a method of self-publication she continued through 1872, adding three more fascicles to the total. Formally, in their rhyme schemes and rhythm, her poems resemble contemporary hymns and ballads, but those features are deceptively simple. Within that framework, her language is enigmatic, a riddling maze of allusions pointing to imagined entities, and presented with deliberately nonstandard capitalization and punctuation that accentuate the poet's strong personal voice.

Whereas Dickinson voluntarily chose a life of seclusion, so that she could be a "Nobody," as she wrote in one of her poems, and create her complex verse statements undisturbed in her own mental universe, Charlotte Perkins Gilman

---

4. Walt Whitman, *Selected Poems*, ed. Harold Bloom (New York: The Library of America, 2003), xxxi.

(1860–1935), a generation later, was forced into seclusion by her male advisers as a supposed remedy for her mental distress. A New Englander like Dickinson, she was a descendant, on her father's side, of the prominent Beecher family (and a kinswoman of Harriet Beecher Stowe); and like several of the Beechers, although raised in poverty and educated erratically, she became a prolific author and social reformer. As a writer, she published novels, stories, and poems, as well as, of her many nonfiction works, innumerable newspaper articles, a pioneering exploration of *Women and Economics* (1898), and an autobiography (published posthumously). As an activist, she advocated for feminism not only in print, but also in her frequent lectures, winning renown both in the United States and Europe. She was married a first time, unhappily, to the father of her one child, from whom she separated and then unusually for that era, divorced. Later, following an intense relationship with a woman, she was married a second time, happily, to the supportive George Houghton Gilman, whose name she bore until her death in 1935, one year after his, by suicide.

Gilman's first important publication was a short story, of which excerpts are given in this chapter, which appeared in 1892 in *The New England Journal*: *The Yellow Wall Paper*. Still widely read today as a fundamental work of modern feminism, it describes the postpartum mental breakdown of a young married woman whose condition is treated, at her husband's direction, by isolation in a room of a spacious and stately house, rented for the purpose. The room, which had previously served as a nursery, is large, airy, and brightly lit by large windows affording splendid views. But the bed is oddly bolted to the floor and the walls are covered in worn yellow wallpaper imprinted with a design of whirling forms that become, in the disturbed narrator's eyes, a bizarre phantasmagoria. In these shifting patterns, she believes she sees a woman trapped behind bars—as she herself is trapped in a children's nursery. To release the prisoner, she creeps around the room, with her bare fingers peeling the lurid yellow paper from the walls; and she creeps over, as well, the inert body of her husband who had entered, and on seeing her, fallen to the floor unconscious. This story, told by a narrator whose disintegration is brilliantly conveyed, encapsulates the message that Gilman would deliver for the next forty years and more: the wrongful control of women's minds, bodies, and energies by husbands and credentialed experts; in sum, by men.

With this sampling of Anglophone American literature by authors born between 1804 and 1860, attention may now turn to Latin American literature. Latin America was a cultural more than a geographical entity, encompassing regions where mostly Romance languages (derived from ancient Latin) were spoken: Mexico, Central America, South America, and the Caribbean. This chapter considers three authors born between 1776 and 1851, representing the three diverse literary cultures of Spanish-speaking Mexico and Argentina, and Portuguese-speaking Brazil.

Latin America, it is often forgotten, having developed earlier than Anglo-America, possessed economic and bureaucratic systems more complex than those of the northern region, and a far greater population.[5] In the colonial era, its political governance was autocratic and monarchical; supported, and was supported by, an ecclesiastical regime, born of Counter-Reformation missionary zeal, intent on maintaining religious conformity. Largely coinciding with the era, in Europe, of the French Revolution and Napoleon Bonaparte's subsequent advance and defeat, independence movements broke out in Latin America, whose revolutionary goal was the liberalization of both state and church.

It was in this milieu that José Joaquín Fernández de Lizardi (1776–1827) came to maturity. Born in Mexico City[6] to a middle-class Creole[7] family, and largely self-educated after dropping out of university studies, the political journalist Lizardi, defying the censors and despite recurrent imprisonments, produced hundreds of pamphlets and articles. He wrote, in addition, poetry, plays, fables, and four novels, composed over the four tense years 1816 to 1819 during Mexico's war of independence (1810–1821). The first of these is the novel *The Mangy Parrot* (*El Periquillo Sarniento*),[8] selections from which appear in this chapter, published serially in 1816.[9] It is, as well, the first novel ever published in Mexico; and equally, the first published in all of Latin America.

The Mangy Parrot is considered a picaresque novel—one of many offshoots of the pioneering Spanish novella *The Life of Lazarillo de Tormes* (1554)[10] featuring the adventures of a *picaro*, or little boy—in that it narrates the varied and shocking adventures of a rebellious young man. But it is also viewed as a nation-building novel, in that it depicts the myriad types of contemporary Mexicans, mostly from the underclass, speaking colloquially in their multifarious dialects. By this means, Lizardi introduces a middle-class audience to its own country, in preparation for the nation's soon-to-come autonomy. He performs, it might be said, the same task performed by America's poet Whitman, who heard America "singing," and, as the "Modern Man,"

---

5. Evident, for example, in the relative populations of Hispanic Mexico City and Anglophone New York City around the year 1800: about 100,000 to 150,000 in the first case, about 20,000 to 30,000 in the second.

6. His career follows a little more than a century after that of an earlier native of Mexico City, the poet Sor Juana Inés de la Cruz (1648–1695; see Volume One, Introduction to Chapter 13 and Text 7).

7. Creole: *criollo*, a person born in the Americas of European ancestry.

8. The title "Mangy Parrot" translates the protagonist's nickname, *El Periquillo*, derived from his birth name Pedro Sarmiento, which becomes Perico (parrot) Sarniento (itching, or "mangy"); the first name diminutized as Periquillo.

9. The last sixteen chapters of fifty-two, stalled by the censors, appeared only posthumously in 1831.

10. See Volume One, Chapter 13, Text 2.

introduced the American people to his compatriots.[11] *The Mangy Parrot* is, further, a political screed, for inserted within the narrative are long discursive passages presenting the author's critical views of government, church, and culture.

The Argentine Eduardo Gutiérrez (1851–1889) bears a certain resemblance to the Mexican Lizardi. Both men were undereducated, having dropped out of the universities that prepared youth for leadership positions. At the same time, both were prolific writers connected to the printing industry, who published rapidly and without revision on a host of topics in a slew of newspapers. Furthermore, both authors excelled in their understanding of underclass norms, language, and values. Their works resonated with an emerging group of readers, literate but unimpressed by the refinements of the elite, and eager to read about alienated heroes not averse to breaking the law. Lizardi's El Periquillo, turning thirty years old, repents of his youthful misdeeds and lives to raise a family that he will instruct in leading a decent life. Juan Moreira, in contrast, the hero of Gutiérrez's fictionalized biography—*The Gaucho Juan Moreira*, excerpted here first published serially in 1879–1880—is defeated in the end by the agents of the state. His legend, however, extolling his prowess, essential nobility, and proud self-determination, lived on for decades. It burst into performance in the circus, the theater, the opera, and on film, celebrating the myth of the Argentinian frontier amid an immigrant surge, urbanization, and rapid modernization.

In clear contrast to the literary products of the Mexican Lizardi and Argentinian Gutiérrez are the meticulous creations of the Brazilian mulatto Joaquim Maria Machado de Assis (1839–1908). The son of a house painter, who was himself the son of freed slaves, and of a Portuguese washerwoman, Machado benefited as a child from the protection of a wealthy widow and her kinsman, and in adolescence from the mentoring of prominent intellectual and political figures. At age fifteen, he became a printer's apprentice, soon after a proofreader, and not much later a published author in various Rio de Janeiro newspapers, acquiring along the way, having had no formal education, knowledge of French, English, German, Latin, and Greek. His publications won him early recognition and, before he turned thirty, employment in the service of Emperor Pedro II, who twice conferred upon him, in 1867 and 1888, the significant imperial titles of knight and officer in the imperial Order of the Rose. In Brazil, where the color line that prevailed in the United States did not exist, persons of mixed race could ascend professional ladders, as did Machado. By the late 1880s, he was acclaimed and revered, and he is still today regarded as Brazil's greatest author, as well as one of the greatest writers of modern times in any language.

---

11. See in this volume Chapter 6, Text 6.

Machado wrote copiously: the 1975 edition of his complete works runs to fifteen volumes, and includes novels, poems, plays, translations, journalism, and short stories. His style is famous for its precision, clarity, and ironic intonation, which gently but piercingly conveys a critique of contemporary Brazilian life. These features of his prose are displayed in the brief short story included here in its entirety: *To Be Twenty Years Old!* Never scolding or scowling, Machado exposes in this story the gestures and attitudes of the privileged youth of Rio de Janeiro, and eviscerates them. Thus may an outsider possessed of abundant talent, but unwilling to arouse antipathies or cause unease of any kind, write about those responsible for his social isolation.

Between Hawthorne's sparse, tense Puritan Boston with which this chapter opens, and the urban elegance of Machado's Rio de Janeiro, lies a long road. The former represents the psychological and cultural germ from which the history of the United States would evolve; the latter the nineteenth-century culmination of the colonized world of Latin America.

1. Nathaniel Hawthorne, *The Scarlet Letter* (1850)

In the selections that follow from the opening scenes of Hawthorne's novel, Hester Prynne emerges from prison, holding her illegitimate child Pearl, exhibiting on her breast a defiantly brilliant scarlet letter; she then mounts the scaffold for the public humiliation that is the crux of her punishment. She is exhorted by the ministerial eminences who, along with the governor of Massachusetts, preside over the ceremony, to reveal the identity of her partner in adultery. She will not; and the younger clergyman, the Reverend Dimmesdale, is oddly relieved. At the same time, Hester recognizes in the crowd her husband, Chillingworth, who has appeared after a long absence. Seven years later, both men will die, Chillingworth's legacy leaving Pearl an heiress. Mother and daughter depart for some years, until, as told in the conclusion, Hester returns to her solitude and the burden, willfully resumed, of the scarlet letter.[12]

THE SCARLET LETTER

The door of the jail being flung open from within, there appeared, in the first place, . . . the grim and grisly presence of the town-beadle, with a sword by his side and his staff of office in his hand. . . . Stretching forth the official staff in

---

12. The original orthography and punctuation of this 1850 publication are retained, as well as the archaic second-person pronouns and verbs—"thou hast," "beside thee"—that would have been used by seventeenth-century Puritans, although no longer in Hawthorne's day.

his left hand, he laid his right upon the shoulder of a young woman, whom he thus drew forward until, on the threshold of the prison-door, she repelled him, by an action marked with natural dignity and force of character, and stepped into the open air, as if by her own free-will. She bore in her arms a child, a baby of some three months old, who winked and turned aside its little face from the too vivid light of day; because its existence, heretofore, had brought it acquainted only with the gray twilight of a dungeon. . . .

When the young woman—the mother of this child—stood fully revealed before the crowd, it seemed to be her first impulse to clasp the infant closely to her bosom; not so much by an impulse of motherly affection, as that she might thereby conceal a certain token, which was wrought or fastened into her dress. In a moment, however, . . . she took the baby on her arm, and, with a burning blush, and yet a haughty smile, and a glance that would not be abashed, looked around at her townspeople and neighbours. On the breast of her gown, in fine red cloth, surrounded with an elaborate embroidery and fantastic flourishes of gold thread, appeared the letter A. It was so artistically done, and with so much fertility and gorgeous luxuriance of fancy, that it had all the effect of a last and fitting decoration to the apparel which she wore; and which was of a splendor in accordance with the taste of the age, but greatly beyond what was allowed by the sumptuary regulations of the colony.[13]

The young woman was tall, with a figure of perfect elegance, on a large scale. She had dark and abundant hair, so glossy that it threw off the sunshine with a gleam, and a face which, besides being beautiful from regularity of feature and richness of complexion, had the impressiveness belonging to a marked brow and deep black eyes. She was lady-like, too, after the manner of the feminine gentility of those days; characterized by a certain state and dignity. . . . And never had Hester Prynne appeared more lady-like . . . than as she issued from the prison. Those who had before known her, and had expected to behold her dimmed and obscured by a disastrous cloud, were astonished, and even startled, to perceive how her beauty shone out, and made a halo of the misfortune and ignominy in which she was enveloped. . . . Her attire, which, indeed, she had wrought for the occasion, in prison, . . . seemed to express the attitude of her spirit, the desperate recklessness of her mood, by its wild and picturesque peculiarity. But the point which drew all eyes, and, as it were, transfigured the wearer . . . was that SCARLET LETTER, so fantastically embroidered and illuminated upon her bosom. It had the effect of a spell, taking her out of the ordinary relations with humanity, and inclosing her in a sphere by herself. . . .

---

13. sumptuary regulations of the colony: the Puritan community established strict regulations to control excessive luxury in dress.

Hester Prynne set forth towards the place appointed for her punishment. . . . [A]nd came to a sort of scaffold, at the western extremity of the market-place. . . . In fact, this scaffold constituted a portion of a penal machine, which . . . was held, in the old time, to be as effectual an agent in the promotion of good citizenship, as ever was the guillotine among the terrorists of France.[14] . . .

On the platform was erected a "contrivance of wood and iron," a pillory, in which the culprit's head and hands might be pinioned by a board affixed to a pole, so as to suffer the punishment of painful immobility and public humiliation.

The unhappy culprit sustained herself as best a woman might, under the heavy weight of a thousand unrelenting eyes, all fastened upon her, and concentrated at her bosom. It was almost intolerable to be borne. Of an impulsive and passionate nature, she had fortified herself to encounter the stings and venomous stabs of public contumely, wreaking itself in every variety of insult; but there was a quality so much more terrible in the solemn mood of the popular mind, that she longed rather to behold all those rigid countenances contorted with scornful merriment, and herself the object. . . . Yet there were intervals when the whole scene, in which she was the most conspicuous object, seemed to vanish from her eyes, or, at least, glimmered indistinctly before them, like a mass of imperfectly shaped and spectral images. Her mind, and especially her memory, was preternaturally active, and kept bringing up other scenes than this roughly hewn street of a little town, on the edge of the Western wilderness.[15] . . . Reminiscences, the most trifling and immaterial, passages of infancy and school-days, sports, childish quarrels, and the little domestic traits of her maiden years, came swarming back upon her. . . .

Lastly, in lieu of these shifting scenes, came back the rude market-place of the Puritan settlement, with all the townspeople assembled and levelling their stern regards at Hester Prynne,—yes, at herself,—who stood on the scaffold of the pillory, an infant on her arm, and the letter A, in scarlet, fantastically embroidered with gold thread, upon her bosom!

Could it be true? She clutched the child so fiercely to her breast, that it sent forth a cry; she turned her eyes downward at the scarlet letter, and even touched it with her finger, to assure herself that the infant and the shame were real. Yes!—these were her realities,—all else had vanished! . . .

---

14. the guillotine among the terrorists of France: the guillotine was a machine designed for the impersonal execution of prisoners during the French Revolution (here Hawthorne names the revolutionaries "terrorists"), operated by a pulley allowing a blade to descend to decapitate the victim.

15. Western wilderness: in this era, the "wilderness," territory not governed by European colonists, began immediately west of the limits of the settlement.

In the distance, Hester sees her long-absent husband, old and deformed, the scholar and physician Chillingworth, who has mysteriously reappeared. From the balcony of the meetinghouse facing the scaffold, the senior minister Wilson calls upon her.

"Hearken unto me, Hester Prynne!" said the voice.

It has already been noticed, that directly over the platform on which Hester Prynne stood was a kind of balcony, or open gallery, appended to the meeting-house. It was the place whence proclamations were wont to be made, amidst an assemblage of the magistracy, with all the ceremonial that attended such public observances in those days. Here, to witness the scene which we are describing, sat Governor Bellingham himself. . . .

Wilson turns to his younger associate, the Reverend Mr. Dimmesdale, a gifted young clergyman educated in "one of the great English universities, bringing all the learning of the age into our wild forest-land." Wilson asks Dimmesdale to question Hester, and elicit from her the name of the adulterous father of her infant. Dimmesdale is reluctant, but at last does as he is bid.

The Reverend Mr. Dimmesdale bent his head, in silent prayer, as it seemed, and then came forward.

"Hester Prynne," said he, leaning over the balcony, and looking down sted-fastly into her eyes, "thou hearest what this good man says. . . . I charge thee to speak out the name of thy fellow-sinner and fellow-sufferer! Be not silent from any mistaken pity and tenderness for him; for, believe me, Hester, though he were to step down from a high place, and stand there beside thee, on thy pedestal of shame, yet better were it so, than to hide a guilty heart through life. What can thy silence do for him, except it tempt him—yea, compel him, as it were—to add hypocrisy to sin?" . . .

The young pastor's voice was tremulously sweet, rich, deep, and broken. . . . So powerful seemed the minister's appeal, that the people could not believe but that Hester Prynne would speak out the guilty name; or else that the guilty one himself, in whatever high or lowly place he stood, would be drawn forth by an inward and inevitable necessity, and compelled to ascend the scaffold.

Hester shook her head.

"Woman, transgress not beyond the limits of Heaven's mercy!" cried the Reverend Mr. Wilson, more harshly than before. "That little babe hath been gifted with a voice, to second and confirm the counsel which thou hast heard. Speak out the name! That, and thy repentance, may avail to take the scarlet letter off thy breast."

"Never!" replied Hester Prynne, looking, not at Mr. Wilson, but into the deep and troubled eyes of the younger clergyman. "It is too deeply branded. Ye cannot take it off. And would that I might endure his agony, as well as mine!"

"Speak, woman!" said another voice,[16] coldly and sternly, proceeding from the crowd about the scaffold. "Speak; and give your child a father!"

"I will not speak!" answered Hester, turning pale as death, but responding to this voice, which she too surely recognized. "And my child must seek a heavenly Father; she shall never know an earthly one!"

"She will not speak!" murmured Mr. Dimmesdale, who, leaning over the balcony, with his hand upon his heart, had awaited the result of his appeal. He now drew back, with a long respiration. "Wondrous strength and generosity of a woman's heart! She will not speak!"

Hester has rescued Dimmesdale, her lover, from public shame, but not from private desperation. For the next seven years, Dimmesdale suffers, knowing his sinfulness and wearing on his own bare chest—Was it real? Or invisible? The work of magic?—a letter "A" that burned mercilessly. Seven years later, after the lovers have reunited and planned to go away together, he cannot execute the plan. He mounts the scaffold in the plain view of the multitude, confesses his sin, and dies. Chillingworth, who has hounded him in pursuit of his revenge, dies within the year, leaving his fortune to young Pearl. Hester and Pearl escape to the Old World, where Pearl, it is inferred, marries. Hester returns to her lonely cottage on the edge of town, by the sea.

The story of the scarlet letter grew into a legend. Its spell, however, was still potent, and kept the scaffold awful where the poor minister had died, and likewise the cottage by the sea-shore, where Hester Prynne had dwelt. Near this latter spot, one afternoon, some children were at play, when they beheld a tall woman, in a gray robe, approach the cottage-door. In all those years it had never once been opened; but either she unlocked it, or the decaying wood and iron yielded to her hand, or she glided shadow-like through these impediments,—and, at all events, went in.

On the threshold she paused,—turned partly round,—for, perchance, the idea of entering, all alone, and all so changed, the home of so intense a former life, was more dreary and desolate than even she could bear. But her hesitation was only for an instant, though long enough to display a scarlet letter on her breast.

And Hester Prynne had returned, and taken up her long-forsaken shame. But where was little Pearl? If still alive, she must now have been in the flush and bloom of early womanhood. None knew—nor ever learned, with the fulness of perfect certainty—whether [she] had gone thus untimely to a maiden grave; or whether her wild, rich nature had been softened and subdued, and made capable of a woman's gentle happiness. But, through the remainder of Hester's life, there were indications that the recluse of the scarlet letter was the object

---

16. another voice: Chillingworth's, demanding that his wife betray the adulterous father.

of love and interest with some inhabitant of another land. Letters came, with armorial seals upon them. . . . In the cottage there were articles of comfort and luxury, such as Hester never cared to use, but which only wealth could have purchased, and affection have imagined for her. There were trifles, too, little ornaments, . . . that must have been wrought by delicate fingers, at the impulse of a fond heart. And, once, Hester was seen embroidering a baby-garment, with such a lavish richness of golden fancy as would have raised a public tumult, had any infant, thus apparelled, been shown to our sombre-hued community.

In fine, the gossips of that day believed . . . that Pearl was not only alive, but married, and happy, and mindful of her mother. . . .

But there was a more real life for Hester Prynne, here, in New England, than in that unknown region where Pearl had found a home. Here had been her sin; here, her sorrow; and here was yet to be her penitence. She had returned, therefore, and resumed,—of her own free will, for not the sternest magistrate of that iron period would have imposed it,—resumed the symbol of which we have related so dark a tale. Never afterwards did it quit her bosom. . . .

2. Herman Melville, *Benito Cereno* (1855)

The excerpts below trace the ark of the unfathomable innocence of Captain Delano from his first arrival on board the Spanish ship until, pages short of the conclusion, the "scales dropped from his eyes" at last, and he sees the Africans "not in misrule, not in tumult, . . . but with mask torn away, flourishing hatchets and knives, in ferocious piratical revolt." He had been unwilling to recognize what was plainly visible: the inversion of what he and his contemporaries saw as the natural condition of the two races, with blacks subject to whites. His incomprehension anticipates the violence of America's imminent struggle in the Civil War and its aftermath.[17]

Benito Cereno

To Captain Delano's surprise, the stranger, viewed through the glass, showed no colors;[18] though to do so upon entering a haven, however uninhabited in its shores, where but a single other ship might be lying, was the custom among peaceful seamen of all nations. Considering the lawlessness and loneliness of the spot, and the sort of stories, at that day, associated with those seas, Captain

---

17. The original orthography, punctuation, and language choices of this 1856 edition are retained.

18. colors: a flag, identifying the ship's nation of origin.

Delano's surprise might have deepened into some uneasiness had he not been a person of a singularly undistrustful good-nature, not liable, except on extraordinary and repeated incentives, and hardly then, to indulge in personal alarms, any way involving the imputation of malign evil in man. . . .

Delano approaches the Spanish ship, the San Dominick, *in the* Rover, *a small whaleboat dispatched from the American ship, the* Bachelor's Delight.

Upon a still nigher approach, this appearance was modified, and the true character of the vessel was plain—a Spanish merchantman of the first class, carrying negro slaves, amongst other valuable freight, from one colonial port to another. A very large, and, in its time, a very fine vessel, such as in those days were at intervals encountered along that main. . . .

Climbing the side, the visitor was at once surrounded by a clamorous throng of whites and blacks, but the latter outnumbering the former more than could have been expected, negro transportation-ship as the stranger in port was. But, in one language, and as with one voice, all poured out a common tale of suffering; in which the negresses, of whom there were not a few, exceeded the others in their dolorous vehemence. The scurvy, together with the fever, had swept off a great part of their number, more especially the Spaniards. Off Cape Horn they had narrowly escaped shipwreck; then, for days together, they had lain tranced without wind; their provisions were low; their water next to none; their lips that moment were baked. . . .

Captain Delano observes groups of Africans, but as he tours the ship deck, he sees only a few white sailors. The occupants are haggard and dejected, starved for water and provisions. He turns "in quest of whomsoever it might be that commanded the ship." Its Spanish captain presents himself.

[T]he Spanish captain, a gentlemanly, reserved-looking, and rather young man to a stranger's eye, dressed with singular richness, but bearing plain traces of recent sleepless cares and disquietudes, stood passively by, leaning against the main-mast, at one moment casting a dreary, spiritless look upon his excited people, at the next an unhappy glance toward his visitor. By his side stood a black of small stature, in whose rude face, as occasionally, like a shepherd's dog, he mutely turned it up into the Spaniard's, sorrow and affection were equally blended.

Struggling through the throng, the American advanced to the Spaniard, assuring him of his sympathies, and offering to render whatever assistance might be in his power. To which the Spaniard returned for the present but grave and ceremonious acknowledgments, his national formality dusked by the saturnine mood of ill-health.

But losing no time in mere compliments, Captain Delano, returning to the gangway, had his basket of fish brought up; and . . . bade his men return to [his own ship] the sealer, and fetch back as much water as the whale-boat could carry, with whatever soft bread the steward might have, all the remaining pumpkins on board, with a box of sugar, and a dozen of his private bottles of cider. . . .

The Spanish captain, Don Benito Cereno, visibly fatigued and ill, is tended by his curiously attentive African servant Babo.

But the debility, constitutional or induced by hardships, bodily and mental, of the Spanish captain, was too obvious to be overlooked. . . . He was rather tall, but seemed never to have been robust, and now with nervous suffering was almost worn to a skeleton. A tendency to some pulmonary complaint appeared to have been lately confirmed. His voice was like that of one with lungs half gone—hoarsely suppressed, a husky whisper. No wonder that, as in this state he tottered about, his private servant apprehensively followed him. Sometimes the negro gave his master his arm, or took his handkerchief out of his pocket for him; . . . [a servant] whom a master need be on no stiffly superior terms with, but may treat with familiar trust; less a servant than a devoted companion. . . . [I]t was not without humane satisfaction that Captain Delano witnessed the steady good conduct of Babo. . . .

Neither were his thoughts taken up by the captain alone. . . . [T]he noisy confusion of the San Dominick's suffering host repeatedly challenged his eye. Some prominent breaches, not only of discipline but of decency, were observed. . . . What the San Dominick wanted was . . . stern superior officers. But on these decks not so much as a fourth-mate was to be seen. . . .

Engaging again with Don Benito, Captain Delano invites him to tell the whole story of his mishaps.

Don Benito faltered; then, like some somnambulist suddenly interfered with, vacantly stared at his visitor, and ended by looking down on the deck. He maintained this posture so long, that Captain Delano, . . . turned suddenly from him, walking forward to accost one of the Spanish seamen for the desired information. But he had hardly gone five paces, when . . . Don Benito invited him back, regretting his momentary absence of mind, and professing readiness to gratify him.

While most part of the story was being given, the two captains stood on the after part of the main-deck, a privileged spot, no one being near but the servant [Babo]. . . .

The San Dominick, *190 days before, had sailed from Buenos Aires [Argentina] bound for Lima [Peru], well-manned, with passengers, a full cargo, and some three hundred African slaves managed by the slavetrader Alexandro Aranda. They met with heavy gales off Cape Horn, at South America's southern tip, as a result of which they lost some seamen and were forced to off-load some supplies. There followed a deadly contagion, which killed all the officers and many seamen, the slave-trader Aranda, and some slaves. Then the ship stalled in a calm. Don Benito recounts these details with difficulty, interrupted by fits of coughing and as though in a haze. Babo, he concludes, had kept order on the ship and saved his life.*

"But it is Babo here to whom, under God, I owe not only my own preservation, but likewise to him, chiefly, the merit is due, of pacifying his more ignorant brethren, when at intervals tempted to murmurings."

"Ah, master," sighed the black, bowing his face, "don't speak of me; Babo is nothing; what Babo has done was but duty."

"Faithful fellow!" cried Captain Delano. "Don Benito, I envy you such a friend; slave I cannot call him." . . .

Having heard Don Benito's story, Captain Delano again promises assistance.

Captain Delano, having heard out his story, not only engaged, as in the first place, to see Don Benito and his people supplied in their immediate bodily needs, but, also, now farther promised to assist him in procuring a large permanent supply of water, as well as some sails and rigging . . . so that without delay the ship might proceed to Conception [Concepción, Peru], there fully to refit for Lima, her destined port.

Such generosity was not without its effect, even upon the invalid. His face lighted up; eager and hectic, he met the honest glance of his visitor. With gratitude he seemed overcome.

"This excitement is bad for master," whispered the servant, taking his arm, and with soothing words gently drawing him aside. . . .

Captain Delano further observes very odd behavior by groups of the Africans, as well as instances of insubordination, including an assault on some of the Spanish sailors that went unpunished—a hint of gross disorder in the management of the ship. Delano begins to suspect some grave disorder: Was the captain mad? Or was there some evil afoot?

The singular alternations of courtesy and ill-breeding in the Spanish captain were unaccountable, except on one of two suppositions—innocent lunacy, or wicked imposture.

But the first idea, though it might naturally have occurred to an indifferent observer, and, in some respect, had not hitherto been wholly a stranger to Captain Delano's mind, yet, now that . . . , he began to regard the stranger's conduct something in the light of an intentional affront, of course the idea of lunacy was virtually vacated. But if not a lunatic, what then? Under the circumstances, would a gentleman . . . act the part now acted by his host? The man was an impostor. Some low-born adventurer, masquerading as an oceanic grandee. . . .

But the Cereno family was well known and of high repute, so Captain Delano rejects the notion of imposture, and assures himself that the captain "was a true off-shoot of a true hidalgo [aristocratic] Cereno." At that point, Don Benito approaches and asks some odd and disturbing questions.

"Señor, may I ask how long you have lain at this isle?"

"Oh, but a day or two, Don Benito."

"And from what port are you last?"

"Canton [China]."

"And there, Señor, you exchanged your sealskins for teas and silks, I think you said?"

"Yes, Silks, mostly."

"And the balance you took in specie, perhaps?"

Captain Delano, fidgeting a little, answered—

"Yes; some silver; not a very great deal, though."

"Ah—well. May I ask how many men have you, Señor?"

Captain Delano slightly started, but answered—

"About five-and-twenty, all told."

"And at present, Señor, all on board, I suppose?"

"All on board, Don Benito," replied the Captain, now with satisfaction.

"And will be to-night, Señor?"

At this last question, following so many pertinacious ones, for the soul of him Captain Delano could not but look very earnestly at the questioner, who, instead of meeting the glance, with every token of craven discomposure dropped his eyes to the deck; presenting an unworthy contrast to his servant, who, just then, was kneeling at his feet, adjusting a loose shoe-buckle; his disengaged face meantime, with humble curiosity, turned openly up into his master's downcast one. . . .

"Your ships generally go—go more or less armed, I believe, Señor?"

"Oh, a six-pounder or two, in case of emergency," was the intrepidly indifferent reply, "with a small stock of muskets, sealing-spears, and cutlasses, you know." . . .

Captain Delano, having observed some more cases of odd behavior among the sailors and African passengers, looks over at Don Benito and Babo, deep in conversation.

They had the air of conspirators. In connection with the late questionings, . . . these things now begat such return of involuntary suspicion, that the singular guilelessness of the American could not endure it. Plucking up a gay and humorous expression, he crossed over to the two rapidly, saying:—"Ha, Don Benito, your black here seems high in your trust; a sort of privy-counselor, in fact."

Upon this, the servant looked up with a good-natured grin, but the master started as from a venomous bite. It was a moment or two before the

Spaniard sufficiently recovered himself to reply; which he did, at last, with cold constraint:—"Yes, Señor, I have trust in Babo."

Here Babo, changing his previous grin of mere animal humor into an intelligent smile, not ungratefully eyed his master.

Finding that the Spaniard now stood silent and reserved. . . , Captain Delano, unwilling to appear uncivil even to incivility itself, made some trivial remark and moved off; again and again turning over in his mind the mysterious demeanor of Don Benito Cereno. . . .

He recalled the Spaniard's manner while telling his story. There was a gloomy hesitancy and subterfuge about it. It was just the manner of one making up his tale for evil purposes, as he goes. But if that story was not true, what was the truth? . . .

But those questions of the Spaniard. There, indeed, one might pause. Did they not seem put with much the same object with which the burglar or assassin, by day-time, reconnoitres the walls of a house? . . .

But once again, Captain Delano refuses to think the worst—until further strange events deepen his suspicions. At this moment, the whaleboat Rover *arrives with supplies. Delano invites Don Benito back to his own ship, but the Spaniard declines. Delano's sealer approaches the San Dominick and the two ships are anchored together. Delano moves to return to his own ship, and Don Benito, disturbed, grabs his hand and makes an anguished farewell.*

Waiting a moment for the Spaniard to relinquish his hold, the now embarrassed Captain Delano lifted his foot, to overstep the threshold of the open gangway; but still Don Benito would not let go his hand. And yet, with an agitated tone, he said, "I can go no further; here I must bid you adieu. Adieu, my dear, dear Don Amasa. Go—go!" suddenly tearing his hand loose, "go, and God guard you better than me, my best friend."

Not unaffected, Captain Delano would now have lingered; but catching the meekly admonitory eye of the servant, with a hasty farewell he descended into his boat, followed by the continual adieus of Don Benito, standing rooted in the gangway.

Seating himself in the stern, Captain Delano, making a last salute, ordered the boat shoved off. The crew had their oars on end. The bowsmen pushed the boat a sufficient distance for the oars to be lengthwise dropped. The instant that was done, Don Benito sprang over the bulwarks, falling at the feet of Captain Delano. . . .

Don Benito's impetuous and astonishing leap into the whaleboat sets off a struggle. Some of the Spanish sailors jump from the ship and swim toward the boat, while the Africans onboard brandish arms—among them Babo who, dagger in hand, jumps into the whaleboat after Don Benito, intent on slaying him before he can escape.

That moment, across the long benighted mind of Captain Delano, a flash of revelation swept, illuminating, in unanticipated clearness, his host's whole mysterious demeanor, with every enigmatic event of the day, as well as the entire past voyage of the *San Dominick.* He smote Babo's hand down, but his own heart smote him harder. With infinite pity he withdrew his hold from Don Benito. Not Captain Delano, but Don Benito, the black, in leaping into the boat, had intended to stab.[19]

Both the black's hands were held, as, glancing up towards the *San Dominick,* Captain Delano, now with scales dropped from his eyes, saw the negroes, not in misrule, not in tumult, not as if frantically concerned for Don Benito, but with mask torn away, flourishing hatchets and knives, in ferocious piratical revolt. . . .

Safely back with Don Benito on his own ship and with Babo held captive, Captain Delano counterattacks, sending out his small boats with armed sailors to board and subdue the San Dominick. *The ship taken, Don Benito and the prisoners are brought to Lima in Peru, where an investigation ensues and the Spanish captain gives a full deposition of the mutiny that had seized his ship. Babo is executed; and Don Benito, who has retired to a monastery, soon dies.*

3. Harriet Beecher Stowe, *Uncle Tom's Cabin* (1852)

Triggering the plot of *Uncle Tom's Cabin* is the decision of the slaveholder Shelby, pressed by financial difficulties, to sell to Haley, a slavetrader, two of his slaves: the beloved Uncle Tom, elderly and sweet-tempered, and the toddler Harry, never before separated from his mother, Eliza—who had previously given birth to two children, both dead and buried on the plantation, and whose slave husband, fearing his own impending sale, had fled to the free state of Ohio. Whereas Tom accepted his fate, leaving his beloved family with the consolation that the same God would reign wherever he was sent, Eliza could not. Her escape with Harry, told in the selections that follow, is one of the most dramatic and heart-wrenching episodes of a novel that is full of tragic and stirring moments.[20]

---

19. Delano had feared that Babo was attacking him, but now realizes that the intended target was Don Benito.

20. The text has been emended to correct orthography and punctuation, with the quoted dialect passages lightly altered for readability and with modern equivalents given in brackets in some cases.

UNCLE TOM'S CABIN

Chapter 7: The Mother's Struggle

It is impossible to conceive of a human creature more wholly desolate and for-lorn than Eliza, when she turned her footsteps from Uncle Tom's cabin.

Her husband's suffering and dangers, and the danger of her child, all blended in her mind, with a confused and stunning sense of the risk she was running, in leaving the only home she had ever known, and cutting loose from the protection of a friend whom she loved and revered. Then there was the part-ing from every familiar object,—the place where she had grown up, the trees under which she had played, the groves where she had walked many an evening in happier days, by the side of her young husband,—everything, as it lay in the clear, frosty starlight, seemed to speak reproachfully to her, and ask her whither could she go from a home like that?

But stronger than all was maternal love, wrought into a paroxysm of frenzy by the near approach of a fearful danger. Her boy was old enough to have walked by her side, and, in an indifferent case, she would only have led him by the hand; but now the bare thought of putting him out of her arms made her shudder, and she strained him to her bosom with a convulsive grasp, as she went rapidly forward.

The frosty ground creaked beneath her feet, and she trembled at the sound; every quaking leaf and fluttering shadow sent the blood backward to her heart, and quickened her footsteps. She wondered within herself at the strength that seemed to be come upon her; for she felt the weight of her boy as if it had been a feather, and every flutter of fear seemed to increase the supernatural power that bore her on. . . .

If it were *your* Harry, mother, or your Willie, that were going to be torn from you by a brutal trader, tomorrow morning—if you had seen the man, and heard that the papers were signed and delivered, and you had only from twelve o'clock till morning to make good your escape—how fast could *you* walk? How many miles could you make in those few brief hours, with the darling at your bosom—the little sleepy head on your shoulder—the small, soft arms trust-ingly holding on to your neck?[21]

For the child slept. At first, the novelty and alarm kept him waking; but his mother so hurriedly repressed every breath or sound, and so assured him that if he were only still she would certainly save him, that he clung quietly round her neck, only asking, as he found himself sinking to sleep,

"Mother, I don't need to keep awake, do I?"

---

21. In this paragraph, Stowe makes a direct appeal to contemporary mothers, a digression announcing that her story is written not just to entertain, but also to persuade to action.

"No, my darling; sleep, if you want to."

"But, mother, if I do get asleep, you won't let him get me?"

"No! so may God help me!" said his mother, with a paler cheek, and a brighter light in her large dark eyes.

"You're *sure*, an't [aren't] you, mother?"

"Yes, *sure!*" said the mother, in a voice that startled herself; for it seemed to her to come from a spirit within, that was no part of her; and the boy dropped his little weary head on her shoulder, and was soon asleep. How the touch of those warm arms, the gentle breathings that came in her neck, seemed to add fire and spirit to her movements! It seemed to her as if strength poured into her in electric streams, from every gentle touch and movement of the sleeping, confiding child. . . .

The boundaries of the farm, the grove, the wood-lot, passed by her dizzily, as she walked on; and still she went, leaving one familiar object after another, slacking not, pausing not, till reddening daylight found her many a long mile from all traces of any familiar objects upon the open highway.

She had often been, with her mistress, to visit some connections, in the little village of T——, not far from the Ohio river,[22] and knew the road well. To go thither, to escape across the Ohio river, were the first hurried outlines of her plan of escape; beyond that, she could only hope in God.

When horses and vehicles began to move along the highway, . . . she became aware that her headlong pace and distracted air might bring on her remark and suspicion. She therefore put the boy on the ground, and, adjusting her dress and bonnet, she walked on at as rapid a pace as she thought consistent with the preservation of appearances. In her little bundle she had provided a store of cakes and apples, which she used as expedients for quickening the speed of the child, rolling the apple some yards before them, when the boy would run with all his might after it. . . .

After a while, they came to a thick patch of woodland, through which murmured a clear brook. As the child complained of hunger and thirst, she climbed over the fence with him; and, sitting down behind a large rock which concealed them from the road, she gave him a breakfast out of her little package. The boy wondered and grieved that she could not eat; and when, putting his arms round her neck, he tried to wedge some of his cake into her mouth, it seemed to her that the rising in her throat would choke her.

"No, no, Harry darling! Mother can't eat till you are safe! We must go on—on—till we come to the river!" And she hurried again into the road, and again constrained herself to walk regularly and composedly forward.

She was many miles past any neighborhood where she was personally known. If she should chance to meet any who knew her, she reflected that

---

22. The Ohio River separated Kentucky, a slave state, from Ohio, a free state.

the well-known kindness of the family would be of itself a blind to suspicion, as making it an unlikely supposition that she could be a fugitive. As she was also so white as not to be known as of colored lineage, without a critical survey, and her child was white also, it was much easier for her to pass on unsuspected.[23] . . .

An hour before sunset, she entered the village of T——, by the Ohio river, weary and footsore, but still strong in heart. Her first glance was at the river, which lay, like Jordan, between her and the Canaan of liberty on the other side.[24]

It was now early spring, and the river was swollen and turbulent; great cakes of floating ice were swinging heavily to and fro in the turbid waters. Owing to the peculiar form of the shore on the Kentucky side, the land bending far out into the water, the ice had been lodged and detained in great quantities, and the narrow channel which swept round the bend was full of ice, piled one cake over another, thus forming a temporary barrier to the descending ice, which lodged, and formed a great, undulating raft, filling up the whole river, and extending almost to the Kentucky shore.

Eliza stood, for a moment, contemplating this unfavorable aspect of things, which she saw at once must prevent the usual ferryboat from running, and then turned into a small public house on the bank, to make a few inquiries.

The hostess, who was busy in various fizzing and stewing operations over the fire, preparatory to the evening meal, stopped, with a fork in her hand, as Eliza's sweet and plaintive voice arrested her.

"What is it?" she said.

"Isn't there any ferry or boat, that takes people over to B——, now?" she said.

"No, indeed!" said the woman; "the boats has stopped running."

Eliza's look of dismay and disappointment struck the woman, and she said, inquiringly,

"May be you're wanting to get over?—anybody sick? Ye [you] seem mighty anxious?"

"I've got a child that's very dangerous,"[25] said Eliza. "I never heard of it till last night, and I've walked quite a piece today, in hopes to get to the ferry."

"Well, now, that's unlucky," said the woman, whose motherly sympathies were much aroused; "I'm re'lly consarned for ye. Solomon!" she called, from

---

23. Eliza was a mulatto, half-black, half-white; and Harry's father was also of mixed race; Harry inherited their lighter skin color.

24. A biblical allusion; the Hebrew people fleeing Egypt as told in Exodus, the second book of the Hebrew Bible, would cross the Jordan River to come to Canaan, the land God had promised them.

25. dangerous: ill; or so Eliza describes him, so as to explain her urgency.

the window, towards a small back building. A man, in leather apron and very dirty hands, appeared at the door.

"I say, Sol," said the woman, "is that ar [there] man going to tote them bar'ls [barrels] over tonight?"

"He said he should try, if it was any way prudent," said the man.

"There's a man a piece down here, that's going over with some truck this evening, if he durs' [dares] to; he'll be in here to supper tonight, so you'd better set down and wait. That's a sweet little fellow," added the woman, offering him a cake.

But the child, wholly exhausted, cried with weariness.

"Poor fellow! he isn't used to walking, and I've hurried him on so," said Eliza.

"Well, take him into this room," said the woman, opening into a small bed-room, where stood a comfortable bed. Eliza laid the weary boy upon it, and held his hands in hers till he was fast asleep. For her there was no rest. As a fire in her bones, the thought of the pursuer urged her on; and she gazed with longing eyes on the sullen, surging waters that lay between her and liberty. . . .

In consequence of all the various delays, it was about three-quarters of an hour after Eliza had laid her child to sleep in the village tavern that the party [group] came riding into the same place. Eliza was standing by the window. . . [when] the whole train swept by the window, round to the front door.

A thousand lives seemed to be concentrated in that one moment to Eliza. Her room opened by a side door to the river. She caught her child, and sprang down the steps towards it. The trader caught a full glimpse of her just as she was disappearing down the bank; and throwing himself from his horse, . . . he was after her like a hound after a deer. In that dizzy moment her feet to her scarce seemed to touch the ground, and a moment brought her to the water's edge. Right on behind they came; and, nerved with strength such as God gives only to the desperate, with one wild cry and flying leap, she vaulted sheer over the turbid current by the shore, on to the raft of ice beyond. It was a desperate leap—impossible to anything but madness and despair; and [her pursuers], Haley, Sam, and Andy,[26] instinctively cried out, and lifted up their hands, as she did it.

The huge green fragment of ice on which she alighted pitched and creaked as her weight came on it, but she stayed there not a moment. With wild cries and desperate energy she leaped to another and still another cake; stumbling—leaping—slipping—springing upwards again! Her shoes are gone—her stockings cut from her feet—while blood marked every step; but she saw nothing, felt nothing, till dimly, as in a dream, she saw the Ohio side, and a man helping her up the bank.

---

26. Haley: the slavetrader; Sam and Andy: Shelby's slaves.

"Yer [you're] a brave gal, now, whoever ye ar [are]!" said the man, with an oath.

Eliza recognized the voice and face for a man who owned a farm not far from her old home.

"O, Mr. Symmes!—save me—do save me—do hide me!" said Eliza.

"Why, what's this?" said the man. "Why, if 'tan't [it isn't] Shelby's gal [girl, i.e., slave]!"

"My child!—this boy!—he'd sold him! There is his Mas'r, [Master]" said she, pointing to the Kentucky shore. "O, Mr. Symmes, you've got a little boy!"

"So I have," said the man, as he roughly, but kindly, drew her up the steep bank. "Besides, you're a right brave gal. I like grit, wherever I see it."

When they had gained the top of the bank, the man paused.

"I'd be glad to do something for ye," said he; "but then there's nowhar [nowhere] I could take ye. The best I can do is to tell ye to go *thar* [*there*]," said he, pointing to a large white house which stood by itself, off the main street of the village. "Go thar; they're kind folks. Thar's no kind o' [of] danger but they'll help you,—they're up to all that sort o' thing."

"The Lord bless you!" said Eliza, earnestly.

"No 'casion [occasion], no 'casion in the world," said the man. "What I've done's of no 'count [account]."

"And, oh, surely, sir, you won't tell any one!"

"Go to thunder, gal! What do you take a feller [fellow] for? In course not," said the man. "Come, now, go along like a likely, sensible gal, as you are. You've arnt [earned] your liberty, and you shall have it, for all me."[27]

The woman folded her child to her bosom, and walked firmly and swiftly away. The man stood and looked after her.

"Shelby, now, mebbe [maybe] won't think this yer [you're] the most neighborly thing in the world; but what's a feller to do? If he catches one of my gals in the same fix, he's welcome to pay back. Somehow I never could see no kind o' critter a strivin' and pantin', and trying to clar [clear] theirselves, with the dogs arter [after] 'em [them] and go agin 'em. Besides, I don't see no kind of 'casion for me to be hunter and catcher for other folks, neither."

So spoke this poor, heathenish Kentuckian, who had not been instructed in his constitutional relations, and consequently was betrayed into acting in a sort of Christianized manner, which, if he had been better situated and more enlightened, he would not have been left to do.[28]

Eliza has escaped to Ohio, where eventually she will be reunited with her husband, and the family will make their way to Canada and freedom—and from there

---

27. for all me: for my part, so far as I am concerned.

28. Stowe suggests that this plain, ordinary man has behaved like a true Christian—and a constitutional scholar—when he has no formal knowledge of such ideologies.

to Liberia.[29] *Meanwhile, Sam and Andy return to the plantation. Sam tells the Shelbys that he had seen Eliza "with my own eyes, a crossin' on the floatin' ice," and that she and the child were now safely in Ohio.*

4. Frederick Douglass, *What to the Slave Is the Fourth of July?* (1852)

Douglass opens his speech, delivered one day after the celebration of the seventy-sixth anniversary of American independence, with cordial words for those who had opposed the tyranny of Britain. They were "brave men," who "preferred revolution to peaceful submission to bondage." But in the central section of his address, from which excerpts follow, he pivots to "the present" and the reality of slavery. He asks: "Are the great principles of political freedom and of natural justice, embodied in that Declaration of Independence, extended to us?" They are not. For the slave, the Fourth of July is "a day that reveals to him, more than all other days in the year, the gross injustice and cruelty to which he is the constant victim." In its continued embrace of slavery, "for revolting barbarity and shameless hypocrisy, America reigns without a rival."

With that incendiary claim these general statements conclude and in the remainder of his speech, Douglass turns to specifics. He deplores the slave trade that still goes on within American borders and the hypocrisy of the churches, which defend slaveholding and deny slaves the religious freedom that they had fought to gain for themselves. The fault is not with the Constitution, which Douglass views as a "glorious liberty document," but with Americans who have not yet realized its ideals. "I do not despair of this country," Douglass closes optimistically, for "the doom of slavery is certain."[30]

WHAT TO THE SLAVE IS THE FOURTH OF JULY?

Fellow-citizens, pardon me, allow me to ask, why am I called upon to speak here to-day? What have I, or those I represent, to do with your national independence? Are the great principles of political freedom and of natural justice, embodied in that Declaration of Independence, extended to us? and am I, therefore, called upon to bring our humble offering to the national altar, and to confess the benefits and express devout gratitude for the blessings resulting from your independence to us?

---

29. Liberia: an African state on the Atlantic coast established by freed American slaves.
30. Minor emendations are made to this original nineteenth-century text.

Would to God, both for your sakes and ours, that an affirmative answer could be truthfully returned to these questions! Then would my task be light, and my burden easy and delightful. . . . But, such is not the state of the case. I say it with a sad sense of the disparity between us. I am not included within the pale of this glorious anniversary! Your high independence only reveals the immeasurable distance between us. . . . The rich inheritance of justice, liberty, prosperity and independence, bequeathed by your fathers, is shared by you, not by me. The sunlight that brought life and healing to you, has brought stripes and death to me. This Fourth of July is yours, not mine. You may rejoice, I must mourn. To drag a man in fetters into the grand illuminated temple of liberty, and call upon him to join you in joyous anthems, were inhuman mockery and sacrilegious irony. Do you mean, citizens, to mock me, by asking me to speak to-day? If so, there is a parallel to your conduct. And let me warn you that it is dangerous to copy the example of a nation whose crimes, lowering up to heaven, were thrown down by the breath of the Almighty, burying that nation in irrecoverable ruin! I can today take up the plaintive lament of a [fallen] and woe-smitten people![31] . . .

Fellow-citizens; above your national, tumultuous joy, I hear the mournful wail of millions! whose chains, heavy and grievous yesterday, are, today, rendered more intolerable by the jubilee shouts that reach them. . . . My subject, then fellow-citizens, is AMERICAN SLAVERY. I shall see, this day, and its popular characteristics, from the slave's point of view. Standing, there, identified with the American bondman, making his wrongs mine, I do not hesitate to declare, with all my soul, that the character and conduct of this nation never looked blacker to me than on this Fourth of July! Whether we turn to the declarations of the past, or to the professions of the present, the conduct of the nation seems equally hideous and revolting. America is false to the past, false to the present, and solemnly binds herself to be false to the future. Standing with God and the crushed and bleeding slave on this occasion, I will, in the name of humanity which is outraged, in the name of liberty which is fettered, in the name of the constitution and the Bible, which are disregarded and trampled upon, dare to call in question and to denounce, with all the emphasis I can command, everything that serves to perpetuate slavery—the great sin and shame of America! "I will not equivocate; I will not excuse;" I will use the severest language I can command; and yet not one word shall escape me that any man,[32] whose judgment is not blinded by prejudice, or who is not at heart a slaveholder, shall not confess to be right and just.

---

31. Douglass alludes to the Babylonian Captivity of the sixth century BCE, when after God allowed the conquest of Jerusalem, the Jewish leaders of the Kingdom of Judah were sent into exile for a period of, according to tradition, seventy years.

32. any man: as was common in his day and until recent times, Douglass uses "man" to mean "person" or "human being," and "manhood" to mean "humanity."

But I fancy I hear some one of my audience say, it is just in this circumstance that you and your brother abolitionists fail to make a favorable impression on the public mind. Would you argue more, and denounce less, would you persuade more, and rebuke less, your cause would be much more likely to succeed. But, I submit, where all is plain there is nothing to be argued. What point in the anti-slavery creed would you have me argue? On what branch of the subject do the people of this country need light? Must I undertake to prove that the slave is a man? That point is conceded already. Nobody doubts it. The slaveholders themselves acknowledge it in the enactment of laws for their government. They acknowledge it when they punish disobedience on the part of the slave. There are seventy-two crimes in the State of Virginia, which, if committed by a black man (no matter how ignorant he be), subject him to the punishment of death; while only two of the same crimes will subject a white man to the like punishment. What is this but the acknowledgement that the slave is a moral, intellectual and responsible being? The manhood of the slave is conceded. It is admitted in the fact that Southern statute books are covered with enactments forbidding, under severe fines and penalties, the teaching of the slave to read or to write. When you can point to any such laws, in reference to the beasts of the field, then I may consent to argue the manhood of the slave. When the dogs in your streets, when the fowls of the air, when the cattle on your hills, when the fish of the sea, and the reptiles that crawl, shall be unable to distinguish the slave from a brute, there will I argue with you that the slave is a man!

For the present, it is enough to affirm the equal manhood of the Negro race.[33] Is it not astonishing that, while we are plowing, planting and reaping, using all kinds of mechanical tools, erecting houses, constructing bridges, building ships, working in metals of brass, iron, copper, silver and gold; that, while we are reading, writing and cyphering, acting as clerks, merchants and secretaries, having among us lawyers, doctors, ministers, poets, authors, editors, orators and teachers; that, while we are engaged in all manner of enterprises common to other men, digging gold in California, capturing the whale in the Pacific, feeding sheep and cattle on the hillside, living, moving, acting, thinking, planning, living in families as husbands, wives and children, and, above all, confessing and worshipping the Christian's God, and looking hopefully for life and immortality beyond the grave, we are called upon to prove that we are men!

Would you have me argue that man is entitled to liberty? That he is the rightful owner of his own body? You have already declared it. Must I argue the

---

33. Negro race: the term "Negro" (which means "black" in Spanish among other languages) was generally used until the 1970s to denote persons of African ancestry and was current in Douglass's day, although in the contemporary United States, the terms "Black" or "African American" are more commonly used.

wrongfulness of slavery? Is that a question for Republicans?[34] Is it to be settled
by the rules of logic and argumentation, as a matter beset with great difficulty,
involving a doubtful application of the principle of justice, hard to be understood? How should I look today, in the presence of Americans, dividing, and
subdividing a discourse, to show that men have a natural right to freedom?
Speaking of it relatively, and positively, negatively, and affirmatively. To do so,
would be to make myself ridiculous, and to offer an insult to your understanding. There is not a man beneath the canopy of heaven who does not know that
slavery is wrong for him.

What, am I to argue that it is wrong to make men brutes, to rob them
of their liberty, to work them without wages, to keep them ignorant of their
relations to their fellow men, to beat them with sticks, to flay their flesh with
the lash, to load their limbs with irons, to hunt them with dogs, to sell them at
auction, to sunder their families, to knock out their teeth, to burn their flesh,
to starve them into obedience and submission to their masters? Must I argue
that a system thus marked with blood, and stained with pollution, is wrong?
No! I will not. I have better employments for my time and strength, than such
arguments would imply. . . .

At a time like this, scorching irony, not convincing argument, is needed.
O! had I the ability, and could I reach the nation's ear, I would, today, pour out
a fiery stream of biting ridicule, blasting reproach, withering sarcasm, and stern
rebuke. For it is not light that is needed, but fire; it is not the gentle shower,
but thunder. We need the storm, the whirlwind, and the earthquake. The feeling of the nation must be quickened; the conscience of the nation must be
roused; the propriety of the nation must be startled; the hypocrisy of the nation
must be exposed; and its crimes against God and man must be proclaimed and
denounced.

What, to the American slave, is your Fourth of July? I answer: a day that
reveals to him, more than all other days in the year, the gross injustice and
cruelty to which he is the constant victim. To him, your celebration is a sham;
your boasted liberty, an unholy license; your national greatness, swelling vanity; your sounds of rejoicing are empty and heartless; your denunciations of
tyrants, brass fronted impudence; your shouts of liberty and equality, hollow
mockery; your prayers and hymns, your sermons and thanksgivings, with all
your religious parade and solemnity, are, to him, mere bombast, fraud, deception, impiety, and hypocrisy—a thin veil to cover up crimes which would disgrace a nation of savages. There is not a nation on the earth guilty of practices,
more shocking and bloody, than are the people of these United States, at this
very hour.

---

34. Republicans: Douglass means citizens of a republic, as the United States was and is, and not
members of a particular political party.

Go where you may, search where you will, roam through all the monarchies and despotisms of the old world, travel through South America, search
out every abuse, and when you have found the last, lay your facts by the side of
the everyday practices of this nation, and you will say with me, that, for revolting barbarity and shameless hypocrisy, America reigns without a rival.

5. Henry David Thoreau, *Walden* (1854)

Thoreau goes into the woods to make himself a home. He lays out the land,
sited by a clear pond, dividing it into orchard, wood, and pasture, and choosing
which trees should remain standing by his door—and then does no more:
"[F]or a man is rich in proportion to the number of things which he can afford to
let alone." He had gone into the woods because he "wished to live deliberately,
to front only the essential facts of life, and see if I could not learn what it had to
teach, and not, when I came to die, discover that I had not lived." He had no
need of a post office to deliver useless messages, or of a newspaper to tell him
news that did not matter, or a railroad to speed him to places he need not go.
We can do without these, Thoreau proposes, and instead thrust our feet down
into "the mud and slush of opinion, and prejudice, and tradition, and delusion,
and appearance, . . . till we come to a hard bottom and rocks in place, which
we can call *reality*, and say, This is, and no mistake; and then begin. . . ." And
there he stayed, for two years, two months, and two days, becoming the hermit
saint of the American tradition.[35]

WALDEN

Where I Lived, and What I Lived For

At a certain season of our life we are accustomed to consider every spot as the
possible site of a house. I have thus surveyed the country on every side within
a dozen miles of where I live. In imagination I have bought all the farms in
succession, for all were to be bought, and I knew their price. . . . Well, there
I might live, I said; and there I did live, for an hour, a summer and a winter
life; saw how I could let the years run off, buffet the winter through, and see
the spring come in. . . . An afternoon sufficed to lay out the land into orchard,
woodlot, and pasture, and to decide what fine oaks or pines should be left to
stand before the door, and whence each blasted tree could be seen to the best

---

35. Minor emendations are made to this original nineteenth-century text.

advantage; and then I let it lie, fallow perchance, for a man is rich in proportion to the number of things which he can afford to let alone. . . .

The real attractions of the Hollowell farm, to me, were; its complete retirement, being, about two miles from the village, half a mile from the nearest neighbor, and separated from the highway by a broad field; its bounding on the river, which the owner said protected it by its fogs from frosts in the spring, though that was nothing to me; the gray color and ruinous state of the house and barn, and the dilapidated fences, which put such an interval between me and the last occupant; the hollow and lichen-covered apple trees, gnawed by rabbits, showing what kind of neighbors I should have; but above all, the recollection I had of it from my earliest voyages up the river, when the house was concealed behind a dense grove of red maples, through which I heard the house-dog bark. . . .

When first I took up my abode in the woods, that is, began to spend my nights as well as days there, which, by accident, was on Independence Day, or the Fourth of July, 1845, my house was not finished for winter, but was merely a defense against the rain, without plastering or chimney, the walls being of rough, weather-stained boards, with wide chinks, which made it cool at night. The upright white hewn studs and freshly planed door and window casings gave it a clean and airy look, especially in the morning, when its timbers were saturated with dew, so that I fancied that by noon some sweet gum would exude from them. . . . This was an airy and unplastered cabin, fit to entertain a travelling god, and where a goddess might trail her garments. The winds which passed over my dwelling were such as sweep over the ridges of mountains, bearing the broken strains, or celestial parts only, of terrestrial music. . . .

I was seated by the shore of a small pond, about a mile and a half south of the village of Concord and somewhat higher than it, in the midst of an extensive wood between that town and Lincoln, and about two miles south of that our only field known to fame, Concord Battle Ground.[36] . . . This small lake was of most value as a neighbor in the intervals of a gentle rain storm in August, when, both air and water being perfectly still, but the sky overcast, mid-afternoon had all the serenity of evening, and the wood-thrush sang around, and was heard from shore to shore. A lake like this is never smoother than at such a time; and the clear portion of the air above it being shallow and darkened by clouds, the water, full of light and reflections, becomes a lower heaven itself so much the more important. . . .

Every morning was a cheerful invitation to make my life of equal simplicity, and I may say innocence, with Nature herself. . . . That man who does not believe that each day contains an earlier, more sacred, and auroral hour than he has yet profaned, has despaired of life, and is pursuing a descending and

---

36. Concord Battle Ground: one of the sites of the first battles against Britain fought in 1775, preliminary to the American Revolution.

darkening way. . . . Why is it that men give so poor an account of their day if they have not been slumbering? They are not such poor calculators. If they had not been overcome with drowsiness, they would have performed something. The millions are awake enough for physical labor; but only one in a million is awake enough for effective intellectual exertion, only one in a hundred millions to a poetic or divine life. To be awake is to be alive. I have never yet met a man who was quite awake. How could I have looked him in the face? . . .

I went to the woods because I wished to live deliberately, to front only the essential facts of life, and see if I could not learn what it had to teach, and not, when I came to die, discover that I had not lived. I did not wish to live what was not life, living is so dear; nor did I wish to practice resignation, unless it was quite necessary. I wanted to live deep and suck out all the marrow of life, . . . to drive life into a corner, and reduce it to its lowest terms, and, if it proved to be mean, why then to get the whole and genuine meanness of it, and publish its meanness to the world; or if it were sublime, to know it by experience, and be able to give a true account of it in my next excursion. . . .

Our life is frittered away by detail. An honest man has hardly need to count more than his ten fingers, or in extreme cases he may add his ten toes, and lump the rest. Simplicity, simplicity, simplicity! I say, let your affairs be as two or three, and not a hundred or a thousand; instead of a million count half a dozen, and keep your accounts on your thumb nail. . . . Simplify, simplify. Instead of three meals a day, if it be necessary eat but one; instead of a hundred dishes, five; and reduce other things in proportion. . . . Men think that it is essential that the *Nation* have commerce, and export ice, and talk through a telegraph, and ride thirty miles an hour . . . ; but whether we should live like baboons or like men, is a little uncertain. If we do not get out sleepers, and forge rails, and devote days and nights to the work, but go to tinkering upon our *lives* to improve *them*, who will build railroads? And if railroads are not built, how shall we get to heaven in season? But if we stay at home and mind our business, who will want railroads? We do not ride on the railroad; it rides upon us. . . .

For my part, I could easily do without the post-office. I think that there are very few important communications made through it. To speak critically, I never received more than one or two letters in my life—I wrote this some years ago—that were worth the postage. . . . And I am sure that I never read any memorable news in a newspaper. If we read of one man robbed, or murdered, or killed by accident, or one house burned, or one vessel wrecked, or one steamboat blown up, or one cow run over on the Western Railroad, or one mad dog killed, or one lot of grasshoppers in the winter,—we never need read of another. One is enough. . . . [A]nd as for England, almost the last significant scrap of news from that quarter was the revolution of 1649. . . . If one may judge who rarely looks into the newspapers, nothing new does ever happen in foreign parts, a French revolution not excepted. . . .

Let us spend one day as deliberately as Nature, and not be thrown off the track by every nutshell and mosquito's wing that falls on the rails. . . . Why should we knock under and go with the stream? . . . Let us settle ourselves, and work and wedge our feet downward through the mud and slush of opinion, and prejudice, and tradition, and delusion, and appearance, that allusion which covers the globe, . . . till we come to a hard bottom and rocks in place, which we can call *reality*, and say, This is, and no mistake; and then begin. . . . If you stand right fronting and face-to-face to a fact, you will see the sun glimmer on both its surfaces, . . . and feel its sweet edge dividing you through the heart and marrow, and so you will happily conclude your mortal career. Be it life or death, we crave only reality. If we are really dying, let us hear the rattle in our throats and feel cold in the extremities; if we are alive, let us go about our business.

Time is but the stream I go a-fishing in. I drink at it; but while I drink I see the sandy bottom and detect how shallow it is. Its thin current slides away, but eternity remains.

6. Walt Whitman, *Leaves of Grass* (1855–1892)

In free verse that leaves Petrarchan formalities[37] a distant memory, Whitman paints a broad canvas weaving together meditations on the self, the universe, and humankind. Some prevailing motifs of Walt Whitman's symphonic *Leaves of Grass* are represented in the selections below: his own existence; nature as energy and spiritual force; the American people and America's democracy; and the war-torn bodies of the soldiers who fell in the epochal Civil War.

LEAVES OF GRASS (1892)

One's-Self I Sing

In this brief lyric, the poet sees himself as a distinct individual within a joyous immensity of the distinct persons, male and female, who comprise Democracy, in which the Modern Man emerges.

One's-Self I sing, a simple separate person,
Yet utter the word Democratic, the word En-Masse.

---

37. Francis Petrarch (1304–1374) developed, among other poetic genres, the form of the sonnet, a strictly organized fourteen-line lyric poem that set the standard for the next several centuries. See Volume One, Introduction to Chapter 8, and Text 1.

Of physiology from top to toe I sing,
Not physiognomy alone nor brain alone is worthy for the Muse, I say the Form
    complete is worthier far,
The Female equally with the Male I sing.

Of Life immense in passion, pulse, and power,
Cheerful, for freest action form'd under the laws divine,
The Modern Man I sing.

Song of Myself, 1

In section 1 of the 52 sections of the sequence Song of Myself, *the poet celebrates his own self, a fourth-generation American, a young man who will speak of "Nature without check with original energy"—and yet equaled by every other self that makes up the whole.*

I celebrate myself, and sing myself,
And what I assume you shall assume,
For every atom belonging to me as good belongs to you.

I loafe and invite my soul,
I lean and loafe at my ease observing a spear of summer grass.

My tongue, every atom of my blood, form'd from this soil, this air,
Born here of parents born here from parents the same, and their parents the
    same,
I, now thirty-seven years old in perfect health begin,
Hoping to cease not till death.

Creeds and schools in abeyance,
Retiring back a while sufficed at what they are, but never forgotten,
I harbor for good or bad, I permit to speak at every hazard,
Nature without check with original energy.

Song of Myself, 16

In section 16 of Song of Myself, *the poet views himself as comprising the diversity of America: young and old, male and female, a southerner and a northerner, a citizen of any state, and of every faith and profession.*

I am of old and young, of the foolish as much as the wise,
Regardless of others, ever regardful of others,
Maternal as well as paternal, a child as well as a man,
Stuff'd with the stuff that is coarse and stuff'd with the stuff that is fine,
One of the Nation of many nations, the smallest the same and the largest the
    same,

A Southerner soon as a Northerner, a planter nonchalant and hospitable down by
    the Oconee I live,
A Yankee bound my own way ready for trade, my joints the limberest joints on
    earth and the sternest joints on earth,
A Kentuckian walking the vale of the Elkhorn in my deer-skin leggings, a
    Louisianian or Georgian,
A boatman over lakes or bays or along coasts, a Hoosier, Badger, Buckeye;
At home on Kanadian snow-shoes or up in the bush, or with fishermen off
    Newfoundland,
At home in the fleet of ice-boats, sailing with the rest and tacking,
At home on the hills of Vermont or in the woods of Maine, or the Texan ranch,
Comrade of Californians, comrade of free North-Westerners, (loving their big
    proportions,)
Comrade of raftsmen and coalmen, comrade of all who shake hands and
    welcome to drink and meat,
A learner with the simplest, a teacher of the thoughtfullest,
A novice beginning yet experient of myriads of seasons,
Of every hue and caste am I, of every rank and religion,
A farmer, mechanic, artist, gentleman, sailor, quaker,
Prisoner, fancy-man, rowdy, lawyer, physician, priest.

I resist any thing better than my own diversity,
Breathe the air but leave plenty after me,
And am not stuck up, and am in my place.

(The moth and the fish-eggs are in their place,
The bright suns I see and the dark suns I cannot see are in their place,
The palpable is in its place and the impalpable is in its place.)

When I Heard the Learn'd Astronomer

*In an eight-line narrative, the poet contrasts the calculations and demonstrations of
the intellectual with his own simplicity and intuitive understanding of nature, in
which he finds spiritual completeness.*

When I heard the learn'd astronomer,
When the proofs, the figures, were ranged in columns before me,
When I was shown the charts and diagrams, to add, divide, and measure them,
When I sitting heard the astronomer where he lectured with much applause in
    the lecture-room,
How soon unaccountable I became tired and sick,
Till rising and gliding out I wander'd off by myself,
In the mystical moist night-air, and from time to time,
Look'd up in perfect silence at the stars.

I Hear America Singing

In eleven rolling lines in which "singing" appears eleven times, the poet not only embraces the diverse peoples of America, but also the joy, potency, and energy heard in "their strong melodious songs."

I hear America singing, the varied carols I hear,
Those of mechanics, each one singing his as it should be blithe and strong,
The carpenter singing his as he measures his plank or beam,
The mason singing his as he makes ready for work, or leaves off work,
The boatman singing what belongs to him in his boat, the deckhand singing on
    the steamboat deck,
The shoemaker singing as he sits on his bench, the hatter singing as he stands,
The wood-cutter's song, the ploughboy's on his way in the morning, or at noon
    intermission or at sundown,
The delicious singing of the mother, or of the young wife at work, or of the girl
    sewing or washing,
Each singing what belongs to him or her and to none else,
The day what belongs to the day—at night the party of young fellows, robust,
    friendly,
Singing with open mouths their strong melodious songs.

The Wound Dresser

In an extended American lament, the poet describes the carnage left behind by the battlefield, whose "unsurpass'd heroes" now lie in anguish as "their priceless blood reddens the grass." He tends the bodies and souls of the wounded, offering them love and sacrifice, saying to one: "[P]oor boy! I never knew you, / Yet I think I could not refuse this moment to die for you, if that would save you."

1
An old man bending I come among new faces,
Years looking backward resuming in answer to children,
Come tell us old man, as from young men and maidens that love me,
(Arous'd and angry, I'd thought to beat the alarum, and urge relentless war,
But soon my fingers fail'd me, my face droop'd and I resign'd myself,
To sit by the wounded and soothe them, or silently watch the dead;)
Years hence of these scenes, of these furious passions, these chances,
Of unsurpass'd heroes, (was one side so brave? the other was equally brave;)
Now be witness again, paint the mightiest armies of earth,
Of those armies so rapid so wondrous what saw you to tell us?
What stays with you latest and deepest? of curious panics,
Of hard-fought engagements or sieges tremendous what deepest remains?

2

O maidens and young men I love and that love me,
What you ask of my days those the strangest and sudden your talking recalls,
Soldier alert I arrive after a long march cover'd with sweat and dust,
In the nick of time I come, plunge in the fight, loudly shout in the rush of
    successful charge,
Enter the captur'd works—yet lo, like a swift running river they fade,
Pass and are gone they fade—I dwell not on soldiers' perils or soldiers' joys,
(Both I remember well—many of the hardships, few the joys, yet I was content.)

But in silence, in dreams' projections,
While the world of gain and appearance and mirth goes on,
So soon what is over forgotten, and waves wash the imprints off the sand,
With hinged knees returning I enter the doors, (while for you up there,
Whoever you are, follow without noise and be of strong heart.)

Bearing the bandages, water and sponge,
Straight and swift to my wounded I go,
Where they lie on the ground after the battle brought in,
Where their priceless blood reddens the grass, the ground,
Or to the rows of the hospital tent, or under the roof'd hospital,
To the long rows of cots up and down each side I return,
To each and all one after another I draw near, not one do I miss,
An attendant follows holding a tray, he carries a refuse pail,
Soon to be fill'd with clotted rags and blood, emptied, and fill'd again.

I onward go, I stop,
With hinged knees and steady hand to dress wounds,
I am firm with each, the pangs are sharp yet unavoidable,
One turns to me his appealing eyes—poor boy! I never knew you,
Yet I think I could not refuse this moment to die for you, if that would save you.

3

On, on I go, (open doors of time! open hospital doors!)
The crush'd head I dress, (poor crazed hand tear not the bandage away,)
The neck of the cavalry-man with the bullet through and through I examine,
Hard the breathing rattles, quite glazed already the eye, yet life struggles hard,
(Come sweet death! be persuaded O beautiful death!
In mercy come quickly.)

From the stump of the arm, the amputated hand,
I undo the clotted lint, remove the slough, wash off the matter and blood,
Back on his pillow the soldier bends with curv'd neck and side falling head,

His eyes are closed, his face is pale, he dares not look on the bloody stump,
And has not yet look'd on it.

I dress a wound in the side, deep, deep,
But a day or two more, for see the frame all wasted and sinking,
And the yellow-blue countenance see.

I dress the perforated shoulder, the foot with the bullet-wound,
Cleanse the one with a gnawing and putrid gangrene, so sickening, so offensive,
While the attendant stands behind aside me holding the tray and pail.

I am faithful, I do not give out,
The fractur'd thigh, the knee, the wound in the abdomen,
These and more I dress with impassive hand, (yet deep in my breast a fire, a
    burning flame.)

4
Thus in silence in dreams' projections,
Returning, resuming, I thread my way through the hospitals,
The hurt and wounded I pacify with soothing hand,
I sit by the restless all the dark night, some are so young,
Some suffer so much, I recall the experience sweet and sad,
(Many a soldier's loving arms about this neck have cross'd and rested,
Many a soldier's kiss dwells on these bearded lips.)

7. Emily Dickinson, *Poems* (c. 1860–c. 1873)

The nine poems appearing below are a sampling—a mere one-half of one percent—of Dickinson's 1,800 poems, illustrating some of the prominent themes characteristic of her production: nature, soul and self, books, death, and immortality. They are given in the standard order with first-line titles, by date of the first known manuscript;[38] the originals were unnumbered, untitled, and undated. Brief introductions are given at the head of each component poem.[39]

---

38. As established by Thomas H. Johnson, editor of *The Poems of Emily Dickinson*, 3 vols. (Cambridge, MA: Belknap Press of the Harvard University Press, 1955).
39. The nonstandard practices of capitalization and punctuation, and some erratic verbs and invented word usage, are a hallmark of Dickinson's style and are retained unaltered.

NINE POEMS

181: I lost a World — the other day! (c. 1860)

Two principal themes are voiced in this brief poem: the poet has lost a "World," perhaps the world of imagination, signaled by a headband of stars; and it cannot be valued by coin (the "ducats" of a vanished age), but only by the "frugal" eye of the poet.

I lost a World — the other day!   A Rich man — might not notice it —
Has Anybody found?   Yet — to my frugal Eye,
You'll know it by the Row of Stars   Of more Esteem than Ducats[40] —
Around its forehead bound.   Oh find it — Sir — for me!

258: There's a certain Slant of light (c. 1861)

The "Slant of light" of the pre-dusk winter afternoon is oppressively heavy, inscrutable, bringing "Despair" from above, and foreboding death.

There's a certain Slant of light,   None may teach it— Any—
Winter Afternoons—   'Tis the seal Despair—
That oppresses, like the Heft   An imperial affliction
Of Cathedral Tunes—   Sent us of the Air—
Heavenly Hurt, it gives us—   When it comes, the Landscape listens—
We can find no scar,   Shadows— hold their breath—
But internal difference—   When it goes, 'tis like the Distance
Where the Meanings, are—   On the look of Death—

288: I'm Nobody! Who are you? (c. 1861)

It is better to be "Nobody" than "Somebody"; the poet bonds with her nobody listener, and mocks self-important somebodies.

I'm Nobody! Who are you?   How dreary — to be — Somebody!
Are you — Nobody — too?   How public — like a Frog —
Then there's a pair of us!   To tell one's name — the livelong
Don't tell! they'd advertise — you   June —
    know!   To an admiring Bog!

328: A Bird came down the Walk (c. 1862)

The poet luxuriates in the boundless splendor of nature encompassed by a single bird, murderous, thirsty, courteous, and anxious, whose flight to safety is mysteriously silken and silent.

---

40. ducat: a gold coin in common use in Renaissance Europe.

A Bird came down the Walk —
He did not know I saw —
He bit an Angleworm in halves
And ate the fellow, raw,

And then he drank a Dew
From a convenient Grass —
And then hopped sidewise to the Wall
To let a Beetle pass —

He glanced with rapid eyes
That hurried all around —
They looked like frightened Beads, I thought —
He stirred his Velvet Head

Like one in danger, Cautious,
I offered him a Crumb
And he unrolled his feathers
And rowed him softer home —

Than Oars divide the Ocean,
Too silver for a seam —
Or Butterflies, off Banks of Noon
Leap, plashless as they swim.

441: This is my letter to the World (c. 1862)

The poet addresses the "World," which has ignored her, telling the truths that she has learned from nature; these she commits to unknown listeners, her compatriots, asking their indulgence.

This is my letter to the World
That never wrote to Me —
The simple News that Nature told —
With tender Majesty

Her Message is committed
To Hands I cannot see —
For love of Her — Sweet — countrymen —
Judge tenderly — of Me

465: I heard a Fly buzz — when I died — (c. 1862)

The poet is poised between life and death, having already given away what she possessed in life; but before the light is finally extinguished, she hears the buzzing of a fly, the signal of death, her last awareness before a certain end.

I heard a Fly buzz — when I died —
The Stillness in the Room
Was like the Stillness in the Air —
Between the Heaves of Storm —

The Eyes around — had wrung them dry —
And Breaths were gathering firm
For that last Onset — when the King
Be witnessed — in the Room —

I willed my Keepsakes — Signed away
What portion of me be
Assignable — and then it was
There interposed a Fly —

With Blue — uncertain stumbling Buzz —
Between the light — and me —
And then the Windows failed — and then
I could not see to see—

657: I dwell in Possibility — (c. 1862)

The world of imagination, of "Possibility," that the poet inhabits, is like a house that has more and better windows, doors, rooms, and roof, than a house built of "Prose," language barren of soul and the hope of "Paradise."

I dwell in Possibility —
A fairer House than Prose —
More numerous of Windows —
Superior — for Doors —

Of Chambers as the Cedars —
Impregnable of Eye —
And for an Everlasting Roof
The Gambrels of the Sky —

Of Visitors — the fairest —
For Occupation — This —
The spreading wide my narrow Hands
To gather Paradise —

712: Because I could not stop for Death — (c. 1863)

The poet "could not stop for Death," so Death itself, a kindly gentleman, stops for her in his horse-drawn carriage to take her gently past familiar sights—children at play, pleasant fields of grain, the setting sun; then cold descends and the team of horses, inexorably, brings her to "Eternity."

Because I could not stop for Death —
He kindly stopped for me —

The Carriage held but just Ourselves —
And Immortality.

We slowly drove —He knew no haste,
And I had put away
My labor and my leisure too,
For His Civility —

We passed the School, where Children strove
At recess —in the ring —
We passed the Fields of Gazing Grain —
We passed the Setting Sun —

Or rather —He passed Us —
The Dews drew quivering and chill —
For only Gossamer, my Gown —
My Tippet —only Tulle —

We paused before a House that seemed
A Swelling of the Ground —
The Roof was scarcely visible —
The Cornice —in the Ground —

Since then —'tis centuries —and yet
Feels shorter than the Day
I first surmised the Horses' Heads
Were toward Eternity —

1263: There is no Frigate like a Book (c. 1873)

The poet celebrates the power of literature to bear the soul delightfully to distant places, painlessly, and at no cost.

There is no Frigate like a Book
To take us Lands away
Nor any Coursers like a Page
Of prancing Poetry —
This Traverse may the poorest take
Without oppress of Toll —
How frugal is the Chariot
That bears the Human soul.

8. Charlotte Perkins Gilman,
The Yellow Wallpaper (1892)

The selections below from *The Yellow Wallpaper*, totaling about one-third of the whole, trace the unnamed narrator's deterioration, told in her own voice, from instability to insanity. They begin with a description of the large, sunny former nursery in which she is confined, and end with her ceaseless creeping around the perimeter of the yellow-papered walls, stripping the paper so as to free the imaginary captive woman within—creeping even over the body of her unconscious husband, who falls in a faint at the sight.[41]

THE YELLOW WALLPAPER

It is a big, airy room, the whole floor nearly, with windows that look all ways, and air and sunshine galore. It was nursery first and then playground and gymnasium, I should judge; for the windows are barred for little children, and there are rings and things in the walls.

The paint and paper look as if a boys' school had used it. It is stripped off—the paper—in great patches all around the head of my bed, about as far as I can reach, and in a great place on the other side of the room low down. I never saw a worse paper in my life.

One of those sprawling flamboyant patterns committing every artistic sin.

It is dull enough to confuse the eye in following, pronounced enough to constantly irritate, and provoke study, and when you follow the lame, uncertain curves for a little distance they suddenly commit suicide—plunge off at outrageous angles, destroy themselves in unheard-of contradictions.

The color is repellant, almost revolting; a smouldering, unclean yellow, strangely faded by the slow-turning sunlight.

It is a dull yet lurid orange in some places, a sickly sulphur tint in others.

No wonder the children hated it! I should hate it myself if I had to live in this room long. . . .

The wall paper, as I said before, is torn off in spots, and it sticketh closer than a brother—they must have had perseverance as well as hatred.

Then the floor is scratched and gouged and splintered, the plaster itself is dug out here and there, and this great heavy bed, which is all we found in the room, looks as if it had been through the wars.

But I don't mind it a bit—only the paper. . . .

This wall paper has a kind of sub-pattern in a different shade, a particularly irritating one, for you can only see it in certain lights, and not clearly then.

---

41. The nonstandard orthography of this 1892 original, along with some unusual verb forms and intentional sentence fragments, are retained unaltered.

But in the places where it isn't faded, and where the sun is just so, I can see a strange, provoking, formless sort of figure, that seems to sulk about behind that silly and conspicuous front design. . . .

I'm getting really fond of the room in spite of the wall paper. Perhaps *because* of the wall paper.

It dwells in my mind so!

I lie here on this great immovable bed—it is nailed down, I believe—and follow that pattern about by the hour. It is as good as gymnastics, I assure you. I start, we'll say, at the bottom, down in the corner over there where it has not been touched, and I determine for the thousandth time that I *will* follow that pointless pattern to some sort of a conclusion.

I know a little of the principles of design, and I know this thing was not arranged on any laws of radiation, or alternation, or repetition, or symmetry, or anything else that I ever heard of.

It is repeated, of course, by the breadths,[42] but not otherwise.

Looked at in one way, each breadth stands alone, the bloated curves and flourishes . . . go waddling up and down in isolated columns of fatuity.

But, on the other hand, they connect diagonally, and the sprawling outlines run off in great slanting waves of optic horror, like a lot of wallowing seaweeds in full chase.

The whole thing goes horizontally, too, at least it seems so, and I exhaust myself in trying to distinguish the order of its going in that direction. . . .

There are things in that paper that nobody knows but me, or ever will.

Behind that outside pattern the dim shapes get clearer every day.

It is always the same shape, only very numerous.

And it is like a woman stooping down and creeping about behind that pattern. I don't like it a bit. I wonder—I begin to think—I wish John[43] would take me away from here!

It is so hard to talk with John about my case, because he is so wise, and because he loves me so.

But I tried it last night.

It was moonlight. The moon shines in all around, just as the sun does.

I hate to see it sometimes, it creeps so slowly, and always comes in by one window or another.

John was asleep and I hated to waken him, so I kept still and watched the moonlight on that undulating wall paper till I felt creepy.

The faint figure behind seemed to shake the pattern, just as if she wanted to get out.

---

42. repeated . . . by the breadths: that is, each strip of wallpaper consists of repeated patterns, and when is cut into shorter pieces that are hung side by side, the repeating pattern is visible.
43. John: her husband, a physician, who has arranged her confinement.

I got up softly and went to feel and see if the paper *did* move, and when I came back John was awake. . . .

She asks her husband if they can go away, but he refuses, urging her to trust him.

So of course I said no more on that score, and we went to sleep before long. He thought I was asleep first, but I wasn't,—I lay there for hours trying to decide whether that front pattern and the back pattern really did move together or separately.

On a pattern like this, by daylight, there is a lack of sequence, a defiance of law, that is a constant irritant to a normal mind.

The color is hideous enough, and unreliable enough, and infuriating enough, but the pattern is torturing.

You think you have mastered it, but just as you get well under way in following, it turns a back somersault, and there you are. It slaps you in the face, knocks you down, and tramples upon you. It is like a bad dream.

The outside pattern is a florid arabesque, reminding one of a fungus. If you can imagine a toadstool in joints, an interminable string of toadstools, budding and sprouting in endless convolutions,—why, that is something like it.

That is, sometimes!

There is one marked peculiarity about this paper, a thing nobody seems to notice but myself, and that is that it changes as the light changes.

When the sun shoots in through the east window—I always watch for that first long, straight ray—it changes so quickly that I never can quite believe it.

That is why I watch it always.

By moonlight—the moon shines in all night when there is a moon—I wouldn't know it was the same paper.

At night in any kind of light, in twilight, candlelight, lamplight, and worst of all by moonlight, it becomes bars! The outside pattern, I mean, and the woman behind it is as plain as can be.

I didn't realize for a long time what the thing was that showed behind,—that dim sub-pattern,—but now I am quite sure it is a woman.

By daylight she is subdued, quiet. I fancy it is the pattern that keeps her so still. It is so puzzling. It keeps me quiet by the hour. . . .

John is so pleased to see me improve! He laughed a little the other day, and said I seemed to be flourishing in spite of my wall paper.

I turned it off with a laugh. I had no intention of telling him it was *because* of the wall paper—he would make fun of me. He might even want to take me away.

I don't want to leave now until I have found it out. There is a week more, and I think that will be enough.

I'm feeling ever so much better! I don't sleep much at night, for it is so interesting to watch developments; but I sleep a good deal in the daytime.

In the daytime it is tiresome and perplexing.

There are always new shoots on the fungus, and new shades of yellow all over it. I cannot keep count of them, though I have tried conscientiously.

It is the strangest yellow, that wall paper! It makes me think of all the yellow things I ever saw—not beautiful ones like buttercups, but old foul, bad yellow things. . . .

I really have discovered something at last.

Through watching so much at night, when it changes so, I have finally found out.

The front pattern *does* move—and no wonder! The woman behind shakes it!

Sometimes I think there are a great many women behind, and sometimes only one, and she crawls around fast, and her crawling shakes it all over.

Then in the very bright spots she keeps still, and in the very shady spots she just takes hold of the bars and shakes them hard.

And she is all the time trying to climb through. . . .

I think that woman gets out in the daytime!

And I'll tell you why—privately—I've seen her!

I can see her out of every one of my windows!

It is the same woman, I know, for she is always creeping, and most women do not creep by daylight.

I see her in that long shaded lane, creeping up and down. I see her in those dark grape arbors, creeping all around the garden.

I see her on that long road under the trees, creeping along, and when a carriage comes she hides under the blackberry vines.

I don't blame her a bit. It must be very humiliating to be caught creeping by daylight! . . .

It is the last day they will stay in that house and John is away overnight. The caged woman in the wallpaper will emerge and they will creep together, stripping the paper from the walls.

As soon as it was moonlight, and that poor thing began to crawl and shake the pattern, I got up and ran to help her.

I pulled and she shook, I shook and she pulled, and before morning we had peeled off yards of that paper.

A strip about as high as my head and half around the room.

And then when the sun came and that awful pattern began to laugh at me I declared I would finish it today! . . .

The lease is now up and they are packed up to leave.

But I must get to work.

I have locked the door and thrown the key down into the front path. . . .

But I forgot I could not reach far without anything to stand on!

This bed will *not* move!

I tried to lift and push it until I was lame, and then I got so angry I bit off a little piece at one corner—but it hurt my teeth.

Then I peeled off all the paper I could reach standing on the floor. It sticks horribly and the pattern just enjoys it! All those strangled heads and bulbous eyes and waddling fungus growths just shriek with derision! . . .

She now believes that there are other women in the wallpaper who come out and creep about—and that she herself is one of them.

I suppose I shall have to get back behind the pattern when it comes night, and that is hard!

It is so pleasant to be out in this great room and creep around as I please!

John comes, retrieves the key she had thrown away, enters, and faints away at the sight before him.

"What is the matter?" he cried. "For God's sake, what are you doing?"

I kept on creeping just the same, but I looked at him over my shoulder.

"I've got out at last," said I, "in spite of you and Jane![44] And I've pulled off most of the paper, so you can't put me back!"

Now why should that man have fainted? But he did, and right across my path by the wall, so that I had to creep over him every time!

9. José Joaquín Fernández de Lizardi, *The Mangy Parrot* (1816/1831)

Our hero El Periquillo, the "Mangy Parrot," has been a gambler, a thief, and a trickster, for some time—but here, in Chapter 46 of the 52 chapters that make up the novel, his perambulations come to an end. He participates in a failed assault on a well-defended merchant caravan and is nearly killed, while two comrades are killed in fact; and he encounters the cadaver of a man hanged for theft, whom he recognizes as the old friend who had introduced him to his errant life. He will repent and turn to God, and as an *hombre de bien*, a decent and respectable old man, leave the account of his adventures to his children, to guide them on a better road.

---

44. Jane: also called Jennie; John's sister, who serves as housekeeper.

THE MANGY PARROT

Chapter 46: IN WHICH OUR AUTHOR TELLS THE ADVENTURES HE HAD IN THE GANG OF THIEVES; THE SAD SPECTACLE PRESENTED BY THE CADAVER OF A HANGED MAN; AND THE BEGINNING OF HIS CONVERSION

Though God often allows the wicked to achieve their intentions, whether to test the righteous or to punish the depraved, He does not always permit their designs to go forward. . . .

So it happened with El Aguilucho ["The Eaglet"] and his companions, the morning that we came out to surprise the traveling merchants.

It was about six in the morning when, from the crest of a hill, we spied them coming down the highway. Three men went in front, with their shotguns in hand; then came four horses with empty saddles, which is to say, without riders; after them came four mules loaded down with trunks, cots, and bedrolls—we could see what the cargo was from far off, even though it was all covered with blue cloaks; and finally the three serving lads were in the rearguard.

As soon as El Aguilucho saw them, he vowed to take his revenge and a large booty, so he made us hide behind a steep slope at the foot of the hill, and he told us, "Now it's time, companions, to show our bravery and take advantage of a lucky situation, because there's no doubt that they're merchants on their way to Veracruz, and their cargo's bound to be made up of cash and fine clothes. The important thing is not to hold back, but to attack them boldly, knowing that the advantage is ours, since we're five and they're just three; because the serving lads are hired hands and cowardly folk who have no reason to give us pause. They'll take off running at the first shots; so you, Perico [Periquillo], and me and the Gobbler will jump out in front of them as soon as they come within a good distance, I mean, within a gunshot; and Lefty and Snubnose will take the rearguard so they'll know they're surrounded. If they give up right away, all we'll have to do is take away their weapons, tie them up, and bring them here to this hill, where we'll let them go after night falls; but if they resist and fire on us, don't give them quarter: they all die."

Between the sight of our enemies, who were coming closer second by second, and thinking about the dangers that threatened me, I was trembling like a hatter, unable to hide my fear, to the point that my terror became noticeable, because my legs were trembling so hard that the little chains on my spurs were jangling perceptibly against the stirrups; this attracted El Aguilucho's attention, and, noting my fear and glaring at me, he said, "What are you trembling for, you shameless pansy? Do you think you're going to go fight against an army of lions? Haven't you noticed, you chicken, that they're men like you, and they're just three against five? Don't you see that you're not going in alone, but with four men—four real men—who are going to be exposed to the same danger, and who'll defend you like the apple of their eyes? You think it's so likely that you'll perish and not one of us? And finally, let's say they hit you with a bullet and kill you: what's so new or unheard of about that? Are you planning to die in childbirth, you spineless lout, or are you expecting to stick around in this world to witness the coming of the Antichrist? What, do you expect to have money, eat well, dress well, and ride good horses if you're a lazy bum, closed up in a shop and never taking any risks? Well, that's too green, brother, you've got to take some risks to pay the rent. If you tell me, as you have, that you've known thieves who rob and stroll down the street without the slightest danger, I'll tell you that's true: but not everybody can rob that way. Some people rob in a military way—I mean, out in the open, risking their necks; others rob in a courteous way, that is, in the cities, living it up and never running the risk of losing their lives; but not everybody can manage to do it that way, though most would like to. So watch your spinelessness, because I'll shoot you myself before you have a chance to turn your horse around."

I was frightened by his harsh rebuke and fearsome threats, so I told him I wasn't afraid, and that if I was trembling, it was just because of the cold; so we should get on with the attack, and then he'd see how brave I was.

"God grant that will happen," El Aguilucho said, "though I doubt it very much."

Meanwhile the travelers had reached the point prescribed by El Aguilucho. Snubnose and Lefty broke off from our group and took on the rearguard, while at the same time, the Gobbler, El Aguilucho, and I came out in front of them pointing our shotguns and shouting: "Everybody stop, if you don't want to die at our hands."

At our shouts, four armed men jumped up out of the packed cargo, immediately mounted the four empty horses, and went after Lefty and Snubnose, who opened fire on them with their carbines, killing one before fleeing like jackrabbits.

The three traveling merchants attacked us, killing our Gobbler in the first volley. I fired my shotgun, aiming to kill, but only managed to get a horse, which bit the dust.

When El Aguilucho saw that he was all alone (because he didn't count me at all), he told me, "This isn't an even match any more; one of us is dead, two ran away, there's nine against us: let's get out of here."

As he said this, he tried to turn his horse and run, but he couldn't, because it shied on him; so in spite of the fact that we were loading and firing as fast as we could, we weren't doing any damage, while bullets kept whizzing by us; and we were afraid they'd catch us with their swords, for the three merchants were galloping toward us full speed, unafraid of our shotguns.

Then El Aguilucho jumped down, killing his horse with a blow from his rifle butt to the head, and while he was leaping onto my horse behind me, they fired a shot at him that was so well aimed it went right through his temples and he fell down dead.

The bullet came close to going through my body, too, for it nipped off a piece of my poncho. The blood of the unhappy Aguilucho spattered my clothes. I had not time to do more than tell him, "Jesus bless you," and, finding myself alone with so many enemies on top of me, I spurred on my horse and fled down the highway faster than an arrow. Fortunately it was an excellent horse, and it galloped as quickly as I could have hoped. . . .

Tired, filled with fear, and riding an exhausted horse, I found myself around noon in an empty and pleasant little wood.

There I got out of the saddle; I loosened the horse's straps, took off his bridle, gave him water in a stream, and let him pasture on the green grass; I sat down under a cool, shady tree, and gave myself over to the most serious considerations.

"No doubt about it," I said; "laziness, licentiousness, and vice cannot be the surest means of achieving our true happiness. True happiness in this life can never consist of anything other than having a tranquil spirit, whatever one's fortunes; and that's something a criminal can never have, no matter how merry a time he has of it when he's satisfying his passions; his ephemeral merriment is succeeded by an unbearable languor, many hours of boredom, and incessant remorse, so that in the end he pays a long and costly tribute for his miserable bit of pleasure, which he perhaps bought at the expense of a thousand crimes, frights, and hazards."

El Periquillo's meditations go on at some length before he winds down to a conclusion.

"Just as those two died, couldn't I have died? Since there were bullets aimed directly at them, couldn't there have been one for me? Did I escape them because of my virtue and agility? Of course not. An invisible and Almighty Hand was what turned them aside from my body, with the pious end that I not be lost forever. . . . Oh, God, how it shames me to recall that my whole life has been an uninterrupted chain of crimes! I have run through childhood and youth like a raving lunatic, . . . and now I have reached manhood, older and with more crimes on my conscience than in my puberty and adolescence.

"I have had thirty some-odd years of life, and a sinful, immortal life it has been. However, it is not too late; I still have time to truly convert and change my conduct. If it saddens me to think how long my life has been immoral, let it console me to know that the Great Father of all families is most liberal and kind. . . . What is done is done; let us reform ourselves." . . .

El Periquillo sets off on the road back to Mexico City, the first night encountering a police lieutenant who tells him of gangs of thieves operating in the area. They part the next day and El Periquillo continues his journey.

That night I slept in Teotihuacán, where I learned that the thieves had been defeated the previous week, and their ringleader had been captured and hanged at the entrance to the town.

Filled with fear by this news, I managed to sleep, and the next day at six in the morning, I saddled my horse, commended myself wholeheartedly to God, and continued on my way.

I had gone a league [about three miles] or a bit farther when I saw, tied to a tree and held up by a stake, the cadaver of a hanged man, with his white sackcloth, his tall hat adorned with a cross made of red cloth, which had fallen forward to cover his forehead, and his hands tied.

I came closer to look at him carefully; but how did I react when I saw and recognized that misshapen corpse as my old unhappy friend Januario? My hairs stood on end; my blood froze in my veins; my heart raced; my tongue became a knot in my throat; my forehead was covered with a deadly sweat; and, having lost the elasticity of my sinews, I was about to fall from my horse due to the distress of my soul.

But God wished to aid my faltering spirit, and, with an extraordinary effort to keep brave on my part, I managed to recover slowly from the turmoil that oppressed me.

At that moment, I recalled his misdeeds, his corrupt advice, his infernal examples and maxims; I greatly mourned his misfortune; I cried for him, for after all he was my friend and we had grown up together; but I also gave hearty thanks to God for separating me from his friendship, since, between that and my evil disposition, I would certainly have become a thief like him, and perhaps at that hour I would have been hanging from the next tree.

I confirmed more and more my resolution to change my life, endeavoring to take advantage thenceforth of the world's lessons, and to profit from the wickedness and adversities of men. . . .

10. Eduardo Gutiérrez, *The Gaucho Juan Moreira* (1879–1880)

In Chapter One of his fictionalized biography of Juan Moreira, the journalist Eduardo Gutiérrez introduces his "true crime" story, telling us about the gaucho himself—whom he had met in person—and about gauchos in general, who roamed the southern cattle ranges of nineteenth-century Argentina like the cowboys of North America's Wild West. In Chapter Seven, he depicts the pivotal moment in Moreira's transformation from respectable cattle rancher to outlaw and, eventually, bandit. In a fair fight in which Moreira, too, is wounded, he has killed a shopkeeper who had cheated him, with the collusion of local government officials. Now he confronts the Assistant Justice of the Peace who pursues Moreira, planning to slaughter him and claim his wife, Vicenta. Moreira dispatches the Assistant Justice "like a dog," along with his two guards. He has killed a government man; now he must roam abroad. His only companions are his little dog Cacique ("Chief") and his champion dappled bay horse. Cacique guards Moreira, signaling with his shrill bark the approach of any threat, as the gaucho sleeps in the rough alongside his horse, always saddled and ready for a quick escape.

JUAN MOREIRA

Chapter One

Juan Moreira is one of those figures who stride into this world, into any walk of life, destined for celebrity, like a walking bronze statue. This gaucho was no twisted, cowardly, blood-thirsty criminal, as some have said.

No, Juan Moreira's instincts were gentle and noble and, had they been properly directed and educated, his life would have turned out differently. At the head of a regiment of cavalry, Moreira would have been a credit to his country, a national glory, but on the slippery slope of crime, viciously pursued and fighting for his life, he turned on his pursuers with heroic fury. The valor of the "bandit" Juan Moreira seems almost super-human, yet he was in most ways no different from most of our gauchos, strong of heart and generous of spirit. . . .

His neighbors also knew him, in earlier years, as a sort of roving troubadour or, as they would say, *payador*. Moreira had a fine voice, and when he tuned his guitar to sing at a country dance, surrounded by friends, he always impressed them with his tender lyrics. . . . All gauchos possess an artistic sensibility, however, and all play the guitar more or less by instinct, without any musical instruction whatsoever. Juan Moreira possessed these qualities in a high degree. When he began to play the guitar at a dance, the assembly fell silent, and his plaintive verses moved men and women alike.

I met Juan Moreira on only one occasion, in 1874, but I've never forgotten the sound of his voice. He was already being called a bandit, and his frightful reputation had already spread to small towns across the pampa. And yet, he had about him something so appealing, that anyone who met him had the same thought as I did: This man *cannot be* a bandit.

Nobility characterized his face, and also the way that he carried himself, and he spoke with profound sincerity, bathing the face of his interlocutor with the light of his sad, dark eyes. . . .

Moreira was thirty-four years old at the time—tall, and not thin. His dress was the picturesque stuff that gauchos wear, more or less the national costume.

He wears wide-legged fringed calzoncillos *as trousers, a wide leather* tirador *around his waist, a white shirt, high boots and spurs; he also carries two* trabucos, *or short-barreled shotguns, a two-foot-long knife, or* facón, *with a gold-trimmed silver handle, a silver-handled riding whip; and across his chest lies a gold watch chain terminating in the pocket of the* tirador.

This was the Juan Moreira about whose daring deeds the gauchos sing their melancholy airs. What powerful motive, what fatal force led this good, upstanding man—a moral exemplar until the age of thirty—to a life of crime? . . .

Our gauchos have only two options, to become bandits, . . . or be drafted into the army as cannon fodder. Gauchos are routinely deprived of their civil rights and even, one could say, of their human rights. Both military and police authorities abuse our gauchos, who have no recourse, because if they resist, it's into the army and off to the southern frontier. Gauchos cannot find honorable work at all, and their crime? To be native sons and citizens of Argentina! . . .

Chapter Seven

In a fair fight, Moreira has killed a shopkeeper who had cheated him—with the collusion of the authorities. He is now pursued by the Assistant Justice of the Peace, Francisco, once a friend, who has designs on Moreira's wife, Vicenta. Evading capture, Moreira goes on the offensive against Francisco and his men, who have entered his house.

It was about eight o'clock when Moreira stopped and dismounted only a few hundred yards from his house. Inside were five men: the Assistant Justice, two soldiers, and two of Moreira's erstwhile neighbors. In the moment when Moreira, slipping through the shadows, pressed his eye to a crack in the door, the men were talking about him. On the table stood a bottle of gin and two glasses.

"He was a good *criollo*,"[45] one of the neighbors was saying. "What he did, you would have done yourself, Francisco, and a good man deserves some consideration. He's suffered enough already."

"No," replied the Assistant Justice. "I'm going to chase him until I catch him, and when I catch him, I'm going to kill him like a dog, but not before he suffers a lot more. I want him to know that I've got Vicenta. He stole her from *me*, you know. And since she didn't want to be my wife, she can be my *comfort*."

The neighbor was about to reply when the words hardened in his mouth, frozen solid by the chill blast of terror that turned all five seated men into icy

---

45. *criollo:* or Creole; originally a person of European descent, but here signifying more broadly an Argentinian native adhering to traditional culture, as opposed to a newcomer or immigrant.

statues in an instant. The chill came from the door, which had opened with a loud kick to reveal, outlined against the black, the figure of Juan Moreira, his head held high, his eyes full of lightning bolts, his poncho on his left arm, and in his right hand, the dreadful blade.

"Do you want to see how a man kills a dog, Francisco?"

Moreira's voice trembled with repressed rage. The Assistant Justice was a hardened fighter, and Moreira's words galvanized him to action. He brought out his pistol and fired, but the shot went wide.

"See? That's why you need pointers," laughed Moreira, who seemed to become calmer as the waiting finally ended and the fighting began. "You like to kill from a safe distance," he added, after dodging a second bullet.

Moreira moved forward slowly, smiling. His calm unnerved Francisco, who had no more bullets in his double-barreled pistol. The Assistant Justice turned to the two soldiers:

"Kill him! What are you waiting for?"

The soldiers' fear, as well as certain natural sympathies toward Moreira, had combined to keep them motionless. At the shouts of the Assistant Justice, they remembered themselves, drew their sabers, and attacked Moreira. The bloody scene that ensued became neighborhood lore.

Like a crouching tiger, Moreira awaited, his awful blade extended toward the advancing soldiers, who raised their swords together, as if to split him in two. Unfortunately for the soldiers, both swung at the same time, and both blows sank uselessly into the wall as Moreira leapt to the right and, as the soldiers struggled to recover a defensive posture, forward, pushing his facón into one of them to the hilt, just below the ribcage. The skewered gendarme dropped silently to the floor, and Moreira turned his attention to the other, just in time to catch another saber stroke in his poncho. Then in went the hungry facón, this time deftly between the ribs. The second soldier stumbled, with an expression of surprise, and went down right in front of the Assistant Justice.

He and Moreira found each other face-to-face for the final showdown, with only the two neighbors and the two dead soldiers, all four equally motionless, as witnesses. Because of Francisco's sword, however, their arms were still not equal.

"Now we'll see how you handle yourself in a fair fight, friend Francisco," said the gaucho with astonishing cool, adding, with a blood-chilling smile: "And then we'll see the color of your insides."

It was a clash of titans, two strong, brave men who hated each other profoundly, both knowing that one was about to die. The dim room flashed with the hot lightening of their eyes and the cold lightening of their steel. Moreira's calm was greater because he recognized his superior ability and because he had so much less to lose. He calmly and skillfully diverted Francisco's slashes and thrusts with his poncho without counterattacking, only brandishing his facón as if indecisive about just how to kill his attacker. When Francisco threw his most violent blow yet, leaving himself off balance, Moreira managed to entangle the sword in his poncho and, passing his facón to his left hand, he pulled the sword out of his enemy's grip.

The surprised Assistant Justice retreated until he found his back against the wall, crying for help to Moreira's two neighbors, who remained frozen in place, filled with admiration for Moreira.

"Don't get so excited," said the gaucho to the Assistant Justice. "I am not going to kill you just yet. There are a few things you have to hear first, 'friend' Francisco, as I once considered you. You've persecuted me unjustly, reducing me to my present disgrace, you've beaten me when I was defenseless in the stocks, and not content with that, you've tried to kill me in order to take my wife, whose pure heart you'll never sully, I promise, because, Francisco, now you are about to die," Moreira smiled broadly, as if relieved at last of the heavy emotional burden, "and not because I'm afraid of you, no, but only because I want to spare Vicenta your nauseating advances in my absence. So get ready because here I come."

His little speech concluded, the gaucho threw Francisco's sword back to him. The Assistant Justice grabbed the weapon avidly, beaming with relief and happiness, and all his energy returned at once. Beside himself, his eyes wide and his mouth, half-open, he did not wait for Moreira's onslaught but, rather, surged forward with a sword thrust so violent that the two remaining onlookers uttered small, woeful exclamations in the belief that the gaucho could not possibly survive it. They were wrong, of course, and suddenly, the duel had ended. Moreira had deflected the sword thrust in a way that left Francisco's chest close and undefended. The opening was all that Moreira needed.

"I've been murdered," cried the Assistant Justice as he fell backward, blood welling from his chest, his sword clattering to the floor.

"You lie," said Moreira. "You died in a fair fight, and I have two witnesses."

Then, looking closely at the dying man's bloody chest, he leaned over and, with an expression of mild distaste, slipped his blade in again, between two ribs and directly into the beating heart of his enemy, which was stilled immediately. With a glance at the two dead soldiers and another at the speechless witnesses, he sheathed his facón and turned to the door, stopping suddenly just as he reached it and stepping back with his hand on his knife again.

Someone else stood outside the doorway, viewing the scene of carnage inside. Moreira relaxed. It was [his friend] Julián. The gaucho extended his hand to Moreira after wiping away a tear.

"You've got guts, friend Moreira," he said, shaking the other's hand. "Too bad you've got a quarrel with the law, because at this rate we'll end up without police."

The two went to where Moreira had left his horse, and they found Julián's horse there, too.

"I need to ask a final favor," said Moreira.

"Say the word," replied Julián, "and I'll do it, whatever it may be."

"Go see if you can talk to Vicenta," explained Moreira, "because all the police are likely to come looking for me when they hear about the little ruckus tonight. There won't be anyone guarding Vicenta. Tell her what I've done and that she has nothing more to fear from Francisco. Tell her that I'll watch out for her, wherever my destiny leads me. Tell her that our compadre [close friend] Giménez will take care of her while I'm gone. And find my dog, Cacique. He's the only one who can accompany me where I'm bound. . . ."

11. Joaquim Maria Machado de Assis, *To Be Twenty Years Old!* (1884)

In a brisk five pages, Machado de Assis presents the sophisticated urban hub of Rio de Janeiro, depicting the fast set of young men destined for leadership positions in state and society. He paints this scene in strokes that are deft, detached, and amused—and they are damning. The twenty-year-old at the forefront of the drama is a spendthrift, obsessed with superficial trappings and trivial pursuits. He and his friends squander countless hours drinking coffee and cognac at an expensive café on the fashionable Rua do Ouvidor, ogling the beautiful women passing by and wafting thoughtless allusions to Aristotle, Wagner, Darwin, Spencer, and "all the other big names."[46] These names, of which they have only superficial knowledge, are proffered to demonstrate their possession of European culture, employed as a social marker establishing rank and privilege. Machado's critique of this elite, conveyed in silken tones, is devastating.

To Be Twenty Years Old!

Gonçalves, insulted and furious, crumpled the sheet of paper and bit his lip. He took five or six steps across the room, lay down on the bed, stared at the ceiling, and thought for a while. Then he went to the window and stood there for ten or twelve minutes, tapping his foot on the floor and looking out at the street, a backstreet in the Lapa district.

---

46. The ancient Greek philosopher Aristotle (384–322 BCE), and the contemporaries Richard Wagner (1813–1883), composer; Charles Darwin (1809–1882), theorist of evolution; and Herbert Spencer (1820–1903), social philosopher.

Surely, there isn't a man reading this, and much less, a woman, who won't assume immediately that the paper that young Gonçalves has crumbled into a ball is a letter, a love letter, expressing a girl's ill temper, for example, or informing him that her father opposes their relationship, that the father is packing her out of Rio that very day for some weeks in the country. Erroneous guesses! It isn't a love letter, not a letter at all, really, even though it is addressed to him and signed and dated at the bottom. Here is what this is about: Gonçalves is a student whose family lives in the provinces. His father has an agent in Rio who doles out the young man's monthly living allowance. Gonçalves gets his allowance punctually every month, he spends it immediately, and most of the time he has no money. He gets along fine, though, because to be twenty years old itself constitutes great wealth. On the other hand, to be twenty also means to be inexperienced and headstrong, so Gonçalves slips here and there and occasionally commits major blunders. Not long ago he saw a coat, a fur coat of the sort that stylish students wear, unbelievably nice, and a walking cane[47] to go with it, nothing fancy, but in excellent taste. He had no money, so he bought them on credit. It wasn't his idea, mind you; a friend encouraged him. That was four months ago, and the store owner won't leave him in peace. Gonçalves decided to send the bill to his father's agent describing the situation in terms that would melt the hardest heart on earth.

The agent did not have a hard heart; being an agent, he had none at all. He went rigidly by the book, or rather, according to the letters of instruction sent to him by the father, who said that his son was a spendthrift and required discipline. When Gonçalves sent him the bill, though, the agent saw that it needed to be paid. How to do so without encouraging the young man to keep buying things on credit? The agent sent word that he would pay the bill, but not without first writing to the father, asking for instructions, and informing him of other, less consequential bills that he had already paid. All this was written in two or three lines at the bottom of the bill itself, which he had returned to Gonçalves.

One understands the young man's unhappiness. The bill had not been paid, and worse, now his father was going to hear about it. If it were for something different, it wouldn't be so bad. But the bill was for an unnecessary luxury, a fur coat, an enormous encumbrance really, heavy and hot . . . Gonçalves swore at the shop owner and even more at his father's agent. Why had the man gone and told his father? What a letter his father was going to write now! What a letter! Gonçalves could just imagine what it would say, because it wouldn't be the first. Last time his father had threatened to cut off his money completely.

---

47. fur coat and cane: accessories prized by the fashionable students of the medical school of Rio de Janeiro.

After swearing at the agent and changing his mind several times about what to do next, Gonçalves decided that the best plan was to go straight to the fellow's house armed with his walking cane, tell him a thing or two, and give him a thrashing if he answered back. It was an energetic and immediate response, a fairly easy one, and (his heart said) it would set an example for the ages.

"Don't bother me, scoundrel, or I'll smash your face!"

Agitated and tremulous, he dressed in a hurry and, wonder of wonders, didn't even put on a necktie until, halfway down the stairs, he noticed its absence and went back to choose one. He brandished his walking cane in the air like a sword to see if it was ready for action. It was.

"Take that, you scoundrel!"

He apparently then delivered several loud blows to the chairs and floorboards, provoking a shout from an irritable neighbor. Finally, he left, his twenty fervent years boiling in his veins, incapable of swallowing the insult and disguising his annoyance.

Once outside, Gonçalves passed the Ocean Walk, Our Lady of Perpetual Help Street, and Goldsmith Street. He went all the way to Ouvidor Street, and it occurred to him he could go that way to the agent's house. So he took Ouvidor, but he didn't turn to look at fellows who waved at him there, or even at the pretty girls who were out for a walk. Like a charging bull, he looked neither left nor right. Someone called his name.

"Gonçalves! Gonçalves!"

He charged ahead as if he hadn't heard. The voice came from the open front of a café. The caller called again, then emerged and grabbed him by the shoulder.

"Where are you going?"

"I'll be right back—"

"Come here for a moment."

And he pulled Gonçalves by the arm into the café where three other young men were sitting at a table. They were his classmates, all the same age as he. They asked where he was going. "To punish an uppity scoundrel," replied Gonçalves, by which his four friends knew that his target was neither church nor state, but, rather, someone to whom he owed money or, very probably, a rival. One of them went so far as to say that he should leave Brito alone.

"What about Brito?"

"What about him? What about Brito, the chosen one, the big man with the mustache, whom Chiquinha Coelho likes better than you? Or don't you remember Chiquinha anymore?"

With a shrug, Gonçalves summoned a waiter and ordered a small cup of black, sweet coffee. This wasn't about Chiquinha, and it wasn't about Brito. It was about something quite serious. The coffee came, and he rolled a cigarette while one of his friends confessed that Chiquinha was the prettiest girl that he'd seen since coming to Rio de Janeiro. Gonçalves said nothing. He smoked his cigarette, drank his coffee in small, slow sips, and gazed into the street. Then he interrupted his friends to declare that Chiquinha was pretty, but not the prettiest, and he cited five or six others. Some of his friends agreed entirely, some partly, and some not at all. Chiquinha, the incomparable. Various analyses. A lengthy debate.

"More coffee," ordered Gonçalves.

"Some cognac?"

They drank coffee and cognac. One of the beauties that they were talking about passed by, at that point, strolling down Ouvidor Street on the arm of her father, a deputy in the National Assembly. The father's appearance turned the debate in a political direction. He was about to be named head of an imperial ministry.

"A minister, imagine! And Gonçalves his future son-in-law!"

"Quit joking around," laughed Gonçalves.

"What's the matter?"

"I don't like jokes. Me, a son-in-law? Anyway, you know my political views. There is a huge gap between us. In politics, I am a radical."

"Yes, but radicals also marry," observed one of his friends.

"They marry radical beauties," added another.

"Exactly, radical beauties."

"She's beautiful, but radical?"

"This coffee is cold!" exclaimed Gonçalves. "Hey, another coffee! Somebody have a cigarette? Me, a radical, the future son-in-law of an imperial minister? That's a good one! Haven't you read Aristotle?"

"I haven't."

"Me, neither."

"They say he's good."

"Excellent," insisted Gonçalves. "Hey, Lamego, do you remember that fellow who wanted a costume for the masked ball, and we put that hat on him and said that his costume was Aristotle?"

And he told the story, which really was funny, and everyone laughed, starting with Gonçalves himself, in long belly laughs. The waiter brought his second coffee, which he found hot enough but too scant, and he asked for a third cup and another cigarette. One of his classmates then told a similar story, and when he happened to mention Wagner, the conversation turned suddenly to music and the Wagnerian revolution underway in Europe. From there, the conversation naturally turned to modern science, to Darwin, Spencer, and all the other big names, and between one thing and another—here a serious note, there a lighthearted one, here a cigarette, there a coffee, and lots of general hilarity—they were surprised to hear a clock strike five.

"Five o'clock!" said two or three of them at once.

"In my stomach it feels more like seven o'clock," considered another.

"Where do you fellows eat supper?"

They decided to pool their funds and eat together. They scraped together six milréis[48] and went to a modest hotel where they ate well and kept the bill in mind. It was half past six o'clock when they stepped outside, dusk on a beautiful summer evening. They walked toward São Francisco Square. They saw some girls still out on Ouvidor Street, only a few stragglers, though, and more girls at the São Cristóvão streetcar stop. One of these really got their attention. She was tall, good-looking, and recently widowed. Gonçalves thought that she looked a lot like Chiquinha Coelho, but the others disagreed. Whether she resembled Chiquinha or not, Gonçalves got excited and proposed that all of them get on whatever streetcar she did. His friends just laughed.

Night was really falling by that time, and they went back to Ouvidor Street. At half past seven, they headed for a theater, not to see the show, because they had only cigarettes and a stray coin or two in their pockets, but to watch the fine ladies arrive. An hour later we could find them at Rocio Square, discussing physics. Then they recited poetry, both well-known works and verses of their own. Next there were more funny stories, puns, horsing around, and general high spirits. Gonçalves was the noisiest and most expansive of all, as if he didn't have a care in the world. At nine o'clock, he was back on Ouvidor Street, now by himself, and since he was out of smokes, he bought a pack for twenty-two milréis, on credit.

To be twenty years old!

---

48. milréis: at this time, the basic currency unit of Brazil.

SECTION III

Modernism and the Crisis

Introduction to Section III

Western literature in the first half of the twentieth century, considered in Section III, has two faces.[1] One is Modernism, treated in Chapter 7: the rejection of the traditional understanding of the text as a nexus of words that say what they mean and can be understood by the intelligent reader. It involves the disruption of meaning, the indulgence in ambiguity and allusion, and the elaboration of complex symbols. These approaches result in communication that is incomplete, prompting readers to supply themselves the missing pieces of the message that has been transmitted.

The other face of twentieth-century literature, treated in Chapter 8, is the response—by authors who were sometimes also actors or eyewitnesses—to crisis: the series of events by which the triumphal advance of Western culture is stalled and shattered. Those events include World War I, in which the nation-states of Europe nearly destroyed themselves for inscrutable purposes; the Russian Revolution and the subsequent establishment of Soviet Communism, in which the state asserted control over all economic and social relations; and World War II, in which a fascist surge, embodied especially by Germany's National Socialists, or "Nazis," threatened to conquer all of Europe and achieved the murder of nine million noncombatants, among them six million Jews.

Chapter 7 opens with poems composed between 1893 and 1925 by William Butler Yeats and T. S. Eliot: poems that build on the work of nineteenth-century predecessors including Giacomo Leopardi, Charles Baudelaire, Walt Whitman, and Emily Dickinson (see Chapters 2, 4, and 6), who employed patterns of sound and meter that defied the traditions of poetic composition. Yeats's poems *When You Are Old, Easter, 1916*, and *The Second Coming*, exemplify these practices, while Eliot's *The Love Song of J. Alfred Prufrock* and *The Hollow Men* further describe a world that has become futile and incoherent. Turning next to drama, Chapter 7 presents Luigi Pirandello as a representative of the same Modernist defiance of prevailing norms. Pirandello's *Six Characters in Search of an Author* inverts the principles of the inherited dramatic

---

1. See Glossary for important persons, events, places, and concepts that recur throughout Section III.

tradition in which a playwright creates characters who are then realized on the stage: here instead, explosively, the characters precede both the actors who will perform them and the author who has created them.

Eight texts follow in Chapter 7 that portray the disintegration of identity, the corollary to the disintegration of the text, that also characterizes Modernism. Works written between 1903 and 1930 by Osip Mandelstam, James Joyce, Ernest Hemingway, William Faulkner, Thomas Mann, Franz Kafka, Virginia Woolf, and W. E. B. Du Bois, in the genres of autobiography, short story, and essay, explore the fragile self at the core of their narratives. *The Noise of Time*, the autobiography of a poet at the center of the Acmeist movement in late-tsarist Russia, reveals the complex intermingling of his Russian and Jewish pasts. Like the child Mandelstam, the young boys featured in short stories by Joyce and Hemingway, respectively *The Sisters* and *Indian Camp*, are as yet in formation, uncertain of who they are as they are shocked by disturbing events. Not a child but an aging recluse, the protagonist of Faulkner's *A Rose for Emily* cannot confront a reality constructed by the loss of her father, her rejection by her lover, and the death of the aristocratic American South that she has outlived. Mann's *Tonio Kröger*, a fictional autobiography of novella length, explores its hero's bifurcated identity, torn by competing northern and southern European tendencies. Mann's contemporary Kafka, also writing in German, deals with a still more fractured sense of self in the epochal story *The Metamorphosis*, which portrays a traveling salesman who awakes one morning to find he has become a giant insect. Woolf and Du Bois, finally, write nonfictional accounts of the social categories that have powerfully shaped their identities: gender and race. Woolf reflects in *A Room of One's Own* on the historical and societal forces that have powerfully denied women the opportunity for self-realization—and specifically, to write. Du Bois examines in *The Souls of Black Folk* the "double-consciousness"—as Americans, the heirs of liberal ideals, and as Blacks, the survivors of slavery—with which African-Americans must struggle in their quest for self-actualization.

The last four works represented in Chapter 7, composed between 1915 and 1947 by Mariano Azuela, Pablo Neruda, Federico García Lorca, and Jean-Paul Sartre, are characterized by cultural despair: the collapse of meaning in the world that they or their characters inhabit. Two Latin American authors struggle with cultural meaning in national settings. In his novel *The Underdogs*, Azuela depicts the combatants for a reborn Mexico as hopelessly mired in corruption and violence. The poet Neruda, a diplomat and global traveler, is consumed by existential despair resolved, in part, by his apprehension of the pre-conquest Incan civilization of his native Chile, experienced as he stands on the heights of Andean Macchu Picchu. In his play *The House of Bernarda Alba*, Lorca depicts the hideous tyranny of traditional Spanish village life, shortly before he falls prey to fascist executioners in the very contemporary Spanish

Civil War. In *No Exit*, the philosopher Sartre as playwright plots the geography of hell: it is where people torment themselves and each other—and since they are already dead, they do so for all eternity.

Even as these Modernist authors remake the literary norms of the Western tradition, that tradition is threatened by epochal catastrophe: a sequence of war, revolution, tyranny, and destruction, lasting from 1914 to 1945—and beyond. The authors included in Chapter 8, participants in these critical events, recorded their alarm and anguish in poetry, drama, essay, letter, speech, memoirs, and novels.

The authors of the first five works represented in Chapter 8, composed or published between 1917 and 1939, respond to the slaughter in World War I that consumed a generation of young men and roughly an equal number of civilians—about ten million dead in each case. The chapter opens with the poets Wilfred Owen and Siegfried Sassoon, whose verses capture the horror of the infamous trench warfare on the European Western Front. Selections follow from Erich Maria Remarque's novel *All Quiet on the Western Front*; Bertolt Brecht's play *Mother Courage and Her Children*; and Simone Weil's essay *The* Iliad *or the Poem of Force*. All three works are profoundly anti-war: Remarque's describing realistically the experience of young German soldiers in the trenches; Brecht's merciless exposure of the evil of warfare based on the exemplary case of a dauntless woman's failed attempt, during the Thirty Years' War three centuries past, to save her children's lives; and Weil's unpacking the Homeric condemnation of violence that accompanied that poet's celebration of ancestral heroes.

Ironically, even as these last three authors excoriate the profession of war as manifested in World War I, a second cataclysm was brewing. All three fled to safety in advance of the outbreak of World War II.

Meanwhile, amid the trauma of the first World War, a cadre of young Russian intellectuals, the Bolsheviks—chafing under tsarist autocracy and utilizing as a theoretical guide, among others, the writings of nineteenth-century philosopher Karl Marx—envisioned a more humane society serving the needs of all citizens. Accordingly, they plotted a revolution: not the first, which had been attempted in 1905 and suppressed, but a successful one, beginning early in 1917 and culminating in the October Revolution (by the old Russian calendar; actually November) of that year.

The next five authors, writing between 1919 and 1940, depict the Russian, or Bolshevik, Revolution and its consequences. John Reed, the first of these, a journalist and socialist who heartily approved the aspiration for a more just and fair society, provides an eyewitness account of the October Revolution in *Ten Days That Shook the World*, published a little more than a year after the event itself and shortly before his own death. In her autobiography *Living My Life*, the Lithuanian-born American anarchist Emma Goldman reports on her return to

Russia in 1920–1921 and sadly concludes that the ideals of the revolution had been betrayed by those who created the new Soviet state. The Russian communist Victor Serge, the author of *Memoirs of a Revolutionary* (1951), was similarly disillusioned: in a letter to the French literary giant André Gide, who was sympathetic to communism and about to embark on a journey to the Soviet Union, Serge enumerates the historians, economists, scholars, and writers, who had been executed or caused to "vanish" by the repressive Soviet regime. Serge's terse account is powerful, but Arthur Koestler's novel *Darkness at Noon* and Anna Akhmatova's poem sequence *Requiem* are bone-chilling responses to the systematic violence of Stalin's Great Purge of 1936–1938. Koestler explores the psychological condition of Old Bolshevik revolutionaries who publicly confess to crimes against the state when their only crime had been to think outside the limits of official ideology. Akhmatova heartbreakingly records her attempts to find and succor her son who was caught up in the Stalinist terror—her first husband having previously been executed by the Bolsheviks in 1921—and dispatched to labor camps.

World War II followed only twenty years after the peace treaty was signed that had put an end, but only temporarily, to World War I. It opens with Nazi Germany's unprovoked invasion of Poland in 1939, followed by, in 1940, its push into western Europe, marked by the occupation of Paris on June 14 that sent Weil and Koestler into exile in the south of France.

Three authors writing between 1940 and 1958 bear witness to the Nazi endeavor. The new British prime minister, Winston Churchill, assumed that title on May 10, 1940, the same day that Germany launched its offensive against Luxembourg, Belgium, the Netherlands, and France. From June 1940 through June 1941, when Germany (now joined in the Axis alliance by Italy and Japan) invaded the Soviet Union, its former ally, Churchill's Britain faced the Nazi threat alone. Churchill rallied the British people and government against the Nazi offensive in three famous speeches, including the rousing *We Shall Fight on the Beaches* (June 4, 1940), appearing in this chapter. In December 1941, following the Japanese assault on Pearl Harbor on December 7, the United States joined Britain and the Soviet Union, the three constituting the principal Allied parties.

As Germany expanded its military operations, it pursued and broadened its offensive against European Jewry. That effort was launched in 1933 with racial laws limiting Jewish professional, economic, and social activity, and accelerated with increasing brutality to the creation of concentration camps during the 1930s and, in 1941, the initiation of the Final Solution, which aimed at the extermination of the Jewish population in Europe and beyond. (Alongside the Jews, defined as the principal enemy, the Nazis also targeted communists, homosexuals, Gypsies, children deemed "defective," and others.)

Chapter 8 includes excerpts from the work of two authors who suffered in the resulting Holocaust. The first is the *Diary* kept by Anne Frank for more than two years during 1942 to 1944 while in hiding with her family in Amsterdam (the Netherlands), prior to her arrest in 1944 and death at age fifteen in the Bergen-Belsen concentration camp. The second is the autobiographical novel *Night* by Elie Wiesel, published in 1958, more than a decade later, drawn from his extensive memoir of his experience during 1944–1945, at age sixteen, in Auschwitz and Buchenwald concentration camps.

The Allied powers gain victory in Europe by the 1943–1944 campaign in Italy, the 1944 D-Day (June 6) landing at Normandy, and the German surrender in 1945 (May 7–9) to Western and Soviet armies converging on Berlin. The war in the Pacific against Japan, however, still raged on fiercely on land and sea. It was brought to a sudden end on August 6 and 9, 1945: two atomic bombs dropped by the United States on the cities of Hiroshima and Nagasaki elicited Japan's surrender on August 14. In his journalistic account *Hiroshima* (1946), John Hersey depicts the horrendous destruction and psychological despair wrought by this newly invented weapon of terrifying force.

The calamities of the early twentieth century did not end in 1945. Out of that maelstrom had emerged the phenomenon of totalitarianism. The total control of economy, society, and culture by an all-powerful state, requiring the restructuring of the human personality, can be aspired to, as history has shown, by adherents of ideologies as different as communism and fascism. The danger it poses is unforgettably presented in the novel *1984* by the democratic socialist George Orwell. Selections from that work, whose importance endures well beyond the era in which it was written, fittingly constitute the final text presented in Chapter 8 and in this second volume of *The Western Literary Tradition*.

Chapter 7

Modernism

Introduction

In the twentieth century, authors who were themselves immersed in the tradition of Western thought and culture queried, challenged, and defied it, cracking out of its shell to hatch a new consciousness: that of Modernism. Chapter 7 presents fifteen authors, among the most important of the twentieth century, who shatter the norms of literary production. They reject traditional poetic forms, wielding a novel palette of sounds and using symbolism, abstraction, and allusion to create an abstruse text whose meaning the reader is challenged to deduce. They question their own identities, disaggregating inheritances of family, ethnicity, and culture. Trapped, deceived, and disillusioned by the events of the age, they despair of a world that is no longer whole.

Chapter 7 opens with two poets writing in English—one Irish, one American by birth: William Butler Yeats and T. S. Eliot. Descended from a prominent Anglo-Protestant Irish family and born in Dublin to striving parents, winner of the Nobel Prize in Literature in 1923, Yeats (1865–1939) wrote strikingly original and insightful poems and plays. In his early years, immersed in Irish myth and folklore, he wrote verse in traditional formats evoking an enchanted, haunted past. In his maturity, he developed a Modernist style, marked by free, rolling rhythms, interspersed accents of rhyme, complex symbols, and abstract ideas. In those later years, as well, the romantic nationalism of his youth evolved into a more pragmatic, though always detached, support of a free and independent Ireland—in the government of which, once achieved, he served two terms as senator. His poems, in tandem, often engaged contemporary events, as do two of the three included in this chapter: *Easter, 1916* (1916), a lament for the revolutionaries executed by the British in response to the Easter Rising; and *The Second Coming* (1919), an ominous prophecy of calamitous change written in the wake of World War I. The first of the three poems, *When You Are Old* (1893), written when Yeats was not yet thirty years old, was addressed to the vibrant actress Maud Gonne whom he loved unrequitedly for more than two decades.

In 1915, the American-born Eliot (1888–1965) published his first poem, *The Love Song of J. Alfred Prufrock*, which exhibits the Modernist features for which Eliot, like Yeats, would be famous: free but rhythmic verse; interspersed unpatterned rhymed lines; and the dense presence of symbols, allusions, and metaphysical concepts—Eliot drawing on the philosophers Aristotle, Plato,

312

Maurras, and Bergson, as well as Dante, Shakespeare, and Joseph Conrad, as Yeats had drawn on the Irish folk tradition.[1] These characteristics of Eliot's verse are evident in *Prufrock* and in *The Hollow Men*, written ten years later, in 1925. *The Hollow Men* responds to the cultural void of the years following World War I that had tormented Yeats as well, and that Eliot had previously confronted in 1922 in his lengthy poem *The Waste Land*. In 1927, two years after *The Hollow Men*, Eliot expressed his unease with the present age not in a poem but with a double conversion: he became a British citizen and an Anglo-Catholic.

Eliot is viewed here primarily as a poet, and it is as a poet that he was awarded the Nobel Prize in Literature in 1948. Yet he, too, again like Yeats, was also a playwright and a literary critic. Writing regularly in the *Criterion*, the literary journal he edited from 1922 to 1939, he contributed importantly to the discussion of Modernist literature, while as the director of the publishing house of Faber & Faber for the forty years from 1925 to 1965, he further helped shape the literary trends of the era.

Like James Joyce (to be introduced shortly) and Eliot, the Italian playwright Luigi Pirandello (1867–1936) defies the norms of literary composition, in this case in the genre of drama—a genre that purports to display real events in real space and time. But Pirandello dematerializes the author, emancipating the characters that he has created, thus inverting the relations of reality and illusion. This is the startling achievement of his play *Six Characters in Search of an Author* (1921), the prototype of the "theater of the absurd" that reached its apogee a generation later in post–World War II Europe.

Born in Sicily to a wealthy family, Pirandello attended universities in Palermo (Sicily), Rome, and Bonn (Germany), becoming expert in both Italian and German literature. From the 1890s, participating in literary circles in Rome, he acquired a stellar reputation as the author of novels, short stories, plays, poems, and journalistic and literary critical essays.[2] His plays, especially, won an enthusiastic reception—the one exception, in its first performance in Rome, being his all-important *Six Characters*, which scandalized the audience. It was "for his bold and ingenious revival of dramatic and scenic art"[3] that he was awarded the Nobel Prize in Literature in 1934.

---

1. Aristotle, etc.: the Greek philosophers Aristotle and Plato, and the French philosophers Charles Maurras (1868–1952) and Henri Bergson (1859–1941); for Dante and Shakespeare, see respectively, Volume One, Introductions to Chapter 3 and 4; for Conrad, see in this volume, Introduction to Chapter 3.

2. Pirandello enjoyed the support of dictator Benito Mussolini (Italian fascist dictator; 1925–1945), but claimed he was apolitical; and the ambivalence of his fascism brought him the close surveillance of the secret police.

3. "Luigi Pirandello Facts," The Nobel Prize (website), https://www.nobelprize.org/prizes/literature/1934/pirandello/facts/.

Six Characters is a play about a play and about theater itself. It features six Characters (Father, Mother, Step-Daughter, Son, Boy, and Child) who have been abandoned by the author who created them. Having by that abandonment become detached from their author and "real," they demand to be enacted, addressing themselves for that purpose to the Manager of the theater. Intrigued, the Manager allows them to present their story, telling the company of Actors, who will need to perform the roles the Characters model, to stand by and observe. The Characters protest: Why do they need Actors when they are themselves Characters?

The drama—the plot—is incidental; a horrific tale of family conflict and sexual perversion that ends in the Child's murder, the Boy's suicide, and the frenzied departure of the key character, the Step-Daughter, leaving on the stage the iconic and miserable nuclear family of Father, Mother, and Son. The Manager declares the whole thing a flop and a waste of his time.

But the point, manifestly, is not the story, but the astonishing resurrection of the Characters from the pages written by the vanished Author. Becoming real, they overcome the reality of the Actors, the Manager, and that machine of illusion, the theater itself.

In contrast to the Characters in Pirandello's play, who though illusory had a firm sense of who they were and for what purpose they existed, the protagonists of the works from which the next eight selections are drawn suffer from a sense of identity that is inchoate or badly compromised.

The Noise of Time (1925), the autobiography of Osip Mandelstam (1891–1938), is a young man's recollection of his childhood and adolescence in tsarist Russia. The selection included in Chapter 7 features the strong contrast between the splendid public life of imperial Russia and the author's private experience as the child of an intellectual Russian mother and a Polish merchant father, both Jews; Mandelstam himself had been born in Poland, but reared mostly in Russia. Mandelstam's sense of himself is riddled by the contradiction between his Polish and Russian, and Russian and Jewish identities.

Aside from his compelling autobiography, Mandelstam is mostly remembered for his poetry; considered one of the greatest Russian poets of his century, he is exceeded, perhaps, only by his contemporary Anna Akhmatova (see Introduction to Chapter 8, and Text 10). Finely educated in Russia and abroad, by 1910 Mandelstam had joined the pre-revolutionary St. Petersburg circle of Acmeist poets. Acmeism advocated a sparse Modernist style, vaunting "beautiful clarity" in contrast to what its proponents saw as the elaborately metaphysical and uncommunicative approach of the rival Symbolists. Mandelstam's essay, *The Morning of Acmeism* (composed 1913, published 1919), defined the movement's values, which he displayed in his highly acclaimed collection of poems, *Stone* (published in 1913, and in expanded versions in 1916 and 1923).

Stone was published shortly before the outbreak of World War I and the Bolshevik Revolution, of 1917. In the coming years, though he had initially supported Bolshevism, Mandelstam refused to put his poetry in its service—by which decision, he invited his eventual fate. He defied the Soviet literary establishment with the publication in 1925 of his highly personal *The Noise of Time*, followed by other publications the regime also found provocative: essays, poems, and an experimental novella. His sharp-tongued 1933 poem mocking the Soviet dictator Stalin,[4] the *Stalin Epigram*, triggered his downfall. Mandelstam was arrested, tortured, and exiled; and after a brief respite, sent off to the gulag of labor camps, where he died the following year. With the post-Stalinist thaw, his widow, the writer Nadezhda Mandelstam, who had shared his exile and preserved his works, was able to publish in the West her account of their experience in *Hope Against Hope* (1970) and *Hope Abandoned* (1974).

Unlike Mandelstam, who looked back in his adulthood on the conflicts that beset him in his youth, the Irish author James Joyce (1882–1941) portrays, in his short story *The Sisters*, a child who apprehends but does not understand the confusion around him, which will shape his identity as he matures. The first story in his story collection entitled *Dubliners, The Sisters* is the revision of an earlier version published in 1904—at that time, Joyce's first published story. It is, on the surface, a realistic description of events: an ailing priest, who has been mentoring a promising boy, has a stroke and dies. While others—the boy's aunt and uncle, their lodger, and the priest's two sisters—seem strangely unconcerned, the boy himself is troubled as he reflects on the priest and their relationship. As narrator, the boy says little about his feelings, but his feelings may be inferred from the discomfiture of all involved. The priest's reaction to an incident in which he accidentally breaks a chalice—a sacred vessel that held transubstantiated wine in the Catholic Mass—radiates with heightened significance. His symptoms, especially his paralysis, suggest syphilis, an evidence of past sexual behavior that would have shaken his familiars and the boy himself. One message that lurks behind the thin, tense fabric of sparse narration is that of the corruption of the church, which is itself morally paralyzed, and a contagious presence dangerous to the boy it pretends to nurture.

Joyce emerged from the world that is depicted in *Dubliners*. Born and raised in Dublin, the eldest surviving child of a downwardly mobile middle-class family, he was educated by Jesuits in the Catholic tradition he renounced but never entirely abandoned. Together with the woman he joyously met in 1904 and loved ever after (although he did not marry her until 1931), he left

---

4. Joseph Vissarionovich Stalin (1878–1953): Bolshevik revolutionary, general secretary of the Russian Communist Party, and Soviet premier from 1924 until his death.

Ireland a few months later to live in Trieste, Rome, Zurich, and Paris.[5] While resident in these capitals, working as a teacher and, briefly, a bank clerk, and surviving on generous subventions from patrons he had impressed, he published all his major and transformative works.

These works identify him as part of the Modernist vanguard. His novels and short stories eliminate the traditional all-seeing narrator, introduce stream-of-consciousness passages that display the interior complexities of his characters, and defy both moral and literary critical norms, setting a new standard for prose fiction. While these Modernist approaches will become fully developed in his monumental novels *Ulysses* (1922) and *Finnegan's Wake* (1939), they are already evident in his autobiographical novel *A Portrait of the Artist as a Young Man* (1916) and in his early short stories collected in *Dubliners* (1914).

Like Joyce, the American author Ernest Hemingway (1899–1961) portrays in the short story *Indian Camp*, the first in his early collection *In Our Time* (1925), an as yet unformed young boy who undergoes an experience that arouses confusion and distress—in this case, a shocking medical procedure on a woman in childbirth. Nick Adams (in whom the reader recognizes the figure of the author) has accompanied his physician father and his Uncle George to an Indian logging camp in Michigan. A woman has been struggling in labor for two days, tormented by pain. Nick's father uses his jack-knife, without anesthesia, to rip open her womb and extract the infant, whom he hands over to an old women standing by. The devastated mother has survived the operation, but the father, lying in the bunk above as she screamed in pain, has cut his own throat. The horrified boy, his father, and his uncle walk off to another world.

Written early in his career, *Indian Camp* already exemplifies the narrative style—taut and unadorned—that will characterize Hemingway's work. A journalist, soldier, and hunter, and at the same time a novelist and short story writer, he deals in hard facts, fierce emotions, and sparse language. He began his career working on a Kansas City newspaper, and as a journalist or a participant, witnessed the major events of the first half of the twentieth century: World War I, in which he served as an ambulance driver for the Red Cross; the expatriate world of the 1920s in Paris, when he lived as one of the "lost generation," as he named it; the Spanish Civil War (1936–1939), which he covered as a correspondent; and even Fidel Castro's[6] takeover in Cuba. During all these events, he wrote: several collections of short stories, a genre in which he dominated; and among ten novels, notably *The Sun Also Rises* (1926) on the 1920s

---

5. Trieste: an important seaport and commercial hub, now Italian, but until the close of World War I, part of the Austro-Hungarian Empire; Rome, Zurich, and Paris: respectively, major Italian, Swiss, and French cities.

6. Fidel Castro (1926–2016): Cuban revolutionary, Communist Party leader, prime minister (1959–1976) and president (1976–2008) of Cuba.

expatriate scene; *A Farewell to Arms* (1929) set during World War I; and *For Whom the Bell Tolls* (1940) set during the Spanish Civil War. He was awarded the Nobel Prize in Literature in 1954, the Prize Committee noting especially "his mastery of the art of narrative . . . [and] the influence that he has exerted on contemporary style."[7]

A Rose for Emily (1930), a short story by a second American author, William Faulkner (1897–1962), also considers the troubled identity of the principal character, a woman whose triple unbearable losses—of her father, her lover, and the traditional culture of the old South—result in her complete isolation and madness. Understated and elusive, it coyly offers a series of clues that challenge the reader to deduce what is happening with Miss Emily, the last survivor of a proud and distinguished family. She is a lady of the old southern gentry class: Why then, after her father's death, would she not release his body? It seemed then that she would marry the northerner Homer Barron: But why and to where had he disappeared? And what was the source of the stench that arose from her house, which town officials, stealthily at night, treated with lime to suppress? When she died, the loyal Black butler who had served her all her life walked out the back door and went away forever: What did he know of what had happened in that house?

Like most of Faulkner's stories, *A Rose for Emily* is a window into southern culture as seen in fictional Yoknapatawpha County in Mississippi—the state where the author, the descendant of an American Civil War hero, was born, lived, and died. After a shiftless youth with scant academic achievement, Faulkner began to write seriously in the mid-1920s, and his career took off with the publication in 1929 of the novella *Sartoris* and the novel *The Sound and the Fury*. Despite his fascination with the legacy of the Old South, Faulkner was a Modernist writer who utilized a stream-of-consciousness technique and multiple narrative voices to probe the complex psychology of his characters, as seen perhaps most forcefully in his 1936 novel *Absalom, Absalom!*

Increasingly acclaimed for his numerous novels and several short story collections in addition to Hollywood screenplays, Faulkner was selected for the 1949 Nobel Prize in Literature, which was conferred a year later. His acceptance speech, given on December 10, 1950, in Stockholm, is famous for the optimism he expressed for the future of humankind in an atomic age: "I believe that man will not merely endure: he will prevail. He is immortal, not because he alone among creatures has an inexhaustible voice, but because he has a soul, a spirit capable of compassion and sacrifice and endurance. The poet's, the writer's, duty is to write about these things."[8]

---

7. "The Nobel Prize in Literature 1954," The Nobel Prize (website), https://www.nobelprize.org/prizes/literature/1954/summary/.

8. William Faulkner, "Banquet Speech," The Nobel Prize (website), https://www.nobelprize.org/prizes/literature/1949/faulkner/speech/.

The German author Thomas Mann (1875–1955) was a young man when he wrote *Tonio Kröger* (1903), a short story closely based on the author's own life: it was very nearly an autobiography, such as that written by the young Osip Mandelstam, and rather like the autobiographical novel, *A Portrait of the Artist as a Young Man*, written by the young James Joyce. In *Kröger*, Mann struggled with the two tendencies of his personality, each an inheritance from one of his parents: his blond, northern, dominant father; and his dark, southern, artistic mother. His happiness, he suspects, would lie in being more like his father; but he is an artist, a writer, excruciatingly involved in his creations, and so remains his mother's son.

The eponymous hero of *Tonio Kröger* mirrors the competing themes of the author's persona. The adolescent Tonio had admired his young blond friend Hans, and fell in love with Ingeborg, a young blond girl—two idols who eventually, one might say inevitably, come together. But in his maturity, a successful author, he has turned from that world of simple normalcy to the stormier one of artistic creation. After a chance encounter with the two blond icons of his youth, he makes explicit the tension between those two worlds in a letter to his close friend (but not lover), the Russian artist Lisaveta:

> I stand between two worlds, am at home in neither, and in consequence have rather a hard time of it. [. . .] While I am writing, the sea's roar is coming up to me, and I close my eyes. I am looking into an unborn and shapeless world that longs to be called to life and order, I am looking into a throng of phantoms of human forms which beckon me to conjure them and set them free [. . .]. But my deepest and most secret love belongs to the blond and blue-eyed, the bright-spirited living ones, the happy, amiable, and commonplace.[9]

Born to a wealthy and cultivated German family, Mann enjoyed the material advantages many writers lack, and was able to devote himself wholly to his art. Best known for his major novels—including *Buddenbrooks* (1924), also dealing with family relations; *The Magic Mountain* (1924); and the immense four-part *Joseph and His Brothers* (1933–1943)—Mann's short stories also have classic status in literary history, foremost among them *Tonio Kröger* and the likewise autobiographical *Death in Venice* (1912). Awarded the Nobel Prize in Literature in 1929 shortly before the Nazi ascendancy in Germany, in 1933 he emigrated to Switzerland; in 1939, when World War II broke out, he fled to the United States, becoming a citizen in 1944; and in 1952, he returned to Switzerland, where he died.

---

9. Thomas Mann, *Tonio Kröger*, trans. Bayard Quincy Morgan, in *German Classics of the Nineteenth and Twentieth Centuries: Masterpieces of German Literature Translated into English*, gen. ed. Kuno Francke (New York: The German Publication Society, 1913), vol. 19, section XV, 249–50.

Whereas Mann could analyze serenely the crosscurrents of his identity, Franz Kafka (1883–1924) was tormented by them. Born in Prague[10] to a German-speaking middle-class Jewish family of hard-working merchants, he studied law and worked for an insurance company, able to write only in brief intervals. Few of his works were published in his brief lifetime—he died of tuberculosis at age forty—and he was little known. Nonetheless, his disturbing and often bizarre novels and short stories, which portray the human suffering caused by oppressive and secretive bureaucracies, tyrannical officials, and persecuting fathers, have assured his reputation as a great twentieth-century author.

Kafka's works reflect the many uncertainties and discomforts of his life: he was shy, quiet, and in poor health; he had many love affairs, but never married; he stood at the intersection of the German, Czech, and Jewish cultural traditions; his childhood was disturbed by the deaths of siblings and, above all, by the anger and expectations of his father. His novels were left unfinished, and even what we have is less than it should be, as he burned many of his manuscripts. He had instructed his friend and executor Max Brod to destroy all his papers on his death, but Brod instead published Kafka's works—finishing the unfinished ones—between 1925 and 1935. Kafka thereby won the fame he never sought in his lifetime.

Kafka is best known for his novels *The Trial* (1914, published 1925), about a man arrested and prosecuted by a mysterious authority for a crime that is not named; *The Castle* (1922, published 1926), about a man who attempts unsuccessfully to gain access to invisible officials who govern from a castle; and, among his numerous short stories, especially *The Metamorphosis* (1915), selections from which appear in this chapter.

The Metamorphosis follows the deterioration of the traveling salesman Gregor, who awakes one morning to find he has been transformed into a giant beetle-like insect, with multiple legs and hard carapace. His shocked family initially tries to understand what has happened to a beloved member of their family who was, moreover, their main breadwinner. Over time, however, as their financial hardships mount, they lose patience with their beetle-son. His talented and sensitive adolescent sister, sympathetic at first, turns callous, then murderous, declaring to her parents: "It must be gotten rid of"; "You must try to get rid of the idea that this is Gregor." Gregor knows he is unloved; he refuses to eat and dies.

The next two authors considered in Chapter 7—the Englishwoman Virginia Woolf and the African-American W. E. B. Du Bois—also struggle with their identities, but for a different reason: not because of the contradictory

---

10. Prague: modern Czech Republic, but at Kafka's birth, the capital of the Kingdom of Bohemia, part of the Austro-Hungarian Empire.

forces at work within their souls and minds, but because of their membership in a particular social group: the group of all women, in Woolf's case, and of American Blacks, in Du Bois's.

Born to a cultivated, liberal, and upper-class British family, the daughter of an eminent scholar, Virginia Woolf (1882–1941) began writing as a child and her literary ambitions never flagged, despite the early deaths of family members and her own mental illness. Joining her brothers and their friends, she was a member of the literary circle known as the Bloomsbury Group (named after the section of London where they resided and worked). Later, with her husband Leonard Woolf, a Jewish intellectual and civil servant from outside her aristocratic circle, she ran the distinguished Hogarth Press (founded 1917), famous for, among other achievements, publishing the English edition of the complete works of Sigmund Freud, the founder of psychoanalysis. In addition to her editorial work and more than five hundred essays and critical reviews, Woolf is known for her Modernist novels, which employ the stream of consciousness technique used also by Eliot and Joyce: among them, *Mrs Dalloway* (1925), *To the Lighthouse* (1927), and *Orlando* (1928).

Even those who have not read Woolf's novels may be aware of her most famous essay, a fundamental document of modern feminism: *A Room of One's Own* (1929). Based on two lectures she delivered in 1928 at Newnham and Girton Colleges, Cambridge, to audiences of eager university women, it confronts the plight—a plight specific to an elite population—of young women who wanted, as she had years before, to be writers. You will need, she told them, two things: a room of your own, set apart from other rooms that impose domestic responsibilities; and an income of 500 pounds a year. That sum of 500 pounds in British currency was sufficient to provide a modest living, and it happened, at the same time, to correspond to the income that Woolf herself received as an inheritance. Beyond the statement of these requirements, Woolf's essay also highlights the history of women's literary activity. It was a history full of holes: although some women authors shone as brightly as male counterparts, many more were never heard from, because their ambitions were consumed by their duties as daughters, wives, and mothers.

Unlike the Black abolitionist Frederick Douglass (see Introduction to Chapter 6 and Text 4) or the Black educator Booker T. Washington, William E. B. Du Bois (1868–1963) was not born in slavery. He was born, rather, in Great Barrington, Massachusetts, the son of two parents of mixed race: his mother the descendant of a freed slave, his father a descendant of French Huguenots.[11] Schooled in Massachusetts alongside white contemporaries, he

---

11. Huguenots: dissenting French Calvinists of the sixteenth and seventeenth centuries, many of whom fled to the Netherlands, Britain, and the American colonies after the 1685 revocation of the Edict of Nantes that had protected their freedom of worship.

went on to study at Fisk University, Harvard University, and the University of Berlin (Germany), completing his education at Harvard in 1895 with a PhD— the first African American awarded that degree by Harvard. He went on to a career as author, academic, social theorist, and civil rights activist, founding the NAACP (National Association for the Advancement of Colored People) in 1909.

Yet although Du Bois was fortunate to have eluded the worst consequences of the system of African slavery, he lived necessarily in two realities, black and white, in a state that he called "double consciousness": he embodied both the burden of the slave experience, and the triumph of liberal values in the American political system. Like Mandelstam and Mann, whose sense of themselves was riven by oppositional forces, Du Bois struggled to understand his dividedness, and in so doing to understand the condition of African Americans—the "souls of black folk." *The Souls of Black Folk* (1903), the collection of essays so named, is the one of his many works for which he is most renowned.

"The problem of the twentieth century is the problem of the color-line,"[12] Du Bois memorably announced at the dawning of that era. The color line was the barrier separating black and white or whites and others not only in the United States, but also across the globe. And the solution for blacks would be education: not just a technical education, leading to employment, but an education of mind and character, to be gained by a deep and serious immersion in the intellectual tradition. Only a fraction, perhaps a "talented tenth"[13] of black folk would be able to pursue that road, but if they could do so, they would lead their fellows to a fuller consciousness and, finally, to freedom and equality.

Chapter 7 next considers the works of four authors, writing from 1915 to 1944, who observe in different settings—two American and two European—a world that has been fatally damaged and corrupted. The physician and novelist Mariano Azuela (1873–1952) writes of the chaotic Mexican Revolution (1910–1920) in which he participated, having been attached from 1914 to 1915 to the army of Pancho Villa.[14] The noble effort to establish a constitutional government following the 1911 ouster of dictator Porfirio Díaz[15] almost immediately broke down in internecine warfare among competing elite strongmen. Of the seven leading competitors, two were eventually exiled, one executed, and four assassinated. Most of Azuela's more than twenty novels written over

---

12. W. E. B. Du Bois, *The Souls of Black Folk*, 2nd ed. (Chicago: A. C. McClurg & Co., 1903), vii.

13. Du Bois, *Souls of Black Folk*, 105.

14. Francisco "Pancho" Villa (1878–1923): prominent landowner and commander of the Northern Division during the Mexican Revolution.

15. Porfirio Díaz (1830–1915): Mexican dictator for thirty-one years between 1876 and 1911, overthrown by the Mexican Revolution.

his more than forty-year career, including six published during the very years of conflict, portray the violence, treachery, and disillusionment the Revolution generated. Of these, the most famous is *The Underdogs* (1915). In it, the peasant proprietor Demetrio Macías, his homestead seized and set on fire by government soldiers, fights for the Revolution and for himself, leading a band of locals who, corrupted, ravage the countryside amid the general chaos. At his right hand is an idealistic physician, a young man from an elite family, modeled on Azuela, the author.

Azuela's novel is reminiscent of works encountered earlier in this volume: José Joaquín Fernández de Lizardi's *The Mangy Parrot* (see Introduction to Chapter 6 and Text 9) about the earlier Mexican War of Independence of 1810–1821, in which that nation threw off its colonial overlords; and Eduardo Gutiérrez's *The Gaucho Juan Moreira* (see Introduction to Chapter 6 and Text 10) about an Argentinian gaucho turned outlaw by unjust government officials and revered as a cultural hero. Azuela clearly drew on these prototypes, embedding them in the novel circumstances of the revolutionary struggle. But in Azuela's work, there is no redemption for the sin-burdened protagonist, as in Lizardi's; and none of the nobility of Gutiérrez's martyred gaucho Moreira. In the maelstrom of early twentieth-century Mexico, all hope and all virtue died.

The Chilean author and diplomat Pablo Neruda (penname of Neftalí Ricardo Reyes Basoalto; 1904–1973) also despaired of the condition of things. The son of a railway worker whose mother died soon after his birth, Neruda became a poet when he was still a child: he published his first work in 1917, at age thirteen. He soon won instant recognition for his second poem collection, a bestseller still today, published in 1924 when he was twenty: *Twenty Love Poems and a Desperate Song*. Over the next half-century, Neruda wrote prolifically and to thunderous applause. The 1968 edition of his *Complete Works* ran to more than three thousand pages in two volumes. He was awarded the Nobel Prize in Literature in 1971, the committee commending the "elemental force" of his poetry.[16]

Neruda's early success as a poet did not solve the problem of his poverty. To support himself, he began a diplomatic career in 1927 that took him to Asian capitals in Burma, Sri Lanka, Java, and Singapore; to Buenos Aires in South America; and to Barcelona and Madrid in Spain. In Madrid in 1935, he joined a brilliant literary circle that included the poet Federico García Lorca (to be introduced shortly). While posted there he witnessed the Spanish Civil War, in which conflict he championed the Republicans, with their array of socialist, anarchist, and communist supporters. Moved in part by Lorca's execution in

---

16. "The Nobel Prize in Literature 1971," The Nobel Prize (website), https://www.nobelprize.org/prizes/literature/1971/summary/.

1936, Neruda joined the Communist Party in 1940, and remained a lifelong communist, undeterred even by Stalin. Recalled home, he served as consul-general in Mexico from 1940 to 1943 (during which term he assisted one of accused assassins of the Old Bolshevik, Leon Trotsky[17]), and returned to Chile to an enthusiastic public reception as a great national poet.

But Neruda had seen much of the world, and he was world-weary. He found renewal in 1945 when, during a visit to Peru, he climbed to the heights of Macchu Picchu, a fifteenth-century Incan cosmopolis that had been unknown until its discovery in 1911. Built on stepped stones cut into the mountainside at an elevation of 7,970 feet, with a population of about 750 mostly immigrant slave laborers, it was a royal administrative center about fifty miles from the Incan capital at Cusco. Neruda commemorates the complex pre-conquest and pre-Christian civilization revealed in its ruins in *The Heights of Macchu Picchu*, a sequence of twelve poems published in 1947. It was later included as part of his *Canto general* (*General Song*), published in 1950, a two-volume collection of more than three hundred poems celebrating the people and past of South America.

Neruda published the *Canto general* in Mexico, during a period of politi-cal exile: he had fled Chile in 1948 during a crackdown on communists, not returning until 1952. In the presidential elections of 1952, he supported the socialist candidate Salvador Allende,[18] who would eventually become Chil-ean president; Allende, in turn, promoted Neruda. Returning to Chile in 1972 from a diplomatic post in Paris, Neruda died in 1973, during the coup d'état of Augusto Pinochet[19] that felled Allende. It may have been poison dis-pensed by Pinochet's lackeys, and not prostate cancer, that caused Neruda's death.

The brilliant Spanish poet, playwright, and theater director Federico García Lorca (1898–1936) had known Neruda in Madrid in 1935, before the outbreak of the Spanish Civil War silenced the literary and artistic ferment of that city—and silenced the rebel Lorca. When the fascist nationalists seized power in Spain in 1936, Lorca was thirty-eight years old and his career was well underway. The son of a wealthy landowning and politically liberal fam-ily based in Granada (southeastern Spain), he studied law and philosophy at the University of Granada, but by 1919 had gravitated to Madrid and devoted himself to writing. He joined Madrid's dynamic literary and artistic circle,

---

17. Leon Trotsky (1879–1940): Bolshevik revolutionary; after Lenin's death the leader of the Left Opposition; expelled from the Party and exiled in 1929; assassinated in exile in Mexico, 1940.
18. Salvador Allende (1908–1973): Chilean socialist politician and physician, president of Chile 1970–1973.
19. Augusto Pinochet (1915–2006): Chilean general and politician, leader of the military coup against socialist Salvador Allende, subsequently president of Chile, 1974–1990.

where he promoted Modernist approaches in literature and theater—and where he found opportunities as well to pursue his homosexual tendencies that were elsewhere impossible in culturally conservative Spain, and which he would daringly report in his *Sonnets of Dark Love* (1935).

Lorca spent the year 1929–1930 in New York City (which he memorialized in his poem collection, *Poet in New York*), studying at Columbia University and observing that city's vibrant cultural scene. He returned to Spain as the liberal Republican Party triumphed in elections and founded the Second Spanish Republic. Over the next six years, he directed a touring theater company, promoted by the Republican government, which aimed to bring classical theater to the town squares of provincial Spain. During these years as well, he wrote his most famous poem, *Lament for the Death of a Bullfighter* (1935), and his most famous plays, including *Blood Wedding* (1932), *Yerma* (1934), and *The House of Bernarda Alba* (1936), which established his reputation as Spain's greatest modern playwright.

Lorca was visiting his family in Granada in the summer of 1936 when nationalist forces burst into that city. He was arrested, questioned, and executed, perhaps on August 19. His remains have not yet been located. The fascist regime banned his works, only relenting years later, in 1953, when it permitted the publication of a censored collection of his *Complete Works*.

The House of Bernarda Alba, completed two months before Lorca's death, is fittingly subtitled *Drama about Women in the Villages of Spain*. The subordination of women and the corollary repression of sexuality, were hallmarks of Spain's conservative Catholic culture that reigned in the countryside—and which the fascists would promote—even as the Spanish cities participated brightly in modern European culture. The "house" of Bernarda Alba is the metonymy of that subordination and repression. Paradoxically, whereas a house in traditional Europe is not so much a building as a family constellation reaching across generations, headed by a male, and sexually reproduced, the house of Alba is headed by Bernarda, a woman who despotically controls her five daughters in order to protect its honor, vulnerable to the merest expression of their sexual desire.

Condemned by the death of Bernarda's husband to an extraordinary eight-year term of mourning, the daughters resist. The eldest, as the daughter of Bernarda's first husband, is equipped with an inheritance, and so inspires the courtship of Pepe el Romano, the one male character in the play (who yet never appears on stage). Yet while courting Angustias, the over-aged eldest daughter, Pepe seduces Adela, the very willing youngest. Adela's sexual adventure discovered, Bernarda grabs a shotgun and shoots Pepe, who runs away. Told that her lover is dead, Adela hangs herself. Her mother, unperturbed by her daughter's death, cares only about her honor: tell everyone, she sternly commands, "The youngest daughter of Bernarda Alba has died a virgin."

Lorca exposes the stifling hypocrisy and sterility of Christian culture on the eve of the fascist takeover that would reinforce it for another generation; but it is already dead for the philosopher, novelist, and playwright Jean-Paul Sartre (1905–1980). Existentialism, an important strand of twentieth-century philosophy, holds that individuals are completely free agents who determine their own existence. Since for Sartre, modern existentialism's leading proponent, there is no Creator—that is, no God—the individual necessarily, by his freely chosen actions, creates himself. This outlook he develops in several theoretical works—among them *Being and Nothingness* (1943) and *Existentialism Is a Humanism* (1946)—and, notably, in his more than twenty novels and plays, among the latter *No Exit*, presented in this chapter.

After 1939, Sartre's career of teaching, philosophizing, and writing took a new turn, toward political activism. As Neruda had been radicalized by the Spanish Civil War, Sartre was by World War II, during which he spent nine months at a prisoner of war camp, and then experienced the horror of the Nazi occupation of Paris. In the post-war era, he supported the goal of worldwide socialist revolution, and although he never joined the Communist Party, he admired a gallery of communist leaders, including Stalin, the Chinese chairman Mao Zedong,[20] as well as the Latin American revolutionaries Fidel Castro and dashing martyr Che Guevara.[21] In 1964, when he heard that he was about to be awarded the Nobel Prize in Literature, he attempted to refuse the honor, although it was bestowed upon him nonetheless. In his public explanation of that attempt, he explained that a writer, to be authentic, must "refuse to let himself be transformed into an institution . . . ,"[22] especially one identified with what he considered to be the decadent culture of bourgeois Europe.

In Sartre is reached, it could be said, the culmination of Modernism: in his detestation, that is, of the European civilization of which he himself was a principal embodiment. His nihilistic message is concisely conveyed in the one-act play *No Exit*, first performed in 1944, while World War II still raged and Paris cringed under Nazi rule, and published the following year. It paints the landscape of a hell made not by God, but by other human beings. In it, three dead souls who had gravely sinned find themselves together in hell—configured as a

---

20. Mao Zedong (1893–1976): Chinese communist revolutionary, founder of the People's Republic of China, which he ruled 1949–1976.

21. Che Guevara (1928–1967): Argentine communist revolutionary and physician, major figure in the Cuban revolution and following his execution, worldwide cultural icon of political resistance.

22. Jean-Paul Sartre and Richard Howard, trans., "Sartre on the Nobel Prize," *The New York Review of Books*, December 17, 1964, https://www.nybooks.com/articles/1964/12/17/sartre-on-the-nobel-prize/.

room in a shabby hotel—where they are tortured not by demons and fearsome instruments, but by each other. Forever.

1. William Butler Yeats, *When You Are Old* (1893); *Easter, 1916* (1916); *The Second Coming* (1919)

The first of the three poems that follow is an early love lyric, both touching and taunting, written when the poet was not yet thirty years old. The second and third are products of his full maturity. *Easter, 1916* is a response to the tragic events of the Irish Easter Rising. *The Second Coming*, written in 1919 when the aftershocks of World War I still resounded, is a portentous reflection on the current age and anticipation of the fearsome one to come.

WHEN YOU ARE OLD

Repudiated by the woman he loves, still in love, but gently spiteful, Yeats invites his beloved to imagine herself in her old age thinking about the lover she has lost—one who truly understood her passionate "pilgrim soul," and who when spurned, powered by sorrow, soared to the mountain tops and hid himself, transformed as "Love" itself, amid the stars.

When you are old and gray and full of sleep,
And nodding by the fire, take down this book,
And slowly read, and dream of the soft look
Your eyes had once, and of their shadows deep;
How many loved your moments of glad grace,
And loved your beauty with love false or true,
But one man loved the pilgrim soul in you,
And loved the sorrows of your changing face;
And bending down beside the glowing bars,
Murmur, a little sadly, how Love fled
And paced upon the mountains overhead
And hid his face among a crowd of stars.

EASTER, 1916

Yeats celebrates the dead heroes of the Easter Rising, shot over ten days in May following their surrender in April. He had known them as ordinary fellows, a bit sensitive, or a bit rough. But now they are utterly changed, transformed by their sacrifice, resurrected, as Christ had been, at Eastertide; their names commemorated in two lilting lines, "Mac-Donagh and MacBride / And Connolly and Pearse"; a "terrible beauty" has been born.

I have met them at close of day
Coming with vivid faces
From counter or desk among grey
Eighteenth-century houses.
I have passed with a nod of the head
Or polite meaningless words,
Or have lingered awhile and said
Polite meaningless words,
And thought before I had done
Of a mocking tale or a gibe
To please a companion
Around the fire at the club,
Being certain that they and I
But lived where motley is worn:
All changed, changed utterly:
A terrible beauty is born.

That woman's days were spent
In ignorant good-will,
Her nights in argument
Until her voice grew shrill.
What voice more sweet than hers
When, young and beautiful,
She rode to harriers?
This man had kept a school
And rode our wingèd horse;
This other his helper and friend
Was coming into his force;
He might have won fame in the end,
So sensitive his nature seemed,
So daring and sweet his thought.
This other man I had dreamed
A drunken, vainglorious lout.
He had done most bitter wrong
To some who are near my heart,
Yet I number him in the song;
He, too, has resigned his part
In the casual comedy;
He, too, has been changed in his turn,
Transformed utterly:
A terrible beauty is born.

Hearts with one purpose alone
Through summer and winter seem
Enchanted to a stone
To trouble the living stream.
The horse that comes from the road,
The rider, the birds that range
From cloud to tumbling cloud,
Minute by minute they change;
A shadow of cloud on the stream
Changes minute by minute;
A horse-hoof slides on the brim,
And a horse plashes within it;
The long-legged moor-hens dive,
And hens to moor-cocks call;
Minute by minute they live:
The stone's in the midst of all.

Too long a sacrifice
Can make a stone of the heart.
O when may it suffice?
That is Heaven's part, our part
To murmur name upon name,
As a mother names her child
When sleep at last has come
On limbs that had run wild.
What is it but nightfall?
No, no, not night but death;
Was it needless death after all?
For England may keep faith
For all that is done and said.
We know their dream; enough
To know they dreamed and are dead;
And what if excess of love
Bewildered them till they died?
I write it out in a verse—
MacDonagh and MacBride
And Connolly and Pearse
Now and in time to be,
Wherever green is worn,
Are changed, changed utterly:
A terrible beauty is born.

September 25, 1916

The Second Coming

There is something frightfully wrong with the present age (and indeed, the poem is written in 1919, only months after the close of the catastrophic World War I): it has fallen apart; it has lost its center. Two thousand years after the birth of Christ, a new spirit is about to be born—this second one a "rough beast" with a "blank and pitiless" gaze, more fearsome than the first.

Turning and turning in the widening gyre
The falcon cannot hear the falconer;
Things fall apart; the centre cannot hold;
Mere anarchy is loosed upon the world,
The blood-dimmed tide is loosed, and everywhere
The ceremony of innocence is drowned;
The best lack all conviction, while the worst
Are full of passionate intensity.
Surely some revelation is at hand;
Surely the Second Coming is at hand.
The Second Coming! Hardly are those words out
When a vast image out of Spiritus Mundi[23]
Troubles my sight: a waste of desert sand;
A shape with lion body and the head of a man,
A gaze blank and pitiless as the sun,
Is moving its slow thighs, while all about it
Wind shadows of the indignant desert birds.
The darkness drops again but now I know
That twenty centuries of stony sleep
Were vexed to nightmare by a rocking cradle,
And what rough beast, its hour come round at last,
Slouches towards Bethlehem to be born?

2. T. S. Eliot, *The Love Song of J. Alfred Prufrock* (1915) and *The Hollow Men* (1925)

The two poems by T. S. Eliot that follow exemplify in turn his youthful and his full-career writing. *Prufrock* offers an internal monologue by the archetypal man of the new, rudderless twentieth century: a man unfulfilled, wandering, and indecisive. *The Hollow Men*, like the lengthier *The Waste Land* (1922) that

---

23. Spiritus Mundi: literally, in Latin, "spirit of the world," the universal mind or repository of thought.

preceded it, is an anguished lament for the current age: it is limping into nonexistence, populated only by hollow men.

The Love Song of J. Alfred Prufrock

Prufrock cannot sing a love song because he cannot love. Through his head run fragmentary thoughts and apperceptions, revealing his inability to act even on his deepest needs. Time hangs heavy on him; he has time for "a hundred indecisions" before tucking in to a formalized afternoon repast of "toast and tea." Does he dare to climb the staircase, or will he turn back, lest he "disturb the universe"? As he walks along the beach he hears the mermaids singing to each other: but "I do not think that they will sing to me."[24]

> *S'io credesse che mia risposta fosse*
> *A persona che mai tornasse al mondo,*
> *Questa fiamma staria senza piu scosse.*
> *Ma percioche giammai di questo fondo*
> *Non torno vivo alcun, s'i'odo il vero,*
> *Senza tema d'infamia ti rispondo.*[25]

Let us go then, you and I,
When the evening is spread out against the sky
Like a patient etherized upon a table;
Let us go, through certain half-deserted streets,
The muttering retreats
Of restless nights in one-night cheap hotels
And sawdust restaurants with oyster-shells:
Streets that follow like a tedious argument
Of insidious intent
To lead you to an overwhelming question . . .
Oh, do not ask, "What is it?"
Let us go and make our visit.

In the room the women come and go
Talking of Michelangelo.[26]

---

24. The ellipses in this poem are the author's, found in the original text.

25. Epigraph is from Dante, *Inferno* XXVII, 61–66, in which Guido da Montefeltro tells his secret story to Dante in the mistaken belief that Dante will not return to earth again from hell and by betraying the narrator's tale, defame him. Prufrock, too, by communicating his thoughts, defames himself. For Dante, see Volume One, Introduction to Chapter 7.

26. Michelangelo: the Italian Renaissance artist. The portrayal is implied of idle women strolling through a gallery speaking in shallow and pretentious tones of the great artist.

The yellow fog that rubs its back upon the window-panes,
The yellow smoke that rubs its muzzle on the window-panes,
Licked its tongue into the corners of the evening,
Lingered upon the pools that stand in drains,
Let fall upon its back the soot that falls from chimneys,
Slipped by the terrace, made a sudden leap,
And seeing that it was a soft October night,
Curled once about the house, and fell asleep.

And indeed there will be time
For the yellow smoke that slides along the street,
Rubbing its back upon the window-panes;
There will be time, there will be time
To prepare a face to meet the faces that you meet;
There will be time to murder and create,
And time for all the works and days of hands
That lift and drop a question on your plate;
Time for you and time for me,
And time yet for a hundred indecisions,
And for a hundred visions and revisions,
Before the taking of a toast and tea.

In the room the women come and go
Talking of Michelangelo.

And indeed there will be time
To wonder, "Do I dare?" and, "Do I dare?"
Time to turn back and descend the stair,
With a bald spot in the middle of my hair—
(They will say: "How his hair is growing thin!")
My morning coat, my collar mounting firmly to the chin,
My necktie rich and modest, but asserted by a simple pin—
(They will say: "But how his arms and legs are thin!")
Do I dare
Disturb the universe?
In a minute there is time
For decisions and revisions which a minute will reverse.

For I have known them all already, known them all:
Have known the evenings, mornings, afternoons,
I have measured out my life with coffee spoons;
I know the voices dying with a dying fall
Beneath the music from a farther room.
          So how should I presume?

And I have known the eyes already, known them all—
The eyes that fix you in a formulated phrase,
And when I am formulated, sprawling on a pin,
When I am pinned and wriggling on the wall,
Then how should I begin
To spit out all the butt-ends of my days and ways?
            And how should I presume?

And I have known the arms already, known them all—
Arms that are braceleted and white and bare
(But in the lamplight, downed with light brown hair!)
Is it perfume from a dress
That makes me so digress?
Arms that lie along a table, or wrap about a shawl.
                And should I then presume?
                And how should I begin?

Shall I say, I have gone at dusk through narrow streets
And watched the smoke that rises from the pipes
Of lonely men in shirt-sleeves, leaning out of windows? . . .

I should have been a pair of ragged claws
Scuttling across the floors of silent seas.

And the afternoon, the evening, sleeps so peacefully!
Smoothed by long fingers,
Asleep . . . tired . . . or it malingers,
Stretched on the floor, here beside you and me.
Should I, after tea and cakes and ices,
Have the strength to force the moment to its crisis?
But though I have wept and fasted, wept and prayed,
Though I have seen my head (grown slightly bald) brought in upon a platter,[27]
I am no prophet—and here's no great matter;
I have seen the moment of my greatness flicker,
And I have seen the eternal Footman hold my coat, and snicker,
And in short, I was afraid.

And would it have been worth it, after all,
After the cups, the marmalade, the tea,
Among the porcelain, among some talk of you and me,
Would it have been worth while,
To have bitten off the matter with a smile,

---

27. head upon a platter: a reference to John the Baptist, whom King Herod has beheaded; John the Baptist's head is then brought to Herodias, who hated him (Matthew 14:3–11).

To have squeezed the universe into a ball
To roll it towards some overwhelming question,
To say: "I am Lazarus, come from the dead,[28]
Come back to tell you all, I shall tell you all"—
If one, settling a pillow by her head
       Should say: "That is not what I meant at all;
       That is not it, at all."

And would it have been worth it, after all,
Would it have been worth while,
After the sunsets and the dooryards and the sprinkled streets,
After the novels, after the teacups, after the skirts that trail along the floor—
And this, and so much more?—
It is impossible to say just what I mean!
But as if a magic lantern threw the nerves in patterns on a screen:
Would it have been worth while
If one, settling a pillow or throwing off a shawl,
And turning toward the window, should say:
       "That is not it at all,
       That is not what I meant, at all."

No! I am not Prince Hamlet,[29] nor was meant to be;
Am an attendant lord, one that will do
To swell a progress, start a scene or two,
Advise the prince; no doubt, an easy tool,
Deferential, glad to be of use,
Politic, cautious, and meticulous;
Full of high sentence, but a bit obtuse;
At times, indeed, almost ridiculous—
Almost, at times, the Fool.[30]

I grow old . . . I grow old . . .
I shall wear the bottoms of my trousers rolled.

Shall I part my hair behind? Do I dare to eat a peach?
I shall wear white flannel trousers, and walk upon the beach.
I have heard the mermaids singing, each to each.

---

28. Lazarus: the poet alludes to one of the two Lazarus figures in the New Testament, both of whom are dead: Jesus's friend, whom he calls for from the tomb and from death (John 11:1–44); and the beggar Lazarus, who when he dies is lovingly sheltered in the bosom of Abraham (Luke 16:19–31).
29. Prince Hamlet: eponymous hero of Shakespeare's tragedy *Hamlet*, a man indecisive like Prufrock, but as a king's son, of much higher rank and dignity. For Shakespeare, see Volume One, Introduction to Chapter 11 and Text 3.
30. the Fool: perhaps the court jester, or more likely, in *Hamlet*, the unctuous official Polonius, who serves the king ("an easy tool," "glad to be of use"), but who is in truth a fool.

I do not think that they will sing to me.
I have seen them riding seaward on the waves
Combing the white hair of the waves blown back
When the wind blows the water white and black.
We have lingered in the chambers of the sea
By sea-girls wreathed with seaweed red and brown
Till human voices wake us, and we drown.

THE HOLLOW MEN

"Hollow men" are the soulless human beings we have all become amid the cata-
strophic events of the early twentieth century: stuffed with straw, like scarecrows,
in our fecklessness leaning on each other. Our words are meaningless; our gestures
motionless; our world is dead—"cactus land," or desert—as it has been drained
of the water of life. This lifeless world will end, "Not with a bang but a whimper."

Mistah Kurtz—he dead[31]
        A penny for the Old Guy[32]

I

We are the hollow men
We are the stuffed men
Leaning together
Headpiece filled with straw. Alas!
Our dried voices, when
We whisper together
Are quiet and meaningless
As wind in dry grass
Or rats' feet over broken glass
In our dry cellar

Shape without form, shade without colour,
Paralysed force, gesture without motion;

---

31. *Mistah Kurtz—he dead*: the words of an African attendant, announcing the death of the
central character of Joseph Conrad's *Heart of Darkness*, an idealist who is corrupted and dies
horribly. For Conrad, see Introduction to Chapter 3.
32. Old Guy: Guy Fawkes, Catholic conspirator; the failure of Fawkes's "Gunpowder Plot" to
blow up the English Parliament and destroy King James I on November 5, 1605 has since been
celebrated in England. In these yearly celebrations, Fawkes and his followers are burned in effigy,
the effigy being a human being stuffed with straw, like Eliot's Hollow Men.

Those who have crossed
With direct eyes, to death's other Kingdom[33]
Remember us—if at all—not as lost
Violent souls, but only
As the hollow men
The stuffed men.

II

Eyes I dare not meet in dreams
In death's dream kingdom
These do not appear:
There, the eyes are
Sunlight on a broken column
There, is a tree swinging
And voices are
In the wind's singing
More distant and more solemn
Than a fading star.

Let me be no nearer
In death's dream kingdom
Let me also wear
Such deliberate disguises
Rat's coat, crowskin, crossed staves
In a field
Behaving as the wind behaves
No nearer—

Not that final meeting
In the twilight kingdom

III

This is the dead land
This is cactus land
Here the stone images
Are raised, here they receive
The supplication of a dead man's hand
Under the twinkle of a fading star.

Is it like this
In death's other kingdom
Waking alone
At the hour when we are

---

33. death's other Kingdom: the afterworld of those who have been redeemed; paradise.

Trembling with tenderness
Lips that would kiss
Form prayers to broken stone.

IV

The eyes are not here
There are no eyes here
In this valley of dying stars
In this hollow valley
This broken jaw of our lost kingdoms

In this last of meeting places
We grope together
And avoid speech
Gathered on this beach of the tumid river

Sightless, unless
The eyes reappear
As the perpetual star
Multifoliate rose[34]
Of death's twilight kingdom
The hope only
Of empty men.

V

Here we go round the prickly pear[35]
Prickly pear prickly pear
Here we go round the prickly pear
At five o'clock in the morning.

Between the idea
And the reality
Between the motion
And the act
Falls the Shadow
　　　　For Thine is the Kingdom[36]

---

34. Multifoliate rose: In *Paradise* XXX, Dante envisions heaven as a rose of many petals formed by the Virgin Mary and the saints.

35. prickly pear: the cactus; "Here we go round the prickly pear" is a negative reiteration of the children's game song "Here we go round the mulberry bush," a celebration of life.

36. For Thine is the Kingdom: phrase from the Lord's Prayer (based on Matthew 6:9–13): "For thine is the kingdom, and the power, and the glory, forever and ever." The speaker utters phrases from the prayer in this and subsequent lines but fails to complete even a sentence.

Between the conception
And the creation
Between the emotion
And the response
Falls the Shadow
      Life is very long

Between the desire
And the spasm
Between the potency
And the existence
Between the essence
And the descent
Falls the Shadow
      For Thine is the Kingdom

For Thine is
Life is
For Thine is the

This is the way the world ends[37]
This is the way the world ends
This is the way the world ends
Not with a bang but a whimper.

3. Luigi Pirandello, *Six Characters in Search of an Author* (1921)

Six Characters arrive in a puff of light and announce that they are in search of an author, the author who created them having disappeared. The Manager thinks they are mad, but the Father, the Characters' main spokesman, argues that what is absurd is often true, and that he and the other Characters are "living beings more alive than those who breathe and wear clothes"; "less real perhaps, but truer!" Since the author, who may be dead, cannot stage their drama, the Characters, who once they are born are immortal, must themselves enact it for the Actors to observe and perform: "The drama is in us," the Father proclaims,

---

37. the world ends: the world of the Hollow Men ends, unlike God's world, which lasts, as stated in the final words of the Lord's Prayer, "for ever and ever."

"and we are the drama." They begin to tell their story—a lurid one—and the Manager, intrigued, will hear them out.[38]

SIX CHARACTERS IN SEARCH OF AN AUTHOR

DOOR-KEEPER (*cap in hand*): Excuse me, sir . . .

THE MANAGER (*rudely*): Eh? What is it?

DOOR-KEEPER (*timidly*): These people are asking for you, sir.

THE MANAGER (*furious*): I am rehearsing, and you know perfectly well no one's allowed to come in during rehearsals! (*Turning to the* CHARACTERS.) Who are you, please? What do you want?

THE FATHER (*coming forward a little, followed by the others who seem embarrassed*): As a matter of fact . . . we have come here in search of an author . . .

THE MANAGER (*half angry, half amazed*): An author? What author?

THE FATHER: Any author, sir.

THE MANAGER: But there's no author here. We are not rehearsing a new piece.

THE STEP-DAUGHTER (*vivaciously*): So much the better, so much the better! We can be your new piece.

AN ACTOR (*coming forward from the others*): Oh, do you hear that?

THE FATHER (*to* STEP-DAUGHTER): Yes, but if the author isn't here . . . (*To* MANAGER) unless you would be willing . . .

THE MANAGER: You are trying to be funny.

THE FATHER: No, for Heaven's sake, what are you saying? We bring you a drama, sir.

THE STEP-DAUGHTER: We may be your fortune.

THE MANAGER: Will you oblige me by going away? We haven't time to waste with mad people.

THE FATHER (*mellifluously*): Oh sir, you know well that life is full of infinite absurdities, which, strangely enough, do not even need to appear plausible, since they are true.

THE MANAGER: What the devil is he talking about?

---

38. Minor changes in punctuation and capitalization have been made to the original text for greater legibility. Bracketed ellipses in the text indicate the editor's deletions; unbracketed ellipses are the author's. To distinguish my notes from the stage directions, I have set them within brackets.

THE FATHER: I say that to reverse the ordinary process may well be considered a madness: that is, to create credible situations, in order that they may appear true. But permit me to observe that if this be madness, it is the sole *raison d'être* of your profession, gentlemen. (*The* ACTORS *look hurt and perplexed.*)

THE MANAGER (*getting up and looking at him*): So our profession seems to you one worthy of madmen then?

THE FATHER: Well, to make seem true that which isn't true . . . without any need . . . for a joke as it were . . . Isn't that your mission, gentlemen: to give life to fantastic characters on the stage?

THE MANAGER (*interpreting the rising anger of the* COMPANY): But I would beg you to believe, my dear sir, that the profession of the comedian is a noble one. If today, as things go, the playwrights give us stupid comedies to play and puppets to represent instead of men, remember we are proud to have given life to immortal works here on these very boards! (*The* ACTORS, *satisfied, applaud their* MANAGER.)

THE FATHER (*interrupting furiously*): Exactly, perfectly, to living beings more alive than those who breathe and wear clothes: beings less real perhaps, but truer! I agree with you entirely. (*The* ACTORS *look at one another in amazement.*)

THE MANAGER: But what do you mean? Before, you said . . .

THE FATHER: No, excuse me, I meant it for you, sir, who were crying out that you had no time to lose with madmen, while no one better than yourself knows that nature uses the instrument of human fantasy in order to pursue her high creative purpose.

THE MANAGER: Very well—but where does all this take us?

THE FATHER: Nowhere! It is merely to show you that one is born to life in many forms, in many shapes, as tree, or as stone, as water, as butterfly, or as woman. So one may also be born a character in a play.

THE MANAGER (*with feigned comic dismay*): So you and these other friends of yours have been born characters?

THE FATHER: Exactly, and alive as you see! (MANAGER *and* ACTORS *burst out laughing.*)

THE FATHER (*hurt*): I am sorry you laugh, because we carry in us a drama, as you can guess from this woman here veiled in black.

THE MANAGER (*losing patience at last and almost indignant*): Oh, chuck it! Get away please! Clear out of here! (*To* PROPERTY MAN.) For Heaven's sake, turn them out!

THE FATHER (*resisting*): No, no, look here, we . . .

THE MANAGER (*roaring*): We come here to work, you know.

LEADING ACTOR: One cannot let oneself be made such a fool of.

THE FATHER (*determined, coming forward*): I marvel at your incredulity, gentlemen. Are you not accustomed to see the characters created by an author spring to life in yourselves and face each other? Just because there is no "book" (*pointing to the* PROMPTER'S box) which contains us, you refuse to believe . . .

THE STEP-DAUGHTER (*advances towards* MANAGER, *smiling and coquett-ish*): Believe me, we are really six most interesting characters, sir; side-tracked however.

THE FATHER: Yes, that is the word! (*To* MANAGER *all at once.*) In the sense, that is, that the author who created us alive no longer wished, or was no longer able, materially to put us into a work of art. And this was a real crime, sir; because he who has had the luck to be born a character can laugh even at death. He cannot die. The man, the writer, the instrument of the creation will die, but his creation does not die. And to live for ever, it does not need to have extraordinary gifts or to be able to work wonders. Who was Sancho Panza? Who was Don Abbondio?[39] Yet they live eternally because—live germs as they were—they had the fortune to find a fecundating matrix, a fantasy which could raise and nourish them: make them live for ever!

THE MANAGER: That is quite all right. But what do you want here, all of you?

THE FATHER: We want to live.

THE MANAGER (*ironically*): For Eternity?

THE FATHER: No, sir, only for a moment . . . in you.

AN ACTOR: Just listen to him!

LEADING LADY: They want to live, in us . . .

JUVENILE LEAD (*pointing to the* STEP-DAUGHTER): I've no objection, as far as that one is concerned!

THE FATHER: Look here! look here! The comedy has to be made. (*To the* MANAGER.) But if you and your actors are willing, we can soon concert it among ourselves.

---

39. Sancho Panza: the comedic sidekick of Don Quixote in the novel of that name by Miguel de Cervantes; Don Abbondio: the cowardly and hypocritical priest in Alessandro Manzoni's *The Betrothed.* For Cervantes, see Volume One, Introduction to Chapter 10; for Manzoni, see in this volume, Introduction to Chapter 2.

THE MANAGER (*annoyed*): But what do you want to concert? We don't go in for concerts here. Here we play dramas and comedies!

THE FATHER: Exactly! That is just why we have come to you.

THE MANAGER: And where is the "book"?

THE FATHER: It is in us! (*The* ACTORS *laugh*.) The drama is in us, and we are the drama. We are impatient to play it. Our inner passion drives us on to this.

THE STEP-DAUGHTER (*disdainful, alluring, treacherous, full of impudence*): My passion, sir! Ah, if you only knew! My passion for him! (*Points to the* FATHER *and makes a pretence of embracing him. Then she breaks out into a loud laugh*.)

THE FATHER (*angrily*): Behave yourself! And please don't laugh in that fashion. [. . .]

[The Step-Daughter performs a sassy song and dance.]

THE MANAGER: Silence! This isn't a café concert, you know! (*Turning to the* FATHER *in consternation*.) Is she mad?

THE FATHER: Mad? No, she's worse than mad.

THE STEP-DAUGHTER (*to* MANAGER): Worse? Worse? Listen! Stage this drama for us at once! Then you will see that at a certain moment I . . . when this little darling here . . . (*Takes the* CHILD *by the hand and leads her to the* MANAGER.) Isn't she a dear? (*Takes her up and kisses her*.) Darling! Darling! (*Puts her down again and adds feelingly*.) Well, when God suddenly takes this dear little child away from that poor mother there; and this imbecile here (*Seizing hold of the* BOY *roughly and pushing him forward*.) does the stupidest things, like the fool he is, you will see me run away. Yes, gentlemen, I shall be off. But the moment hasn't arrived yet. After what has taken place between him and me (*indicates the* FATHER *with a horrible wink*), I can't remain any longer in this society, to have to witness the anguish of this mother here for that fool . . . (*Indicates the* SON.) Look at him! Look at him! See how indifferent, how frigid he is, because he is the legitimate son. He despises me, despises him (*pointing to the* BOY), despises this baby here; because . . . we are bastards. (*Goes to the* MOTHER *and embraces her*.) And he doesn't want to recognize her as his mother—she who is the common mother of us all. He looks down upon her as if she were only the mother of us three bastards. Wretch! (*She says all this very rapidly, excitedly. At the word "bastards" she raises her voice, and almost spits out the final "Wretch!"*)

THE MOTHER (*to the* MANAGER, *in anguish*): In the name of these two little children, I beg you . . . (*She grows faint and is about to fall*.) Oh God!

THE FATHER (*coming forward to support her as do some of the* ACTORS): Quick, a chair, a chair for this poor widow!

THE ACTORS: Is it true? Has she really fainted?

THE MANAGER: Quick, a chair! Here! (*One of the* ACTORS *brings a chair, the* OTHERS *proffer assistance. The* MOTHER *tries to prevent the* FATHER *from lifting the veil which covers her face.*)

THE FATHER: Look at her! Look at her!

THE MOTHER: No, no; stop it please!

THE FATHER (*raising her veil*): Let them see you!

THE MOTHER (*rising and covering her face with her hands, in desperation*): I beg you, sir, to prevent this man from carrying out his plan which is loathsome to me.

THE MANAGER (*dumbfounded*): I don't understand at all. What is the situation? Is this lady your wife? (*To the* FATHER.)

THE FATHER: Yes, gentlemen: my wife!

THE MANAGER: But how can she be a widow if you are alive? (*The* ACTORS *find relief for their astonishment in a loud laugh.*)

THE FATHER: Don't laugh! Don't laugh like that, for Heaven's sake. Her drama lies just here in this: she has had a lover, a man who ought to be here.

THE MOTHER (*with a cry*): No! No!

THE STEP-DAUGHTER: Fortunately for her, he is dead. Two months ago as I said. We are in mourning, as you see.

THE FATHER: He isn't here you see, not because he is dead. He isn't here— look at her a moment and you will understand—because her drama isn't a drama of the love of two men for whom she was incapable of feeling anything except possibly a little gratitude—gratitude not for me but for the other. She isn't a woman, she is a mother, and her drama—powerful sir, I assure you— lies, as a matter of fact, all in these four children she has had by two men.

THE MOTHER: I had them? Have you got the courage to say that I wanted them? (*To the* COMPANY.) It was his doing. It was he who gave me that other man, who forced me to go away with him.

THE STEP-DAUGHTER: It isn't true.

THE MOTHER (*startled*): Not true, isn't it?

THE STEP-DAUGHTER: No, it isn't true, it just isn't true.

THE MOTHER: And what can you know about it?

THE STEP-DAUGHTER: It isn't true. Don't believe it. (*To* MANAGER.) Do you know why she says so? For that fellow there. (*Indicates the* SON.) She tortures herself, destroys herself on account of the neglect of that son there; and she wants him to believe that if she abandoned him when he was only two years old, it was because he (*indicates the* FATHER) made her do so.

THE MOTHER (*vigorously*): He forced me to it, and I call God to witness it. (*To the* MANAGER.) Ask him (*indicates* HUSBAND) if it isn't true. Let him speak. You (*to* DAUGHTER) are not in a position to know anything about it.

THE STEP-DAUGHTER: I know you lived in peace and happiness with my father while he lived. Can you deny it?

THE MOTHER: No, I don't deny it . . .

THE STEP-DAUGHTER: He was always full of affection and kindness for you. (*To the* BOY, *angrily*.) It's true, isn't it? Tell them! Why don't you speak, you little fool?

THE MOTHER: Leave the poor boy alone. Why do you want to make me appear ungrateful, daughter? I don't want to offend your father. I have answered him that I didn't abandon my house and my son through any fault of mine, nor from any wilful passion.

THE FATHER: It is true. It was my doing.

LEADING MAN (*to the* COMPANY): What a spectacle!

LEADING LADY: We are the audience this time.

JUVENILE LEAD: For once, in a way.

THE MANAGER (*beginning to get really interested*): Let's hear them out. Listen!

4. Osip Mandelstam, *The Noise of Time* (1925)

In the third and fourth chapters of his autobiography, excerpts from which follow here, Mandelstam recalls his youthful experiences in St. Petersburg, the official and cultural capital of Russia, and in his family home. St. Petersburg is portrayed as a city at peace and at leisure, where nothing of great importance happens and the inhabitants—among them numerous French governesses—engage in gala ceremonies and showy promenades, attending well-policed riots announced in advance. Yet Petersburg was only an "elegant mirage," around which "sprawled the chaos of Judaism": a chaos concretized in the apartment where the young Osip lived with his Russian mother and Polish-born leather-merchant father. The family's story can be known by its bookcase: its lower shelf containing "Jewish ruins"—a Russian history of the Jews, Osip's unused Hebrew primer; one shelf higher, his father's books, the German classics, in fine bindings; above that, his mother's treasured works by Russian authors in prized editions—Pushkin, Turgenev, Dostoevsky.[40] Mandelstam himself was forged from the shelves of the family bookcase.

NOISE OF TIME

III. Riots and French Governesses

It was always known in advance when the students would riot in front of the Kazan Cathedral.[41] Every family had its student informer. The result was that these riots were attended—at a respectful distance, to be sure—by a great mass of people: children with their nurses, mamas and aunts who had been unable to keep their insurrectionaries at home, old civil servants, and simply people who happened to be walking idly about. On the day appointed for the riot the side-walks of the Nevsky teemed with a dense throng of spectators all the way from Sadovaya to the Anichkov Bridge. This mob was afraid to approach the Kazan Cathedral. The police were hidden in courtyards—for example, in the court-yard of the Roman Catholic Church of St. Catherine. The Kazan Square itself was relatively empty; across it would pass small knots of students and actual working men, the latter being pointed at with fingers. Suddenly, from the di-rection of the Kazan Square, there would burst forth a protracted, crescendoing yell, something on the order of a steady "oo" or "ee," which became an ominous howling, growing nearer and nearer. At that moment the spectators scattered and the crowd was crushed back by the horses. "Cossacks! Cossacks!"—the cry spread like lightning, faster than the Cossacks themselves. The "riot" itself, strictly speaking, was cordoned off and led away to the Mikhaylovsky Manège, and the Nevsky emptied as if it had been swept with a broom.

My first conscious, sharp perceptions were of gloomy crowds of people in the streets. I was exactly three years old. It was 1894 and I had been brought from Pavlovsk to Petersburg for the purpose of seeing the funeral of [Tsar] Alexander III. A furnished room had been rented on the fourth floor of some house on the Nevsky, opposite Nikolaevskaya Street. On the evening of the

40. Alexander Pushkin, Ivan Turgenev, and Fyodor Dostoevsky: all major nineteenth-century Russian authors. For Pushkin and Dostoevsky, see respectively in this volume, Introductions to Chapter 2 and Chapter 5.
41. Kazan Cathedral, etc.: throughout this account, Mandelstam names buildings, monuments, and streets of St. Petersburg that were generally known to his contemporaries.

day before the ceremonies, having crawled up on the windowsill and seen the crowd-darkened street, I asked, "When will they start?" and was told, "tomorrow." It profoundly impressed me that all these throngs of people were spending the entire night in the street. Even death first appeared to me in a totally unnatural, elegant, and festive guise. Once I was walking with Mother and my nurse on the street along the Moyka past the chocolate building of the Italian Embassy. Suddenly the doors there were wide open and everyone was freely admitted inside, and there issued forth a smell of resin, incense, and something sweet and pleasant. Black velvet was draped over the entrance and the walls, which glistened with silver and tropical plants. Very high on his bier lay the embalmed Italian ambassador. What had all that to do with me? I do not know, but these impressions were strong and clear and I cherish them to this day.

The ordinary life of the city was poor and monotonous. Every day at about five o'clock there was promenading on the Bolshaya Morskaya from Gorokhovaya Street to the General Staff Arch. All the foppish and idle elements of the city then proceeded slowly back and forth along the sidewalks bowing and exchanging smiles: the ring of spurs, the languages of England and France—a living exhibit from the English Store and the Jockey Club.[42] Hither also the nursemaids and governesses, young-looking Frenchwomen, brought the children, in order to sigh and compare it all to the Champs Elysées.[43]

So many French governesses were hired to look after me that all their features have become blurred and resolved into one general patch of portraiture. It is my opinion that the little songs, models of penmanship, anthologies, and conjugations had ended by driving all these French and Swiss women themselves into an infantile state. At the center of their worldview, distorted by anthologies, stood the figure of the great emperor Napoleon[44] and the War of 1812; after that came Joan of Arc (one Swiss girl, however, turned out to be a Calvinist),[45] and no matter how often I tried, curious as I was, to learn something from them about France, I learned nothing at all, save that it was beautiful. . . .

But what had I to do with the Guards' festivals, the monotonous prettiness of the host of the infantry and its steeds, the stone-faced battalions flowing with hollow tread down the Millionnaya, gray with marble and granite?

---

42. the ring of spurs . . . the Jockey Club: affluent Russians imitated the fashions and culture of western Europe, especially France and England.

43. Champs Elysées: "Elysian Fields," the name of the famous, broad, and fashionable Paris avenue.

44. Napoleon: Napoleon Bonaparte, the French emperor who invaded Russia in 1812.

45. Joan of Arc: the fifteenth-century Catholic saint and martyr, a national heroine, who was revered by French Catholics, but not by French or Swiss Calvinists (Protestants).

All the elegant mirage of Petersburg was merely a dream, a brilliant covering thrown over the abyss, while round about there sprawled the chaos of Judaism—not a motherland not a house, not a hearth, but precisely a chaos, the unknown womb world whence I had issued, which I feared, about which I made vague conjectures and fled, always fled.

The chaos of Judaism showed through all the chinks of the stone-clad Petersburg apartment: in the threat of ruin, in the cap hanging in the room of the guest from the provinces, in the spiky script of the unread books of Genesis, thrown into the dust one shelf lower than Goethe and Schiller,[46] in the shreds of the black-and-yellow ritual.

The strong, ruddy, Russian year rolled through the calendar with decorated eggs, Christmas trees, steel skates from Finland, December, gaily bedecked Finnish cabdrivers, and the villa. But mixed up with all this there was a phantom—the new year in September—and the strange, cheerless holidays, grating upon the ear with the harsh names: Rosh Hashanah and Yom Kippur.[47]

IV. The Bookcase

As a little bit of musk fills an entire house, so the least influence of Judaism overflows all of one's life. Oh, what a strong smell that is! Could I possibly not have noticed that in real Jewish houses there was a different smell from that in Aryan [gentile] houses? And it was not only the kitchen that smelled so, but the people, things, and clothing. To this day I remember how that sweetish Jewish smell swaddled me in the wooden house of my grandfather and grandmother on Klyuchevaya Street in German Riga [modern Latvia]. My father's study at home was itself unlike the granite paradise of my sedate strolls; it led one away into an alien world, and the mixture of its furnishings, the selection of the objects in it were strongly knitted together in my consciousness. First of all, there was the handmade oak armchair bearing the image of a balalaika and a gauntlet and, on its arched back, the motto "Slow but Sure"—a tribute to the pseudo-Russian style of [Tsar] Alexander III. Then there was a Turkish divan completely overwhelmed with ledgers, whose pages of flimsy paper were covered over with the minuscule gothic hand of German commercial correspondence. . . . [A]ll this, plus the bourgeois writing table with its little marble calendar, swims in a tobacco haze and is seasoned with the smells of leather. And in the drab surroundings of this mercantile room there was a bookcase that I should like to speak of now. The bookcase of early childhood is a man's companion for life. The arrangement of its shelves, the choice of books, the

---

46. Goethe and Schiller: the classic German authors Johann Wolfgang von Goethe and Friedrich von Schiller, for whom see in this volume the Introduction to Section I, Chapter 2.
47. Rosh Hashanah and Yom Kippur: the two most important of the Jewish religious holy days.

colors of the spines are for him the color, height, and arrangement of world literature itself. And as for the books which were not included in that first bookcase—they were never to force their way into the universe of world literature. Every book in the first bookcase is, willy-nilly, a classic, and not one of them can ever be expelled.

There was nothing haphazard in the way that strange little library had been deposited, like a geological bed, over several decades. The paternal and maternal elements in it were not mixed, but existed separately, and a cross section of the strata showed the history of the spiritual efforts of the entire family, as well as the inoculation of it with alien blood.

I always remember the lower shelf as chaotic: the books were not standing upright side by side but lay like ruins: reddish five-volume works with ragged covers, a Russian history of the Jews written in the clumsy, shy language of a Russian-speaking Talmudist. This was the Judaic chaos thrown into the dust. This was the level to which my Hebrew primer, which I never mastered, quickly fell. . . . The Hebrew primer was illustrated with pictures which showed one and the same little boy, wearing a visored cap and with a melancholy adult face, in all sorts of situations—with a cat, a book, a pail, a watering can. I saw nothing of myself in that boy and with all my being revolted against the book and the subject. . . .

Above these Jewish ruins there begins the orderly arrangement of book; those were the Germans—Schiller, Goethe, Kerner,[48] and Shakespeare in German[49]—in the old Leipzig and Tübingen editions, chubby little butterballs in stamped claret-colored bindings with a fine print calculated for the sharp vision of youth and with soft engravings done in a rather classical style. . . . All this was my father fighting his way as an autodidact into the German world out of the Talmudic wilds.

Still higher were my mother's Russian books—Pushkin in Isakov's 1876 edition. I still think that was a splendid edition and like it more than the one published by the Academy. It contained nothing superfluous, the type was elegantly arranged, the columns of poetry flowed freely as soldiers in flying battalions, and leading them like generals were the clear reasonable years of composition, right up to 1837. . . .

My Isakov Pushkin was in a cassock of no color at all, in a binding schoolboy calico, in a brownish, faded cassock with a tinge of earth and sand; he feared neither spots, nor ink, nor fire nor kerosene. For a quarter of a century the black-and-sand cassock had lovingly absorbed everything into itself—so vividly do I sense the everyday spiritual beauty, the almost physical charm of

---

48. Kerner: Justinus Kerner, German poet, spiritualist, and medical writer.
49. Shakespeare in German: the plays of William Shakespeare (for whom see Volume One, Introduction to Chapter 11) were frequently translated into German, including by Schiller, who translated *Macbeth*.

my mother's Pushkin. It bore an inscription in reddish ink: "For her diligence as a pupil of the Third Form." The Isakov Pushkin is bound up with stories about ideal schoolmasters and schoolmistresses, ruddy with consumption and shod in ragged boots: the 1880s in Vilno [modern Lithuania]. The word "intellectual" was pronounced by my mother, and especially by my grandmother, with pride. . . .

And how about Turgenev and Dostoevsky? . . . They were bound in boards covered with a thick leather. Prohibition lay upon Dostoevsky like a gravestone: it was said that he was "heavy." Turgenev was altogether sanctioned and open, with his Baden-Baden, *Spring Torments,* and languid conversations. But I knew that the tranquil life in Turgenev had already vanished and was nowhere to be found. . . .

What a meager life, what poor letters, what unfunny jokes and parodies! I used to have pointed out to me in the family album a daguerreotype of my uncle Misha, a melancholiac with swollen and unhealthy features, and it was explained that he had not merely gone out of his mind—he had "burnt up," as that generation put it. . . .

Semyon Afanasich Vengerov, a relative of mine on my mother's side (the family in Vilno and school memories), understood nothing in Russian literature and studied Pushkin as a professional task, but "one thing" he understood. His "one thing" was: the heroic character of Russian literature. . . .

5. James Joyce, *The Sisters,* from *Dubliners* (1914)

Opening the collection *Dubliners, The Sisters* is a terse story in which everything is left unsaid. The narrator, an unnamed boy, has been mentored by a priest who has now died, his death arousing some reflections and unclear reactions. The boy is told of the death; the next day, he reads the posted death announcement; and that night, with his aunt, he visits the priest's surviving sisters, and views the body. The story ends in mid-air, with sister Eliza's account of an incident that had made the observers think that "something [had] gone wrong with him . . ." What kind of person the priest was and the nature of his relationship with the boy are not detailed, but the boy's uneasiness as events unfold is eloquent. Some malevolence is suggested; perhaps a hint of something unsavory in the priest's tutoring of the child, or, more broadly, of the malignant effect of the church on youth, the paralysis of the priest signaling the paralysis of a church-ridden culture.[50]

---

50. Bracketed ellipses in the text indicate the editor's deletions; unbracketed ellipses are the author's.

THE SISTERS

There was no hope for him this time: it was the third stroke. Night after night I had passed the house (it was vacation time) and studied the lighted square of window: and night after night I had found it lighted in the same way, faintly and evenly. If he was dead, I thought, I would see the reflection of candles on the darkened blind for I knew that two candles must be set at the head of a corpse. He had often said to me: "I am not long for this world," and I had thought his words idle. Now I knew they were true. Every night as I gazed up at the window I said softly to myself the word paralysis. It had always sounded strangely in my ears. [. . .]

Old Cotter[51] was sitting at the fire, smoking, when I came downstairs to supper. While my aunt was ladling out my stirabout he said, as if returning to some former remark of his:

"No, I wouldn't say he was exactly . . . but there was something queer . . . there was something uncanny about him. I'll tell you my opinion. . . ." He began to puff at his pipe, no doubt arranging his opinion in his mind. [. . .]

He began to puff again at his pipe without giving us his theory. My uncle saw me staring and said to me:

"Well, so your old friend is gone, you'll be sorry to hear."

"Who?" said I.

"Father Flynn."

"Is he dead?"

"Mr. Cotter here has just told us. He was passing by the house."

I knew that I was under observation so I continued eating as if the news had not interested me. My uncle explained to old Cotter.

"The youngster and he were great friends. The old chap taught him a great deal, mind you; and they say he had a great wish for him."

"God have mercy on his soul," said my aunt piously.

Old Cotter looked at me for a while. I felt that his little beady black eyes were examining me but I would not satisfy him by looking up from my plate. He returned to his pipe and finally spat rudely into the grate. "I wouldn't like children of mine," he said, "to have too much to say to a man like that."

"How do you mean, Mr. Cotter?" asked my aunt.

"What I mean is," said old Cotter, "it's bad for children. My idea is: let a young lad run about and play with young lads of his own age and not be . . . Am I right, Jack?"

"That's my principle, too," said my uncle. "Let him learn to box his corner." [. . .]

---

51. Old Cotter: a cotter is a laborer, often one who is given lodging in exchange for work; old Cotter lodges with the family.

I crammed my mouth with stirabout for fear I might give utterance to my anger. Tiresome old red-nosed imbecile!

It was late when I fell asleep. Though I was angry with old Cotter for alluding to me as a child, I puzzled my head to extract meaning from his unfinished sentences. In the dark of my room I imagined that I saw again the heavy grey face of the paralytic. I drew the blankets over my head and tried to think of Christmas. But the grey face still followed me. It murmured; and I understood that it desired to confess something. [. . .] It began to confess to me in a murmuring voice [. . .].

The next morning after breakfast I went down to look at the little house in Great Britain Street. [. . .] A crape bouquet was tied to the door-knocker with ribbon. Two poor women and a telegram boy were reading the card pinned on the crape. I also approached and read:

July 1st, 1895
The Rev. James Flynn (formerly of S. Catherine's Church,
Meath Street), aged sixty-five years.
R. I. P.

The reading of the card persuaded me that he was dead and I was disturbed to find myself at check. Had he not been dead I would have gone into the little dark room behind the shop to find him sitting in his arm-chair by the fire, nearly smothered in his great-coat. [. . .] I wished to go in and look at him but I had not the courage to knock. I walked away slowly along the sunny side of the street, reading all the theatrical advertisements in the shop-windows as I went. I found it strange that neither I nor the day seemed in a mourning mood and I felt even annoyed at discovering in myself a sensation of freedom as if I had been freed from something by his death. I wondered at this for, as my uncle had said the night before, he had taught me a great deal. He had studied in the Irish college in Rome and he had taught me to pronounce Latin properly. He had told me stories about the catacombs and about Napoleon Bonaparte, and he had explained to me the meaning of the different ceremonies of the Mass and of the different vestments worn by the priest. Sometimes he had amused himself by putting difficult questions to me, asking me what one should do in certain circumstances or whether such and such sins were mortal or venial or only imperfections. His questions showed me how complex and mysterious were certain institutions of the Church which I had always regarded as the simplest acts. The duties of the priest towards the Eucharist and towards the secrecy of the confessional seemed so grave to me that I wondered how anybody had ever found in himself the courage to undertake them [. . .].

In the evening my aunt took me with her to visit the house of mourning. It was after sunset; but the window-panes of the houses that looked to the west reflected the tawny gold of a great bank of clouds. Nannie received us in the hall [. . .]. The old woman pointed upwards interrogatively and, on my aunt's nodding, proceeded to toil up the narrow staircase before us, her bowed head being scarcely above the level of the banister-rail. At the first landing she stopped and beckoned us forward encouragingly towards the open door of the dead-room. My aunt went in and the old woman, seeing that I hesitated to enter, began to beckon to me again repeatedly with her hand.

I went in on tiptoe. The room through the lace end of the blind was suffused with dusky golden light amid which the candles looked like pale thin flames. He had been coffined. Nannie gave the lead and we three knelt down at the foot of the bed. [. . .] The fancy came to me that the old priest was smiling as he lay there in his coffin.

But no. When we rose and went up to the head of the bed I saw that he was not smiling. There he lay, solemn and copious, vested as for the altar, his large hands loosely retaining a chalice. His face was very truculent, grey and massive, with black cavernous nostrils and circled by a scanty white fur. There was a heavy odour in the room—the flowers.

We crossed ourselves and came away. In the little room downstairs we found Eliza seated in his arm-chair in state. I groped my way towards my usual chair in the corner while Nannie went to the sideboard and brought out a decanter of sherry and some wine-glasses. She set these on the table and invited us to take a little glass of wine. Then, at her sister's bidding, she filled out the sherry into the glasses and passed them to us. [. . .] No one spoke: we all gazed at the empty fireplace.

My aunt waited until Eliza sighed and then said:

"Ah, well, he's gone to a better world."

Eliza sighed again and bowed her head in assent. My aunt fingered the stem of her wineglass before sipping a little.

"Did he . . . peacefully?" she asked.

"Oh, quite peacefully, ma'am," said Eliza. "You couldn't tell when the breath went out of him. He had a beautiful death, God be praised."

"And everything . . . ?"

"Father O'Rourke was in with him a Tuesday and anointed him and prepared him and all."

"He knew then?"

"He was quite resigned." [. . .]

"He looks quite resigned," said my aunt. [. . .]

She sipped a little more from her glass and said:

"Well, Miss Flynn, at any rate it must be a great comfort for you to know that you did all you could for him. You were both very kind to him, I must say."

Eliza smoothed her dress over her knees. "Ah, poor James!" she said. "God knows we done all we could, as poor as we are—we wouldn't see him want anything while he was in it."

Nannie had leaned her head against the sofa-pillow and seemed about to fall asleep.

"There's poor Nannie," said Eliza, looking at her, "she's wore out. All the work we had, she and me, getting in the woman to wash him and then laying him out and then the coffin and then arranging about the Mass in the chapel. Only for Father O'Rourke I don't know what we'd done at all. It was him brought us all them flowers and them two candlesticks out of the chapel and wrote out the notice for the *Freeman's General* and took charge of all the papers for the cemetery and poor James's insurance."

"Wasn't that good of him?" said my aunt.

Eliza closed her eyes and shook her head slowly.

"Ah, there's no friends like the old friends," she said, "when all is said and done, no friends that a body can trust."

"Indeed, that's true," said my aunt. "And I'm sure now that he's gone to his eternal reward he won't forget you and all your kindness to him."

"Ah, poor James!" said Eliza. "He was no great trouble to us. You wouldn't hear him in the house any more than now. Still, I know he's gone and all to that. . . ." [. . .]

She stopped, as if she were communing with the past and then said shrewdly:

"Mind you, I noticed there was something queer coming over him latterly. Whenever I'd bring in his soup to him I'd find him with his breviary fallen to the floor, lying back in the chair and his mouth open."

She laid a finger against her nose and frowned: then she continued:

"But still and all he kept on saying that before the summer was over he'd go out for a drive one fine day just to see the old house again where we were all born down in Irishtown and take me and Nannie with him. [. . .] He had his mind set on that. . . . Poor James!"

"The Lord have mercy on his soul!" said my aunt.

Eliza took out her handkerchief and wiped her eyes with it. Then she put it back again in her pocket and gazed into the empty grate for some time without speaking.

"He was too scrupulous always," she said. "The duties of the priesthood was too much for him. And then his life was, you might say, crossed."

"Yes," said my aunt. "He was a disappointed man. You could see that."

A silence took possession of the little room and, under cover of it, I approached the table and tasted my sherry and then returned quietly to my chair in the corner. Eliza seemed to have fallen into a deep revery. We waited respectfully for her to break the silence: and after a long pause she said slowly:

"It was that chalice he broke. . . . That was the beginning of it. Of course, they say it was all right, that it contained nothing, I mean. But still. . . . They say it was the boy's fault. But poor James was so nervous, God be merciful to him!"

"And was that it?" said my aunt. "I heard something. . . ."

Eliza nodded.

"That affected his mind," she said. "After that he began to mope by him-self, talking to no one and wandering about by himself. So one night he was wanted for to go on a call and they couldn't find him anywhere. They looked high up and low down; and still they couldn't see a sight of him anywhere. So then the clerk suggested to try the chapel. So then they got the keys and opened the chapel and the clerk and Father O'Rourke and another priest that was there brought in a light for to look for him. . . . And what do you think but there he was, sitting up by himself in the dark in his confession-box, wide-awake and laughing-like softly to himself?"

She stopped suddenly as if to listen. I too listened; but there was no sound in the house: and I knew that the old priest was lying still in his coffin as we had seen him, solemn and truculent in death, an idle chalice on his breast.

Eliza resumed:

"Wide-awake and laughing-like to himself. . . . So then, of course, when they saw that, that made them think that there was something gone wrong with him. . . ."

6. Ernest Hemingway, *Indian Camp,* from *In Our Time* (1925)

Nick Adams, his father, and his uncle are led at night to a crude shanty in a Michigan logging camp where a woman suffers in labor, unable after two days to birth her baby. Nick's father sterilizes some implements in boiling water poured from a kettle, wields his jackknife to open an incision, rescues the infant, then sews up the incision—while the mother, held down by Uncle George and three Indians, screams in agony. Nick's father had no anesthetic, he explained; "But her screams are not important. I don't hear them because they are not important." Proud of his work when the operation has been successfully accomplished, Nick's father turns to the man in the upper bunk—who amid the cacophony of torment, has cut his throat. The story's intensity derives from the utter sparseness of the narrative of these horrific events that the child Nick, without comment, has witnessed.

INDIAN CAMP

At the lake shore there was another rowboat drawn up. The two Indians stood waiting.

Nick and his father got in the stern of the boat and the Indians shoved it off and one of them got in to row. Uncle George sat in the stern of the camp rowboat. The young Indian shoved the camp boat off and got in to row Uncle George.

The two boats started off in the dark. Nick heard the oar-locks of the other boat quite a way ahead of them in the mist. The Indians rowed with quick choppy strokes. Nick lay back with his father's arm around him. It was cold on the water. The Indian who was rowing them was working very hard, but the other boat moved further ahead in the mist all the time.

"Where are we going, Dad?" Nick asked.

"Over to the Indian camp. There is an Indian lady very sick."

"Oh," said Nick.

Across the bay they found the other boat beached. Uncle George was smoking a cigar in the dark. The young Indian pulled the boat way up the beach. Uncle George gave both the Indians cigars.

They walked up from the beach through a meadow that was soaking wet with dew, following the young Indian who carried a lantern. Then they went into the woods and followed a trail that led to the logging road that ran back into the hills. It was much lighter on the logging road as the timber was cut away on both sides. The young Indian stopped and blew out his lantern and they all walked on along the road.

They came around a bend and a dog came out barking. Ahead were the lights of the shanties where the Indian bark-peelers lived. More dogs rushed out at them. The two Indians sent them back to the shanties. In the shanty nearest the road there was a light in the window. An old woman stood in the doorway holding a lamp.

Inside on a wooden bunk lay a young Indian woman. She had been trying to have her baby for two days. All the old women in the camp had been helping her. The men had moved off up the road to sit in the dark and smoke out of range of the noise she made. She screamed just as Nick and the two Indians followed his father and Uncle George into the shanty. She lay in the lower bunk, very big under a quilt. Her head was turned to one side. In the upper bunk was her husband. He had cut his foot very badly with an ax three days before. He was smoking a pipe. The room smelled very bad.

Nick's father ordered some water to be put on the stove, and while it was heating he spoke to Nick.

"This lady is going to have a baby, Nick," he said.

"I know," said Nick.

"You don't know," said his father. "Listen to me. What she is going through is called being in labor. The baby wants to be born and she wants it to be born. All her muscles are trying to get the baby born. That is what is happening when she screams."

"I see," Nick said.

Just then the woman cried out.

"Oh, Daddy, can't you give her something to make her stop screaming?" asked Nick.

"No. I haven't any anæsthetic," his father said. "But her screams are not important. I don't hear them because they are not important."

The husband in the upper bunk rolled over against the wall.

The woman in the kitchen motioned to the doctor that the water was hot. Nick's father went into the kitchen and poured about half of the water out of the big kettle into a basin. Into the water left in the kettle he put several things he unwrapped from a handkerchief.

"Those must boil," he said, and began to scrub his hands in the basin of hot water with a cake of soap he had brought from the camp. Nick watched his father's hands scrubbing each other with the soap. While his father washed his hands very carefully and thoroughly, he talked.

"You see, Nick, babies are supposed to be born head first but sometimes they're not. When they're not they make a lot of trouble for everybody. Maybe I'll have to operate on this lady. We'll know in a little while."

When he was satisfied with his hands he went in and went to work.

"Pull back that quilt, will you, George?" he said. "I'd rather not touch it."

Later when he started to operate Uncle George and three Indian men held the woman still. She bit Uncle George on the arm and Uncle George said, "Damn squaw bitch!" and the young Indian who had rowed Uncle George over laughed at him. Nick held the basin for his father. It all took a long time.

His father picked the baby up and slapped it to make it breathe and handed it to the old woman.

"See, it's a boy, Nick," he said. "How do you like being an intern?"

Nick said, "All right." He was looking away so as not to see what his father was doing.

"There. That gets it," said his father and put something into the basin.

Nick didn't look at it.

"Now," his father said, "there's some stitches to put in. You can watch this or not, Nick, just as you like. I'm going to sew up the incision I made."

Nick did not watch. His curiosity has been gone for a long time.

His father finished and stood up. Uncle George and the three Indian men stood up. Nick put the basin out in the kitchen.

Uncle George looked at his arm. The young Indian smiled reminiscently.

"I'll put some peroxide on that, George," the doctor said.

He bent over the Indian woman. She was quiet now and her eyes were closed. She looked very pale. She did not know what had become of the baby or anything.

"I'll be back in the morning," the doctor said, standing up. "The nurse should be here from St. Ignace by noon and she'll bring everything we need."

He was feeling exalted and talkative as football players are in the dressing room after a game.

"That's one for the medical journal, George," he said. "Doing a Caesarian with a jack-knife and sewing it up with nine-foot, tapered gut leaders."

Uncle George was standing against the wall, looking at his arm.

"Oh, you're a great man, all right," he said.

"Ought to have a look at the proud father. They're usually the worst sufferers in these little affairs," the doctor said. "I must say he took it all pretty quietly."

He pulled back the blanket from the Indian's head. His hand came away wet. He mounted on the edge of the lower bunk with the lamp in one hand and looked in. The Indian lay with his face toward the wall. His throat had been cut from ear to ear. The blood had flowed down into a pool where his body sagged the bunk. His head rested on his left arm. The open razor lay, edge up, in the blankets.

"Take Nick out of the shanty, George," the doctor said.

There was no need of that. Nick, standing in the door of the kitchen, had a good view of the upper bunk when his father, the lamp in one hand, tipped the Indian's head back.

It was just beginning to be daylight when they walked along the logging road back toward the lake.

"I'm terribly sorry I brought you along, Nickie," said his father, all his postoperative exhilaration gone. "It was an awful mess to put you through."

"Do ladies always have such a hard time having babies?" Nick asked.

"No, that was very, very exceptional."

"Why did he kill himself, Daddy?"

"I don't know, Nick. He couldn't stand things, I guess."

"Do many men kill themselves, Daddy?"

"Not very many, Nick."

"Do many women?"

"Hardly ever."

"Don't they ever?"

"Oh, yes. They do sometimes."

"Daddy?"

"Yes."

"Where did Uncle George go?"

"He'll turn up all right."

"Is dying hard, Daddy?"

"No, I think it's pretty easy, Nick. It all depends."

They were seated in the boat, Nick in the stern, his father rowing. The sun was coming up over the hills. A bass jumped, making a circle in the water. Nick trailed his hand in the water. It felt warm in the sharp chill of the morning.

In the early morning on the lake sitting in the stern of the boat with his father rowing, he felt quite sure that he would never die.

7. William Faulkner, *A Rose for Emily* (1930)

Miss Grierson was the last of the Griersons—an aristocratic family of Jefferson, Mississippi, in Yoknapatawpha County, the fictional setting of most of Faulkner's stories and novels. Her father was a Civil War hero (of the Southern Confederacy, of course), who enjoyed the respect of the townsfolk, as well as fiscal privileges that descended, upon his death, to Miss Emily. While she was still young, she had many suitors; but they all vanished, impelled, perhaps, by her jealous father who conspicuously held a horsewhip in his hand even when he sat in his front parlor. The summer after his death, when she was well past thirty, she took up with Homer Barron, the boisterous Yankee[52] foreman of the construction team brought in to build sidewalks for the antiquated town. The two could be seen buggy riding together on Sunday afternoons; there was speculation about marriage—yet at the same time, speculation about Barron's sexual proclivities. Miss Emily was known to have purchased a handsome, silver-plated, and monogrammed toilet set that had all the appearance of a wedding gift. And then, sometime later, she was known to have purchased arsenic at the druggist's shop. Barron disappeared. An overwhelming stench issued from her house. Thirty years later, when she died at age seventy-four, the townsfolk find out why.

A ROSE FOR EMILY

III

After her father's death—

She was sick for a long time. When we saw her again, her hair was cut short, making her look like a girl, with a vague resemblance to those angels in colored church windows—sort of tragic and serene.

The town had just let the contracts for paving the sidewalks, and in the summer after her father's death they began the work. The construction company came with n———s[53] and mules and machinery, and a foreman named Homer Barron, a Yankee—a big, dark, ready man, with a big voice and eyes

---

52. Yankee: a term used in the South for a Union soldier during the Civil War and thereafter for anyone from a northern state.

53. n———s: Southern colloquial form of "Negro" now considered derogatory and avoided in speech and in print.

lighter than his face. The little boys would follow in groups to hear him cuss the n——s, and the n——s singing in time to the rise and fall of picks. Pretty soon he knew everybody in town. Whenever you heard a lot of laughing anywhere about the square, Homer Barron would be in the center of the group. Presently we began to see him and Miss Emily on Sunday afternoons driving in the yellow-wheeled buggy and the matched team of bays from the livery stable.

At first we were glad that Miss Emily would have an interest, because the ladies all said, "Of course a Grierson would not think seriously of a Northerner, a day laborer." But there were still others, older people, who said that even grief could not cause a real lady to forget *noblesse oblige*—without calling it *noblesse oblige*.[54] They just said, "Poor Emily. Her kinsfolk should come to her." She had some kin in Alabama; but years ago her father had fallen out with them over the estate of old lady Wyatt, the crazy woman, and there was no communication between the two families. They had not even been represented at the funeral. And as soon as the old people said, "Poor Emily," the whispering began. "Do you suppose it's really so?" they said to one another. "Of course it is. What else could . . ." This behind their hands; rustling of craned silk and satin behind jalousies closed upon the sun of Sunday afternoon as the thin, swift clop-clop-clop of the matched team passed: "Poor Emily."

She carried her head high enough—even when we believed that she was fallen. It was as if she demanded more than ever the recognition of her dignity as the last Grierson; as if it had wanted that touch of earthiness to reaffirm her imperviousness. Like when she bought the rat poison, the arsenic. That was over a year after they had begun to say "Poor Emily," and while the two female cousins were visiting her.

"I want some poison," she said to the druggist. She was over thirty then, still a slight woman, though thinner than usual, with cold, haughty black eyes in a face the flesh of which was strained across the temples and about the eye sockets as you imagine a lighthouse-keeper's face ought to look. "I want some poison," she said.

"Yes, Miss Emily. What kind? For rats and such? I'd recom—"

"I want the best you have. I don't care what kind."

The druggist named several. "They'll kill anything up to an elephant. But what you want is—"

"Arsenic," Miss Emily said. "Is that a good one?"

"Is . . . arsenic? Yes, ma'am. But what you want—"

"I want arsenic."

---

54. *noblesse oblige*: a French phrase meaning the sense of obligation the privileged should have toward the less privileged.

The druggist looked down at her. She looked back at him, erect, her face like a strained flag. "Why, of course," the druggist said. "If that's what you want. But the law requires you to tell what you are going to use it for."

Miss Emily just stared at him, her head tilted back in order to look him eye for eye, until he looked away and went and got the arsenic and wrapped it up. The Negro[55] delivery boy brought her the package; the druggist didn't come back. When she opened the package at home there was written on the box, under the skull and bones: "For rats."

IV

So the next day we all said, "She will kill herself"; and we said it would be the best thing. When she had first begun to be seen with Homer Barron, we had said, "She will marry him." Then we said, "She will persuade him yet," because Homer himself had remarked—he liked men, and it was known that he drank with the younger men in the Elks' Club—that he was not a marrying man. Later we said, "Poor Emily" behind the jalousies as they passed on Sunday afternoon in the glittering buggy, Miss Emily with her head high and Homer Barron with his hat cocked and a cigar in his teeth, reins and whip in a yellow glove.

Then some of the ladies began to say that it was a disgrace to the town and a bad example to the young people. The men did not want to interfere, but at last the ladies forced the Baptist minister—Miss Emily's people were Episcopal—to call upon her. He would never divulge what happened during that interview, but he refused to go back again. The next Sunday they again drove about the streets, and the following day the minister's wife wrote to Miss Emily's relations in Alabama.

So she had blood-kin under her roof again and we sat back to watch developments. At first nothing happened. Then we were sure that they were to be married. We learned that Miss Emily had been to the jeweler's and ordered a man's toilet set in silver, with the letters H. B. on each piece. Two days later we learned that she had bought a complete outfit of men's clothing, including a nightshirt, and we said, "They are married." We were really glad. We were glad because the two female cousins were even more Grierson than Miss Emily had ever been.

So we were not surprised when Homer Barron—the streets had been finished some time since—was gone. We were a little disappointed that there was not a public blowing-off, but we believed that he had gone on to prepare for Miss Emily's coming, or to give her a chance to get rid of the cousins. (By

---

55. Negro: a term meaning simply "black" in Romance languages, formerly in general use but now largely discontinued in the United States, replaced by "African American" or simply "Black."

that time it was a cabal, and we were all Miss Emily's allies to help circumvent the cousins.) Sure enough, after another week they departed. And, as we had expected all along, within three days Homer Barron was back in town. A neighbor saw the Negro man admit him at the kitchen door at dusk one evening.

And that was the last we saw of Homer Barron. And of Miss Emily for some time. The Negro man went in and out with the market basket, but the front door remained closed. Now and then we would see her at a window for a moment, as the men did that night when they sprinkled the lime, but for almost six months she did not appear on the streets. Then we knew that this was to be expected too; as if that quality of her father which had thwarted her woman's life so many times had been too virulent and too furious to die.

When we next saw Miss Emily, she had grown fat and her hair was turning gray. During the next few years it grew grayer and grayer until it attained an even pepper-and-salt iron-gray, when it ceased turning. Up to the day of her death at seventy-four it was still that vigorous iron-gray, like the hair of an active man.

From that time on her front door remained closed, save for a period of six or seven years, when she was about forty, during which she gave lessons in china-painting. She fitted up a studio in one of the downstairs rooms, where the daughters and granddaughters of Colonel Sartoris's contemporaries were sent to her with the same regularity and in the same spirit that they were sent to church on Sundays with a twenty-five-cent piece for the collection plate. Meanwhile her taxes had been remitted.

Then the newer generation became the backbone and the spirit of the town, and the painting pupils grew up and fell away and did not send their children to her with boxes of color and tedious brushes and pictures cut from the ladies' magazines. The front door closed upon the last one and remained closed for good. When the town got free postal delivery, Miss Emily alone refused to let them fasten the metal numbers above her door and attach a mailbox to it. She would not listen to them.

Daily, monthly, yearly we watched the Negro grow grayer and more stooped, going in and out with the market basket. Each December we sent her a tax notice, which would be returned by the post office a week later, unclaimed. Now and then we would see her in one of the downstairs windows—she had evidently shut up the top floor of the house—like the carven torso of an idol in a niche, looking or not looking at us, we could never tell which. Thus she passed from generation to generation—dear, inescapable, impervious, tranquil, and perverse.

And so she died. Fell ill in the house filled with dust and shadows, with only a doddering Negro man to wait on her. We did not even know she was sick; we had long since given up trying to get any information from the Negro.

He talked to no one, probably not even to her, for his voice had grown harsh and rusty, as if from disuse.

She died in one of the downstairs rooms, in a heavy walnut bed with a curtain, her gray head propped on a pillow yellow and moldy with age and lack of sunlight.

V

The Negro met the first of the ladies at the front door and let them in, with their hushed, sibilant voices and their quick, curious glances, and then he disappeared. He walked right through the house and out the back and was not seen again.

The two female cousins came at once. They held the funeral on the second day, with the town coming to look at Miss Emily beneath a mass of bought flowers, with the crayon face of her father musing profoundly above the bier and the ladies sibilant and macabre; and the very old men—some in their brushed Confederate uniforms—on the porch and the lawn, talking of Miss Emily as if she had been a contemporary of theirs, believing that they had danced with her and courted her perhaps, confusing time with its mathematical progression, as the old do, to whom all the past is not a diminishing road but, instead, a huge meadow which no winter ever quite touches, divided from them now by the narrow bottle-neck of the most recent decade of years.

Already we knew that there was one room in that region above stairs which no one had seen in forty years, and which would have to be forced. They waited until Miss Emily was decently in the ground before they opened it.

The violence of breaking down the door seemed to fill this room with pervading dust. A thin, acrid pall as of the tomb seemed to lie everywhere upon this room decked and furnished as for a bridal: upon the valance curtains of faded rose color, upon the rose-shaded lights, upon the dressing table, upon the delicate array of crystal and the man's toilet things backed with tarnished silver, silver so tarnished that the monogram was obscured. Among them lay a collar and tie, as if they had just been removed, which, lifted, left upon the surface a pale crescent in the dust. Upon a chair hung the suit, carefully folded; beneath it the two mute shoes and the discarded socks.

The man himself lay in the bed.

For a long while we just stood there, looking down at the profound and fleshless grin. The body had apparently once lain in the attitude of an embrace, but now the long sleep that outlasts love, that conquers even the grimace of love, had cuckolded him. What was left of him, rotted beneath what was left of the nightshirt, had become inextricable from the bed in which he lay; and upon him and upon the pillow beside him lay that even coating of the patient and biding dust.

Then we noticed that in the second pillow was the indentation of a head. One of us lifted something from it, and leaning forward, that faint and invisible dust dry and acrid in the nostrils, we saw a long strand of iron-gray hair.

8. Thomas Mann, *Tonio Kröger* (1903)

At age fourteen, as told in the first section of Mann's story, the shy, uncertain, and sensitive Tonio Kröger, who resembles his exotic, black-haired mother, unsuccessfully seeks the friendship of his bluff and confident classmate Hans Hansen, a strong, blond, blue-eyed figure like Tonio's father. Two years later, as told in the second section, he is in love with the pretty blond and blue-eyed Ingeborg Holm, but cannot win her affection. Yet in time, he overcomes his disappointment, for he knows he will be a writer and leave the world of Hans and Ingeborg behind—for he "felt in himself the desire and the ability to accomplish in his fashion a quantity of remarkable things in the world."[56]

TONIO KRÖGER

I

THE winter sun, only a poor make-believe, hung milky pale behind cloud strata above the cramped city. Wet and draughty were the gable-fringed streets, and now and then there fell a sort of soft hail, not ice and not snow.

School was out. Over the paved yard and from out the barred portal streamed the throngs of the liberated. Big boys dignifiedly held their books tightly under their left armpits, while their right arms rowed them against the wind toward the noon meal; little fellows set off on a merry canter, so that the icy slush spattered, and the traps of Science rattled in their knapsacks of seal leather. [. . .]

"Is it you at last, Hans?" said Tonio Kröger, who had long been waiting on the drive; and with a smile he stepped up to his friend, who was just coming out of the gate in conversation with other comrades, and who was on the point of going off with them.

"What is it?" asked the latter, looking at Tonio;—"Oh yes, that's so; well, let's take a little walk, then."

Tonio was silent, and his eyes grew sad. Had Hans forgotten, not to think of it again until this minute, that they were going to walk a bit together this

---

56. Bracketed ellipses in the text indicate the editor's deletions; unbracketed ellipses are the author's.

noon? And he himself had been looking forward to it almost uninterruptedly since the plan was made.

"Well, so long, fellows," said Hans Hansen to his comrades. "I'm going to take a little walk with Kröger." And they turned to the left, while the others sauntered off to the right.

Hans and Tonio had time to go walking after school, because they both belonged to houses in which dinner was not eaten until four o'clock. Their fathers were great merchants who held public offices and were a power in the city. For many a generation the Hansens had owned the extensive lumber yards down along the river, where mighty steam saws cut up the logs amid buzzing and hissing. And Tonio was Consul Kröger's son, whose grain sacks were carted through the streets day after day, with the broad black trade mark on them; the big ancient house of his ancestors was the most princely of the whole town. The two friends had to take off their caps constantly, because of their many acquaintances, and indeed these fourteen-year-old boys did not always have to bow first.

Both had hung their school-bags over their shoulders, and both were dressed warmly and well; Hans in a short seaman's jacket, over the shoulders and back of which lay the broad blue collar of his sailor suit, Tonio in a gray belted top-coat. Hans wore a Danish sailor's cap with short ribbons, a tuft of his flaxen hair peeping out from under it. He was extraordinarily handsome and well formed, broad of shoulder and narrow of hip, with unshaded, keen, steel-blue eyes. From under Tonio's round fur cap, on the other hand, there looked out of a swarthy face, with very clearly marked southern features, dark and delicately shaded eyes under excessively heavy lids, dreamy and a trifle timid. Mouth and chin were both fashioned with uncommonly soft lines. He walked carelessly and unevenly, whereas Hans's slender legs in their black stockings moved so elastically and rhythmically.

Tonio did not speak. He was grieved. Drawing together his rather slanting eyebrows, and holding his lips pursed for whistling, he looked into space with his head on one side. This attitude and expression were peculiar to him.

Suddenly Hans thrust his arm under that of Tonio with a sidelong glance at him, for he understood quite well what the matter was. And although Tonio persisted in silence during the next few steps, yet he was all at once amazingly softened.

"You know I hadn't forgotten, Tonio," said Hans, looking down at the walk before him, "but I simply thought probably nothing could come of it today, because it's so wet and windy, you know. But that doesn't bother me at all, and I think it's fine that you waited for me in spite of it. I had begun to think you had gone on home, and was vexed . . ."

At these words Tonio's entire being began to leap and shout. [. . .]

The fact was that Tonio loved Hans Hansen and had already suffered much for his sake. He who loves most is the weaker and must suffer—this simple and bitter doctrine of life his fourteen-year-old spirit had already accepted; and he was so constituted that he marked well all such experiences, and as it were jotted them down inwardly, and indeed he had a certain pleasure in them, though to be sure without ordering his conduct accordingly and so deriving practical benefit from them. Furthermore, his nature was such that he deemed such teachings much more important and interesting than the knowledge which was forced upon him in school; during the class hours in the vaulted Gothic school-rooms he applied himself mostly to tasting the sensations of such bits of insight to the lees, and thinking them out in their entirety. This occupation afforded the same kind of satisfaction as when he would walk up and down his room with his violin (for he played the violin), letting the soft tones, as soft as he could produce them, mingle with the plashing of the fountain which rose in a flickering jet under the branches of the old walnut-tree in the garden below.

The fountain, the old walnut, his violin, and far away the sea, the Baltic, whose summer dreams he could listen to in the long vacation—these were the things he loved, with which he encompassed himself, as it were, and among which his inward life ran its course; things whose names may be employed with good effect in verse, and which did actually ring out time and again in the verses which Tonio Kröger occasionally composed. [. . .]

As he wasted his time at home, was slow and generally inattentive in class hours, and had a bad record with his teachers, he always brought home the most wretched reports; at which his father, a tall, carefully dressed gentleman with meditative blue eyes, who always wore a wild flower in his button-hole, showed himself both incensed and distressed. But to his mother, his beautiful mother with the black hair, whose name was Consuelo and who was altogether so different from the other ladies of the town, because Tonio's father had once fetched her from clear down at the bottom of the map[57]—to his mother his reports were absolutely immaterial.

Tonio loved his dark, passionate mother, who played the piano and the mandolin so wonderfully, and he was happy that she did not grieve over his doubtful position among men. On the other hand, however, he realized that his father's anger was much more estimable and respectable, and although he was censured by his father, he was at bottom quite in agreement with him, whereas he found the cheerful indifference of his mother a trifle unprincipled. At times his thoughts would run about thus: "It is bad enough that I am as I am, and will not and cannot alter myself, negligent, refractory, and intent on things that nobody else thinks of. At least it is proper that they should seriously chide and punish me for it, and not pass it over with kisses and music. After

---

57. bottom of the map: that is, from South America.

all, we aren't [Gypsies] in a green wagon, but decent folks, Consul Krögers, the Kröger family" . . . And not infrequently he would think: "Well, why am I so peculiar and at outs with everything, at loggerheads with my teachers and a stranger among the boys? [. . .] How proper they must feel, how satisfied with everything and everybody. That must be nice . . . But what ails me, and how will all this end?" [. . .]

After these reflections, Tonio returns to describing his encounter with Hans.

"I've just been reading something wonderful, something splendid," he said. They were walking along, eating fruit tablets from a bag which they had purchased at Iverson's on Mill Street for ten pfennig.[58] "You must read it, Hans, it is *Don Carlos* by Schiller.[59] I'll lend it to you, if you wish."

"No, no," said Hans Hansen, "never mind, Tonio, that's not my style. I stick to my horse-books, you know. Splendid illustrations in them, I tell you. Sometime I'll show them to you at the house. They are snap-shots, and you see the horses trotting and galloping and jumping, in every position, such as you would never see in life because they move too fast."

"In all positions?" asked Tonio politely. "Yes, that's fine, but as for *Don Carlos*, it is beyond all comprehension. There are passages in it, you'll see, that are so beautiful that it gives you a jerk, as if something had suddenly burst."

"Burst?" asked Hans Hansen. "How do you mean?"

"For example, there is the passage where the king has wept because he has been deceived by the marquis—but the marquis has only deceived him for love of the prince, you understand, for whom he is sacrificing himself. And now the news that the king has wept comes out of his cabinet into the ante-room. 'Wept? The king has wept?' All the courtiers are terribly taken aback, and it just goes through you, for he's an awfully stiff and strict king. But you understand so clearly that he did weep, and I really feel sorrier for him than for the marquis and the prince together. He's always so utterly alone and without love, and now he thinks he has found a friend, and the friend betrays him . . ."

Hans Hansen cast a sidelong glance into Tonio's face, and something in that face must surely have won him over to this subject, for he suddenly thrust his arm into Tonio's again and asked,

"Why, how does he betray the king, Tonio?"

Tonio was stirred to action.

"Why, the fact is," he began, "that all letters to Brabant and Flanders . . ."

"There comes Erwin Immerthal," said Hans. [. . .]

---

58. pfennig: penny; a coin of small value in common use in Central Europe.
59. *Don Carlos*: play by Friedrich von Schiller, for which see Introduction to Chapter 2 and Text 5.

II

Two years after the preceding awkward interaction with Hans, Tonio is equally unsuccessful in approaching the attractive Ingeborg.

Fair-haired Inga, Ingeborg Holm, daughter of Doctor Holm who lived on the market-place where the Gothic fountain stood, lofty, many-pointed, and of varied form, she it was whom Tonio Kroger loved at sixteen.

How did that happen? He had seen her a thousand times; but one evening he saw her in a certain light, saw how in conversing with a girl friend she laughingly tossed her head in a certain saucy fashion, and carried her hand, a little-girl's hand, by no means especially slender or dainty, up to her back hair in a certain fashion, so that the white gauze sleeve slipped down from her elbow; heard how she pronounced a word, an insignificant word, in a certain fashion, with a warm ring in her voice,—and a rapture seized upon his heart, far stronger than that which he had formerly felt at times when he looked at Hans Hansen, in those days when he was a small, silly boy. [. . .]

This loss of Tonio Kröger's heart to merry Inga Holm occurred in the empty drawing-room of Mrs. Consul Husteede, whose turn it was that evening to have the dancing class; for it was a private class, to which only members of the first families belonged, and they assembled in turn in the parental houses in order to receive instruction in dancing and deportment. For this special purpose dancing-master Knaak came over every week from Hamburg. [. . .]

Tonio embarrasses himself in the dancing class, ending up in the row of girls instead of with the boys, to the amusement of all present.

Had she too laughed at him, like all the rest? Yes, she had done so, gladly as he would have denied it for her and his own sake. And yet he had only danced *"moulinet des dames"* because absorbed in her presence. And what did it matter? Perhaps they would stop laughing some time. Had not a magazine a short while before accepted one of his poems, though it was discontinued before the poem could appear? The day would come when he would be famous, when everything he wrote would be printed, and then it was to be seen whether that wouldn't make an impression on Inga Holm . . . But it wouldn't make any impression, no, that was just the trouble. On Magdalen Vermehren, who was always falling down, yes, on her it would. But never on Inga Holm, never on the blue-eyed, merry Inga. And so was it not in vain? [. . .]

But even if his love is not reciprocated, Tonio will continue to love Ingeborg.

"Faithfulness!" thought Tonio Kröger. "I will be faithful and love you, Ingeborg, as long as I live." So good were his intentions. And yet a secret fear and sadness whispered: "You know you have forgotten Hans Hansen altogether, although you see him daily." And the hateful and pitiful thing was that this soft and slightly malicious voice had the right of it, that time went on and days came when Tonio Kröger was no longer so unconditionally ready to die for the merry Inga as formerly, because he felt in himself the desire and the ability to accomplish in his fashion a quantity of remarkable things in the world.

And he cautiously circled about the altar of sacrifice on which the pure and chaste flame of his love was blazing, knelt before it, and stirred and fed it in every way, because he wanted to be faithful. Yet after a time, imperceptibly, without sensation or noise, it went out nevertheless.

But Tonio Kröger stood yet awhile before the chilled altar, full of wonder and disappointment to find that faithfulness was impossible on earth. Then he shrugged his shoulders and went his way.

9. Franz Kafka, *The Metamorphosis* (1915)

The following selections from the first and third parts of Kafka's *Metamorphosis* track the experience of the traveling salesman Gregor Samsa from his transformation into a giant beetle-like creature to his repudiation by his family, as they gradually cease to think of him as a human being, a son, and a brother. He had loved them and sustained them in his human form; and now that he has become hideous and burdensome, an "animal," he compliantly starves himself, and dies.[60]

THE METAMORPHOSIS

I.

One morning, as Gregor Samsa was waking up from anxious dreams, he discovered that in bed he had been changed into a monstrous verminous bug. He lay on his armour-hard back and saw, as he lifted his head up a little, his brown, arched abdomen divided up into rigid bow-like sections. From this height the blanket, just about ready to slide off completely, could hardly stay in place. His numerous legs, pitifully thin in comparison to the rest of his circumference, flickered helplessly before his eyes.

"What's happened to me," he thought. It was no dream. His room, a proper room for a human being, only somewhat too small, lay quietly between the four well-known walls. [. . .] "Why don't I keep sleeping for a little while

---

60. Bracketed ellipses in the text indicate the editor's deletions; unbracketed ellipses are the author's.

longer and forget all this foolishness," he thought. But this was entirely impractical, for he was used to sleeping on his right side, and in his present state he couldn't get himself into this position. No matter how hard he threw himself onto his right side, he always rolled again onto his back. He must have tried it a hundred times, closing his eyes so that he would not have to see the wriggling legs, and gave up only when he began to feel a light, dull pain in his side which he had never felt before.

"O God," he thought, "what a demanding job I've chosen! Day in, day out, on the road. The stresses of selling are much greater than the work going on at head office, and, in addition to that, I have to cope with the problems of travelling, the worries about train connections, irregular bad food, temporary and constantly changing human relationships, which never come from the heart. To hell with it all! [. . .] If I didn't hold back for my parents' sake, I'd have quit ages ago. I would've gone to the boss and told him just what I think from the bottom of my heart. He would've fallen right off his desk! [. . .] Anyway, I haven't completely given up that hope yet. Once I've got together the money to pay off my parents' debt to him—that should take another five or six years— I'll do it for sure. Then I'll make the big break. In any case, right now I have to get up. My train leaves at five o'clock."

Gregor hears a knock on the door.

"Gregor," a voice called—it was his mother!—"it's quarter to seven. Don't you want to be on your way?" The soft voice! Gregor was startled when he heard his voice answering. It was clearly and unmistakably his earlier voice, but in it was intermingled, as if from below, an irrepressibly painful squeaking, which left the words positively distinct only in the first moment and distorted them in the reverberation, so that one didn't know if one had heard correctly. Gregor wanted to answer in detail and explain everything, but in these circumstances he confined himself to saying, "Yes, yes, thank you mother. I'm getting up right away." [. . .]

Not really understanding, his mother turns away, but now his father and sister realize he is still at home. His sister begs him to open the door and Gregor rejoices that he had locked the door.

First he wanted to stand up quietly and undisturbed, get dressed, above all have breakfast, and only then consider further action [. . .]. It was very easy to throw aside the blanket. He needed only to push himself up a little, and it fell by itself. But to continue was difficult, particularly because he was so unusually wide. He needed arms and hands to push himself upright. Instead of these, however, he had only many small limbs which were incessantly moving with very different motions and which, in addition, he was unable to control. [. . .]

At first he wanted to get out of bed with the lower part of his body, but this lower part—which, by the way, he had not yet looked at and which he also couldn't picture clearly—proved itself too difficult to move. [. . .] Thus, he tried to get his upper body out of the bed first and turned his head carefully toward the edge of the bed. He managed to do this easily, and in spite of its width and weight his body mass at last slowly followed the turning of his head. [. . .] And he made an effort then to rock his entire body length out of the bed with a uniform motion. [. . .]

He had already got to the point where, by rocking more strongly, he maintained his equilibrium with difficulty, and very soon he would finally have to decide, for in five minutes it would be a quarter past seven. Then there was a ring at the door of the apartment. "That's someone from the office," he told himself, and he almost froze while his small limbs only danced around all the faster. [. . .] Must the manager himself come, and in the process must it be demonstrated to the entire innocent family that the investigation of this suspicious circumstance could be entrusted only to the intelligence of the manager? And more as a consequence of the excited state in which this idea put Gregor than as a result of an actual decision, he swung himself with all his might out of the bed. There was a loud thud, but not a real crash. [. . .]

"Gregor," his father now said from the neighbouring room on the left, "Mr. Manager has come and is asking why you have not left on the early train. We don't know what we should tell him. Besides, he also wants to speak to you personally. So please open the door. He will be good enough to forgive the mess in your room." [. . .]

Gregor pushed himself slowly towards the door, with the help of the easy chair, let go of it there, threw himself against the door, held himself upright against it—the balls of his tiny limbs had a little sticky stuff on them—and rested there momentarily from his exertion. Then he made an effort to turn the key in the lock with his mouth. Unfortunately it seemed that he had no real teeth. How then was he to grab hold of the key? But to make up for that his jaws were naturally very strong; with their help he managed to get the key really moving. He didn't notice that he was obviously inflicting some damage on himself, for a brown fluid came out of his mouth, flowed over the key, and dripped onto the floor. [. . .]

The door was now open and Gregor was partially visible. Alarmed, the manager backs off and leaves. His mother looks frantically at his father, who then attempts to drive Gregor back into his room.

With his left hand, his father picked up a large newspaper from the table and, stamping his feet on the floor, he set out to drive Gregor back into his room by waving the cane and the newspaper. No request of Gregor's was of any use; no request would even be understood. No matter how willing he was to turn his head respectfully, his father just stomped all the harder with his feet. [. . .]

Now, Gregor had no practice at all in going backwards—it was really very slow going. [. . .] But when he finally was successful in getting his head in front of the door opening, it became clear that his body was too wide to go through any further. [. . .] Now it was really no longer a joke, and Gregor forced himself, come what might, into the door. [. . .] His one flank was sore with the scraping. On the white door ugly blotches were left. Soon he was stuck fast and would have not been able to move any more on his own. The tiny legs on one side hung twitching in the air above, and the ones on the other side were pushed painfully into the floor. Then his father gave him one really strong liberating push from behind, and he scurried, bleeding severely, far into the interior of his room. The door was slammed shut with the cane, and finally it was quiet.

The family still thinks of Gregor as Gregor, their son. His sister, especially, brings him food, adjusting the offerings to match his taste for rotten things. Gregor adjusts to his new form and learns to scurry up and down the walls and to hang from the ceiling. As time goes on, however, hardship sets in, as Gregor had been the family's sole supporter. His father and his sister take jobs and the full-time maid is dismissed. On one occasion, Gregor comes out of his room, and his father drives him back by bombarding him with apples—one of which penetrates a gap in his hard shell and decomposes in the wound.

III.

Gregor's serious wound, from which he suffered for over a month—since no one ventured to remove the apple, it remained in his flesh as a visible reminder—seemed by itself to have reminded the father that, in spite of his present unhappy and hateful appearance, Gregor was a member of the family, something one should not treat as an enemy, and that it was, on the contrary, a requirement of family duty to suppress one's aversion and to endure— nothing else, just endure. And if through his wound Gregor had now apparently lost for good his ability to move and for the time being needed many, many minutes to crawl across his room, like an aged invalid—so far as creeping up high was concerned, that was unimaginable—nevertheless for this worsening of his condition, in his opinion, he did get completely satisfactory compensation, because every day towards evening the door to the living room, which he was in the habit of keeping a sharp eye on even one or two hours beforehand, was opened, so that he, lying down in the darkness of his room, invisible from the living room, could see the entire family at the illuminated table and listen to their conversation, to a certain extent with their common permission, a situation quite different from what had happened before. [. . .]

But then he was in no mood to worry about his family. He was filled with sheer anger over the wretched care he was getting, even though he couldn't imagine anything which he might have an appetite for. Still, he made plans about how he could take from the larder what he at all account deserved, even if he wasn't hungry. Without thinking any more about how they might be able to give Gregor special pleasure, the sister now kicked some food or other very quickly into his room in the morning and at noon, before she ran off to her shop, and in the evening, quite indifferent to whether the food had perhaps only been tasted or, what happened most frequently, remained entirely undisturbed, she whisked it out with one sweep of her broom. The task of cleaning his room, which she now always carried out in the evening, could not be done any more quickly. Streaks of dirt ran along the walls; here and there lay tangles of dust and garbage. At first, when his sister arrived, Gregor positioned himself in a particularly filthy corner in order with this posture to make something of a protest. But he could have well stayed there for weeks without his sister's changing her ways. In fact, she perceived the dirt as much as he did, but she had decided just to let it stay. [. . .]

Gregor is deeply depressed by his treatment and hardly eats any more. One night, though, he hears his sister playing the violin "so beautifully . . . her gaze follow[ing] the score intently and sadly," and he creeps into the living room to listen. But he is a sight to behold—

because as a result of the dust which lay all over his room and flew around with the slightest movement, he was totally covered in dirt. On his back and his sides he carted around with him dust, threads, hair, and remnants of food. His indifference to everything was much too great for him to lie on his back and scour himself on the carpet, as he often had done earlier during the day. In spite of his condition he had no timidity about inching forward a bit on the spotless floor of the living room. [. . .] The violin fell silent. [. . .]

Appalled by the sight of Gregor, the three lodgers who had been taken in to help cover expenses angrily leave, without paying for their room and board. The family is desperate.

"My dear parents," said the sister banging her hand on the table by way of an introduction, "things cannot go on any longer in this way. Maybe if you don't understand that, well, I do. I will not utter my brother's name in front of this monster, and thus I say only that we must try to get rid of it. We have tried what is humanly possible to take care of it and to be patient. I believe that no one can criticize us in the slightest. [. . .] It must be gotten rid of," cried the sister. "That is the only way, father. You must try to get rid of the idea that this is Gregor. The fact that we have believed for so long, that is truly our real misfortune. But how can it be Gregor? If it were Gregor, he would have long ago realized that a communal life among human beings is not possible with such an animal and would have gone away voluntarily. Then we would not have a brother, but we could go on living and honour his memory. But this animal plagues us. It drives away the lodgers, will obviously take over the entire apartment, and leave us to spend the night in the alley." [. . .]

Gregor retreats to his room and his sister jumps up to lock the door after him.

"What now?" Gregor asked himself and looked around him in the darkness. He soon made the discovery that he could no longer move at all. He was not surprised at that. On the contrary, it struck him as unnatural that up to this point he had really been able to move around with these thin little legs. Besides he felt relatively content. True, he had pains throughout his entire body, but it seemed to him that they were gradually becoming weaker and weaker and would finally go away completely. The rotten apple in his back and the inflamed surrounding area, entirely covered with white dust, he hardly noticed. He remembered his family with deep feelings of love. In this business, his own thought that he had to disappear was, if possible, even more decisive than his sister's. He remained in this state of empty and peaceful reflection until the tower clock struck three o'clock in the morning. From the window he witnessed the beginning of the general dawning outside. Then without willing it, his head sank all the way down, and from his nostrils flowed out weakly his last breath.

10. Virginia Woolf, *A Room of One's Own* (1929)

In this famous essay, Woolf concisely defines the preconditions for a woman's literary career: "[A] woman must have money and a room of her own if she is to write fiction." Domestic responsibilities—performed in other rooms that are shared by family members—stifle literary creation. So, too, does poverty, and women are often poor, for all sorts of reasons: because of "this or that," writes Woolf. Women's real historical condition, despite the appearance in fiction of towering female characters, was likely to have been isolated, exploited, or "locked up, beaten and flung about the room." In consequence, few women have become authors. Why did William Shakespeare astound, while his sister, Judith Shakespeare, never had the chance to excel?

A ROOM OF ONE'S OWN

Chapter One

But, you may say, we asked you to speak about women and fiction—what has that got to do with a room of one's own? I will try to explain. When you asked me to speak about women and fiction I sat down on the banks of a river and began to wonder what the words meant. They might mean simply a few remarks about Fanny Burney; a few more about Jane Austen; a tribute to the Brontës . . . ; a respectful allusion to George Eliot.[61] . . . But at second sight the words seemed not so simple. The title women and fiction might mean, and you may have meant it to mean, women and what they are like; or it might mean women and the fiction that they write; or it might mean women and the fiction that is written about them; or it might mean that somehow all three are inextricably mixed together and you want me to consider them in that light. But when I began to consider the subject in this last way, . . . I soon saw that it had one fatal drawback. I should never be able to come to a conclusion. I should never be able to fulfil what is, I understand, the first duty of a lecturer—to hand you after an hour's discourse a nugget of pure truth to wrap up between the pages of your notebooks and keep on the mantel-piece for ever. All I could do was to offer you an opinion upon one minor point—a woman must have money[62] and a room of her own if she is to write fiction. . . .

Chapter Three

Arguing that poverty, among other things, has prevented women from writing, Woolf has sought, unsuccessfully, an answer to the question: Why are women poor?

Women are poorer than men because—this or that. Perhaps now it would be better to give up seeking for the truth, and . . . to narrow the enquiry and to ask the historian, who records not opinions but facts, to describe under what conditions women lived, not throughout the ages, but in England, say, in the time of Elizabeth.[63]

For it is a perennial puzzle why no woman wrote a word of that extraordinary literature when every other man, it seemed, was capable of song or sonnet. What were the conditions in which women lived, I asked myself; for fiction . . . is not dropped like a pebble upon the ground . . . , [but] is like a spider's web, attached ever so lightly, perhaps, but still attached to life at all four corners. . . . But when the web is pulled askew, hooked up at the edge, torn in the middle, one remembers that these webs are not spun in mid-air by incorporeal creatures, but are the work of suffering human beings, and are attached to grossly material things, like health and money and the houses we live in. . . .

---

61. Burney, etc.: Woolf names five important English women authors of the nineteenth century: Frances Burney, Jane Austen, Charlotte and Emily Brontë, and George Eliot. For Austen and Charlotte Brontë, see Introduction to Chapter 3 and Texts 1 and 4.
62. Woolf will later specify the sum of five hundred pounds per year, the income she has inherited, as permitting a middling existence.
63. the time of Elizabeth: a reference to Elizabeth the Great, Queen of England (r. 1558–1603), who reigned in the era of William Shakespeare.

Woolf concedes, as the historian she consults had commented, that women as portrayed in literature—such as the Shakespearean characters Cleopatra, Lady Macbeth, and Rosalind, as well as a stream of others—were given strong personalities, yet real women were viewed as insignificant and regularly abused.

Not being a historian, one might go even further and say that women have burnt like beacons in all the works of all the poets from the beginning of time— Clytemnestra, Antigone, Cleopatra, Lady Macbeth, Phèdre, Cressida, Rosalind, Desdemona, the Duchess of Malfi, among the dramatists; then among the prose writers: Millamant, Clarissa, Becky Sharp, Anna Karenina, Emma Bovary, Madame de Guermantes—the names flock to mind. . . .[64] Indeed, if women had no existence save in the fiction written by men, one would imagine her a person of the utmost importance; very various; heroic and mean; splendid and sordid; . . . as great as a man, some think even greater. But this is woman in fiction. In fact, . . . she was locked up, beaten and flung about the room.

A very queer, composite being thus emerges. Imaginatively she is of the highest importance; practically she is completely insignificant. She pervades poetry from cover to cover; she is all but absent from history. . . . Some of the most inspired words, some of the most profound thoughts in literature fall from her lips; in real life, she could hardly read, could scarcely spell, and was the property of her husband. . . .

I could not help thinking, as I looked at the works of Shakespeare on the shelf, that . . . it would have been impossible, complete and entirely, for any woman to have written the plays of Shakespeare in the age of Shakespeare. Let me imagine . . . what would have happened had Shakespeare had a wonderfully gifted sister, called Judith, let us say. Shakespeare himself went, very probably . . . to the grammar school, where he may have learnt Latin . . . and the elements of grammar and logic. He was, it is well known, a wild boy who poached rabbits, perhaps shot a deer, and had, rather sooner than he should have done, to marry a woman in the neighbourhood, who bore him a child rather quicker than was right. That escapade sent him to seek his fortune in London. He had, it seemed, a taste for the theatre; he began by holding horses at the stage door. Very soon he got work in the theatre, became a successful actor, and lived at the hub of the universe, meeting everybody, knowing everybody, practicing his art on the boards, exercising his wits in the streets, and even getting access to the palace of the queen. Meanwhile, his extraordinarily gifted sister, let us suppose,

---

64. Clytemnestra, etc.: Woolf names a series of literary heroines in no particular order from works by ancient Greek and modern English, French, and Russian authors: Aeschylus, Sophocles, William Shakespeare, Jean Racine, John Webster, William Congreve, Samuel Richardson, William Thackeray, Leo Tolstoy, Gustave Flaubert, and Marcel Proust. For Aeschylus and Sophocles, see Volume One, Introduction to Chapter 2; for Shakespeare, see Volume One, Introduction to Chapter 11; and for Tolstoy, see in this volume, Introduction to Chapter 5.

remained at home. She was as adventurous, as imaginative, as agog to see the world as he was. But she was not sent to school. She had no chance of learning grammar and logic, let alone of reading Horace and Virgil. She picked up a book now and then, one of her brother's perhaps, and read a few pages. But then her parents came in and told her to mend the stockings or mind the stew and not moon about with books and papers. . . . Perhaps she scribbled some pages up in an apple loft on the sly, but was careful to hide them or set fire to them. Soon, however, before she was out of her teens, she was to be betrothed to the son of a neighbouring wool-stapler. She cried out that marriage was hateful to her, and for that she was severely beaten by her father. Then he ceased to scold her. He begged her instead not to hurt him, not to shame him in this matter of her marriage. . . . How could she disobey him? How could she break his heart? The force of her own gift alone drove her to it. She made up a small parcel of her belongings, let herself down by a rope one summer's night and took the road to London. . . . Like [her brother], she had a taste for the theatre. She stood at the stage door; she wanted to act, she said. Men laughed in her face. The manager— a fat, loose-lipped man, guffawed. He bellowed something about poodles dancing and women acting—no woman, he said, could possibly be an actress. He hinted—you can imagine what. . . . At last . . . Nick Greene the actor-manager took pity on her; she found herself with child by that gentleman and so—who shall measure the heat and violence of the poet's heart when caught and tangled in a woman's body?—killed herself one winter's night and lies buried at some cross-roads where the omnibuses now stop outside the Elephant and Castle.[65]

That, more or less, is how the story would run, I think, if a woman in Shakespeare's day had had Shakespeare's genius. . . . [B]ut what is true . . . is that any woman born with a great gift in the sixteenth century would certainly have gone crazed, shot herself, or ended her days in some lonely cottage outside the village, half witch, half wizard, feared and mocked at. . . .

After an extended discussion of women's participation in literary production and the impediments to their success, Woolf concludes her essay with a plea to women to pursue the career that Shakespeare's sister could not.

How can I further encourage you to go about the business of life? Young women, I would say, and please attend, for the peroration is beginning, you are, in my opinion, disgracefully ignorant. You have never made a discovery of any sort of importance. You have never shaken an empire or led an army into battle. The plays of Shakespeare are not by you, and you have never introduced a barbarous race to the blessings of civilization. What is your excuse? It is all very well for you to say . . . we have had other work on our hands. . . . We have borne and bred and washed and taught, perhaps to the age of six or seven years,

---

65. Elephant and Castle: a major traffic hub in London.

the one thousand six hundred and twenty-three million human beings who are, according to the statistics, at present in existence, and that, allowing that some had help, takes time.

There is truth in what you say—I will not deny it. But at the same time may I remind you that there have been at least two colleges for women in existence in England since the year 1866;[66] that after the year 1880 a married woman was allowed by law to possess her own property; and that in 1919—which is a whole nine years ago—she was given a vote? May I also remind you that most of the professions have been open to you for close on ten years now? When you reflect upon these immense privileges and the length of time during which they have been enjoyed, . . . you will agree that the excuse of lack of opportunity, training, encouragement, leisure and money no longer holds good. . . .

Thus, with some time on your hands and with some book learning in your brains . . . surely you should embark upon another stage of your very long, very laborious and highly obscure career. . . .

I told you in the course of this paper that Shakespeare had a sister. . . . She died young—alas, she never wrote a word. She lies buried where the omnibuses now stop, opposite the Elephant and Castle. Now my belief is that this poet who never wrote a word and was buried at the crossroads still lives. She lives in you and in me, and in many other women who are not here tonight, for they are washing up the dishes and putting the children to bed. But she lives; for great poets do not die; they are continuing presences; they need only the opportunity to walk among us in the flesh. This opportunity, as I think, is now coming within your power to give her. For my belief is that if we live another century or so—I am talking of the common life which is the real life and not of the little separate lives which we live as individuals—and have five hundred a year each of us and rooms of our own; if we have the habit of freedom and the courage to write exactly what we think; if we escape a little from the common sitting-room and see human beings not always in their relation to each other but in relation to reality . . . , then the opportunity will come and the dead poet who was Shakespeare's sister will put on the body which has so often laid down. Drawing her life from the lives of the unknown who were her forerunners, as her brother did before her, she will be born. As for her coming without that preparation, without that effort on our part, without that determination that when she is born again she shall find it possible to live and write her poetry, that we cannot expect, for that would be impossible. But I maintain that she would come if we worked for her, and that so to work, even in poverty and obscurity, is worth while.

---

66. Woolf here recounts the legal and material improvements in women's condition realized in quite recent years.

11. W. E. B. Du Bois, *The Souls of Black Folk* (1903)

In the first chapter of *The Souls of Black Folk*, Du Bois describes his own discovery of what it means to be identified as Black and diagnoses the problem his fellow African Americans face as a "double consciousness," an inability to see themselves except through the eyes of white America. "The history of the American Negro,"[67] he writes, "is the history of this strife,—this longing to attain self-conscious manhood, . . . to make it possible for a man to be both a Negro and an American, without being cursed and spit upon by his fellows, without having the doors of Opportunity closed roughly in his face." But to become a part of American culture, he argues, African Americans must throw off "the weight of [their] ignorance," and acquire a thorough and classical education. Then they will be able to lead their fellows "toward that vaster ideal that swims before the Negro people, . . . the ideal of fostering and developing the traits and talents of the Negro, not in opposition to or contempt for other races, but rather in large conformity to the greater ideals of the American Republic. . . ."

THE SOULS OF BLACK FOLK

I. Of Our Spiritual Strivings

Between me and the other world there is ever an unasked question: unasked by some through feelings of delicacy; by others through the difficulty of rightly framing it. All, nevertheless, flutter round it. They approach me in a half-hesitant sort of way, eye me curiously or compassionately, and then, instead of saying directly, How does it feel to be a problem? they say, I know an excellent colored man in my town; or, I fought at Mechanicsville; or, Do not these Southern outrages make your blood boil? At these I smile, or am interested, or reduce the boiling to a simmer, as the occasion may require. To the real question, How does it feel to be a problem? I answer seldom a word.

And yet, being a problem is a strange experience,—peculiar even for one who has never been anything else, save perhaps in babyhood and in Europe. It is in the early days of rollicking boyhood that the revelation first bursts upon one, all in a day, as it were. I remember well when the shadow swept across me. I was a little thing, away up in the hills of New England, where the dark Housatonic[68] winds between Hoosac and Taghkanic[69] to the sea. In

---

67. Negro: a term meaning simply "black" in Romance languages, regularly used in English in Du Bois's era, but one whose use has been largely discontinued in the United States in recent decades and replaced by "African American" or simply "Black."
68. Housatonic: a river flowing south-southeast through western Massachusetts and Connecticut and into Long Island Sound.
69. Hoosac and Taghkanic: towns in New York State not far west of the Massachusetts border and somewhat north of Great Barrington, Massachusetts, where Du Bois was born.

a wee wooden schoolhouse, something put it into the boys' and girls' heads to buy gorgeous visiting-cards—ten cents a package—and exchange. The exchange was merry, till one girl, a tall newcomer, refused my card,—refused it peremptorily, with a glance. Then it dawned upon me with a certain suddenness that I was different from the others; or like, mayhap, in heart and life and longing, but shut out from their world by a vast veil. I had thereafter no desire to tear down that veil, to creep through; I held all beyond it in common contempt, and lived above it in a region of blue sky and great wandering shadows. That sky was bluest when I could beat my mates at examination-time, or beat them at a foot-race, or even beat their stringy heads. Alas, with the years all this fine contempt began to fade; for the words I longed for, and all their dazzling opportunities, were theirs, not mine. But they should not keep these prizes, I said; some, all, I would wrest from them. Just how I would do it I could never decide: by reading law, by healing the sick, by telling the wonderful tales that swam in my head,—some way. With other black boys the strife was not so fiercely sunny: their youth shrunk into tasteless sycophancy, or into silent hatred of the pale world about them and mocking distrust of everything white; or wasted itself in a bitter cry, Why did God make me an outcast and a stranger in mine own house? The shades of the prison-house[70] closed round about us all: walls strait and stubborn to the whitest, but relentlessly narrow, tall, and unscalable to sons of night who must plod darkly on in resignation, or beat unavailing palms against the stone, or steadily, half hopelessly, watch the streak of blue above.

After the Egyptian and Indian, the Greek and Roman, the Teuton and Mongolian, the Negro is a sort of seventh son, born with a veil, and gifted with second-sight in this American world,—a world which yields him no true self-consciousness, but only lets him see himself through the revelation of the other world. It is a peculiar sensation, this double-consciousness, this sense of always looking at one's self through the eyes of others, of measuring one's soul by the tape of a world that looks on in amused contempt and pity. One ever feels his twoness,—an American, a Negro; two souls, two thoughts, two unreconciled strivings; two warring ideals in one dark body, whose dogged strength alone keeps it from being torn asunder.

The history of the American Negro is the history of this strife,—this longing to attain self-conscious manhood, to merge his double self into a better and truer self. In this merging he wishes neither of the older selves to be lost. He would not Africanize America, for America has too much to teach the world and Africa. He would not bleach his Negro soul in a flood of white

---

70. shades of the prison-house: Du Bois alludes to William Wordsworth's *Ode: Intimations of Immortality*: "Shades of the prison-house begin to close / Upon the growing Boy." See Chapter 2, Text 2.

Americanism, for he knows that Negro blood has a message for the world. He simply wishes to make it possible for a man to be both a Negro and an American, without being cursed and spit upon by his fellows, without having the doors of Opportunity closed roughly in his face.

This, then, is the end of his striving: to be a co-worker in the kingdom of culture, to escape both death and isolation, to husband and use his best powers and his latent genius. These powers of body and mind have in the past been strangely wasted, dispersed, or forgotten. The shadow of a mighty Negro past flits through the tale of Ethiopia the Shadowy and of Egypt the Sphinx. Through history, the powers of single black men flash here and there like falling stars, and die sometimes before the world has rightly gauged their brightness. Here in America, in the few days since Emancipation, the black man's turning hither and thither in hesitant and doubtful striving has often made his very strength to lose effectiveness, to seem like absence of power, like weakness. And yet it is not weakness,—it is the contradiction of double aims. The double-aimed struggle of the black artisan—on the one hand to escape white contempt for a nation of mere hewers of wood and drawers of water, and on the other hand to plough and nail and dig for a poverty-stricken horde— could only result in making him a poor craftsman, for he had but half a heart in either cause. By the poverty and ignorance of his people, the Negro minister or doctor was tempted toward quackery and demagogy; and by the criticism of the other world, toward ideals that made him ashamed of his lowly tasks. The would-be black savant was confronted by the paradox that the knowledge his people needed was a twice-told tale to his white neighbors, while the knowledge which would teach the white world was Greek to his own flesh and blood. The innate love of harmony and beauty that set the ruder souls of his people a-dancing and a-singing raised but confusion and doubt in the soul of the black artist; for the beauty revealed to him was the soul-beauty of a race which his larger audience despised, and he could not articulate the message of another people. This waste of double aims, this seeking to satisfy two unreconciled ideals, has wrought sad havoc with the courage and faith and deeds of ten thousand thousand people,—has sent them often wooing false gods and invoking false means of salvation, and at times has even seemed about to make them ashamed of themselves.

Away back in the days of bondage they thought to see in one divine event the end of all doubt and disappointment; few men ever worshipped Freedom with half such unquestioning faith as did the American Negro for two centuries. To him, so far as he thought and dreamed, slavery was indeed the sum of all villainies, the cause of all sorrow, the root of all prejudice; Emancipation was the key to a promised land of sweeter beauty than ever stretched before the eyes of wearied Israelites. In song and exhortation swelled one refrain—Liberty; in his tears and curses the God he implored had Freedom in his right hand. At last it came,—suddenly, fearfully, like a dream. With one wild carnival of blood and passion came the message in his own plaintive cadences:—

"Shout, O children!
Shout, you're free!
For God has bought your liberty!"

Years have passed away since then,—ten, twenty, forty; forty years of national life, forty years of renewal and development, and yet the swarthy spectre sits in its accustomed seat at the Nation's feast. . . .

The Nation has not yet found peace from its sins; the freedman has not yet found in freedom his promised land. Whatever of good may have come in these years of change, the shadow of a deep disappointment rests upon the Negro people,—a disappointment all the more bitter because the unattained ideal was unbounded save by the simple ignorance of a lowly people.

The first decade was merely a prolongation of the vain search for freedom, the boon that seemed ever barely to elude their grasp,—like a tantalizing will-o'-the-wisp, maddening and misleading the headless host. The holocaust of war, the terrors of the Ku-Klux Klan,[71] the lies of carpet-baggers,[72] the disorganization of industry, and the contradictory advice of friends and foes, left the bewildered serf with no new watchword beyond the old cry for freedom. As the time flew, however, he began to grasp a new idea. The ideal of liberty demanded for its attainment powerful means, and these the Fifteenth Amendment[73] gave him. The ballot, which before he had looked upon as a visible sign of freedom, he now regarded as the chief means of gaining and perfecting the liberty with which war had partially endowed him. And why not? Had not votes made war and emancipated millions? Had not votes enfranchised the freedmen? Was anything impossible to a power that had done all this? A million black men started with renewed zeal to vote themselves into the kingdom. So the decade flew away, the revolution of 1876[74] came, and left the half-free serf weary, wondering, but still inspired. Slowly but steadily, in the following years, a new vision began gradually to replace the dream of political power,—a powerful movement, the rise of another ideal to guide the unguided, another pillar of fire by night after a

---

71. Ku-Klux Klan: formed after the Civil War, a secret society promoting and enforcing white supremacy.

72. carpet-baggers: a northerner in the post-Civil War South who sought private gain by taking advantage of reconstruction rules.

73. Fifteenth Amendment: amendment to the US Constitution (1870) effectively granting Black Americans the right to vote, which was not to be denied on grounds of "race, color, or previous condition of servitude."

74. revolution of 1876: the point when federal US troops were withdrawn from the South, ending the effort of Reconstruction.

clouded day. It was the ideal of "book-learning"; the curiosity, born of compulsory ignorance, to know and test the power of the cabalistic letters of the white man, the longing to know. Here at last seemed to have been discovered the mountain path to Canaan; longer than the highway of Emancipation and law, steep and rugged, but straight, leading to heights high enough to overlook life.

Up the new path the advance guard toiled, slowly, heavily, doggedly; only those who have watched and guided the faltering feet, the misty minds, the dull understandings, of the dark pupils of these schools know how faithfully, how piteously, this people strove to learn. It was weary work. The cold statistician wrote down the inches of progress here and there, noted also where here and there a foot had slipped or some one had fallen. To the tired climbers, the horizon was ever dark, the mists were often cold, the Canaan was always dim and far away. If, however, the vistas disclosed as yet no goal, no resting-place, little but flattery and criticism, the journey at least gave leisure for reflection and self-examination; it changed the child of Emancipation to the youth with dawning self-consciousness, self-realization, self-respect. In those sombre forests of his striving his own soul rose before him, and he saw himself,—darkly as through a veil; and yet he saw in himself some faint revelation of his power, of his mission. He began to have a dim feeling that, to attain his place in the world, he must be himself, and not another. For the first time he sought to analyze the burden he bore upon his back, that dead-weight of social degradation partially masked behind a half-named Negro problem. He felt his poverty; without a cent, without a home, without land, tools, or savings, he had entered into competition with rich, landed, skilled neighbors. To be a poor man is hard, but to be a poor race in a land of dollars is the very bottom of hardships. He felt the weight of his ignorance,—not simply of letters, but of life, of business, of the humanities; the accumulated sloth and shirking and awkwardness of decades and centuries shackled his hands and feet. . . .

So dawned the time of *Sturm und Drang*:[75] storm and stress to-day rocks our little boat on the mad waters of the world-sea; there is within and without the sound of conflict, the burning of body and rending of soul; inspiration strives with doubt, and faith with vain questionings. The bright ideals of the past,—physical freedom, political power, the training of brains and the training of hands,—all these in turn have waxed and waned, until even the last grows dim and overcast. Are they all wrong,—all false? No, not that, but each alone was over-simple and incomplete,—the dreams of a credulous race-childhood, or the fond imaginings of the other world which does not know and does not want to know our power. To be really true, all these ideals must be melted and welded into one. The training of the schools we need to-day more

---

75. *Sturm und Drang*: Du Bois alludes to the German moment so-named, a turbulent cultural shift that marks the first phase of German Romanticism. See Introduction to Chapter 2.

than ever,—the training of deft hands, quick eyes and ears, and above all the broader, deeper, higher culture of gifted minds and pure hearts. The power of the ballot we need in sheer self-defence,—else what shall save us from a second slavery? Freedom, too, the long-sought, we still seek,—the freedom of life and limb, the freedom to work and think, the freedom to love and aspire. Work, culture, liberty,—all these we need, not singly but together, not successively but together, each growing and aiding each, and all striving toward that vaster ideal that swims before the Negro people, the ideal of human brotherhood, gained through the unifying ideal of Race; the ideal of fostering and developing the traits and talents of the Negro, not in opposition to or contempt for other races, but rather in large conformity to the greater ideals of the American Republic, in order that some day on American soil two world-races may give each to each those characteristics both so sadly lack. . . .

12. Mariano Azuela, *The Underdogs* (1915)

This brutal, disheartening story begins when government soldiers, for no reason, kill Demetrio's dog Palomo, dishonor his wife, and burn his house. The proud peasant proprietor and expert marksman takes to the hills, where he summons his rebel band, and is soon joined by the aristocratic physician and zealous liberal Cervantes, the author's alter ego. They are fighting for the Revolution and a new Mexico, but they turn into killers, looters, and rapists. The following excerpts tell how, in Part One, Demetrio's band sets out on its exploits, and how, in Part Three, it all tragically ends.[76]

UNDERDOGS

Part One: I

"It's not an animal. . . . Just hear Palomo bark. . . . It's got to be a person."

The woman's eyes searched the darkness of the sierra.

"Maybe Federales,"[77] answered the man who squatted, eating in a corner, a clay pot in his right hand and three rolled *tortillas*[78] in the other.

The woman did not answer; her senses were concentrated outside the hut.

---

76. Bracketed ellipses indicate material omitted by the editor; unbracketed ellipses are the author's.

77. Federales: federal or government soldiers or agents

78. *tortilla*: thin corn pancake, a staple of the Mexican diet.

They heard the sound of hooves in the nearby gravel, and Palomo barked more furiously.

"You should hide just in case, Demetrio."

Calmly, the man finished eating, grabbed a *cántaro* [water jug], and lifting it with both hands, drank water in gulps. Then he stood.

"Your rifle is under the mat," she whispered.

The small room was lit by a tallow candle. A yoke, a plow, a goad and other farming tools rested in a corner. From the roof hung ropes holding up an old adobe mold that served as a bed, and on blankets and faded rags a child slept.

Demetrio buckled on the cartridge belt and picked up the rifle. Tall, strong, red-faced, beardless, he wore a white cotton shirt and trousers, a wide-brimmed straw *sombrero* [hat] and *huaraches* [sandals].

He walked out slowly, fading into the impenetrable darkness of the night.

Palomo, furious, jumped the corral fence. Suddenly a shot was heard, the dog let out a dull cry and barked no more.

Some men on horseback arrived shouting and cursing. Two got down and another remained to mind the animals.

"Women . . . something to eat! . . . Eggs, milk, beans, whatever you've got, we're starving."

"Damned sierra! Only the devil could find his way!"

"He'd get lost, sergeant, if he were as drunk as you. . . ."

One of them had braid on his shoulders, the other red stripes on his sleeves.

"Where the hell are we, woman? . . . Anybody home?"

"Then why the light? . . . What about the kid? Woman, we want to eat, now! Are you coming out or do we make you come out?"

"Wicked men, you killed my dog! . . . What did my poor Palomo ever do to you?"

The woman went into the house dragging the dog, white, fat, only the whites of his eyes showed now and his body was limp. [. . .]

"*Señora* [Ma'am], what do they call this place?" the sergeant asked.

"Limón," the woman replied sharply, as she blew on the embers and placed more wood on the fire.

"So this is Limón . . . home of the famous Demetrio Macías! . . . Hear that, lieutenant? We're in Limón."

"Limón? . . . I couldn't give a hoot!" [. . .]

"You must know that bandido,[79] *señora*. . . . I was in the Escobedo Penitentiary with him." [. . .]

"Sergeant, bring me a bottle of tequila. I've decided to spend the night in the charming company of this little brunette. . . . That's what I want. Sergeant,

---

79. *bandido*: bandit, outlaw, rascal.

my bottle, my bottle of tequila. Honey, you're too far, come over have a drink. What do you mean, no? . . . Afraid of your . . . husband . . . or whatever he is? . . . If he's in some hole tell him to come out. . . . I don't care! . . . Rats don't bother me."

A white silhouette immediately filled the dark mouth of the door.

"Demetrio Macías!" cried the sergeant fearfully stepping back.

The lieutenant stood, suddenly silent, cold and motionless like a statue.

"Kill them!" shouted the woman, her throat dry.

"Forgive me, *amigo!*[80] . . . I didn't know. . . . But I respect really brave men."

Demetrio stood there looking at them, an insolent smile of disdain wrinkling his features.

"I not only respect them, I also like them. . . . I'm poor and I've got a large family to support! Sergeant, let's go. I always respect the house of a brave man, a real man."

After they disappeared, the woman hugged Demetrio tightly.

"Holy Virgin of Jalpa! What a scare! I thought it was you they'd shot."

"Go straight to my father's," Demetrio said.

She tried to stop him, begged, cried, but pushing her away sweetly, he answered somberly:

"I've got a feeling they'll all be back."

"Why didn't you kill them?"

"I guess their time hadn't come!"[81]

They went out together, she holding the child in her arms. At the door they went in opposite directions.

The moon peopled the mountain with vague shadows.

At every ridge and every bush, Demetrio still saw the sad silhouette of a woman with a child in her arms.

After many hours of climbing, when he turned to look, at the bottom of the canyon near the river, huge flames rose. His house was burning. . . .

II

All was still shadows when Demetrio Macías started his descent to the bottom of the ravine. [. . .] During his swift and agile descent he thought:

"Now the Federales are sure to pick up our scent and track us like dogs. Lucky they don't know the trails, entrances or exists. [. . .] The people from Limón, Santa Rosa and other mountain villages are loyal. They'd never betray us. . . ."

---

80. *amigo*: friend; colloquial, "buddy."

81. their time hadn't come: a wry allusion to John 7:30 and 8:20; Jesus would be caught and crucified, but his time "had not yet come."

And he got to the bottom of the ravine just as it was becoming daylight. He threw himself on the stones and fell asleep. [. . .]

Demetrio woke up startled, forded the river and made for the opposite slope of the canyon. Tenacious like an ant, he climbed up the crest, his hands clasped the rocks and branches, the soles of his feet clasped the stones of the trail. [. . .]

Demetrio stopped at the summit, reached back with his left hand and grabbed the horn slung on his back. He raised it to his thick lips and, filling his cheeks, blew three times. Three whistles beyond the facing slope answered his signal.

In the distance, from a conical cluster of reeds and rotten straw, one by one emerged many men with bare chests and legs; they were dark and polished like old bronze. They rushed to meet Demetrio.

"They burned my house!" was his answer to their questioning looks. There were curses, threats and boasts.

Demetrio let them get it off their chests; then he drew a bottle from his shirt, took a swig, wiped it with the back of his hand and passed it to the man next to him. The bottle made its way from mouth to mouth and was emptied. The men licked their lips.

"God willing," Demetrio said, "tomorrow or even tonight we'll look the Federales in the eyes. We'll show them around, what do you say, *muchachos?*"[82]

The half-naked men jumped, shouting for joy. Then their insults, curses and threats multiplied.

"We don't know how many they are," Demetrio observed, searching their faces. "In Hostotipaquillo, Julián Medina and half a dozen field hands with knives sharpened on their *metates* [knife grinders] stood up to all the cops and Federales in the town and kicked them out. . . ."

"What do Medina's men have that we don't?" said a strong, compact man with thick, black eyebrows and beard and a sweet look in his eyes.

"All I know is," he added, "My name ain't Anastasio Montañés if tomorrow I ain't got a Mauser rifle, a cartridge belt, trousers, and shoes. I mean it! [. . .] Bullets scare me as much as a little ball of candy. Wait and see."

"*Viva* [long live!] Anasasio Montañés!" shouted Manteca.

"No," Anastasio replied, "*viva* Demetrio Macías, our leader, and God in Heaven and his Holy Mother."

"*Viva* Demetrio Macías!" they all shouted.

They lit a fire with dry grass and wood, and over the glowing embers they stretched pieces of fresh meat. They gathered around the flames, sitting on their haunches, sniffing hungrily as the meat twisted and crackled in the fire. [. . .]

---

82. *muchachos*: boys, fellows.

"Well," said Demetrio, "beside my thirty-thirty, we've only got twenty rifles. If there are few Federales, we won't leave a single one alive, if there are many at least we'll give them a good scare." [. . .]

III

Amid the brush of the sierra, Demetrio Macías' twenty-five men slept until the signal horn woke them. Pancracio sounded the alarm from the top of a ridge.

"This is it, *muchachos,* look alive!" said Anastasio Montañés, checking the action on his rifle. [. . .]

When the white of the moon glow faded into the slightly pink stripe of dawn, the outline of the first soldier stood out against the highest edge of the trail. After him others appeared, then ten more, then a hundred more, but they all disappeared quickly into the shadows. The first rays of the sun revealed that the precipice was covered with people: tiny men on miniature horses.

"Ain't they pretty!" Pancracio exclaimed. "Come on *muchachos,* let's play with the toy soldiers!"

The little moving figures would disappear into the dense chaparral and then show up black against the ochre boulders.

The voices of the officers and the soldiers could be heard distinctly.

Demetrio made a signal, and the bolts of the rifles clicked.

"Now!" he ordered in a whisper.

Twenty-one men fired as one, and twenty-one Federales fell from their horses. The rest, surprised, were motionless, like bas-reliefs carved into the boulders.

A new volley, and another twenty-one men rolled from rock to rock, their heads split open.

"Come out, *bandidos!* . . . Peasant scum!" [. . .]

"Die, you cattle rustlers!" . . .

The Federales shouted at their enemies, who from their hiding places calmly and quietly continued to display the marksmanship for which they were already famous.

"Look, Pancracio," said Meco, who was all dark except for the whites of his eyes and teeth, "this is for the one just passing the *pitahaya* [dragonfruit] bush! [. . .] Now for the one on the dapple-gray horse. . . . Down you go, *pelón!*"[83]

"I'm gonna give the one riding on the edge of the trail a bath . . . I'll dunk you in the river, damn *mocho.*"[84] [. . .]

Suddenly, Codorniz showed himself, buck naked, holding his trousers like a bullfighter's cape, taunting the Federales. Then a rain of bullets fell on Demetrio's men.

---

83. *pelón*: literally, bald; in Spanish slang, "baldy" or "shifty."
84. *mocho*: literally, without horns; in Spanish slang, a prude or "without balls."

"Ay! Ay! A swarm of bees is coming at my head," said Anastasio Montañés, already flat against the rocks, not daring to look up.

"Codorniz, you son of a . . . ! Now go where I told you!" Demetrio roared.

And, crawling, they took new positions.

The Federales stopped firing and were loudly celebrating their triumph, when a new hail of bullets confused them.

"Now there's more of them!" the soldiers shouted.

In a panic, many turned their horses around ready to flee, others dismounted and scrambled over the rocks looking for refuge. The officers had to fire on the fleeing soldiers to restore order.

"Shoot the ones below, the ones below!" Demetrio shouted, pointing his thirty-thirty toward the crystal thread of the river. [. . .]

The comrades now shared weapons, picking targets and making hefty bets.

"My leather belt if I don't hit the one on the dark horse on the head. Lend me your rifle, Meco. . . ."

"Twenty Mauser rounds and half a *chorizo* [sausage] if you let me knock down the one on the black horse with a white star on its forehead. Good. . . . Now! . . . See him jump! Like a deer!"

"Don't run *mochos*! . . . Come meet your father, Demetrio Macías." [. . .]

Demetrio continued firing, and warning the others about the impending danger, but they did not heed his desperate voice until they felt the whizzing of the bullets on their flank.

"They got me!" Demetrio cried, and ground his teeth, "Sons of . . . !"

And he quickly let himself slide toward a gully.

Part Three: VII

Demetrio recovers from his wound and his band wreaks havoc in a tour through central-western Mexico that is at once a revolutionary sortie and a piratic raid, in search of booty and women. He sees his wife and young son for the first time in two years, then despite her pleas, rejoins the fight.

It was a real wedding morning. On the eve, it had rained all night and the morning sky was covered with white clouds. [. . .] Trees, cacti and ferns, everything seems freshly washed. The rocks, their ochre looking like the rust of old armors, drip large drops of transparent water.

Macías' men are silent for a moment. It seems they have heard a familiar sound: the bursting of a distant rocket, but a few minutes go by and nothing more is heard.

"In this very sierra," says Demetrio, "I, with only twenty men, inflicted more than five hundred casualties on the Federales. . . ."

And when Demetrio begins to recount that famous feat of arms, the men realize the grave danger they are in. What if the enemy weren't two days' travel away? What if they turned out to be hiding in the brush of that formidable gully along whose bottom they have ventured? But who's going to say he's afraid? When did Demetrio's men ever say: "We won't go there?"

And when the shooting breaks out up ahead, where the vanguard is, no one is surprised. The recruits turn tail and desperately seek the exit to the canyon.

A curse escapes from Demetrio's dry throat:

"Shoot them! . . . Shoot any who run away! . . ."

"Drive them from the high ground!" he then roars like a beast.

But the enemy, hiding by the thousands, unleash their machine guns, and Demetrio's men fall like sheaves cut by a sickle.

Demetrio sheds tears of rage and pain when Anastasio slides slowly from his horse, without uttering a complaint, and lies motionless. Venancio falls by his side, his chest horribly torn by a machine gun, and Meco falls over the edge and rolls to the bottom of the abyss. Suddenly Demetrio finds himself alone. The bullets buzz in his ears like hail. He dismounts, crawls over the rocks until he finds cover, places a rock to protect his head, and chest to the ground, he begins to fire.

The enemy fans out, in pursuit of the few fugitives who are still hiding in the chaparral.

Demetrio aims and he doesn't miss a single shot. . . . Paf! . . . Paf! . . . Paf!

His famous marksmanship fills him with joy; wherever he aims the bullet finds its mark. He empties a clip and he inserts another. And aims. . . .

The smoke of the rifles still has not dissipated. The cicadas intone their imperturbable and mysterious song; the doves coo sweetly from the nooks of the rocks; the cows browse peaceably. [. . .]

And at the foot of a crevice, enormous and sumptuous like the portico of an ancient cathedral, Demetrio Macías, his eyes forever fixed, continues to aim with the barrel of his rifle.

13. Pablo Neruda, *The Heights of Macchu Picchu* (1947)

The following selections from Poems I, II, VI, X, and XII trace Neruda's journey from despair to hope. Before his climb begins, in Poem I, it is autumn,[85] "with the leaves' / proffer of currency," and he "like a blind man" looks back on "our exhausted human spring." In Poem II, he reflects on his longing for truth—how often he has "wanted to pause and look for the eternal,

---

85. autumn: in the southern hemisphere, in which most of South America resides, autumn lasts from March to June; spring lasts from September to November.

unfathomable / truth's filament"—and has wondered "What was man?"; in which of his ordinary words and deeds exists the real "quality of life"?

In Poem VI, Neruda begins the ascent to Macchu Picchu—"up the ladder of the earth I climbed"—and comes to the site where "the fat grains of maize grew high"; here the wool of the Andean vicuña was carded, and here men slept, while "with gentle footstep hurricanes" cleansed "the lonely precinct of the stone." In Poem X, he thinks back in time to the lives of the human beings, hungering, who had worked here to build these walls: "Let me have back the slave you buried here!" In the final Poem XII, he summons up the dead: "Arise to birth with me, my brother"; "Give me your hand out of the depths / sown by your sorrows." He asks them to tell him of their lives—farmers, weavers, masons, jewelers, potters—"your ancient buried sorrows." He will speak for them to the current age: "I come to speak for your dead mouths"; "Speak through my speech and through my blood."[86]

THE HEIGHTS OF MACCHU PICCHU

I

From air to air, like an empty net,
dredging through streets and ambient atmosphere, I came
lavish, at autumn's coronation, with the leaves'
proffer of currency and—between spring and wheat ears—
that which a boundless love, caught in a gauntlet fall,
grants us like a long-fingered moon.

. . . .

Leaning my forehead through unfathomed waves
I sank, a single drop, within a sleep of sulphur
where, like a blind man, I retraced the jasmine
of our exhausted human spring.

. . . .

II

Flower to flower delivers up its seed
and rock maintains its blossom broadcast
in a bruised garment of diamond and sand
yet man crumples the petal of the light he skims
from the predetermined sources of the sea

---

86. Bracketed ellipses in the text indicate the editor's deletions; unbracketed ellipses are the author's.

and drills the pulsing metal in his hands.
Soon, caught between clothes and smoke, on the sunken floor,
the soul's reduced to a shuffled pack,
quartz and insomnia, tears in the sea,
like pools of cold—yet this is not enough:
he kills, confesses it on paper with contempt,
muffles it in the rug of habit, shreds it
in a hostile apparel of wire. [. . .]

How many times in wintry city streets, or in
a bus, a boat at dusk, or in the denser solitude
of festive nights, drenched in the sound
of bells and shadows, in the very lair of human pleasure,
have I wanted to pause and look for the eternal, unfathomable
truth's filament I'd fingered once in stone, or in the flash a kiss released.
. . . .

What was man? In what layer of his humdrum conversation,
among his shops and sirens—in which of his metallic movements
lived on imperishably the quality of life?

VI

Then up the ladder of the earth I climbed
through the barbed jungle's thickets
until I reached you Macchu Picchu.

Tall city of stepped stone,
home at long last of whatever earth
had never hidden in her sleeping clothes.
In you two lineages that had run parallel
met where the cradle both of man and light
rocked in a wind of thorns.

Mother of stone and sperm of condors.
High reef of the human dawn,
Spade buried in primordial sand.
This was the habitation, this is the site:
here the fat grains of maize grew high
to fall again like red hail.

The fleece of the vicuña was carded here
to clothe men's loves in gold, their tombs and mothers,
the king, the prayers, the warriors.

Up here men's feet found rest at night
near eagles' talons in the high
meat-stuffed eyries. And in the dawn
with thunder steps they trod the thinning mists,
touching the earth and stones that they might recognize
that tough come night, come death.

. . . .

And the air came in with lemon blossom fingers
to touch those sleeping faces:
a thousand years of air, months, weeks of air,
blue wind and iron cordilleras[87]—
these came with gentle footstep hurricanes
cleansing the lonely precinct of the stone.

X

Stone within stone, and man, where was he?
Air within air, and man, where was he?
Time within time, and man, where was he?
Were you also the shattered fragment
of indecision of hollow eagle
which, through the streets of today, in the old tracks,
through the leaves of accumulated autumns,
goes pounding at the soul into the tomb?
Poor hand, poor foot and poor, dear life . . .
The days of unraveled light
in you, familiar rain
falling on feast-day banderillas,[88]
did they grant, petal by petal, their dark nourishment
to such an empty mouth?

       Famine, coral of mankind,
hunger, secret plant, root of the woodcutters,
famine, did your jagged reef dart up
to those high, side-slipping towers?

I question you, salt of the highways,
show me the trowel; allow me, architecture,
to fret stone stamens with a little stick,
climb all the steps of air into the emptiness,

---

87. cordilleras: mountain range.
88. banderillas: the darts thrust into the bull's shoulder during a bullfight.

scrape the intestine until I touch mankind.
Macchu Picchu, did you lift
stone upon stone on a groundwork of rags?
coal upon coal and, at the bottom, tears?
fire-crested gold, and in that gold, the bloat
dispenser of this blood?

Let me have back the slave you buried here!
Wrench from these lands the stale bread
of the poor, prove me the tatters
on the serf, point out his window.
Tell me how he slept when alive,
whether he snored,
his mouth agape like a dark scar
worn by fatigue into the wall.
That wall, that wall! If each stone floor
weighed down his sleep, and if he fell
beneath them, as if beneath a moon, with all that sleep!

Ancient America, bride in her veil of sea,
your fingers also,
from the jungle's edges to the rare height of gods,
under the nuptial banners of light and reverence,
blending with thunder from the drums and lances,
your fingers, your fingers also—
that bore the rose in mind and hairline of the cold,
the blood-drenched breast of the new crops translated
into the radiant weave of matter and adamantine hollows—
with them, with them, buried America, were you in that great depth,
the bilious gut, hoarding the eagle hunger?

XII

Arise to birth with me, my brother.

Give me your hand out of the depths
sown by your sorrows,
You will not return from these stone fastnesses.
You will not emerge from subterranean time.
Your rasping voice will not come back,
nor your pierced eyes rise from their sockets.

Look at me from the depths of the earth,
tiller of fields, weaver, reticent shepherd,

groom of totemic guanacos,[89]
mason high on your treacherous scaffolding,
iceman of Andean tears,
jeweler with crushed fingers,
farmer anxious among his seedlings,
potter wasted among his clays—
bring to the cup of this new life
your ancient buried sorrows.
Show me your blood and your furrow;
say to me: here I was scourged
because a gem was dull or because the earth
failed to give up in time its tithe of corn or stone.
Point out to me the rock on which you stumbled,
the wood they used to crucify your body.
Strike the old flints
to kindle ancient lamps, light up the whips
glued to your wounds throughout the centuries
and light the axes gleaming with your blood.

I come to speak for your dead mouths.
Throughout the earth
let dead lips congregate,
out of the depths spin this long night to me
as if I rode at anchor here with you.

And tell me everything, tell chain by chain,
and link by link, and step by step;
sharpen the knives you kept hidden away,
thrust them into my breast, into my hands,
like a torrent of sunbursts,
an Amazon of buried jaguars,
and leave me cry: hours, days and years,
blind ages, stellar centuries.

And give me silence, give me water, hope,
Give me the struggle, the iron, the volcanoes.
Let bodies cling like magnets to my body.
Come quickly to my veins and to my mouth.
Speak through my speech, and through my blood.

---

89. guanacos: animals of the camel family, from which the domesticated llama is bred.

14. Federico García Lorca, *The House of Bernarda Alba* (1936)

In the last scenes of the final act of *The House of Bernarda Alba*, the fourth-eldest sister Martirio[90] discovers Adela's sexual involvement with Pepe el Romano and reveals it to the others. Mother Bernarda seizes a shotgun and shoots Pepe, who escapes. But Martirio tells Adela that Pepe is dead and Adela hangs herself. Bernarda sheds no tears for Adela, caring only for the honor of her house: no one must know of Adela's seduction. "The youngest daughter of Bernarda Alba has died a virgin," she declares. "Does everyone hear me? Silence, I say! Silence!"

HOUSE OF BERNARDA ALBA

Act III

Martirio, the fourth eldest sister, goes to the door that leads to the yard, and calls for her sister, Adela, the youngest. Adela enters, "her hair disheveled."

ADELA: What do you want with me?

MARTIRIO: Leave that man alone!

ADELA: Who are you to tell me what to do?

MARTIRIO: That is no place for a decent woman.

ADELA: Wouldn't you just love to occupy it!

MARTIRIO: *(Raising her voice.)* The time has come to speak. This can't go on.

ADELA: This is just the beginning. I've taken charge now, with all the resolution and capability you lack. I've had enough of the death beneath this roof. I'm leaving to claim what's mine, what belongs to me.

MARTIRIO: That soulless man out there came for another woman. You've crossed the line.

ADELA: He came for the money, but his eyes have always been on me.

MARTIRIO: I won't allow you to snatch him away. He will marry Angustias.

ADELA: You know as well as I do he doesn't love her.

MARTIRIO: Yes.

ADELA: You know because you've seen the truth: he loves me.

---

90. Bernarda Alba has five daughters, ages twenty to thirty-nine: in ascending order by age, Adela, Martirio, Amelia, Magdalena, and Angustias. Poncia is a domestic servant.

MARTIRIO: *(Desperately.)* Yes.

ADELA: *(Drawing closer.)* He loves *me*. He loves *me*.

MARTIRIO: Stab me with a dagger if you like, but stop saying that!

ADELA: That's why you can't bear the thought of us together. You don't care if he embraces a woman he doesn't love, and neither do I. He could be with Angustias forever, but a single glimpse of him wrapping his arms around me is poison to your soul because you love him too. *You love him too.*

MARTIRIO: *(Dramatically.)* Yes! Do you want me to shout it from the rooftop? Slice my breast open like a bitter pomegranate? Yes, I love him!

ADELA: *(Embracing MARTIRIO in a fit of emotion.)* Martirio, oh Martirio, it's not my fault!

MARTIRIO: Don't touch me! You won't get me to shed one tear for you. My blood is no longer yours. I'd like to look upon you as a sister, but all I see is another woman.

(She pushes ADELA away.)

ADELA: So be it. If I must drown, I'll drown. Pepe el Romano is mine, and he's taking me to the reeds at the river's edge.

MARTIRIO: It won't happen!

ADELA: I can't bear the horror of this house after tasting the sweetness of his mouth. I'll be whatever he wants me to be. The whole village can rise up against me. Let the self-appointed guardians of decency come after me and sear me with their fiery fingertips. I'll stand before them all and don the adulteress' crown of thorns.

MARTIRIO: Stop it!

ADELA: Yes. Yes.

(Whispering.)

Let's go back to bed, let's let him marry Angustias. I don't care anymore. But I'm going to go away and live by myself in a little shack where he can come and see me any time he likes, whatever his pleasure.

MARTIRIO: That will never happen as long as I have a drop of blood left in my body!

ADELA: You have no power over me, you little weakling. I could bring a runaway horse to its knees with the strength of my little finger.

MARTIRIO: Lower that grating voice of yours. I'm choking on the evil spilling from my heart.

ADELA: They teach us to love our sisters. But God must have forgotten me in the shadows, because I see you now as never before.

(A whistle sounds. ADELA rushes toward the door, but MARTIRIO blocks her way.)

MARTIRIO: Where do you think you're going?

ADELA: Get away from the door!

MARTIRIO: Just try getting through!

ADELA: Out of my way!

(They struggle.)

MARTIRIO: *(Shouting.)* Mother! Mother!

ADELA: Get your hands off me!

(Enter BERNARDA [with her staff] in a petticoat and black shawl.)

BERNARDA: Calm down, calm down. By god, if I had a lightning bolt I'd smite you both!

MARTIRIO: *(Pointing to ADELA.)* She was with him! Look at the straw in her petticoat!

BERNARDA: That's the bed of a sinful woman!

(She rushes furiously toward ADELA.)

ADELA: *(Standing her ground.)* I've had it with this prison house!

(She grabs the staff from her mother and breaks it in two.)

That's what I think of the tyrant's rod. Don't take another step toward me. I take orders from no one but Pepe.

(Enter MAGDALENA.)

MAGDALENA: Adela!

(Enter PONCIA and ANGUSTIAS.)

ADELA: I am his.

(To ANGUSTIAS.)

Get it through your head, then go out to the yard and tell him. He will rule over this whole house. You'll find him out there, raging like a lion.

ANGUSTIAS: My god!

BERNARDA: The shotgun! Where's the shotgun?

(BERNARDA rushes out. Enter AMELIA in the background, a look of terror on her face as she cringes against the wall. Exit MARTIRIO, following BERNARDA.)

ADELA: No one can stop me now!

(She makes a move to exit.)

ANGUSTIAS: *(Grabbing her.)* You're not going anywhere with your thieving little body, so triumphant! You've brought shame on our whole house!

MAGDALENA: Let her go so we'll never have to look at her again!

(A gunshot sounds.)

BERNARDA: *(Entering.)* Go look for him now.

MARTIRIO: *(Entering.)* That's the end of Pepe el Romano.

ADELA: Pepe! Oh god! Pepe!

(She rushes offstage.)

PONCIA: You killed him?

MARTIRIO: No! He got away on his horse!

BERNARDA: It was my fault. A woman's aim is worthless.

MAGDALENA: So why did you say that?

MARTIRIO: To spite her! I would have poured a river of blood over her head!

PONCIA: Damn you, child.

MAGDALENA: You're possessed!

BERNARDA: No, it's good she said it!

(A dull thud shakes the stage.)

Adela! Adela!

PONCIA: *(At the door.)* Adela, open the door!

BERNARDA: Open up! You can't hide your shame behind walls!

MAID: *(Entering.)* We've woken the neighbors!

BERNARDA: *(In a low growl.)* Open up or I'll break the door down!

(Pause. Total silence.)

Adela!

(BERNARDA steps away from the door.)

Bring a hammer!

(PONCIA pushes against the door and enters. She screams and rushes back onstage.)

What?

PONCIA: *(Raising her hands to her throat.)* May we never come to such an end!

(The DAUGHTERS recoil in horror. The MAID crosses herself. BERNARDA lets out a cry and steps forward.)

PONCIA: Don't go in there!

BERNARDA: No, I won't! Pepe, you may have escaped into the darkness of the forest, but one day you'll fall. Take her down! My daughter has died a virgin! Take her to her room and dress her as such. And not a word from anyone! She has died a virgin! Send word for the bells to toll twice at sunrise.

MARTIRIO: So fortunate she was to get what she wanted.

BERNARDA: And I won't tolerate any crying. Death must be faced head on. Silence!

(To one daughter.)

Silence I say!

(To another.)

You can cry when you're alone! We'll all drown in a sea of mourning. The youngest daughter of Bernarda Alba has died a virgin. Does everyone hear me? Silence, I say! Silence!

CURTAIN

15. Jean-Paul Sartre, *No Exit* (1944)

A ghostly attendant has conducted Garcin, Estelle, and Inez to their room in hell, the destination they have merited for their crimes. Garcin, a revolutionary and editor of a pacifist newspaper who, when the war began, had fled, was caught, and was executed for desertion—an embarrassment, since he had always pretended to be a "real man"—causing the death of the wife he had, incidentally, betrayed and abused. The seductive adulteress Estelle had drowned her illegitimate baby, which triggered the death of her lover. The lesbian Inez had seduced her cousin's wife, who then, when her husband committed suicide, killed both Inez and herself. In the concluding scene of *No Exit* that follows, Garcin, who has repelled Estelle's advances and has come to fear Inez's insight into his character, bangs furiously on the door, demanding to get out: "Open the door! Open, blast you! I'll endure anything, your red-hot tongs and molten lead, your racks and prongs and garrotes—all your fiendish gadgets. . . . Anything, anything would be better than this agony of mind. . . ." The door flies open—but he cannot leave. The three characters finally realize that they are dead indeed, that they *are* in hell, and that they *are* hell, and will torment each other eternally.[91]

No Exit

GARCIN [*to the two women*]: You disgust me, both of you.

[*He goes towards the door.*]

ESTELLE: What are you up to?

GARCIN: I'm going.

INEZ [*quickly*]: You won't get far. The door is locked.

GARCIN. I'll *make* them open it. [*He presses the bell-push. The bell does not ring.*]

ESTELLE: Please! Please!

INEZ [to ESTELLE]: Don't worry, my pet. The bell doesn't work.

GARCIN: I tell you they shall open. [*Drums on the door.*] I can't endure it any longer, I'm through with you both. [ESTELLE *runs to him; he pushes her away.*] Go away. You're even fouler than she. I won't let myself get bogged in your eyes. You're soft and slimy. Ugh! [*Bangs on the door again.*] Like an octopus. Like a quagmire.

ESTELLE: I beg you, oh, I beg you not to leave me. I'll promise not to speak again, I won't trouble you in any way—but don't go. I daren't be left alone with Inez, now she's shown her claws.

GARCIN: Look after yourself. I never asked you to come here.

ESTELLE: Oh, how mean you are! Yes, it's quite true you're a coward.

INEZ [*going up to* ESTELLE]: Well, my little sparrow fallen from the nest, I hope you're satisfied now. You spat in my face—playing up to him, of course—and we had a tiff on his account. But he's going, and a good riddance it will be. We two women will have the place to ourselves.

---

91. Ellipses in the text that follows are the author's.

ESTELLE: You won't gain anything. If that door opens, I'm going, too.

INEZ: Where?

ESTELLE: I don't care where. As far from you as I can. [GARCIN *has been drumming on the door while they talk.*]

GARCIN: Open the door! Open, blast you! I'll endure anything, your red-hot tongs and molten lead, your racks and prongs and garrotes—all your fiendish gadgets, everything that burns and flays and tears—I'll put up with any torture you impose. Anything, anything would be better than this agony of mind, this creeping pain that gnaws and fumbles and caresses one and never hurts quite enough. [*He grips the door-knob and rattles it.*] Now will you open? [*The door flies open with a jerk, and he just avoids falling.*] Ah! [*A long silence.*]

INEZ: Well, Garcin? You're free to go.

GARCIN [*meditatively*]: Now I wonder why that door opened.

INEZ: What are you waiting for? Hurry up and go.

GARCIN: I shall not go.

INEZ: And you, Estelle? [ESTELLE *does not move.* INEZ *bursts out laughing.*] So what? Which shall it be? Which of the three of us will leave? The barrier's down, why are we waiting? . . . But what a situation! It's a scream! We're—inseparables!

[ESTELLE *springs at her from behind.*]

ESTELLE: Inseparables? Garcin, come and lend a hand. Quickly. We'll push her out and slam the door on her. That'll teach her a lesson.

INEZ [*struggling with* ESTELLE]: Estelle! I beg you, let me stay. I won't go, I won't go! Not into the passage.

GARCIN: Let go of her.

ESTELLE. You're crazy. She hates you.

GARCIN: It's because of her I'm staying here.

[ESTELLE *releases* INEZ *and stares dumbfoundedly at* GARCIN.]

INEZ: Because of me? [*Pause.*] All right, shut the door. It's ten times hotter here since it opened. [GARCIN *goes to the door and shuts it.*] Because of me, you said?

GARCIN: Yes. *You*, anyhow, know what it means to be a coward.

INEZ: Yes, I know.

GARCIN: And you know what wickedness is, and shame, and fear. There were days when you peered into yourself, into the secret places of your heart, and what you saw there made you faint with horror. And then, next day, you didn't know what to make of it, you couldn't interpret the horror you had glimpsed the day before. Yes, you know what evil costs. And when you say I'm a coward, you know from experience what that means. Is that so?

INEZ: Yes.

GARCIN: So it's you whom I have to convince; you are of my kind. Did you suppose I meant to go? No, I couldn't leave you here, gloating over my defeat, with all those thoughts about me running in your head.

INEZ: Do you really wish to convince me?

GARCIN: That's the one and only thing I wish for now. I can't hear them any longer, you know. Probably that means they're through with me. For good and all. The curtain's down, nothing of me is left on earth—not even the name of coward. So, Inez, we're alone. Only you two remain to give a thought to me. She—she doesn't count. It's you who matter; you who hate me. If you'll have faith in me I'm saved.

INEZ: It won't be easy. Have a look at me. I'm a hard-headed woman.

GARCIN: I'll give you all the time that's needed.

INEZ: Yes, we've lots of time in hand. *All* time.

GARCIN [*putting his hands on her shoulders*]: Listen! Each man has an aim in life, a leading motive; that's so, isn't it? Well, I didn't give a damn for wealth, or for love. I aimed at being a real man. A tough, as they say. I staked everything on the same horse. . . . Can one possibly be a coward when one's deliberately courted danger at every turn? And can one judge a life by a single action?

INEZ: Why not? For thirty years you dreamt you were a hero, and condoned a thousand petty lapses—because a hero, of course, can do no wrong. An easy method, obviously. Then a day came when you were up against it, the red light of real danger—and you took the train to Mexico.[92]

GARCIN: I "dreamt," you say. It was no dream. When I chose the hardest path, I made my choice deliberately. A man is what he wills himself to be.

INEZ: Prove it. Prove it was no dream. It's what one does, and nothing else, that shows the stuff one's made of.

GARCIN: I died too soon. I wasn't allowed time to—to do my deeds.

---

92. Garcin was in Rio de Janeiro and fled to Mexico when Brazil entered World War II in 1942.

INEZ: One always dies too soon—or too late. And yet one's whole life is complete at that moment, with a line drawn neatly under it, ready for the summing up. You are—your life, and nothing else.

GARCIN: What a poisonous woman you are! With an answer for everything.

INEZ: Now then! Don't lose heart. It shouldn't be so hard, convincing me. Pull yourself together, man, rake up some arguments. [GARCIN *shrugs his shoulders.*] Ah, wasn't I right when I said you were vulnerable? Now you're going to pay the price, and what a price! You're a coward, Garcin, because I wish it. I wish it—do you hear?—I wish it. And yet, just look at me, see how weak I am, a mere breath on the air, a gaze observing you, a formless thought that thinks you. [*He walks towards her, opening his hands.*] Ah, they're open now, those big hands, those coarse, man's hands! But what do you hope to do? You can't throttle thoughts with hands. So you've no choice, you must convince me, and you're at my mercy.

ESTELLE: Garcin!

GARCIN: What?

ESTELLE: Revenge yourself.

GARCIN: How?

ESTELLE: Kiss me, darling—then you'll hear her squeal.

GARCIN: That's true, Inez. I'm at your mercy, but you're at mine as well.

[*He bends over* ESTELLE. INEZ *gives a little cry.*]

INEZ: Oh, you coward, you weakling, running to women to console you!

ESTELLE: That's right, Inez. Squeal away.

INEZ: What a lovely pair you make! If you could see his big paw splayed out on your back, rucking up your skin and creasing the silk. Be careful, though! He's perspiring, his hand will leave a blue stain on your dress.

ESTELLE: Squeal away, Inez, squeal away! . . . Hug me tight, darling; tighter still—that'll finish her off, and a good thing too!

INEZ: Yes, Garcin, she's right. Carry on with it, press her to you till you feel your bodies melting into each other; a lump of warm, throbbing flesh. . . . Love's a grand solace, isn't it, my friend? Deep and dark as sleep. But I'll see you don't sleep.

ESTELLE: Don't listen to her. Press your lips to my mouth. Oh, I'm yours, yours, yours.

INEZ: Well, what are you waiting for? Do as you're told. What a lovely scene: coward Garcin holding baby-killer Estelle in his manly arms! Make your stakes, everyone. Will coward Garcin kiss the lady, or won't he dare? What's the betting? I'm watching you, everybody's watching, I'm a crowd all by myself. Do you hear the crowd? Do you hear them muttering, Garcin? Mumbling and muttering. "Coward! Coward! Coward! Coward!"—that's what they're saying. . . . It's no use trying to escape, I'll never let you go. What do you hope to get from her silly lips? Forgetfulness? But I shan't forget you, not I! "It's I you must convince." So come to me. I'm waiting. Come along, now. . . . Look how obedient he is, like a well-trained dog who comes when his mistress calls. You can't hold him, and you never will.

GARCIN: Will night never come?

INEZ: Never.

GARCIN: You will always see me?

INEZ: Always.

[GARCIN *moves away from* ESTELLE *and takes some steps across the room. He goes to the bronze ornament.*]

GARCIN: This bronze. [*Strokes it thoughtfully.*] Yes, now's the moment; I'm looking at this thing on the mantelpiece, and I understand that I'm in hell. I tell you, everything's been thought out beforehand. They knew I'd stand at the fire-place stroking this thing of bronze, with all those eyes intent on me. Devouring me. [*He swings round abruptly.*] What? Only two of you? I thought there were more; many more. [*Laughs.*] So this is hell. I'd never have believed it. You remember all we were told about the torture-chambers, the fire and brimstone, the "burning marl." Old wives' tales! There's no need for red-hot pokers. Hell is—other people!

ESTELLE: My darling! Please—

GARCIN: [*thrusting her away*]: No, let me be. She is between us. I cannot love you when she's watching.

ESTELLE: Right! In that case, I'll stop her watching. [*She picks up the paper-knife from the table, rushes at* INEZ *and stabs her several times.*]

INEZ: [*struggling and laughing*]: But, you crazy creature, what do you think you're doing? You know quite well I'm dead.

ESTELLE: Dead?

[*She drops the knife. A pause.* INEZ *picks up the knife and jabs herself with it regretfully.*]

INEZ: Dead! Dead! Dead! Knives, poison, ropes—all useless. It has happened *already*, do you understand? Once and for all. So here we are, forever. [*Laughs.*]

ESTELLE [*with a peal of laughter*]: Forever. My God, how funny! Forever.

GARCIN [*looks at the two women, and joins in the laughter*]: For ever, and ever, and ever.

[*They slump onto their respective sofas. A long silence. Their laughter dies away and they gaze at each other.*]

GARCIN: Well, well, let's get on with it. . . .

CURTAIN

Chapter 8

The Crisis

Introduction

As seen in Chapter 7, Modernist authors introduced new methods and outlooks at the outset of the twentieth century not only in reaction to the traditional forms of the nineteenth, but also, in many cases, to the disastrous conditions of their contemporary world. The years from 1914 to 1945 were shaken by recurrent war and revolution, and with these came totalitarian rule, usurpation, persecution, invasion, famine, and genocide. Most of the authors considered in the previous chapter—among them Yeats, Eliot, Mandelstam, Mann, Kafka, Hemingway, Azuela, Neruda, Lorca, and Sartre—were markedly affected by these events. Chapter 8 now considers fifteen authors who engaged with them directly, as participants, eyewitnesses, critics, or victims. This single generation offers a unique case of the intersection of literary production and political, military, social, and economic crisis.

A first cluster of five authors were either participants themselves in World War I or, in the post-war era, cast a sharply critical eye on war and its effects. Two young British poets found themselves in the trenches on the Western Front, engaged in an especially brutal form of combat: the British soldiers fighting from trenches almost as deep as a man faced, across a strip of territory called No Man's Land, an equivalent line of entrenched German soldiers. At the command of an officer, they would be ordered to go "over the top," cut through any barbed wire barriers set up by the enemy, and kill or be killed. The casualty rates were extraordinary, and over four years of such battles, little land was won or lost.

Owen and Sassoon describe their experience on the Western Front in unforgettable, impassioned verse. Wilfred Owen (1893–1918), born to downwardly mobile middle-class Welsh parents, was already committed to poetry as a vocation at age twenty, when he composed a first book of poems, never published. In 1915, he enlisted in the British army, and in 1916, commissioned as a lieutenant, he was sent to fight in France. Wounded, he was sent home in June 1917, but returned to the front in August 1918 as a company commander. By this time, his initial enthusiasm had turned to fierce anger at those who had sent the uncomprehending young to the battlefront to face the devastation of trauma, pain, and death. He did not survive the war, dying at age twenty-five on November 4, 1918, seven days before the armistice that brought World War I to a close.

Chapter 8 presents three of Owen's war poems, all composed between August 1917 and September 1918: *The Send-Off*; *Anthem for Doomed Youth*; and *Dulce et Decorum Est*. *The Send-Off* describes a trainload of new recruits on their way to the battlefield, from which few will return. *Anthem for Doomed Youth* imagines the funerals of those "who die as cattle," for whom no bells toll, or choirs sing, or candles glow. *Dulce et Decorum Est* is a withering response to the ode of the ancient Roman poet Horace, entitled *Sweet and Proper It Is to Die for the Fatherland*, which hails the nobility of those who sacrifice themselves for Rome—"the old Lie," as Owen calls it. This poem has an iconic reputation as the single most cutting and desperate expression of the anti-war sentiments of those compelled to fight one.

Twenty-three of the war poems composed by Wilfred Owen were collected and published in 1920 by Siegfried Sassoon (1886–1967), whom Owen had met in the hospital while on medical leave in 1917. The son of a wealthy Jewish merchant (who died when Siegfried was nine) and an Anglo-Catholic mother, Sassoon was able to introduce Owen to the London literary circles in which he traveled. Reared as a country gentleman who played cricket and loved to hunt, Sassoon had already published several books of poems by the time war broke out in 1914—published, but all privately, in editions for himself and close friends. His early poems were about the beauties of nature and the joys of sport. Their tone changed sharply by 1917: his verse now bitterly laments the dead and wounded, and mercilessly lambastes the powerful men in government and the military who let the slaughter go on.

In 1917, Sassoon was sent for treatment to the same hospital where Owen was recuperating; and like Owen, despite his disgust with the war, he would return to the front so as to stand with his comrades. But he would survive combat, while distinguishing himself for exceptional bravery, write a shelfful of novels and memoirs, and live to an old age. Yet he is best remembered for the nearly one hundred war poems he wrote during his youth, of which four from the collection *Counter-Attack and Other Poems*, published in 1918, are included in this chapter: *Counter-Attack*, *The Rear-Guard*, *Dreamers*, and *Suicide in the Trenches*.

Tougher and less sonorous than Owen's, but just as graphic, Sassoon's poems depict the full horror of the trenches. *Counter-Attack* describes the hopeless and senseless counter-offensive with which British soldiers respond to a ferocious German attack and are destroyed. *The Rear-Guard* follows the soldier who stumbles through a darkened trench to find the officer in charge, and asks a man to point the way—a man who had died in agony ten days before. *Dreamers* contrasts the soldier's responsibility to achieve some "flaming, fatal climax with their lives," with the dreams that fill their heads "of firelit homes, clean beds, and wives." *Suicide in the Trenches* tells in a sparse twelve lines the whole tale of a British soldier: a simple, wholesome boy who, overcome by life in the trenches, "put a bullet through his brain." The war poems of Owen and Sassoon are essential reading for those who think too lightly about the purported necessity of war between nations.

Readers of Owen and Sassoon may feel they have all they need to know about trench warfare; but in *All Quiet on the Western Front* (1929) by German novelist Erich Maria Remarque (1898–1970), the story is told again, this time in prose, and from the German vantage point. At age eighteen, the son of working-class Catholics, Remarque was drafted into the army and sent to the Western Front. Seriously wounded in July 1917, he spent the rest of the war in a military hospital. After the war, he worked as a teacher, librarian, and editor while writing his first books. In 1932, ahead of the Nazi takeover, Remarque left Germany for Switzerland; the following year, having seized power, the Nazis banned his books. In 1939, just before World War II broke out, Remarque left Europe altogether for the United States, where he became a citizen in 1947, soon thereafter returning to Switzerland where he spent the rest of his life.

Remarque wrote more than a dozen novels about World War II and its aftermath, several bestsellers among them, but none more successful than *All Quiet on the Western Front*, a sensation since its first publication in German and in English in 1929. Its crisp, spare narration of the daily horrors of the trenches punctures the rhetorical excess and patriotic embellishment of the standard accounts of the war. It tells the story of a group of classmates who, urged on by their teacher, a fervent nationalist, enlisted together to fight in the German army. Very few survived; even the protagonist will die in the last pages of the book; and they suffer terribly from wounds, from shortages of food and supplies, and from the cruelty inflicted even by members of their own company. Strikingly, and contrary to the usual pattern of war novels, it does not villainize the enemy. Remarque underscores the humanity and suffering of the young on both sides who were cruelly sent to die by those they had trusted—the old, the secure, and the powerful.

Writing a decade later, in 1939, the German dramatist Bertolt Brecht (1898–1956) addressed not only the war just past, but also war as a universal, the cumulus of all wars, which he saw as intrinsically dehumanizing and essentially evil, a tool used by the powerful to keep the powerless in subjection. In 1941, the Frenchwoman and philosopher Simone Weil (1909–1943) similarly pinpointed the violent exercise of power as the principal cause of human suffering. Like Remarque, these anti-war authors, who had witnessed World War I and the troubled interwar years, fled Nazism to shelter in the United States, Scandinavia, and Britain.

Brecht was a conscientious Marxist and communist loyalist (though he never joined the Communist Party) for whom the goal of drama was to enlist an audience of ordinary workers in the effort to transform the social and political order. His anti-war outlook was but a part of this more comprehensive message. But in his play *Mother Courage and Her Children: A Chronicle of the*

Thirty Years' War (1939), he spotlights the stark horror, the awful sin of war, which consumes innocents by killing them in battle; by starving them of the wherewithal for survival; by deceiving, corrupting, and twisting them; and by destroying the human bonds that are the matrix of what it is to be human.

Mother Courage, the female protagonist of the drama of that name, is essentially a mother, and she embodies, in its essence, courage. Her character is drawn from contemporary texts from the period of the Thirty Years' War (1618–1648), one of the most destructive conflicts of all European history, anticipating by three centuries the global wars of the twentieth century. Mother Courage struggles to nurture and protect her children amid the wartime havoc by operating a canteen in the rear of the Finnish army (Finnish forces were attached to those of Sweden, a principal combatant); it is mounted on a wagon drawn not by horses, but by her two sturdy sons—while they live. From it, she buys and sells goods, food, and drink, shrewdly driving hard bargains and not always observing niceties. But her three children will all die; and the magnitude of her bereavement is scarcely to be borne.

Mother Courage is one of Brecht's most famous plays, and arguably one of the most important produced in the twentieth century. But it is only one of the more than fifty he wrote (in addition to stories, poems, and theoretical essays). He produced his early plays, including *Edward II*, *The Threepenny Opera*, and *Saint Joan of the Stockyards*, in Berlin in the 1920s and 1930s, where he experimented with innovative theatrical techniques that were as groundbreaking as his dramatic compositions. When the Nazis came to power in 1933, they banned his plays and stripped his German citizenship. Brecht fled to Scandinavia, where he wrote the most famous plays of his maturity: in addition to *Mother Courage*, also *The Life of Galileo*, *The Good Person of Szechwan*, and *The Caucasian Chalk Circle*. In 1941, he left war-torn Europe for the United States. In 1947, pressured because of his communist views, he returned to Europe, and, in Berlin in the 1950s, to his theatrical experimentation. In 1954, he journeyed to Moscow to be awarded the Stalin Peace Prize,[1] a tribute to his stalwart communism.

Brecht wrote the iconic anti-war drama *Mother Courage* in Stockholm (Sweden) during the period September to November 1939, coincident with the German invasion of Poland launched on September 1 of that year. Similarly, two years later in Marseille (southern France), having fled Paris on June 14, 1941, moments before the Nazi takeover of that city, Simone Weil turned to Homer's *Iliad* as the consummate statement of the case against war—ironically, as it is all about war.

An idealistic socialist (and Christian mystic, though born a Jew) who did not merely preach fellowship with the dispossessed but joined them and served

---

1. Stalin Peace Prize: the Soviet counterpart of the Swedish Nobel Peace Prize and named for the premier Joseph Stalin.

them, Weil identified violence as the driving force in history. Violence, she argues, is the central theme of the *Iliad*, the most important epic of the Western literary tradition, which at once celebrates violence and deplores it. She makes this case in her 1941 essay *The* Iliad *or the Poem of Force*, her best-known work.

Weil's essay on *The Poem of Force* is firstly a work of literary criticism: a close reading of Homer's *Iliad* in its original language—she had mastered ancient Greek by the time she was twelve—in which arguments are supported by textual passages in her own translations. She explores the depictions of violent deeds, which captivated Homer's audience; and she equally explores those passages where Homer reveals his compassionate awareness of the cost of war: where unblinkingly he sympathizes with those who suffer and shows how force dehumanizes the human being. In this analysis, however, she is not only a literary critic: she is a historian, a philosopher, and a moralist.

Weil's many other works (her complete works run to sixteen volumes) discuss not only the primal impulse to violence, but also the formation of oppressive bureaucracies in complex societies, and the brutalization of workers by industrial practices, as causes of the subjugation of ordinary people. But war remained a paramount concern, especially as a new one loomed. By 1939, World War II had indeed exploded into being, despite the hopes of pacifists, with the German invasion of Poland. When the German army occupied Paris on June 14, 1940, Weil fled with her family to Marseille. While there she wrote *The Poem of Force*, an explanation of the war to those caught up in its toils. From Marseille, by way of New York City in 1942, she came eventually to London in 1943, where she supported the Free French cause ("free" because it had found safety in Britain). There, at age thirty-four, she died: perhaps of tuberculosis but arguably of starvation, for she had refused to eat when the poor she cherished could not do so.

Their experience of World War I shaped the vision of Owen, Sassoon, Remarque, Brecht, and Weil, who spoke for a generation that rejected their elders' glorification of war to dwell on its grievous consequences. Their generation, as well, would witness the rise of two major political movements of the twentieth century, both responding to the trauma of World War I: communism and fascism. Chapter 8 next considers a group of five authors who observed the Bolshevik Revolution of 1917 and, in its aftermath, the consolidation of the Soviet Union, with its mission to achieve world revolution and global communism. Their voices veer from initial enthusiasm to increasing disillusionment and despair.

Marxism, the philosophical foundation of communism, elaborated from the daring analysis of nineteenth-century thinker Karl Marx[2] and his associates, appealed to many intellectuals and artists who welcomed its promise of

---

2. Karl Marx (1818–1883): German philosopher, economist, and political theorist, whose many works supported the theorization of socialism and communism.

a more just society and the expansion of human freedom and welfare. Those possibilities had beckoned Mann, Neruda, Lorca, and Sartre among authors considered in the previous chapter, and Brecht and Weil, as has been seen, among those already encountered in this one. The Russian intelligentsia, as its members called its politically aware creative elite, earnestly studied Marxist theory and were ready to enact its principles as the increasingly intolerable tsarist regime devolved. In 1905, revolutionary outbursts by workers, peasants, and members of the military swept the country, resulting in partial measures—the establishment of a constitution and a parliament, among others—to calm the underlying unrest. When Russia's engagement in World War I proved disastrous, conditions were ripe for the Bolsheviks, a minority political party with inspired leadership, to take over in the October Revolution of 1917.

The socialist son of a wealthy and prominent family, the American journalist John Reed (1887–1920), who had supported the Mexican Revolution and opposed America's entering World War I, set sail for Russia in 1917 to observe the revolution then in progress. He arrived in Petrograd[3] in August of that year. The previous February, the tsar had suppressed an eruption of protests and strikes; in March, the tsar was himself forced to abdicate. An official provisional government then formed to replace the tsarist government, while an unofficial body of rebellious workers and soldiers declared themselves to be the Petrograd Soviet.[4] In June, soldiers returned in droves from the battlefront, refusing to participate in the war now being waged by the provisional government. More protests broke out in July, and a Russian army commander attempted a counter-revolutionary coup in August, shortly before Reed's arrival. The revolutionary leaders—an assemblage from a variety of political parties—now met continually. From November 7 to November 8 (October 25 to October 26 in the traditional Russian calendar), the Bolsheviks seized the Winter Palace, formerly the tsar's residence and later the seat of the provisional government, and took charge.

In *Ten Days That Shook the World* (1919), his account of this insurrection, Reed closely follows unfolding events by the day and even the hour, embedding in his narrative the speeches, proclamations, and press releases generated by the members of the revolutionary assembly.[5] It is clear the author shares the excitement and aspirations of the revolutionary leaders, yet his report consists mainly of words and events that he himself witnessed or were repeated to him by participants. As he writes in his Preface, "In the struggle my sympathies

---

3. Petrograd: from 1914 to 1924, the renamed former city St. Petersburg.
4. Petrograd Soviet: a *soviet* is any Russian council or parliament, at the local or national level; the Petrograd Soviet formed spontaneously during 1917, and acted as the unofficial governing body that guided the Bolshevik takeover and establishment of power.
5. Reed's *Ten Days* was the basis of, among other derivatives, Russian filmmaker Sergei Eisenstein's *October* (1927) and American director and actor Warren Beatty's *Reds* (1981).

were not neutral. But in telling the story of those great days I have tried to see events with the eye of a conscientious reporter, interested in setting down the truth." The British historian A. J. P. Taylor, in his introduction to Reed's work first appearing in the 1977 Penguin edition and subsequently reprinted, deemed it "not only the best account of the Bolshevik revolution, it comes near to being the best account of any revolution."[6] The Russian leader Lenin,[7] too, had appreciated Reed's book: "Unreservedly do I recommend it to the workers of the world."[8]

Reed wrote *Ten Days* during three weeks in late 1918 from the extensive notes that had been confiscated by customs officials upon his return to the United States the previous April, and eventually restored to him. He died in Russia of typhus two years later in 1920, at age thirty-two. He is one of only three Americans buried in the Kremlin Wall Necropolis in Moscow.

Reed looked to a great future for Soviet communism, hoping that people would rise up everywhere and bring about "a red world-tide." His friend, the anarchist Emma Goldman (1869–1940), who lived in Soviet Russia from January 1920 to December 1921, found that the dream had failed. There with her lifelong partner, fellow activist Alexander Berkman,[9] she eagerly sought out old friends—John Reed among them—and key actors in the new Soviet regime—including the novelist Maxim Gorky[10] and Lenin himself, the head of state. When she spoke with Reed, who "had burst into [her] room like a sudden ray of light," she questioned the brutal repression by the Cheka, the secret police, of those critical of the regime. Reed replied, to Goldman's horror: "'To the wall with them!' . . . He was surprised to see me so worked up over the death of a few plotters."

Goldman was a writer, political activist, and anarchist theorist—the author of, among numerous other works, the important collection *Anarchism and Other Essays* (1910). Born in Lithuania, she came to the United States in 1885, at age sixteen, and moved to New York City in 1887. She supported industrial labor strikes, participated in a failed assassination coup, and was arrested in 1893 for incitement to riot, for which offense she spent a year in prison. Later, she advocated for the legalization of birth control and, as World War I approached, against war preparation and conscription. Arrested for promoting draft resistance, she spent two years in prison from 1917 to 1919. In

---

6. John Reed, *Ten Days That Shook the World* (London: Penguin, 1977), vii.

7. Lenin (Vladimir Ilyich Ulyanov; 1870–1924), the principal Bolshevik leader and premier of the Russian state created by the revolution.

8. Reed, *Ten Days*, xxi.

9. Alexander Berkman (1870–1936): anarchist activist, partner and lover of Emma Goldman.

10. Maxim Gorky (Gorki; 1868–1936): Russian author, supporter of the Bolshevik Revolution and Soviet state.

1920, she and Berkman were deported to Soviet Russia with 248 other aliens.[11] After leaving Russia in 1921, Goldman lived in Germany, Britain, and elsewhere in Europe, settling finally (barred from returning to the United States) in Canada, where she died in 1940.

In some 200 pages of her 1,000-page autobiography *Living My Life* (1931), Goldman describes what she saw in Soviet Russia. Those who had helped put the Bolsheviks in power spoke of "the slavery forced upon the toilers, the emasculation of the soviets, the suppression of speech and thought, the filling of prisons with recalcitrant peasants, workers, soldiers, sailors, and rebels of every kind," and reported "wholesale executions without hearing or trial." Heroes of the revolution were persecuted and broken. The Kronstadt sailors, famous for their participation in the revolutions of both 1905 and 1917, were massacred at the order of Soviet officials.[12] As an anarchist, Goldman was committed to the liberation and advancement of all people; the Soviet experiment, she believed, had abandoned that goal to create a state that existed to perpetuate itself and consolidate its power. She departed Russia; and in her autobiography writes, "My dreams crushed, my faith broken, my heart like a stone."

The persecution of those who had helped achieve the Bolshevik triumph also troubled Victor Serge (penname of Victor Lvovich Kibalchich; 1890–1947), born in Belgium of Russian parents who had opposed the tsarist regime. Imprisoned twice in France as an anarchist committed to world revolution, upon his release Serge arrived in Petrograd to join the Bolsheviks and become a writer and translator for the Comintern.

Yet like Goldman, Serge came to oppose the repressive machinery of Bolshevism, the secret police, the gulag,[13] and the show trials.[14] He was perhaps the first to use the term "totalitarian" to characterize the Soviet regime and to name the places to which prisoners were exiled "concentration camps." In 1923, Serge joined the "Left Opposition" (of which Leon Trotsky,[15] Lenin's former colleague, was the principal member), a faction of Old Bolsheviks who

---

11. aliens: foreign-born residents in the United States, often suspected, as in the 1920s, of illicit political activity.

12. Kronstadt rebellion: insurrection (March 7–17, 1921) of sailors of the port city of Kronstadt (on a Baltic Sea island just west of St. Petersburg), brutally suppressed by the Bolshevik regime.

13. gulag: the network of Soviet forced-labor camps in which many died, including political prisoners, from the 1920s to the 1950s.

14. show trials: trials conducted whose outcomes are predetermined, designed to influence public opinion rather than to achieve justice; specifically, the Moscow Trials under Soviet premier Stalin, 1936–1938, which purged the Communist Party leadership of Trotskyist and other discredited factions.

15. Leon Trotsky (1879–1940): Bolshevik revolutionary, after Lenin's death the originator of the Left Opposition, eventually expelled from the party, exiled in 1929, and assassinated in exile in Mexico in 1940.

resisted the totalitarian features of the new Soviet state, especially after Lenin's death in 1924 and the ascension of Stalin.

The "Left Opposition," expanded to the "United Opposition," was suppressed in 1927; Trotsky was exiled and Serge expelled from the Communist Party. In 1933, he was imprisoned and harshly pressured to "capitulate" to the regime. He did not capitulate and so was sent into internal "administrative exile." In 1936, he was permitted to leave for Belgium, although Soviet censors confiscated all of his manuscripts. From there, in 1940, ahead of the Nazi invasion, he fled to Mexico. Trotsky had settled in Mexico in 1929, where not long before Serge's arrival, he was assassinated at Stalin's command on August 21, 1940. In collaboration with Trotsky's widow, Serge wrote the biography of this most feared of the Old Bolsheviks—one with whom Serge had not always agreed. In 1947, Serge died in Mexico, penniless and stateless, seven years after Trotsky's murder, and thirty years after the Russian Revolution.

A masterful writer, Serge wrote ceaselessly throughout his career. His novels, histories, poems, and essays, most famously his *Memoirs of a Revolutionary* (French original, 1951), expound his socialist but firmly anti-Stalinist views. He was supported during his imprisonment by a broad spectrum of European intellectuals, including the celebrated novelist André Gide[16] to whom, in May 1936, Serge wrote a famous "open letter." In it, Serge urged the French thinker to look with "eyes wide open" and see the atrocities committed by Stalin's regime, especially those against intellectuals whose only "crime" was to think forbidden thoughts. Gide would soon journey to the Soviet Union to speak at the funeral of the novelist Maxim Gorky, who died on June 18 of that year. What he saw there moved Gide to repudiate the Soviet regime, objecting especially to its limits on free expression—precisely the issue that Serge had raised in his eloquent letter.

Even as he denounced the Soviet dictatorship, Serge remained committed to a humane and democratic communism, in the same way that Goldman never abandoned her anarchist hopes. In contrast, the Hungarian author Arthur Koestler (1905–1983), who had joined the Communist Party in 1931 and actively pursued its mission through 1937, later wholly rejected Soviet communism as brutal and totalitarian. His sensationally successful novel *Darkness at Noon* (1940) is important, beyond its literary value, for its exposure of the psychological mechanisms making possible the self-destructive confessions of those prosecuted in the Soviet show trials of the Stalinist era.

Koestler was born to a wealthy Hungarian Jewish family that was impoverished during World War I and which, for that reason, supported the ill-fated 1919 Hungarian revolution led by the communist Béla Kun. As a young man,

---

16. André Gide (1869–1951): major French author of numerous novels, essays, autobiographical works, and winner of the Nobel Prize for Literature in 1947.

he worked as a journalist in Palestine and Paris. In 1931, he joined the Communist Party and actively pursued its goals. In 1937, serving the party as a spy during the Spanish Civil War, he was arrested, imprisoned, and sentenced to death—an experience that would inform his later writing on both communism and the prison experience.

Released through the efforts of high-placed supporters, Koestler moved to Paris, from where, ahead of the Nazi invasion in 1940, he fled to Marseille. Once again, he was arrested, interned, and released, finally taking refuge in Britain. There he worked during World War II for the Ministry of Information and later as a journalist and author, writing, in all, several major novels, two autobiographies, and a multitude of articles and essays on a variety of topics including euthanasia, mysticism, and the paranormal. He lectured worldwide on what he identified as the peril of communism, while he married and remarried, conducted numerous affairs, and participated in elite literary circles.

In Paris on the eve of the Nazi invasion, Koestler wrote his most important work, *Darkness at Noon*, in German. His English lover Daphne Hardy, a young student, translated it from the German and mailed the manuscript to the London publisher Jonathan Cape, which published it in December 1940. For seventy-five years, Hardy's English version was the only one known to exist. It became an international bestseller and, although a translation from the German, was ranked eighth on the Modern Library's list of the one hundred best English novels of the twentieth century, in the company of works by such masters as Faulkner, Joyce, and Orwell.[17] In the meantime, Koestler had sent a carbon copy of the German original to a publisher in neutral Switzerland, a manuscript that was lost until 2015. A revised English translation, based on the original German, appeared in 2019.

Darkness at Noon exposes the campaign of intimidation, torture, and slaughter of Stalin's alleged enemies during the Great Purge of 1936–1938. Koestler wrote the novel soon after those events and soon after the humiliation and execution in March 1938 of Nikolai Bukharin, the political theorist and editor of the Bolshevik newspaper *Pravda* who had aided Stalin's rise to power—and whom Koestler had met and admired in 1932 when he visited the Soviet Union. The novel does not name any historical figures, nor even the Soviet Union, although the protagonist and victim is named the Russian-sounding Nikolai Salmanovich Rubashov. It thus universalizes its message, detailing the program of psychological manipulation and physical torment inflicted by any and every totalitarian state.

The Russian poet Anna Akhmatova (penname of Anna Andreyevna Gorenko; 1889–1966), perhaps the greatest of all Russian woman poets, experienced

---

17. See the ranked list, "100 Best Novels," Modern Library (website), http://www.modern library.com/top-100/100-best-novels/.

the Stalinist repression that Koestler condemned. Her first husband, Nikolai Gumilev, was executed as a counter-revolutionary in 1921. Her son Lev Gumilev (1912–1992), and her lover, the art historian Nikolai Punin, were arrested in 1935, and then released. Punin later was sent to the gulag where he died in 1953. Lev Gumilev was arrested a second time in 1938 and sent to the gulag for a five-year term; released in 1942 to fight in World War II, he was returned to the gulag in 1949 and freed only in 1956. In 1950, in an unsuccessful attempt to save him, Akhmatova compromised herself by writing poems celebrating Stalin.

Akhmatova's own genuine work was censored, controlled, and silenced from 1923 until the post-Stalinist thaw in the 1950s. There was a brief respite during wartime, but afterward, in 1946, she was expelled from the Union of Soviet Writers, denounced as an aristocrat, "half harlot, half nun," and placed under secret police surveillance. Her major works were published in the Soviet Union only after her death: the epic *Poem Without a Hero* not until 1976; *Requiem* not until 1987.[18] *Requiem*, a poem sequence composed between 1935 and 1940 recording the trauma of her son's imprisonment and of the Stalinist terror, existed for two decades only in her memory and that of close friends. She was able to commit it to writing only in 1957.

This grim career could not have been foreseen in 1910 when the elegant and talented Akhmatova joined the vibrant circle of St. Petersburg poets associated with Acmeism, the literary movement led by, among others, her friend (and later lover) Osip Mandelstam (see Introduction to Chapter 7 and Text 4) and her new husband Nikolai Gumilev.[19] Her talent was immediately recognized, and her first poem collections, *Evening* (1912) and *Rosary* (1914), were instant successes. But World War I, breaking out in 1914, disrupted Petersburg's cultural florescence, and the October Revolution of 1917 put an end to it. Civil war, impoverishment, and repression followed.

The communist society installed by the Russian Revolution of 1917 promised to offer a better life for citizens and workers. It turned out otherwise, as Emma Goldman and Victor Serge observed. Nonetheless, it won the support of many intellectuals, writers, and creative artists, both initially in Russia itself and subsequently more widely in Europe and beyond. The fascist movements that developed in the 1930s, in contrast, rather than attracting the support of intellectuals, generally repelled them. Fascism appealed to nationalists who believed their nation had been abused or betrayed: to cultural and religious traditionalists and to those who felt threatened by the currents of modernity.

---

18. It had been published earlier in Russian, however, in Munich (Germany) in 1963.

19. Mandelstam and Gumilev would both later be victims of the Soviet regime: Gumilev executed in 1921, as said earlier; Mandelstam, arrested in Akhmatova's presence, died in a labor camp in 1938.

Where fascists came to power, whether by violent coup or normal elections, they formed authoritarian and totalitarian states. They did so in Italy, Spain, Germany, and elsewhere. In Germany, the fascist party was named the National Socialist German Workers' Party—the Nazi party.

Superficially, communist and fascist states resembled each other, although their policies and theoretical foundations were quite different. But communists and liberals would join together to oppose fascism. They did so during the Spanish Civil War of 1936–1939, where the Spanish nationalists, the fascist party, faced, and triumphed over, a motley coalition of liberals, anarchists, socialists, and communists. They did so again in June 1941, when the Nazi invasion of the Soviet Union undid the opportunistic and unusual alliance forged in 1939 between the Nazis and the Soviet leaders, Adolf Hitler[20] and Joseph Stalin. The Soviet Union thereupon joined in alliance with Britain, which previously had stood alone against Nazi aggression—the other liberal nations having themselves suffered invasion or declared neutrality. By December 1941, when Hitler's ally Japan attacked the US naval base at Pearl Harbor (Hawaii), that nation joined Britain and the Soviets to form the core of the Allied forces that would, after four more years, defeat Germany and its Axis partners.

While fighting the war, the Nazis also pursued a violent campaign against groups of noncombatants—primarily the Jews, but also other groups, including homosexuals and the Roma people (Gypsies), who were deemed inferior and fit for extermination. The Nazi slaughter of some nine million victims, some six million of them Jews, mostly in their system of concentration camps but also in wartime actions, went far beyond the "little blood-letting" Lenin had dismissed in conversation with Goldman and Berkman. Without pursuing a genocidal strategy, however, the Soviets also killed tens of millions of their own people during the Civil War, in the collectivization of the countryside, in the Great Purge, and during World War II—as did other communist regimes, including that of Mao Zedong in China. Ironically and tragically, the United States, one of the key Allies in the struggle against Hitler, dropped two atomic bombs[21] on busy Japanese cities to force a rapid ending to the war in Asia. The bombs did not kill millions of people, but they killed well over one hundred thousand and wounded and disabled more. Still worse, the deployment of the atom bomb introduced into global politics the possibility of mass extinction through nuclear power.

---

20. Adolf Hitler (1889–1945): leader of the Nazi Party and German dictator 1933–1945, led the German war effort during World War II; he is the key figure responsible for the genocide of European Jews in the Holocaust.

21. atomic bombs: weapons of unprecedented potency, resulting from nuclear fission, developed by scientists working in the United States during World War II and deployed for the first time against Japanese cities Hiroshima and Nagasaki on August 6 and August 9, 1945.

Chapter 8 closes by examining a last group of five authors whose works offer a kaleidoscope of responses to the catastrophe brought on by the fascist surge: the catastrophe of World War II, a clash between free and totalitarian regimes, marked by the use of horrific weaponry, culminating in the deployment of the first atomic bomb and the Nazi institutionalization of mass murder.

During the 1930s, while European diplomats raced to appease Hitler, one British statesman warned ceaselessly of the danger of Nazi aggression: Winston Churchill (Sir Winston Leonard Spencer-Churchill; 1874–1965). In May 1940, when the Germans invaded the Low Countries (Belgium, the Netherlands, and Luxembourg), dividing and isolating the British and French forces that had attempted to stop their surge, Churchill, now prime minister, stood alone against the Nazi behemoth. The Nazis, with their allies, had bought off the Soviet Union, conquered much of Europe, and threatened to invade Britain. In three memorable speeches delivered on May 13, June 4, and June 18, 1940, Churchill rallied the British to stand up to Hitler and defend their country. From that moment, until June 1941, only Churchill among world leaders, and only Britain among the nations, fended off the Nazi storm.

Winston Churchill was an aristocrat, a military officer, a member of the British Parliament, and ultimately that nation's prime minister from May 10, 1940, at the outset of World War II, until its close in 1945, and again in 1951 to 1955. He was also a journalist, a historian, and an orator of the first order, for which activities he was awarded the Nobel Prize in Literature in 1953. His three wartime speeches—the second of which, *We Shall Fight on the Beaches*, is included in this chapter—are elegantly wrought compositions, as well as powerful tools in rallying his nation to face deliberately and courageously the Nazi menace that he was one of the first to identify and oppose.

The British won the "Battle of Britain," the air war with Germany waged from July to October 1940. From mid-1941, the Allied forces, the "grand alliance" of Britain, the United States, and the Soviet Union, gained a costly victory over the Axis powers, principally Germany, Italy, and Japan. Churchill would exit as prime minister with the war's end in Europe (three months before its close in Asia), reentering global politics in 1946 to warn against the aggressions now of the Soviet Union, a former ally. A staunch and unapologetic imperialist, perhaps a racist (as some have asserted), Churchill has been hated by many; yet for his brilliant achievements, especially during World War II when he perceived and withstood the menace of Nazism, he remains an outstanding twentieth-century figure.

Even as Winston Churchill prepared the British people to resist a Nazi invasion, the Nazis invaded the Netherlands, where they imposed increasingly harsh restrictions on Dutch Jews, preparatory to a wholesale evacuation of the Jewish population to concentration camps in Germany and Poland. The family of Otto Frank, a prosperous Jewish merchant, anticipated what was to come and arranged a sealed-off refuge on the top floor of his company building—the "Secret Annex." There, provisioned and protected by loyal gentile employees, they might survive the onslaught. On July 9, 1942, the Frank family and that of his associate, Hermann van Pels,[22] moved into the safe house, where they remained in hiding for two years and twenty-six days. On August 4, 1944, German soldiers breached the secret entrance, arrested all the occupants, and deported them to different concentration camps. Only Otto Frank survived.

Anne Frank (1929–1945), Otto's daughter, was thirteen years old when the family went into hiding, fifteen when she was arrested, and not yet sixteen when, in February or March 1945, she died of typhus in the German concentration camp at Bergen-Belsen, a few weeks before its liberation on April 15. During her two years in hiding, she kept a diary, written in the form of letters addressed to "Kitty," an alter ego, copiously documenting the family's experience. In lively prose, her acute observations of group life tell of close and fraught relationships, food scarcity, amusing mishaps, the trials of adolescence, and the terrifying news transmitted in radio broadcasts.

On March 29, 1944, the Dutch minister for Education, Art, and Science, then in exile in London, urged his compatriots in a news broadcast to keep memoirs and documents of their experience under occupation. Anne accordingly revised her diary with its official preservation in view. Immediately following the arrest, the Frank family's gentile supporters discovered the original diary and notebooks (Version A) and the revised version in loose scattered manuscript sheets (Version B). After the war, they conveyed these materials to Anne's father, who arranged for the diary's posthumous publication in Amsterdam in 1947, entitled *The Diary of a Young Girl*. One of the most important firsthand accounts of the events of World War II, and "one of the most read, most important and most inspiring books in the world," it was subsequently published in multiple editions in Dutch, German, French, and English, and translated into more than seventy languages.[23]

In the same winter of 1945 that Anne Frank fell fatally ill at Bergen-Belsen, Elie Wiesel (1928–2016), as Eliezer, the protagonist of his fictionalized autobiography *Night*, watched his worn, sick, and wretched father die at Buchenwald (Germany), just weeks before its liberation. Wiesel composed *Night* in Paris, more than a decade after these events. Based on his 862-page memoir (composed in Yiddish in 1954) of his wartime experience, it was published in French in 1958, and in English in 1960. It is considered the most important account of the Holocaust, the Nazi effort to annihilate European Jewry in a Final Solution, to be realized in a network of concentration camps in Germany and Poland.

---

22. In her diary, using pseudonyms, Anne Frank refers to the van Pels family as van Daan.
23. Anne Frank House (website), https://www.annefrank.org/en/anne-frank/diary/.

Night also explores the father-son relationship, one central to the human condition and especially important in Judaism. As the story begins, Wiesel's father is a strong man, not easily daunted. When the Jews of their native Transylvania (modern Romania) were ordered to wear a yellow star announcing their membership in a despised group, he shook it off: "The yellow star? So what? It's not lethal . . ." Wiesel then comments: "Poor Father! Of what then did you die!"[24] Indeed, he would die of Jew-hatred in January 1945, pleading for the aid of a son who had abandoned him. The two themes—the horror of the camps, the son's abandonment of his father—are interconnected: the Nazi terror did not only kill bodies but also souls, disrupting all human relationships, and dissolving the humanity of those it would destroy.

From Paris, Wiesel moved to the United States. The author of dozens of books, he was a professor at several universities, a founder of the United States Holocaust Memorial Museum in Washington, DC, and spokesperson for the oppressed everywhere. Awarded the Nobel Peace Prize in 1986, Wiesel spoke memorably of the need to always remember the Holocaust, and never to remain silent when anyone—not just Jews—suffer oppression; and "more people are oppressed than free": the world knew of the Holocaust and yet "remained silent. And that is why I swore never to be silent whenever and wherever human beings endure suffering and humiliation."[25]

When Allied troops liberated Buchenwald concentration camp on April 11, 1945, and Elie Wiesel, the survivor, walked free, World War II was drawing to a close in Europe, but still raged in the Pacific theater. US forces had invaded Iwo Jima and Okinawa, the two major Japanese islands on the path to the Japanese mainland, which was targeted for invasion on November 1. At the Potsdam Conference in Germany (July 17–August 2, 1945), the three Allied leaders, US president Harry S. Truman,[26] British prime minister Winston Churchill, and Soviet premier Joseph Stalin, demanded Japan's unconditional surrender—a demand the Japanese repeatedly refused.

The death toll anticipated from an American invasion of Japan was enormous: in taking Iwo Jima and Okinawa, the United States had realized nearly 100,000 military deaths, the Japanese nearly 200,000 combatants and noncombatants. To avoid further catastrophic loss, by President Truman's decision, the United States dropped an atomic bomb, a newly developed weapon of unprecedented force, on the Japanese city of Hiroshima[27] on August 6, 1945.

---

24. Elie Wiesel, *Night*, trans. Marion Wiesel (New York: Hill and Wang, 2006), 11.

25. Wiesel, Nobel Peace Prize Acceptance Speech, December 10, 1986, *Night*, 119, 118.

26. Harry S. Truman (1884–1972), US President (1945–1953), succeeded on death of Franklin Delano Roosevelt, then reelected in 1948; presided during closing phase of World War II, making the decision to drop two atomic bombs on Japan.

27. Hiroshima: a manufacturing city and seaport of military importance with a wartime population of about 250,000. Figures for the casualties of the Hiroshima bombing are highly variable and uncertain; these that follow are estimates.

To offer roughly approximate numbers, the blast killed some 70,000 people initially, another 100,000 in the following months from burns and radiation, and a further 100,000 over the next five years from radiation poisoning. Yet the Japanese refused to surrender. Three days later, on August 9, the United States dropped a second bomb on Nagasaki,[28] killing tens of thousands more civilians. On August 15, Japan surrendered without conditions; the surrender officially concluded on September 2.

The American war correspondent and Pulitzer Prize winning novelist John Hersey (1914–1993), son of Protestant missionaries in China, a graduate of Yale University and the University of Cambridge, had already written three books (the first of many more) when he went to Japan in 1945 to 1946 to observe that nation's reconstruction following its attack by two atomic bombs. Identifying six survivors of the attack, Hersey described their experience: where they were when the bomb fell, their actions immediately following, how they came to understand what had occurred, and what was the final outcome in each case. He wove their stories together like a novelist, but the hard facts on which they rested had been gleaned from diligent reporting and extensive interviews of the survivors of the blast.

Hersey published *Hiroshima*, the finely crafted account of his research, in the popular magazine *The New Yorker*, which devoted to the work most of its issue of August 31, 1946. The following November, it was published as a book by Alfred A. Knopf. It was and has remained a bestseller. In 1999, it was recognized as the best work of journalism of the twentieth century by a panel of thirty-six judges organized by the New York University journalism department.[29] It has left the world a predicament. Although few would fail to recognize the heroic military achievement of the Allies in staunching the tide of totalitarianism, the tragic end of World War II in the bombing of the non-combatant inhabitants of two thriving cities, so brilliantly told by John Hersey, casts a shadow on that victory.

Yet inarguably the outcome of World War II was the defeat of Nazism. It would be followed by the Cold War, in which western European democracies resisted Soviet communism, another totalitarianism. But totalitarianism was not defeated. George Orwell's novel *1984*, published in 1949, capsulizes the persistent danger of totalitarianism even to an ostensibly free society and civilization.

George Orwell (penname of Eric Arthur Blair; 1903–1949), seeking the greatest welfare for the greatest number of people, was a lifelong democratic

---

28. Nagasaki: large seaport city and producer of military equipment with a population of more than 200,000.

29. Felicity Barringer, "Journalism's Greatest Hits," March 1, 1999, The *New York Times*: https://www.nytimes.com/1999/03/01/business/media-journalism-s-greatest-hits-two-lists-of-a-century-s-top-stories.html

socialist. He opposed colonialism abroad and championed workers' movements at home. He fought for the Republican cause in the Spanish Civil War, staunchly opposing the fascist nationalists, but became at the same time disillusioned by the machinations of the communist factions on the Republican side. He abhorred both Nazism and Stalinism. These views he expressed in six novels, many short stories, critical essays, and book-length works of nonfiction. His best-known works include, on the experience of poverty, *The Road to Wigan Pier* (1937); on the Spanish Civil War, *Homage to Catalonia* (1938); on communism, *Animal Farm* (1945); and on totalitarianism's threat to human freedom and dignity, *1984* (1949), published the year he died of tuberculosis at age forty-six. Translated into dozens of languages, ranking near the top on several lists of best novels, *1984* is one of the most important and influential books of the twentieth century.

Orwell's *1984* expands and transforms Koestler's *Darkness at Noon*, which Orwell had hailed as a "masterpiece."[30] Like Koestler, he describes the surveillance, sudden arrest, harsh confinement, physical torture, and psychological manipulation of the victims of an all-powerful state—one blending features of Nazism and communism but not naming any existing political entity or living individuals. In both works, moreover, the prisoner is coerced to welcome his own extinction. But Orwell goes further in four principal ways.

First, Orwell describes not a plausible contemporary state, but an imagined future one: Oceania, one of three intercontinental superstates (the others are Eurasia and Eastasia) born of global war, and ruled by the Party. Yet, though Oceania is a fiction, it is eerily, comfortably British—the protagonist, Winston Smith, and other characters have familiar English names and live in a city like London—suggesting that the danger is present, that all this could happen right here and now.

Second, the goal of the (unnamed) Party is explicitly to gain and hold onto power. It pretends to pursue the greater good of human welfare, but in truth it seeks only to control. "The Party seeks power entirely for its own sake," says the interrogator; "We are not interested in the good of others; we are interested solely in power." Power has its own thrill—that of crushing a helpless enemy: "If you want a picture of the future, imagine a boot stamping on a human face—forever."

Third, to achieve that unbreakable hold on power, the Party seeks the destruction of meaning, and thereby the capacity for human thought. In the language of "Newspeak," things mean their opposites: thus the three slogans of the party are WAR IS PEACE; FREEDOM IS SLAVERY; IGNORANCE IS STRENGTH. These oxymorons are inscribed on the surface of the glistening

---

30. In "Arthur Koestler," Orwell's evaluation of that author's works in *Critical Essays* (London: Secker and Warburg, 1946), online at https://orwell.ru/library/reviews/koestler/english/e_ak

white pyramidal edifice of the Ministry of Truth, which produces propaganda and negates historical memory. Any documents reporting events that should not have happened, according to the censors, are thrust into the nothingness of the "memory hole."

Fourth, to remain in power, the Party aims to control minds, especially those of the professional, that is, the intellectual class (who constitute 13 percent of the population, a stratum below that of Party officials, who constitute 2 percent). Everyone else—the Proletariat (constituting 85 percent of the population)—exists simply to be controlled, a control exerted by the Thought Police, who eradicate "thoughtcrimes." Surveillance is everywhere, announced by oversized posters blaring out the warning BIG BROTHER IS WATCHING YOU! The result of surveillance is the total control, not just of politics and society, but also of the soul and body, the annihilation of personality, and the creation of a new form of soulless humanity, a condition of "unpersonhood."

Orwell's *1984* is the distillation of the West's cultural condition at the end of the first half of the twentieth century. Perhaps it will not be forgotten—or erased, by some Ministry of Truth—before the end of the first half of the twenty-first.

1. Wilfred Owen, *The Send-Off; Anthem for Doomed Youth; Dulce et Decorum Est* (1917–1918)

The emotional power of Owen's war poems derives from their meticulous artistry. As seen in the three poems that follow, the author pairs, recalls, repeats, and contrasts sounds to create a musical as much as a verbal message about the slaughter of young men and the arrogance of those who sacrifice them to the horrors of war. *The Send-Off* depicts the departure of new recruits to the front, and anticipates the sorrow that will be felt when only a few return. *Anthem for Doomed Youth* evokes the lonely deaths of those who fall in battle, unsung and uncelebrated. *Dulce et Decorum Est* is a retort to the ancient Roman poet Horace, who had written "sweet and proper it is to die for the fatherland": that is nothing but a lie, Owen says, that the old tell to deceive the young.

THE SEND-OFF

The Send-Off *opens with a stark contrast between the phrases "sang their way," suggesting the joyous mood of the soldiers about to depart for war, and "grimly gay," describing their faces. At the close, the rhyming phrases of "great bells," "drums and yells," and "village wells"—the bells that will not ring, the drums and yells that will*

*not be heard, and the village wells that run dry—convey the sadness of lives lost,
and consternation at the scant number of those who will return.*

Down the close, darkening lanes they sang their way
To the siding-shed,
And lined the train with faces grimly gay.

Their breasts were stuck all white with wreath and spray
As men's are, dead.

Dull porters watched them, and a casual tramp
Stood staring hard,
Sorry to miss them from the upland camp.
Then, unmoved, signals nodded, and a lamp
Winked to the guard.

So secretly, like wrongs hushed-up, they went.
They were not ours:
We never heard to which front these were sent.

Nor there if they yet mock what women meant
Who gave them flowers.

Shall they return to beatings of great bells
In wild trainloads?
A few, a few, too few for drums and yells,
May creep back, silent, to still village wells
Up half-known roads.

ANTHEM FOR DOOMED YOUTH (1917)

In Anthem for Doomed Youth—*in form a sonnet,*[31] *a genre more often employed
to express sexual longing—the shocking first line governs the rest: "What passing-
bells for these who die as cattle?" The answers follow, in rolling, alliterative phrases:
the only orison to be heard is "the stuttering rifles' rapid rattle," and the only hymns
are sung by "shrill, demented choirs of wailing shells"; while faraway, at home,
bugles call for the dead from "sad shires," and at each nightfall, in each bereaved
home, there is "a drawing-down of blinds."*

What passing-bells for these who die as cattle?
Only the monstrous anger of the guns.
Only the stuttering rifles' rapid rattle

---

31. sonnet: a fourteen-line poem, employing a variety of rhyme schemes, though often consisting
of an octave (set of eight lines) followed by a sestet (set of six lines), as does this one.

Can patter out their hasty orisons.
No mockeries now for them; no prayers nor bells;
Nor any voice of mourning save the choirs,
The shrill, demented choirs of wailing shells;
And bugles calling for them from sad shires.
What candles may be held to speed them all?
Not in the hands of boys, but in their eyes
Shall shine the holy glimmers of good-byes.
The pallor of girls' brows shall be their pall;
Their flowers the tenderness of patient minds,
And each slow dusk a drawing-down of blinds.

DULCE ET DECORUM EST (1918)

The famous Dulce et Decorum Est, *a parody of Horace's ode to Roman piety and valor, describes a squad attacked by poison gas, one of the nightmare weapons deployed in World War I. The soldiers put on their gas masks, but one man is hit and could be seen "flound'ring like a man in fire or lime" (the sounds of "flound'ring" matched by those of "fire" and "lime"); and "Dim, through the misty panes and thick green light, / As under a green sea, I saw him drowning" ("through" the "green light" matched by "under a green sea"). He is laid in a wagon and followed by the men who could hear his blood "gargling from the froth-corrupted lungs, / Obscene as cancer, bitter as the cud / Of vile, incurable sores on innocent tongues" ("obscene" and "bitter," "cancer" and "cud," and "incurable" and "innocent" form striking chords of sound). If you had heard this ghastly gargling, the poet observes, you would not repeat to children "the old Lie": that it is noble and fitting to die for one's country. Rebuking the ancient poet Horace, Owen indicts not only the modern politicians and generals who had brought this war down upon his generation, but also the whole Western tradition—one among others—that had fostered a cult of militarism.*

Bent double, like old beggars under sacks,
Knock-kneed, coughing like hags, we cursed through sludge,
Till on the haunting flares we turned our backs
And towards our distant rest began to trudge.
Men marched asleep. Many had lost their boots
But limped on, blood-shod. All went lame; all blind;
Drunk with fatigue; deaf even to the hoots
Of tired, outstripped Five-Nines[32] that dropped behind.
Gas! Gas! Quick, boys!—An ecstasy of fumbling,
Fitting the clumsy helmets just in time;

---

32. Five-Nines: German artillery shells, containing poison gas.

But someone still was yelling out and stumbling
And flound'ring like a man in fire or lime . . .
Dim, through the misty panes and thick green light,
As under a green sea, I saw him drowning.
In all my dreams, before my helpless sight,
He plunges at me, guttering, choking, drowning.
If in some smothering dreams you too could pace
Behind the wagon that we flung him in,
And watch the white eyes writhing in his face,
His hanging face, like a devil's sick of sin;
If you could hear, at every jolt, the blood
Come gargling from the froth-corrupted lungs,
Obscene as cancer, bitter as the cud
Of vile, incurable sores on innocent tongues,—
My friend, you would not tell with such high zest
To children ardent for some desperate glory,
The old Lie: *Dulce et decorum est*
Pro patria mori.

2. Siegfried Sassoon, *Counter-Attack; The Rear-Guard; Dreamers; Suicide in the Trenches* (1918)

In these four sketches of scenes from the Western Front, Sassoon is enraged by those in power who permit the purposeless killing to continue and is consumed by sorrow for the pain and loss he has witnessed.

COUNTER-ATTACK

The detachment has "gained [its] first objective," so things "seemed all right"— even though the trench "was rotten with dead" and dismembered bodies. An attack was expected and soon came from the German line, with deadly accurate fire of shells "spouting dark earth and wire with gusts from hell." The British soldiers are ordered to counter-attack: but it is hopeless, the enemy fire is overwhelming. A soldier is hit: "Down, and down, and down, he sank and drowned, / Bleeding to death." Immediately following this vivid and ghastly scene, four terse words, idiotically uncommunicative, end the poem: "The counter-attack had failed."

We'd gained our first objective hours before
While dawn broke like a face with blinking eyes,

Pallid, unshaved and thirsty, blind with smoke.
Things seemed all right at first. We held their line,
With bombers posted, Lewis guns[33] well placed,
And clink of shovels deepening the shallow trench.
    The place was rotten with dead; green clumsy legs
    High-booted, sprawled and grovelled along the saps;
    And trunks, face downward, in the sucking mud,
    Wallowed like trodden sand-bags loosely filled;
    And naked sodden buttocks, mats of hair,
    Bulged, clotted heads slept in the plastering slime.
    And then the rain began,—the jolly old rain!

A yawning soldier knelt against the bank,
Staring across the morning blear with fog;
He wondered when the Allemands[34] would get busy;
And then, of course, they started with five-nines[35]
Traversing, sure as fate, and never a dud.
Mute in the clamour of shells he watched them burst
Spouting dark earth and wire with gusts from hell,
While posturing giants dissolved in drifts of smoke.
He crouched and flinched, dizzy with galloping fear,
Sick for escape,—loathing the strangled horror
And butchered, frantic gestures of the dead.

An officer came blundering down the trench:
"Stand-to and man the fire-step!" On he went . . .
Gasping and bawling, "Fire-step . . . counter-attack!"
    Then the haze lifted. Bombing on the right
    Down the old sap: machine-guns on the left;
    And stumbling figures looming out in front.
    "O Christ, they're coming at us!" Bullets spat,
And he remembered his rifle . . . rapid fire . . .
And started blazing wildly . . . then a bang
Crumpled and spun him sideways, knocked him out
To grunt and wriggle: none heeded him; he choked
And fought the flapping veils of smothering gloom,
Lost in a blurred confusion of yells and groans . . .
Down, and down, and down, he sank and drowned,
Bleeding to death. The counter-attack had failed.

———————————

33. Lewis guns: a type of machine gun used regularly by the British in World War I.
34. Allemands: the Germans
35. five-nines: see p. 423 note 32.

THE REAR-GUARD (HINDENBURG LINE, APRIL 1917)

A soldier feels his way through a dark trench deep below the battlefield, looking
for the commanding officer. He comes across a sleeping man, as he thinks, while he
himself has not slept for days. Impatient, he kicks the inert body and finds that it
is a corpse that has been dead some ten days, its bruised face contorted in the final
agony of death, its fingers clutching the fatal wound.

Groping along the tunnel, step by step,
He winked his prying torch with patching glare
From side to side, and sniffed the unwholesome air.

Tins, boxes, bottles, shapes too vague to know,
A mirror smashed, the mattress from a bed;
And he, exploring fifty feet below
The rosy gloom of battle overhead.

Tripping, he grabbed the wall; saw some one lie
Humped at his feet, half-hidden by a rug,
And stooped to give the sleeper's arm a tug.
"I'm looking for headquarters." No reply.
"God blast your neck!" (For days he'd had no sleep.)
"Get up and guide me through this stinking place."
Savage, he kicked a soft, unanswering heap,
And flashed his beam across the livid face
Terribly glaring up, whose eyes yet wore
Agony dying hard ten days before;
And fists of fingers clutched a blackening wound.

Alone he staggered on until he found
Dawn's ghost that filtered down a shafted stair
To the dazed, muttering creatures underground
Who hear the boom of shells in muffled sound.
At last, with sweat of horror in his hair,
He climbed through darkness to the twilight air,
Unloading hell behind him step by step.

DREAMERS

The first six lines of Dreamers *portray the heroic soldiers who are "citizens of*
death's grey land," standing "[i]n the great hour of destiny"; they are "sworn to
action," expected to "win / Some flaming, fatal climax with their lives"—the tone
is elevated and celebratory. But the real soldiers are ordinary men whose minds are
elsewhere: on the "firelit homes, clean beds, and wives" they left behind; "dreaming

of things they did with balls and bats." They will never get to go home, the poem
suggests.

Soldiers are citizens of death's grey land,
  Drawing no dividend from time's to-morrows.
In the great hour of destiny they stand,
  Each with his feuds, and jealousies, and sorrows.
Soldiers are sworn to action; they must win
  Some flaming, fatal climax with their lives.
Soldiers are dreamers; when the guns begin
  They think of firelit homes, clean beds, and wives.
I see them in foul dug-outs, gnawed by rats,
  And in the ruined trenches, lashed with rain,
Dreaming of things they did with balls and bats,
  And mocked by hopeless longing to regain
Bank-holidays, and picture shows, and spats,
  And going to the office in the train.

SUICIDE IN THE TRENCHES

An ordinary and untroubled boy is sent to the Front and, unable to bear the sham-
bles of the trenches, he "put a bullet through his brain." His suffering is untold and
unrecognized; "No one spoke of him again." You folks at home, the poet hisses, "[w]ho
cheer when soldier lads march by," do not know and do not seek to know the truth
of war. Sneering, the poem ends with a devastating, jingling couplet: "Sneak home
and pray you'll never know / The hell where youth and laughter go."

I knew a simple soldier boy
Who grinned at life in empty joy,
Slept soundly through the lonesome dark,
And whistled early with the lark.

In winter trenches, cowed and glum,
With crumps and lice and lack of rum,
He put a bullet through his brain.
No one spoke of him again.
* * * * *
You smug-faced crowds with kindling eye
Who cheer when soldier lads march by,
Sneak home and pray you'll never know
The hell where youth and laughter go.

3. Erich Maria Remarque,
All Quiet on the Western Front (1929)

The following selections from Remarque's novel trace the experience of a group of schoolmates who enlisted together to fight in the German army. Chapter One introduces Kantorek, their teacher, who had urged them to enlist, one of those who "let us down so badly": "While they continued to write and talk, we saw the wounded and dying." In Chapter Two, the young men whose heads were full of romantic notions of wartime heroics—they were so young they had just begun shaving—learned that what really matters in the army is that they keep their buttons brightly shined: "[N]ot the mind but the boot brush, not intelligence but the system, not freedom but drill." In Chapter Four, the soldiers learn, at the first bursting of the shells, to throw themselves upon the ground—because the earth itself, that primal element, "is [their] only friend, [their] brother, [their] mother." In Chapter Six, they are attacked and they fight back: "We have become wild beasts. We do not fight, we defend ourselves against annihilation." Then at last, they are sent home for a short time of leave. They are only 32 of the original company of 150 men: "A line, a short line trudges off into the morning."

ALL QUIET ON THE WESTERN FRONT

Chapter One

Kantorek had been our schoolmaster, a stern little man in a grey tail-coat, with a face like a shrew mouse. . . . During drill-time Kantorek gave us long lectures until the whole of our class went, under his shepherding, to the District Commandant and volunteered. I can see him now, as he used to glare at us through his spectacles and say in moving voice: "Won't you join up, Comrades?" . . .

There was, indeed, one of us who hesitated and did not want to fall into line. That was Joseph Behm, a plumb, homely fellow. But he did allow himself to be persuaded, otherwise he would have been ostracized. . . . Strange to say, Behm was one of the first to fall. He got hit in the eye during an attack, and we left him lying for dead. . . .

Naturally we couldn't blame Kantorek for this. Where would the world be if one brought every man to book? There were thousands of Kantoreks, all of whom were convinced that they were acting for the best—in a way that cost them nothing.

And that is why they let us down so badly.

For us lads of eighteen they ought to have been mediators and guides to the world of maturity, the world of work, of duty, of culture, of progress—to the future. . . . But the first death we saw shattered this belief. . . . The first bombardment showed us our mistake, and under it the world as they had taught it to us broke in pieces.

While they continued to write and talk, we saw the wounded and dying. While they taught that duty to one's country is the greatest thing, we already knew that death-throes are stronger. . . .

Chapter Two

When we went to the district commandant to enlist, we were a class of twenty young men, many of whom proudly shaved for the first time before going to the barracks. . . . We were still crammed full of vague ideas which gave to life, and to the war also an ideal and almost romantic character. We were trained in the army for ten weeks and in this time more profoundly influenced than by ten years at school. We learned that a bright button is weightier than four volumes of Schopenhauer.[36] At first astonished, then embittered, and finally indifferent, we recognized that what matters is not the mind but the boot brush, not intelligence but the system, not freedom but drill. . . . We had fancied our task would be different, only to find we were to be trained for heroism as though we were circus-ponies. But we soon accustomed ourselves to it. We learned in fact that some of these things were necessary, but the rest merely show. Soldiers have a fine nose for such distinctions. . . .

Chapter Four

To me the front is a mysterious whirlpool. Though I am in still water far away from its centre, I feel the whirl of the vortex sucking me slowly, irresistibly, inescapably into itself.

From the earth, from the air, sustaining forces pour into us—mostly from the earth. To no man does the earth mean so much as to the soldier. When he presses himself down upon her long and powerfully, when he buries his face and his limbs deep in her from the fear of death by shell-fire, then she is his only friend, his brother, his mother; he stifles his terror and his cries in her silence and her security; she shelters him and releases him for ten seconds to live, to run, ten seconds of life; receives him again and often for ever.

Earth!—Earth!—Earth! . . .

At the sound of the first droning of the shells we rush back, in one part of our being, a thousand years. By the animal instinct that is awakened in us we are led and protected. . . . A man is walking along without thought or heed;—suddenly he throws himself down on the ground and a storm of fragments flies harmlessly over him;—yet he cannot remember either to have heard the shell coming or to have thought of flinging himself down. But had he not abandoned himself to the impulse he would now be a heap of mangled flesh.

---

36. Arthur Schopenhauer (1788–1860): nineteenth-century German philosopher.

Chapter Six

We wake up in the middle of the night. The earth booms. Heavy fire is falling on us. We crouch into corners. We distinguish shells of every caliber.

Each man lays hold of his things and looks again every minute to reassure himself that they are still there. The dug-out heaves, the night roars and flashes. We look at each other in the momentary flashes of light, and with pale faces and pressed lips shake our heads. . . .

Slowly the grey light trickles into the post and pales the flashes of the shells. Morning is come. The explosion of mines mingles with the gunfire. That is the most dementing convulsion of all. The whole region where they go up becomes one grave. . . .

The bombardment does not diminish. It is falling in the rear too. As far as one can see spout fountains of mud and iron. A wide belt is being raked. . . .

Our trench is almost gone. At many places it is only eighteen inches high, it is broken by holes, and craters, and mountains of earth. A shell lands square in front of our post. At once it is dark. We are buried and must dig ourselves out. After an hour the entrance is clear again, and we are calmer because we have had something to do. . . .

We have become wild beasts. We do not fight, we defend ourselves against annihilation. It is not against men that we fling our bombs, what do we know of men in this moment when Death is hunting us down. . . . No longer do we lie helpless, waiting on the scaffold, we can destroy and kill, to save ourselves, to save ourselves and to be revenged.

We crouch behind every corner, behind every barrier of barbed wire, and hurl heaps of explosives at the feet of the advancing enemy before we run. The blast of the hand-grenades impinges powerfully on our arms and legs; crouching like cats we run on, overwhelmed by this wave that bears us along, that fills us with ferocity, turns us into thugs, into murderers . . . ; this wave that multiplies our strength with fear and madness and greed of life, seeking and fighting for nothing but deliverance. . . .

The forward trenches have been abandoned. Are they still trenches? They are blown to pieces, annihilated. . . . But the enemy's casualties increase. They did not count on so much resistance. . . .

Suddenly the shelling begins to pound again. Soon we are sitting up once more with the rigid tenseness of blank anticipation.

Attack, counter-attack, charge, repulse—these are words, but what things they signify! We have lost a good many men, mostly recruits. Reinforcements have again been sent up to our sector. They are one of the new regiments, composed almost entirely of young fellows just called up. They have had hardly any training, and are sent into the field with only a theoretical knowledge. They do know what a hand-grenade is, it is true, but they have very little idea of cover, and what is most important of all, have no eye for it. A fold in the ground has to be quite eighteen inches high before they can see it. . . .

The young recruits of course know none of these things. They get killed simply because they hardly can tell shrapnel from high-explosive, they are mown down because they are listening anxiously to the roar of the big coal-boxes falling in the rear, and miss the light, piping whistle of the low spreading daisy-cutters. They flock together like sheep instead of scattering, and even the wounded are shot down like hares by the airmen.

Their pale turnip faces, their pitiful clenched hands, the fine courage of these poor devils, the desperate charges and attacks made by the poor brave wretches, who are so terrified that they dare not cry out loudly, but with battered chests, with torn bellies, arms and legs only whimper softly for their mothers and cease as soon as one looks at them. . . .

Between five and ten recruits fall to every old hand.

A surprise gas-attack carries off a lot of them. They have not yet learned what to do. We found one dug-out full of them, with blue heads and black lips. Some of them in a shell-hole took off their masks too soon; they did not know that the gas lies longest in the hollows; when they saw others on top without masks they pulled theirs off too and swallowed enough to scorch their lungs. Their condition is hopeless, they choke to death with haemorrhages and suffocation. . . .

How long has it been? Weeks—months—years? Only days. We see time pass in the colourless faces of the dying, we cram food into us, we run, we throw, we shoot, we kill, we lie about, we are feeble and spent, and nothing supports us but the knowledge that there are still feebler, still more spent, still more helpless ones there who, with staring eyes, look upon us as gods that escape death many times.

In the few hours of rest we teach them. "There, see that waggle-top? That's a mortar coming. Keep down, it will go clean over. But if it comes this way, then run for it. You can run from a mortar."

We sharpen their ears to the malicious, hardly audible buzz of the smaller shells that are not easily distinguishable. They must pick them out from the general din by their insect-like hum—we explain to them that these are far more dangerous than the big ones that can be heard long beforehand. . . .

We show them how to take cover from aircraft . . . ; we put them wise to the sound of gas shells;—show them all the tricks that can save them from death.

They listen, they are docile—but when it begins again, in their excitement they do everything wrong. . . .

We see men living with their skulls blown open; we see soldiers run with their two feet cut off, they stagger on their splintered stumps into the next shell-hole; a lance-corporal crawls a mile and a half on his hands dragging his smashed knee after him; another goes to the dressing station and over his clasped hands bulge his intestines; we see men without mouths, without jaws, without faces; we find one man who has held the artery of his arm in his teeth for two hours in order not to bleed to death. The sun goes down, night comes, the shells whine, life is at an end.

Still the little piece of convulsed earth in which we lie is held. We have yielded no more than a few hundred yards of it as a prize to the enemy. But on every yard there lies a dead man.

***

We have just been relieved. The wheels roll beneath us, we stand dully, and when the call "Mind—wire" comes, we bend our knees. It was summer when we came up, the trees were still green, now it is autumn and the night is grey and wet. The lorries stop, we climb out—a confused heap, a remnant of many names. On either side stand people, dark, calling out the numbers of the brigades, the battalions. And at each call a little group separates itself off, a small handful of dirty, pallid soldiers, a dreadfully small handful, and a dreadfully small remnant.

Now someone is calling the number of our company, it is, yes, the Company Commander. . . . And we hear the number of our company called again and again. He will call a long time, they do not hear him in the hospitals and shell-holes.

Once again: "Second Company, this way!" And then more softly: "Nobody else, Second Company?"

He is silent, and then huskily he says: "Is that all?" he gives the order: "Number!"

The morning is grey, it was still summer when we came up, and we were one hundred and fifty strong. Now we freeze, it is autumn, the leaves rustle, the voices flutter out wearily: "One—two—three—four"—and cease at thirty-two. And there is a long silence before the voice asks: "Anyone else?"—and waits and then says softly: "In squads—" and then breaks off and is only able to finish: "Second Company—" with difficulty: "Second Company—march easy!"

A line, a short line trudges off into the morning.

Thirty-two men.

4. Bertolt Brecht, *Mother Courage and Her Children* (1939)

Mother Courage is a tough, cagey entrepreneur who drives a canteen wagon in the rear of the Finnish regiment, buying and selling to support her three children. In the course of twelve years of the Thirty Years' War (1624–1636), as told in the excerpts that follow from six of the play's twelve scenes, all three are killed: the boisterous Eilif for his poaching; the honest Swiss Cheese for his diligence; and the warmhearted Kattrin for her heroic defiance.[37]

Mother Courage

[MOTHER COURAGE is introduced in Scene One. It is 1624, the sixth year of the Thirty Years' War, and she manages a canteen wagon in the rear of the Finnish Second Regiment (fighting under the Protestant Swedish king Gustavus Adolphus), from which she sells merchandise, food, and drink. She scrounges up her stock here and there, sells it high and bargains hard in order to support her three children by different fathers: the high-spirited Eilif, always spoiling for a fight; her second son, Swiss Cheese, characterized by his honesty; and her mute daughter Kattrin, characterized by her compassion for the weak and suffering. The two boys are harnessed to the heavy-laden wagon that they pull, which is stopped by a Sergeant.]

Scene One

MOTHER COURAGE: A good day to you, Sergeant!

SERGEANT (*barring the way*): Good day to *you*! Who d'you think *you* are?

MOTHER COURAGE: Tradespeople.
> *She sings:*
> Stop all the troops: here's Mother Courage!
> Hey, Captain, let them come and buy!
> For they can get from Mother Courage
> Boots they will march in till they die!
> Your marching men do not adore you
> (Packs on their backs, lice in their hair)
> But it's to death they're marching for you
> And so they need good boots to wear!
>> Christians, awake! Winter is gone!
>> The snows depart! Dead men sleep on!
>> Let all of you who still survive
>> Get out of bed and look alive!

---

37. To distinguish my notes from the stage directions, I have set them within brackets

SERGEANT: Halt! Where are you from, riffraff?

EILIF: Second Finnish Regiment!

SERGEANT: Where are your papers?

MOTHER COURAGE: Papers?

SWISS CHEESE: But this is Mother Courage!

SERGEANT: Never heard of her. Where'd she get a name like that?

MOTHER COURAGE: They call me Mother Courage 'cause I was afraid I'd be ruined, so I drove through the bombardment of Riga like a madwoman, with fifty loaves of bread in my cart. They were going moldy, what else could I do?

SERGEANT: No funny business! Where are your papers?

Scene Two

[Eilif has been recruited into the army, where he has impressed his Commander with his daring. The two stop by to see his mother. She cuffs him on the cheek for having risked his life.]

EILIF: To see you again! Where are the others?

MOTHER COURAGE (*in his arms*): Happy as ducks in a pond. Swiss Cheese is paymaster with the Second Regiment, so at least he isn't in the fighting. I couldn't keep him out altogether. . . .

The COMMANDER *has come over.*

COMMANDER: So you're his mother! I hope you have more sons for me like this fellow.

EILIF: If I'm not the lucky one: to be feasted by the Commander while you sit listening in the kitchen!

MOTHER COURAGE: Yes. I heard all right. (*She gives him a box on the ear.*)

EILIF (*his hand on his cheek*): Because I took the oxen?

MOTHER COURAGE: No. Because you didn't surrender when the four peasants let fly at you and tried to make mincemeat of you! Didn't I teach you to take care of yourself? You Finnish devil, you!

Scene Three

[Honest Swiss Cheese is, appropriately, paymaster for the Finnish Second Regiment and does all he can to save the cash box when Catholic forces advance. He will bury

the cash box near the river's edge to save it; and will be captured and shot for not having surrendered it.]

MOTHER COURAGE (*to Swiss Cheese*): What have you got there?

SWISS CHEESE: The regimental cash box.

MOTHER COURAGE: Throw it away! Your paymastering days are over!

SWISS CHEESE: It's a trust! . . . I thought I'd just put it in the wagon.

MOTHER COURAGE (*horrified*): What! In my wagon? God punish you for a prize idiot! If I just look away for a moment! They'll hang all three of us!

SWISS CHEESE: Then I'll put it somewhere else. Or escape with it.

MOTHER COURAGE: You'll stay where you are. It's too late. . . .

SWISS CHEESE: I don't like it. How will the sergeant pay his men?

MOTHER COURAGE: Soldiers in flight don't get paid.

SWISS CHEESE: Well, they could claim to be. No pay, no flight. They can refuse to budge.

MOTHER COURAGE: Swiss Cheese, your sense of duty worries me. I've brought you up to be honest because you're not very bright. But don't overdo it. And now I'm going with the chaplain to buy a Catholic flag and some meat. . . .

[Mother Courage goes off, and Kattrin and her brother Swiss Cheese talk. Two men, a Sergeant and the Man with the Badge over his eye, come in search of Swiss Cheese. He kisses Kattrin good-bye and heads off to save the cash box. Mother Courage returns, and Kattrin runs to meet her, distressed.]

MOTHER COURAGE: Now, Kattrin, calm down and tell all about it, your mother understands you. What, that little bastard of mine's taken the cash box away? I'll box his ears for him, the rascal! Now take your time and don't try to talk, use your hands. . . . A man with one eye was here? . . .

   Voices off. The two men bring in SWISS CHEESE.

SWISS CHEESE: Let me go. I've nothing on me. You're breaking my shoulder! I am innocent.

SERGEANT: This is where he comes from. These are his friends.

MOTHER COURAGE: Us? Since when?

SWISS CHEESE: I don't even know 'em. I was just getting my lunch here. . . .

SERGEANT: Who *are* you people, anyway?

MOTHER COURAGE: Law-abiding citizens! It's true what he says. He bought his lunch here. . . .

SERGEANT: We're after the regimental cash box. And we know what the man looks like who's been keeping it. We've been looking for him two days. It's you.

SWISS CHEESE: No, it's not!

SERGEANT: And if you don't shell out, you're dead, see? Where is it?

MOTHER COURAGE (*urgently*): 'Course he'd give it to you to save his life. He'd up and say, *I've* got it, here it is, you're stronger than me. He's not *that* stupid. Speak, little stupid, the sergeant's giving you a chance.

SWISS CHEESE: What if I haven't got it?

SERGEANT: Come off with us. We'll get it out of you. (*They take him off.*)

MOTHER COURAGE (*shouting after them*): He'd tell you! He's not *that* stupid! And don't you break his shoulder! . . .

[*Mother Courage arranges through her intermediary Yvette to pawn her wagon for two hundred guilders*[38] *so that she can bribe the Catholic soldiers: "Thanks be to God they're corruptible," she observes. "They're not wolves, they're human and after money. God is merciful, and men are bribable, that's how His will is done on earth as it is in Heaven." She plans to recoup her loss from the cash box when it is recovered. She haggles, trying to bring down the cost of the bribe to one hundred and twenty guilders. But she has haggled too long. Swiss Cheese will be shot; and to save herself and Kattrin, Mother Courage will not identify him as her son. His body is consigned to a mass grave.*]

> In the distance, a roll of drums. . . . MOTHER COURAGE *remains seated. It grows dark. It gets light again.* MOTHER COURAGE *has not moved.* YVETTE *appears, pale.*

YVETTE: Now you've done it—with your haggling. You can keep the wagon now. He got eleven bullets in him. I don't know why I still bother about you, you don't deserve it, but I just happened to learn that they don't think the cash box is really in the river. They suspect it's here, they think you're connected with him. I think they're going to bring him here to see if you'll give yourself away when you see him. You'd better not know him or we're in for it. And I'd better tell you straight, they're just behind me. Shall I keep Kattrin away? (MOTHER COURAGE *shakes her head.*) Does she know? Maybe she never heard the drums or didn't understand.

---

38. guilder: a Dutch coin, usually silver, in use into the late twentieth century.

MOTHER COURAGE: She knows. Bring her.

> YVETTE *brings* KATTRIN, *who walks over to her mother and stands by her.* MOTHER COURAGE *takes her hand. Two men come on with a stretcher; there is a sheet on it and something underneath. Beside them, the* SERGEANT. *They put the stretcher down.*

SERGEANT: Here's a man we can't identify. But he has to be registered to keep the records straight. He bought a meal from you. Look at him, see if you know him. (*He pulls back the sheet.*) Do you know him? (MOTHER COURAGE *shakes her head.*) What? You never saw him before he took that meal? (MOTHER COURAGE *shakes her head.*) Lift him up. Throw him in the carrion pit. He has no one that knows him.

> *They carry him off.*

Scene Eight

[*Gustavus Adolphus, king of Sweden, has died, and peace is declared—a peace that lasts only three days. Mother Courage hies off to market to "get rid of this stuff" before prices fall. In the meantime, her son Eilif has stolen some cattle from a peasant and killed a peasant's wife, a predation allowable in time of war, but not in peacetime. He is brought to say a final goodbye to Mother Courage before he is executed. The Chaplain and the Cook decide they will not tell her of her son's fate. Mother Courage returns, rejoicing that the war is back on and prices are up. She learns that Eilif has visited—but not that he has been killed, and that now, both her sons are dead.*]

> *Followed by two soldiers with halberds,* EILIF *enters. His hands are fettered. He is white as chalk.*

CHAPLAIN: What's happened to you?

EILIF: Where's mother?

CHAPLAIN: Gone to town.

EILIF: They said she was here. I was allowed a last visit.

COOK (*to the* SOLDIERS): Where are you taking him?

A SOLDIER: For a ride.

> *The other* SOLDIER *makes the gesture of throat cutting.*

CHAPLAIN: What has he done?

SOLDIER: He broke in on a peasant. The wife is dead.

CHAPLAIN: Eilif, how could you?

EILIF: It's no different. It's what I did before.

COOK: That was in war time.

EILIF: Shut your hole. Can I sit down till she comes?

SOLDIER: No.

CHAPLAIN: It's true. In war time they honored him for it. He sat at the Commander's right hand. It was bravery. Couldn't we speak with the military police?

SOLDIER: What's the use? Stealing cattle from a peasant, what's brave about that?

COOK: It was just stupid.

EILIF: If I'd been stupid, I'd have starved, smarty.

COOK: So you were bright and paid for it.

CHAPLAIN: At least we must bring Kattrin out.

EILIF: Let her alone. Just give me some brandy.

SOLDIER: No.

CHAPLAIN: What shall we tell your mother?

EILIF: Tell her it was no different. Tell her it was the same. Oh, tell her nothing.

   The SOLDIERS *take him away.* . . .

COOK (*calling after him*): I'll have to tell her, she'll want to see him!

CHAPLAIN: Better tell her nothing. . . .

Scene Eleven

[Catholic troops advance on the Protestant town of Halle. On the outskirts, three soldiers stop at a prosperous farmhouse and force the son of the family to show them the way, threatening to burn down the house. Mother Courage has gone off to market to buy at bargain prices the goods dumped by evacuating townspeople, but Kattrin, who stays with the wagon, hears the prayers of the terrified peasants. She takes a drum from the wagon, climbs up a ladder onto the roof, and beats it to warn the townspeople of the enemy's approach. She will not stop. And her drumming will save the town.]

PEASANT WOMAN: Heavens, what's she doing?

OLD PEASANT: She's out of her mind!

PEASANT WOMAN: Get her down, quick.

> *The* OLD PEASANT *runs to the ladder but* KATTRIN *pulls it up on the roof.*

She'll get us in trouble.

OLD PEASANT: Stop it this minute, you silly cripple! . . .

PEASANT WOMAN: Have you no pity, have you no heart? We have relations there too, four grandchildren, but there's nothing we can do. If they find us now, it's the end, they'll stab us to death!

> KATTRIN *is staring into the far distance, toward the town. She goes on drumming.*

PEASANT WOMAN (*to the* PEASANT): I told you not to let that riffraff on your farm. What do *they* care if we lose our cattle?

LIEUTENANT (*running back with* SOLDIERS *and the* YOUNG PEAS-ANT): I'll cut you all to bits!

PEASANT WOMAN: We're innocent, sir, there's nothing we can do. She did it, a stranger!

LIEUTENANT: Where's the ladder?

OLD PEASANT: On the roof.

LIEUTENANT (*calling*): Throw down the drum. I order you! (KATTRIN *goes on drumming.*) . . .

FIRST SOLDIER (*to the* LIEUTENANT): I beg leave to make a suggestion. (*He whispers something to the* LIEUTENANT, *who nods.*) Listen, you! We have an idea—for your own good. Come down and go with us to the town. Show us your mother and we'll spare her.

> KATTRIN *goes on drumming.* . . .

LIEUTENANT: We must set fire to the farm. Smoke her out.

OLD PEASANT: That's no good, Captain. When they see fire from the town, they'll know everything.

> *During the drumming* KATTRIN *has been listening again. Now she laughs.*

LIEUTENANT: She's laughing at us, that's too much. I'll have her guts if it's the last thing I do. Bring a musket!

> *Two* SOLDIERS *off.* KATTRIN *goes on drumming.*

PEASANT WOMAN: I have it, Captain. That's their wagon over there, Captain. If we smash that, she'll stop. It's all they have, Captain.

LIEUTENANT (*to the* YOUNG PEASANT): Smash it! (*Calling:*) If you don't stop that noise, we'll smash your wagon!

The YOUNG PEASANT *deals the wagon a couple of feeble blows with a board.*

PEASANT WOMAN (*to* KATTRIN): Stop, you little beast!

KATTRIN *stares at the wagon and pauses. Noises of distress come out of her. But she goes on drumming.* . . . *The* SOLDIERS *arrive with the musket.* . . .

LIEUTENANT: Set it up! Set it up! (*Calling while the musket is set up on forks:*) Once and for all: stop that drumming!

Still crying, KATTRIN *is drumming as hard as she can.*

Fire!

The SOLDIERS *fire.* KATTRIN *is hit. She gives the drum another feeble beat or two, then slowly collapses.*

LIEUTENANT: That's an end to the noise.

But the last beats of the drum are lost in the din of cannon from the town. Mingled with the thunder of cannon, alarm bells are heard in the distance.

FIRST SOLDIER: She made it.

Scene Twelve

[*Mother Courage returns to find Kattrin's dead body. As the Catholic troops retreat, she sings a lullaby to her daughter, arranges for her burial, and heads off to find Eilif, her third child. She does not know that he, too, is dead.*]

MOTHER COURAGE: She's asleep now.

PEASANTS: She's not asleep, it's time you realized. She's gone. You must get away. There are wolves in these parts. And the bandits are worse.

MOTHER COURAGE: That's right. (*She goes and fetches a cloth from the wagon to cover up the body.*)

PEASANT WOMAN: Have you no one now? Someone you can go to?

MOTHER COURAGE: There's one. My Eilif.

PEASANT (*while* MOTHER COURAGE *covers the body*): Find him then. Leave *her* to us. We'll give her a proper burial. You needn't worry.

MOTHER COURAGE: Here's money for the expenses.

She pays the PEASANT. *The* PEASANT *and his son shake her hand and carry* KATTRIN *away.*

PEASANT WOMAN (*also taking her hand, and bowing, as she goes away*): Hurry!

MOTHER COURAGE (*harnessing herself to the wagon*): I hope I can pull the wagon by myself. Yes, I'll manage, there's not much in it now. I must get back into business.

> *Another regiment passes at the rear with pipe and drum.* MOTHER COURAGE *starts pulling the wagon.*

MOTHER COURAGE: Hey! Take me with you!

> *Soldiers are heard singing:*

Dangers, surprises, devastations!
The war moves on, but will not quit.
And though it last three generations,
We shall get nothing out of it.
Starvation, filth, and cold enslave us.
The army robs us of our pay.
But God may yet come down and save us:
His holy war won't end today.
   Christians, awake! Winter is gone!
   The snows depart! Dead men sleep on!
   Let all of you who still survive
   Get out of bed and look alive!

5. Simone Weil, *The* Iliad *or the Poem of Force* (1941)

For Weil, Homer's *Iliad*[39] is the West's first and last genuine epic, in which today's victors are tomorrow's victims, and destiny transforms triumph into devastation. In Homer's telling, the epochal battle for the city of Troy was an orgy of violence, featuring innumerable encounters between mighty heroes with details of thrusts and parries, heads burst open, limbs severed, and organs eviscerated. These violent clashes memorialize the deeds of the ancestors of Homer's generation. But this is not the whole of Homer's message according to Weil's unique, original, and highly persuasive interpretation. Rather than glorifying the slaughter, he conveys the essential Greek vision that no later era has grasped: no one escapes suffering; all are toys of destiny; death awaits both the strong and the weak; and the individual's momentous exertion of will, on the canvas of eternity, amounts to nothing whatsoever. The force displayed in the *Iliad*, the

---

39. For Homer and the *Iliad*, see Volume One, Introduction to Chapter 2 and Text 1.

poem of force, the force exercised by the states, armies, and bureaucracies that in all prior centuries have oppressed humankind will not, ultimately, prevail. The *Iliad*, the poem of force, exposes the powerlessness of force.

The *Iliad* or the Poem of Force

1. The true hero, the true subject matter, the center of the *Iliad* is force. The force that men wield, the force that subdues men, in the face of which human flesh shrinks back. The human soul seems ever conditioned by its ties with force, swept away, blinded by the force it believes it can control, bowed under the constraint of the force it submits to. Those who have supposed that force, thanks to progress, now belongs to the past, have seen a record of that in Homer's poem; those wise enough to discern the force at the center of all human history, today as in the past, find in the *Iliad* the most beautiful and flawless of mirrors.

2. Force is that which makes a thing of whoever submits to it. Exercised to the extreme, it makes the human being a thing quite literally, that is, a dead body. Someone was there and, the next moment, no one. . . .

7. The force that kills is summary and crude. How much more varied in operation, how much more stunning in effect is that other sort of force, that which does not kill just yet. It will kill for a certainty, or it will kill perhaps, or it may merely hang over the being it can kill at any instant; in all cases, it changes the human being into stone. . . .

34. Though all are destined from birth to endure violence, the realm of circumstances closes their minds to this truth. The strong is never perfectly strong nor the weak perfectly weak, but neither knows this. They believe they are of different species; the weak man does not consider himself like the strong, nor is he regarded as such. He who possesses force moves in a frictionless environment; nothing in the human matter around him puts an interval for reflection between impulse and action. Where reflection has no place, there is neither justice nor forethought; hence the ruthless and mindless behavior of warriors. Their sword plunges into a disarmed opponent at their knees; they vaunt over a dying man, telling him the insults his body will undergo. . . . In wielding their power they never suspect that the consequences of their actions will affect them in turn. . . . When Achilles delights to see the wretched Greeks flee, can he grasp that this flight, which will continue and end at his whim, will cost his friend and even himself their lives? Those to whom fate has loaned force perish through their over-reliance on it.

35. It is impossible that they should not perish, since they neither consider their own force to be limited nor recognize that their relations with others are a balance of unequal forces. Other men do not pause in their actions to have some regard for their fellow man; they conclude that destiny has granted them every license and none to their inferiors. From this point, they overstep the force at their disposal—inevitably for they fail to see its limits. They are then surrendered ineluctably to chance, and things no longer obey them. Chance sometimes helps, sometimes hurts them; they are exposed quite naked to sorrow, without the armor of power that had shielded their spirit, with nothing to insulate them any longer from tears.

36. This geometrically stringent chastisement, which spontaneously punishes the abuse of force, was the primary issue in Greek thought. . . . The concept is familiar wherever the spirit of Greek thought has penetrated. . . .

61. Such is the character of force. Its power to transform human beings into things is twofold and operates on two fronts; in equal but different ways, it petrifies the souls of those who undergo it and those who ply it. This characteristic reaches its extreme form in the milieu of arms, at the instant when a battle begins to incline toward a decision. Battles are not determined among men who calculate, devise, take resolutions and act on them but among men stripped of these abilities, transformed, fallen to the level either of purely passive inert matter or of the blind forces of sheer impetus. This is the ultimate secret of war, which the *Iliad* expresses in its similes. In these, warriors are likened either to fire, flood, wind, fierce beasts, and whatever blind cause of disaster or to frightened animals, trees, water, sand, whatever is affected by the violence of outside forces. . . .

63. The thoughtlessness of those that wield force with no regard for men or things they have or believe they have at their mercy, the hopelessness that impels the soldier to devastate, the crushing of the enslaved and the defeated, the massacres, all these things make up a picture of unrelieved horror. Force is its sole hero. A tedious gloom would ensue were there not scattered here and there some moments of illumination—fleeting and sublime moments when men possess a soul. The soul thus roused for an instant, soon to be lost in the empire of force, wakes innocent and unmarred; no ambiguous, complex, or anxious feeling appears in it; courage and love alone have a place there. . . .

71. These moments of grace are infrequent in the *Iliad*, but they suffice to convey with deep regret just what violence has killed and will kill again.

72. However, such an amassing of violent acts would leave one cold but for an accent of incurable bitterness that constantly makes itself felt, even in a single word, turn of a verse, or run-on line. This is what makes the *Iliad* unique, this bitterness emerging from tenderness and enveloping all men equally, like the bright light of the sun. The tone always is imbued with bitterness but never descends to lamentation. Justice and love, totally out of place in this depiction of extremes and unjust violence, subtly and by nuance, drench all with their light. Nothing of value, whether doomed to die or not, is slighted; the mystery of all is revealed without dissimulation or condescension; no man is set above or below the human condition; all that is destroyed is regretted. Victors and victims are equally close to us, and thereby akin to both poet and listener. . . .

79. The cold brutality of war's deeds is disguised not one iota, since neither victors nor victims are idolized, reviled, or despised. Destiny and the gods almost always determine the shifting fortune of battles. Within the limits imposed by destiny, the gods highhandedly dispense victory and ruin. They are always the ones to provoke the stupidities and betrayals that, time and again, preclude peace; war is their true *métier* [profession], whim and malevolence their only motives. As for the warriors, the similes that liken them—victors and victims—to beasts or objects can elicit neither admiration nor scorn but only sorrow that men may be so transfigured.

80. The exceptional impartiality that pervades the *Iliad* may have parallels unknown to us, but it has had no imitators. It is difficult to detect that the poet is Greek and not Trojan. The tone of the poem seems to attest directly to the source of its oldest parts; history will perhaps never shed a clear light on this. If one believes with Thucydides that eighty years after the fall of Troy the Achaeans suffered conquest in their turn, one may ask whether these songs, in which iron is seldom mentioned, are not those of the exiled remnants of a conquered people. Constrained to live and die "far from their homeland," like the Greeks fallen at Troy, and having like the Trojans lost their cities, they identified both with the victors, who had been their fathers, and with the victims, whose misery was like their own. The reality of this still-recent war appeared to them across the years, tainted neither by the intoxication of arrogance nor by disgrace. Able to envisage themselves at once as victors or vanquished, they therefore understood what the blinded victors and vanquished could not. This is only a conjecture; one may hardly do more than guess about times so remote.

81. Whatever the case may be, this poem is a miraculous thing. Its bitterness rests on the only just cause for bitterness—the subjection of the human spirit to force, that is, in the last analysis, to inert matter. This subjection is the same for all mortals, though souls bear it differently according to their goodness. No one in the *Iliad* is spared it, just as no one on earth is spared. No one who yields to it is regarded as contemptible for this reason. All who escape the empire of force in their innermost being and in their relations with their fellow men are loved, but loved in grief at the threat of constantly impending destruction. Such is the spirit of the only true epic that the West possesses. The *Odyssey* seems only a good reproduction of the *Iliad* in some places, of oriental poems in others. The *Aeneid* is an imitation, granted a brilliant one, marred by frigidity, ostentation, and poor taste. The *chansons de geste*, lacking impartiality, fall short of grandeur; the author and the reader of the *Chanson de Roland* do not feel the death of an enemy as they do that of Roland. . . .[40]

83. . . . The Greeks had a force of soul that allowed them, for the most part, to avoid self-delusion; they were compensated for this by understanding how to attain in all things the highest degree of insight, purity, and simplicity. But the spirit transmitted from the *Iliad* to the Gospels via the philosophers and tragic poets hardly ever breached the borders of Greek civilization; and, after the fall of Greece, nothing remained but reflections of that spirit.

84. The Romans and Hebrews both thought themselves exempt from common human misfortune, the former as a nation destined to be master of the world, the latter by the favor of their God and precisely in proportion as they were obedient to him. The Romans despised foreigners, enemies, the vanquished, their subjects, their slaves; thus they had neither epics nor tragedies. They substituted gladiators for tragedies. The Hebrews saw misfortune as indicative of sin and consequently a proper justification for contempt. They considered their beaten foes repellent to God himself and damned to atone for crimes; this made cruelty permissible, even mandatory. . . . Throughout twenty centuries of Christianity, Romans and Hebrews have been admired, read, emulated in deeds and words, cited whenever a crime needed justification.

85. Moreover, the spirit of the Gospels was not handed down uncontaminated though successive generations of Christians. From the beginning, the joyful willingness of martyrs to suffer and die was deemed a sign of grace, as if grace could do more for men than for Christ. Those who consider that even God himself, once he had become human, contemplated the severity of destiny with a tremor of anguish ought to know that human misery may be disregarded only by those who have camouflaged the severity of destiny in their own eyes by an illusion, an intoxication, or a figment of the imagination. . . . Having forgotten it so thoroughly, the Christian tradition has only very seldom recovered the simplicity that makes each phrase of the Passion narratives so poignant. . . .

86. Notwithstanding the brief intoxication with rediscovered Greek literature during the Renaissance, the Greek genius has not revived in twenty centuries . . . [and] nothing the peoples of Europe have produced matches their first known

---

40. The *Odyssey*, etc.: Weil names a series of other epics that do not match Homer's *Iliad* in significance of message: Homer's *Odyssey*; Virgil's *Aeneid*; and the medieval *chansons de geste*, the *Chanson de Roland* (*Song of Roland*) principal among them. For Homer, Virgil, and the *Song of Roland*, see in Volume One respectively, Introduction to Chapter 2; Introduction to Chapter 3 and Text 4; and Introduction Chapter 6 and Text 3.

poem. They will perhaps rediscover epic genius when they learn to believe nothing is protected from fate, learn never to admire force, not to hate the enemy nor to scorn the unfortunate. It is doubtful whether this will soon occur.

6. John Reed, *Ten Days That Shook the World* (1919)

On November 2, 1917, the Bolsheviks summoned representatives from all the Russian Soviets to meet in Petrograd and take over the Russian Provisional Government, headed by Alexander Kerensky.[41] Over the next ten days, Kerensky would resign, and the Soviets, led by Bolshevik commissars, would seize the Winter Palace (the tsar's former residence), fend off a counter-revolutionary assault, and declare the victory of the Russian Revolution. Selections from Reed's detailed account of these events follow, focused on the critical period of November 5 through November 8.[42]

TEN DAYS THAT SHOOK THE WORLD

Preface

This book is a slice of intensified history—history as I saw it. It does not pretend to be anything but a detailed account of the November Revolution, when the Bolsheviki [Bolsheviks], at the head of the workers and soldiers, seized the state power of Russia and placed it in the hands of the Soviets. [. . .]

Instead of being a destructive force, it seems to me that the Bolsheviki were the only party in Russia with a constructive program and the power to impose it on the country. If they had not succeeded to the Government when they did, there is little doubt in my mind that the armies of Imperial Germany would have been in Petrograd [St. Petersburg] and Moscow in December, and Russia would again be ridden by a Tsar. . . .

No matter what one thinks of Bolshevism, it is undeniable that the Russian Revolution is one of the great events of human history, and the rise of

---

41. Alexander Kerensky (1881–1970): socialist revolutionary, head of the Russian provisional government, July to November 1917.
42. Minor changes in punctuation and formatting have been made to the original text, which is otherwise retained. Bracketed ellipses in the text indicate the editor's deletions; unbracketed ellipses are the author's. Dates are given according to the modern calendar. The events from November 2 to November 8 correspond to October 20 to October 28 in the traditional Russian calendar; hence the term "October Revolution."

the Bolsheviki a phenomenon of world-wide importance. . . . [H]istorians will want to know what happened in Petrograd in November 1917, the spirit which animated the people, and how the leaders looked, talked and acted. It is with this in view that I have written this book.

In the struggle my sympathies were not neutral. But in telling the story of those great days I have tried to see events with the eye of a conscientious reporter, interested in setting down the truth.

New York, January 1st 1919   J. R.

Chapter 3: On the Eve

November 5

Outside a chill, damp wind came from the west, and the cold mud underfoot soaked through my shoes. . . . At the first cross-street I noticed that the City Militiamen were mounted, and armed with revolvers in bright new holsters; a little group of people stood silently staring at them. At the corner of the Nevsky[43] I bought a pamphlet by Lenin, "Will the Bolsheviki be Able to Hold the Power?" paying for it with one of the stamps which did duty for small change. [. . .]

An armoured automobile went slowly up and down, siren screaming. On every corner, in every open space, thick groups were clustered; arguing soldiers and students. Night came swiftly down, the wide-spaced street-lights flickered on, the tides of people flowed endlessly. [. . .]

From there I hurried to Smolny.[44] [. . .] A steady stream of couriers and Commissars came and went. [. . .] In the hall I ran into some of the minor Bolshevik leaders. One showed me a revolver. "The game is on," he said, and his face was pale. "Whether we move or not the other side knows it must finish us or be finished. . . ."

The Petrograd Soviet[45] was meeting day and night. As I came into the great hall Trotzky [Trotsky] was just finishing. [. . .] "We feel that our Government, entrusted to the personnel of the Provisional Cabinet, is a pitiful and helpless Government, which only awaits the sweep of the broom of History to give way to a really popular Government. But we are trying to avoid a conflict, even now, to-day. We hope that the All-Russian Congress will take . . . into its hands that power and authority which rests upon the organised freedom of the people. If, however, the Government wants to utilise the short period it is expected to live—twenty-four, forty-eight, or seventy-two hours—to attack us, then we shall answer with counter-attacks, blow for blow, steel for iron!" [. . .]

---

43. Nevsky: the Nevsky Prospect, the main street of St. Petersburg.
44. Smolny: originally a convent with a school, a complex of buildings in central St. Petersburg where the revolutionary leaders met during the critical months of the Bolshevik Revolution.
45. Petrograd Soviet: see p. 409 note 4.

November 6

As I left Smolny, at three o'clock in the morning, I noticed that two rapid-firing guns had been mounted, one on each side of the door, and that strong patrols of soldiers guarded the gates and the near-by street-corners. [. . .]

As I crossed the Palace Square[46] several batteries of *yunker*[47] artillery came through the Red Arch at a jingling trot, and drew up before the Palace. The great red building of the General Staff was unusually animated, several armoured automobiles ranked before the door, and motors full of officers were coming and going. . . . The censor was very much excited, like a small boy at a circus. Kerensky, he said, had just gone to the Council of the Republic to offer his resignation. I hurried down to the Marinsky Palace, arriving at the end of that passionate and almost incoherent speech of Kerensky's, full of self-justification and bitter denunciation of his enemies. [. . .]

November 7

Toward four in the morning I met Zorin in the outer hall, a rifle slung from his shoulder.

"We're moving!" said he, calmly but with satisfaction. "We pinched the Assistant Minister of Justice and the Minister of Religions. They're down cellar now. One regiment is on the march to capture the Telephone Exchange, another the Telegraph Agency, another the State Bank. The Red Guard is out. . . ."

On the steps of Smolny, in the chill dark, we first saw the Red Guard— a huddled group of boys in workmen's clothes, carrying guns with bayonets, talking nervously together. [. . .] Behind us great Smolny, bright with lights, hummed like a gigantic hive. . . .

Chapter 4: The Fall of the Provisional Government

Wednesday, November 7th, I rose very late. The noon cannon boomed from [the Saints Peter and Paul Cathedral] as I went down the Nevsky. It was a raw, chill day. In front of the State Bank some soldiers with fixed bayonets were standing at the closed gates.

"What side do you belong to?" I asked. "The Government?"

"No more Government," one answered with a grin, "*Slava Bogu!* Glory to God!" That was all I could get out of him. [. . .]

---

46. Palace Square: open space in front of the Winter Palace, the tsar's residence when in Petersburg.
47. *yunker*: the revolutionaries' term for the forces of the counter-revolutionary military.

Reed and his companions go to the Winter Palace, now in Soviet hands, and gain admittance by showing their American passports.

Just inside a couple of soldiers stood on guard, but they said nothing. At the end of the corridor was a large, ornate room with gilded cornices and enormous crystal lustres [. . .]. On both sides of the parquetted floor lay rows of dirty mattresses and blankets, upon which occasional soldiers were stretched out; everywhere was a litter of cigarette-butts, bits of bread, cloth, and empty bottles with expensive French labels. [. . .] The place was all a huge barrack, and evidently had been for weeks, from the look of the floor and walls. Machine guns were mounted on window-sills, rifles stacked between the mattresses. [. . .]

They leave the Winter Palace and return to Smolny.

The massive facade of Smolny blazed with lights as we drove up, and from every street converged upon it streams of hurrying shapes dim in the gloom. [. . .] The extraordinary meeting of the Petrograd Soviet was over. I stopped Kameniev[48]—a quick moving little man, with a wide, vivacious face set close to his shoulders. Without preface he read in rapid French a copy of the resolution just passed:

> The Petrograd Soviet of Workers' and Soldiers' Deputies, saluting the victorious Revolution of the Petrograd proletariat and garrison, particularly emphasises the unity, organisation, discipline, and complete cooperation shown by the masses in this rising; rarely has less blood been spilled, and rarely has an insurrection succeeded so well.
>
> The Soviet expresses its firm conviction that the Workers' and Peasants' Government which, as the government of the Soviets, will be created by the Revolution, and which will assure the industrial proletariat of the support of the entire mass of poor peasants, will march firmly toward Socialism, the only means by which the country can be spared the miseries and unheard-of horrors of war.
>
> The new Workers' and Peasants' Government will propose immediately a just and democratic peace to all the belligerent countries.
>
> It will suppress immediately the great landed property, and transfer the land to the peasants. It will establish workmen's control over production and distribution of manufactured products, and will set up a general control over the banks, which it will transform into a state monopoly.
>
> The Petrograd Soviet of Workers' and Soldiers' Deputies calls upon the workers and the peasants of Russia to support with all their energy and all their devotion the Proletarian Revolution. The Soviet expresses

---

48. Kameniev (Lev Kamenev; 1883–1936): Bolshevik revolutionary, one of the seven members of the first governing Politburo.

its conviction that the city workers, allies of the poor peasants, will assure complete revolutionary order, indispensable to the victory of Socialism. The Soviet is convinced that the proletariat of the countries of Western Europe will aid us in conducting the cause of Socialism to a real and lasting victory.

"You consider it won then?"

He lifted his shoulders. "There is much to do. Horribly much. It is just beginning. [. . .]

Lenin had appeared, welcomed with a mighty ovation, prophesying world-wide Social Revolution. . . . And Zinoviev,[49] crying, "This day we have paid our debt to the international proletariat, and struck a terrible blow at the war, a terrible body-blow at all the imperialists and particularly at Wilhelm the Executioner.[50] [. . .]

So we came into the great meeting-hall, pushing through the clamorous mob at the door. In the rows of seats, under the white chandeliers, packed immovably in the aisles and on the sides, perched on every window-sill, and even the edge of the platform, the representatives of the workers and soldiers of all Russia waited in anxious silence or wild exultation the ringing of the chairman's bell. There was no heat in the hall but the stifling heat of unwashed human bodies. A foul blue cloud of cigarette smoke rose from the mass and hung in the thick air. [. . .] It was 10.40 P. M. [. . .]

But suddenly a new sound made itself heard, deeper than the tumult of the crowd, persistent, disquieting—the dull shock of guns. People looked anxiously toward the clouded windows, and a sort of fever came over them. [. . .] Always the methodical muffled boom of cannon through the windows, and the delegates, screaming at each other. . . . So, with the crash of artillery, in the dark, with hatred, and fear, and reckless daring, new Russia was being born. [. . .]

When we came into the chill night, all the front of Smolny was one huge park of arriving and departing automobiles, above the sound of which could be heard the far-off slow beat of the cannon. A great motor-truck stood there, shaking to the roar of its engine. Men were tossing bundles into it, and others receiving them, with guns beside them.

"Where are you going?" I shouted.

"Down-town—all over—everywhere!" answered a little workman, grinning, with a large exultant gesture.

We showed our passes. "Come along!" they invited. "But there'll probably be shooting—" [. . .]

---

49. Grigory Zinoviev (1883–1936): Bolshevik revolutionary and later Soviet official.
50. Wilhelm the Executioner: mocking appellation for Kaiser Wilhelm (William) II, the last German emperor and king of Prussia, who would abdicate toward the end of World War I, on November 9, 2018.

They return to the Winter Palace, now in Soviet hands.

By this time, in the light that streamed out of all the Winter Palace windows, I could see that the first two or three hundred men were Red Guards, with only a few scattered soldiers. [. . .] On both sides of the main gateway the doors stood wide open, light streamed out, and from the huge pile came not the slightest sound.

Carried along by the eager wave of men we were swept into the right hand entrance, opening into a great bare vaulted room, the cellar of the East wing, from which issued a maze of corridors and stair-cases. A number of huge packing cases stood about, and upon these the Red Guards and soldiers fell furiously, battering them open with the butts of their rifles, and pulling out carpets, curtains, linen, porcelain plates, glassware. . . . [. . .] The looting was just beginning when somebody cried, "Comrades! Don't touch anything! Don't take anything! This is the property of the People!" [. . .] Through corridors and up stair-cases the cry could be heard growing fainter and fainter in the distance, "Revolutionary discipline! Property of the People. . . ." [. . .]

In the meanwhile unrebuked we walked into the Palace. [. . .] The paintings, statues, tapestries and rugs of the great state apartments were unharmed; in the offices, however, every desk and cabinet had been ransacked, the papers scattered over the floor, and in the living rooms beds had been stripped of their coverings and ward-robes wrenched open. The most highly prized loot was clothing, which the working people needed. In a room where furniture was stored we came upon two soldiers ripping the elaborate Spanish leather upholstery from chairs. They explained it was to make boots with [. . .]

November 8

We came out into the cold, nervous night, murmurous with obscure armies on the move, electric with patrols. [. . .] It was now after three in the morning. On the Nevsky all the street-lights were again shining, the cannon gone, and the only signs of war were Red Guards and soldiers squatting around fires. The city was quiet—probably never so quiet in its history; on that night not a single hold-up occurred, not a single robbery. [. . .]

They return to Smolny.

The windows of Smolny were still ablaze, motors came and went, and around the still-leaping fires the sentries huddled close, eagerly asking everybody the latest news. The corridors were full of hurrying men, hollow-eyed and dirty. In some of the committee-rooms people lay sleeping on the floor, their guns beside them. In spite of the seceding delegates, the hall of meetings was crowded with people, roaring like the sea. [. . .]

Trotzky was gesturing for silence. "These 'comrades' who are now caught plotting the crushing of the Soviets with the adventurer Kerensky—is there any reason to handle them with gloves? After July 16th and 18th they didn't use much ceremony with us!" With a triumphant ring in his voice he cried, "Now that the *oborontsi*[51] and the faint-hearted have gone, and the whole task of defending and saving the Revolution rests on our shoulders, it is particularly necessary to work—work—work! We have decided to die rather than give up!" [. . .]

So. Lenin and the Petrograd workers had decided on insurrection, the Petrograd Soviet had overthrown the Provisional Government, and thrust the *coup d'état* upon the Congress of Soviets.[52] Now there was all great Russia to win—and then the world! Would Russia follow and rise? And the world—what of it? Would the peoples answer and rise, a red world-tide?

7. Emma Goldman, *Living My Life* (1931)

Emma Goldman expected to like what she would see when she arrived in Soviet Russia in January 1920. But she soon was made aware of many problems. Paramount among these was the brutal repression by the Cheka, the secret police, of persons critical of the government—persons who had committed no crime against the state to which they remained loyal. Heroes of the revolution were hounded and broken. Prisoners were abused. Workers were exploited and pushed beyond endurance. The inspirational novelist Maxim Gorky now believed that the people were incompetent and could be governed only by coercion. The brilliant Lenin, craftsman of the Revolution, now thought that free speech was a bourgeois phantom. Horribly, the Kronstadt sailors, courageous defenders of the Revolution, were massacred when they stood in solidarity with striking workers. The dream is shattered.

LIVING MY LIFE

Emma Goldman and her longtime partner Sasha (Alexander) Berkman arrive in Russia in January 1920, along with 248 other aliens deported from the United States.

---

51. *oborontsi*: the "defenders," identifying the moderate socialists in favor of continuing the war effort.

52. Congress of Soviets: the All-Russian Congress of Soviets, consisting of representatives from more than three hundred local governing councils from all over Russia, which ratified the October Revolution and would be summoned to meet in January 1918; but effectively, the Bolsheviks, a small minority, held control.

Soviet Russia! Sacred ground, magic people! You have come to symbolize humanity's hope, you alone are destined to redeem mankind. I have come to serve you, beloved *matushka* [mother]. Take me to your bosom, let me pour myself into you, mingle my blood with yours, find my place in your heroic struggle, and give to the uttermost to your needs! . . .

Goldman at first hears enthusiastic reports of life in Soviet Russia—and soon some dissenting voices.

Soon, however, other voices rose from the depths, harsh, accusing voices that greatly disturbed me. I had been asked to attend a conference of anarchists in Petrograd, and I was amazed to find that my comrades were compelled to gather in secret in an obscure hiding-place. . . . Why should people with such a record, I wondered, be driven under cover.

Presently came the answer—from workers in the Putilov Ironworks, from factories and mills, from the Kronstadt sailors, from Red Army men, and from an old comrade who had escaped while under sentence of death. The very brawn of the revolutionary struggle was crying out in anguish and bitterness against the people they had helped place in power. They spoke of the Bolshevik betrayal of the Revolution, of the slavery forced upon the toilers, the emasculation of the soviets, the suppression of speech and thought, the filling of prisons with recalcitrant peasants, workers, soldiers, sailors, and rebels of every kind. They told of the raid with machine-guns upon the Moscow headquarters of the anarchists by the order of Trotsky; of the Cheka and the wholesale executions without hearing or trial. These charges and denunciations beat upon me like hammers and left me stunned. . . .

Goldman talks with her old friend John Reed, who had celebrated the Bolshevik October Revolution of 1917 (see in this chapter, Text 6), and now defends the use of harsh measures in the service of the Revolution.

John Reed had burst into my room like a sudden ray of light, the old buoyant, adventurous Jack that I used to know in the States. He was about to return to America, by way of Latvia. Rather a hazardous journey, he said, but he would take even greater risks to bring the inspiring message of Soviet Russia to his native land. "Wonderful, marvellous, isn't it, E.G.?" he exclaimed. "Your dream of years now realized in Russia, your dream scorned and persecuted in my country, but made real by the magic wand of Lenin and his band of despised Bolsheviks. Did you ever expect such a thing to happen in the country ruled by the tsars for centuries?"

"Not by Lenin and his comrades, dear Jack," I corrected, "though I do not deny their great part. But by the whole Russian people, preceded by a glorious revolutionary past. No other land of our days has been so literally nurtured by the blood of her martyrs, a long procession of pioneers who went to their death that new life may spring from their graves." . . .

"Look at your old pioneers . . .," he cried heatedly; "see where they are now! . . . I don't give a damn for their past. I am concerned only in what the treacherous gang has been doing during the past three years. To the wall with them! I say. I have learned one mighty expressive Russian word, '*razstrellyat*'!" (execute by shooting).

"Stop, Jack! Stop!" I cried; "this word is terrible enough in the mouth of a Russian. In your hard American accent it freezes my blood. Since when do revolutionists see in wholesale execution the only solution of their difficulties? In time of active counter-revolution it is no doubt inevitable to give shot for shot. But cold-bloodedly and merely for opinion's sake, do you justify standing people against the wall under such circumstances?" . . . He was surprised to see me so worked up over the death of a few plotters. As if that mattered in the scales of the world revolution! . . .

She also talks with the great novelist Maxim Gorky, who lionizes Lenin, and will not fault his leadership.

I had looked forward with much anticipation to the chance of talking to Gorki [Gorky], yet now I did not know how to begin. . . . At last . . . I proceeded to tell him of my faith in the Bolsheviki [Bolsheviks] from the very beginning of the October Revolution, and my defence of them and of Soviet Russia at a time when even very few radicals dared speak up for Lenin and his comrades. . . .

He stopped me with a gesture of his hand. "If that is so, and I do not doubt you, how can you be so perplexed at the imperfections you find in Soviet Russia? As an old revolutionist you must know that revolution is a grim and relentless task. Our poor Russia, backward and crude, her masses, steeped in centuries of ignorance and darkness, brutal and lazy beyond any other people in the world!" I gasped at his sweeping indictment of the entire Russian people. . . . Somewhat irritated, he replied that the . . . Revolution had dispelled the bubble of the goodness and naïveté of the peasantry. It had proved them shrewd, avaricious, and lazy, even savage in their joy of causing pain. . . . They have no cultural traditions, no social values, no respect for human rights and life. They cannot be moved by anything except coercion and force. . . .

I protested vehemently against these charges. I argued that . . . it was the ignorant and crude Russian people that had risen first in revolt. They had shaken Russia by three successive revolutions within twelve years, and it was they and their will that gave life to "October."

"Very eloquent," Gorki retorted, "but not quite accurate." He admitted the share of the peasantry in the October uprising, though even that, he thought, was not conscious social feeling, but mere wrath accumulated for decades. If not checked by Lenin's guiding hand, it would have surely destroyed rather than advanced the great revolutionary aims. Lenin, Gorki insisted, was the real parent of the October Revolution. It had been conceived by his genius, nurtured by his vision and faith, and brought to maturity by his far-sighted and patient care. . . . Since the birth of October it was again Lenin who was steering its development and growth.

"Miracle-worker, your Lenin," I cried; "but I seem to remember that you have not always thought him a god or his comrades infallible." I reminded Gorki of his scathing arraignment of the Bolsheviki . . . in the days of Kerensky. What had caused his change? He had attacked the Bolsheviki, Gorki acknowledged, but the march of events had convinced him that a revolution in a primitive country with a barbarous people could not survive without resort to drastic methods of self-defence. . . .

Goldman also has an interview with Lenin himself. She and Berkman are brought into his presence.

Two slanting eyes were fixed upon us with piercing penetration. Their owner sat behind a huge desk, everything on it arranged with the strictest precision, the rest of the room giving the impression of the same exactitude. A board with numerous telephone switches and a map of the world covered the entire wall behind the man; glass cases filled with heavy tomes lined the sides. . . .

The background seemed most fitting for one reputed for his rigid habits of life and matter-of-factness. Lenin, the man most idolized in the world and equally hated and feared, would have been out of place in surroundings of less severe simplicity. . . .

His sharp scrutiny having bared us to the bone, we were treated to a volley of questions, one following the other, like arrows from his flint-like brain. America, her political and economic conditions—what were the chances of revolution there in the near future? . . . He had just finished reading our speeches in court. "Great stuff! Clear-cut analysis of the capitalist system, splendid propaganda!" Too bad we could not have remained in the United States, no matter at what price. We were most welcome in Soviet Russia, of course, but such fighters were badly needed in America to help in the approaching revolution, "as many of your best comrades had been in ours." . . . Well, you're here. Have you any thought of the work you want to do? . . .

Berkman responds with a question: Why are there anarchists in Soviet prisons?

"Anarchists?" [Lenin] interrupted; "nonsense! Who told you such yarns, and how could you believe them? We do have bandits in prison, . . . but no . . . anarchists." . . . Free speech is a *bourgeois* prejudice, a soothing plaster for social ills. In the Workers' Republic economic well-being talks louder than speech, and its freedom is far more secure. The proletarian dictatorship is steering that course. . . . In the present state of Russia all prattle of freedom is merely food of the reaction trying to down Russia. Only bandits are guilty of that, and they must be kept under lock and key. . . ."

We had fought in America for the political rights even of our opponents, we told him, the denial of them to our comrades was therefore no trifle to us. I, for one, felt, I informed him, that I could not co-operate with a régime that persecuted anarchists or others for the sake of mere opinion. . . . His reply was that my attitude was *bourgeois* sentimentality. The proletarian dictatorship was engaged in a life-and-death struggle, and small consideration could not be permitted to weigh in the scale. Russia was making giant strides at home and abroad. It was igniting world revolution, and here I was lamenting over a little blood-letting. . . .

Traveling through Ukraine, Goldman and Berkman visit the local prison and detention camp.

The camp . . . occupied an old building without any provisions for sanitation and not half large enough for its thousand inmates. The dormitories, overcrowded and smelly, were barren except for wide boards that served as beds and had to be shared by two and sometimes three persons. During the day they had to squat on the floor and even eat their meals in that position. For an hour they were taken out in sections to the yard, the rest of the time being kept indoors without anything to occupy their time and minds. Their offences ranged from sabotage to speculation, and they were all counter-revolutionists, as our stern guide impressed upon us. . . .

The occupants of locked cells were dangerous criminals, she assured us, one, a woman, was a member of the counter-revolutionary bandit army of Makhno, and the man occupying the adjoining cell had been caught in a counter-revolutionary plot. Both deserved severest treatment and the supreme penalty. . . .

The Makhnovka, an old peasant woman, was crouching in the corner of her cell like a frightened hare. She blinked stupidly when the door was opened. Suddenly she threw herself headlong before me and shrieked: "*Barinya* [madam], let me out, I know nothing, I know nothing!" . . . In the corridor I told our guide that it seemed absurd to consider that stupefied old creature dangerous to the Revolution. She was half-crazed with the solitary and the fear of execution, and if kept locked up much longer, she would surely go stark mad. "It is mere sentimentality on your part," the guide upbraided me; "we live in a revolutionary period, with enemies on all sides."

The man in the next cell was sitting on a low stool, his head bent. With a sudden jerk he turned his eyes on the door, a terrorized and hunted look in their anticipation. Just as quickly he pulled himself together, his body stiffened, and his look fastened on our guide with concentrated contempt. Two words, no more audible than a sigh, yet petrifying in their effect, broke the silence. "Scoundrels! Murderers!" A horrible feeling overcame me that he believed us to be officials. I took a step towards him to explain, but he turned his back upon us and was standing erect and forbidding beyond my reach. With heavy heart I followed my companions out of the corridor. . . .

Back in Petrograd, a strike is brewing. The workers' demands won the support of the Kronstadt sailors, loyal communists who had come to the aid of the revolutionaries of 1905 and 1917. Those they had helped bring to power would destroy them during the terrible Kronstadt rebellion (March 1–17, 1921).

Into this tense and desperate situation there was presently introduced a new factor that held out the hope of some settlement. It was the sailors of Kronstadt. True to their revolutionary traditions and solidarity with the workers, so loyally demonstrated in the revolution of 1905, and later in the March and October upheavals of 1917, they now again took up the cudgels in behalf of the harassed proletarians in Petrograd. . . . They further demanded freedom of assembly for labour unions and peasant organizations and the release of all labour and political prisoners from Soviet prisons and concentration camps. . . .

The regime's response . . .

An order signed by Lenin and Trotsky spread like wildfire through Petrograd. It declared that Kronstadt had mutinied against the Soviet Government, and denounced the sailors as "tools of former tsarist generals who together with Socialist-Revolutionist traitors staged a counter-revolutionary conspiracy against the proletarian Republic." . . .

Trotsky assembles a huge force of seasoned strategists and trusted troops to suppress the Kronstadt rebellion.

Kronstadt was forsaken by Petrograd and cut off from the rest of Russia. It stood alone. . . . But, forced to defend itself against unprovoked military attack, it fought like a lion. During ten harrowing days and nights the sailors and workers of the besieged city held out against a continuous artillery fire from three sides and bombs hurled from aeroplanes upon the non-combatant community. . . .

The cannonade of Kronstadt continued without let-up for ten days and nights and then came to a sudden stop on the morning of March 17. The stillness that fell over Petrograd was more fearful than the ceaseless firing of the night before. It held everyone in agonized suspense. . . . In the late afternoon the tension gave way to mute horror. Kronstadt had been subdued—tens of thousands slain—the city drenched in blood. . . . The heroic sailors and soldiers had defended their position to the last breath. Those not fortunate enough to die fighting had fallen into the hands of the enemy to be executed or sent to slow torture in the frozen regions of northernmost Russia. . . .

Their fellow anarchists and other heterodox groups, people who had enthusiastically supported the October Revolution, were being arrested, deported, and executed. Goldman and Berkman must leave. Goldman reflects on what her hopes had been on her arrival, and what she now knows.

Belo-Ostrov,[53] January 19, 1920. O radiant dream, O burning faith! *O Matushka Rossiya* [Mother Russia], reborn in the travail of the Revolution, purged by it from hate and strife, liberated for true humanity and embracing all. I will dedicate myself to you, O Russia!

In the train, December 1, 1921! My dreams crushed, my faith broken, my heart like a stone. *Matushka Rossiya* [Mother Russia] bleeding from a thousand wounds, her soil strewn with the dead.

8. Victor Serge, *Open Letter to André Gide* (1936)

At the International Congress of Writers for the Defense of Culture held in Paris in 1935, intellectuals of all stripes protested Victor Serge's imprisonment and internal exile in the Soviet Union as part of a broader statement about the importance of free speech. Among them was the French novelist and public intellectual André Gide, a figure of monumental stature. In May 1936, in advance of Gide's planned journey to the Soviet Union, Serge (who had been released and was now in Brussels) wrote the public letter that follows, intending its further circulation. In it, he informs the Frenchman in impassioned tones of the Soviet regime's silencing of authors, scientists, literary critics, journalists, and scholars, including those, like himself, who had been ardent supporters of the Bolshevik Revolution in 1917. Three times, he urges Gide to attend to his "bitter letter" and look critically at what he sees—to keep his eyes "wide open"—concluding with this plea: "Grant me that we not serve [the revolution] by being silent about its illness or by covering our eyes in order not to see it." How can we block the surging threat of fascism, Serge urgently asks, "with so many concentration camps behind us?"[54]

OPEN LETTER TO ANDRÉ GIDE

Brussels, May 1936

Dear André Gide:
You once presided in Paris at an international writer's congress gathered for the defense of culture, where the question of the freedom of thought in the USSR was brought up only insofar as it concerns me and, it seems, against the will of the majority of those at the congress. I have learned that at that time you

---

53. Belo-Ostrov: Beloostrov, Russia, the first railway station on the Russian side of the Russian-Finnish border.
54. Minor emendations in punctuation, grammar, and the transcription of Russian names have been made to this text. The ellipses shown are Serge's.

attempted several steps to save some of my manuscripts that were being held by the censor in Moscow. They are still there, along with all my personal papers, all my keepsakes, all the works I'd begun, all that one gathers of precious papers during a lifetime . . . I thank you for all that you have done for me, as well as the impartiality you have shown towards the friends who defend me and who have been refused the right to speak. If my case interests you, you will find some information about it in a letter to Magdeleine Paz,[55] a copy of which I've attached. In any event, I am at your disposal.

In the great drama in which we participate it is in reality very little a question of you and me. You have come to assume a place among revolutionaries, André Gide, so allow a communist to speak to you frankly of that which is most important to us. I remember the pages of your *Journal*[56] in which you noted in 1933 your adherence to communism because it assures the free development of the personality. (I am reconstituting your thought from memory; not a single book remains to me and I don't have the leisure to look for your text.) I read these pages in Moscow with contradictory feelings. At first I was happy to see you come to socialism, you whose thought I'd followed—from afar—since my days of youthful enthusiasm. And then I was saddened by the contrast between your affirmations and the reality in which I was plunged. I read the pages of your *Journal* at a period when no one around me would have risked keeping a journal, convinced as we were that the political police would without fail have come looking for it some night. Reading you I felt a sentiment very much like that of combatants who, in the trenches, received the gazettes from the rear and found lyrical prose about the war, etc. Is it possible, I asked myself, that you know nothing of our struggle, nothing of the tragedy of a revolution ravaged from within by reaction? It was no longer possible for a worker to express any kind of an opinion, even in a whisper, without being immediately chased from the party, from the union, from the workshop, imprisoned, deported . . . Three years have passed since then, and what years they've been! Marked by the hecatomb that followed the end of Kirov,[57] by the deportation en masse of a part of the population of Leningrad [St. Petersburg], by the imprisonment of several thousand communists of the first hour, by the overpopulating of the concentration camps that are without any doubt the most vast in the whole world.

If I correctly understand you, dear André Gide, your courage has always been that of living with your eyes wide open. You cannot close them today on

---

55. Magdeleine Paz (1889–1973): French journalist and left-wing intellectual, instrumental in obtaining Serge's release from prison, 1936.

56. *Journal*: Serge refers to the journal Gide kept throughout his life, eventually totaling more than one thousand pages.

57. Sergei Kirov (1886–1934): Kirov's assassination in 1934 signaled the launching of Stalin's Great Purge.

this reality, or you would no longer have the moral right to say a word to workers for whom socialism is much more than a concept; it's the work of their flesh and their spirit, the very meaning of their lives.

What is the condition of thought? A dry doctrine, emptied of all its content, strictly imposed in all domains, and reduced in all it prints, without any exceptions, to the word for word repetition or to the flattest commentaries on the statements of one man alone. History completely revised every year, encyclopedias rewritten, libraries purged in order to cross out the name of Trotsky, to suppress or soil the names of other companions of Lenin, putting science at the service of the agitation of the moment, making it yesterday denounce the League of Nations[58] as a low instrument of Anglo-French imperialism, and today making it revere in the League of Nations an instrument of peace and human progress . . .

What is the condition of the writer, i.e., that of the man whose profession is speaking for all those others who have no voice? We have seen Gorky[59] revise his memories of Lenin[60] in order to have Lenin say in the latest edition the exact opposite of what he said on certain pages of the first. A literature guided in its least manifestations. A literary mandarinate[61] admirably organized, royally remunerated, *bien-pensant* [right-thinking], as could be expected. As for the others . . . What has become of the brother in spirit of our great Alexander Blok,[62] [or] the author of a *History of Contemporary Russian Thought* [History of Russian Social Thought, 1907], Ivanov-Razumnik?[63] He was in prison at the same time as me in '33. Is it true, as has been said, that the old symbolist poet Vladimir Piast[64] ended up committing suicide in deportation? His crime was great: he tended towards mysticism. But there are materialists of various nuances: what has become of Herman Sandormirsky,[65] author of highly thought of works on Italian fascism, condemned to death under the ancien régime?[66] In what penitentiary, in what deportation is he passing his time, and why? Where is

---

58. League of Nations: worldwide organization created in 1920, in the aftermath of World War I, to maintain world peace. In 1945, replaced by the United Nations.

59. See p. 410 note 10.

60. Lenin (Vladimir Ilyich Ulyanov; 1870–1924): principal leader of Bolshevik revolution and first premier of the Soviet Union (constituted 1923).

61. mandarinate: the rule by bureaucrats, implicitly of those who have become conscienceless representatives of authority.

62. Alexander Blok (1880–1921): Russian writer, literary critic, and publicist.

63. Razumnik Ivanov-Razumnik (1878–1946): Russian writer, literary critic, and philosopher.

64. Vladimir Piast (1886–1940): Russian writer and Symbolist poet associated with Alexander Blok.

65. Herman Sandormirsky: anarchist and historian of Italian fascism, mentioned by Serge in his *Memoirs of a Revolutionary*, trans. Peter Sedgwick (New York: New York Review of Books, 2012), 319.

66. ancien régime: Serge is eliding the autocratic "Old Regime" of pre-revolutionary France with the repressive Soviet state.

Novomiski,[67] he, too, a prisoner under the ancien régime, initiator of the first Soviet encyclopedia, recently condemned to ten years of concentration camp. Why? These two are veteran anarchists. Allow me to name as well communists, fighters of October[68] and intellectuals of the first rank (it pains me to name them): Anychev,[69] to whom we owe the only *Essay on the History of the Civil War* that we have in Russian; Gorbachev, Lelevich, Vardin,[70] all three of them critics and historians of literature. These last four were suspected of sympathizing with the Zinoviev tendency:[71] concentration camp. The following are Trotskyists, the worst treated because they are the firmest, imprisoned or deported for eight years: Fedor Dingelstedt,[72] professor of agronomy in Leningrad, Grigory Yakovin,[73] professor of sociology, our young and great Solntsev[74] died in January as a result of a hunger strike. I limit myself to naming writers, André Gide, when it would whole pages would be covered with the names of heroes. It humiliates me to make this concession to the caste feelings of men of letters, so forgive me. What has become of the exemplary Bazarov,[75] pioneer of Russian socialism, who disappeared five years ago? What has become of the founder of the Marx-Engels Institute, Ryazanov?[76] Dead or alive after his long struggles in the prison of Verkhneouralsk [Verkhne-Uralsk], the historian Soukhanov[77] who gave us a monumental history of the revolution of February 1917? What price is he paying for the sacrifice of his conscience that was demanded of him and that he consented to?

---

67. Novomiski: not identified; perhaps Novominsky, b. Moissaye Joseph Olgin (1878–1939): Russian writer, journalist, translator, early supporter of socialist revolution in Russia, later emigrated to the United States.

68. fighters of October: the Bolsheviks, who led the October, or Bolshevik, Revolution of November 1917.

69. Anychev: not identified.

70. Gorbachev, etc.: Russian writers Grigory Lelevich (1901–1945) and Ilya Vardin (1890–1941); Gorbachev, not to be confused with the later Russian politician and last leader of the Soviet Union Mikhail Gorbachev (b. 1931), is not identified.

71. Zinoviev tendency: alludes to a faction within the communist leadership led by Grigory Zinoviev (1883–1936), Bolshevik revolutionary and Soviet official, and in 1936, chief defendant in the Trial of the Sixteen during the Great Purge.

72. Fedor Dingelstadt: Bolshevik revolutionary who had written on the agrarian question in India; ardent member of the Left Opposition, disappeared without record.

73. Grigory Yakovin: member of Left Opposition, in prison in 1929.

74. Eleazar Solntsev (1901?–1935): member of Left Opposition, imprisoned 1928–1933, then exiled, and sentenced again in 1935, at which point he died of self-starvation.

75. Vladimir Bazarov (Vladimir Alexandrovich Rudnev; 1874–1939): Russian revolutionary, journalist, philosopher, and economist, involved in the economic planning of the Soviet Union.

76. David Ryazanov (David Borisovich Goldendach; 1870–1938): anti-Tsarist revolutionary, then Bolshevik, made director of Marx-Engels Institute in 1920.

77. Nikolai Sukhanov (Nikolai Himmer; 1882–1940): Social Revolutionary, participant in 1905 revolution; later a founding member of the Petrograd Soviet in revolution of February 1917, about which he wrote a seven-volume history; exiled for ten years following a show trial in 1931 and executed in 1940.

What is the human condition? You see full well that we must stop. No internal threat justifies this senseless repression, if not that which is invented in the shadows for the needs of the security forces. It is striking that the gratuitous functioning of a formidable police apparatus, causing a multitude of victims, establishes veritable schools of counter-revolution in Soviet penitentiaries, where the citizens of yesterday are tempered into enemies of tomorrow. Only one explanation is possible, and that's that, frightened by the consequences of its own policies, and used to the exercise of absolute power over a mass without rights, the ruling bureaucracy has lost control of itself. Here we must talk about the problem of real wages, which have generally fallen to an extremely low level; about labor legislation, into which constraint scandalously intervenes; about the system of internal passports, which deprives the populace of the right to move about; about special laws instituting the death penalty against workers and even against children; about the system of hostages, which pitilessly strikes an entire family for the fault of one alone; about the law that punishes with death any worker who attempts to cross the border of the USSR without a passport (keep in mind that it is impossible for him to obtain a passport for overseas travel), and orders the deportation of those close to him.

We are confronting fascism, but how can we block its path with so many concentration camps behind us? Duty is no longer simple, as you see, and it is up to no one to simplify it. No new conformism, no sacred lie can prevent the oozing of this wound. The line of defense of the revolution is no longer only on the Vistula and the Manchurian border.[78] The obligation to defend the revolution from within against the reactionary regime that has installed itself in the proletarian city, little by little frustrating the working class of the greatest part of its conquests, is no less imperious. In one way alone does the USSR remain the greatest hope of the men of our time; it's that the Soviet proletariat has not said its last word.

Dear André Gide, it's possible that this bitter letter will teach you something. I hope so. I beg of you not to close your eyes. Look behind the new Marshals,[79] the ingenious and costly propaganda, the parades, the congresses—how old world[80] all this is—and see the reality of a revolution wounded in its living work and calling on all of us for help. Grant me that we not serve it by being silent about its illness or by covering our eyes in order not to see it.

No one better than you represents that great Western intelligentsia which, even if it has done much for civilization, has much to ask forgiveness of the

---

78. Vistula and Manchurian border: Serge alludes to the military front in the Russian Civil War, 1918–1920.
79. Marshals: Serge refers to the Soviet commissars.
80. old world: Serge again is aligning the Soviet dictatorship with older European autocracies, particularly the tsarist regime.

proletariat for not having understood what the war of 1914[81] was; for having misunderstood the Russian revolution at its beginnings, in its grandeur; for not having sufficiently defended the freedoms of the workers. Now that it turns with sympathy towards the socialist revolution incarnated in the USSR, it must choose in its heart of hearts between blindness and lucidity. Allow me to say that only with lucidity can one serve the working class and the USSR. Allow me to ask you, in the name of those there who are full of courage, to have the courage of that lucidity.

Your fraternally devoted,
Victor Serge

9. Arthur Koestler, *Darkness at Noon* (1940)

In the middle of the night, the secret police come to Rubashov's apartment, arrest him, and put him in solitary confinement. Rubashov knows from the start he will be shot. All that remains is the process. Rubashov's old acquaintance Ivanov, who had gently urged the prisoner to confess, comes to Rubashov's cell with a bottle of brandy to share, and they spend the night in philosophical conversation. At its end, Ivanov again urges Rubashov to sign a statement of capitulation (the term used for a confession that submits to the judgment of the regime). "Now go and get some sleep, you old warhorse . . . you're already halfway convinced that you'll sign." Alone in his cell, Rubashov composes his capitulation. In a third interrogation, Gletkin (for Ivanov has been arrested and appears no more) informs Rubashov that it is his duty to confess, for the sake of the Communist Party. Rubashov signs the statement. As he awaits execution, he reflects on the "grammatical fiction" that is the flaw in communist theory: it erases the individual, the conscience, the pronoun "I." Rubashov is shot.[82]

DARKNESS AT NOON

The First Interrogation

Rubashov has been arrested and put in a cell in isolation. He knows he will not leave alive.

---

81. war of 1914: World War I (1914–1918).

82. The original text is altered by rendering Rubashov's thinking to himself with quotation marks rather than italics, to avoid confusion with the italicized transitional notes. Bracketed ellipses in the text indicate the editor's deletions; unbracketed ellipses are the author's.

Rubashov knew he was in an isolation cell and that he'd remain there until they shot him. . . .

"So they're going to shoot you," he thought. He blinked and stared at his foot [. . .]. He felt warm, snug, and secure—and very tired; he didn't mind the idea of dozing off into death, as long as they let him lie under the warm blanket. [. . .] "So they're going to snuff us out," he said to himself quietly, and lit a new cigarette, although he only had three left. [. . .] He felt a warm wave of sympathy with his body, which he otherwise did not love, and his impending destruction filled him with a compassionate lust. "The old guard is dead," he said out loud, "we are the last ones." [. . .]

The Second Interrogation

In his first interrogation, Ivanov had urged Rubashov to confess, and he now comes to Rubashov's cell in person to conduct a second one. He presses Rubashov to capitulate by confessing to the crimes with which Rubashov is charged. Ivanov speaks:

"I realize you're convinced you won't capitulate. But just answer this one question: if you could persuade yourself of the logical correctness and objective expedience of capitulating, would you do it?"

Rubashov didn't answer right away. He had a hollow sensation that the conversation had taken a turn he should not have allowed. [. . .]

"Go," he said to Ivanov. "There's no use. Go . . ." Only now did he realize that he was no longer leaning against the wall but had for some time been pacing up and down the cell while Ivanov stayed sitting on the cot. [. . .]

Ivanov and Rubashov engage in an extended philosophical discussion, touching on the rightness of the communist cause.

"I'm against mixing ideologies," Ivanov continued. "There are only two concepts of human ethics and they are polar opposites. One is Christian-humanitarian and declares that the individual is sacred and maintains that no calculations may be done with blood. The other is based on the principle that the collective goal justifies the means, and this not only allows but requires that the individual be subordinated to the collective in every way, including as a guinea pig or sacrificial lamb. [. . .] The first time anyone in a position of power and responsibility is faced with a decision, he immediately realizes he must make a choice, and the dreadful thing is that he is impelled to choose the second alternative. [. . .]

"Until now all revolutions were made by moralizing dilettantes; they were always well-intentioned, and were invariably ruined by their dilettantism. We are the first to be consistent."

"So consistent," said Rubashov, "that in the interest of just distribution of land we purposely let some five million large and middle landowners die of starvation. So consistent that in order to free people from the shackles of capitalist wage labor, we sent some ten million people to forced labor in the Arctic and the taiga,[83] in conditions akin to those of the ancient galley slaves. So consistent that in the name of removing differences of opinion we recognize only one argument: death, whether it is a question of submarine tonnage or fertilizer or which party line should be pursued in [Indochina]. Our engineers labor under the constant fear that one mistaken calculation could send them to prison or to the gallows; our administrative officials mercilessly destroy their subordinates because they know they must account for their actions and otherwise will be destroyed themselves; our writers carry out their debates on stylistic matters through denunciations to the secret police, because the Expressionists consider the naturalist style counterrevolutionary and vice versa. [. . .] The living conditions of the masses are worse than they were before the revolution; the working conditions are harsher, the discipline less humane, the drudgery of piecework worse than in colonial countries with indigenous coolies. . . . Our newspapers and schools breed chauvinism, militarism, dogmatism, conformism, and empty-headedness. The power and arbitrariness of the regime is unchecked and unmatched in history, with freedom of the press, freedom of opinion, freedom of movement so utterly stamped out as though there had never been a Declaration of the Rights of Man.[84] We have constructed the largest police state in history, the most gigantic stool-pigeon apparatus, the most sophisticated scientific system of physical and psychological torture." [. . .]

After further discussion, as daylight comes, Ivanov reaches the point.

"Don't be a fool, Rubashov. What I've been arguing is nothing new to you—it's pretty basic wisdom. Your nerves were shot, but now it's over. [. . .] Now go and get some sleep, you old warhorse; tomorrow your time is up, and both need our wits about us to compile the statement. Don't shrug your shoulders—you're already halfway convinced that you'll sign. It would be intellectual cowardice to refuse. And you wouldn't be the first to become a martyr out of intellectual cowardice." [. . .]

"I'll think about it," Rubashov said after a while.

When the door clanged shut behind Ivanov, he knew that with this sentence he had already half capitulated.

The Third Interrogation

Rubashov will confess; on the wall of his cell he taps a message, using the prisoners' code, to #402, the old tsarist counter-revolutionary in the adjacent cell; then he drafts his statement of capitulation.

---

83. taiga: coniferous forest found in northern latitudes of both hemispheres.
84. *Declaration of the Rights of Man*: the statement of principles (1789) guiding the first stage of the French Revolution.

I AM CAPITULATING.

He was curious to see the effect.

For a while there was nothing. 402 was suddenly mute. After a full minute the ticking resumed:

BETTER TO DIE.

Rubashov smiled. He tapped:

TO EACH HIS OWN.

Actually he had expected an outburst of rage. Instead the tapping sounded muted, as though resigned:

I WAS INCLINED TO THINK YOU WERE AN EXCEPTION. DON'T YOU HAVE EVEN A SPARK OF HONOR?

Rubashov lay on his back, holding his pince-nez. He felt a sensation of peace, a serene contentment. He tapped:

WE HAVE DIFFERENT CONCEPTS OF HONOR.

402 answered quickly and precisely:

THERE IS ONLY ONE KIND OF HONOR: TO LIVE AND DIE FOR ONE'S IDEALS.

Rubashov wrote back just as quickly.

HONOR MEANS BEING USEFUL WITHOUT VANITY.

402 replied, this time louder and more vehemently:

HONOR IS DECENCY—NOT UTILITY. [. . .]

WE HAVE REPLACED DECENCY WITH LOGICAL CONSIS-TENCY, he tapped back.

Number 402 stopped answering.

***

Before the evening meal was doled out, Rubashov reread what he had written. He made a few corrections and copied the entire text in the form of a letter addressed to the state prosecutor of the republic. He underscored the closing paragraphs describing the alternatives for oppositionists, and ended the document with a final sentence:

"For the above-cited reasons the undersigned, N. S. Rubashov, former member of the Central Committee, former people's commissar, former commander of the Second Division of the Revolutionary Army and bearer of the Revolutionary Order for Bravery in the Face of the Enemy, has decided to sign his capitulation, to publicly acknowledge his mistakes, and to forswear his oppositional attitude."

The young interrogator Gletkin explains to Rubashov that the revolution demands conformity and that Rubashov must conform to serve the party.

"Once our revolution had attained its goal on one-sixth of the earth, we believed that the rest of the world would soon follow us. In its stead came a reactionary wave, which threatened to sweep us away as well. Within the party there were two currents of thought. One consisted of adventurers willing to risk everything to help the world revolution to victory outside the country. You belonged to that group. We recognized this direction as harmful and stamped it out. [. . .]

"The leader of the party," Gletkin's voice continued, "had a broader perspective and tougher tactics. He recognized that everything depended on holding the fort, withstanding and outlasting the period of global reaction. He recognized that it might take ten, twenty, or possibly fifty years until the world was ready for a new revolutionary wave. Until that time we would have to stand alone. Until then we had only one single duty: not to perish [. . .].

"The bastion must be held at any price, any sacrifice. [. . .] Whoever did not recognize this necessity had to be exterminated. [. . .]

"Your faction, Citizen Rubashov, has been beaten and destroyed. You followed the policy of an adventurer, a policy that would lead the country to ruin. Your motives do not interest us. What we are interested in is the restoration of party unity, which has been threatened by your actions. [. . .]

"Your task will be simple. . . . Your task is to make the opposition appear contemptible, to make clear to the masses that opposition is a crime and oppositionists are criminals. [. . .]

"I hope, Comrade Rubashov, that you have understood the task the party is assigning you."

The Grammatical Fiction

In his cell just prior to his execution, Rubashov identifies the fallacy of the communist vision: it extinguishes the individual, and with that, all morality. The grammatical fiction is the pronoun "I."

Infinity was a politically suspect quantity and the "I" a suspect quality. The party wanted nothing to do with the existence of such an entity. The definition of the individual was: a mass of one million divided by one million.

The party denied the free will of the individual—and at the same time it demanded that the individual bend his will to the party; it required absolute self-sacrifice. It denied the individual's ability to decide between two alternatives, and at the same time demanded that he always decide on the correct one. It denied his power to choose between good and evil, and at the same time it solemnly declaimed about guilt and betrayal. [. . .]

For forty years he had lived strictly by the rules of the party order. He had always followed its logical calculus, thought and acted everything through to the end. He had taken the caustic pencil of reason and burned the vestiges of the old, illogical moral laws out of his consciousness. [. . .]

Looking back, it seemed he had spent forty years in a mad frenzy—in a rampage of pure reason. . . .

Inside the cell was quiet: Rubashov could hear nothing but the grating of his steps on the tiles. [. . .] Soon it would be over. But when he asked himself, "What are you really dying for?" he could find no answer.

There was an error in the system, perhaps even in the proposition he had hitherto accepted as incontestable, in whose name he had sacrificed others and now he himself would be sacrificed—the proposition that the end justifies the means. It was this tenet that had killed the great fraternity of the revolution and had turned them all into mad, frenzied people. [. . .]

Perhaps herein lay the core of the malady. Perhaps it was not healthy to sail without ethical ballast. And perhaps reason alone was a faulty compass, which indicated such a long, tortuous, circuitous course that the destination got fully lost in the fog . . .

Perhaps now came the time of the great darkness.

Perhaps only later, much later, would a new movement arise, with new banners, a new spirit [. . .]. Perhaps members of the new party would wear monks' cowls and teach that only purity of means can justify the end. Perhaps they will disprove the theorem that a human being is the quotient of one million divided by one million and introduce a new arithmetic, based on multiplication: on the merger of millions of *I*s to form a new unity that is no longer an amorphous mass but maintains its I-character, the oceanic feeling reinforced a millionfold, within a universe that was boundless and yet closed within itself . . .

Rubashov is taken from his cell and shot.

10. Anna Akhmatova, *Requiem* (1935–1940)

Of the ten poems that make up Akhmatova's *Requiem*, poems 1–5, 8, and 10 appear here (poems 5 and 8 abridged), plus the Prologue and Epilogue. They do not constitute a continuous narrative, but reveal Akhmatova's state of mind as she witnesses the Stalinist terror, and expresses her grief for her son's fate and that of all the Russian people.[85]

---

85. Bracketed ellipses in the text indicate the editor's deletions; unbracketed ellipses are the author's.

REQUIEM

Prologue

The poet evokes the time of terror when "only the dead smiled," and "innocent Russia / Writhed under bloodstained boots."

In those years only the dead smiled,
Glad to be at rest:
And Leningrad[86] city swayed like
A needless appendix to its prisons.
It was then that the railway-yards
Were asylums of the mad;

Short were the locomotives'
Farewell songs.
Stars of death stood
Above us, and innocent Russia
Writhed under bloodstained boots, and
Under the tyres of Black Marias.[87]

1

The poet recalls the arrest of her son. She must now "creep to our wailing wall," and beg for his release or succor.

They took you away at daybreak. Half wak-
ing, as though at a wake, I followed.
In the dark chamber children were crying,
In the image-case, candlelight guttered.
At your lips, the chill of an ikon,
A deathly sweat at your brow.
I shall go creep to our wailing wall,
Crawl to the Kremlin towers.

2

She depicts herself in her grief: "[A] woman stretched alone," "[s]on in irons and husband clay."

Gently flows the gentle Don,[88]
Yellow moonlight leaps the sill,

Leaps the sill and stops astonished as it sees the shade

Of a woman lying ill,
Of a woman stretched alone.

Son in irons and husband clay.[89]
Pray. Pray.

---

86. Leningrad: previously Petrograd (1914–1924); before that, and since 1991, St. Petersburg.
87. Black Marias: police vehicles, typically black, for transporting prisoners.
88. Don: one of Europe's longest rivers, flowing north to south in Russia into the Black Sea.
89. husband clay: her husband Nikolai Gumilev had been shot by the Cheka (the secret police) in 1921.

3

It really couldn't be her—it must be "someone else"—"I could not have borne it."

No, it is not I, it is someone else who is suffering.
I could not have borne it. And this thing which has happened,
Let them cover it with black cloths,
And take away the lanterns . . .
                    Night.

4

She was never told, when an innocent child, that one day she would wait, "the three hundredth in a queue," weeping burning tears for her son.

Someone should have shown you—little jester,
Little teaser, blue-veined charm-
er, laughing-eyed, lionised, sylvan-princessly
Sinner—to what point you would come:
How, the three hundredth in a queue,
You'd stand at the prison gate
And with your hot tears
Burn through the New-Year ice.
How many lives are ending there! Yet it's
Mute, even the prison-poplar's
Tongue's in its cheek as it's swaying.

5

She has pleaded for his release for seventeen months and is now lost in confusion, feeling the "tightening vice"[90]—the likelihood of his execution.

For seventeen months I've called you   Simply the flowers of dust,
To come home, I've pleaded   Censers ringing, tracks from a far
—O my son, my terror!—groveled   Settlement to nowhere's ice.
At the hangman's feet,   And everywhere the glad
All is confused eternally—   Eye of a huge star's
So much, I can't say who's   Still tightening vice.
Man, who's beast any more, nor even
How long till execution.   [. . .]

---

90. vice: here and in the text; "vise" is the more usual American spelling of the British "vice."

8: To Death

She is ready for her own death—"I have turned off the lights and thrown the door wide open"—as her son faces the "final horror."

You will come in any case, so why not now?
Life is very hard: I'm waiting for you.
I have turned off the lights and thrown the door wide open
For you, so simple and so marvelous.
Take on any form you like.
Why not burst in like a poisoned shell,
Or steal in like a bandit with his knuckleduster,
Or like a typhus-germ?
Or like a fairy-tale of your own invention—
Stolen from you and loathsomely repeated,
Where I can see, behind you in the doorway,
The police-cap and the white-faced concierge?
I don't care how. The Yenisei[91] is swirling,
The Pole Star glittering. And eyes
I love are closing on the final horror.

[. . .]

10: Crucifixion[92]

When he was crucified, Jesus reproached God the Father for abandoning him and begged his Mother, the Virgin Mary, not to weep. Those watching were grief-stricken, but none more than his Mother, whose anguish was so terrible that no one "dared to look that way."

I

Angelic choirs the unequalled hour exalted,
And heaven disintegrated into flame.
Unto the Father: 'Why hast Thou forsaken . . . !'
But to the Mother: 'Do not weep for me . . .'

---

91. Yenisei: one of three rivers flowing north from Siberia to the Arctic Ocean.
92. The two parts of this poem allude to the crucifixion of Jesus Christ as told in the four Gospels of the New Testament, attended by his grieving mother Mary, his faithful follower Mary Magdalene, and his disciple John. See Matthew 27:1–54, Mark 15:1–40, Luke 23:1–48, and John 19:1–30.

II

Magdalina[93] beat her breast and wept, while
The loved disciple[94] seemed hammered out of stone.
But, for the Mother, where she stood in silence,—
No one as much as dared to look that way.

Epilogue

The poet prays "not only for myself," but also for all the other mothers, fathers, sons,
and daughters "who stood there / In bitter cold, or in the July heat, / Under that
red blind prison-wall." She would like to call to each one of them by name, but,
sardonically, "they have lost the lists." She will weave for them "a great shroud" out
of the words she heard them say. And if ever a bronze monument is built for her, the
poet and the mother, "may the melting snow drop like tears / From my motionless
bronze eyelids."

I

There I learned how faces fall apart,
How fear looks out from under the eyelids,
How deep are the hieroglyphics
Cut by suffering on people's cheeks.
There I learned how silver can inherit
The black, the ash-blond, overnight,
The smiles that faded from the poor in spirit,
Terror's dry coughing sound.
And I pray not only for myself,
But also for all those who stood there
In bitter cold, or in the July heat,
Under that red blind prison-wall.

II

Again the hands of the clock are nearing
The unforgettable hour. I see, hear, touch

All of you: the cripple they had to support
Painfully to the end of the line; the moribund;

And the girl who would shake her beautiful head and
Say: 'I come here as if it were home.'

I should like to call you all by name,
But they have lost the lists. . . .

---

93. Magdalina: Mary Magdalene, one of the women present at Christ's crucifixion.
94. loved disciple: John the Apostle.

I have woven for them a great shroud
Out of the poor words I overheard them speak.

I remember them always and everywhere,
And if they shut my tormented mouth,

Through which a hundred million of my people cry,
Let them remember me also. . . .

And if ever in this country they should want
To build me a monument

I consent to that honour,
But only on condition that they

Erect it not on the sea-shore where I was born:
My last links there were broken long ago,

Nor by the stump in the Royal Gardens,
Where an inconsolable young shade is seeking me,

But here, where I stood for three hundred hours
And where they never, never opened the doors for me.

Lest in blessed death I should forget
The grinding scream of the Black Marias,

The hideous clanging gate, the old
Woman wailing like a wounded beast.

And may the melting snow drop like tears
From my motionless bronze eyelids,

And the prison pigeons coo above me
And the ships sail slowly down the Neva.[95]

11. Winston Churchill, *We Shall Fight on the Beaches* (1940)

From May 13 to June 18, 1940, Winston Churchill delivered three rousing speeches. The first, delivered on May 13, rallied the public in his first speech to Parliament as British prime minister, promising victory while offering, as he memorably puts it, nothing but "blood, toil, tears, and sweat." The second,

---

95. Neva: the river that flows through St. Petersburg (here Leningrad, previously Petrograd).

delivered on June 4, given here nearly in its entirety, retells the disastrous stranding and brilliant evacuation of British troops at Dunkirk (France), on the English Channel coast, pledging unflagging defiance in the event of an invasion: "We shall fight on the beaches, we shall fight on the landing grounds, we shall fight in the fields and in the streets, we shall fight in the hills, we shall never surrender. . . ." The third, delivered on June 18, predicts Germany's imminent invasion of Britain and calls for stalwart resistance: "Let us therefore brace ourselves to our duty and so bear ourselves that if the British Commonwealth and Empire lasts for a thousand years, men will still say: 'This was their finest hour.'"

We Shall Fight on the Beaches

Churchill opens with a description of the developing military situation. The Germans have invaded Belgium and cut the French forces in two: "[T]he German eruption swept like a sharp scythe around the right and rear of the Armies of the north. . . ." The French remnant and the small British Expeditionary Force (BEF) take refuge at Dunkirk.

Eight or nine armoured divisions, each of about 400 armoured vehicles of different kinds, . . . cut off communications between us and the main French Armies. . . . Behind this armoured and mechanised onslaught came a number of German divisions in lorries, and behind them again there plodded comparatively slowly the dull brute mass of the ordinary German Army and German people, always so ready to be led to the trampling down in other lands of liberties and comforts which they have never known in their own.

I have said this armoured scythe-stroke almost reached Dunkirk—almost but not quite. . . . Thus it was that the port of Dunkirk was kept open. . . . [O]nly one choice remained. It seemed, indeed, forlorn. The Belgian, British and French Armies were almost surrounded. Their sole line of retreat was to a single port and to its neighbouring beaches. They were pressed on every side by heavy attacks and far outnumbered in the air.

When a week ago to-day I asked the House to fix this afternoon as the occasion for a statement, I feared it would be my hard lot to announce the greatest military disaster in our long history. I thought—and some good judges agreed with me—that perhaps 20,000 or 30,000 men might be re-embarked. But it certainly seemed that the whole of the French First Army and the whole of the British Expeditionary Force north of the Amiens-Abbeville gap, would be broken up in the open field or else would have to capitulate for lack of food and ammunition. These were the hard and heavy tidings for which I called upon the House and the nation to prepare themselves a week ago. The whole root and core and brain of the British Army, on which and around which we were to build, and are to build, the great British Armies in the later years of the war, seemed about to perish upon the field or to be led into an ignominious and starving captivity.

That was the prospect a week ago. But another blow which might well have proved final was yet to fall upon us.

The king of Belgium, without warning, has surrendered to the Germans, leaving the British eastern flank and passage to the sea exposed.

The surrender of the Belgian Army compelled the British at the shortest notice to cover a flank to the sea more than 30 miles in length. Otherwise all would have been cut off, and all would have shared the fate to which King Leopold had condemned the finest Army his country had ever formed. . . .

The enemy attacked on all sides with great strength and fierceness, and their main power, the power of their far more numerous air force, was thrown into the battle or else concentrated upon Dunkirk and the beaches. Pressing in upon the narrow exit, both from the east and from the west, the enemy began to fire with cannon upon the beaches by which alone the shipping could approach or depart. They sowed magnetic mines in the channels and seas; they sent repeated waves of hostile aircraft, sometimes more than 100 strong in one formation, to cast their bombs upon the single pier that remained, and upon the sand dunes upon which the troops had their eyes for shelter. Their U-boats, one of which was sunk, and their motor launches took their toll of the vast traffic which now began. For four or five days an intense struggle reigned. . . .

Meanwhile, the Royal Navy, with the willing help of countless merchant seamen, strained every nerve to embark the British and Allied troops. Two hundred and twenty light warships and 650 other vessels were engaged. They had to operate upon the difficult coast, often in adverse weather, under an almost ceaseless hail of bombs and an increasing concentration of artillery fire. Nor were the seas, as I have said, themselves free from mines and torpedoes. It was in conditions such as these that our men carried on, with little or no rest, for days and nights on end, making trip after trip across the dangerous waters, bringing with them always men whom they had rescued. The numbers they have brought back are the measure of their devotion and their courage. The hospital ships, which brought off many thousands of British and French wounded, being so plainly marked were a special target for Nazi bombs; but the men and women on board them never faltered in their duty.

Meanwhile, the Royal Air Force . . . struck at the German bombers, and at the fighters which in large numbers protected them. This struggle was protracted and fierce. Suddenly the scene has cleared, the crash and thunder has for the moment—but only for the moment—died away. A miracle of deliverance, achieved by valour, by perseverance, by perfect discipline, by faultless service, by resource, by skill, by unconquerable fidelity, is manifest to us all. The enemy was hurled back by the retreating British and French troops. . . . The Royal Air Force engaged the main strength of the German Air Force, and inflicted upon them losses of at least four to one; and the Navy, using nearly 1,000 ships of all kinds, carried over 335,000 men, French and British, out of the jaws of death and shame, to their native land and to the tasks which lie immediately ahead. We must be very careful not to assign to this deliverance the attributes of a victory. Wars are not won by evacuations. But there was a victory inside this deliverance, which should be noted. It was gained by the Air Force. . . .

This was a great trial of strength between the British and German Air Forces. Can you conceive a greater objective for the Germans in the air than to make evacuation from these beaches impossible, and to sink all these ships which were displayed, almost to the extent of thousands? Could there have been an objective of greater military importance and significance for the whole purpose of the war than this? They tried hard, and they were beaten back; they were frustrated in their task. We got the Army away; and they have paid four-fold for any losses which they have inflicted. . . .

When we consider how much greater would be our advantage in defending the air above this island against an overseas attack, I must say that I find in these facts a sure basis upon which practical and reassuring thoughts may rest. I will pay my tribute to these young airmen. May it not also be that the cause of civilisation itself will be defended by the skill and devotion of a few thousand airmen? There never had been, I suppose, in all the world, in all the history of war, such an opportunity for youth. . . . [T]hese young men, going forth every morn to guard their native land and all that we stand for, holding in their hands these instruments of colossal and shattering power, . . . deserve our gratitude, as do all of the brave men who, in so many ways and on so many occasions, are ready, and continue ready, to give life and all for their native land.

I return to the Army. In the long series of very fierce battles, now on this front, now on that, fighting on three fronts at once, battles fought by two or three divisions against an equal or somewhat larger number of the enemy, and fought fiercely on some of the old grounds that so many of us knew so well, in these battles our losses in men have exceeded 30,000 killed, wounded and missing. . . .

Churchill offers condolences to those who have lost family members and expresses hope for many of those still missing.

Against this loss of over 30,000 men, we can set a far heavier loss certainly inflicted upon the enemy. But our losses in material are enormous. . . . This loss will impose a further delay on the expansion of our military strength. That expansion had not been proceeding as fast as we had hoped. . . . And now here is this further delay. How long it will be, how long it will last, depends upon the exertions which we make in this island. An effort the like of which has never been seen in our records is now being made. Work is proceeding everywhere, night and day, Sundays and week-days. Capital and labour have cast aside their interests, rights, and customs and put them into the common stock. Already the flow of munitions has leapt forward. There is no reason why we should not in a few months overtake the sudden and serious loss that has come upon us, without retarding the development of our general programme.

Nevertheless, our thankfulness at the escape of our Army and so many men, whose loved ones have passed through an agonising week, must not blind us to the fact that what has happened in France and Belgium is a colossal military disaster. The French Army has been weakened, the Belgian Army has been lost, a large part of those fortified lines upon which so much faith had been reposed is gone, many valuable mining districts and factories have passed into the enemy's possession, the whole of the Channel ports are in his hands, with all the tragic consequences that follow from that, and we must expect another blow to be struck almost immediately at us or at France. . . .

The whole question of home defence against invasion is, of course, powerfully affected by the fact that we have for the time being in this island incomparably more powerful military forces than we have ever had at any moment in this war or the last. But this will not continue. We shall not be content with a defensive war. . . .

Churchill cautiously describes preparations that are underway for defending the island.

Turning once again, and this time more generally, to the question of invasion, I would observe that there has never been a period in all these long centuries of which we boast when an absolute guarantee against invasion, still less against serious raids, could have been given to our people. . . . There was always the chance, and it is that chance which has excited and befooled the imaginations of many Continental tyrants. Many are the tales that are told. We are assured that novel methods will be adopted, and when we see the originality of malice, the ingenuity of aggression, which our enemy displays, we may certainly prepare ourselves for every kind of novel stratagem and every kind of brutal and treacherous manœuvre. I think that no idea is so outlandish that it should not be considered and viewed with a searching, but at the same time, I hope, with a steady eye. We must never forget the solid assurances of sea power and those which belong to air power if it can be locally exercised.

I have, myself, full confidence that if all do their duty, if nothing is neglected, and if the best arrangements are made, as they are being made, we shall prove ourselves once again able to defend our island home, to ride out the storm of war, and to outlive the menace of tyranny, if necessary for years, if necessary alone. At any rate, that is what we are going to try to do. That is the resolve of His Majesty's Government—every man of them. That is the will of Parliament and the nation. The British Empire and the French Republic, linked together in their cause and in their need, will defend to the death their native soil, aiding each other like good comrades to the utmost of their strength.

Even though large tracts of Europe and many old and famous States have fallen or may fall into the grip of the Gestapo[96] and all the odious apparatus of Nazi rule, we shall not flag or fail. We shall go on to the end. We shall fight in France, we shall fight on the seas and oceans, we shall fight with growing confidence and growing strength in the air, we shall defend our island, whatever the cost may be. We shall fight on the beaches, we shall fight on the landing grounds, we shall fight in the fields and in the streets, we shall fight in the hills; we shall never surrender, and even if, which I do not for a moment believe, this island or a large part of it were subjugated and starving, then our Empire beyond the seas, armed and guarded by the British Fleet, would carry on the struggle, until, in God's good time, the new world, with all its power and might, steps forth to the rescue and the liberation of the old.

12. Anne Frank, *The Diary of a Young Girl* (1942–1944)

Three weeks before the Frank family went into hiding in their "Secret Annex" to escape Nazi persecution, Anne Frank, then thirteen years old, began a diary, structured as a series of letters to an imaginary correspondent, "Kitty." During the two years and more of the family's confinement, as seen in the excerpts that follow, Anne reflects on the purpose of keeping a record of events; describes the safe house in which she lives; learns of the deportation of Dutch Jews; hears the announcement of the D-Day invasion; and three weeks before her arrest, finding it "utterly impossible for me to build my life on a foundation of chaos, suffering and death," imagines a future of peace and tranquility.[97]

THE DIARY OF A YOUNG GIRL

Saturday, June 20, 1942

Anne begins the third letter of her collection reflecting on the new experience of writing a diary.

Writing in a diary is a really strange experience for someone like me. Not only because I've never written anything before, but also because it seems to me that later on neither I nor anyone else will be interested in the musings of a thirteen-year-old schoolgirl. Oh well, it doesn't matter. I feel like writing, and I have an even greater need to get all kinds of things off my chest. [. . .]

---

96. Gestapo: the German secret police during the Nazi era, infamous for its brutality.
97. Bracketed ellipses in the text indicate the editor's deletions; unbracketed ellipses are the author's.

Now I'm back to the point that prompted me to keep a diary in the first place: I don't have a friend.

Let me put it more clearly, since no one will believe that a thirteen-year-old girl is completely alone in the world. And I'm not. I have loving parents and a sixteen-year-old sister, and there are about thirty people I can call friends. [. . .] I have a family, loving aunts and a good home. No, on the surface I seem to have everything, except my one true friend.

At this point, Anne records the family history: her father and mother's marriage, the birth of their two children, their flight to Amsterdam in 1933, along with other German Jews following the Nazi ascendancy. But by May 1940, with the German occupation of the Netherlands, persecution of Dutch Jews begins.

After May 1940 the good times were few and far between: first there was the war, then the capitulation and then the arrival of the Germans, which is when the trouble started for the Jews. Our freedom was severely restricted by a series of anti-Jewish decrees: Jews were required to wear a yellow star; Jews were required to turn in their bicycles; Jews were forbidden to use streetcars; Jews were forbidden to ride in cars, even their own; Jews were required to do their shopping between 3 and 5 P.M.; Jews were required to frequent only Jewish-owned barbershops and beauty parlors; Jews were forbidden to be out on the streets between 8 P.M. and 6 A.M.; Jews were forbidden to go to theaters, movies or any other forms of entertainment; Jews were forbidden to use swimming pools, tennis courts, hockey fields or any other athletic fields; [. . .] Jews were forbidden to sit in their gardens or those of their friends after 8 P.M.; Jews were forbidden to visit Christians in their homes; Jews were required to attend Jewish schools, etc. You couldn't do this and you couldn't do that, but life went on.

Sunday, July 5, 1942

Anne's father reveals that he has been making plans for their going into hiding.

A few days ago, as we were taking a stroll around our neighborhood square, Father began to talk about going into hiding. He said it would be very hard for us to live cut off from the rest of the world. I asked him why he was bringing this up now.

"Well, Anne," he replied, "you know that for more than a year we've been bringing clothes, food and furniture to other people. We don't want our belongings to be seized by the Germans. Nor do we want to fall into their clutches ourselves. So we'll leave of our own accord and not wait to be hauled away."

"But when, Father?" He sounded so serious that I felt scared.

"Don't you worry. We'll take care of everything. Just enjoy your carefree life while you can."

That was it. Oh, may these somber words not come true for as long as possible.

Wednesday, July 8, 1942

Only three days after Anne's father's talk about going into hiding, circumstances dictate that they must do so immediately.

At three o'clock [. . .] the doorbell rang. I didn't hear it, since I was out on the balcony, lazily reading in the sun. A little while later Margot appeared in the kitchen doorway looking very agitated. "Father has received a call-up notice from the SS," she whispered. "Mother has gone to see Mr. van Daan." (Mr. van Daan is Father's business partner and a good friend.)

I was stunned. A call-up: everyone knows what that means. Visions of concentration camps and lonely cells raced through my head. How could we let Father go to such a fate? "Of course he's not going," declared Margot [. . .]. "Mother's gone to Mr. van Daan to ask whether we can move to our hiding place tomorrow. The van Daans are going with us. There will be seven of us altogether." Silence. We couldn't speak. [. . .]

Anne's mother and Mr. van Daan have arrived and are in consultation. Margot reveals to Anne that the call-up was not for their father, but for Margot.

At this second shock, I began to cry. [. . .] Hiding . . . where would we hide? In the city? In the country? In a house? In a shack? When, where, how . . . ? These were questions I wasn't allowed to ask, but they still kept running through my mind.

Margot and I started packing our most important belongings into a school-bag. The first thing I stuck in was this diary, and then curlers, handkerchiefs, schoolbooks, a comb and some old letters. Preoccupied by the thought of going into hiding, I stuck the craziest things in the bag, but I'm not sorry. Memories mean more to me than dresses.

Thursday, July 9, 1942

They walk to Anne's father's office building, within which, on the first two floors, were his company's warehouse and offices. On the third was a doorway (which they would later conceal with a hinged bookcase) to a "Secret Annex," consisting of several rooms. The space was adequate for the Frank and van Daan families, joined a few weeks later by an eighth resident, a friend of the van Daans.

The door to the right of the landing leads to the "Secret Annex" at the back of the house. No one would ever suspect there were so many rooms behind that plain gray door. [. . .] Straight ahead of you is a steep flight of stairs. To the left is a narrow hallway opening onto a room that serves as the Frank family's living room and bedroom. Next door is a smaller room, the bedroom and study of the two young ladies of the family. To the right of the stairs is a windowless washroom with a sink. The door in the corner leads to the toilet and another to Margot's and my room. If you go up the stairs and open the door at the top, you're surprised to see such a large, light and spacious room in an old canalside house like this. It contains a stove and a sink. This will be the kitchen and bedroom of Mr. and Mrs. van Daan, as well as the general living room, dining room and study for us all. A tiny side room is to be Peter van Daan's bedroom. Then, just as in the front part of the building, there's an attic and a loft. So there you are. Now I've introduced you to the whole of our lovely Annex!

Saturday, July 11, 1942

[. . .] You no doubt want to hear what I think of being in hiding. Well, all I can say is that I don't really know yet. I don't think I'll ever feel at home in this house, but that doesn't mean I hate it. It's more like being on vacation in some strange pension [small hotel]. [. . .] The Annex is an ideal place to hide in. It may be damp and lopsided, but there's probably not a more comfortable hiding place in all of Amsterdam. No, in all of Holland.

Friday, October 9, 1942

Anne has heard reports of Dutch Jews being taken to camps and gassed and of innocents held hostage.

Today I have nothing but dismal and depressing news to report. Our many Jewish friends and acquaintances are being taken away in droves. The Gestapo is treating them very roughly and transporting them in cattle cars to Westerbork, the big camp in Drenthe[98] to which they're sending all the Jews. [. . .] It must be terrible in Westerbork. The people get almost nothing to eat, much less to drink, as water is available only one hour a day, and there's only one toilet and sink for several thousand people. Men and women sleep in the same room, and women and children often have their heads shaved. [. . .]

    If it's that bad in Holland, what must it be like in those faraway and uncivilized places where the Germans are sending them? We assume that most of them are being murdered. The English radio says they're being gassed. Perhaps that's the quickest way to die. [. . .]

    Have you ever heard the term "hostages"? That's the latest punishment for saboteurs. It's the most horrible thing you can imagine. Leading

---

98. Drenthe: a province in the northeastern Netherlands. Camp Westerbork, located there, was used as a staging ground for the further deportation of Jews.

citizens—innocent people—are taken prisoner to await their execution. If the Gestapo can't find the saboteur, they simple grab five hostages and line them up against the wall. You read the announcements of their death in the paper, where they're referred to as "fatal accidents."

Wednesday, March 29, 1944

Anne's family and friends have been in hiding twenty-one months when Anne hears a broadcast from London in which the Dutch minister of Education Art, and Science urges the preservation of memoirs and other documents for an eventual archive of the war experience. Anne begins to see her diary as a product of conscious composition. She will revise it with publication in mind: the original notebooks will later be known as Version A and the loose pages of the revision as Version B.

Mr. Bluestein, the Cabinet Minister, speaking on the Dutch broadcast from London, said that after the war a collection would be made of diaries and letters dealing with the war. Of course, everyone pounced on my diary. Just imagine how interesting it would be if I were to publish a novel about the Secret Annex. The title alone would make people think it was a detective story.

Seriously, though, ten years after the war people would find it very amusing to read how we lived, what we ate and what we talked about as Jews in hiding. Although I tell you a great deal about our lives, you still know very little about us. How frightened the women are during air raids; last Sunday, for instance, when 350 British planes dropped 550 tons of bombs on Ijmuiden, so that the houses trembled like blades of grass in the wind. Or how many epidemics are raging here. [. . .]

Tuesday, June 6, 1944

The BBC broadcast announces the Allied invasion of Normandy.

"This is D Day,"[99] the BBC announced at twelve. "This is *the* day." The invasion has begun!

This morning at eight the British reported heavy bombing of Calais, Boulogne, Le Havre and Cherbourg, as well as Pas de Calais (as usual). Further, as a precautionary measure for those in the occupied territories, everyone living within a zone of twenty miles from the coast was warned to prepare for bombardments. Where possible, the British will drop pamphlets an hour ahead of time. [. . .]

---

99. D-Day: June 6, 1944; day of Allied invasion of Normandy (France) and beginning of the military march to Berlin and victory in the European theater of World War II.

German news reports the landing of British craft at Normandy. At 10:00 a.m., in German, Dutch, French, and other languages, it is announced that the invasion has begun.

BBC broadcast in English: "This is D Day." General Eisenhower said to the French people: "Stiff fighting will come now, but after this the victory. The year 1944 is the year of complete victory. Good luck!" [. . .]

A huge commotion in the Annex! Is this really the beginning of the long-awaited liberation? The liberation we've all talked so much about, which still seems too good, too much of a fairy tale ever to come true? Will this year, 1944, bring us victory?

Saturday, July 15, 1944

Anne has been reading a book on "the modern young girl," whose writer criticizes "today's youth." She feels the writer's criticism and counters that the young are worse off than the old.

"Deep down, the young are lonelier than the old." I read this in a book somewhere and it's stuck in my mind. As far as I can tell, it's true.

So if you're wondering whether it's harder for the adults here than for the children, the answer is no, it's certainly not. [. . .]

Anyone who claims that the older folks have a more difficult time in the Annex doesn't realize that the problems have a far greater impact on *us.* [. . .]

It's utterly impossible for me to build my life on a foundation of chaos, suffering and death. I see the world being slowly transformed into a wilderness, I hear the approaching thunder that, one day, will destroy us too, I feel the suffering of millions. And yet, when I look up at the sky, I somehow feel that everything will change for the better, that this cruelty too will end, that peace and tranquility will return once more. In the meantime, I must hold on to my ideals. Perhaps the day will come when I'll be able to realize them!

That day never came. Anne writes these thoughts in her antepenultimate letter. Twenty days later, she and all her family will be arrested, and they will die in the camps of exhaustion, starvation, and disease. Of those with whom Anne lived for twenty-five months in the Secret Annex, only Anne's father, Otto Frank, will survive. He dedicates the rest of his life to publicizing her Diary *to the ends of the earth.*

13. Elie Wiesel, *Night* (1958)

The fifteen-year-old Eliezer, in the first of the selections given here, recalls his first night—it is May or June 1944—in the concentration camp at Auschwitz: "Never shall I forget the small faces of the children whose bodies I saw transformed into smoke under a silent sky." Some months later, he and his father barely survive a forced march through a blizzard en route from Auschwitz to Buchenwald. At Buchenwald, his father is deathly ill, groaning for help that Eliezer cannot give. Lying in the upper bunk, the boy hears but does not act when a guard strikes his father a deadly blow, leaving the invalid whimpering and gasping for breath. The next morning—it is January 29, 1945—Eliezer's father has died; a new occupant lies in the lower bunk.[100]

NIGHT

In May or June 1944, they arrive at Auschwitz-Birkenau (Poland), the center of the universe for the Final Solution. Eliezer's mother and sisters are sent to the right, to be gassed, and he and his father Shlomo to the left, to labor. Eliezer sees ahead of him the smoke rising from the crematoria, into which trucks were dumping their loads of infant bodies.

Never shall I forget that night, the first night in camp, that turned my life into one long night seven times sealed.

Never shall I forget that smoke.

Never shall I forget the small faces of the children whose bodies I saw transformed into smoke under a silent sky.

Never shall I forget those flames that consumed my faith forever.

Never shall I forget the nocturnal silence that deprived me for all eternity of the desire to live.

Never shall I forget those moments that murdered my God and my soul and turned my dreams to ashes.

Never shall I forget those things, even were I condemned to live as long as God Himself.

Never.

In January 1945, as the Red Army closes in on Auschwitz, Eliezer with his father and thousands of fellow prisoners are driven in a death march through icy wind and snow from Auschwitz to Gleiwitz (Gliwice, Poland); from there they will be taken to Buchenwald concentration camp in Germany. Midway on the march, they stop for rest. Eliezer and his father take shelter in a shed.

One more hour of marching and, at last, the order to halt.

---

100. Bracketed ellipses in the text indicate the editor's deletions; unbracketed ellipses are the author's.

As one man, we let ourselves sink into the snow.

My father shook me. "Not here . . . Get up . . . A little farther down. There is a shed over there . . . Come . . ." [. . .]

Inside, too, the snow was thick. [. . .] The snow seemed to me like a very soft, very warm carpet. I fell asleep. [. . .] When I woke up, a frigid hand was tapping my cheeks. I tried to open my eyes: it was my father. [. . .]

"Don't let yourself be overcome by sleep, Eliezer. It's dangerous to fall asleep in snow. One falls asleep forever. Come, my son, come . . . Get up." [. . .]

I got up, with clenched teeth. [. . .]

We were outside. The icy wind whipped my face. [. . .] My head was reeling. I was walking through a cemetery. Among the stiffened corpses, there were logs of wood. Not a sound of distress, not a plaintive cry, nothing but mass agony and silence. Nobody asked anyone for help. One died because one had to. [. . .]

"Come, Father, let's go back to the shed . . ."

He didn't answer. He was not even looking at the dead.

"Come, Father, it's better there. You'll be able to lie down. We'll take turns. I'll watch over you and you'll watch over me. We won't let each other fall asleep. We'll look after each other."

He accepted. After trampling over many bodies and corpses, we succeeded in getting inside. We let ourselves fall to the ground.

"Don't worry, son. Go to sleep. I'll watch over you."

"You first, Father. Sleep." [. . .]

Heavy snow continued to fall over the corpses.

The door of the shed opened. An old man appeared. [. . .] It was Rabbi Eliahu, who had headed a small congregation in Poland. [. . .] A very kind man, beloved by everyone in the camp [. . .]. He looked like one of those prophets of old, always in the midst of his people when they needed to be consoled. [. . .] As he entered the shed, his eyes, brighter than ever, seemed to be searching for someone.

"Perhaps someone here has seen my son?"

He had lost his son in the commotion. He had searched for him among the dying, to no avail. Then he had dug through the snow to find his body. In vain. [. . .]

When he came near me, Rabbi Eliahu whispered, "It happened on the road. We lost sight of one another during the journey. I fell behind a little, at the rear of the column. I didn't have the strength to run anymore. And my son didn't notice. That's all I know. Where has he disappeared? Where can I find him? Perhaps you have seen him somewhere?"

"No, Rabbi Eliahu, I haven't seen him."

And so he left, as he had come: a shadow swept away by the wind.

He had already gone through the door when I remembered that I had noticed his son running beside me. I had forgotten and so had not mentioned it to Rabbi Eliahu!

But then I remembered something else: his son *had* seen him losing ground, sliding back to the rear of the column. He had seen him. And he had continued to run in front, letting the distance between them become greater.

A terrible thought crossed my mind: What if he had wanted to be rid of his father? He had felt his father growing weaker and, believing that the end was near, had thought by this separation to free himself of a burden that could diminish his own chance for survival.

It was good that I *had* forgotten all that. And I was glad that Rabbi Eliahu continued to search for his beloved son.

And in spite of myself, a prayer formed inside me, a prayer to this God in whom I no longer believed.

"Oh God, Master of the Universe, give me the strength never to do what Rabbi Eliahu's son has done." [. . .]

Arrived at Gleiwitz, they are loaded into cattle cars, one hundred to a car, and brought to Buchenwald. Eliezer and his father are two of the twelve survivors of the hundred who had begun the ten-day, 385-mile journey with them. They are assigned to barracks and fall asleep.

When I woke up, it was daylight. That is when I remembered that I had a father. During the alert, I had followed the mob, not taking care of him. I knew he was running out of strength, close to death, and yet I had abandoned him.

I went to look for him. [. . .]

I walked for hours without finding him. Then I came to a block where they were distributing black "coffee." People stood in line, quarreled.

A plaintive voice came from behind me:

"Eliezer, my son . . . bring me . . . a little coffee . . ."

I ran toward him.

"Father! I've been looking for you for so long . . . Where were you? Did you sleep? How are you feeling?"

He seemed to be burning with fever. I fought my way to the coffee cauldron like a wild beast. And I succeeded in bringing back a cup. I took one gulp. The rest was for him.

I shall never forget the gratitude that shone in his eyes when he swallowed this beverage. The gratitude of a wounded animal. [. . .]

He was lying on the boards, ashen, his lips pale and dry, shivering. I couldn't stay with him any longer. We had been ordered to go outside to allow for cleaning of the blocks. Only the sick could remain inside.

We stayed outside for five hours. We were given soup. When they allowed us to return to the blocks, I rushed toward my father:

"Did you eat?"

"No."

"Why?"

"They didn't give us anything . . . They said that we were sick, that we would die soon, and that it would be a waste of food . . . I can't go on . . ."

I gave him what was left of my soup. But my heart was heavy. I was aware that I was doing it grudgingly.

Just like Rabbi Eliahu's son, I had not passed the test.

Every day, my father was getting weaker. His eyes were watery, his face the color of dead leaves. [. . .]

Eliezer's father is sick with dysentery, getting weaker every day. He won't eat, wanting only water—which was "the worst poison for him." He imagines he is being robbed, that his barracks-companions are beating him.

A week went by like that.

"Is this your father?" asked the *Blockälteste*.[101]

"Yes."

"He is very sick."

"The doctor won't do anything for him."

He looked me straight in the eye:

"The doctor *cannot* do anything more for him. And neither can you."

He placed his big, hairy hand on my shoulder and added:

"Listen to me, kid. Don't forget that you are in a concentration camp. In this place, it is every man for himself, and you cannot think of others. Not even your father. In this place, there is no such thing as father, brother, friend. Each of us lives and dies alone. Let me give you good advice: stop giving your ration of bread and soup to your old father. You cannot help him anymore. And you are hurting yourself. In fact, you should be getting *his* rations . . ."

I listened to him without interrupting. He was right, I thought deep down, not daring to admit it to myself. Too late to save your old father . . . You could have two rations of bread, two rations of soup . . .

It was only a fraction of a second, but it left me feeling guilty. I ran to get some soup and brought it to my father. But he did not want it. All he wanted was water. [. . .]

In front of the block, the SS were giving orders. An officer passed between the bunks.[102] My father was pleading:

"My son, water . . . I'm burning up . . . My insides . . ."

"Silence over there!" barked the officer.

"Eliezer," continued my father, "water . . ."

---

101. *Blockälteste*: "block elder," an inmate put in charge of a concentration camp block, or barrack.

102. At this point, Eliezer is occupying the upper bunk above his father's.

The officer came closer and shouted to him to be silent. But my father did not hear. He continued to call me. The officer wielded his club and dealt him a violent blow to the head.

I didn't move. I was afraid, my body was afraid of another blow, this time to *my* head.

My father groaned once more, I heard:

"Eliezer . . ."

I could see that he was still breathing—in gasps. I didn't move.

When I came down from my bunk after roll call, I would see his lips trembling; he was murmuring something. I remained more than an hour leaning over him, looking at him, etching his bloody, broken face into my mind.

Then I had to go to sleep. I climbed into my bunk, above my father, who was still alive. The date was January 28, 1945.

I woke up at dawn on January 29. On my father's cot there lay another sick person. They must have taken him away before daybreak and taken him to the crematorium. Perhaps he was still breathing . . .

No prayers were said over his tomb. No candle lit in his memory. His last word had been my name. He had called out to me and I had not answered.

14. John Hersey, *Hiroshima* (1946)

The dramatic opening words of Hersey's *Hiroshima* announce the explosion of the atomic bomb and set the stage for the introduction of the six survivors Hersey will track throughout the book: "At exactly fifteen minutes past eight in the morning, on August 6, 1945, Japanese time, at the moment when the atomic bomb flashed above Hiroshima, Miss Toshiko Sasaki . . . Dr. Masakazu Fujii . . . Mrs. Hatsuyo Nakamura . . . Father Wilhelm Kleinsorge . . . Dr. Terufumi Sasaki . . . and the Reverend Mr. Kiyoshi Tanimoto. . . . They still wonder why they lived when so many others died. . . ." They are a clerk in a factory personnel office, a tailor's widow, two physicians, a Jesuit priest, and a Methodist pastor. The rest of the book tells their story in taut, lucid, and faultlessly restrained prose. Excerpts follow from the first two chapters, which describe the moment the bomb fell, and the fires that quickly spread, scattering inhabitants to places of refuge.

HIROSHIMA

The atomic bomb exploded soundlessly on Hiroshima, a city of about 250,000 people, on August 6, 1945, the blast killing approximately seventy thousand people and injuring one hundred thousand. Hersey's report opens by introducing the six survivors whose experience he will detail.

I. A Noiseless Flash

At exactly fifteen minutes past eight in the morning, on August 6, 1945, Japanese time, at the moment when the atomic bomb flashed above Hiroshima, Miss Toshiko Sasaki, a clerk in the personnel department of the East Asia Tin Works, had just sat down at her place in the plant office and was turning her head to speak to the girl at the next desk. At that same moment, Dr. Masakazu Fujii was settling down cross-legged to read the Osaka *Asahi* on the porch of his private hospital . . . ; Mrs. Hatsuyo Nakamura, a tailor's widow, stood by the window of her kitchen, watching a neighbor tearing down his house because it lay in the path of an air-raid-defense fire lane; Father Wilhelm Kleinsorge, a German priest of the Society of Jesus, reclined in his underwear on a cot on the top floor of his order's three-story mission house, reading a Jesuit magazine, *Stimmen der Zeit*; Dr. Terufumi Sasaki, a young member of the surgical staff of the city's large, modern Red Cross Hospital, walked along one of the hospital corridors with a blood specimen for a Wassermann test in his hand; and the Reverend Mr. Kiyoshi Tanimoto, pastor of the Hiroshima Methodist Church, paused at the door of a rich man's house in Koi, the city's western suburb, and prepared to unload a handcart full of things he had evacuated from town in fear of the massive B-29 raid which everyone expected Hiroshima to suffer. A hundred thousand people were killed by the atomic bomb, and these six were among the survivors. They still wonder why they lived when so many others died. . . . And now each knows that in the act of survival he lived a dozen lives and saw more death than he ever thought he would see. At the time, none of them knew anything. . . .

II. The Fire

Atop a hill, Mr. Tanimoto looks down on Hiroshima, as fires break out everywhere.

From the mound, Mr. Tanimoto saw an astonishing panorama. Not just a patch of Koi, as he had expected, but as much of Hiroshima as he could see through the clouded air was giving off a thick, dreadful miasma. Clumps of smoke, near and far, had begun to push up through the general dust. He wondered how such extensive damage could have been dealt out of a silent sky; even a few planes, far up, would have been audible. Houses nearby were burning. . . .

Mr. Tanimoto . . . thought of his wife and baby, his church, his home, his parishioners, all of them down in that awful murk. Once more he began to run in fear—toward the city.

Mrs. Hatsuyo Nakamura, the tailor's widow, having struggled up from under the ruins of her house after the explosion, and seeing Myeko, the youngest of her three children, buried breast-deep and unable to move, crawled across the debris, hauled at timbers, and flung tiles aside, in a hurried effort to free the child. Then, from what seemed to be caverns far below, she heard two small voices crying, "*Tasukete! Tasukete!* Help! Help!"

She called the names of her ten-year-old son and eight-year-old daughter: "Toshio! Yaeko!"

The voices from below answered.

Mrs. Nakamura abandoned Myeko, who at least could breathe, and in a frenzy made the wreckage fly above the crying voices. . . .

She struggles to extract the two children from under the wreckage.

The children were filthy and bruised, but none of them had a single cut or scratch.

Mrs. Nakamura took the children out into the street. . . . The children were silent, except for the five-year-old, Myeko, who kept asking questions: "Why is it night already? Why did our house fall down? What happened?" Mrs. Nakamura, who did not know what had happened (had not the all-clear sounded?), looked around and saw through the darkness that all the houses in her neighborhood had collapsed. . . .

Mrs. Nakamura takes her family to Asano Park, designated as an evacuation site for their neighborhood.

The only building they saw standing on their way to Asano Park was the Jesuit mission house. . . . As they passed it, she saw Father Kleinsorge, in bloody underwear, running out of the house with a small suitcase in his hand. . . .

That suitcase was the sole intact item in his office at the mission house and a very important one, containing his breviary and irreplaceable financial documents.

Dr. Masakazu Fujii's hospital was no longer on the bank of the Kyo River; it was in the river. After the overturn, Dr. Fujii was so stupefied and so tightly squeezed by the beams gripping his chest that he was unable to move at first, and he hung there about twenty minutes in the darkened morning. Then a thought which came to him—that soon the tide would be running in through the estuaries and his head would be submerged—inspired him to fearful activity. . . .

In pain and with great difficulty, Dr. Fujii pulls himself out of the river.

Dr. Fujii, who was in his underwear, was now soaking and dirty. His undershirt was torn, and blood ran down it from bad cuts on his chin and back. In this disarray, he walked out onto Kyo Bridge, beside which his hospital had stood. The bridge had not collapsed. He could see only fuzzily without his glasses, but he could see enough to be amazed at the number of houses that were down all around. . . . New fires were leaping up, and they spread quickly, and in a very short time terrible blasts of hot air and showers of cinders made it impossible to stand on the bridge any more. . . .

With so many physicians and surgeons dead or injured, and medical offices and hospitals destroyed, many of the wounded were left untended.

Of a hundred and fifty doctors in the city, sixty-five were already dead and most of the rest were wounded. Of 1,780 nurses, 1,654 were dead or too badly hurt to work. In the biggest hospital, that of the Red Cross, only six doctors out of thirty were able to function, and only ten nurses out of more than two hundred. The sole uninjured doctor on the Red Cross Hospital staff was Dr. Sasaki. After the explosion, he hurried to a storeroom to fetch bandages. This room, like everything he had seen as he ran through the hospital, was chaotic—bottles of medicines thrown off shelves and broken, salves spattered on the walls, instruments strewn everywhere. He grabbed up some bandages and an unbroken bottle of mercurochrome, hurried back to the chief surgeon, and bandaged his cuts. Then he went out into the corridor and began patching up the wounded patients and the doctors and nurses there. . . .

In a city of two hundred and forty-five thousand, nearly a hundred thousand people had been killed or doomed at one blow; a hundred thousand more were hurt. At least ten thousand of the wounded made their way to the best hospital in town, which was altogether unequal to such a trampling. . . . Tugged here and there in his stockinged feet, bewildered by the numbers, staggered by so much raw flesh, Dr. Sasaki . . . became an automaton, mechanically wiping, daubing, winding, wiping, daubing, winding.

Some of the wounded in Hiroshima were unable to enjoy the questionable luxury of hospitalization. In what had been the personnel office of the East Asia Tin Works, Miss Sasaki lay doubled over, unconscious, under the tremendous pile of books and plaster and wood and corrugated iron. She was wholly unconscious (she later estimated) for about three hours. Her first sensation was of dreadful pain in her left leg. . . . At the moments when it was sharpest, she felt that her leg had been cut off somewhere below the knee. Later, she heard someone walking on top of the wreckage above her, and anguished voices spoke up, evidently from within the mess around her: "Please help! Get us out!"

Eventually, several men were able to rescue Miss Saski. Her leg, although not severed, was badly broken, leaving her disabled. Meanwhile, Mr. Tanimoto sets out to find his family.

Mr. Tanimoto, fearful for his family and church, at first ran toward them by the shortest route, along Koi Highway. He was the only person making his way into the city; he met hundreds and hundreds who were fleeing, and every one of them seemed to be hurt in some way. The eyebrows of some were burned off and skin hung from their faces and hands. Others, because of pain, held their arms up as if carrying something in both hands. Some were vomiting as they walked. Many were naked or in shreds of clothing. . . .

He thought he would skirt the fire, . . . [but] as he turned left to get around it, he met, by incredible luck, his wife. She was carrying their infant son. Mr. Tanimoto was now so emotionally worn out that nothing could surprise him. He did not embrace his wife; he simply said, "Oh, you are safe." . . .

His wife tells how she had been buried under the parsonage with her baby in her arms, but managed to work her way out.

She said she was now going out to Ushida again. Mr. Tanimoto said he wanted to see his church and take care of the people of his Neighborhood Association. They parted as casually—as bewildered—as they had met. . . .

The wounded and dislocated gathered for refuge at Asano Park.

All day, people poured into Asano Park. This private estate was far enough away from the explosion so that its bamboos, pines, laurel, and maples were still alive, and the green place invited refugees. . . . Mrs. Nakamura and her children were among the first to arrive, and they settled in the bamboo grove near the river. They all felt terribly thirsty, and they drank from the river. At once they were nauseated and began vomiting, and they retched the whole day. . . . When Father Kleinsorge and the other priests came into the park, nodding to their friends as they passed, the Nakamuras were all sick and prostrate. . . . The priests went farther along the river and settled down in some underbrush. . . .

When Mr. Tanimoto . . . reached the park, it was very crowded, and to distinguish the living from the dead was not easy, for most of the people lay still, with their eyes open. . . . He walked to the riverbank and began to look for a boat in which he might carry some of the most severely injured across the river from Asano Park and away from the spreading fire. . . . Soon he found a good-sized pleasure punt drawn up on the bank. . . . The punt was heavy, but he managed to slide it into the water. There were no oars, and all he could find for propulsion was a thick bamboo pole. He worked the boat upstream to the most crowded part of the park and began to ferry the wounded. . . .

Early in the afternoon, the fire swept into the woods of Asano Park. The first Mr. Tanimoto knew of it was when, returning in his boat, he saw that a great number of people had moved toward the riverside. On touching the bank, he went up to investigate, and when he saw the fire, he shouted, "All the young men who are not badly hurt come with me!" . . . Mr. Tanimoto sent some to look for buckets and basins and told others to beat the burning underbrush with their clothes; when utensils were at hand, he formed a bucket chain from one of the pools in the rock gardens. The team fought the fire for more than two hours, and gradually defeated the flames. As Mr. Tanimoto's men worked, the frightened people in the park pressed closer and closer to the river, and finally the mob began to force some of the unfortunates who were on the very bank into the water. . . .

It began to rain. Mrs. Nakamura kept her children under the umbrella. . . . [T]he wind grew stronger and stronger, and suddenly—probably because of the tremendous convection set up by the blazing city—a whirlwind ripped through the park. Huge trees crashed down; small ones were uprooted and flew into the air. Higher, a wild array of flat things revolved in the twisting funnel—pieces of iron roofing, papers, doors, strips of matting. . . .

After the storm, . . . when he went ashore for a while, Mr. Tanimoto, upon whose energy and initiative many had come to depend, heard people begging for food. He consulted Father Kleinsorge, and they decided to go back into town to get some rice from Mr. Tanimoto's Neighborhood Association shelter and from the mission shelter. . . . They got out several bags of rice and gathered up several . . . pumpkins [cooked by the fire] and dug up some potatoes that were nicely baked under the ground, and started back. . . . Altogether, the rice was enough to feed nearly a hundred people.

Just before dark, Mr. Tanimoto came across a twenty-year-old girl, Mrs. Kamai, the Tanimotos' next-door neighbor. She was crouching on the ground with the body of her infant daughter in her arms. The baby had evidently been dead all day. Mrs. Kamai jumped up when she saw Mr. Tanimoto and said, "Would you please try to locate my husband?"

Mr. Tanimoto knew that her husband had been inducted into the Army just the day before. . . . Kamai had reported to the Chugoku Regional Army Headquarters . . . where some four thousand troops were stationed. Judging by the many maimed soldiers Mr. Tanimoto had seen during the day, he surmised that the barracks had been badly damaged by whatever it was that had hit Hiroshima. He knew he hadn't a chance of finding Mrs. Kamai's husband, even if he searched, but he wanted to humor her. "I'll try," he said.

"You've got to find him," she said. "He loved our baby so much. I want him to see her once more."

15. George Orwell, *1984* (1949)

Winston Smith, imprisoned for thoughtcrime, is being reeducated by O'Brien, an official of the so-called Ministry of Love, tasked to eradicate dissent by coercive means. Winston has been starved, tortured, and humiliated for an untold length of time. Intellectually, he has accepted the Party's version of truth; emotionally, he still resists, as seen in this episode, where he is at once tormented and instructed by O'Brien. But Winston's full conversion will come soon: he will conquer himself and ecstatically confess, "he loved Big Brother." And then he will be freed by the executioner's bullet.

1984

Part Two, section III

"There are three stages in your reintegration," said O'Brien. "There is learning, there is understanding, and there is acceptance. It is time for you to enter upon the second stage."

As always, Winston was lying flat on his back. But of late his bonds were looser. They still held him to the bed, but he could move his knees a little and could turn his head from side to side and raise his arms from the elbow. The dial, also, had grown to be less of a terror. He could evade its pangs if he was quick-witted enough; it was chiefly when he showed stupidity that O'Brien pulled the lever. Sometimes they got through a whole session without use of the dial. He could not remember how many sessions there had been. The whole process seemed to stretch out over a long, indefinite time—weeks, possibly—and the intervals between the sessions might sometimes have been days, sometimes only an hour or two.

"As you lie there," said O'Brien, "you have often wondered—you have even asked me—why the Ministry of Love should expend so much time and trouble on you. . . ."

O'Brien knows about Winston's study of a forgiven book—"the book"—which exposed the workings of the Party, and envisioned a more humane society.

"Is it true, what it says?"

"As description, yes. The program it sets forth is nonsense. The secret accumulation of knowledge—a gradual spread of enlightenment—ultimately a proletarian rebellion—the overthrow of the Party. . . . It is all nonsense. The proletarians will never revolt, not in a thousand years or a million. . . . If you have ever cherished any dreams of violent insurrection, you must abandon them. There is no way in which the Party can be overthrown. The rule of the Party is forever. Make that the starting point of your thoughts."

He came closer to the bed. "Forever!" he repeated. . . . "Now tell me *why* we cling to power. What is our motive? Why should we want power? Go on, speak," he added as Winston remained silent.

Nevertheless Winston did not speak for another moment or two. . . . He knew in advance what O'Brien would say: that the Party did not seek power for its own ends, but only for the good of the majority. . . . That the Party was the eternal guardian of the weak, a dedicated sect doing evil that good might come, sacrificing its own happiness to that of others. . . .

"You are ruling over us for our own good," he said feebly. "You believe that human beings are not fit to govern themselves, and therefore—"

He started and almost cried out. A pang of pain had shot through his body. O'Brien had pushed the lever of the dial up to thirty-five.

"That was stupid, Winston, stupid!" he said. "You should know better than to say a thing like that."

He pulled the lever back and continued:

"Now I will tell you the answer to my question. It is this. The Party seeks power entirely for its own sake. We are not interested in the good of others; we are interested solely in power. . . . We are different from all the oligarchies of the past in that we know what we are doing. All the others, even those who resembled ourselves, were cowards and hypocrites. The German Nazis and the Russian Communists came very close to us in their methods, but they never had the courage to recognize their own motives. They pretended, perhaps they even believed, that they had seized power unwillingly and for a limited time, and that just round the corner there lay a paradise where human beings would be free and equal. We are not like that. We know that no one ever seizes power with the intention of relinquishing it. Power is not a means; it is an end. One does not establish a dictatorship in order to safeguard a revolution; one makes the revolution in order to establish the dictatorship. The object of persecution is persecution. The object of torture is torture. The object of power is power. Now do you begin to understand me?" . . .

He turned away from the bed and began strolling up and down again, one hand in his pocket.

"We are the priests of power," he said. . . . "It is time for you to gather some idea of what power means. The first thing you must realize is that power is collective. The individual only has power in so far as he ceases to be an individual. . . . Alone—free—the human being is always defeated. It must be so, because every human being is doomed to die, which is the greatest of all failures. But if he can make complete, utter submission, if he can escape from his identity, if he can merge himself in the Party so that he *is* the Party, then he is all-powerful and immortal. The second thing for you to realize is that power is power over human beings. Over the body—but, above all, over the mind. Power over matter—external reality, as you would call it—is not important. Already our control over matter is absolute."

For a moment Winston ignored the dial. He made a violent effort to raise himself into a sitting position, and merely succeeded in wrenching his body painfully.

"But how can you control matter?" he burst out. "You don't even control the climate or the law of gravity. And there are disease, pain, death—"

O'Brien silenced him by a movement of the hand. "We control matter because we control the mind. Reality is inside the skull. . . . You must get rid of those nineteenth-century ideas about the laws of nature. We make the laws of nature."

"But you do not! You are not even masters of this planet. What about Eurasia and Eastasia? You have not conquered them yet."

"Unimportant. We shall conquer them when it suits us. And if we did not, what difference would it make? We can shut them out of existence. Oceania[103] is the world."

"But the world itself is only a speck of dust. And man is tiny—helpless! How long has he been in existence? For millions of years the earth was uninhabited."

"Nonsense. The earth is as old as we are, no older. How could it be older? Nothing exists except through human consciousness." . . .

"But the whole universe is outside us. Look at the stars! Some of them are a million light-years away. They are out of our reach forever."

"What are the stars?" said O'Brien indifferently. "They are bits of fire a few kilometers away. We could reach them if we wanted to. Or we could blot them out. The earth is the center of the universe. The sun and the stars go round it." . . .

Winston shrank back upon the bed. Whatever he said, the swift answer crushed him like a bludgeon. And yet he knew, he *knew*, that he was in the right. The belief that nothing exists outside your own mind—surely there must be some way of demonstrating that it was false. . . . A faint smile twitched the corners of O'Brien's mouth as he looked down at him.

"I told you, Winston," he said, "that metaphysics is not your strong point. . . . All this is a digression," he added in a different tone. "The real power, the power we have to fight for night and day, is not power over things, but over men." He paused, and for a moment assumed again his air of a schoolmaster questioning a promising pupil: "How does one man assert his power over another, Winston?"

Winston thought. "By making him suffer," he said.

"Exactly. By making him suffer. Obedience is not enough. Unless he is suffering, how can you be sure that he is obeying your will and not his own? Power is in inflicting pain and humiliation. Power is in tearing human minds to pieces and putting them together again in new shapes of your own choosing. Do you begin to see, then, what kind of world we are creating? It is the exact opposite of the stupid hedonistic Utopias that the old reformers imagined. . . . Progress in our world will be progress toward more pain. The old civilizations claimed that they were founded on love or justice. Ours is founded upon hatred. In our world there will be no emotions except fear, rage, triumph, and self-abasement. Everything else we shall destroy—everything. Already we are breaking down the habits of thought which have survived from before the Revolution. We have cut the links between child and parent, and between man and man, and between man and woman. No one dares trust a wife or a child or a friend any longer. But in the future there will be no wives

---

103. Oceania: one of the three superstates that would in the future dominate the globe.

and no friends. Children will be taken from their mothers at birth, as one takes eggs from a hen. The sex instinct will be eradicated. Procreation will be an annual formality like the renewal of a ration card. We shall abolish the orgasm. Our neurologists are at work upon it now. There will be no loyalty, except loyalty toward the Party. There will be no love, except the love of Big Brother. There will be no laughter, except the laugh of triumph over a defeated enemy. There will be no art, no literature, no science. . . . But always—do not forget this, Winston—always there will be the intoxication of power, constantly increasing and constantly growing subtler. Always, at every moment, there will be the thrill of victory, the sensation of trampling on an enemy who is helpless. If you want a picture of the future, imagine a boot stamping on a human face—forever."

He paused as though he expected Winston to speak. Winston had tried to shrink back into the surface of the bed again. He could not say anything. His heart seemed to be frozen. O'Brien went on:

"And remember that it is forever. The face will always be there to be stamped upon. The heretic, the enemy of society, will always be there, so that he can be defeated and humiliated over again. Everything that you have undergone since you have been in our hands—all that will continue, and worse. The espionage, the betrayals, the arrests, the tortures, the executions, the disappearances will never cease. It will be a world of terror as much as a world of triumph. . . . Always we shall have the heretic here at our mercy, screaming with pain, broken up, contemptible—and in the end utterly penitent, saved from himself, crawling to our feet of his own accord. That is the world that we are preparing, Winston. . . . You are beginning, I can see, to realize what that world will be like. But in the end you will do more than understand it. You will accept it, welcome it, become part of it."

Winston had recovered himself sufficiently to speak. "You can't!" he said weakly.

"What do you mean by that remark, Winston?"

"You could not create such a world as you have just described. It is a dream. It is impossible."

"Why?"

"It is impossible to found a civilization on fear and hatred and cruelty. It would never endure."

"Why not?"

"It would have no vitality. It would disintegrate. It would commit suicide."

"Nonsense. You are under the impression that hatred is more exhausting than love. . . . The Party is immortal." . . .

As usual, the voice had battered Winston into helplessness. . . . Feebly, without arguments, with nothing to support him except his inarticulate horror of what O'Brien had said, he returned to the attack.

"I don't know—I don't care. Somehow you will fail. Something will defeat you. Life will defeat you."

"We control life, Winston, at all its levels. You are imagining that there is something called human nature which will be outraged by what we do and will turn against us. But we create human nature. Men are infinitely malleable. Or perhaps you have returned to your old idea that the proletarians or the slaves will arise and overthrow us. Put it out of your mind. They are helpless, like the animals. Humanity is the Party. The others are outside—irrelevant."

"I don't care. In the end they will beat you. Sooner or later they will see you for what you are, and then they will tear you to pieces."

"Do you see any evidence that that is happening? Or any reason why it should?"

"No. I believe it. I *know* that you will fail. There is something in the universe—I don't know, some spirit, some principle—that you will never overcome." . . .

"Then what is it, this principle that will defeat us?"

"I don't know. The spirit of Man."

"And do you consider yourself a man?"

"Yes."

"If you are a man, Winston, you are the last man. Your kind is extinct; we are the inheritors. Do you understand that you are *alone*? You are outside history, you are nonexistent." His manner changed and he said more harshly: "And you consider yourself morally superior to us, with our lies and our cruelty?"

"Yes, I consider myself superior." . . .

"Get up from that bed," he said.

The bonds had loosened themselves. Winston lowered himself to the floor and stood up unsteadily.

"You are the last man," said O'Brien. "You are the guardian of the human spirit. You shall see yourself as you are. Take off your clothes." . . .

O'Brien has Winston strip and look at himself in a three-panel mirror: he is emaciated, mangled, and filthy, the outcome of starvation and torture.

"You are rotting away," he said; "you are falling to pieces. What are you? A bag of filth. Now turn round and look into that mirror again. Do you see that thing facing you? That is the last man. If you are human, that is humanity. Now put your clothes on again." . . .

"You did it!" sobbed Winston. "You reduced me to this state."

"No, Winston, you reduced yourself to it. This is what you accepted when you set yourself up against the Party." . . .

"Tell me," he said, "how soon will they shoot me?"

"It might be a long time," said O'Brien. "You are a difficult case. But don't give up hope. Everyone is cured sooner or later. In the end we shall shoot you."

CREDITS

Except where noted below, all texts are in the public domain or were newly translated for this volume by Margaret L. King. Credits are listed in order of appearance.

Chapter 1

Jean-Jacques Rousseau. *Discours sur l'origine et les fondements de l'inégalité parmis les hommes.* Translated by Margaret L. King, based on King's previous translation in her *Enlightenment Thought: An Anthology of Sources.* Indianapolis, IN: Hackett, 2019. Excerpt from pp. 181–85.

Voltaire. *Candide.* In *Candide and Related Texts.* Edited and translated by David Wootton. Indianapolis, IN: Hackett, 2000. Excerpt from Chapter 5 (pp. 10–12).

Gotthold Ephraim Lessing. *Nathan der Weise.* Translated by Margaret L. King, based on King's previous translation in her *Enlightenment Thought: An Anthology of Sources.* Indianapolis, IN: Hackett, 2019. Excerpt from pp. 106–10.

Denis Diderot. *Rameau's Nephew.* In *Rameau's Nephew and Other Works.* Translated by Jacques Barzun and Ralph H. Bowen. Indianapolis, IN: Hackett, 1956; reprint 2001. Selections from pp. 8–12, 28–29, 33–35, 71–74, 87.

Chapter 2

Adam Mickiewicz. *Ode to Youth and To a Polish Mother.* In *Polish Romantic Literature: An Anthology.* Edited and translated by Michael J. Mikoś. Bloomington, IN: Slavica Publishers, 2002. Used by permission.

Alexander Pushkin. *The Bronze Horseman: A St. Petersburg Story.* In *Translation and Literature* 7.1 (1998). Translated with commentary and notes by John Dewey. Reproduced with permission of the Licensor through PLSclear.

Chapter 4

Charles Baudelaire. In *Paris Spleen and La Fanfarlo.* Translated by Raymond N. MacKenzie. Indianapolis, IN: Hackett, 2008. Selections from *Paris Spleen,* ##2, 7, 17, 19, 33, and 48 (pp. 6, 13, 32, 36–37, 73, 96–97).

Émile Zola. *Germinal.* Translated by Raymond N. MacKenzie. Indianapolis, IN: Hackett, 2011. Excerpts from V.3, VI.1, VII.6 (pp. 291–99, 344–45, and 471–74).

Chapter 5

Fyodor Dostoevsky. *Notes from the Underground.* Translated by Constance Garnett. Translation reprinted in Dostoevsky, *Notes from the Underground.* Edited with an Introduction by Charles Guignon and Kevin Aho. Indianapolis, IN: Hackett, 2008. Excerpts from Part One, prefatory note and Chapters 1, 3, 7, 9, and 10 (pp. 1, 3–5, 10–11, 15–20, 24–27).

Anton Chekhov. *The Cherry Orchard.* Edited and translated by Sharon Marie Carnicke. Indianapolis, IN: Hackett, 2010. Excerpts from Acts I, II, and III (pp. 10–12, 14, 25, 27–28, 32, 46–47).

Chapter 6

José Joaquín Fernández de Lizardi. *The Mangy Parrot*. Translated by David Frye. Introduction by Nancy Vogeley. Indianapolis, IN: Hackett, 2004. Selections from Chapter 46 (pp. 479–81, 482, 484).

Eduardo Gutiérrez. *The Gaucho Juan Moreira: True Crime in Nineteenth-Century Argentina*. Translated by John Charles Chasteen; edited with an Introduction by William G. Acree Jr. Indianapolis, IN: Hackett, 2014. Selections from Chapters One and Seven (pp. 3–6, 24–27).

Joaquim Maria Machado de Assis. *To Be Twenty Years Old!* In *The Alienist and Other Stories of Nineteenth-Century Brazil*. Edited and translated, with an Introduction by John Charles Chasteen (Indianapolis, IN: Hackett, 2013). Excerpt from pp. 1–6.

Chapter 7

Osip Mandelstam. *The Noise of Time* (1925). First published 1965 by Princeton University Press as *The Prose of Osip Mandelstam*. Copyright © 1965 by Princeton University Press. Expanded edition published 1986 by North Point Press as *The Noise of Time*. Copyright © 1986 by Clarence Brown. Published 1993 by Penguin Books. Northwestern University Press edition published 2002 by arrangement with Clarence Brown. All rights reserved. Selections from pp. 74–81.

William Faulkner. "A Rose for Emily" (1930) from *Collected Stories of William Faulkner*. Copyright 1930 and © renewed 1958 by William Faulkner. Used by permission of Random House, an imprint and division of Penguin Random House LLC and W.W. Norton & Company, Inc. All rights reserved. Selections from Sections III and IV (pp. 396–402).

Virginia Woolf. *A Room of One's Own* (1929). Copyright © 1929 by Houghton Mifflin Harcourt Publishing Company, renewed 1957 by Leonard Woolf. Reprinted by permission of Houghton Mifflin Harcourt Publishing Company and the Society of Authors. All rights reserved. Excerpts from Chapters One, Three, and Six (pp. 3–4, 41–43, 46–49, 110–12).

Mariano Azuela. *The Underdogs: Pictures and Scenes from the Present Revolution* (1915). Translated and edited by Gustavo Pellón. Indianapolis, IN: Hackett, 2006. Excerpts from Part One, I–III and Part Three, VII (pp. 1–7, 86–87).

Pablo Neruda. *The Heights of Macchu Picchu*. Translated by Nathaniel Tarn. Translation copyright © 1966, renewed © 1994 by Nathaniel Tarn. Originally published as "Alturas de Macchu Picchu" in *Canto General* © Pablo Neruda, 1950 and Fundación Pablo Neruda. Reprinted by permission of Farrar, Straus and Giroux, Random House, and Agencia Literaria Carmen Balcells, S.A. All Rights Reserved. Selections from poems I, II, VI, X, and XII (pp. 3, 7, 9, 27, 29, 57, 59, 67, 69, 71).

Federico García Lorca. *The House of Bernarda Alba* (1936). In *Four Key Plays*. Translated with an Introduction by Michael Kidd. Indianapolis, IN: Hackett, 2019. Excerpt from Act III (pp. 205–9).

Jean-Paul Sartre. Excerpt(s) from *No Exit and the Flies*. Translated by Stuart Gilbert; copyright © 1946 by Stuart Gilbert, copyright renewed 1974, 1975 by Maris Agnes Mathilde Gilbert. Originally published as *Huis Clos* © Editions Gallimard, Paris, 1945. Used by permission of Alfred A. Knopf, an imprint of the Knopf Doubleday Publishing Group, a division of Penguin Random House LLC and Editions Gallimard. All rights reserved. Excerpt from pp. 40–46.

Chapter 8

Erich Maria Remarque. *All Quiet on the Western Front* (1929). Translated by A. W. Wheen. New York: Fawcett Columbine, 1958; reprinted Ballantine Books, a division of Random House, 1996. Used by permission of New York University Press. Selections from Chapters One, Two, Four, and Six (pp. 10–13, 21–22, 55–56, 104–7, 113–14, 129–36).

Bertolt Brecht. *Mother Courage* (1939). In *Mother Courage and Her Children: A Chronicle of the Thirty Years' War*. Translated by Eric Bentley. New York: Grove Press, 1966. © Methuen Drama, an imprint of Bloomsbury Publishing Plc. Selections from Scenes 1, 2, 3, 8, 11, and 12 (pp. 25, 41, 50–52, 55–57, 61, 64, 91–92, 106–11).

Simone Weil. *The* Iliad *or The Poem of Force*, Pendle Hill Pamphlet 91. Wallingford, PA: Pendle Hill Publications. Used by permission. Selections from paragraphs 1–2, 7, 34–36, 61, 63, 71–72, 79–81, 83–86.

Arthur Koestler. *Darkness at Noon*. Translated by Daphne Hardy. Copyright © 1941 by Macmillan Publishing Company. Copyright renewed © 1968 by Mrs. F.H.H. Henrica (Daphne Hardy). Reprinted with the permission of Scribner, a division of Simon & Schuster, Inc. and Sterling Lord Literistic, Inc. All rights reserved. Selections from pp. 12, 131–32, 139–41, 144, 154–56, 209–212, 229–32.

Anna Akhmatova. *Requiem* (1940). In Akhmatova, *Requiem and Poem without a Hero*. Translated by D. M. Thomas. Athens, OH: Swallow Press, Ohio University Press, 1976. Used by permission. Selections from Prologue, poems 1–5, 8, 10, and Epilogue (pp. 25–32).

Anne Frank. *The Diary of a Young Girl: The Definitive Edition*. Edited by Otto H. Frank and Mirjam Pressler. Translated by Susan Massotty. Copyright © The Anne Franke - Fonds, Basle, Switzerland, 1991, 2002. Translation copyright © 1995 by Penguin Random House LLC. Used by permission of Doubleday, an imprint of the Knopf Doubleday Publishing Group, a division of Penguin Random House LLC and Penguin Books Limited. All rights reserved. Excerpts from letters of June 20, July 5, 8, 9, and 11, and October 9, 1942; and March 29, June 6, and July 15, 1944 (pp. 6, 8, 18–20, 23–26, 54–55, 244–45, 311–12, 332–33).

Elie Wiesel. *Night*. Translated by Marion Wiesel. Copyright © 1972, 1985 by Elie Wiesel. English translation copyright © 2006 by Marion Wiesel. Originally published as *La Nuit* by Les Editions de Minuit. Copyright © 1958 by Les Editions de Minuit. Reprinted by permission of Hill and Wang, a division of Farrar, Straus and Giroux, and Georges Borchardt, Inc., for Les Editions de Minuit. All Rights Reserved. Excerpts from pp. 34, 88–91, 106–7, 110–12.

John Hersey. *Hiroshima* (1946). *The New Yorker*. August 24, 1946. New York: Knopf, 1946. Used by permission of BN Publishing.

George Orwell. *Nineteen Eighty-Four*. Copyright © 1949 by Houghton Mifflin Harcourt Publishing Company, renewed 1977 by Sonia Brownell Orwell. Reprinted by permission of Houghton Mifflin Harcourt Publishing Company and A.M. Heath Literary Agents. © 1949 the Estate of the late Sonia Brownell Orwell. All rights reserved. Excerpts from Part Two, section III (pp. 232–44).

INDEX